Muriel Spark

OMNIBUS 3

MURIEL SPARK

OMNIBUS 3

•

THE TAKEOVER

•

NOT TO DISTURB

•

THE MANDELBAUM GATE

•

CONSTABLE • LONDON

The Takeover
first published in Great Britain 1976
by Macmillan & Co
Copyright © Copyright Administration Ltd, 1976

Not to Disturb
first published in Great Britain 1971
by Macmillan & Co
Copyright © Copyright Administration Ltd, 1971

The Mandelbaum Gate
first published in Great Britain 1965
by Macmillan & Co
Copyright © Muriel Spark, 1965

This edition first published in Great Britain 1996
by Constable and Company Ltd
3 The Lanchesters
162 Fulham Palace Road
London W6 9ER
ISBN 0 09 472580 2
Set in Monophoto Imprint 11pt by
Servis Filmsetting Ltd, Manchester
Printed in Great Britain by
St Edmundsbury Press Ltd
Bury St Edmunds, Suffolk

A CIP catalogue record for this book
is available from the British Library

Contents

THE TAKEOVER

ONE

At Nemi, that previous summer, there were three new houses of importance to the surrounding district. One of them was new in the strict sense; it had been built from the very foundations on cleared land where no other house had stood, and had been planned, plotted, discussed with an incomprehensible lawyer, and constructed, over a period of three years and two months ('and seven days, three hours and twenty minutes,' the present occupant would add. 'Three years, two months, seven days, three hours and twenty minutes from the moment of Maggie giving the go-ahead to the moment we moved in. I timed it. God, how I timed it!')

The other two houses were reconstructions of buildings already standing or half-standing; both had foundations of Roman antiquity, and of earlier origin if you should dig down far enough, it was said. Maggie Radcliffe had bought these two, and the land on which she had put up the third house.

One was intended eventually for her son, Michael; that was the farm-house. He was to live in it when he got married.

Maggie herself was never there that previous summer, was reputed to be there, was never seen, had been, had gone, was coming soon, had just departed for Lausanne, for London.

Hubert Mallindaine, in the new-built house, had news of Maggie; had seen, had just missed, Maggie; had had a long discussion with Maggie; was always equipped to discuss knowledgeably the ins and outs of Maggie's life. He had been for years Maggie's friend number one and her central information agent.

The third house had been a large villa in bad repair. It was now in good repair, sitting in handsome grounds, with a tennis court, a swimming-pool, the old lily-pond made wholesome and the lawns newly greened. Maggie could do everything. But it had taken years and years. The Italian sense of time and Maggie's lack of concentration due to her family troubles and involvements had held things up. But the villa, too, was ready that previous summer. In an access of financial morality, although it was quite unnecessary, Maggie had decided to let this house for a monthly rent to a rich business-man. She didn't need the money, but it put Maggie in a regular sort of position. Her present husband, Ralph Radcliffe, who also had money and never thought of anything else, had less justification to resent the whole idea when he could be reminded that Maggie was drawing a rent from one of the houses. This was the summer when it was said Maggie's marriage was going on the rocks.

Hubert Mallindaine's terrace had a view of the lake and the Alban hills folding beyond.

Hubert needed the best view: he had so encamped himself in his legend that Maggie had not questioned that he was entitled to the view. His secretaries from their bedrooms also had splendid views.

There were four secretaries that summer: Damian Runciwell, Kurt Hakens, Lauro Moretti, Ian Mackay. Only one, Damian, did the secretarial work.

'We can't stay here all summer, darling.'
'Darling, why not? I hate to travel.'
'Take off those earrings before you open the door to the butcher.'
'Darling, why?'
'Did you remember the garlic?'
'My dear Kurt-o, we do not need garlic today.'
'Ian, we do . . . The salad.'
'Dearie, we have a clove of garlic for the salad. More garlic we do not need today.'
'Oh, get out of my kitchen. Go on. You make me nervous.'

'My boredom,' said Hubert Mallindaine, the master of the house, 'makes you all look so tawdry.' He was addressing the others at the lunch table. 'Forgive me that I feel that way.'

'Feel what you like,' said one of them, 'but you shouldn't say it.'

'The mushrooms are soggy. They have been done in oil. Too much oil, too. They should have been done in butter and oil. Very little butter, very little oil.'

*

There was a heatwave so fierce you would have thought someone had turned it on somewhere by means of a tap, and had turned it too high, and then gone away for the summer.

Hubert lay on the sofa in his study and deplored Maggie's comparative lack of chivalry. It was siesta time and his room had been made dark. Hubert decided to talk to Maggie about air-conditioning. But this decision annoyed him. One should not find oneself in the position, he thought, of having to ask, having to wait for the opportunity to talk on practical matters with a woman of no routine. She might progress into the neighbourhood, looking gorgeous, at any moment, without advance notice. She had no sense of chivalry. A protectress of chivalry would not have left him dependent on her personal bounty for little things; Maggie should have made a settlement. Even the house, he thought, as he lay on the sofa at the onslaught of that previous summer, is not in one's own name but in Maggie's. One has no claim to anything. Something might happen to Maggie and one would have no claim. She could be killed in an air crash. Hubert, staring at the ceiling, pulled a hair from his beard, and the twinge of pain confirmed and curiously consoled the thought. It was unlikely that anything would happen to Maggie. She was indestructible.

TWO

'Miss Thin,' Hubert said, 'I wish you would not try to use your intelligence because you have so little of it. Just do as I say. Put them in date order.'

'I thought you would want to keep the personal separate from the professional,' said Pauline Thin belligerently. 'That would be the logical way.'

'There is no distinction between the two so far as I'm concerned,' Hubert said, looking, with a horror that had no connection whatsoever with Pauline Thin, at the great trunkfuls of old letters still to be gone through. Masses of old, old letters are very upsetting to contemplate, each one containing a world of past trivialities or passions forever pending. The surprise of words once overlooked and meanings newly realized, the record of debts unpaid or overpaid, of boredom unrequited or sweetness forever lost, came rising up to Hubert from the open boxes.

'Put them in chronological order,' Hubert said, 'a bundle for each year, then break each bundle up into three months. That's all you have to do. Don't read them through and through, it's a waste of your working hours.'

'Mine not to reason why,' Pauline Thin answered, pulling towards her a pile of letters which she had set on the table.

'Yours *is* to reason why,' Hubert said. 'You can reason as much as you like if you know how to do it. You're free and I'm free to reason about anything. Only keep it to yourself. Don't waste my time. Don't ask me for the reasons. Just put them in order of dates.'

Hubert walked to the door and went out to the shady verandah overlooking the lake. It was a warm day for March. Spring was ready. He thought maybe he had better try to get on well with the girl and start calling her Pauline. She already called him Hubert without asking. His nerves were edgy since, at the beginning of the year, a sequence of financial misfortunes had begun to fall upon him, unexpectedly, shock after shock. Hubert thought of these setbacks as 'curious' and 'unexpected' although, he would presently be brought to reflect, they had not been actually unforeseeable and were linked by no stronger force of coincidence than Maggie's second divorce and a new marriage to an Italian nobleman, probably jealous, and to the deterioration of money in general, and the collapse of a shady company in Switzerland where Hubert had put some of his personal money in the hope of making a fortune. He didn't know quite what to do. But he had one resource. Its precise application was still forming in his mind and wandering lonely as a cloud, and meantime he was short of funds.

The very panorama of Nemi, the lake, the most lush vegetation on earth, the scene which had stirred the imagination of Sir James Frazer at the beginning of his massive testament to comparative religion, *The Golden Bough*, all this magical influence and scene which had never before failed in their effects, all the years he had known the place and in the months he had lived there, suddenly was too expensive. I can't afford the view, thought Hubert and turned back into the room.

The sight of Pauline stacking the papers gave him a slight euphoric turn. There, among the letters and documents of his life, he had that one secret resource and he had decided to exploit it. Maggie could never take Nemi away from him because, spiritually if not actually, the territory of Nemi was his.

Actually, of course, not even the house was his. Maggie was . . . Maggie had been . . . Maggie, Maggie . . .

Pauline Thin was reading one of the letters. Sometimes when a letter was undated it was necessary for her to read it for a clue as to its appropriate place in the various piles of correspondence set out on the table. But Pauline was reading with a happy sort of interest and Hubert was not sure that he could afford Pauline Thin's happiness in her work, seeing she was theoretically paid by the hour. He was not sure, because on the one hand she was paid very little by the hour, and, further, she was greatly to be trusted and he relied on her now more than ever; he was not sure, on the other hand, if he could afford her at all, because, moreover, he owed her a lot of hours' pay, the debt increasing every hour in proportion as the likelihood decreased of his ever discharging it.

Hubert glanced back again at Pauline with her tiny face and her curly hair and felt the absence, now, of Ian, the boy from Inverness, and Damian, the Armenian boy with the curious surname of Runciwell who, as secretary, had been the best secretary, and he missed the other two with their petulance and their demands, their talents for cooking or interior design, their earrings and their neck-chains and their tight blue jeans and twin-apple behinds, fruit of the same tree. He felt their absence without specified regret; it was their kind he missed. Their departure was a fact which still paralysed him, belonging to a time so recent and yet so definitely last summer, in the past.

The morning news had announced the death of Noël Coward, calling it 'the passing of an era.' Everything since Maggie's sudden divorce and equally sudden Italian marriage last year had been to Hubert the passing of an era. Eras pass, thought Hubert. They pass every day. He felt dejected. He cheered up. Then he felt dejected again.

He glanced back at Miss Thin. She had finished reading the apparently absorbing letter and was bending with her back to him over the table stacking the piles of documents neatly. She was broad in the behind, too large. Where is the poetry of my life? Hubert thought. He retained an inkling that the poetry was still there and would return. Wordsworth defined poetry as 'emotion recollected in tranquillity'. Hubert took a tranquillizer, quite a mild one called Mitigil, and knew he would feel better in about ten minutes. To make sure, he took another. In the meantime a familiar white car turned into the drive and stopped before it reached the door. 'Oh God, it's him,' Hubert said and turning to Pauline Thin he called out, 'Miss Thin, this is a tiresome person. Please hang around and keep on bothering me with letters to sign. Remind me emphatically that I have a dinner date this evening. I'll give him one drink. This man's a pathological pest.'

The girl came out to see who had arrived. A medium-sized thin man in a clerical suit had got out of the car, had slammed the door and was walking towards them, smiling and waving.

'He's a Jesuit,' said Hubert, 'from Milwaukee.'

'I've seen him before,' Pauline said. 'He pesters everyone.'

'I know,' Hubert said, feeling friendly towards Miss Thin. He stepped forward a little way to meet the priest.

'Oh, Hubert, this is wonderful to find you in,' said the priest in a voice that twanged like a one-stringed guitar. 'I just drove from Rome as I wanted to talk to you.'

'How are you?' said Hubert politely. 'I'm afraid I'm going to be a bit pressed for time. If you'd have phoned me I could have made a date for you to come to dinner.'

'Oh, oh, are you going out . . . ?'

'About sevenish,' said Hubert putting on a weak smile. It was then sixish. 'I have to go and change soon' – Hubert indicated his old clothes – 'out of these things. Have you met Pauline Thin? – Pauline, this is Father Cuthbert Plaice.'

'Why, I think I know you, Pauline,' said the priest, shaking her hand and, it seemed, trying to locate her in his social register.

'I worked for Bobby Lester in Rome,' Pauline said.

'Why, of course! Yes. Well, now you're here?'

'Yes, I'm here.'

'Hubert, I've got a Jesuit friend down there in the car,' said the priest, 'that I want you to meet. I thought you would like to meet him, he's been studying the ancient ecological cults and in fact he's taken some tape recordings of modern nature-cultists which you have to hear. There are the conscious and the unconscious. It's fascinating. I thought we could have dinner together but anyway I'll just go and call him and we can have a drink. I just wanted to tell you before you meet him, you see, that he's on your wave-length.' The priest made away towards the car stretching one arm behind him as if Hubert were straining away from him at the end of an invisible cord.

'Bloody pest,' said Hubert to Pauline. 'Why should I give them my drinks? He knows – I've told him – that I can't afford those lavish entertainments any more. And dinner – he wanted to stay with his friend for dinner. – He marches in, and one's house isn't one's own. Priests can be very rough people, you know. Such a bore.'

'This one's an awful bore,' said Pauline. 'Bobby Lester couldn't stand him.'

Father Cuthbert was returning with a younger Jesuit of the same size to whom he was talking eagerly.

'Hubert,' he said, when he had reached the verandah, 'I want you to meet Father Gerard Harvey. Gerard has been doing studies of ecolog-

ical paganism and I've told him all about you. Oh, this is Pauline Thin.
She's working for Hubert. I knew Pauline before. She –'

'Come in and have a drink,' said Hubert.

'We can sit right here on the terrace. I want Gerard to see the view.
What marvellous weather! That's the thing about Italy. You can sit
outside in March, and –'

Hubert left them sitting on the terrace and went inside to fetch the
drinks. Pauline followed him. 'Do you want me to stay with them?'
she said.

'Yes, make a nuisance of yourself. Hang around looking silly so
they can't speak freely. Remember I'm supposed to get ready for
dinner in about half an hour's time. These people need to be house-
trained.'

Pauline went out on the terrace and sat down with the two men.

'Have you been in Italy long?' she said to the younger man.

'I've been here six months.'

She looked at her watch. 'Hubert has to go and change very soon,'
she said. 'He's got a long drive ahead to arrive for eight. He has some
letters to sign first.'

'Oh, where's he going?' said Father Cuthbert.

'You shouldn't ask,' she said.

'Well, now, that's not the way to talk,' said Cuthbert, looking very
amazed.

'I guess she isn't a Catholic,' said Gerard soothingly.

'I'm a Catholic,' said Pauline. 'But that's got nothing to do with it.
One doesn't tell people all one's business and all one's employer's
business.'

Hubert appeared with a tray of drinks. The whisky bottle was one
third full and the gin was slightly less. There was a box of ice and a
bottle of mineral water.

'It's terrorism,' said Pauline.

'What's this?' Hubert said, setting down the tray.

'Priests,' said Pauline. 'They're terrorists. They hold you to
ransom.'

The Jesuits looked at each other with delight. This was the sort of
thing they felt at home with, priests being their favourite subject.

'Times have changed,' Hubert said to Pauline, 'since you were at
school at the Sacred Heart, I'm afraid.'

'It isn't so long ago,' Pauline said, 'since I was at school. My last years, I went to Cheltenham.'

Father Gerard said, 'What goes on at Cheltenham?'

'Ladies' College,' said Hubert. 'If you look closely, it's written all over her face.'

'What do you have against us?' Father Cuthbert said, shifting about with excitement in his chair as if he were sexually as much as pastorally roused.

'It seems to me,' Hubert said, turning with gentle treachery towards Pauline, 'a bit inhospitable to carry on this conversation.' His Mitigil had started to work. He had put ice in the glasses. 'What will you drink?' he said to the guests.

'Whisky,' said both priests at once. Hubert looked sadly at his whisky bottle, lifted it and poured.

'Hubert,' said Pauline, 'that's all the whisky we have.'

'Yes,' said Hubert. 'I'm having gin. What about you, Miss Thin?'

'Plain tonic,' said Pauline.

The younger priest sipped his drink and looked out over the still lake in its deep crater and the thick wildwood of Nemi's fertile soil. 'Terrific ecology!' he said.

'You mean the view?' Pauline said.

Hubert sat in a chair with his back to the grand panorama and he sighed. 'I have to give it up,' he said. 'There's nothing for it. The house isn't mine and Maggie's changed so much since her new marriage. They're insisting on charging me rent. A high rent. I have to go.'

'Remember your dinner date,' Pauline said, 'and Hubert, would you sign some letters, please?'

'Dinner date . . . ?' said Hubert. Since Maggie's marriage following on her son Michael's marriage, and since the trouble with his money in Switzerland, he had been asked out less and less. He looked into his little drop of gin, while Father Cuthbert seized on the doubt about dinner. 'You're going to go out for dinner?'

'We've already told you so,' said Pauline.

'Oh, I didn't know if you meant it,' said the priest.

Hubert, remembering, said, 'Oh, yes, I am. I have to go and change very soon, I'm afraid. They eat early, these people.'

'What people?' said Father Cuthbert. 'Do I know them? Could we come along?'

His companion the ecologist began to show embarrassment. He said, 'No, no, Cuthbert. We can go back to Rome. Really, we mustn't intrude like this. Unexpectedly. We have to . . .' He rose and looked nervously towards the car where it was parked half-way down the drive.

'Why don't you go and see Michael?' Hubert said, meaning Maggie's son, whose house was nearby.

Father Cuthbert looked eager. 'Do you know if he's home?'

'I'm sure he is,' said Hubert. 'They're both in Nemi just now. He got married himself recently. Marriage does seem to be a luxury set apart for the rich. I'm sure they'll be delighted to see you.'

While Hubert explained to the excited priest how to get there by car, his friend, Father Gerard, looked around him and across the lake. 'The environment,' he said. 'This is a wonderful environmental location.'

'It's your duty to visit Michael and Mary, really,' Pauline egged them on. 'They have sumptuous dinners. They had a shock when Maggie got divorced and married again, you know. It's been an upset for the Radcliffes. Her new husband's a pig.'

'Don't they see his father?'

'Oh, I dare say,' Hubert said. 'Radcliffe was Maggie's second husband, of course. The new one's the third. But it was so sudden. The family's all right financially of course. But I must say it's left me in a mess, personally speaking.'

When the priests had left, Hubert went with Pauline into the kitchen. He opened a tin of tuna fish while she made a potato salad. They then sat down to eat at the kitchen table, silently, reflectively.

It seemed as if Hubert had forgotten the priests. Pauline, as if anxious that he should not forget a subject that had served to bring them closer, assiduously said, 'Those priests . . .'

At first he didn't respond to the tiny needle. He merely said dreamily, 'It's not too much to wonder if they're not a bit too much,' and took in a mouthful of food.

'But so pressing, so insufferably pushy,' Pauline said, at which Hubert was so roused into agreement, chummily communicating it: 'It's an extraordinary fact,' he said, 'that just at the precise moment when you're at your wits' end it's always the last people in the world you want to see who turn up, full of themselves, demanding total attention. It's always the exceptionally tiresome who barge in at the exceptionally difficult moment. Would you believe there was a time when a Jesuit was a gentleman, if you'll forgive the old-fashioned expression?'

Pauline passed him the potato salad. It had onion, too, in it, and mayonnaise. 'Forget them, Hubert,' she said, plainly intending him not to do so.

But Hubert smiled. 'Miss Thin,' he said as he took the salad bowl from her hand, 'I have inside me a laughter demon without which I would die.'

THREE

'Demons frequented these woods, protectors of the gods. Nymphs and dryads inhabited the place. Have you seen the remains of Diana's temple down there? It's terribly overgrown and the excavations are all filled in, but there's a great deal more to see than you might think.'

'No, I haven't seen it,' said Mary, curling her long legs as she sat, yoga-style, on a cushion on the pavement of the terrace. She was a young long-haired blonde girl from California, newly married to Michael Radcliffe. The priests were entertaining her enormously. She didn't want them to leave and pressed them to stay on for a late dinner. Michael had gone to Rome and wouldn't be back till nine. 'He said nine, which most probably will be ten,' she said.

'Pius the Second,' said Father Gerard, 'said that Nemi was the home of nymphs and dryads, when he passed through this area.'

'Really?'

An Italian manservant, young and dark-skinned in a white coat with shining buttons and elaborate epaulettes, brought in a tray of canapés and nuts which he placed on the terrace table beside the bottles. He looked with recognition at Father Cuthbert who, without looking at the manservant, took a handful of nuts, as also did Father Gerard. The ice clinked in the glasses, and they helped themselves to the drinks when their glasses were empty, refilling Mary's glass too. They were Americans together, abroad, with the unwatchful attitude of co-nationals who share some common experiences, however few.

'I majored in social science,' said Mary, who had been to college in California.

'Did you come to Italy before?' said Father Gerard.

'No, never. I met Michael in Paris. Then we settled here. I love it.'

'How's your Italian?' said the other priest, beaming with idle pleasure – as who would not after two months' continuous residence in the priests' bleak house in Rome, anonymous and detached in its laws of life?

'Oh, my Italian's coming along. I took a crash course. I guess I'll get more fluent. How about yours?'

'Gerard's is pretty good,' said Father Cuthbert. 'He doesn't get enough practice. There are Italians at the Residence of course, but we only talk to the Americans. You know the way it gets. Or maybe the French –'

'Cuthbert speaks almost perfect Italian,' said Father Gerard. 'He's a great help when I'm talking to the locals around the country about their legends and beliefs.'

'Gerard,' said Father Cuthbert, 'is doing a study on pagan ecology.'

'Really? I thought the Italians were mostly all Catholics.'

'On the surface, yes, but underneath there's a large area of pagan remainder to be explored. And absorbed into Christianity. A very rich seam.'

'Well,' said the girl, 'I don't know if you've talked to Hubert Mallindaine about that . . .'

Hubert was a whole new subject, vibrating to be discussed. The priests began to speak in unison, questions and answers, then the girl broke in with laughing phrases and exclamation marks, until Father Cuthbert's voice, being the highest and most excitable, attained the first hearing. The manservant hovered at the terrace door, his eyes upon them, waiting to serve. Mary stretched her fine long suntanned legs and listened. 'We arrived this evening,' said Cuthbert, 'without letting him know in advance. Well, that's nothing new. As a matter of fact the last time I saw him, about six weeks ago, in Rome, he said, "Come to dinner any time. Sure, bring a friend, you're always welcome. There's no need to call me. I never go out. Just get into that car and come." That's what he said. Well. We arrived this evening – didn't we, Gerard?'

'We did,' said Gerard.

A person with a good ear might have questioned the accuracy of Cuthbert's report on the grounds that Hubert, not being American, was not likely to have used a phrase like, 'Sure, bring a friend . . .' But it did seem that the priest had been in the habit of dropping in on Hubert from time to time, whether welcome or not. Clearly he regarded it as his right to do so, anywhere.

'I was embarrassed for Gerard,' Cuthbert was saying, 'especially as this was his first visit, you know. He had an awful secretary, a girl who used to work for another friend of mine in Rome. A terribly –'

Here Gerard broke in, and so did Mary. When they had finished exclaiming over Pauline, Cuthbert continued, 'I think she's got a problem. Then she kept telling Hubert he had to go out to dinner, which I'm sure wasn't true because of the way it was said, you know.' He finished his drink and the manservant came out of the shadows to replenish it. This time Cuthbert recognized the man's face but couldn't at first place it.

The servant lifted the glass with a well-paid and expert air and smiled.

'I know you, don't I?' said Cuthbert to the man.

'It's Lauro,' said Mary. 'He was one of Hubert's secretaries last summer.'

'Why, Lauro, I didn't recognize you in that uniform! Why Lauro!' The priest seemed confused, realizing the man had understood their conversation.

Lauro answered in easy, accented English. 'You surprised to see me here? I lost my job with Hubert and I went to a bar on the Via Veneto then I came back to Nemi to work for Mary and Michael.'

'Lauro's on first-name terms with us,' Mary said. 'The Embassy crowd are shocked. But we don't care.'

Lauro smiled and slipped back to his doorway.

'Lauro could tell you everything you wanted to know about Hubert,' Mary said. Lauro's shadowed form stooped to adjust a rose in a vase. Cuthbert looked carefully at Mary as if to see quite what she had meant by her words, but she had evidently meant far less than she might have done.

'Oh, I like Hubert. Don't misunderstand me,' said Cuthbert, and he looked towards Gerard who gave it as his opinion that Hubert had seemed very likeable.

'Well, I used to like him too,' said Mary. 'And I still do. But when Maggie and her husband number three got kind of mad at him we had to take her part; after all, she's Michael's mother. What can you do? There's been a bad feeling between the houses since Maggie got into this marriage. She wants Hubert to go. He says he won't and he can't pay rent. She's going to put him out. The furniture belongs to Maggie as well. But my, she's finding it difficult. The laws in this country . . . Hubert might get around them forever.'

They sat down to dinner soon after Mary's husband, Michael arrived. They spoke of Hubert most of the time. Hubert was a subject sufficiently close to them to provide a day-to-day unfolding drama and yet it was sufficiently remote, by reason of their wealth, not to matter very much. Hubert himself, since the young couple had ceased to see him, had become someone else than the large-living and smart-spoken old friend they used to know when he was Maggie's favourite. Now that Maggie had turned against him he was, in their mythology, a parasite on society. 'He's not like the old Hubert at all,' Michael said. 'Something's changed him.'

'I dread one day maybe bumping into him in the village,' said Mary. 'I don't know what I'd say.'

First one Jesuit and then the other offered advice as to the coping with this eventuality. So dark, rather short but somehow splendid, Lauro served the meal, assisted by a good-looking maid. The spring evening air from the terrace stood around them like another ubiquitous servant, tendering occasional wafts of a musky creeper's scent. The wine had been sent by Maggie's new husband from his own vineyards in the north.

'Hubert,' said Michael, 'of course considers he is a direct descendant of the goddess Diana of Nemi. He considers he's mystically and spiritually, if not actually, entitled to the place.'

'No kidding!' said Gerard.

'No kidding,' Mary said. 'That's what Hubert believes. It's a family tradition. All the Mallindaines have always believed it. Michael and I met an aunt of his in Paris. She was convinced of it. But I think her health had broken up.'

'She was old,' Michael said.

'Well,' said Gerard, 'I should look into this for my research.'

The other Jesuit said, 'I always thought, you know, the Diana mythology was just an interest of his. I didn't know it was in the family. We'll have to go see him again.'

*

One of the stories to be read from the ancient historians of Imperial Rome is that the Emperor Caligula enjoyed sex with the goddess Diana of Nemi. And indeed, two luxurious Roman ships, submerged for centuries in the lake and brought to land in recent times, have been attributed variously to the purpose of Imperial orgies on the lake of Nemi, and to service in the worship of Diana. These ships were brought to land in reconstructable condition only to be destroyed by some German soldiers during the Second World War; however, their remaining contents and fittings testified to the impression that something highly ritualistic took place on board, well into Christian times, although the worship of Diana at Nemi reaches back into the mythological childhood of the race. Hubert's ancestors . . .

But it is time, now, to take a closer look at Hubert on that spring evening, seeing that he had provided a full and wonderful stream of conversation for the party over there in the other house, where the frank spirits rose higher, Lauro glowed in the shadows and Mary, with her golden Californian colouring, her dark blue eyes and white teeth, was so far stimulated as to repeat for good measure a recent saying of Maggie's: 'The goddess Diana presents her compliments, and desires the company of her kinsman Mr Hubert Mallindaine at the Hunt Ball to be held at Nemi . . .'

Meanwhile, then, Hubert watched Pauline Thin wash up the plates. He carried their coffee through the sitting-room and out to the terrace. 'At my age,' Hubert said, 'I shouldn't drink coffee at night. But, Miss Thin, it doesn't always bear to think of what one should or shouldn't drink. There's a limit to everything.'

'I can see that,' said Pauline, looking out over the marvellous lake.

'Miss Thin,' said Hubert, 'I have decided, I will not leave this house.' Hubert had shaved off his beard shortly after hearing of Maggie's divorce last year in the December of 1972. Then, a week after he had heard, in the following January, that she had married the northern Marquis, he had shaved off his moustache. Not that he felt these actions were in any way connected with Maggie's. It does, however, obscurely seem that in these two shavings he was express-ing some reaction to her divorce and marriage, or, more probably, preparing himself for something, maybe an ordeal, requiring a clean-cut appearance.

He looked younger, now. Pauline Thin who had come to work for him this February, had never known him with his hairy maestro's face. She described him to her best friend in Italy, another English girl who was working in Rome, as 'dishy'.

Hubert was now forty-five. His generally good looks varied from day to day. Sometimes, when she went into Rome for shopping and stopped to lunch with her girlfriend, Pauline described him as 'a bit fagoty'. However that may be, Hubert undoubtedly had good looks, especially when anguished. By a system of panic-action whenever he started to be overweight, he had managed to keep his good line. The panic-system, which consisted of a total fast for a sufficient number of days, never more than twelve, to make him thoroughly skinny and underweight, allowed him then to put on weight comfortably with small indulgences in food and drink which otherwise he would never have enjoyed. Hubert had been told, much earlier in his life, that eventually this course would ruin his health but the event had never happened. Indeed, most of his active life was formed by panic-action and in the interludes he was content to dream or fret or for long periods simply enjoy sweet life. One such of these interludes was just coming to an end, which accounted for the especially good looks of his worried face. He was fairly dark-skinned with light blue eyes and sandy-grey hair. His features were separately nothing much, but his face and the way his head was set on his body were effective. Quite often, he was conscious of his physical assets, but more often he simply forgot them.

This house, with the best view of all Maggie's three houses in the neighbourhood, was furnished richly. After only a year's occupancy this new house still had newness penetrating its bones. Even the antiques, many of them, were new. Maggie had brought back across the water from an apartment high in the air, on the east-sixties of Manhattan, large lifts of itinerant European furniture and pictures. The drawing-room furniture was Louis XIV; there had been six fine chairs, at present only five; one was away in a clever little workshop on the Via di Santa Maria dell'Anima in Rome, being sedulously copied. Hubert was short of money and, almost certain that Maggie would at least succeed in removing the furniture from the house, he was taking reasonable precautions for his future. The new chair was almost finished, and it only remained for the upholstery on the

original to be tenderly removed and fitted on to the fake before
Pauline should be ordered to go into Rome and fetch the chair. She
had been told only that it was being mended. The original would
remain in Rome for a while at Hubert's disposal. Like money in the
bank. Hubert thought of switching and rearranging, perhaps, a few
more items, and maybe, if there was time, another chair. Maggie had
put on the drawing-room floor a seventeenth-century rug; Isfahan.
Hubert brooded upon it: not at all possible to copy with excellence.
He didn't use the drawing-room much these days; the heart had gone
out of it.

Maggie's withdrawal from Hubert had taken place quite slowly. It
was only to him that it seemed abrupt. To him it was the heedless by-
product of a too-rich woman's whim or the effect of her new
husband's influence, the new husband also being rich. But Hubert's
memory was careless. As we have seen, as far back as the previous
summer he was privately lamenting Maggie's lack of chivalry. His
protectress had already started, even before that, to recede. She had
let him occupy the new house, as one silently honouring a bad
bargain; the house had been ordered to his taste more than three
years before it was ready. But it was during those three years and
more while the house was being made that she had gradually stopped
confiding in him and even before that, perhaps, the disaffection and
boredom of the relationship had set in for Maggie.

Hubert had been uneasy about his position, really, for many years
more than he now admitted when he thought or spoke of Maggie.
'Like any other spoilt moneybags she used me when she needed me
and then suddenly told me to go, to clear out of her house and her
life. All my projects were based on her promises. We had an understanding . . .' So he dramatized it in a nutshell, first to himself, then,
later, to Pauline Thin.

Pauline assumed there had been a love affair till one night, when
he was confiding in her for the sheer lack of anyone else to talk to
about himself, he remarked, 'I never touched a woman. I love women
but I never went near one. It would break the spell. There's a magic
. . . women are magic. I can't live without women around me. Sex is
far, far away out of the question in my mind where women are concerned.'

Which bewildered Pauline. Quickly rearranging her ideas, and in the spirit of the missionaries of old who held that conversion was only a matter of revealing the true doctrine, she ended with the conviction that he had not yet met a truly appetizing, faithful woman and decided more than ever to stick by Hubert in these reduced days of his.

FOUR

'Lo, Nemi! navell'd in the woody hills
So far, that the uprooting wind which tears
The oak from his foundation, and which spills
The ocean o'er its boundary, and bears
Its foam against the skies, reluctant spares
The oval mirror of thy glassy lake;
And calm as cherish'd hate, its surface wears
A deep cold settled aspect nought can shake,
All coil'd into itself and round, as sleeps the snake.'

'It's a perfect description,' said Nancy Cowan, the English tutor. 'Can you imagine what Byron meant by "calm as cherished hate"? – It's mysterious, isn't it? – Yet perfectly applicable. One can see that in the past, the historic long-ago, there was some evil hidden under the surface of the lake. Many evils, probably. Pagan customs were cruel. "Cherished hate" is a great evil, anyway.'

Her pupils pondered, perhaps being nice enough to feel they had missed the point. Letizia, a girl of eighteen, was not quite sure what the phrase meant. 'Hatred,' explained the tutor, 'which has been kept hidden, secret, never expressing itself behind its impassive face. That's why the poet wrote "calm as cherished hate".'

'It's very good,' said Pietro. He was twenty. Both Letizia and Pietro were cramming for entrance exams to American colleges.

The villa at Nemi where they sat in early summer with the English teacher had no view at all of the lake. One could only glimpse the castle tower from one of the windows. It was the third of Maggie Radcliffe's houses, the newly-restored one, recently let to the family. Letizia, a passionate Italian nationalist with an ardour for folklore and the voluntary healing of youthful drug-addicts, resented very much the fact that her father rented the house from an American. She was

against the foreign ownership of Italian property, held that the youth
of Italy was being corrupted by foreigners, especially in the line of
drugs, and asserted herself, with her light skin and hair, large-boned
athletic shapelessness, and religious unbelief, to be a representative of
the new young Italy. The father, who was divorced from the mother,
was extremely rich. Letizia was in no accepting frame of mind to
study for an American university entrance, and had already almost
converted Miss Cowan, the tutor, to her view. Her brother Pietro,
dark-eyed, long-lashed, with a pale oval face, wanted very much to be
in a film and then to direct a film, and whenever he was free he spent
his time among the courtiers of famous film directors, skimming the
speed-routes by day and by night in his Porsche, his St Christopher
medal dangling on his chest, speeding the length of the boot of Italy
and back to be with some group of young men who clustered round
the film director wherever the film should be in the making. Italy is a
place much given to holding court. Pietro, when he was not at one or
another court, was happier at home now than he had been in recent
years because of the presence of Nancy Cowan.

She was thirty-six, well-informed, rather thin, long-nosed, tender-
hearted towards anyone within her immediate radius at any one time.
She had come in answer to an advertisement in *The Times*, bringing
her Englishness, her pale summer dresses, her sense of fair play, and
many other foreign things with her. Letizia had been at first delighted
to find that the English tutor was so easy to walk all over in intellectual matters; it was as if Miss Cowan had anything you like instead
of views of society or political stands. But at times she suspected that
Nancy Cowan really didn't feel it worth while to give her own opinions; sometimes it almost seemed, in fact, as if Nancy was making
herself agreeable to either the brother or the sister simply because
they mattered very little to her. Letizia, when this feeling struck her,
would force her own views the more strongly, and would sometimes
speak her mind to the point of insult. Pietro thought Nancy's malle-
ability to be very feminine, and with an intuitive artistic sense of
economy, he set out to get his father's money's worth out of her in his
studies. It seemed likely that their father was already sleeping with
her. It would have been possible to find out for sure, but Pietro felt
too young and sex-free to make the effort; it would have been
unhealthy, indelicate, but Pietro one night when they were taking

their coffee after dinner in the garden, from the way Nancy Cowan responded to the night-beauty, decided that his father had wooed and won her there. She was also better-looking in the moonlight, quite handsome as in a film; and then, again, the manner towards Nancy of the big fat whiney parlour maid, Clara, told Pietro something. He supposed it also told Letizia something, but he didn't expect Letizia to acknowledge any such unsevere facts about their father or their English tutor. It was thoroughly in keeping, though, that Papa was getting as full value out of Nancy Cowan, as was she from the job.

The brother and sister sat reading Byron with Nancy in the shady garden a few yards from the house. It was six in the afternoon. To humour Letizia, Nancy had bent her English lessons in the direction of local lore. A poor rescued drug-addict in the wreckage of his twenties was cleaning out the swimming-pool under the direction of a gardener and fat Clara. This simple operation made a terrific background noise since Clara's only tone for all occasions was one of lament, and the gardener, in trying to make a simple instruction penetrate the saved youth's brain, treated him as if he were hard of hearing. The youth, who had been brought in by Letizia from Rome that morning, would be given a meal and an old pair of Pietro's trousers for his services before he was taken back to the welfare centre. A few such garden chores got done in this way; only garden chores, since Letizia did not bring these strange people into the house for fear of what they might see and be tempted either to take away or send their friends to procure. To her father, Letizia's protégés were more or less what in the old days were gypsies. To the eyes of Nancy Cowan they were young drug-addicts just like the London variety. Letizia referred to them as 'our new social phenomena' and this, oddly enough, was the title they liked best; they seemed to respond to Letizia, to her statistics and her sociological language which apparently gave them a status in life, and it was rarely that any one of them attempted to take undue advantage of her or ask her for money. Mostly they demonstrated an allergy to Pietro with his Bulgari steel watch, his Gucci shoes and belt, his expensive haircut, and with his Porsche being endlessly cleaned by the house's young lodge-keeper in overalls.

Big Clara lumbered up from the pool to the house, clutching her heart. She was not yet fifty but she looked much older and yet behaved like a child of twelve which evidently she still felt herself to be. 'A headache,' she said in her babyish whine. 'It's too hot. You need a professional to clean out the pool. He'll never understand the chlorine. I've got a headache. He has no capacity. You need a man, a real man. He'll never learn.'

Letizia sprang up from her seat beside Nancy Cowan, full of what it took to cope with Clara in their native tongue. Letizia's young skin glowed in the late afternoon, her pale blue eyes had a fishy bulge. She swung around in her folklore skirt, her red platform clogs and smocked blouse, gesticulating with her healthy arms. As a specimen, Letizia at eighteen was rounded-off and complete; the finishing touches were already put, there was no room for further contention between character and contours, there was scope only, now, for wear and tear. She was much as she would be, she thought much as she would think, and looked not much different from what she would look, at forty-eight.

The grumbling servant having been coped with, Letizia returned to her garden chair beside her brother and Nancy, with a grin full of healthy teeth.

Nancy Cowan held out her hand for the copy of Byron which Pietro had taken to look at.

'He must have come here in winter,' Pietro said, 'since he wrote about the wind tearing up the oak tree.'

Letizia leaned over Nancy Cowan to examine the lines. 'He says the wind spares the lake, which is true. Nemi is a very secluded spot. Was Byron at Nemi in winter, then?'

'Look, you'll have to get a Life of Byron . . .'

'I think Papa has a biography of Byron. Pietro, do you know?'

'. . . something you ought to know about, though. Byron's always –'

'He was a lame lord . . .' Pietro had taken the book from Nancy and was reading aloud from the biographical foreword to the poems: '. . . a spendthrift and a rake . . .'

'What is that – spendthrift . . . ?' Pietro reached for the dictionary. Nancy Cowan began explaining Byron while the air grew cooler, the light faded over the lawn and Letizia suddenly recollected a bit of Byron's history from her earlier schooldays.

Just then Letizia was called to the telephone and cursing in Italian went indoors to answer it.

Nancy caught Pietro looking closely at her, and turned her head to look back into his face.

'Would it embarrass you if I asked you a question?' he said.

'You've just asked me an embarrassing one,' she said to gain ground, and was never to know what Pietro's other embarrassing question might be, for Letizia returned by way of the kitchen door to say, 'Papa has asked our landlady to dinner. She phoned Papa at the office. Her name was Mrs Radcliffe but she got married again to an Italian. La Radcliffe wants to see us.'

'What's she like?' Nancy said.

'We've never seen her. She rents the house through an agent. She's a rich American, Madame Radcliffe, and now she's a Marchesa married to a nobleman from the north. I hate Papa for renting a house from an American in our own country. It should be round the other way. Why doesn't Papa buy a villa?'

'Italians own property in England,' said Nancy.

'That is different. They settled there for two, three generations. They was poor.' Letizia looked angry, unable to clarify her thoughts, if indeed her feelings existed in thought-form. She slightly lost her grip on correct English. 'There is many reasons,' she said. 'Here in Italy the foreigners takes everything.'

'Maybe you're right,' said Nancy. 'I really hadn't thought of it before.' She thought of it now, looking with purely formal anxiety into the distance.

'This was an old Italian villa, the foundations are ancient Roman,' said the girl calming down a little, 'then along came an American woman with the money. She restores the house. She's got other houses, all over Nemi, full of foreigners. We're the only Italians and we pay her rent. Papa pays a huge rent. We had to put in a downstairs sitting-room. Before there was no sitting-room downstairs. We had to make over one of the garages at Papa's expense. Papa likes the house so he pays and pays.'

The large maid came out with a tray of drinks and ice, wearing a baleful expression. Nancy smiled at her but this made Clara close her eyes as if in pain.

'You shouldn't criticize foreigners in Nancy's presence,' said Pietro. He was hoping to get a part in a foreign film just at that time and although it was unlikely that their English tutor had many friends among the thousands of foreigners in Italy, far less the Americans who were making the film, he felt there was nothing to lose by shutting his sister up a bit.

'But Papa pays her to help us with our English and we're talking English,' Letizia said. 'And tonight we have to talk English at dinner for our landlady.'

Their father's car could be heard coming up the drive, whereupon Nancy Cowan smiled.

A sixteenth-century refectory table with some antique chairs from Tuscany waited for the party in a green damask dining-room. Some special-looking green and gold china was arranged on shelves in four flood-lit alcoves. The candles were all ready to be lit in the silver candlesticks, the table was set for six, which meant that the seats were twice as far apart as they need have been. Letizia looked sulkily over the table, said nothing one way or another to the waiting manservant, then left the room through folding doors which led to the drawing-room. The manservant slipped out of another door to report, apparently, no complaints.

In the drawing-room Letizia's father sat back on a sofa with his contented drink. Nancy Cowan sat by his side, tentatively and upright, near the edge of the seat. Letizia, coming in from the dining-room, said, 'We should have dined in the north room. The green dining-room is far too formal for six.'

The father, Dr Emilio Bernardini, elegantly thin with a pale skin and rather beautiful, very dark eyes behind a pair of scholarly spectacles, black-glossy hair and sharply defined eye-brows, had a look of the portraits of the Stuart monarchs. He was a business lawyer occupied between Rome, Milan and Zürich; in fact, a good part of his business was real estate, and the reason he had yet to sell his own family villa and had chosen to rent from Maggie Radcliffe the one in which he now sat was presumably known only to himself. Although it annoyed his daughter she was too well-fabricated within the business world of Italy to believe she could persuade the father to buy rather than rent. Whatever his reason, it was definitely in his own interest.

He replied in Italian, carelessly, that the dining-room was best for their landlady's visit. Pietro, in the meantime, was telling Nancy he admired her dress.

Nancy answered, in correct Italian, that it was a new one. She added, 'After my first long stay in Italy when I saw how Italians dressed, I felt I was underdressed in my London things, so I always get some clothes for the evening when I come to stay here.'

'Do you mean we're overdressed?' said the charming father of the family.

'In England, at this moment, for this occasion, we would be quite overdressed.'

The father contemplated his children and then herself with some happiness. 'I think we all look very elegant,' he said. 'I'm glad we overdo it. Not long ago we overdid it far more.'

A new young man was shown in, whom Letizia had hastily summoned to dinner to make a respectable number. He, at least, had not overdone it, but was wearing a dingy, grey cotton round-necked shirt and dark trousers, both very much too tight. He was small and plump, bulging with little rolls of flesh under the arms, above the belly, all over; it seemed he had never even started to care what he looked like; Letizia introduced him as Marino Vesperelli, adding, for her father's sake, that he was a Professor of Psychology. Dr Bernardini took him in good part, cast a hand to indicate a seat, rose to ask him what he would drink. At which Letizia took over, and the young man followed her to the wagon of bottles and ice at the far end of the room. Emilio Bernardini then murmured to Nancy, 'I hate to think of *him* breathing all over my daughter.'

'Maybe he's just a friend.'

'Where does she pick them up?'

'I expect this one works with her in her welfare work.'

'He needs a bit of welfare himself,' said the father.

However, as soon as the young psychologist had sat down with his drink Dr Bernardini tried to engage him in conversation as to his profession. The young man answered briefly and asked no return questions; plainly he felt that his odd-looking presence was sufficient social contribution to the evening; which, in its decided oddity, it rather was.

'There's a car arriving; it must be *her*,' said Pietro.

Maggie Radcliffe was so much in the long, long habit of making heads swim when she came into view that she still did so. She looked somewhere in her late forties but the precise age was irrelevant to the effect which was absolutely imperious in its demands for attention; and what was more, Maggie achieved it carelessly. She cared only, and closely, about what was going on around her. And so, as soon as she had given her hand to everyone in the room, she started to admire the Bernardinis' pictures whose authors she recognized, one by one. Still administering her entrance like drops of heart-medicine, she turned to the owner and reminded him how the Klimt over the mantelpiece had very nearly remained in the Austrian collection, thus establishing with him the higher market-place communion that exists between rich and rich.

Nancy Cowan stood waiting for the special guest to sit down. She pulled, through her dress, at the top of her panty-hose, setting herself to rights like a schoolgirl. She then moved her finger under her hair at the nape of her neck. Maggie sat down. The men sat down. Maggie, on being asked what she would drink, turned to the uncomely young psychologist and asked him what he was drinking.

'Sherry on the rocks,' he said.

Maggie gave a soundless laugh, looking towards her host in merry collusion, and said she would have a vodka-tonic. She had overdressed very tastefully, with a mainly-white patterned dress, brilliant against her shiny sun-tan. Her hair was silver-tipped, her eyes large and bright. She had a flood-lit look up to the teeth.

The air-conditioner was turned off before dinner seeing that the evening was cool. The windows of the dining-room were opened to the breeze of the Alban hills. They sat at the long refectory table, spaced out, murmuring pleasantly one to the other, waiting to be served. Emilio Bernardini at the top of the table had Maggie on his right, Nancy on his left. Letizia sat facing him with Pietro on her left and her boy-friend in his chair on her right.

Wine, water, avocado, sauce. 'What do you think of your villa, Marchesa, now that we're in it?'

'You've made it charming, more delightful than I remembered having seen it before,' Maggie said.

'We made some alterations,' Letizia said. 'We had to get workmen. One of the garages is now a downstairs sitting-room. Otherwise, there wasn't –'

'I know,' said Maggie. 'My agent mentioned it.'

'The Marchesa must see it later,' said the father.

'Yes, I must,' said Maggie.

'If we're speaking English why do you say "Marchesa",' said Letizia, '"Marchioness" is English.'

Pietro said, 'Because it sounds nicer.'

'Oh, yes, it does,' Maggie said and laid down her little spoon to drink some water. 'And "Signora" would be better. "Mrs" and "Miss" make you close your mouth for the ms but for "Signora" and "Signorina" you don't shut your mouth. "Mrs" and "Miss" form a sneer but "Signora" and "Signorina" are a hiss.'

Marino the psychologist leaned forward to catch Maggie's drift, puzzled. The others laughed while Letizia explained the point to Marino in rapid Italian undertones. He said, 'Why is a hiss better than a sneer?'

'It's better,' said the father as the glasses were filled with his good wine.

'Anyway,' said Maggie, 'Signora is perfectly all right for me as I'm now married to an Italian and Italy's a republic.'

'The Signora is of course the Marchesa di Tullio-Friole,' said Dr Bernardini with his cool good manners, at the same time drawing a line at any excess of a tiresome subject arising from Maggie's logic.

'Oh, Marchesa is so formal. It suits me only when I'm with my husband.'

'I was at school with his son, Pino,' said Dr Bernardini. 'I remember your husband very well. I stayed at the villa up in the Veneto, often. I've hunted there.'

'Then you must come again,' said Maggie. 'He's there now, seeing to the alterations to my bathroom.'

The candles flickered. Came the spinach soufflé, the crumbed veal and salad, the lemon ice and the fruit, while Maggie talked on about the two other houses she owned in the neighbourhood, her son's and Hubert Mallindaine's.

'Mr Mallindaine's is new,' said Letizia sharply, 'but your son's house is a sixteenth-century farm-house.'

Pietro said he had always admired the old farm-house. He seemed uneasy about his sister.

'It should be in Italian hands,' Letizia said. 'Our national patrimony.'

'It cost a fortune to put right,' Maggie said.

The father intercepted Letizia's foreseen reaction to say that he understood Maggie had restored the old house beautifully, and built the new house beautifully as well.

Pietro, it seemed, knew the young Radcliffes and had been to their house.

'Oh, those are the Americans you spoke of?' This was Letizia again, so much so that her boy-friend laughed. 'What's funny?' said Letizia, seeing that the others were laughing.

'Something,' said Maggie, 'about the way you said "Americans".'

'Letizia, don't be silly,' said the father.

Letizia said, 'Shall we have coffee outside, Papa?' Then, as she led the way through the french windows to the upper terrace, she said, 'I believe in Italy for the Italians.'

'Letizia!' said Emilio.

'You are so impolite,' said her brother.

'What about the English?' said Nancy. 'Are we unwanted here?'

'The English the same,' Letizia said as she waited for her guests to be seated.

The father was explaining to Maggie. 'It's only a toy gun she's playing with, or at least, a gun filled with blanks.'

Letizia said 'Oh!' protestingly.

Maggie said, 'Oh, I agree with her, really I do. I think the Americans soon won't be able to afford to stay in Italy. You know, since I married an Italian, I feel myself to be an Italian.'

The young psychologist said to the father, 'You talk of guns, Dr Bernardini. Playing with guns. That's interesting.'

'It's a sexual image,' Maggie said, and they all laughed except Letizia and her boy-friend.

Letizia sat down and the coffee was brought to the terrace table. Letizia started pouring while Nancy took round the cups. 'And the third house?' Letizia said.

'An Englishman,' Maggie said. 'As a matter of fact, Dr Bernardini, he's my problem. He's the problem I wanted to ask you about.'

'It's a beautiful house,' said the father. 'It must have a wonderful view.'

'It has the best view of all three houses,' Maggie said looking one by one at her rings. 'And what's more, the furniture is mine. Every piece. I've given him notice to quit.'

'But he belongs to Nemi,' said Letizia.

'Who belongs to Nemi?' said Pietro.

'The occupant. The Englishman. He has an ancestral claim.'

Emilio Bernardini called for the brandy and liqueurs.

'He has to quit,' Maggie said. 'My husband insists.' She turned to Emilio. 'You know,' she said, 'what Italians are like, of the old school. Very conservative. And really, I admire it.'

'In our country it's difficult to get rid of tenants,' Emilio said, not anxious to take the landlady's part against a tenant so near at hand. 'Very difficult indeed.'

'He pays no rent,' Maggie said. 'He has been a guest for a year and now his welcome is outworn.'

'I'm not sure we can help you,' Emilio said, as if reinforced by the rest of the company.

'I thought we might, perhaps, get up a neighbourhood petition,' said Maggie, prompt, too, with her 'we'. She added, 'My son and daughter-in-law, of course, will –'

'It would make a scandal,' Pietro said.

'But he himself is quite a scandalous person,' said Maggie. 'I'm sure you must have heard –'

'There is a secretary but no scandal. Miss Cowan knows her, don't you, Nancy?'

'Well, I wouldn't say I know her,' Nancy said. 'I believe I met her in Rome one time at the house of some English friends. She had a job in Rome.'

'Well,' said Maggie, 'before this secretary there were boys.'

'It's a Mediterranean custom and in Italy not a crime,' the host said. 'I sympathize with you, Marchesa, but a petition . . .' – he spread his hands – '. . . a petition to get a man out of his house because of boys . . . The scandal would fall on us, definitely, as Pietro says.'

'What does your lawyer say?' said the psychologist.

'Oh, he's working on it,' said Maggie, somewhat vaguely and without conveying much enthusiasm for her lawyer.

'But Mr Mallindaine has a claim to Nemi,' said Letizia. 'His ancestry goes back to ancient times. He can prove it.'

'You know him well?' Maggie said.

'No, I don't know him at all, but I heard –'

'Well, I,' said Maggie, bending her head sorrowfully, 'know him well.' Since the subject of Hubert had been discussed, she seemed to have been unexpectedly put in the position of asking for an unwelcome favour; her looks seemed to have lost their sensational quality.

In bed that night Emilio Bernardini said to Nancy, 'She's an animal.'

'She looked stunning when she came in.'

'Animals can look stupendous. I wonder what she really wanted to see me about. She rang me in the office this afternoon and said she'd like to see me. I asked her to dinner. I wonder if she just wanted to see what we'd done to her house.'

'I think she wanted you to help her get the other tenant out.'

'He was probably her lover.'

'No. No, he wasn't. He likes boys.'

'He could take women too, I suppose.'

'No, they had a long relationship but there wasn't any sex in it,' Nancy said, lying beside him in the cool of the summer night, under the thin white sheet.

'I don't believe it. Who would believe it?'

Nancy cast aside her half of the sheet and stretched her body. Her underdeveloped skinniness and boniness was, if it was not regarded as a defect, her considerable speciality; so that without her clothes she was changed, in Emilio's view, from a nobody into a somebody. 'What are you thinking of?' she asked her lover.

'I'm admiring your non-figure,' said Emilio. 'You look so much as if you need a good dinner.'

'I had a good dinner,' she said. 'Maybe I don't look very lovable but I don't care.'

'How seldom one falls in love with the lovable!' he said. 'How seldom . . . Hardly ever.'

'How do you know when you're in love?' she said.

'The traffic in the city improves and the cost of living seems to be very low.'

'A typical business-man, about forty-three, I should imagine rather conceited,' said Maggie, 'with a son who looks like a gigolo, a daughter, a kind of Girl Guide, I couldn't stand the girl; then there was a downtrodden English governess and the girl's boy-friend, awful little fellow from under some stone. The only good thing about them was their house, which isn't theirs, it's mine.'

'Oh, but I know Pietro and Michael likes him,' her daughter-in-law said.

'I admit the son was the best of the lot,' Maggie said, 'but it isn't saying much. Very bourgeois; of course they were terrified of lifting a finger to help me get Hubert out.'

'I'll do everything I can to help you,' Mary said eagerly. She was terribly anxious to make a success of her marriage, as she would put it; her father was a success and her mother was a well-known success in advertising although she didn't by any means need the job; moreover, Mary's elder sister was busy making a success of her marriage. Mary had been successfully brought up, neither too much nor too little indulged. And so, still half under the general anaesthetic of her past years, Mary was not disposed to regard Maggie as critically as she would have done had Maggie not been her mother-in-law; it was part of making a success of her marriage. 'So long as I'm here on the spot, Maggie,' Mary said, 'I'll do my best.'

'I know I was foolish to let things get this way,' Maggie said. 'I realize that. It was just that when I was married to Ralph Radcliffe I got just so bored, I just took on a number of artists and intellectuals in a number of cities, and I just . . . Well, Hubert of course was really sort of someone, I really helped him to be what he was, but he's not all that a somebody. He's better known in Paris, of course, or rather was a few years back – after *Ce Soir Mon Frère*, that play, you know –'

'Oh yes! Did Hubert produce it?' Mary said.

'No, Hubert wrote it. Well, I took –'

'Was it a success?' Mary said.

'Well, in Paris it was. So I took Hubert on more and more. He was doing this play. And after a couple of years he was doing another. I helped him a lot with funds and so on, the rent. Sometimes he'd give me a bit of advice about pictures, when we went to the galleries, New York and Paris. Then, well, there was advice and counsel about so much furniture and rugs. He has taste and knowledge, but of course that's not everything. Then you know he kind of took over my life; even when I was away I felt dependent, I felt trapped, and I couldn't rely on Michael's father as a husband, not at all; no, Ralph Radcliffe couldn't have cared less. Of course, Hubert's friendship with me was only platonic.'

'So what were you getting out of it?' Mary said.

'Exactly. In the end, that's what I asked. But who would believe it if there was a scandal? And you know these houses at Nemi, it was Hubert's idea to invest in this way; he found two houses for me, and of course he wanted one for himself on that piece of land. I don't regret the houses, they're all good properties and appreciating in value, only I want out, out, out, where Hubert is concerned. When I remarried I told Berto about Hubert still occupying one of my houses, and all the best furniture in it. Berto said, "You're crazy, Maggie, crazy. He's a hanger-on. Just get him out. Tell him to go." But it's difficult, you know.'

'Hubert has the nerve!' said Mary. 'The nerve of him! I heard that he had a house full of queers last summer.'

'Yes, but I stopped the money. When I married Berto he said, "Stop sending money. Stop the money order at the bank." I didn't really know what to do. It's really hypnotic when you get in someone's clutches. Berto said, "Why are you hesitating? What are you afraid of? Just write and tell him you're stopping the money." Berto said he would write it himself, if I wanted. I said, "Well, Berto, he knows you don't need the money and neither do I, and I don't give him very much." So –'

'That's not the point,' Mary said.

'Right. That's precisely what Berto said. It isn't the point. But now Hubert's being so stubborn, I don't want a scandal, especially as you and Michael live here and like it so much. It's a problem.'

'It's a very, very big problem,' said Mary, eager to be entirely with Maggie. 'It's a tremendous problem.'

'And there's that lesbian secretary living with him,' Maggie said.

'Is she lesbian?'

'I guess so. What else would she be?'

'I guess that's right,' said Mary.

'She couldn't be normal, living there with him.'

'Well, it could be platonic like when you were friends with him,' Mary said, 'but I guess it isn't.'

'A lesbian,' Maggie said, adding, as if to make her real point, 'a penniless lesbian.' With that much off her chest, Maggie now started to praise Hubert by little bits, placing Mary, who also had a few pleasant memories of Hubert, in a state of assenting duplicity.

'He has been careful of the furniture,' Maggie said. 'He appreciates fine furniture and understands it. In fact he helped me choose it. And now I hear he still sends the Louis XIV chairs to an antique expert in Rome to be checked regularly and put right if there's any little thing loose or frayed, you know, and maybe the wood treated. I heard only the other day. In some ways, Hubert was very thoughtful for me.'

'It's expensive, the maintenance of antiques,' Mary said. 'My father's –'

'Oh, I know. He can't be all that short of money, can he?'

Mary said, 'I'll find out what I can.'

'Not that it matters to me,' Maggie said. 'Only, I mean, he can't be all that badly off if he's looking after my furniture, can he?'

'No, he can't.'

'He didn't open the door to the official whom my lawyer sent with a notice to quit. Pretended he was out.'

'But he'd have to let *you* in,' Mary said. 'Why don't you go yourself and have it out with him? A confrontation is always the best.'

'Do you think so?'

'Well, maybe. I don't know. I mean, most of the time a confrontation is healthy when a relationship goes wrong.'

'There's nothing wrong with the relationship,' Maggie said. 'On my side, everything's the same. I just don't want to go on keeping him, that's all. No explanation necessary. I just don't want to go on.'

'I hear he changed the locks on all the doors.'

'Who told you that?' Maggie said.

'Pietro, the Bernardini son. He told us their tutor learned it from Hubert's secretary. They changed all the locks so your keys won't fit.'

'I wouldn't dream,' Maggie said wildly, 'of breaking into the house without his permission. What's he think I am? He's not all that bad.'

'Sure, he's got very good points. Very, very good points.'

'It would be nice,' Maggie said speaking softly now, 'to think he wasn't in need of actual food. I hope he has enough to eat.'

'He couldn't afford a secretary if he hasn't enough to eat,' Mary said in an equally low voice.

'Well, I don't know,' Maggie said, 'and it makes me thoughtful. There are young secretaries foolish enough to work free for a man if they believe in him. And Hubert's secretary, the little time I saw her passing in that station-wagon of his, it was only once, for a second, I don't know . . . She may have ideas for the future.'

'But she's a lesbian!' Mary said.

'Who knows? Lesbians like to hook a man too, you know. Sex isn't everything. She might want a cover. And so might he.'

'Well, if he hasn't enough to eat he'll be starved out,' Mary said.

'Then there's the electricity, the gas and the telephone. They'll be cut off if the bills aren't paid,' Maggie said, and her voice had taken completely to a whisper, as if an utterance of such things could be unlucky.

'That will solve your problem, then,' Mary said. 'He'll have to leave.'

'Do you believe in the evil eye?' said Maggie still speaking very low.

'Well, no,' said Mary whispering back in concert, 'I believe I don't.' She bent closer to Maggie.

'It's possible,' Maggie breathed, 'that if there is such a thing, Hubert has the evil eye. His name, Mallindaine, is supposed to be derived from an old French form, "malline" which means of course malign, and "Diane" with the "i" and the "a" reversed. He told me once, and as he explained it, the family reversed those syllables as a kind of code, because of course the Church would have liquidated the whole family if their descent from a pagan goddess was known. And they always worshipped Diana. It was a stubborn family tradition, apparently.'

'It sounds very superstitious,' Mary said in her hush.

'I wouldn't think Hubert was malign, would you?' Maggie whispered.

'No, I wouldn't think that, I think he's a bum, that's all,' Mary said, shifting in her garden chair, while the treetops on the slope below their house rustled in a sudden warm gust of air and the dark lake showed through the branches, calm, sheltered by the steep banks.

'It makes me uneasy,' Maggie said. 'Could you keep a secret?' She moved her chair a little nearer to the daughter-in-law.

'Sure.'

'Even from Michael?'

'Well, if it wouldn't make any difference to our marriage . . .' Mary said.

'I don't see how it could as it only concerns Hubert and me,' Maggie whispered.

'Oh, sure I can keep a secret,' the girl whispered back eagerly, as if the confidence might otherwise be withdrawn altogether.

'I want to send Hubert money from time to time. But he mustn't know it comes from me,' Maggie said. 'I also have to think of my marriage. Berto insists that I throw Hubert out. Well, I have to keep trying, and in a way I want to.'

'You don't have to tell Berto everything, do you?'

'He wants to know everything,' Maggie said. 'He's the old-fashioned Italian, it's part of the charm.'

'I can see that,' said the girl.

'How can I get this money to Hubert without him guessing?'

'Is it a lot of money?'

'Well, if I decide on a sum . . . enough for him to live on here at Nemi while I'm trying to get him out of the house.'

'I don't think I follow, really,' said Mary. 'But I see what you mean in a way.'

'It's a paradox,' Maggie said. 'But Hubert mustn't know how I feel.'

'He'd think you were frightened of him.'

They talked in hushes late into the afternoon.

'We're going a long way but we aren't getting anywhere,' Maggie said as the air grew cooler.

'I wish I could talk it over with Michael.'

'No! Michael would put a stop to it.'

'So he would, I guess. I'll try to think of a scheme.'

'You have to help me.'

'I'll help you, Maggie.'

They looked down on the incredible fertility beneath them. A head and small flash of face every now and again bobbed out of the trees as the country people came and went; one of these, approaching up a path through the dense woodland, presently emerged clearly as Lauro returning. He appeared and disappeared ever larger, seeming to spring from the trees a fuller person at every turn. A little to the north was a corner of Hubert's roof, and under the cliff below him at a point where the banks of the lake spread less steeply into a small plain lay the cultivated, furrowed and planted small fields of flowers and the dark green density of woodland that covered what Frazer in *The Golden Bough* described as 'the scene of the tragedy'.

The scene of the tragedy lay directly but far below Hubert's house, and meanwhile the stars contended with him. 'Hoping to inherit the earth as I do,' he said, 'I declare myself meek.'

This tragedy was only so in the classical and dramatic sense; its participants were in perfect collusion. In the historic sense it was a pathetic and greedy affair. The recurrent performance of the tragedy began before the dates of knowledge, in mythology, but repeating itself tenaciously well into known history.

The temple of the goddess Diana was, from remote antiquity, a famous pilgrim resort. To guard her sanctuary, Diana Nemorensis, Diana of the Wood, had a court of attendants ruled over by a powerful high priest. Legends and ancient chronicles have described this figure and it was upon him that J. G. Frazer's great curiosity was centred. Here is Frazer's celebrated account of the priesthood of Diana and its 'tragedy':

In the sacred grove there grew a certain tree round which at any time of the day, and probably far into the night, a grim figure might be seen to prowl. In his hand he carried a drawn sword, and he kept peering warily about him as if at every instant he expected to be set upon by an enemy. He was a priest and a murderer; and the man

for whom he looked was sooner or later to murder him and hold
the priesthood in his stead. Such was the rule of the sanctuary. A
candidate for the priesthood could only succeed to office by slaying
the priest, and having slain him, he retained office till he was
himself slain by a stronger or craftier.

The post which he held by this precarious tenure carried with it
the title of king; but surely no crowned head ever lay uneasier, or
was visited by more evil dreams, than his. For year in year out, in
summer and winter, in fair weather and in foul, he had to keep his
lonely watch, and whenever he snatched a troubled slumber it was
at the peril of his life. The least relaxation of his vigilance, the
smallest abatement of his strength of limb or skill of fence, put
him in jeopardy; grey hairs might seal his death-warrant . . .
According to one story the worship of Diana at Nemi was institu-
ted by Orestes, who, after killing Thoas, king of the Tauric
Chersonese (the Crimea), fled with his sister to Italy, bringing with
him the image of the Tauric Diana hidden in a faggot of sticks.
After his death his bones were transported from Aricia to Rome
and buried in front of the temple of Saturn, on the Capitoline
slope, beside the temple of Concord. The bloody ritual which
legend ascribed to the Tauric Diana is familiar to classical readers;
it is said that every stranger who landed on the shore was sacrificed
on her altar. But transported to Italy, the rite assumed a milder
form. Within the sanctuary at Nemi grew a certain tree of which
no branch might be broken. Only a runaway slave was allowed to
break off, if he could, one of its boughs. Success in the attempt
entitled him to fight the priest in single combat, and if he slew him
he reigned in his stead with the title of King of the Wood (*Rex
Nemorensis*). According to the public opinion of the ancients the
fateful branch was that Golden Bough which, at the Sibyl's
bidding, Aeneas plucked before he essayed the perilous journey to
the world of the dead. The flight of the slave represented, it was
said, the flight of Orestes; his combat with the priest was a remi-
niscence of the human sacrifices once offered to the Tauric Diana.
This rule of succession by the sword was observed down to imperial times; for amongst his other freaks Caligula, thinking that the
priest of Nemi had held office too long, hired a more stalwart
ruffian to slay him; and a Greek traveller, who visited Italy in the

age of the Antonines, remarks that down to his time the priesthood was still the prize of victory in a single combat.

Rigid and frigid as was the statue of Diana the huntress, still, after all, it became personified as a goddess of fertility. But how, Hubert would demand of his listeners, did the mad Emperor Caligula have sex with a statue? It was an orgy on a lake-ship: there must have been something more than a statue. Caligula took Diana aboard his ship under her guise as the full moon, according to Suetonius. Diana the goddess, Hubert explained, was adept at adding years to the life of a man – she had done so with her lover Hippolytus. She bore a child to the madly enamoured Emperor, added years to the infant's life so that he became instantly adult, and it was this young man, and not a Roman hireling, whom Caligula sent to supplant the reigning King of the Wood, the priest of Diana.

Hubert descended, then, from the Emperor, the goddess, and from her woodland priest; in reality this was nothing more than his synthesis of a persistent, yet far more vague, little story fostered by a couple of dotty aunts enamoured of the author-image of Sir James Frazer and misled by one of those quack genealogists who flourished in late Victorian times and around the turn of the century, and who still, when they take up the trade, never fail to flourish.

Modern Nemi, at the end of the last century, as more recently when Hubert Mallindaine settled there, appeared to Frazer to be curiously an image of Italy in the olden times; 'when the land was still sparsely peopled with tribes of savage hunters or wandering herdsmen'. Diana's temple had been feared by the Church. The long wall of high arched niches, once part of the temple-life, have perfectly survived antiquity, and these, at a later time, had been named 'the Devil's Grottoes'. Hubert, beating his way through the undergrowth along the rows of remaining cliff-chapels, would come upon the relics of traditional disrespect and of outcast life. There was a rubbish dump, incredibly rubbishy with the backs of yellow plastic chairs, petrol tins, muddy boots and cast-off rags piled up in those enormous Roman votive alcoves which soared above their desecration with stony dignity. And from this view the plateau was beautiful; it contained the rectangular site of the sanctuary itself, now filled up with the earth and cultivated with a chrysanthemum crop.

Very few people now visited this spot as a temple. Hubert had seen reported in a recent article that it was 'still lost as far as the ordinary tourist is concerned'. 'No local folk,' complained the author of the article, 'seem to know where it is.' Which, of course, was instinctively the way with local people. Chrysanthemums enjoyed a commercial popularity in Italy on one day of the year, the Day of the Dead; otherwise they were considered unlucky.

The site of the rectangular sanctuary was marked unobtrusively by a withered tree in one corner. A rim of the temple wall still protruded a few inches from the ground on three of its sides. The reason the peasants had cultivated the soil once more over the late dig was that 'the money for the excavations had stopped', as one of them explained to Hubert.

One spring, when he was supervising the building of the house then destined by Maggie to be his, Hubert had walked down the cliff-path and talked to a man who was pruning a pear tree on the site of Diana's temple. The man was about forty-two. He remembered the excavations, he said, when he was a boy. Very beautiful. Red brick paving. A fireplace. Yes, said Hubert, that was for the vestal virgins; it was an everlasting flame. The man went on with his pruning. My ancestress, Diana, was worshipped here, Hubert said. The man continued his work, no doubt thinking Hubert's Italian was at fault.

Again, standing one winter day alone among the bare soughing branches of those thick woodlands, looking down at the furrowed rectangle where the goddess was worshipped long ago, he shouted aloud with great enthusiasm, 'It's mine! I am the King of Nemi! It is my divine right! I am Hubert Mallindaine the descendant of the Emperor of Rome and the Benevolent-Malign Diana of the Woods . . .' And whether he was sincere or not; or whether, indeed, he was or was not connected so far back as the divinity-crazed Caligula – and if he was descended from any gods of mythology, purely on statistical grounds who is not? – at any rate, these words were what Hubert cried.

SIX

Mary had not yet got used to the Italian afternoon repose. Her hours were the Anglo-Saxon eight in the morning till midnight with a two-hour break for lunch. That Maggie went to bed between three and five in the afternoon she attributed to Maggie's middle-age. That nearly all Italians rested during that period of the day she attributed to Latin laziness. What her husband did with himself in Rome during these hours she had not begun to wonder; if she had done so she would have assumed that he regularly returned to his office after lunch, keeping American hours in lonely righteousness. In fact, Michael had a mistress in Rome in whose flat he spent the customary hours of repose; it was not unusual for Italian businessmen to spend the long free hours of lunch and after-lunch with their mistresses, but if Mary had suspected that Michael had acquired the habit, especially so early in their married life, she would have considered her marriage a failure beyond redemption.

Maggie was sleeping successfully that afternoon. Mary had, with some scruple, for she was a girl of many scruples, plied her mother-in-law with white wine. They had lunched together on the terrace, talking of next week. Then Maggie had given Mary the smart jewel-case of black calf-skin, slightly wider than a shoe-box, which, when opened, was dramatically and really very beautifully packed with gold coins of various sizes, dates and nationalities. 'There are no absolute collectors' items,' Maggie explained. Their two heads – Maggie's shimmering silver and Mary's long and fair – bent over the glittering and chinking hoard. 'But,' said Maggie, 'the collection as a whole is of course worth more than its weight in gold. Coins always are. My real collection is worth a great deal.' Mary's long fingers shifted the coins about. She lifted one, examined it, put it down and took up another, then another. 'Queen Victoria half-sovereign, King Edward sovereign, South African sovereign – whose head is that?'

'Kruger,' said Maggie. 'Kruger. Are these worth a lot of money, then?' 'Well,' Maggie said, 'it depends who you are, whether they are.'

The coins tinkled through Mary's hands, then hearing the coffee-cups being brought she shut the box, put it on her lap and looked over her shoulder. Lauro appeared, his eyes intent on the tray although he must have seen the black box on Mary's lap.

When he had left, Maggie said, 'Hubert mustn't have a clue who sent them.'

Mary said, 'I really don't see why he should have all these.'

'I have my own important collection,' Maggie said, 'and I can get more. Any time I want.'

'I know. But it's crazy . . .'

'Yes, it's crazy. But it's a way of getting rid of him in my own mind.'

'Oh, I do see that.'

'A cheque would tie him to me more. I could never get rid of him.'

'No, I see that. He'd think he was in with you again. But gold is appreciating in value, isn't it?'

'Such a damn cheek,' Maggie said. 'I hate him.'

Later, in Maggie's room, they counted the coins and made a list. It was Mary's idea to make a list. She made lists of everything. A good part of her mornings was spent on list-making. She had lists for entertaining and for shopping. She listed her clothes, her expenditure and her correspondence. She kept lists of her books and music and furniture. She wrote them by hand, then typed them later in alphabetical or chronological order according as might be called for. Sometimes she made a card index when the subject was complex, such as the winter season's dinner parties, whom she had dined with and whom she had asked, what she had worn and when. Now she was making a list of the coins while Maggie took off her clothes, and got right into bed for her afternoon rest. Mary took her unfinished list and the coin-box quietly out of the room when Maggie fell asleep, and now she was in her own room sorting and writing seriously. She felt useful. Even though it was to be a secret from Michael, this help she was giving to Maggie was almost like helping Michael. Maggie, asleep in the next room, was much the same as if Michael were laying down there, having an afternoon sleep.

'Q. Vict.,' she wrote, '½ sov. 1842.'

She grasped quickly that there were no numismatic rarities; the value of the coins was largely commercial. At that, they added up to a considerable amount. They were mostly English half-sovereigns, early and late Victorian, bearing the Queen's young head and her older head. Mary found a sovereign of the reign of George IV and, realizing its extra value, wondered if Maggie had put it in by mistake. She put the coin aside, then, on the thought that Maggie might think her critical or stingy, put it back in the box and marked it on her list. The main idea was to please Maggie and show she understood her position. Maggie, after all, was being very delicate in her treatment of Hubert. Mary began to consider various means of conveying this treasure to him without betraying its origin. When she realized how impossible it would be for her to simply drive or walk over to the house herself and hand it over to him, she felt a waif-like longing to do so; she saw herself for a brief moment as an outcast from what appeared to her as a world of humour and sophistication which Hubert had brought with him during those few months she had known him, when he was still in Maggie's good favour. At the same time she disapproved of him as a proposition in Maggie's life. He really had no right to this golden fortune. Her mood swivelled and she imagined with satisfaction a dramatic little scene of handsome Hubert being thrown out of Maggie's house by the police.

Her list was complete. She closed the box and stood up. From the window she caught sight of a shining black head in the greenery below. She recognized Lauro and at the same time the idea came to her that, obviously, Lauro would be the person to carry this box to Hubert. She was convinced of his discretion and, after all, he had worked for Hubert once.

Mary went immediately to Maggie's room clutching the box. Maggie was still asleep. Her mouth was open and she slept noisily. The girl felt guilty, watching this uncomely sleep. Maggie, if wakened, would know she had been watched. Mary retreated, deciding to act on her own and rightly perceiving how gratified Maggie would be to wake up and find her plan accomplished; she would feel free in her heart and mind to turn Hubert out and give him hell and know that at least he wasn't starving. Mary was already on her way back to meet Lauro, leaving the house by the back door. His white

coat was hanging on the back of a kitchen chair. Mary swung down
the hot winding path with her long brown legs and sandals and, seeing
Lauro's black head once more below her, called to him, 'Lauro!'

He stopped and waited. She found him sitting down in the shade
of the woods just off the path. 'Lauro,' she said, 'I've got something
important to ask you. I want you to do something.'

She expected him to stand up immediately she approached but he
let a moment pass before doing so. He was smiling as if he enjoyed
the lonely scene, and as if the woods belonged to him. She felt
strangely awkward as she had not been before when she had been
alone with him in the house or in the car, or walking with him to the
shops in the village street.

She spoke rapidly, as if giving some domestic instructions while
her free mind, as it might be, was on something weightier. 'You have
to keep a secret, Lauro,' she said. 'I have something here for Mr
Mallindaine but he must not be told who sent it.'

'Okay,' said Lauro.

'I want you to take this box to Mr Mallindaine's house. He mustn't
see you as he mustn't know where the box has come from. Find some
way of leaving it where he's sure to find it. Do you know the lay-out
of the house?'

'Sure, I know the house well. I lived there all last summer. What's
in the box please, Mary?'

Mary opened it, trembling at what she was doing. 'They're old
coins,' she was saying. 'I've made a list.' She displayed the rich
tumble of gold with an expression which conveyed both her naïvety
and the pleasure of showing off to the boy.

The sight of so much golden money in the rich, very rich, tall girl's
hands inflamed him instantly with sexual desire. He grabbed the box
and pulled her into the thick green glade. He pulled her down to the
ground and with the box spilling beside them he would have raped
her had she not quite yielded after the first gasp, and really, in the end,
although she protested in fierce whispers, her eyes all over the green
shrubbery lest someone should see, she put up no sort of struggle.
'That wasn't no good because you didn't relax,' Lauro said, his face,
satyr-like, closing in on hers, his eyes gleaming with automatic hyp-
notism as he had seen it done on the films and television from his
tiniest years, and acquired as a habit.

Mary, in a crisis of breath-shortage and an abundance of tears, pulled at her few clothes and managed to articulate, 'My husband will kill you.'

'He sooner screw me,' Lauro said.

'That, too, I'll tell him,' she said. 'I would hit you on the face if you were not a servant.'

He jumped up; flash and flutter went his eyes closing on her face, and tight went his hands on her bare arms, as if he were directing the film as well as playing the principal part. 'Next time, you relax,' Lauro said, smiling through his teeth. 'For the first time, no good.'

Mary closed her mouth tight and pushed back her hair with a gesture of every-day indifference. He turned and took up the jewel-box whose contents were half-spilled on the earth, and with her help scooped up the lurking gold. He laughed as if the coins were some sort of counters in a party-game, while Mary, still trembling and crying, stood up; she tugged at her clothes and smoothed her hair; she said, 'Give me that box.'

'I'll take it to Hubert,' he said, and started off in that direction.

Mary caught up with him. 'Are you sure you'll find the right place to leave it? It's not mine, it's Maggie's. Hubert mustn't know.'

He smiled, and turned to put his face close to hers again, smiling. 'Leave it to me, Mary,' he said. He clutched the box under his arm as if it were a man's business, and looked as if he had earned the takings within.

She turned and ran back to the house, not sure how far she was guilty, or what she must do next. She became uncertain whether Lauro could be trusted with those coins. She was perplexed about the relationship in which she stood with Lauro now, and above all she was anxious to take a shower.

Hubert was at that moment counting some coins which he had found in a curious way at six o'clock that afternoon.

Pauline had gone in to Rome in Hubert's station-wagon, taking with her, wrapped in lengths and strips of sackcloth, a second Louis XIV chair of Maggie's to be delivered to the address in Via di Santa Maria dell'Anima where the copies were made. Of these transactions Pauline knew nothing, thinking only that the chairs were being examined and repaired, and that the bill for this service

would be sent to their mysterious all-pervasive owner, Maggie.
Pauline had never seen Maggie; to Pauline she was a hovering
name, an absent presence in Hubert's house and his life.

She delivered the chair, with its penitential sackcloth secured by a
winding string round its beautiful legs and tied over its seat and
back, ordering the man who carried it up the stairs to take care, great
care. She left it with him while she went to find a legitimate parking
place for the car. When she returned the man was with a younger
man, tall, in blue jeans and a smart shirt; the chair had already been
unshrouded and they were examining it with pride.

As Pauline approached the younger man disappeared into a back
room from where he carried a chair identical in appearance to the one
Pauline had brought. She had been instructed to fetch this back to
the house; apparently it was the first of Maggie's best chairs to be
sent for inspection and overhaul and, apparently, it was now in
perfect order. In reality, it was a new and very clever fake; one of its
legs was all that remained of Maggie's former chair. Most of these
clever fakes contained at least one limb of the original, and in that
way the dealer was entitled, or felt entitled, to proclaim it 'Louis
XIV'. To Pauline, it did not matter very much what period the chair
belonged to. She had her orders to collect it and she was anxious to
get back to Hubert quickly. She asked the men to wrap the chair carefully, which they duly did, with new rags, and much wadding placed
over the sparkling green silk of the seat. It was carried to the car.

'Tell Mr Mallindaine to pass by early next week,' said the smart
young man in blue jeans.

'He isn't leaving Nemi much, at the moment,' Pauline said, thinking of Hubert, how he was afraid to leave the house in case Maggie
should come and reclaim it in his absence.

But the man repeated his request.

Meantime Hubert, at Nemi, was counting the gold coins he had
found at six o'clock. It was his usual tea time and he had gone into
the kitchen to make it. As he had fetched down the teapot from the
shelf he heard a strange rattling inside it. He took off the lid. He had
found a quantity of gold money inside the pot.

He sat down at the kitchen table, looking inside the teapot. Then
he looked round the kitchen to see what else, if anything, was amiss.
Nothing seemed to be out of place. He wished for Pauline to return.

He had emptied the gold coins on the table, and now was counting them.

There were, in fact, far fewer than the amount entrusted to Lauro who had kept the black box and more than half the gold. Indeed, his sense of prudence in carrying out Mary's orders was mixed with a feeling of decided benevolence that he had deposited any of these coins in Hubert's teapot. It had sunk into his mind that Mary had told him she had made a list of the coins. It had seemed to him both a fruitless thing to do and a suspicious thing, as touching on his honour.

By the time Hubert, at his customary hour for tea, was puzzling over and re-counting the coins, Lauro was back at the Radcliffes' house, and had changed into his smart houseman's coat. He filled the ice-buckets, arranged the drinks and the glasses, set the terrace furniture to rights, then, chatting with the cook in the pantry, he waited for the cocktail hour.

On her return to the house, after her careful shower and before going down to dinner, Mary had sat for a long while in her room, with her head in her hands, thinking God knows what. Then she skipped to her feet and changed into a long skirt and a blouse. She took up her list of coins, where it was lying on the writing table, and put it down again. She sat down at the table, and pulled out another piece of her list paper. At the top of the page she wrote 'Michael' and underneath it she wrote 'Lauro'. She settled for the thought that she could not have been faithful to Michael all her life, but she felt it was too soon because a year had not passed since her marriage. But then she considered how she had not herself planned the incident with Lauro. One way and another, she tidied up her mind, aligned the beauty preparations in their bottles on the dressing table, and put away the paper she had just written Lauro's name on with Michael's together with the coin-list, her guest-lists and her other lists, locking them up in her desk. Mary had then patted her face with a paper tissue, and had gone down, passing Michael, home from the office, on the stairs. Maggie was already sitting on the terrace waiting for her husband to arrive and her son to come down. Lauro came forward to hover till they were ready to say what they wanted to drink.

'Oh, Lauro,' Mary said very uppishly, 'did you remember that errand?'

'Yes, Mary,' he said in his usual friendly tone, 'how could I forget?'

Mary turned to Maggie and said in a decidely natural voice, 'He's delivered the box. You see, Lauro knows the house so well, I sent it by him.'

'Oh!' said Maggie. 'But then Hubert will know where it came from and who sent it, and –'

'He didn't see me,' Lauro said. 'I got in through the bathroom window while he was sleeping upstairs. I put the box beside the teapot, so when he came to make his tea he'd be sure to find it.'

'That's brilliant. Lauro, you're brilliant,' Maggie said. 'Mary, darling, you're brilliant. I feel so much relieved now he's at least not likely to starve, because you know I have to get him out of the house. How I've been in the past to Hubert is no guide to how I shall be in the future.'

'Get the police and have him thrown out,' said Mary rather impatiently. 'Lauro, a Campari-soda, please.'

'Well, in our position we can't have a scandal. You know what the Italian papers are like, and all those Communists,' Maggie said.

'We do it discreet,' Lauro said.

'That's right, Lauro. A gin and tonic. Lauro's got the right ideas. Lauro, you're brilliant.'

Hubert, meanwhile, having counted the coins and made his tea, taking it outside on the handsome terrace, gazed out on the panoramic view and pondered. He then began an inspection of the house and decided that one of the ground-floor windows had been entered. There was a narrow pantry window and a narrow bathroom window. The bathroom window was open. It had not been forced. He decided to put bars on the ground-floor windows. He went on a tour of the whole house, opening drawers and cupboards. Nothing was disarranged, nothing missing; it seemed to Hubert that his burglar had been motivated by sheer benevolence towards him. It was a pity to have to bar the windows. Nothing could have been more clearly intended as a personal and rather touching present than those gold coins in his own teapot. For the first time for nearly a year, Hubert started to feel, singing within him, innocence and happiness.

He spread out the coins on the terrace table in the late bright sunlight: Queen Victoria still with a firm young profile and high curly

bun, on the coin which was dated 1880 although she was born in
1819. St George and the dragon, 1892, whose Queen Victoria on the
reverse had now been minted with an incipient extra chin, a little
coronet and a veil. Gulielmus III D: G: Britanniar: Rex F: D:,
drooping jowls, a thick neck, a curly quiff on top of his head, 1837.
Who, thought Hubert, adores me enough to send me all this glittering mint? And here's Nero wearing a laurel wreath tied with a pretty
ribbon at the nape of his neck, or rather, it's Georgius IIII D: G:
Britanniar: Rex F: D: 1833. And now, Sub. Hoc. Signo. Militamus –
a Knights of Malta ten scudi, 1961. Another juicy young Victoria D:
G: Britanniar: Reg: F: D: – darling Victoria, 1880, and that poor
downtrodden dragon on the reverse. Render unto Caesar the things
that are Caesar's and I wonder, thought Hubert, what utterly charming gentleman hath rendered these things unto me? It then occurred
to Hubert that the actual bearer of the coins was hardly likely to be
the sender. Hubert had instantly formed an image of largeness, if
only of heart, for the sender; he was certainly rich, anyway, and
would most likely have young men at his beck and call. Only a young
man and slim could have got through the bathroom window so
silently and softly. Then, it was someone who knew Hubert's habits
and who knew the house. Someone rich. Who? He scooped up the
many dozens of coins and took them into the kitchen, where he
spread them out and looked at them again.

Pauline returned with the fake chair which they placed in the
drawing-room and admired. 'He wants you to call in and see him.
Better go soon,' Pauline said. 'I hope it isn't about the bill.'

'I hope not,' Hubert said. 'Maggie gets the bills for this servicing
of her stuff. However, if you'll hold the fort I'll go and see him very
soon. Always hold the fort. Let no one into the house. I'm thinking
of getting bars put in these lower back windows as it seems to me
someone might easily get in that way. Once they're in, they can take
possession of the house and we're done for.'

It was in any case his intention to call on the furniture restorers
and collect payment for the genuine parts of Louis XIV. It would be
a considerable sum. Hubert looked at Pauline in a kind of dream,
wondering how he could explain to her the good supply of drinks and
food he intended to bring back from Rome with him. She had
brought back a chicken and some meat and wine from Rome, the

good girl; she had spent her own money and was about to prepare a special supper.

After a glass of wine he was moved to tell her about the gold coins.

'It's my opinion,' he said, 'that the spirit of my ancestors Caligula and Diana are responsible for this.' He gave Pauline two sovereigns.

She accepted them after a little hesitation. 'They could have been stolen' she had said.

'Well, *we* didn't steal them. They were in my teapot, so they're plainly mine. My dear, they are our crock of gold and we have come to the end of the rainbow.'

'Someone must have got into the house.'

'Through the bathroom window,' Hubert said. 'So tomorrow we arrange to have the windows barred.'

'Then your ancestors won't be able to come again,' Pauline said, looking at her sovereigns.

'Those are not on account of wages,' said Hubert. 'Wages I'll pay later and in good measure. I don't like that touch of scepticism in your voice. Remember that my ancestor Diana is very much alive and she doesn't like being mocked. But of course if you're going to express doubts and behave like a French village atheist –'

'It could have been one of those boys who worked for you last summer,' Pauline said, looking at the pile of gold on the table and touching the coins tentatively from time to time.

'Not on your life,' said Hubert.

'It's someone who wants to help you,' Pauline said. 'A well-wisher. Why didn't they send you a cheque?'

Hubert found himself suddenly irritated by this speech. Her kindergarten teacher's tone, he thought. All this being penniless, he thought, has lowered my standards. I should have better company, witty, good minds around me. I find a pile of sovereigns in the teapot and all the silly bitch can say is, 'Someone wants to help you. Why didn't they send a cheque?'

He took up the newspapers and weeklies she had brought in with her, and, leaving the gold coins littering the kitchen table, went off to his study to take a couple of tranquillizers and further hypnotize himself with the current American government scandals of which everyone's latent anarchism drank deep that summer.

*

Lauro left for Rome very early next morning with his list of shopping at the supermarket. His first stop, however, was at one of the
little cave-like shops in the village, filled, as they were, with the
richest of fruits, plants and cut flowers. It was perhaps unusual, but
not noticeably so, that he locked the car when he left it outside the
door on the village street. Lauro went in and waited his turn.

Figs, peaches, strawberries, all so local and proudly selected, there
was not one inferior fruit to be seen. The flowers were mainly of the
aster family, huge, medium-sized and smallish, in white, yellow,
mauve and pink. Among them were some deeply-coloured small
roses and a variety of ferns and leafy plants. The woman who was
serving and she who had just been served looked at Lauro with the
look of curiosity which comes over the faces of people to whom
nothing much happens, and which, to people of more elaborate lives,
looks like hostility. The Radcliffes had their own orchards and rarely
shopped here. However, the local people knew very well who Lauro
was, and of his recent transference from Hubert's mysterious home
to Mary Radcliffe's spectacularly rich one. Lauro, in his smart
clothes, the transparent beige shirt and fine-striped pink trousers,
was to be treated with a touch of deference. What would he desire?
Grapes, peaches fresh this morning, fine tomatoes . . . ?

Lauro desired some plants, strong and lasting, with the roots, for
transplanting.

What type of plants? What did the gardeners at the Radcliffes'
advise.

'Oh, no,' Lauro said, rather impatiently, almost as if to suggest
that not any roots, not any plants, would do, 'they're for my mother's
grave. I'm going to visit her at the cemetery.'

The woman who had been served, although she had received her
change, made no sign of leaving, but entered the discussion. Surely
the Radcliffes had plenty of plants and to spare . . . ?

'For Mama,' said Lauro with a haughty masculine bark that sent
the women scurrying. 'I prefer to pay.' And he bought four chrysanthemum plants not yet in flower and rattled his money while they
were being carefully wrapped in newspaper and placed in an orange-
coloured plastic shopping bag. He left, and was watched to his car.
It was only when he was seen to unlock the empty car, there on the
harmless street, that he looked behind him and saw the two women

exchanging glances. Carefully, he spat on the pavement. Then he got
into his car and drove away too fast. Suspicious old fat cows, what
did it matter if they knew what he might be up to, and he knew that
they knew that he knew, since, if he put his mind to it he could easily
make as many accurate guesses about their doings as they about his.
It was for this reason that he had not even bothered to take the pre-
caution of buying his plants in Rome: in Rome they were twice the
price, whereas in Nemi they were cheap and he didn't need to care
what the people thought. So ended one of those telepathic encounters that go on all the time among compatriots who have foreigners
in their midst.

Arriving in Rome, Lauro made first for the cemetery. He found his
mother's grave, well-tended and neat, with its hovering marble angel
and the little inset photograph. There was room here for his father;
their five children would later buy their own burial-plots in the new
cemetery, since this one would then be fully occupied. 'Cara Mama,'
said Lauro. He had brought his packages in the bright orange plastic
shopping bag from the car. He had unpacked the healthy plant-roots,
the little strong trowel and another newspaper-wrapped package
containing the black leather box with most of the coins that Mary
had given over to him the afternoon before.

Some people passed, old people on the way to visit their dead.
They gave Lauro a muted 'Buon giorno', inclining their heads
towards him with approving piety. Lauro, on his knees, dutifully
digging and tending his mother's flower-bed, looked up and
returned the greeting with wistful repetition, one quiet 'Buon
giorno' for each of the three figures who passed. He was a nice boy
in their eyes, which made him feel nice as he dug. The figures, a fat
woman in black, a thin man and another, less fat woman with diffi-
cult-walking feet, passed from his life. When he had dug enough and
laid on the grass verge some of the flowers and plants he had dis-
lodged in the process, he opened up the sheets of newspaper which
contained the black leather box. He had almost thrown away the
box, keeping only the coins to bury, but it was such a well-made, a
well-bred box, such as Lauro sometimes saw in the shops and boutiques of Rome, and it was so connected, now, with the desirable
coins and the casual and exclusive quality of Mary and Maggie in
their inherited wealthiness, that he had decided to bury the box

along with the coins, despite the nuisance. He opened the box, lifted the paper-tissues which he had stuffed inside to keep the coins from rattling, sifted a few of the beautiful golden disks through his brown fingers, quickly replaced the lot, put the black box in the orange plastic bag for safe preservation and, seeing that it was well-covered, he buried it deep. On top of this he replaced some of the short shrubs he had dug up.

He began also to plant the new chrysanthemum roots he had brought, working his way around the grave and, tidying up the border, tastefully arranged the colours; there were already a few nasturtiums, some asters in pink and purple shades and some dark green shoots the nature of which would not be revealed till the autumn. While he was at it he dug up, examined, and replaced two well-wrapped little parcels, one containing a huge sapphire ring and the other a pair of monogrammed cuff-links, these being objects he had picked up somewhere along the line from two earlier periods and encounters of his young life.

When the grave was ready, Lauro stood up and looked at the picture of his mother whom he remembered as deserving and energetic. Her huge voice had commanded until she died. She looked out unsmiling with her bold eyes and her short hair shining and fresh from the hairdresser's. The costly angel who spread his wings above her little oval picture looked frightened by comparison, and the downcast eyes of that pale, church-going, feathered adherent of the New-fangled Testament seemed shiftily afraid to meet those of the living Lauro.

Nobody except the family was permitted to touch the grave. Lauro had taken on this work exclusively to himself; the rest of the family, from whom, in any case, he had nothing to fear, were all too busy elsewhere to tend it. His father had married again and lived in Milan; his two sisters were married with children and lived in Turin. One brother was married in America, and the other, who lived with his father in Milan, was a student. Once a year at the beginning of November, on the Day of the Dead, those of the family and their spouses who were not in America or, as it might happen, confined in labour wards, came to visit Lauro's mother at the cemetery, bearing with them large bunches of long-petalled white and yellow chrysanthemums. These would be piled on the grave. The family would hover and weep, some lustily, some merely wetly. They would say now nicely Lauro kept it, how good he was, sparing them the expense of the cemetery-attendant's services. They kissed Mama's picture but did not touch the grave and asked no questions, not even of themselves. They felt Lauro was getting on quite well and admired his clothes. After the visit to the cemetery on the Day of the Dead the family would troop out with the other thousands of ancestor-visitors, get into their cars and proceed to a trattoria where they had booked a long table for a five-course family meal. Once a year.

Lauro looked round the cemetery, now, in early August, nearly deserted. Only one or two heads moved behind one or two tombstones. Lauro wrapped the leafy rubbish in a piece of his newspaper and the trowel in another. An attendant passed and wished him good morning. Lauro looked around with pleasure. What secrets lay buried in these small oblong territorial properties of the family dead!

SEVEN

Dear Hubert,

We are leaving for Sardinia next week – out of this frightful heat! I expect you too will have plans to go to the sea. After Sardinia I plan to return with Mary to the U.S. to spend some time on our own beautiful Atlantic beaches. Berto (my husband – he looks forward to the pleasure of meeting you one day!) plans to join me on the Emerald Coast for a few weeks and then goes on to Le Touquet to join his brother. They plan to look over some horses he plans to buy. I plan to join him in Rome, then Nemi for a week on October first after which our plans take us back to the Veneto.

What I am writing about mainly is, if you can plan to vacate the house during the summer so that we can occupy it from October first, that would suit our plans. Will you let me know, please? Address your letter up to the end of August:

La Marchese Adalberto di Tullio-Friole,
Villa Stazzu,
Liscia di Vacca,
Costa Smeralda,
Sardegna.

After that my New York address (address me there as Mrs Maggie Radcliffe as the apartment is still in my old name!) till the end of September. Please leave the key with Mary's maid Agata, if you vacate in the month of August. Agata is coming in every day to feed the cat and dust. September, Lauro will be back so please leave the key with him if you have to vacate as late as the month of September. August would be preferable as this would enable me to plan for the decorators to come in from Rome in September so the house would be in shape for us.

A little bird told me you have been looking after my precious chairs! It was thoughtful of you and very, very simpatico. Bill me with the cost, of course. Maintenance is so very, very important.

One day when all the trivialities of life are settled I hope you will come and visit with me and Adalberto and tell us about your big project that you plan as I am sure you do. I hope it's shaping up!

Happy summer!

As ever, love,

Maggie.

Hubert took a large whisky and two Mitigils. He re-read the letter, paying less attention to what she actually said than to the tone and implication. A mass of ideas moved like nebulae in his mind. It was not until later in the day, after lunch, that he was able to isolate the germ: it was Maggie who, two days ago, had caused the gold coins to be placed in the teapot. The reason: plain guilt. But why buy him off in such an exotic manner?

And why, if she really wanted to make it easy for him to leave the house, had she sent so comparatively little? For, after all, small fortune though they amounted to, they were hardly the value and dimension of what one would call a settlement.

A settlement. In any case, for no money at all would he leave the house.

Again he read the letter. Over lunch he had read it out to Pauline Thin. 'Does she always go on like that about her plans?' Pauline said.

'Not in conversation so much as in her letters. She has an epistolary style which denotes an hysterical need for stability and order. In conversation she counts on her remarkable appearance to hypnotize the immediate environment into a kind of harmony. She learned about planning at college, I should think. It's a useful word in American education. She never understands the rules of anything, however, and her emphatic use of the word "plan" when she writes a letter is nothing but self-reassurance. Naturally, she will not stick to her plans. If she goes to Sardinia at all, she'll probably only stay one night. That's Maggie.'

Pauline said, 'If you look at things in her light, you wonder why she doesn't get her lawyer to press on with the eviction.'

'She doesn't want a scandal and it's difficult to evict.' Hubert, who was always impatient with others who failed to keep pace with his leaps of logic, conveyed impatience now.

Pauline found herself regretting the appearance of the gold coins; Hubert had been sweeter during their recent weeks of meagre living.

'Well, we should still go very carefully,' Pauline said. 'It may be a trick to lure us into carelessness. We mustn't leave the house unguarded in case they suddenly swoop and stage a takeover.'

Hubert considered this. 'You're a clever girl,' he said.

'And we should still be careful with the money. Are you going to sell the coins?'

'Tomorrow,' Hubert said, 'I shall go into Rome and sell a few. You'll have another present, too.'

'Oh, no,' Pauline said.

'Why not?' said Hubert. His mind was on the money he was going to collect for the chairs. He would have to leave early for Rome to give him time to collect the money comfortably and, in the event they didn't pay in cash, change the cheque before the banks closed. It was an exceptionally hot August. He didn't like Rome in the heat. 'I'll leave early in the morning,' Hubert said.

'Then I'll iron those shirts of yours,' she said, the wifely girl.

'Shirts? I've got plenty of shirts,' Hubert said absently, for his head had lifted to hear the sound of a car coming up the drive. A green Volkswagen that he did not recognize presently drew up at the door.

Pauline said, 'It's the Bernardini daughter.' She stood beside Hubert behind the glass doors of the terrace.

'Those people who live in one of Maggie's other houses?'

'Yes, she's the daughter, Letizia.'

Letizia had evidently brought a friend. She got out of the car in front of the house and went round to the other door. Presently, partly by persuasion and partly by force she brought out of the front seat before the eyes of Hubert and Pauline a tall lanky young man with a mop of reddish hair very like a giant chrysanthemum out of which peered a peaked and greyish face. He was trembling and wobbling, and obviously was in a bad way.

'That's Kurt Hakens,' Hubert said.

'Who?'

'One of my secretaries from last summer.' Hubert locked the

terrace door. 'He looks drugged, and my laughter demon, which resides somewhere inside me, has ceased to laugh.' He stood back from the glass door of the terrace. 'Let them in,' he said. 'See what they want. Tell them I'm busy and can't be disturbed.'

The secretaries from last summer were not, in themselves, of any particular account to Hubert. There had been other secretaries and other summers in plenty. And other winters.

Once, at a New Year party, in those days when Maggie was discovering the wonders of Bohemian life through him, one of his secretaries deliberately burnt Maggie's hand, that right hand with which she had signed the cheques, and such grand and frequent cheques. 'Hold this,' had said the young man who, Hubert reflected as he recalled the scene, must now be thirty, maybe with a secretary of his own. 'Hold this,' he had said, out on the terrace of that other villa of those days. It was a firework. He put it in Maggie's hand then lit it; it was the live end of the firecracker that she held in her hand. It flared in her palm before she dropped it. She looked at the young man's smiling face and fuming eyes. 'He burnt my hand!' she screamed out to Hubert across the dark terrace. 'He did it purposely. I'm in agony.' She bent with pain. Hubert was dancing to the distant bells. He seemed to have lost his head to the New Year, and it was another secretary who took Maggie away to treat her hand with some type of cream. Helplessly, Maggie asked for her chauffeur. Another young man joined them. Both secretaries said the chauffeur was asleep in the servants' quarters. They wouldn't call the chauffeur. It was recounted thus later to Hubert first by Maggie and then by the two young men who had helped dress her burns.

'Where were you, Hubert?' Maggie had said. 'Why didn't you help me?'

'I didn't realize what had happened. I thought you were throwing a temperament,' Hubert replied. And he asked her, 'Why didn't you go into the kitchen yourself and demand your chauffeur if you wanted to go home.'

'I couldn't. I felt paralysed. Something just prevented me.'

Maggie had slept in Hubert's bed. They had given her a strong pill. She slept till the party was over at five in the morning, then had got into the car with her bandaged hand, without having seen Hubert around anywhere. The rooms had been littered with used glasses and piled-up ashtrays. Hubert had gone to someone else's bed long before.

When he heard this story later, he saw it all swiftly from Maggie's point of view; he weighed up her nightmare-like experience of being unable to move of her own will to call her chauffeur, and her retiring to a deep sleep on his bed, and decided she was fairly hypnotized by him. For about five years after that, apparently indispensable to Maggie in practical affairs, he had been able to do what he liked with her until that time when gradually, at first unnoticed by him, she began to withdraw. In the meantime there had been secretaries, waves upon waves, season upon season of them. Last summer Kurt Hakens was a secretary, but that was when Maggie had already begun to retreat and was vaguely nowhere to be found. It was plain, now, that last summer she had actually been plotting. She was already getting rid of her ineffectual and purely nominal husband, preparing to marry the new one, and was emerging as a society woman, well-groomed, fully using her enormous wealth which had been lurking there in her favour all the time.

Pauline Thin was at the drawing-room door, apologetically. Hubert looked vexed but in reality he was relieved to see her, imprisoned as he had been, merely sitting it out on one of the still unfaked chairs, out of sight and earshot of his visitors. He had a paranoiac feeling that he was being discussed behind his back and, at the same time as he was very eager to know what was going on between the Bernardini girl, the very ill-looking Kurt Hakens and Pauline, he was afraid to know. Pauline came softly over to him, apologizing in low tones. She pointed to the floor and said, 'They're still down there. Letizia says couldn't you please come down a minute. It's very urgent.'

'What do they want?'

'She says Kurt used to be your secretary and he's an old friend of yours. He needs help.'

'I can't have him here,' Hubert said.

'I'm awfully sorry,' Pauline said.

'You mean you can't cope with them yourself?' Hubert said nastily, rising.

'Yes,' said Pauline humbly.

Hubert took his reading glasses from his pocket and followed her downstairs, looking very much as if he had been torn from his desk.

Letizia was on the terrace, drinking tea. Kurt was stretched out on the long canvas chair beside her, his eyes closed, his mouth quivering. 'How do you do?' Hubert said to the girl.

Letizia stood up, affably showing her teeth and fixing her clear eyes steadily on his face. 'I did not phone,' she said, 'because we haven't met. It was less complicated to come. My father is your neighbour, Emilio Bernardini. I am Letizia.'

Hubert said again, 'How do you do?'

They sat down, looking at the view which seemed always to ask to be looked at like a much-photographed actress. Kurt Hakens continued to lie with closed eyes and quivering lips.

In a while Hubert said, 'What's the matter with him?'

'He's taken an overdose of a drug. I occupy myself with these cases. Now I find me in a predicament because we leave tomorrow for our vacation. This man is a foreigner and he's a friend of yours –'

'Yes, in a way,' Hubert said. 'I gave him a job last summer. A few weeks, then he left. You shouldn't abandon your patients, you know.'

'Papa has made arrangements.'

'Is he getting treatment?'

'I don't know.'

'How does he live?'

'I don't know.'

'Then you want to leave him with me?'

'Yes.'

Pauline said, 'We'll have to call a doctor.'

'Do you know what would happen?' Letizia stood up, agitated. 'They would take him to the Neuro.' The 'Neuro' was the mental hospital in Rome where all cases of mental, nervous, psychopathic and psychotic sufferers who could not afford private clinics were indiscriminately housed in conditions, it was said, rather worse than the Rome prisons, which were reputedly infernal.

'What can I do with him? My dear girl, it's a year since I last saw him,' Hubert said, looking down at Kurt. 'He needs treatment and care. I have no money, my dear. Are the police looking for him? Nemi is in fact my ancestral home. It may be difficult for an Italian to realize, but it is so. My landlady is trying to put me out of the house. How can I take in this poor boy? – I can't do it.'

'Well, yes, as I say, we will do our best,' Hubert said.

Kurt had been helped, half-pushed, upstairs, crying, and without any resistance; he did not seem to know where he was but he knew his way instinctively to the bedroom he had occupied last summer. From time to time a small noise would come from his room to the three sitting downstairs on the terrace; he was faintly whining through his nose; he sounded like a young horse or a dog dreaming in its sleep. Hubert looked at the cheque Letizia had given him. He passed it to Pauline.

'I really don't like taking it,' he said.

'It's from our fund,' Letizia said. 'Papa gave me it for our funds, because I had Kurt on my hands and I didn't know what to do with him for the vacation. I would have had to send him to a clinic, then they would ask him questions and maybe he would be in trouble.'

'It will go straight from your fund into ours,' Hubert said. 'I assure you we have a fund, too, for our unfortunates. Pauline, please put it in the fund.'

'All right,' Pauline said. 'Do you want a receipt, Letizia?'

'Oh, no!' She made a gesture of pushing away the offer with her open palms as if alarmed lest the exchange of any document should continue to bind her to the bought-off Kurt. She said, 'Papa was only too happy to help him. We leave tomorrow on the boat for Greece and Turkey. Then we go to Ischia. Papa wants you to visit us when we come back.'

'If I'm still here,' Hubert said. 'Our padrona is trying to put us out.'

Pauline was upstairs trying to converse softly with Kurt and at the same time to persuade him to stay in bed. She sat near the door in a soft armchair, in a casual attitude, but ready to flee because Kurt, from time to time, demanded his clothes. Pauline had agreed with Hubert in family-type whispers to keep watch over him while Hubert continued his conversation with Letizia downstairs. Letizia had begun to interest him on the subject of Maggie and this, together with the good big cheque she had handed over, made up for the actual infliction of Kurt upon him; the actual problem of Kurt could be solved later.

The intermittent sound of Kurt's argumentative demands and Pauline's soothing replies seeped down to them. Letizia had accepted a sherry. Her face was lightly tanned, her eyes clear blue.

She paused in her account of the night that Maggie dined at her house, and Hubert, thinking she was troubled about Kurt, said, 'Oh, don't worry. We'll calm him down. I know a couple of Jesuits who'll give me advice. American Jesuits. They'll know how to cope with him.'

But Letizia was not, apparently, at all troubled by Kurt; he had become yesterday's problem. She had paused to consider whether, after all, it was wise of her to repeat how Maggie had tried to get her father's help to put Hubert out of the house. 'Yes, Jesuits, that's good,' she said.

'I suppose she wants your father to gang up with her,' Hubert said, coaxingly. The phrase 'gang up' was beyond her, and after it was explained she rattled on obligingly. 'Of course,' she said, 'we've no intention of making the gang with her. I mean, I have no intention and Papa will listen to me. At Casa Bernardini we're on your side. Papa has to think this way: if she can get one tenant out then we'll be the next.'

'This has the best view of all three houses,' Hubert said, wishing to establish a banal, greedy reason why Maggie should want to be rid of him.

'Oh, is that why she wants it? Well, Papa has spent a fortune in reconstruction so our house is now more worth than it was when we rented it.'

'Maggie,' pressed Hubert, 'covets the view.'

'She says you must go because her husband insists.'

'I dare say. He, too, appreciates the situation of the house. But I shan't go. I have an ancestral claim, you know, my dear.'

'I know! I know!' The girl jumped up and sat down again. 'Tell me more, please, about yourself, how you belong to Nemi and your —'

'Nemi . . .' said Hubert, leaning back in the chair with his legs stretched out wide in front of him. 'Nemi is mine. It belongs to me, as a matter of fact. The offspring of Diana and Caligula became the high priest of Diana's sanctuary and I am his descendant.'

Kurt's voice could be heard in some sharp protest from above, joined with Pauline's impatient tones. It appeared, now, that Pauline had left the bedroom and was turning the key in the lock. Her footsteps could be heard coming down.

'I'm interested, so interested, Mr Mallindaine. Our English tutor and your English secretary have talked of your family tradition. I love so much the traditions. You shouldn't be sent away from your house.' She made her hands into fists and thumped one on top of another in a way most alarming to see in a young girl. 'My friends and I,' she shouted coarsely, 'will put the son of that American Marchesa out of his house. They will not send you away from your house. The farm-house of the son is Italian property. The Curia had no right to sell it to her. The land where she built this house for you is Italian property. We want things Italian kept in the hands of the Italian people, we must remember our origins!'

Her oration finished, she breathed heavily with an overflow of indignation. Pauline had entered in the course of this speech and looked rather impatient of the rhetoric, in her English way. But Hubert, whatever he felt, looked impressed. He said, 'More Italian in origin than me you could not be . . . a direct descendant of a union between the Roman Emperor Caligula and the goddess Diana, here at Nemi. She must, of course, have been more than an idea; she was flesh, miraculous flesh, be sure of that. – Pauline, my dear, refill our glasses and help yourself. Letizia looks so like the very Diana of the Woods, she looks a true goddess of ancient Latium.' He shoved his glass towards Pauline who had sulkily fetched the sherry bottle. 'Diana, huntress, chaste and fair . . .' Hubert said. 'It's true. She remained chaste at heart even after she became the great goddess of fertility of all Italy.'

'Do you have documents,' said practical Letizia, 'relating to the family?' Pauline was holding out the refilled glass of sherry; her hand wobbled and a few drops fell on Letizia's pink cotton skirt.

'Documents!' Hubert said, over and above the exchange of Pauline's squeal of apologies, Letizia's reassurances, and the sound of Kurt upstairs banging on his bedroom door. 'Documents! I have an avalanche of family letters and documents. We are working on

them now. We're working against time. What do you think Pauline's
here for?'

Pauline looked downcast, and indeed she felt so. Letizia, so very
young and full of opinion, so very rich and so planted on her home
ground, simply by her presence put Pauline in the position of an
inferior. Upstairs, minding Kurt like the employee she was, while
Letizia relaxed with Hubert on the terrace, Pauline had felt
aggrieved. Letizia did not know quite how much *au pair* Pauline was;
Pauline had been lending Hubert money to live on. She had paid his
electricity bill. She had filled up the station-wagon with petrol to go
back and forwards to Rome with those chairs.

Pauline sat silent, not being at all helpful to Hubert on the subject
of the documents, because in the first place the documents she was
putting in order had so far failed to prove, really, Hubert's ancestral
claim, and secondly she did not feel in the mood to support him by so
much as a misleading grunt. Hubert thought her obtuse. 'Pauline's
been working on the documents,' he said. 'And I have sent for the
important ones, which have been kept in England and in Malta. The
Mallindaines lived for a long time in Malta.'

'It sounds most interesting,' said Letizia.

'It is most interesting,' said Hubert Mallindaine, and the words
brought once more to mind his two aunts having passed the window
on Lady Day. 'It sounds most interesting,' said the vicar who stood
looking straight out from the bow-window with his hands in the
pockets of his summer-grey clergyman's suit, rocking to and fro from
his heels to his toes, while his mother sat sewing in the window-seat.
The aunts had passed, without hats, which was strange for ladies in
Hubert's childhood; their hair, moreover, was cut short, straight,
grey and untidy. They were walking hand in hand, and his mother
had finished explaining to the vicar that her sisters-in-law were convinced 'Mallindaine' was a corruption of 'maligne Diane'. 'Which is
Old French,' his mother said. The aunts had not cared to turn their
heads towards them as they passed the window. '. . . on their way to
Hampstead Heath; they do it every Lady Day,' his mother said, still
intent on her embroidery. 'They light a bonfire and offer up prayers
to the goddess Diana, and I expect there are other rites. They could
be had up. Very eccentric. My poor husband could do nothing with
them.'

'It sounds most interesting,' said the vicar.

'I dare say it is most interesting,' said his mother, 'but it's embarrassing for me, because of the boy.'

'Have they means?' said the vicar, gazing out on the sunny Hampstead pavement.

Hubert had a few letters referring to these aunts and their special eccentricity. He had come across the letters some years ago in Paris, while sorting the first batch of his papers for his memoirs. From that moment he had cultivated the fact of these long-neglected aunts, one of whom had died in the meantime, allowing their fantasy to grow upon him. It may be that in those days he had felt a premonition, even before he had any outward sign, of Maggie's ultimate defection. Those were the years when he still had full control of Maggie's mind and it was he who convinced her to acquire the houses at Nemi 'where Diana, my ancestress, got laid by my ancestor the Roman Emperor'. It wasn't every woman whose escort and protector could make such claims. Submissively and carelessly Maggie had acquired two of the houses at Nemi and had the third built to Hubert's special stipulations; in the meantime she started an affair with a fine-looking young man who was a plain-clothes policeman and part-time actor, the very scourge of those other young men preferred by Hubert. She handed over the fretful details of the purchase of land and buildings at Nemi and had telephoned to Hubert from Rome in that special jargon used by people who at that time woke and took breakfast, as it might be, in Monte Carlo, flew to Venice for a special dinner, Milan next evening for the opera, Portugal for a game of golf and Gstaad for the week-end. 'J'ai compris – toute è Nemi – un avocat . . . called Dante de Lafoucauld, yes, really. – What do you mean, "my policeman lover", Hubert? – Il était gendarme, c'est vrai mais, mais . . . Well, darling, he's handsome. I have to sleep with someone, je dois – ma vie . . . Va bene, va bene, Hubert, ma cosa vuoi, tu? I tuoi ragazzi . . . I don't say a word about your boys, do I? Hubert, after all these years pensando che siamo sempre d'accordo . . . Look, I have to go . . . My maid has the luggage . . .' Maggie always travelled with her maid and now, for a short while, until the affair of course ended, with her policeman.

Hubert's aunts, in the meantime, grew in the grace of his imagination. They sprouted ancestors before them, springing from nowhere into the ever more present past, until Hubert had a genealogy behind him. He started corresponding with the surviving aunt who in her poverty and dotage was greatly consoled by Hubert's complicity in her life-long belief. He had brought the aunt to meet Maggie in her flat in Paris. Maggie's son, Michael, was there, and Mary whom he was shortly to marry. 'Our forebear Diana,' said Hubert's aunt, 'sets us rather apart. That is why I never married, nor my sister. Hubert will always be a bachelor, too.'

He sat, now, on the terrace of the house at Nemi, secure in this lineage in which he could truly be said to have come to believe, seeing that his capacity for belief was in any case not much. He managed very well without sincerity and as little understood the lack of it as he missed his tonsils and his appendix which had been extracted long since.

He sat half-facing Letizia. 'Documents . . . Yes,' he said, 'the documents exist, of course. Pauline is sorting out the documents. I'm writing my memoirs, you know.'

Letizia turned her head to look uncomfortably inside the house where Kurt's noise was coming from.

'You know how to handle him?' she said.

'Of course. Don't worry,' said Hubert.

Pauline helped herself to sherry and sat down.

Hubert said, 'I was good to him before. He wasn't on drugs then.'

Kurt sounded as if he would break down his door. Pauline did not move. She was watching Letizia who was ready to leave, and was standing, now, a little way off, gazing up at Hubert with her young face. They walked off to the car, talking. The girl obviously was extremely relieved to get rid of Kurt, and was gratefully attributing to Hubert a kind of broad-shouldered glamour which Pauline just for that moment realized he did not possess. That Hubert, walking Letizia to her car, was assiduously playing up to this role made Pauline impotently furious. She could not hear what Hubert was saying as he smiled down at Letizia, held her hand, kissed her hand, laid his hand reassuringly on the girl's arm, and held open the door of the car for her. Letizia turned to wave to Pauline who, after a slight pause, waved back in the laziest way she could manage. Then Letizia was off, back to her sheltered privilege, her Papa and

her holidays by the sea, while Hubert, really looking very handsome, strode back and up the steps to the verandah. Kurt was
shouting and banging louder still. Hubert looked for help towards
Pauline.

'What'll we do with him?' Hubert said.

'Get a doctor, I suppose,' Pauline said, not moving. 'It's your job.
You've been paid to look after him.'

'Look, Pauline, we can't get a doctor. You know he'll be put
straight into the loony-bin; my house will be searched; I'll be questioned by the police; you'll be questioned –'

'Oh, no I won't,' Pauline said. 'I'm leaving tonight. Going back to
Rome tonight and tomorrow I'm going to the sea. If your bouncy
admirer can get rid of her responsibilities and flip off to Greece
tomorrow morning, why shouldn't I?'

'Pauline, it would be very dishonourable of you to let me down at
this moment. Listen to him, up there!'

'How honest are you?' Pauline said, the words coming out in an
unpremeditated access of insight. She had never questioned his
honesty before.

Possibly suspecting that she already knew more about him than
she actually did, he said, 'Dishonest I may be when pushed to it; it's
a relative thing. But dishonourable, no.'

Pauline was by now very much upset, and this verbiage confused
her. She said, 'We should go up and get him. Bring him down, and
try to do something with him.'

'Come on, then,' said Hubert, loftily and pained. 'Let's see what
we can do.'

The boy's panic subsided when they opened his door. He was
laughing and crying as they brought him downstairs, Pauline
holding him by the arm and Hubert following, exhorting him to keep
calm, not to worry and to relax.

There was a canvas chair on the terrace that converted into a full-
length couch. Hubert arranged this and they got Kurt stretched out
on it crowing through his tears. His voice had the effect of ventrilo-
quism, sounding sometimes from a point above and behind him,
sometimes from the ground beside him. No words were distinguish-
able among these doom-like cries and sob-like spasms of laughter.
He bayed like an animal. He fell back exhausted. Hubert fetched him

a glass of mineral water and two of his Mitigil tranquillizers which
the boy took with upturned mad eyes.

Pauline was trembling. 'Either you call a doctor or I do,' she said.

'He can't be seen by a doctor here in my house.'

In the end Hubert agreed to take him to Rome to see a doctor he
knew who might even get Kurt into a private clinic. 'It will cost a
fortune,' Hubert said roughly.

'Isn't Letizia's cheque enough for the clinic?' Pauline was eager to
know how much.

'Barely,' Hubert said. 'We must hope for the best.'

It was nearly eleven that night when Hubert arrived in Rome with
Kurt, who was somewhat stunned by a further dose of tranquillizers
and trembling at the wrists and knees, in the front seat beside him.
Hubert drew up at the foot of the Spanish Steps in the Piazza di
Spagna, pressed a golden Victorian half-sovereign into Kurt's hand,
told him it was exchangeable for a week's lodgings, and put the young
man out on the pavement. Kurt made his way without looking back
to a crowd of young vagrants and hippies who were sitting or reclining on the steps in the warm young night.

'That's that,' said Hubert when he returned. Pauline had waited
up for him.

'A clinic?' she said.

'Yes, a clinic.'

'What clinic?'

'It's better you shouldn't know what clinic. If there are any questions, you know nothing. Just mind your own business, my dear.'

'It's Letizia Bernardini's problem. You should phone and let her
know what's happened before she leaves for Greece.'

'Don't be disagreeable, Pauline. Let the girl go in peace.'

'She hates foreigners, actually. She's that type of Italian. She's
only using you.'

'She appeared to be very charming. She's entitled to her bit of
folk-schmaltz, it's fashionable among the young.'

'I don't need to be told by you what it feels like to be young.'

'But you can be taught by me, I see, what it feels like to be jealous.'

'How could I be jealous,' said Pauline, 'when you don't care for
women, anyway? That's what you told me.'

'I do care for women. I don't have sex with them.'

Pauline started to cry. 'There was something passed between you and Letizia. I could see it. All that tenderness. I don't know what to believe.'

Hubert put his arm patiently around her shoulders, meting out an almost equal balance of tenderness. 'You can't leave me,' he said, 'because we're friends, and I need you.'

EIGHT

'Now you priests,' Hubert said, 'give me my money's worth. Ours is a friendship based on mutual advantage and so I expect some intellectual recompense for this materially superb dinner that we are about to receive.'

Father Cuthbert Plaice said coyly, 'Oh, Hubert!' Father Gerard gave a jocular smile to Pauline and lifted his fork.

'Pass the wine,' said Hubert. Pauline was wearing a long lavender-blue dress of floating chiffon; Hubert wore a deep purple patterned shirt of transparent cotton with expensive-looking blue jeans; the smart dining-room had been opened and the silver and fine glasses brought out; a cold buffet of elegant rarities was laid on the sideboard.

Cuthbert, having tasted his chilled salmon mousse, looked at Pauline across the candlelit table and said, 'Everything looks very sumptuous this evening.'

'He means opulent,' Hubert said, for no other reason than to be difficult.

'It's only a semblance of opulence,' said Pauline, warily; she was evidently thinking that their golden windfall must inevitably reach a point of exhaustion.

'But what is opulence,' said Hubert, 'but a semblance of opulence?'

'Well,' said Gerard, 'I would say there is a very, very great difference.'

'How ingenuous you are!' said Hubert.

'I don't understand,' said the young priest. 'How "ingenuous"? . . .'

'If you imagine,' Hubert said, 'that appearance may belie the reality, then you are wrong. Appearances *are* reality.'

'Oh, come, Hubert,' said Father Cuthbert. 'Pauline has just said that you have here a semblance of opulence. "Semblance" was her word – wasn't it, Pauline?'

'Yes, it was,' said Pauline, 'and Hubert knows what I mean.'

'A vulgar concept,' Hubert said. 'Tonight we have opulence.'

'But it might not be everybody's idea of opulence,' ventured Gerard. 'I mean of course you're making reality out to be something very subjective, aren't you? People differ in their perceptions.'

'Reality is subjective,' said Hubert. 'In spite of what your religion claims, I say that even your religion is based on the individual perception of appearances only. Apart from these, there is no reality.'

'Try having a scientist agree with you,' said Cuthbert, making little excited movements in his chair.

'The most advanced scientists do agree with me; in fact they're almost mystics,' Hubert said. 'As am I.'

'Can you come to the sideboard?' said Pauline. 'Take your own plates and help yourselves.'

'It looks delicious,' said Gerard, following her to the sideboard. 'And you look very nice in that gown, Pauline.'

'It's new,' she said.

'Is Maggie back from her holidays?' Cuthbert meanwhile inquired softly of Hubert, as if treading a mined field.

But Hubert ignored the question, standing back and beckoning the guests towards the spread of cooked meats and the choiceworthy range of salads. When they were seated Hubert produced a different wine, recommending it with a grand and far-away voice.

It was mid-September and still the heat of summer hovered far into the nights of Rome and its surroundings. Tonight at Nemi there was a faint hill breeze, hardly enough to flicker the candles through the open doors of the dining-room balcony.

'Delicious,' said Cuthbert. 'Delicious wine.'

'Delicious,' said Gerard.

'And Maggie,' Cuthbert plodded on, '. . . have you heard from her?'

'Not a word,' Pauline said, warming up to communicability which, with a little more wine, would presently become volubility. 'We had a letter from her before she left Nemi. She told us all her movements up to the end of this month. She should have been in America at the moment but I believe she didn't go. She's still in Italy. She wants us to get out of this house by the end of September, but –'

'Pauline!' said Hubert. 'Don't you think you might be boring these learned Fathers with this trivial gossip?'

'No, it isn't boring at all,' Cuthbert said.

'Isn't your chair comfortable, Cuthbert?' Hubert said.

'My chair? – Oh, yes, thank you kindly, it's quite comfortable, Hubert.'

'Cuthbert very often motionizes,' Gerard explained with well-wined pleasantness, 'while verbalizing, depending upon the emotive force of the topic in its relation to the scope and limitations inherent in the process of verbalization.'

'I see,' said Hubert, inclining himself very slightly in aristocratic acknowledgement of this exposition and with the same movement lifting his glass of deep red wine. He sipped and looked at a point above Pauline's head, as one who savours.

'Well, I wasn't being boring,' Pauline said. 'I was only saying that Maggie – and I've never seen her, mind you, I haven't met her at all – is simply impossibly spoilt. Too much money. She had a gentleman's agreement with Hubert and –'

'Maggie is not a gentleman,' Hubert said, 'and I find personalities a boring topic of conversation, Pauline, if you please.'

'What else is there to talk about?' Pauline said. 'Everyone reads the papers and we hear the news; I think it's boring to discuss what everyone's heard already. The point about Maggie is that she's holding this threat over our heads while she's sunning herself on some beach. We only have two weeks to go, and –'

'Pauline, enough!' Hubert said, loudly.

'Maybe we could be of help?' Cuthbert said. 'We found Mary, her daughter-in-law, a very charming, human person. Could I have a word with her? Gerard was in Ischia with them the beginning of August, you know. He –'

'Ischia – I thought they were going to Sardinia,' Pauline said.

'Maggie changed her plans,' said Gerard. 'I had an invitation from Mary to go study the surviving ecological legends of Ischia,' Father Gerard said. 'I stayed with them, it was very comfortable. And I must say that area is rich in legends of nature worship. Mary listed for me many cases of surviving nature-practices and superstitions in that area. They're devout Catholics, of course. I'm not saying anything against their faith; those peasants are great Catholics.'

'But they worship the tree-spirits and the water-spirits,' said Hubert.

'No, no, I wouldn't say worship. You've got it wrong. The Church continues to absorb many pagan nature-rituals because the Church is ecology-conscious.'

Pauline, who had been engaged in conversation with Cuthbert while the other priest was expounding all this to Hubert, suddenly broke in and, hurling the words across the table, said, 'Hubert – listen to this! Lauro, that Italian boy who was your secretary and works for the Radcliffes – well, he went to join them in Ischia and he's sleeping with Mary *and* Maggie. What d'you think of that?'

'Well, perhaps,' said Cuthbert, bouncing in his chair, 'I shouldn't have mentioned it. But, well, maybe – don't you think, Gerard? – it's something that Hubert and Pauline ought to know.'

Gerard, somewhat shaken, said hastily, 'Why, yes, in confidence, of course. As I told Cuthbert on my return from Ischia, this state of affairs arises from an impression, as it was indicated to me by primary coadjunctive factors, that formed in that location with the Radcliffes. But still, as I said, I found Mary very intelligent to be with and very, very helpful. I think, in her case, it's only a passing phase and that young Lauro should never have been allowed the freedom that he has. Mary was very helpful with her documentational listings.' When he had finished this speech he looked at Pauline reproachfully, as if by her outburst she had been a confessor who had burst out of the confessional proclaiming the outrage of a penitent's sins.

Pauline was not apparently concerned with his feelings. She was looking intently at Hubert. He looked back in aloof silence.

'Gerard,' said Father Cuthbert, 'is really very perceptive; since he told me about it, I thought about it and I decided this is something that you ought to know, Hubert, because both Lauro and Maggie have been friends of yours.'

'Personalities bore me,' said Hubert. 'I've spent too much of my life on perishable gossip. Cuthbert, let me change chairs with you; I can see that there's really something wrong with yours.' He got up and started moving his chair. Cuthbert looked bewildered.

'It's only a reflex of Cuthbert's,' said Father Gerard.

Hubert replaced his chair and before he sat down refilled their glasses. He said, 'Gossip and temporal trivialities. Whereas the intellectual principle endures. Cuthbert, be intellectual, for God's sake.'

Pauline took up her plate, holding it at arm's length from her new dress, and moved to the sideboard for a second helping.

'I thought you'd be interested, Hubert,' said Cuthbert, getting up to follow Pauline.

Pauline said, 'We've been hard at work all day. It's nice to relax at night.'

'Do you find it relaxing to think of Lauro busying himself with Maggie and Mary by turns?' Hubert said.

The priests giggled coyly.

Pauline said, 'I do.'

'Then you have a sexual problem, my dear,' Hubert said.

'Whose fault is that?' said Pauline.

'Maybe we'd better keep off personalities, as Hubert suggests,' Gerard said. 'There was a lot of that going on in Ischia, I'm afraid.'

'There always has been,' Hubert said. 'That's where your studies in pagan ecology should begin. Copulation has always been part of the worship and propitiation of nature.'

'Well, Christianity has given all that a very, very, new meaning,' said Cuthbert.

'To us,' said Hubert, 'who are descended from the ancient gods, your Christianity is simply a passing phase. To us, even the God of the Old Testament is a complete upstart and his Son was merely a popular divergence. Diana the huntress, the goddess of nature, and ultimately of fertility, lives on. If you poison her rivers and her trees she takes her revenge in a perfectly logical way. The God of the Christians and the Jews – where's the logic in him?'

'Hubert,' said Pauline, 'you know I'm a Catholic. I don't mind helping you but I won't have my religion insulted.'

Father Cuthbert said, 'Good, Pauline!'

'My dear, I knew you would take it personally,' Hubert said, 'and you look adorable tonight in your new dress. Go and get the sherbet ice out of the refrigerator and mind your frock.'

When the visitors had left, greatly cheered by the wine and liqueurs, the pleasant food, the physical prettiness of the evening and Hubert's exciting insults, Pauline went to change out of her new dress into a cotton nightdress in which she descended to join Hubert at the kitchen sink where he was stacking the dishes into the dish-washer. They started the machine buzzing, then Hubert poured whisky for both, and they sat at the kitchen table, sipping and sizing each other up for a silent while. Eventually Hubert said, 'Lauro and Maggie. Lauro and Mary. When will it be Lauro and Michael?'

'Just what I was wondering myself,' Pauline said. 'Only a few months ago I wouldn't have thought of it. But now since being here alone with you, Hubert, and sharing the trouble, we seem to think the same thoughts. I feel there's a real bond between us. An ever-lasting bond.'

'Everlasting!' said Hubert. 'A bond, my dear Miss Thin, is not very far from bondage. Don't frighten me, please.'

'Well, Hubert, you don't have to go back to calling me Miss Thin, suddenly, just at this moment. It's not very nice of you after all we've been through.'

'When I feel the bonds tightening, Miss Thin,' said Hubert, 'I break loose from them.'

'All right, I'll go away,' said Pauline.

'What have I done?' said Hubert. 'What have I done to deserve this?'

'Nothing,' said Pauline. 'That's the trouble. You've done nothing at all because you're a confirmed queer. Proximity to a man who does nothing gets on one's nerves after a time. I'm at the end of my tether and I'm leaving.'

'Before one speaks of sex I should have thought one considered the aspect of love,' Hubert said.

'I've got a boy-friend in Brussels working for the Common Market,' Pauline said. 'I can go to Brussels and consider the aspect of love with him.'

'Pauline, Pauline, how heartless you are! Love takes time,' Hubert said. 'And if you think you have a right to describe me as a queer when you don't know the first thing about my physical inclinations, then you've got a stupid and a common mind. If I were to impart to you the erotic details of what goes on in my mind they would excite you but *per se* would consequently cease to excite me.'

Pauline, successfully perplexed by this collage of clues, replied sulkily. 'Well, you once told me that you'd never slept with a woman; you said so yourself –'

'Which is not to say I can't.'

'Well, if you haven't, how do you know if you can?'

'Have you ever eaten blubber?'

'No,' said Pauline, ready to be very annoyed.

'Whale-blubber. I ate some once in a little fisherman's café in Normandy. It was on the menu so I thought I'd try it,' Hubert said. It tasted all right – fat and fishy – but I suppose there might be ways in which one could prepare it to make it an absolutely delicious dish. However, you say you can't eat it –'

'I said I'd never eaten it. What's whale-blubber got to do with sex?'

'Practically everything, if you're an Eskimo. Survival first, sex second.' As he spoke Hubert, noticing a two-inch quantity of champagne at the bottom of the bottle, poured it into his own glass. He now drank it and waited for Pauline to snap back some reply to him, which she failed to do.

Hubert reported dreamily, 'Blubber!'

'Do you mean to insult women by saying they're like blubber to sleep with?' Pauline said.

'I don't know what they're like to sleep with. But just because you haven't done a thing doesn't imply you can't.'

'Well, I've never eaten blubber and I'm damn sure I couldn't,' Pauline said. 'What has all this got to do with sex?'

'I thought we were talking about love,' Hubert said, persuasively. He considered it was time to go to bed but on the whole he decided another bottle of champagne between them would be a good investment and a good idea. It was appalling, he thought as he undid the cork, how much she wanted a lover and how much he needed a secretary-accomplice.

'What are you doing?' said Pauline, sitting winefully and sulkily in the corner of the big sofa.

'Opening another bottle of expensive champagne. With you in this mood, Miss Thin, I can't afford not to.'

'May I bring my lover in Brussels to stay with us for a while? He gets leave soon,' Pauline said.

'No,' he said, crossly. If she can try to be clever, he thought, I can be really clever. He filled their glasses, sank into his chair and raised his glass slightly to her before he sipped.

'You're using me,' she said.

'Of course. You'll be paid as soon as I have the money, Pauline.'

'I don't want to be paid.'

'You want to use me?' he said.

'No, I want to leave. Your behaviour . . .'

'You want,' said Hubert, 'to use me to satisfy your dreams. Which is wicked. I only want to use you as a secretary, which is perfectly reasonable behaviour. Are you in love with your lover in Brussels?'

'That's my business. Why do you keep talking about love?'

'My dear, it was you who started –'

'No, it was you.'

'Look,' said Hubert, 'one can't have sex with one's secretary. It doesn't work.'

'Now you're talking about sex,' she said.

'Well, it was you who started talking about sex, Miss Thin,' Hubert said, and refilled their glasses.

'We have to get new locks put on the doors tomorrow. The man's coming,' Pauline said, sleepily.

'Why are we getting new locks?'

'You told me to have them changed every month in case Maggie got hold of a key or something. Tomorrow's the sixteenth. I told the man to come tomorrow. Shall I put him off?'

'It's expensive, everything's expensive,' Hubert said, 'but no, my dear, don't put him off. You're very efficient.'

'Thank you,' she said. She put down her glass and started to walk carefully to the door, weaving only a little from her surplus intake of wine.

'Aren't you going to kiss me goodnight?' Hubert said when she reached the door. He made no motion to get up.

She looked back and felt the start of a drunken haze. She decided to use what lucidity remained to her to climb the stairs, clutching the banisters. 'No, of course not,' she said. 'What do you think I am? A piece of blubber?' She achieved an exit, leaving him to think over what she had said.

What he thought was that the worst was over for the time being. She had got out what was in her mind and might even regret having done so. However, the air was a little cleared and he could count on the *status quo* continuing until it was possible for him to develop a better and more stable *status quo*. Hubert finished the champagne, so musing, and enjoying the solitude of the night. He thought of Maggie in Ischia. She had not told him of her change of plans. He didn't know her house in Ischia. 'Maggie . . .' mused Hubert, 'Maggie . . .' At about three in the morning he had a sudden desire to telephone Maggie and wake her up, hear her voice. The Marchese would probably be snoring by her side in one of those huge matrimonial beds so prized by Italian families. Hubert felt he didn't care. He half rose from his chair to go into the study, get her number from the exchange and ring her up. Then he recalled with great sadness that the telephone of his house had long since been cut off.

NINE

'No reply from Hubert,' Maggie said. 'I should have had the phone bill paid if only to keep in touch with him. But I didn't see why he should have the use of it free, calling San Francisco, Hong Kong, Cape Town, you name it. And that lesbian, I had the phone cut off. Anyway I sent him a telegram two days ago to ask if he's ready to vacate the house, and he hasn't replied.'

Her husband, Berto di Tullio-Friole, was intent on listening to a Beethoven symphony on the gramophone and frowned across the room at Maggie to keep her voice down; he made an irritable gesture with his hand to accompany the frown; he was not in the least dis-enthralled with Maggie; he only wanted very much to savour the mighty bang-crash and terror of sound which would soon be fol-lowed by the sweet 'never mind', so adorable to his ears, of the finale. He was a sentimental man. Maggie and Mary lowered their voices.

Berto closed his eyes till the record came to an end. Then he went to join the women at the other part of the long paved room with its windows opened to the sunlight of October and the sea beyond. Lauro appeared from nowhere and was ordered to fetch a whisky and soda for Berto. 'Si, Signor Marchese,' said Lauro. No first names with Berto, nor would Berto have tolerated his wife, her son and her daughter-in-law to be addressed by their first names by any servant in his presence. Lauro, understanding this perfectly, had not even tried. They were nearly ready for lunch, already missing the past summer's days with their morning rhythm of laze and swim, laze and swim, on and off their private rocky beach. This beach, a small promontory, was not entirely private by law, only the elevated rock was private. The pebbly shore where the waves lapped was like all other beaches in Italy, public property, a fact well-known to the blithe visitors who ostentatiously intruded whenever the whim seized them to bring their little boats ashore. It had happened that, one day during the summer, Maggie's swim had been disturbed by a girl in a rowing boat; she was washing her long hair over the side with a shampoo which bubbled Maggie's way. Maggie, aware of her impotence in territorial rights, shouted at the girl, 'You can't wash your hair in sea-water.' Whereupon the girl shouted back, 'It's a special sea-water shampoo.'

Maggie had been very upset and after a hard day's work on the telephone to the mainland had procured five private coastguards who still lounged along the rim of the shore below and on the rock and in front of Maggie's house, dressed up as 'intruders', thus to keep at a distance the real ones. 'The time is coming,' Maggie said severely, 'when we'll have to employ our own egg-throwers to throw eggs at us, and, my God, of course, miss their aim, when we go to the opera on a gala night.' She had sighed; a deep sigh, from the heart.

Meanwhile they sat in the room with the blinds lowered against both the fairly bright sunshine and those hired intruders, who Maggie thought were making a noise beyond the call of realism, while Berto waited for his drink and the two women continued their discussion of Hubert.

Berto, who was less rich than Maggie, but rich enough to understand the excessive and rather mysterious concerns of rich women of Maggie's generation, and did not object to them, listened with a touch of tolerance and another touch of jealousy. The war of 1973 in the Middle East was just coming to an end. Things would never be the same again, as Berto had been told by the owner of the only newspaper he read. Once when he had entertained at a shooting-party a journalist of considerable fame, descendant of a noble family from Verona, who had ordered the delivery of three newspapers of conflicting politics, Berto had been highly indignant; his roof had been insulted and his hearth befouled; how could anyone read a Communist or a slightly left-wing newspaper, how could any friend of his read anything but the established paper of the right wing with its news reported fairly and its list of important deaths? The mild and middle-aged gentleman of Verona had tried very hard to point out that his profession required him to read all slants of opinion, but had not succeeded in conveying this to Berto who was convinced that all the needs of objectivity were supplied by the one and only newspaper permitted within his walls and whose owner he had known all his life. The journalist gave in and cancelled his wild order, being a man of agreeable temperament, and a desire to shoot some animals being one of the purposes of his visit.

'By law,' Maggie was saying to Mary, 'when you turn someone out of a furnished house in Italy, you send a certain number of warnings, then the authorities send a van for the stuff. By law they have to leave behind the bed, the washing machine and the contents of the files. I would love to take everything away and leave him with the bed, the washing machine and his ridiculous papers and let him share them with Miss Thin.'

'What about the man himself?' Mary said. 'How do you get rid of the person?'

'It's a different process and it's difficult because first of all the neighbours gang up to protect the guy, and then you have the Press and the photographers and the police. But before it comes to all that you have to –'

'Maggie dear!' Berto said. 'Maggie, my love, you'll just have to forget it, you know. Leave him alone; starve him out. He'll leave of his own accord one day, you'll see.'

'Now, Berto, you know you advised me to turn him out!' Maggie said.

'Yes,' said Mary. 'Berto – you did say to turn him out.'

'But,' said Berto slowly, exasperated by their lack of his local logic which he fully thought to be the universal logic, 'if the lawyer has told you the law, and it's going to make a scandal, then you can't succeed. You have to face the fact that the man has tricked you and has stolen your property. And you have to put that man right out of your mind because you can't put him out of your house and make a scandal for the Communists to make capital of in the papers.'

'Italy is a strange place,' Maggie said.

'It's the same everywhere,' Berto said. 'Times are changing rapidly and things will never be the same again.'

'I hate Hubert Mallindaine!' Maggie cried out. 'I loathe Hubert Mallindaine!' And as she exploded further about her feelings against Hubert, her husband was overcome by a tremendous jealousy; Maggie's emotions against Hubert were stronger by far than any she displayed towards himself; and Berto, suspecting in his jealous anxiety that she did not love him with the intensity that she hated

Hubert, was too agitated to care whether she expressed love or hate; he cared only lest Maggie felt something for Hubert and nothing for him.

'Hubert,' Maggie said, 'is a man that I despise, loathe and hate, and absolutely detest.'

'He is very contemptible,' Mary said.

'The servants will hear you, Maggie,' Berto said aimlessly, while staring at her as one appalled at his own fate. Lauro, representing the servants, appeared to inquire if he should serve more drinks. Berto had cancelled his trip to Le Touquet to buy horses. He had thought well before doing so; he had thought well, all the time knowing that he would decide to cancel the trip. Maggie had watched this process of decision with the eye of one watching a horse race, knowing full well which horse ought to win, and seeing it win.

'I'm thinking of getting married,' Lauro said.

'Really? To anyone in particular?' said Maggie.

Lauro looked put out. 'She's a fine girl from a very fine family. She did a year at the University of Pisa studying sociology, and she's only twenty.'

'And what does she do now, then?'

'She works in a boutique in Rome. Her mother also works in a boutique. Her father is dead; I don't know where he is.'

'What do you mean . . . ?'

'I don't know anything of the father. Maybe there isn't a father. The mother's family has land at Nemi, two fields.'

'Well, Lauro,' said Maggie, 'you're a lucky man. Is she beautiful?'

'Oh, yes,' said Lauro as if it went without saying.

'Well, why don't you bring her here to see us?' Maggie said.

'The Marchese wouldn't mix,' Lauro said with a laugh.

Lauro was sitting on the arm of one of the blue cotton-covered armchairs in the long paved room. He had opened the blinds to let in the mild sunlight of the late October afternoon. Berto was upstairs asleep. Mary and Michael had also disappeared upstairs where their voices sounded faintly in a continuous everyday tone. The rest of the staff had dispersed, some to the cottages behind the villa where their quarters were, others to hang around with their local friends at the bars which stretched along the quayside and where the incoming

ferries brought ever-new talkative life from Naples, and the outgoing
ferries carried away those multilingual visitors who had done their
day, or stayed their weeks, on the islands of Ischia. Lauro perched at
his ease, in a fresh shirt and blue jeans, sipping from a glass of cloudy
grapefruit juice and talking to Maggie. She sat back in her immacu-
late bright-coloured house-pyjamas, against the blue cotton covers of
her chair, and smiled through her bright eyes and even as it seemed
through the deep bronze of her skin.

Maggie was wondering whether Lauro had decided to talk of the
girl he wanted to marry from the sheer naturalness of his kind, or
whether he wanted to assert his male pride and put her in her place
in some way, since he made love to her often in Berto's absence and
when Berto returned was so very much the old-fashioned servant; or
did he, thought Maggie, smiling still, want a sum of money on the
excuse that he needed it for his wedding and in the knowledge that,
so far, she had always been generous to him with money? Maggie
pondered on these alternatives as Lauro spoke in his casual manner
about his girl and the boutique where she worked, and how she was
unaware that he was employed as a domestic. 'I am Mary's secretary,'
Lauro advised Maggie, who murmured gaily, 'Quite right, Lauro.'
Meantime Maggie's mind ran on the alternatives of Lauro's motives,
mistakenly assuming that they were in fact alternatives and that
Lauro was capable of analysing his own motives, or bothered to do
so, since it had never been in the least necessary for him to find one
reason only for doing any one thing.

Then Lauro said, 'I hope that Mary will not take it to heart.'

'Oh,' said Maggie, 'she won't object to calling you her secretary.
She'll play along. What's the difference?'

'I mean that I hope my marriage will not upset Mary?'

Maggie was about to ask, 'Why should it?' But, thinking quickly,
she refrained. She gave a little laugh instead and said, 'There's no
question of upsetting Mary.' And she was gratified to see that Lauro
was put out. He's trying to upset me, she thought.

'You know about Mary and me?' Lauro said.

'I know you're a very active boy,' said Maggie, laughing softly
again and gazing openly in his face.

'Well, you Americans . . .' Lauro said, gazing back.

'What about us?'

'Strange women,' he said, and in Italian repeated, 'donne strane.'

'Look, Lauro, I'll give you a wedding present, a handsome one. Mary, too, will give you a present; from her and Michael. Isn't that what you're talking about?'

'No, it isn't what I'm talking about,' said Lauro. He was furious and began to shout, 'You think you can buy everything, don't you? I was a secretary to Hubert Mallindaine and now I'm only the butler.'

'Well, I wouldn't say "butler",' Maggie said. 'A butler is a very special type of professional with a very special training. You would-n't fit in as a butler, really. I always thought of you as our friend who looked after us, as –'

'As a servant,' Lauro shouted. 'I have to wear that white coat, those black pants.'

'Well, Lauro, that's the custom and we pay you well. You do better with us than you ever did with Hubert, and besides you were only his houseman, really, among other things. The word "secretary" –' She stopped and motioned towards the staircase where footsteps descended.

Lauro stood up and Berto appeared in the bend of the staircase. 'What's going on?' he said to Maggie. 'Who's shouting?'

'Lauro wants to be known as our secretary from now on,' Maggie said. 'I don't see why he shouldn't be a secretary. He's going to get married.'

'Secretary? What do you mean? I don't understand,' Berto said.

Lauro stood in a state of confusion. He was exasperated by Maggie's coolness and quickness of mind and by the fact that he had put himself in the wrong by raising his voice. Maggie, smiling in her chair, was fully conscious that even if the younger man burst out at this moment with the wildest truths about his relations with Maggie and, possibly, Mary, he would be disbelieved on principle; and in fact he would be in deep trouble.

Lauro stood looking at Berto's angry face. 'I finish being a servant,' is what he said.

'All right, all right,' said Berto. 'You can go. Take your things and go. Come back tomorrow morning and I'll give you your wages and your severance pay and your holiday pay and all your other damned communistic rights for domestics, but don't stand there abusing the Marchesa. You don't raise your voice in my house, understand.'

The thought flitted into Maggie's mind that Berto was behaving out of character, but then the thought flitted away in the heat of things.

'Now, you listen a minute,' screamed Lauro, ready for a long hysteria-match such as he had been involved in several times before in his life, not only with Hubert but with the owner of a nightclub, with another Marchese, with a policeman known familiarly as Contessa, with his late mother and very many others. In torrential Italian he listed the indignities he had been subjected to in the service of the Radcliffes and threatened to denounce to the Minister of Inland Revenue the family's faulty tax returns, this being a safe guess; he said he would sue for being overworked and having to keep late hours with the result that he now suffered a nervous crisis. Tears came to his eyes as he bawled his accusations, convincing himself by his own voice, more and more, how humiliated he had been and how Berto had even done the unspeakable by addressing him with the familiar 'tu' instead of the third person 'lei' required by the law.

'Go!' screamed Berto and gave him the 'tu' again: 'Vai!'

Maggie now stood up majestically, spreading her golden arms in a peace-appeal. From upstairs Mary called down, 'Maggie!'

Maggie went to the foot of the staircase, leaving the two men glaring at each other, and called up, 'It's all right, Mary.'

Michael looked over the banisters. 'What's wrong?'

'Stay there, both of you,' Maggie said. 'Nothing's wrong.' Then she returned to the combatants. 'I haven't understood a word of all this Italian,' she said, 'but it sounds awful. Berto, I have to speak with you privately. Lauro's only a young man and they're all like that these days.'

Lauro spat on the floor between them and left the scene, mounting the main staircase to his room where he banged the door hard. Against the further banging of Lauro's cupboard door and his suitcases, Maggie settled once again in her chair with her hand to her head.

'I'm sorry, Maggie,' said Berto gently and quite surprisingly.

'Oh, these things happen.'

'Can I get you a drink?'

'Yes. Anything.'

He brought her a whisky and soda and she could hear the clink of ice in the glass as he brought it over. His hand was trembling.

Upstairs, Michael could now be heard in urgent conversation with Lauro, possibly trying to calm him down.

Berto brought over his own drink and perched where Lauro had lately perched. The ice in his glass pelted against the sides. He was agitated. 'I'm sorry,' he said.

'Well, Berto, it's sweet of you to feel sorry for me, but really he wasn't so bad before you appeared.'

'I'm sorry.'

'I don't want him to leave,' Maggie said. 'At least not yet. He might start saying things and cause a scandal.'

'Did he say anything about me? What did he say about me?'

'Nothing,' Maggie said, smiling again, 'except what he said to your face, and that was enough.'

'Oh, I just wondered if the little swine had said anything about me, as you say he might go around talking –'

'I mean Mary. He might talk about Mary.'

'What can he say about Mary?'

'I don't know. Between ourselves, Berto, I don't know if Mary hasn't been foolish with Lauro. He seemed to hint something like that.'

'Mary!' he said.

'Yes, Mary.'

'I can't believe that. These boys are capable of saying anything. They're dangerous. What did he want? Money?'

'I guess so. But you know he's proud and he went a long way round to ask for it.'

'He went the wrong way round.'

'I guess so.'

'He has to leave this house,' Berto said, rather factually and with a melancholy tone which invited contradiction.

'Maybe it will blow over,' Maggie said. 'I don't mind calling him our secretary. I don't see that it makes any difference what he's called. He says he's going to get married and the girl thinks he's a secretary.'

'I don't believe there's a girl.'

'No? Why not?'

'There are things you don't understand, Maggie. You know, at least, that he was Mallindaine's boy.'

'I dare say he goes with boys and girls regardless.'

'Amazing,' said Berto, obviously not much amazed.

'You should talk to him like a father, Berto.'

'Me?' he said. 'Look, I don't want any more to do with him. He's a whore. Coming into my house and raising his voice to my wife . . . Are you sure of what he said about Mary?'

'Well, he hinted. I don't remember the actual words.'

'He's a liar. I'm sorry.'

Maggie, suddenly unable to resist the impression that Berto had said 'I'm sorry' rather often, threw out a small bait. 'If we let him go, what could he say against *you*, Berto?'

'Anything,' he said. 'Anything. But it wouldn't be true, naturally.'

'Then we'll throw him out,' she said. 'Servants are a boring subject. So that's settled. Michael can drive him to the ferry.'

'He'll make a scandal of it,' Berto said. 'I think, in fact, he'll calm down.' He looked up to the ceiling. 'Michael seems to be dealing with him.' Berto was agitated, speaking softly and loudly by turns. Loudly now, he said, 'And he'd better apologize.'

Maggie said, 'I'm going to have a shower.' She put down her glass and got up, looking back at her empty chair. Berto stood up politely beside her, hovering and anxious to please. What a lot one can learn, she thought, just by sitting still for one hour in a chair. She recalled the long gaze of anger that had passed between Lauro and her husband a short while ago. It had been a knowing anger. She said to herself that she had not seen Berto lose his temper with the other servants or with any of his business employ-ees whatever their stupidity, or however much they lost theirs; Berto habitually subdued them by placing a thousand miles of ice between himself and them. On the other hand, she had seen him involved in brief shouting and glaring exchanges, like that with Lauro, when discussing a horse with his brother or politics with an acquaintance.

'Michael seems to have done the trick,' Maggie said, smiling as she went to the stairs. There was silence above. 'I'm sorry, Maggie,' said Berto as she left him.

Lauro came along the passage from the farther end, where his room was, and confronted her before she could reach her room. She put a finger to her lips. Michael threw open the door of his room, meanwhile. 'Mother,' he said, 'you upset Lauro.'

Mary appeared behind him. 'We have to call Lauro our secretary, Maggie,' she said. 'It's only fair.'

'I quite agree,' Maggie said. 'After all, Lauro is our secretary in a very real sense. A secretary is one who keeps secrets. What is the Italian for "secretary" anyway?'

Nobody answered her. She went into her room, glancing swiftly at Michael. God knows, she thought, what next to expect; anything might have been going on under my nose, anything. She took off her clothes and went to turn on her shower. But of course, she thought, it hasn't been under my nose. It's been somewhere I wasn't. Lauro with Mary. Lauro with Berto, of all people; Berto. Michael . . . God knows.

Berto, she mused to herself as she took her shower, is in love with me all the same. Mary and Michael I suppose love each other. Who loves Lauro? Who cares? And he knows he isn't loved in this little family; that's what the row was really about, I guess. She soaped her breasts and pummelled them between her fingers luxuriously. Lauro, she thought, knows a lot, and a man like that is useful to know.

By the evening their holiday guests, the Bernardinis, had returned with their English tutor from a three-day progress to various friends along the Amalfi coast. By the time Berto returned from the chemists with medicine for Lauro's migraine, the visitors were sitting out on the terrace overlooking the sea. Berto handed the bottle of tablets to one of the maids and told her to take it to Lauro in his room: two with a glass of water; then he rubbed his hands, cheered up and kissed Letizia Bernardini and Nancy Cowan, once on each cheek, both girls. Then he went and fetched a shawl for Maggie.

At dinner they spoke of Hubert, and of Nemi to where they were all planning shortly to return. It was not in their minds at the time that this last quarter of the year they had entered, that of 1973, was in fact the beginning of something new in their world; a change in the meaning of property and money. They all understood these were changing in value, and they talked from time to time of recession and inflation, of losses on the stock-market, failures in business, bargains in real-estate; they habitually bandied the phrases of the newspaper economists and unquestioningly used the newspaper writers' figures of speech. They talked of hedges against inflation, as if mathematics could contain actual air and some row of hawthorn could stop an army of numbers from marching over it. They spoke of the mood of the stock-market, the health of the economy as if these were living creatures with moods and blood. And thus they personalized and demonologized the abstractions of their lives, believing them to be fundamentally real, indeed changeless. But it did not occur to one of those spirited and in various ways intelligent people round Berto's table that a complete mutation of our means of nourishment had already come into being where the concept of money and property were concerned, a complete mutation not merely to be defined as a collapse of the capitalist system, or a global recession, but such a sea-change in the nature of reality as could not have been envisaged by Karl Marx or Sigmund Freud. Such a mutation that what were assets were to be liabilities and no armed guards could be found and fed sufficient to guard those armed guards who failed to protect the properties they guarded, whether hoarded in banks or built on confined territories, whether they were priceless works of art, or merely hieroglyphics registered in the computers. Innocent of all this future they sat round the table and, since all were attached to Nemi, talked of Hubert. Maggie had him very much on her mind and the wormwood of her attention focused on him as the battle in the Middle East hiccuped to a pause in the warm late October of 1973.

Letizia Bernardini, with her youth dedicated to an ideal plan of territorial nationalism, had she been able to envisage at that moment the reality to come would have considered it, wrongly, to be a life not worth living. At any rate, at Berto's table in Ischia that evening, Letizia conversationally embarked once more on the leaky ship of Hubert.

'There's a certain magic about him,' Letizia said, causing Maggie to glare at her and her father to smile. 'There's something of the high priest about him,' Letizia went on. 'I want to see more of him when we return to Nemi.'

Nancy Cowan said, 'I think he's pure fake.'

'What!' said Letizia.

'Why?' said Maggie at the same time as her husband said 'Fake what?'

One way and another, Nancy's quiet little words produced an uproar of argument, all about Hubert, so that they hardly noticed the good food they were eating or heard the very professional robbery of

Maggie's summer jewels going on upstairs in the meantime. Here are the details of the burglary:

Maggie's summer collection of jewellery was worth a vast fortune, even although it was far less valuable than her winter jewels, and considerably less again than the jewellery she kept in the bank summer and winter, except for the rarest and most important occasions. Her jewellery was difficult to insure against theft in any way that meant business; the insurance companies' requirements for so large a risk were not only so expensive as to defeat the purpose of insurance, but inconvenient as well. The companies insisted on the jewellery being housed in all types of safes and secured by innumerable safeguards, and even then were becoming more and more unwilling to insure jewellery of Maggie's sort. Generally, she avoided hotels and when she did stay in one she took very little jewellery, which she lodged in the hotel safe when she was not wearing it. Maggie's main problem was to prevent jewel-robberies at home. Burglar-alarms had become less and less effective as the burglars themselves became more and more adept at inventing, patenting, selling and subsequently exploiting them.

Two summers ago, Maggie had thought up a scheme to outwit the burglars, provoked as she had been at that time by a passing thief's discovery that she kept some of her jewels in a hot-water bottle. Her new scheme was to have a tiny kitchen built on an upper landing of every house she owned and frequented. This kitchen, complete with stove, refrigerator and sink, was ostensibly for the use of house-guests who wanted to be independent and who might take it into their heads to cook bacon and eggs in the middle of the night, or mix a drink. These upper kitchens were never used but were always elaborately stocked up with food and drinks. They were always approached by a little step about four inches in height. This step was in reality a drawer, and in this drawer went Maggie's jewellery, unlocked and unnoticed.

Maggie had not been robbed for two years until this evening at Ischia during dinner. Lauro was sleeping off his migraine, heavily dosed with the pain-relieving drugs that Berto had brought from the chemist. The other servants were occupied downstairs with the serving. A boat drew up quietly and unremarked on the rocks below Maggie's villa from where a lift ascended to the top of the house. One man was left in the boat on the look-out. Two others, young in their T-shirts and blue jeans, went up in the lift with fixed and sad expressions on their faces. They got out precisely at the landing where the little upper kitchen stood. The dinner proceeded downstairs and Lauro slept heavily in his room.

They left the lift door open, went straight to the kitchen door and within a few seconds had opened the drawer in the step. They emptied it and stuffed most of it bulgily under their shirts. All the rest, enclosed in their leather cases, they held in their hands and tucked under their arms as they sadly and expertly descended to the waiting boat. This operation was the fruit of six weeks' research into Maggie's habits, casual questioning at local bars connected with the latest construction of Maggie's upper kitchens, of boatmen connected with the villa, of unwitting servants who chattered about how ridiculous it was that the Marchesa had kitchens built at the top of her houses, always unused, and of simple deduction from a builder's boy's remark that she had quite unnecessarily called in a different builder from Milan to construct the step up to the kitchen. Summer jewellery though it was, the haul was high in the chronicles of summer robberies that year.

It was just towards the end of the dinner, with feelings and exchanges still vibrating across the table on the subject of Hubert, and Nancy Cowan quietly insisting that he was a fake, and Letizia rowdily defending him, with a murmur of scorn and an exclamation of despair here and there from Maggie, that the sound of an outboard-motor rapidly leaving the site of their landing-stage caused one of the servants to run out on the terrace and look over the cliff at the departing boat below. Suspicious of what he had seen he called out to one of the maids and ran to the lift. He pressed the button. Nothing happened. It was stuck down at sea-rock level, with the doors open.

It was when the maid returned to the terrace outside the dining-room window and started calling down vainly to Maggie's house-guards that the diners at the table were aware that something had happened.

'What's going on?' said Maggie, waving her arm towards the beautiful night outside the open french windows.

The maid and the manservant both appeared together in the

dining-room, worried. 'There's a boat seems to have just left here, Marchesa. It left with great speed and we can't find the house-guards. Those boys are terrible. I always say they're negligent. They must have gone to a bar, Signora Marchesa.'

'Go down and find them,' said Maggie.

'And the lift doors have been left open,' said the girl. 'The lift's stuck downstairs.'

'Then go down the steps,' said Berto, rising, bothered by the fuss. The man and the girl made off across the terrace to the winding steps that led down the cliff to Maggie's rock-beach. Berto stood looking after them.

The boat had already disappeared across the bay, heading proba-bly for another island or some remote inlet of the Neapolitan shore. Maggie said to the others at the table, 'Don't get up. Letizia, Nancy, go and get the fruit, please, will you? These servants are hysterical.' The cook had joined Berto on the terrace and was shouting inquiries to the maid and the manservant who had now reached the rock-beach. They were presently joined by those two of the five house-guards who were supposed to be on duty; they were amazed that their absence should have caused such a stir. Berto called roughly down to them to ask where they had been while the cook sent down vilifica-tions of a rich and strange Italian variety.

Nancy and Letizia brought fruit and cheese to the table, but Maggie was standing now, and Emilio Bernardini with her, his pale smooth oval face gleaming beside her brown and splendid one. She looked from the terrace to him, then to the terrace again, and then back to Emilio, into his brown eyes behind his judicious spectacles. 'Do you know,' she said, 'I'm going upstairs to check my jewellery.' Emilio looked anxious but he smiled and said, 'Oh, I hardly think . . .'

Maggie was still upstairs when another visitor arrived, by car at the front door. He rang several times before Emilio let him in. A short man with very black dyed-looking hair and a taut, very cosmetically-surgeoned face. He seemed understandably surprised that no ser-vants had appeared at the door to take his luggage and he greeted Emilio, who was obviously an old friend, with an absent-eyed genial-ity.

'Maggie's upstairs; she'll be down soon. The servants have made some mystery about an unknown boat that took off from the landing-stage in a hurry. Berto's down at the shore, investigating. Leave everything in the hall. Come in. Have you had dinner?'

The man said he had already eaten in Naples. Nancy and Letizia had left the table and were on their way down the sea-steps to join Berto and the servants. Emilio took his friend into the drawing-room where his son Pietro sat, sulkily uninterested in the fuss and ostentatiously unmoving. Emilio helplessly pressed a bell. As if in answer to it, Maggie appeared with her arms waving and her lips moving silently up and down in an effort of dumbstruck wild speech. Her arms waved and her dress glittered. On her arms and round her neck she wore the jewellery she had put on for dinner: bracelets and long necklaces of sea-shells which she had taken the whim to have set by a jeweller in conjunction with rubies and diamonds. These jewels, which were now all the summer jewellery she had left, made a sound like little dolls' teacups being washed up in some toy kitchen as her arms waved and her mouth gasped. She sat down on a sofa as Emilio came to help her. His friend had also stood up, quite bewildered by the whole business. Pietro sat still with a supercilious air.

'What happened, Maggie?' said Emilio, sitting down beside her.

Maggie pointed at the stranger, and this time her voice came through. 'Who is that?' she said, her pointing arm outstretched with its expensive shells.

'Maggie, what's happened? You've had a shock.'

'Who is he?' Maggie said. 'Call the police. Arrest him.'

'Maggie, don't you remember, you asked him to stay. He was expected, Maggie. What's wrong with you, my dear? This is my friend Coco de Renault.'

Berto returned followed by Letizia and Nancy. 'Nothing down there,' he reported. 'Someone took the lift down to the water and left the doors open. Must have been one of the servants, though of course they deny it.'

'Arrest him!' Maggie said, still pointing to Coco de Renault, who said, 'What the –'

'He's stolen my jewellery!' Maggie said.

At this moment Coco de Renault took charge. 'This lady,' he said gently, 'has had a shock.'

'I think so,' said Berto, while Emilio said, 'What's happened, Maggie?'

'My jewellery has gone,' Maggie said. 'It was upstairs in the kitchen step and it's gone. Call the police and arrest this man.'

But Coco de Renault was already pouring out a brandy and soda for Maggie. He came and stood over her like a doctor and said in a firm, almost harsh, voice, 'Drink this.' Maggie took the glass and drank. Monsieur de Renault then ordered the two girls to help Maggie stretch out on the sofa; on the strength of Maggie's words, 'My jewellery . . . the upstairs kitchen . . .' and assuming his hostess was unbalanced by nature and a mixed-up mood, he ordered Berto to go up to Maggie's room and investigate, and he ordered Emilio into the kitchen to investigate. He then ordered Pietro to have his luggage taken to his room and unpacked. Maggie lay on the sofa, moaning. Looking cross, Berto none the less went upstairs and Emilio with alacrity went into the kitchen where the servants were complaining and arguing loudly amongst themselves. Pietro did not move from his chair but stretched out his hand and tinkled a little china bell which was to hand. 'The servants are spoilt in this house,' Pietro remarked.

Monsieur de Renault stood in the middle of the room watching his orders being executed. His head was poised like the conductor of an orchestra. Lauro then appeared in the doorway, bare-chested and bare-foot, wearing only his day-time jeans. 'Who are you?' said Coco de Renault.

'I'm the Marchesa's personal secretary,' said Lauro.

'Then go and put on some respectable clothes,' barked the stranger-in-charge. Lauro fled.

At this moment, Berto's voice preceded his footsteps down the staircase. 'There's been a robbery! Maggie's jewels have been taken from their hiding-place. Call the police, call the −'

'Call the police,' Coco de Renault said to Pietro. 'Quickly, your mother's jewellery −'

'She isn't my mother,' Pietro said.

'Then who are you?' said de Renault as if he owned the place, and his question was so imperative that it seemed to include Berto himself who had now appeared in a state of agitation. Pietro said, 'I'm Bernardini's son,' and Berto said, 'I'm Tullio-Friole, the Marchesa's husband.' Pietro dialled the emergency number.

'How do you do,' said Coco de Renault to Berto. 'I'm Emilio's friend −'

'Oh, yes, Maggie was expecting you. I'm sorry about all this . . .'

Emilio returned from the kitchen and said, 'There's nothing missing from there. The servants are –'

'Please come immediately,' Pietro said into the telephone. 'Casa Tullio-Friole, the Marchese. There's been a robbery.'

Lauro appeared again, still half-dressed, and this time ready to express his summoned-up indignation. Maggie feebly pointed at Coco de Renault. 'He stole my jewellery . . .' she murmured.

'Maggie,' said Emilio patiently, 'this is Monsieur Coco de Renault, my friend from the Argentine whom you invited here. Your jewellery has been stolen by someone, probably common thieves who have got away by boat. Monsieur de Renault has just arrived in this distressing situation, but I'm naturally very embarrassed –'

'Maggie, Monsieur de Renault is our guest,' Berto said, while Nancy pressed a table napkin folded round ice from the drinks-trolley on to Maggie's forehead, and Letizia held her hand.

'I really am not embarrassed,' said de Renault. 'I understand shock. It's hardly conceivable that anyone would seriously take me for a jewel thief.'

The servants were questioned by the two policemen who presently arrived. Coco de Renault's documents were looked over as were Nancy Cowan's. The police took the numbers of the passports. They looked with a certain scorn at the drawer in the upstairs kitchen step. They expressed their doubts that the thieves would ever be found: 'The jewels will likely be broken up by now somewhere in the *quartieri* of Naples.' They inquired if the jewellery had been insured. Then they inquired why not. And on learning that its value was beyond the range of the insurance companies, exchanged glances. They assured Berto they would do their best, and Berto assured them, quietly, that there would of course be a reward if the jewellery should be found. The elder of the policemen exchanged some wry Italian colloquialisms with Berto: the stuff would never be found, and they knew it. Lauro, however, was taken away to the police station, in a fuming rage, to be questioned, much against Maggie's protestations but very much with Coco de Renault's approval.

'You can't trust *anybody*,' said de Renault when the police car had gone. And there was in fact this much in what he said, that he himself, within the year, was to trick Maggie into handing over to him the

bulk of her fortune, such a bulk as to make the more entirely absurd
her concern about Hubert's occupancy of the house, or the little
earnings of Lauro, or the theft, that evening, of her summer jewellery.

None the less, later that evening Maggie had so far recovered as to
sit clanking her remaining bracelets on her arm as she reached for her
drink, and asked Coco de Renault's advice as to how Hubert should
be removed from the house at Nemi. Lauro returned from the police
station by this time, soothed by the fact that Berto had followed the
police car and had gone right into the office of the Commissioner
himself to vouch for him, and had telephoned to the Prefect at
Naples, and had altogether given Lauro such a good name as to be
almost equal to promotion from private to general in the army. Lauro
sat, now, in his jeans and in the light cotton sweater he had put on to
go to the police. He sat arrogantly, as arrogant as young Pietro.

TEN

'Truth,' said Hubert, 'is not literally true. The literal truth is a common little concept, born of the materialistic mind.' He raised his right arm gracefully from the lectern before him, and with it the sleeve of his green and silver liturgical vestment. The raised arm seemed to signal an expectancy; the congregation obediently drew its breath; Hubert's eye rested on Pauline Thin in the third row, and he proceeded as if uttering a prophecy directed to all the world, but aimed especially at her.

'Brothers and sisters of Apollo and Diana,' Hubert went on, with his eyes focused defiantly on Pauline, 'we hear on all sides about the evil effects of inflation and the disastrous state of the economy. Gross materialism, I say. The concepts of property and material possession are the direct causes of such concepts as perjury, lying, deception and fraud. In the world of symbol and the worlds of magic, of allegory and mysticism, deceit has no meaning, lies do not exist, fraud is impossible. These concepts are impossible because the materialist standards of conduct from which they arise are non-existent. Ponder well on these words. Hail to the sacred Diana! Hail to Apollo!'

'Hail!' responded the assembly. 'All hail to Diana and Apollo!'

In the second row, the Jesuit Fathers Cuthbert and Gerard whispered together excitedly.

A little over a year had passed since the Middle East war of 1973, and Hubert was fairly flourishing on the ensuing crisis. He had founded a church. It cultivated the worship of Diana according to its final phases when Christianity began to overcast her image with Mary the Mother of God. It was the late Diana and the early Mary that Hubert now preached, and since the oil trauma had inaugurated the Dark Ages II he had acquired a following of a rich variety and ever more full of numbers.

It was the autumn of 1974 and Maggie had not succeeded in

turning Hubert out of her villa, partly because she had been distracted throughout that year by little thumps of suspicion within her
mind at roughly six-week intervals concerning the manipulation of
her fortune, with all its ramifications from Switzerland to the Dutch
Antilles and the Bahamas, from the distilleries of Canada through
New York to the chain-storedom of California, and from the military
bases of Greenland's icy mountains to the hotel business of India's
coral strand. Brilliant Monsieur de Renault was now the overlord of
Maggie's network. Mysterious and intangible, money of Maggie's
sort was able to take lightning trips round the world without ever
packing its bags or booking its seat on a plane. Indeed, money of any
sort is, in reality, unspendable and unwasteable; it can only pass
hands wisely or unwisely, or else by means of violence, and, colour-
less, odourless and tasteless, it is a token for the exchange of colours,
smells and savours, for food and shelter and clothing and for representations of beauty, however beauty may be defined by the person
who buys it. Only in appearances does money multiply itself; in
reality it multiplies the human race, so that even money lavished on
funerals is not wasted, neither directly nor indirectly, since it nour-
ishes the undertaker's children's children as the body fertilizes the
earth.

Anyway, back to Maggie's fortune: Coco de Renault had reorga-
nized her financial network throughout the past year; he had made
something of a masterpiece of it. Like so many others in that year he
began using the new crisis terminology introduced by the current
famous American Secretary of State; Coco de Renault's favourite
word was 'global'. He produced an appealing global plan for
Maggie's fortune, so intricate that it might have been devised pri-
mordially by the angels as a mathematical blueprint to guide God in
the creation of the world. It was quite unfathomable, but Maggie,
whose rich contemporaries were beginning to look at each other with
wild alarm, at first felt a great satisfaction at having acted in time. She
felt that brilliant Monsieur de Renault from the Argentine was a sort
of perfected bomb-shelter. But as the months of 1974 passed from
those of spring and summer into the autumn, she had experienced
these intervals of anxiety, sudden little shocks. On one occasion she
realized that her administration headquarters, which previously
occupied an entire floor of offices in a New York block, with three

full-time lawyers, twelve accountants and a noisy number of filing
clerks and secretaries who fell silent on the few occasions that Maggie
made a visitation thereupon, was now all disbanded. Pensions and
parting gifts had been bestowed on the staff. The lately administering lawyers had lawsuits pending against Maggie for breach of contract, but Coco de Renault was dealing with such trivial nuisances
out of court. Coco explained to Maggie, the first time she had one of
her little shocks on realizing her estate had no business headquarters
any more, that a headquarters was the very thing she had to avoid.
He was her headquarters and she must realize he was dealing with
her affairs globally. Maggie calmed down. Another time, she failed
to find him on any of his telephone numbers on the globe. She went
frantic, rattling the receiver for long hours over a period of three days
and a half, in the course of which a strike of the international telephone service took place in the Veneto, from where she was calling.
Vainly dialling the Minister of Posts and Telegraphs in Rome,
Maggie looked out of the window of Berto's Palladian villa and saw
her husband talking to the groom as if the world were not coming to
an end. It came to her that if she were to die there would be an enormous lachrymose funeral with the Italian nobility speeding up to the
Veneto to attend it and lay her in Berto's family tomb; then two days
later Berto would be out in the garden as usual talking to the groom,
while her son Michael would be busy on the question of her fortune.
Maggie drove off to Venice and booked into an hotel from where she
tried to telephone to Coco. The strike on the international exchange
still prevailed. She looked out of the window and saw a placard which
said 'The Postal Strike of the Veneto Must Be Confronted Globally.'
She remained frantic after the strike was over, and still in the hotel
room tried one number after another in search of Coco and her
power of attorney. She tried San Diego, California, Port au Prince,
Hong Kong, London, Zürich, Geneva and St Thomas in the Virgin
Islands. Then she tried Madras. She had been in Venice two days
when Berto called her to ask what she was doing. Had she been to the
del Macchis' masked ball? How was Peggy? She said she was trying
to find Coco de Renault. He replied that he thought there had been
a call from de Renault if he wasn't mistaken. Maggie returned to the
villa and located Coco within a few more agonizing days. The fear
passed once more. 'I've been at Nemi, at Emilio Bernardini's,' he

said, and laughed at the news that she had looked for him every-where.

These distractions took her mind off Hubert but every now and again she was brought back to her frustration over his stubborn occupancy of the house. At the beginning of the summer of 1974 unknown to Berto she had handed the whole story of Hubert, in her own revised version, to an obscure lawyer in Rome, with instructions to get Hubert out of the house and to do it without a scandal. The lawyer promptly agreed to do it, and not only did he point out that the new Italian laws made it difficult to turn anyone out of any habitation whatsoever, but had exaggerated the difficulties. Maggie duly paid the man the large deposit he demanded to match the exceptional difficulties of the job he had undertaken. As it happened, this lawyer, having sentimental sympathies towards the political left wing, although no longer the extreme leftist he had been in his poor student days, loathed what he conceived Maggie to stand for at the same time as he was put into an ambivalent state of excitement by her glowing and wealthy presence. The one time she presented herself with her case in his absolutely ordinary office became an obsessive memory; as the months passed and the unseen presence of Maggie lingered here and there, with her voice on the phone to remind him on the one hand of his undertaking and, on the other, of her vital self and her money, his office and his life seemed in his eyes to be even more sad and ordinary. So that he was more short-tempered now, with his wife and with his secretary, than before. The secretary, indeed, left and he had to make do with another, inferior one; meantime Maggie was living her life all unaware of the effect she had produced on the lawyer. As to getting Hubert out of the house, the lawyer had written him a letter in a somewhat vague manner. Hubert had sent it back scrawled at the bottom with the message, 'Mr Hubert Mallindaine is at a loss to understand this missive and, assuming that it is misdirected, returns it to the sender.'

'You see,' explained the lawyer on the telephone to Maggie, 'he knows well the Italian laws. If you take out a court order even, this makes two years before you can disencumber him. He will make the newspaper scandal that your husband fears and he might win the case if he proves that the house was built by his instructions for his own use. The laws are now on the side of the tenant, always. And if he loses the case everyone will assume he has been your *amante* and you are tired of him.'

'Don't you know,' Maggie said, 'there's a big recession on? We can't afford to give away houses and there is valuable furniture inside. My Louis XIV furniture . . .'

'You have said he had them restored?'

'I believe he's looking after my things. Yes. There's a Gauguin painting, too. I want it.'

'If he is spending money to care for the property he could argue that the property was his, else why should he spend the money?'

'Are you my lawyer or his?' Maggie said.

'Marchesa, I see the case objectively and I will try. I have my heart's sympathy with your side. Everyone knows what our laws are like in the world of today. I have landlords and proprietors at my office lamenting every day that they cannot remove their tenants and they cannot raise the rents —'

'But he's paying no rent, and it's fully furnished, my house.'

'That is all the more argument for him. Marchesa, you permitted him to stay too long. Now is probably too late, in effect. In effect, I will try and I can only promise to continue to try. If you are not satisfied with my efforts, Marchesa —'

'Oh, please carry on. Please do. I quite understand the difficulties,' Maggie said. 'But I have many problems just at this terrible moment in the economical situation of the world and I do wish to have the house to be near my son.'

'The law says that if you already have a habitation, Marchesa, you cannot evict a tenant on the grounds that you need the house. Only if you are homeless —'

'I know. I know. Go ahead, please; I have complete faith in you —'

'If you would care to lunch with me on your visit to Rome, I could better explain my plan of next procedure, or you could call in again at my office —'

'No, it won't be necessary —'

'It would be a pleasure. Or could I come to visit you at the Veneto? It is a country I well know —'

'What do you mean, "country"? It's still in Italy.'

'That is our manner of speaking. In Italy are many countries. I would be happy to visit —'

'Just at the moment I can't make plans,' Maggie said. 'Please go on trying and keep in touch with me.'

The lawyer wrote again to Hubert, a strong firm letter, cunningly phrased with many citations of law, number this and section that, including the commas. It was the sort of letter that would send the civil courts of Italy into a frenzy of sympathy for the tenant, at the same time as it left the lawyer professionally irreproachable. To this bureaucratic communication Hubert replied from the local bar at Nemi, by telephone.

'Look,' he said to the lawyer, 'this house is mine. The lady gave it to me. I've nowhere else to go. Why don't you just take me to court?'

'What number are you calling from?' said the wary lawyer, anxious about a possible telephone tap.

'The bar,' said Hubert, 'here at Nemi. Can't you hear the noise? I can't afford a telephone at my house. The Marchesa had it cut off.'

'Tell me the number and I'll call you back,' said the lawyer. He checked the number that Hubert gave him, and rang back to the bar.

'Now,' said the lawyer, 'it's like this. I have to do my duty, and I have sent you a letter. You have nothing to worry about.'

'I have plenty of things to worry about,' Hubert said, 'but the house isn't one of them. Why do you send me these absurd letters?'

'I am at the Marchesa's command,' the lawyer said. 'You want my advice? You write me a reply that you are not well and enclose a medical certificate. When you are recovered you will see your lawyer.'

'I'm in the best of health,' Hubert said. 'No doctor would give me a certificate, and anyway, I don't know any doctor in Italy.'

'Write me the letter,' said the lawyer, 'and I will arrange for the certificate.'

'This is unusually kind of you,' Hubert said. 'Why don't you come here and have a chat? I should be delighted to show you my house and my wooded grounds. And then, after all, I don't know how far involved you are with Maggie. I'd like to be reassured.'

The lawyer, who was fat, laughed with the full fruition of the fat. 'Sunday,' he said, 'I could make a little escape and getaway. After lunch, Sunday. Good?'

'Good,' said Hubert.

*

By the autumn, all the Louis XIV chairs had been replaced by very beautiful fakes, the Gauguin had been replaced by a copy for which Hubert had paid a very high price, but not, of course, a price of such an altitude as that fetched by the Gauguin, now safely smuggled into Switzerland. He had also replaced a Constable with a fair enough copy, the original of which, in any case, had been kept in a dark corner, so that the many fine points of difference between this and the fake were obscured by the gloom. A Sickert painting still awaited treatment because the price of a good copy was by now reaching excessively blackmail proportions and Hubert was investigating another organization which provided a discreet art-copyist and export service. He had similar plans for an inoffensive Corot in the lavatory, with its little red blot in the right foreground, and also an umbrageous Turner which, although it was small, overpowered the wall of the upstairs landing, but this, one of the experts in clandestinity had informed Hubert, was already a fake; an expensive fake, but not marketable enough to have copied.

In this way, Hubert was very comfortably off by the time the collapse of money as a concept occurred. 'I refuse,' he said, 'to eke out my existence or change my philosophy of life according to the cost of oil per barrel –'

All the same, he took care to continue changing the locks on the doors of the house frequently. He did not flaunt his newly-acquired money. The telephone remained cut off, the garden was weeded to the minimum and the paint on the outside doors and windows was left to peel and flake with poverty.

The expert self-faker usually succeeds by means of a manifest self-confidence which is itself by no means a faked confidence. On the contrary, it is one of the few authentic elements in a character which is successfully fraudulent. To such an extent is this confidence exercised that it frequently over-rides with an orgulous scorn any small blatant contradictory facts which might lead a simple mind to feel a reasonable perplexity and a sharp mind to feel definite suspicion.

Pauline Thin's mind was not particularly sharp. But in her second year as Hubert's companion and secretary she had acquired enough experience of him, of his documents and his daily sayings, that she couldn't fail to realize that something was amiss between Hubert's claims and the facts. It was just when, with the aid of his new ally, Maggie's plump lawyer, Hubert had founded his religious organization that Pauline had discovered among Hubert's papers clear evidence that his aunts, infatuated by Sir James Frazer and his *Golden Bough*, had been in correspondence with the quack genealogist; they had instructed him in the plainest terms to establish their descent from the goddess Diana.

Hubert had looked Pauline straight in the eyes and with some arrogance informed her that she was misreading his aunts' intention, that she was terribly ignorant on some matters, but that he entertained many fond feelings for her, none the less.

Impressed by his cool confidence Pauline read the letters again, and was again dumbfounded. And once more, Hubert, actually looking over the batch of letters that Pauline had placed in his very hands, said only that she was a nice little fool, threw them aside, and went off about some other business.

It was the next day, at the meeting of the Brothers and Sisters of Diana and Apollo, that Hubert was preaching his sermon on the nature of truth. He had turned the dining-room, which led off the entrance hall beyond the terrace, into a chapel. The new world which was arising out of the ashes of the old, avid for immaterialism, had begun to sprout forth its responsive worshippers.

'Truth,' Hubert repeated as he wound up his sermon, his eyes bending severely on Pauline, 'is not literally true. Truth is never the whole truth. Nothing but the truth is always a lie. The world is ours; it is in metaphorical terms our capital. I remember how my aunts, devotees as they were of Diana and Apollo, used always to say, "Never, never, touch the capital. Live on the interest, not on the capital." The world is ours to conserve, and ours are the fruits thereof to consume. We should never consume the capital, ever. If we do, we are left with the barren and literal truth. Let us give praise to Diana, goddess of the moon, goddess of the tides, the Earth-mother of fertility, and to Apollo, the sun and the ripener, her brother. Hail to Diana! Hail to Apollo!'

'Hail!' said the majority of his congregation, while Father Cuthbert Plaice whispered to his fellow-Jesuit Gerard, 'There's a lot of truth in what he says.'

'I like the bit about the earth being our capital,' replied Gerard, ever ecologically minded, 'but he mixes it up with a lot of shit, doesn't he?'

'Oh, well,' said Cuthbert, 'it's like manure and even if it's shit it gets people thinking about religion, doesn't it?'

'Yes, I suppose it's an experience, isn't it?'

Hubert, splendid as a bishop *in pontificalibus*, folded in his vestments of green and silver, proceeded up the aisle giving his benediction to right and left before disappearing into the downstairs bathroom which had now been transformed into a vestry.

'Miss Thin,' said Hubert as Pauline came in behind him, 'remind me to apply for an unlisted, repeat unlisted, telephone number.'

ELEVEN

'The trouble with Berto,' Maggie said quietly to Mary, 'is that his *tempo* is all wrong. He starts off *adagio*, *adagio*. Second phase, well, you might call it *allegro ma non troppo* and pretty nervy. Third movement, a little passage *con brio*. Then comes a kind of righteous and dutiful *larghetto*, sometimes accompanied by a bit of high-pitched *recitativo*, and he goes on, *lento*, you know, *andante*, *andante* until suddenly without warning three grunts and it's all over. What kind of an art of love is that?'

'Rhythm is very, very important,' said Mary reflectively, 'in every field of endeavour. What is the *recitativo* bit?'

'I don't understand dialect Italian,' Maggie said. 'Ordinary Italian is difficult enough, but this is some sort of dialect that Berto uses on these particular occasions. Afterwards he talks about horses, how a horse may go off his feed from too much exercise or too little or how sometimes horses get lumps on their skin from over-exercise or under-exercise, I forget which. Anyway, he frequently talks about horses afterwards. What kind of an art of love is that?'

'I could tell you a lot about Michael,' Mary said, 'but as he's your son it makes an obstacle.'

'I hardly think of him as my son any more,' Maggie said. 'Michael can be very inconsiderate. I think of him more as his father's son and if he's anything like Ralph Radcliffe then you have a problem there. Ralph was a problem but very, very attractive. Berto is no problem at all, but it's boring to go to bed with him, especially when you're my age. In your case you have your whole lifetime in front of you.'

'Not all of it,' Mary said. 'I feel I'm wasting my best years sometimes, and I know Michael's got a girl in Rome, too. But I want to make a success of my marriage, I really do.'

'You can always take time off,' said Maggie, 'while Michael's in Rome with the girl.'

'Well, I wouldn't like to.'

'You must think I'm pretty dumb,' said Maggie, 'if you think I don't know that you take time off with Lauro.'

Mary said, 'Oh, no! This is terrible. You mustn't say such a thing.'

'Keep calm,' said Maggie. 'Nobody else knows anything about you and Lauro.'

The girl started to cry. 'I wanted my marriage to be a success.'

'Go on wanting it, is my advice,' said Maggie, while Mary dried her tears on a paper tissue from the box beside her and drank a large gulp of her vodka and soda, spilling some of it on her body.

They were in bathing suits on the concealed sun-terrace of Berto's Palladian villa in the Veneto in the spring sunshine of 1975. They lay side by side on the dark blue mattresses soaking up the sunny vitamins of May in the hours between noon and lunch at two. Maggie reached out for her body lotion and smeared it over her legs, her breasts and shoulders, then, playfully, she smeared the remainder on her hands over Mary's belly, so that the girl became less nervy; she lay back somewhat becalmed and murmured solemnly, 'Lauro doesn't mean anything to me.'

'He satisfies the appetite,' said Maggie, 'but not the passions, I agree.'

A bright smile came suddenly to her face as Lauro himself appeared on the terrace, carrying a mute transistor radio and a bottle of Vermouth. 'Why, Lauro!' she said. 'I thought you were taking the morning off.'

'I shouldn't have come to this house at all. I repent it. The staff is terrible. They are vulgar domestics. They hate me. I came to help you out. I should have stayed at Nemi where I work for Mary and Michael. I am not obliged to follow the family.'

'Oh, Lauro, you can go back to Nemi any time you like,' Mary said.

He removed his white coat, put the bottle on the drinks trolley and stretched on a mattress beside them, and then got some pop music on his radio.

'God, Berto, will see you, Lauro!' said Maggie. 'And I'll get the blame for fraternizing.'

Lauro threw the radio to the other end of the terrace where it stopped playing; he jumped up in a neurotic fit, spitting Italian obscenities, put on his white coat, and left.

'Well, I've finished with him as a person,' Mary said. 'He really means to get married to that girl in Nemi.'

'You'd better keep him on as a houseman,' Maggie said. 'Trained servants are hard to get. And he is well trained, you know.'

So much could be recounted about the winter past, so many sudden alarms as to the whereabouts of Coco de Renault and so many frantic messages sent by telex to non-existent offices far away; always, Coco turned up with an explanation and enough ready money to put Maggie back in a stable frame of mind.

He had on one occasion gently and consolingly hinted that she was the victim of the menopause, and this act of stupidity on his part nearly finished his relationship with Maggie, so violently did she react. Berto had to intervene and explain away Coco's mistake. He told Maggie that Coco was probably in love with her. 'This is a way in which a man in love tries to provoke a woman,' he told Maggie. 'When there is no hope for him, he provokes.' And to Coco, privately, he said, 'If what you think is true, as it probably is, then the last thing you should suggest is the truth, since the truth is the original irritant.' Coco meekly humoured Maggie and presently told her that her financial affairs were blooming only a little less than her lovely self.

There had been so many bad scenes that past winter with Lauro, and a cruise with Mary and Michael for Christmas in the Caribbean, followed by a week together in New York where Berto joined them. Berto now expressed strong doubts about Coco's integrity and escorted them home. Maggie defended Coco expansively; Coco was nagging her to have her portrait painted by a young artist friend of his.

And all along, Maggie had reverted to her passion for evicting Hubert from the house at Nemi. So much could be recounted.

'Eras pass,' said Hubert, in the new comfort of his life, 'they pass.' He had just read in the newspaper of 15 February that year that Julian Huxley and P. G. Wodehouse were dead: 'The passing of an era . . .' the newspapers had commented.

But this day in May 1975, in the sun of the north Italian spring, chose itself from among those others to be that sort of day when complications ripen, since inevitably there is always one particular day when discoveries come into being, when incidents put out shoots and start to bring into force from the winter's potentialities the first green blades of a crisis. Maggie and Mary stretched out on the sun-terrace before lunch while downstairs the probabilities foregathered to form what are the most probable events of all, which is to say, the improbable ones.

Meantime, Maggie said to Mary, 'We should go off to Nemi soon. I have to get Hubert out of the house. The Church authorities should be on my side. He's committing a great sacrilege in my house with that cult of his. He's got to be exposed, because of course he's sheer fake.'

'I'd like to go to one of the meetings,' Mary said. 'If only I could do so in disguise. You know, Letizia Bernardini says the services are terribly elating, really like magic.'

'Could we both go in disguise?' Maggie said.

'He'd be sure to find out. He's very, very discerning,' Mary said.

'I could kill that man, I really could,' said Maggie. 'It isn't so much the property, it's the idea of being done down that makes me furious with him.'

'Yes, and he wasn't even your lover,' said Mary, egging her on as usual, since the theme of Hubert had become one of Mary's favourite serialized entertainments.

'He wouldn't know what to do with a woman,' Maggie said. Twelve guests for dinner tonight; with Michael, Mary, herself and Berto that made sixteen. There were dinner parties practically every night. New friends, old friends visiting Italy from America, old and new friends of Berto's. Maggie sat for Coco's young artist; then it was Mary's turn. 'He's got you both out of focus,' Berto had said. In a world of jumping sequences, the problem of Hubert was a point of continuity, although Maggie herself had no idea how gratefully she clung to it.

Berto's Palladian villa was a famous one. It had been photographed from the beginning of photography and, before that, etched, sketched, painted, minutely described inside and out, poetically laboured upon, visited by scholars and drooled over by the world's architects. The Villa Tullio was indeed a beauty; the Villas Foscari, Emo, Serego, D'Este, Barbaro, Capra, with their elegant and economical delights still in comparison with the smaller Villa Tullio, seemed to some tastes to be more in the nature of architectural projects and propositions. The Villa Tullio was somehow magically complete and at rest. It was a farm-house built for the agricultural industry of the original Tullios, for the charm of its position beside a reclaimed waterway and the civilized comfort of Berto's prosperous ancestors. Now, the plans of this house, every angle, every detail of its structure, being known throughout the world, photographs of the interior and exterior, and the original plan of the lay-out from every side having been published for centuries in studious manuals and picture books, it was hardly worth the while or the price for a gang of expert thieves to send their men to case the lay-out. However, they did.

It was ten minutes past twelve when two smart-looking men drove up to the marvellous front door in a white touring car. On to the upper balcony came Berto from the library where he had been glooming behind the french windows. Out he came into the shadows cast by the sweetness and light of that harmonious pediment. He did not recognize the people. They were too early for lunch, and therefore probably were not friends of Maggie's. Most likely, then, they were visitors come to inquire if they could see the house. Berto's arrangements for sightseers were very haphazard. He kept no porter at the lodge. While he was away his old butler was accustomed to use his sixth sense as to whom he admitted into the house and whom he sent away. There were no regular visiting days as had been established in the grand and more famous buildings of Palladio. Mostly, the visitors who wanted to see over the villa wrote in advance, or were written for by their universities or, as it might be, some friend of Berto's family. It was well known that Berto had changed nothing of the structure; only, over the years, in the interior, had new drainage systems been installed and bathrooms fitted in.

Berto was proud of his Palladian jewel, and his heart bent towards the two arrivals with such a desire that they should be educated tourists wanting to see the house that he invested them at first sight with various nice qualities. They mounted the fine steps, a tall, white-haired man and an equally tall youth, presentably dressed in fresh shirts and pale trousers; they approached the house with the right visitors' modesty and lost themselves under the balcony where Berto hovered and awaited their ring of the door-bell.

After a few seconds, during which Berto imagined them to be

admiring the portico, that harmonious little temple, and the well-cal-
culated panorama therefrom, the bell rang. Berto withdrew from the
porch into the library and heard below the shuffle of Guillaume
going to open the door. Guillaume was the old butler, who had been
brought as a small boy from Marseilles sixty-two years ago by
Berto's father and who, having had no surname that he knew of, was
long since equipped with one: Marsigliese; he fairly ran the villa, and
Berto who had grown up under his eye rarely questioned his judgement. Berto enjoyed with Guillaume a kind of reciprocal telepathy
by which Berto understood precisely which of his friends Guillaume
meant when he said that the French had telephoned, or the Germans
had called, or that the Romans might be arriving, although, in fact,
Berto had a good number of friends who might fit each definition.
Guillaume Marsigliese likewise knew exactly which Americans were
expected to dinner when Berto said he had invited 'the Americans';
no doubt there was a slightly different inflection of their voices for
each designation, but no friend discussed between them in that way
was ever confused with another. 'The Americans' also covered Mary
and Michael, and, before her marriage to Berto, Maggie.

Now Guillaume had started to climb the beautiful sweeping staircase and Berto, to save him the fatigue, came out of the library door
to meet him, leaning over the well of the circling banister.

Guillaume looked up. 'People,' he announced, without further
elaboration – '*Genté*', by which he conveyed that the visitors were, as
Berto plainly expected, people who wanted to see over the house.
And the fact that he had invited them to wait inside and given them
some hope that Berto would receive them demonstrated that he considered the newcomers not, so far, unworthy, without committing
himself further to the road of positive approval.

'A few moments,' Berto said, giving himself time to put away the
papers he had been studying and the visitors time, no doubt, to
admire the care that had gone into the maintenance of the villa inside
and out, starting with the hall and its superb outlook.

'Go down and tell them to wait.' His commands to the servants
always struck Maggie and Mary as being on the abrupt and haughty
side: they felt embarrassed and guilty when Berto gave orders to his
old butler especially. But to Guillaume's ears Berto's tone was perfectly normal; the old man judged only what his master said, whether

it was sensible or not sensible. Guillaume's life had been considerably upset by the fraternization that went on between Lauro and the Americans. Now, he turned and shuffled to the hallway, deeming Berto's orders to be sensible.

Berto descended in his own time and, courteously shaking hands with each of the men, inquired their names. At the same time he took in the well-silvered hair and the interesting light blue and white fine stripes of his trousers, the jacket of which he held over his arm. The younger man, who wore well-tailored fawn trousers of some uncrushable and impeccable material, was holding a shiny slim catalogue of an artistic nature. They gave their names, apologized for the intrusion, and asked if they might see over the exquisite villa. They bore no resemblance whatsoever to Caliban the beast, with intent to rape and destroy Prospero's daughter who, some have it, represents the precious Muse of Shakespeare. 'Come along,' said Berto. 'With pleasure, come along.' The younger man left his catalogue on the hall table, while Guillaume came forward to take the older man's jacket from his arm.

Meanwhile Maggie, on the sun-terrace, turned over her splendid body, winter-tanned from the Caribbean, and lay on her belly; she continued smoothing her arms with suntan oil. 'I want my house at Nemi and my furniture and my pictures,' she said. 'It's a simple thing to ask. That man makes me have bloody thoughts; they drip with blood.'

'Do you think he's practising some kind of magic?' Mary said.

'We ought to go to the police. But Berto's so conservative,' Maggie said. 'Berto would prefer magic to a scandal.'

Lauro appeared once more, and sulkily ambled over to where he had thrown the transistor radio. He picked up the battered object, tried it, shook it, opened it and readjusted the batteries, but apparently it was dead from violence. He threw it back on the terrace floor and went to pour himself a drink.

'Where is my husband?' Maggie said, nervously.

'Showing visitors over the house.'

'What visitors?'

'I don't know. They just came and asked to see the house. Guillaume let them in. Two men, well-dressed.'

'Berto will get us all killed one day,' Maggie said. 'They are all well-dressed. They could be armed. We could all be tied up and shot through the head while they loot the place.'

Mary dipped into her bag for her powder-compact and lipstick. She combed her long hair.

'Your husband is too much a gentleman,' Lauro told Maggie, 'and old Guillaume is too much an old bastard in all the senses of the word. He never knew his parents. He was off the streets. No family.'

'What recommendations do they have?' Maggie said. 'Who sent them?'

'I don't know. Perhaps nobody. They are art historians.'

'They are all art historians,' Maggie said. 'You read about them every day in the papers. And look what happened to me the summer before last at Ischia.'

'Those were boys from Naples,' Lauro said. 'These men here are Americans.'

'I wouldn't be surprised if Berto doesn't ask them to stay to lunch,' said Maggie.

Mary closed her powder-compact. 'There are only six of us for lunch today. Two more won't make any difference.'

'They could tie us all up, shoot us, take everything,' Maggie said.

'I got a gun,' Lauro said. 'Don't worry. I go now and get my gun.'

'Oh, we don't want any shooting!' said Mary. 'Please don't start carrying revolvers in the house. It makes me jumpy.'

'Lauro's wonderful,' said Maggie, standing up like a brown statue in her gleaming white two-piece bathing suit. She swung her orange striped towel wrap from the back of a chair and put it on, haughtily. Mary got up too, lean and long. 'I'm going down to the pool for a swim,' she said as she too wrapped herself up neatly in a bathrobe.

'I'm going to my room,' Maggie said. 'One thing they can't do is see over my bedroom. I just won't have it, even if it is one of the most interesting sections of the upper floor.'

'I bring you a drink at the pool, Mary,' Lauro said.

'Lauro, you're sweet.'

They descended from the sun-terrace together, listening for voices but hearing none.

'In fact,' Mary said, 'I think I heard them outside. Berto must be showing them the grounds.'

'Well, if you're keen to see them try to get rid of them before lunch,' said Maggie. 'I don't want them to stay.' She swung into the little lift that descended to her room.

'Maggie,' said Berto, 'these gentlemen are staying to lunch.'

Two middle-aged women, Berto's cousins who were expected to lunch, had already arrived and Maggie saw the two unfamiliar men chatting easily with them in the hall. The younger man was saying 'Byzantium was a state of mind . . .'

Maggie came over regally to be introduced, on her way passing the console table where the young man had left his catalogue. Mary stood with her back to it and when she saw Maggie she murmured, 'The damn pool water wasn't heated – the gardener forgot –'

'How are you? Come on in,' said Maggie to her husband's cousins, and then she held out her hand to welcome the new visitors who stood with Berto. The little group at the console table parted and Maggie's eye caught the picture on the cover of the catalogue just as she had her hand in the elder art historian's. She let her hand drop and her smiling mouth formed a gasp. 'What's this?' she said, grabbing the catalogue.

It bore on its lovely cover, in tasteful print, the name Neuilles-Pfortzheimer, a Swiss auction house famous among collectors of paintings and fine arts. Under this was a reproduction of an Impressionist painting. 'What's this?' Maggie shrieked, and the circle of friends around her stood back a little as if in holy dread. 'What's *what*?' said Berto looking over her shoulder.

'My Gauguin!' Maggie said. 'It was in my house at Nemi. What is it doing in this catalogue? Is it up for sale?'

The younger of the visiting art historians said, 'Why, that was sold last week. We were there. You must be mistaken, ma'am.'

'How can I be mistaken?' Maggie screamed. 'Don't I know my own Gauguin? There's the garden seat and the shed.'

Everyone spoke at once with ideas pouring forth: ring the police; no, never the police, you don't want *them* to know what you've got; get your lawyer; ring the gallery, yes, call Neuilles-Pfortzheimer, I know the director well; I know Alex Pfortzheimer; call your home at Nemi, who is the caretaker? . . . 'Art-thieves!' Maggie screamed, pointing at the two visitors who looked decidedly uncomfortable,

having come predominantly to find the best means of entry to the
little Chinese sitting-room with its rare collection of jade, to plan a
future jewel-robbery at least, and certainly they were alert also to
where Maggie's room, with its wall-safe, was situated, since it was
known she had taken her large ruby pendant, part of the diaspora of
the Hungarian crown jewels, out of the bank to wear to one or two of
the season's balls, even though she ostentatiously insisted, as was the
fashion, that it was a fake. The visitors had also noted, with an eye to
its whereabouts, Berto's sublime Veronese about which they had
already heard, at the top of the staircase. They were innocent,
however, of Maggie's Gauguin and the more she cried out against
them, there in the graceful hall among the astonished friends, the
more it seemed how demonstrably wronged the strangers were; the
only discomfort in the affair, for them, was the risk involved should
the police be called in, for they were already in some embarrassment
in France.

Berto looked at them and said, quietly, 'I *am* sorry. I do apologize.
My wife is distraught,' at the same time as he put his arm round
Maggie as if to protect her from the menaces of a malignant spirit.

Mary joined the group and, shortly, Michael too, seeming, as he
more and more frequently did, that he had too much on his mind to
take notice of a domestic emergency. He eyed his watch. Mary was
looking rather enviously at Berto's gesture of concern for Maggie, for
in fact he looked very handsome at those moments of spontaneous
charm belonging as it did to his own type and generation; it did not
occur to Mary how silly Michael would have looked, how affected,
bending his eyes upon herself as Berto bent his, so frankly with love,
over Maggie. She only admired handsome Berto and envied Maggie
who, pouring out her accusations, did not, in Mary's view, really
deserve so fine a solicitude. If Mary had suspected the theft of any
of her property she would have gone about it silently and with a well-
justifiable slyness. Maggie, in the meantime, shrieked on, and Berto
murmured over her as if she greatly mattered in the first place, the
guests in his house next, and the Gauguin not at all.

Lunch was delayed forty minutes, but the hubbub had been
whisked away little by little by Berto's tactics, and the guests had
been waved into the green sitting-room, had been served drinks and

their several troubled souls variously feather-dusted, while Maggie, refusing her room, lay on a sofa and allowed herself also to be somewhat becalmed. Berto was considerably aided in his efforts by the two cousins, women of authority and many wiles, who had pulled themselves together quickly for the purpose of family solidarity and the pressing need to avoid any threat of a lawsuit against themselves for defamation of character. Quite soon the embarrassed art historians were given new courage, full explanations, and were begged to stay; the elder remained slightly nervous, but both magnanimously overlooked Maggie's accusations which, from her sofa, she blurted out from time to time, ever more feebly, for thirty-odd minutes. A short space, and they went into lunch.

Berto had refused to do anything whatsoever about the Gauguin mystery before lunch. 'Later, later, it must wait,' he said. 'If the picture is stolen . . . well, first we have to make a plan of inquiry, and first we sit down and have a drink before lunch. Maggie, my dear . . . Love, be tranquil. We have a drink, all. Only the worst can happen. Only the worst . . . It is not so very terrible . . . The worst is always happening to many people everywhere. And only the worst can happen, Maggie, my dear.'

Now they sat in the perfect dining-room overlooking the artificial lake. Berto looked attentively towards his cousin Marisa; she was the newsbearer, grand as a Roman statue and anxious to get these pettifogging hysterics of Maggie's over and done with so that she could impart news of the world that mattered to the assembled company, whether they understood what she was talking about or not; for Marisa's world concerned the heavily populated cousinship of their family, and only she could know which of their Colonna cousins was in love with which Lancelotti, and how much the dowry would be; only Marisa could know who was expected to inherit when the ancient Torlonia should die, probably within the next few days; she alone knew that the Baring nephews had been staying in Paris with the Milanese Pignatellis in an endeavour to find a settlement about the companies in Switzerland; all this Marisa only was able to know since only she had the mornings on the telephone with a family information service from all parts. Very often, when the family themselves failed to telephone or were not to be found at home, she would get the required information from an old housekeeper. All these facts she was waiting to impart to Berto and her other cousin, the thin religious widow Viola, at lunch, for she had a strong sense of what was right for lunch, what to eat, what to wear, what to say; she expected fully that these family concerns would enthral every listener; if not, what were the strangers doing at Berto's table? She was as confident of the fascination of her subject to everyone as were the ancient dramatists who held their audiences with incessant variations on the activities of the gods and heroes of legend. And indeed, such was her confidence that she did manage to hold the attention of the outsider, for however unintelligible the substance of her talk she brought a sense of glamorous realism to the Italian mythology of the old families.

Maggie had brought her glass of strong rye whisky to the table, trembling still, but settling somewhat under the influence of Berto's solicitude and induced into an effort of self-control by a determination not to be overborne by the tourist-attraction, Marisa. Maggie now sat gleaming in her shaken beauty at the top of the oval table. On her right was the elder of the intruders who had been pressed to stay for lunch, and who went by the name of Malcolm Stuyvesant. Next to him, Mary, with Berto on her other hand, and next to Berto at the other end of the table his other cousin, the black-dressed pale little Princess Viola Borgognona, very thin of neck among her strings of seed-pearls; Viola was agog to hear Marisa's new serial in the family saga, for it always gave her an excuse to be morally scandalized and to recall the family scandals, misalliances and intrigues of the past. She, like Berto, was aware that this inter-family talk had little relevance to the world of foreign visitors or of newcomers to the family, but she felt that it should be common knowledge even if it wasn't and, anyway, it was plain that people were not bored by it. Marisa had already started talking. 'Dino is sure to get married again when the year is up. He goes every morning to the cemetery, and then rides with Clementine, but of course the parents think he's too old. What can one say?' She turned appealingly to her neighbours, Michael on her left and then, on her right, to the younger of the two intruders, George Falk by name. 'What can one say?' she asked first one and then the other.

Berto, however, was still concerned for Maggie, and now started on a course that was distinctively his own and which he reserved for occasions when the atmosphere required to be soothed. It consisted of the introduction of certain words into the conversation which formed a magic circle of sweet suggestiveness, and, such was his instinct and skill, that he managed to do this without definitely changing the subject. 'When I was young,' Berto now said, 'I was very much in love with a Spanish girl who had been married to a man much older than herself; he was killed in the war. But although I was very much in love I didn't marry her because I felt that she would always desire an older man, and I, of course, was not much older.'

'Well, in the case of Dino,' Marisa went on, 'let me tell you that he does ride with her every morning after visiting poor Lidia's tomb.'

'It is so fragrant and cool in that cemetery,' Berto said. 'You know, it's quite romantic. I went once to visit our German aunts who are buried in that little cemetery, tucked away in the Vatican, and I heard the nightingale, suddenly, as if paradise were there among the tree-tops. I also would have liked, afterwards, to have gone riding with a beautiful lady and kiss her.'

So he went on with his groups of 'I was in love' and his 'fragrants', his 'heaven' and his 'beautiful lady' and all the pleasant numbers of romantic poetry – trite in themselves but accumulatively evocative of a better life than the actual and present one; so he went on, and presently he could see Maggie's wrists relaxing on the table and her shoulders responding as a cat which has been upset responds to the soft stroking hand.

He could see that the danger was past that she should again open her mouth and let forth accusations like the dead pouring out of their tombs, crazed, on All Souls' Night. If she had been a cat she would by now have started, against her better judgement, to purr, and if an analytical critic had been taking a careful note of all that was said, Berto's magic technique would have been a feast more special than the very good lunch they were eating. Mary looked at Michael who alone among the company was brooding over whatever it was he had on his mind, and then she looked at Berto and once more thought how attractive he was in spite of his age; she hadn't noticed before how good-looking was Berto, what marvellous eyes he had.

'And before they went to Baden they were getting that new pool in the garden,' Marisa was saying. 'They had to dig much deeper, and do you know they found a marble head of the first century? Dino says they are now digging deeper to find the rest of it.'

'The Belle Arti will stop everything,' said Cousin Viola. 'They'll take it for the nation and someone will steal it and smuggle it abroad.'

'Well, they had to leave for Baden,' said Marisa. 'But I'm sure, I'm sure, that they haven't breathed a word to the Belle Arti.' Again she appealed to her neighbours. 'The Belle Arti,' she said to Michael on her left and to the young criminal who went by the name of George Falk on her right, 'is our cultural protection agency, but they stop work on anything the moment you report a find. In Italy you only have to dig up a few metres and you have a find. If one reported every find to the Belle Arti nobody would get a house built or a swimming pool.'

'Can they trust the servants?' said Cousin Viola.

'It happened once to me,' Berto said, 'that I was helping Guillaume to put up a rabbit hutch as he was sure the rabbits we bought to eat were poisonous and he wanted to breed our own rabbits. We were digging a trench out there behind the orchard and I felt my spade touch on a stone, but not a stone. It felt not like the stones of the garden. So I put aside the spade and went down on my knees. Guillaume was amazed and he said, "But what are you doing, Marchese!" I scratched at the earth with my hands and I saw a colour, blue, then another, red. It was a moment I could never forget, such a moment of all my dreams – you remember, Viola, the Byzantine vase. It was in fragments, of course.'

'It's in the museum in Verona,' said Viola, calmly eating.

'Oh, yes, it went to the museum.'

'You could have kept it,' Marisa said.

'How could I have kept it? But the moment of discovery, it's a moment that no one can take away from me, not even the Communists. I went back that night to look at the pieces in the moon-light. We left them where we found them, afraid to break them, and Guillaume constructed a little wire fence around them. I looked up at the clouds passing over the moon thinking of Guillaume's tender-ness as he made the fence. It was *una cosa molto bella, molto bella –*'

'You have many fine things in this house,' said the younger crimi-nal.

'Exquisite,' said Mr Stuyvesant, the older one, for whom under another name Interpol were looking to help them with their inquiries. 'It must have been wonderful to grow up with them.'

'I was not here very much as a child,' Berto said. 'I was a great deal in Switzerland, and then at school. But when I was a very young man just before the outbreak of the war I remember we had a masked ball here. It was considered a small house for a masked ball, but it was a summer night, you can imagine for young people in those days how exciting . . .'

The troubadour host turned inquiringly to Lauro who stood quietly by his chair waiting for him to finish speaking. Lauro had appeared unexpectedly, for he did not serve at table here in Berto's villa, clashing so much as he did with Guillaume and the cook. Berto looked up at the brown face with a little questioning smile. Lauro spoke in rapid Italian, very excited and happy and Berto listened with his eyes on Maggie till Lauro had finished, and had turned and left the dining-room.

'The masked ball,' said Marisa across the table to her cousin Viola, 'was where Mimi de Bourbon met Aunt Clothilde. She had just broken off from the Thurn und Taxis –'

'Maggie!' said Berto, 'do you know what Lauro has just told me? Your Gauguin is perfectly safe at Nemi; it's there in your house and hasn't been moved.'

'Oh, darling!' said Maggie, who was by now sweetly mellowed by the fragrant distillations of Berto's talk.

Viola, more mesmerized by her cousin Marisa than by her cousin Berto, set her pale head at a saintly angle, and said, 'Aunt Clothilde is still President of the Orphans of St Joachim. She does good work. She has not changed since the old days.'

'Well, she should have,' said Marisa, 'but that's a different topic. I remember –' Meanwhile, Berto recounted how Lauro had telephoned to his girl-friend at Nemi, and she had gone on a pretext to Hubert's house, and there had seen the leafy Gauguin in its usual place.

'How did she know,' said Mary, 'where to look for that picture?'

'Apparently Lauro's fiancée goes to Mallindaine's dreadful meetings regularly. Moon-worshippers. You can imagine –'

Maggie turned to Mr Stuyvesant, '*Your* Gauguin must be a fake,' she said, happily.

'It isn't my Gauguin,' said the art-thief. 'It belonged to Neuilles-Pfortzheimers' client, and it has been sold as an authentic. One should inform them.'

'Could it possibly be,' said George Falk, the younger crook, 'that the Gauguin at your home is a fake?'

'It is authentic,' said Maggie, and rose to lead her guests into the garden-room for coffee.

Michael woke from his self-absorbed dream and said, 'Mallindaine could have had a copy made. He could have sold the original.'

'Oh, come,' said Berto, as he stood aside to let his guests move out of the dining-room.

'We should get the experts,' Michael said, 'and, anyway, get the picture out of Hubert Mallindaine's hands.'

'That I do agree,' said Maggie.

Berto was about to catch Maggie's arm, to waylay her before she left, and whisper in her ear that she really might, now that she knew her picture was safe, and her initial shock had blown over, apologize to Mr Stuyvesant and Mr Falk. He was about to say she really should, when he was himself waylaid by Guillaume, Maggie in the meantime sailing ahead. Guillaume, alone with Berto in the dining-room, now confided his change of mind about the two visitors of whom he had earlier approved. 'I think they're up to no good,' said Guillaume.

'But why, Guillaume? What makes you say so?'

Guillaume seemed uncertain what precisely to reply. 'The senior visitor spilled *ragoût* on his trousers,' he ventured somewhat wildly. 'It's embarrassing him – a great red stain, and he's trying to cover it up. Right in the front.'

Berto, stifling all reasonable thoughts, and only recalling that it is the easiest thing in the world to splash on one's clothes some of that tomato sauce swimming in which Italian cooks love to present their pasta, was immediately troubled. Plainly, Guillaume had merely only offered an outward symbol for an inward insight, and it was the insight that Berto trusted.

'See if you can do anything for his trousers,' Berto said. 'Offer him some talcum powder. *Ragoût* is always a messy dish. I don't see what it has remotely to do with trusting the unfortunate man, anyway. An accident can happen to the best of us. No reflection whatsoever on his character.'

In the garden-room Berto found Mr Stuyvesant sitting in a

crouched position, leaning well forward, with his legs crossed, holding his coffee. But one could still see, on the pale thin-striped trousers that Berto had so much admired, numerous red blotches and smears. He was glad he had not asked Maggie to apologize to these men. It struck him, now, that it was strange how neither of them had seemed to expect an apology, even after the news had arrived that Maggie's picture was still in her house. They had not been offended, only embarrassed, by Maggie's outburst. That could be a sign of guilt. One had to be careful who one let into one's house. He looked out of the french windows to where the young Mr Falk was walking on the lawn between Maggie and Cousin Viola, and he looked again at Mr Stuyvesant crouched over his coffee. Guillaume had come in to hover. 'Why don't you go with Guillaume to the pantry,' said Berto, 'and let him do something to your trousers?'

Mr Stuyvesant looked helplessly at his splashed suit and gave a short laugh. 'Not the pantry,' Guillaume said. 'If the gentleman will go to the guest cloakroom I will bring some materials to clean.'

Ah, yes, yes, thought Berto. Guillaume is thinking of the silver depository. Not the pantry, not the pantry. Stuyvesant rose to follow Guillaume while Berto, Knight of the Round Table, courteously remarked, 'Beastly stuff, *ragoût.*'

He hung around the window watching his guests and his wife wandering around the garden in the May sunlight. Lauro and Michael stood under the lovely portico which gave off to the back of the house. Lauro was talking quietly but urgently, Michael listening sullenly. Lauro glanced towards the french window, caught Berto's eye where he stood watching, grinned, and resumed his talk. Berto watched Lauro with tolerant resignation; he had little doubt that Lauro was raising a moderate sum of money every so often from Michael; not much, but a moderate amount, just to keep quiet about the mistress in Rome. Berto looked at Lauro's shining head with its expensive hair-cut. It was difficult to think of him keeping a secret or doing anything free of charge. 'Once a whore,' Berto mused to himself, 'always a whore. That's my philosophy.'

Guillaume's efforts to clean the trousers were not a great success. Mr Stuyvesant asked for his coat, saying he would hold it over the stain to hide it. So his coat was brought, and holding it draped over his arm he collected his friend and said good-bye to the party very quickly. Berto, with Guillaume hovering behind, watched them leave from the front door. They revved up and left with unusual speed. 'Guillaume,' said Berto, 'I think you're right about those people. They drove off as if it was a getaway from a bank robbery.'

Guillaume muttered to himself in his French-Italian. Berto went to telephone to Alex Pfortzheimer.

TWELVE

Dear Marchesa Tullio-Friole,

Having written in capacity your legal advocate to Mr Hubert Mallindaine at Nemi with regarding the opera of art painted by Paul Gauguin in view of your righteous inquiry in light of the sale of said painting in Switzerland, and having myself accompanied our expert to examine said painting at Nemi by Mr Hubert Mallindaine's request I have to report as it is suspected by the distinguished House Neuilles-Pfortzheimer that this picture at Nemi is a copy of the original.

From which arises the complication which I myself have foreseen but not wishing to disturb without necessity have not mentioned to you since this moment. That is, the above-written Mr Mallindaine is hoping to claim of you the cost of original which he is declaring to be part of agreement settled upon him at your handing over to him in the year of 1968 the land and promise of house which he undertook for three years plus house-building to his requirements personally in accordance his needs; and the above-written Mallindaine was given contents in the year 1972, July 1, which makes, combined, the remuneration of his services of ten years adviser in your affairs. Always according to Mr Mallindaine's advice, the opera of Paul Gauguin was said at your moment of gift to be original which he has been accepting as such. This is the situation which naturally I hold off with every means from making a confrontation at the present time, as Mr Mallindaine has not yet employed legal offices in the case.

It is my hope you will approve my actions which I should explain you if you should be disposed to be my guest for lunch at the good restaurant that I most admire when we can discuss in tranquillity on the day of your choice.

Very soon hoping to have your telephonic communication my
dear Marchesa,

Yours cordially,

Massimo de Vita.

Massimo de Vita, the obscure lawyer whom Maggie had engaged
to evict Hubert from his house, sat in one of the copies of Maggie's
Louis XIV chairs and looked out at the lake below, while Hubert read
through this letter which the lawyer proposed to post from Rome
next morning. As he gazed at the still green lake he thought of
Maggie, and pictured her, perhaps bursting into his office, Queen of
Sheba, making the secretary even more indignant than she constitu-
tionally was, and demanding, with the rings flashing on her fingers,
that Hubert be denounced to the police; whereupon, so the lawyer
day-dreamed while Hubert studied the letter, one could have a
beautiful time calming her down.

'Excellent,' said Hubert. 'The sentiments are accurate and the
English is wrong just right. You must understand that with a woman
like the Marchesa everything must be done in style. If your style
wavers she takes immediate advantage of it and walks all over you.
No doubt she believes the Gauguin is genuine. Certainly, she had it
smuggled into the country along with many others, in the first place,
so she can hardly make a public fuss. I myself have never doubted its
authenticity or naturally I would never have accepted it in part settlement.'

'Style, style,' said Massimo de Vita grasping at the idea as if it were
a crust, and he starving for it, as indeed he was. He was a brutally
ugly man, which in itself could not be counted a disadvantage if he
had not made it so by a continual unconscious betrayal of his
thoughts which were low-pitched all the time and really quite base.
He thought, in fact, that he exercised a quality which he called style,
but was in reality an aggressive cynicism. Style, in the sense that he
believed himself to possess it, needs a certain basic humility; and
without it there can never be any distinction of manner or of anything whatsoever. 'Style,' he repeated, smiling at Hubert who, on
occasion, did have a certain style.

'Send her this letter,' Hubert said, handing it back.

Some people could be heard coming up the stairs and presently

Pauline entered the drawing-room with a lanky young man. Massimo de Vita got up and greeted her warmly while Hubert sat on in an expressionless way.

Pauline introduced the young man to the lawyer as Walter. He was her boy-friend from the Common Market Headquarters at Brussels, taking his vacation in Italy now that May was passing into June, and was staying in the house as Hubert's guest. He had yellow hair and a moustache of a darker yellow. Hubert tolerated him even though, as he said to Pauline, 'Walter is too occidental for my taste.' At first she thought he had said 'accidental', and was puzzled. He had repeated 'occidental', whereupon she was still puzzled but rather less so.

Walter now plonked himself, tired from his walk, on the sofa, while Pauline busied herself with the letter which the lawyer offered her for a second opinion.

'The English is all wrong. I'll put it right,' she said when she had read it through.

'You will leave the English alone,' Hubert said. 'It expresses Massimo's personality, and besides, if there's any real unpleasantness one can always fall back on the plea that there was some linguistic misunderstanding.'

'What misunderstanding could there be?' Pauline said. 'We thought all along the Gauguin was genuine. We could have counted on it for our bread and butter. Now it turns out to be a fake. I think that woman knew all along it was a fake.'

'I wouldn't be surprised,' Hubert said.

'And we spent all that money on getting it cleaned,' Pauline said.

'You had it cleaned?' the lawyer said.

'Yes, I took it into Rome myself. I was terrified of a hold-up and being robbed or kidnapped on the way. I needn't have been,' Pauline said.

'You needn't say anything to anyone about the cleaning,' Hubert said. 'It would make people laugh. Spending good money on cleaning a fake. It could damage the work of the Brothers and Sisters of Diana and Apollo. The Movement comes first.'

'If the picture went to be cleaned,' said the lawyer, 'this should not be mentioned. The Marchesa must not believe you have money to burn.'

'It's a really lovely picture,' Pauline said. 'It's real to me, anyway.'

Walter said, 'That's all that matters,' and he looked at Hubert with an expression a little more sour than befits a guest.

Bulging Clara, the Bernardinis' chronically victimized maid, stopped in the main street of Nemi, and put down her plastic shopping bags, bulging like herself as they were. Agata, the pretty housemaid from the Radcliffes' house, stopped too. She had approached from the end of the narrow street where the grey castle stood bulkily with its tall and ancient tower, looking like a crazed and bulging woman wearing an absurd top hat, ready to dive off over the cliff into the lake far away below her. Agata was decidedly swollen round the hips and belly, pregnant as a well-founded good hope.

'Well,' said Clara. 'Well, Agata, any news?'

Agata stood into the wall to let the men who were unloading fruit cases from a truck go about their business. She looked back up the haphazard street of fertile Nemi which, by some long-ago access of euphoria or wishful thinking, when Italy was still a kingdom, had been named, doubtless to the peal of bells and the high notes of trumpets, the Corso Vittorio Emmanuele. She already had her paper-tissue handkerchief to her eyes. Agata then named the private parts of numerous animals, including humans, and ended the litany by declaring that, to sum it up, the man was a ne'er-do-well.

'And all his dead!' responded Clara, meaning precisely that all the dead relations of the man in question should by rights endure damnation alike with him.

They stood talking in the sunny main street of Nemi while life bustled by them, the machines in the smithy went on grinding, the electrician skimmed by in his bright Opel, the fruit van backed up and then manoeuvred forward, backed up again and then was off while the fruit shop assistants noisily discussed where the fruit should go in the banked-up crates outside the tiny shop. Clara, with her sly eyes moving occasionally towards the fruit shop, to see how the prices were set on the newly-graded qualities, listened to the young wronged Agata; she listened with her sly ears and puffed out her breath with sympathetic paranoia. Across the street outside the recreation centre stood a carabiniere in his brown uniform, the town clerk in his pressed suit and clean collar and tie, looking on at an exchange of banter between a schoolboy and a white-frocked friar.

The two women were greeted occasionally by busy shoppers who
passed and swept a glance, along with their smiles, at Agata's hard-
done-by belly of shame, while the whole of eternal life carried on
regardless, invisible and implacable, this being what no skinny
craving cat with its gleaming eyes by night had ever pounced upon,
no tender mole of the earth in the hills above had ever discovered
down there under the damp soil, no lucky spider had caught, nor the
white flocks of little clouds could reveal when they separated continually, eternal life untraceable and persistent, that not even the excavators, long-dead, who had dug up the fields of Diana's sanctuary
had found; they had taken away the statues and the effigies, the votive
offerings to the goddess of fertility, terracotta replicas of private
parts and public parts, but eternal life had never been shipped off
with the loot; and even the lizard in the cliff-rocks in its jerky fits had
never been startled by the shadow or motion of that eternal life which
remained, past all accounting, while Clara and Agata chattered on,
tremendously blocking everyone's path although no one cared in the
slightest that they did so.

'Could it be anyone else's?' Clara said.

'No, it could only be Lauro's,' said Agata. 'He wants me to put it
on Mr Michael but Mr Michael wasn't there at the time. It couldn't
have been Mr Michael, but Mr Michael offered to pay for an abortion and Lauro says the offer is a proof of responsibility, and he's
getting married to his fiancée right soon; anything to save himself the
responsibility. I said, "Lauro, there will be a blood test and I can
prove the paternity," but Lauro said, "Well, Michael's group O and
I'm group O, so you can just go to *that country* and prove paternity."
It was terrible to hear him swearing at me like that after all those
times I was good to him when he needed it.'

Clara looked judicious about this. 'You shouldn't have been good
to him.' And she added, 'I'm never good to them,' as if she had
plenty of opportunities. Then she observed the obvious: 'If Mr
Michael wants to pay for an abortion he must have a reason.'

'I never went with him,' said Agata. 'But I know about his woman
in Rome. I know all about that. He even brought her to the house
once.'

'What did the Signora Mary say?'

'She was away. Anyway, he wants to help me, and maybe he wants me to keep quiet, too. Maybe he just wanted to help me, to be kind; I don't know. Anyway, I wouldn't have had an abortion, not even –'

'They never do anything just to be kind. Imagine it, just figure to yourself!' Clara said.

'Well, maybe Michael will give me something to help.'

'He'll have to. He'll have to,' Clara said. 'He has no option. The master of the house . . . Work it out for yourself and take my advice. Be advised by me.'

Lauro sat in the sitting-room of the new bungalow high on the terraced cliffs among the woods and caves of Nemi, one of a new group of small houses that looked as if they belonged to tidy Snow White. His relations-to-be sat around him, a good-looking, long-legged set, modern and, with the exception of his fiancée, slender. His future mother-in-law had a fine tanned face and streaked short hair, a woman who could pass, at sight, for any of the Radcliffes' friends. The same was not quite true of his fiancée with her long dark hair and slightly over-ripe figure dressed in a shirt and blue jeans; Lauro considered that he could slim her down after they were married. The two uncles, however, brothers on the mother's side, were also good-looking; one, in his late thirties, with lightish hair, well-tinted and cared for and of a length to cover his ears; and the other, about fifty years old, grey-haired, bespectacled and professorial of appearance. The latter's wife was a fashionably skinny woman with a close-cropped silvered hairstyle. They all looked as if they worked in the fashion business or the film industry or else ran a night club, and went to the hairdresser a great deal for tints and cuts and for manicures. Lauro, gloomily perceptive, was proud enough of his new family's appearance, now that it had come to the point where he was goaded into actual marriage by the demands of the wretched servant-girl, Agata. It would have been unthinkable for him to marry Agata, a man of considerable pride like Lauro who had been accepted into the familiar confidences and the beds of the Radcliffes and the Tullio-Frioles, not to mention the distinguished and equally care-free company of the past. It was the lack of that very heart-easy quality in his new family, fine-looking as they were, that depressed Lauro. He flicked ash from his cigarette into a clean ceramic ash-tray, and as he did so his impending mother-in-law, good woman that she was, rose and took the ash-tray and shook the

frail ash out of the window, so that Lauro was left with a clean ash-
tray again to finish his cigarette with. It was like eating from a plate
where they gave you a clean one half-way through the dish. To the
tips of her red varnished finger-nails, the mother-in-law was spick-
and-span. It made Lauro unhappy although he could not precisely
say why, since Maggie, too, and Mary and all the others were always
neat and well-groomed enough. It bothered him too that his fiancée,
Elisabetta by name, called herself Betty. It troubled him deeply that
these people were talking about the wedding-feast in the best trattoria in Nemi with grade one French champagne, seven courses, and at
least two hundred people, counting all cousins and friends on both
sides, at the expense of the bride's family, no matter how much per
head, money no object on such an occasion and seven courses; seven,
eight courses, light courses, Betty's sleek, smart aunt was saying, just
as if she was a fat country woman, seven courses so that you start with
antipasto, maybe ham and melon; then the soup, a cold consommé
very chic for summer; and for pasta you want two, three kinds, say a
fine cannelloni of game or spinach and cream cheese inside and a
lovely ravioli with tomato sauce and a good fettucine al burro with
parmigiano over it, a choice; then you have to have the fish, scampi
dipped in a batter; and then a salad, tomatoes and endives with condi-
ments; you have to have the cold meat next, like for instance veal
sliced thin and chicken breasts, or pheasant and for the next course
something original, maybe a shish kebab which is to say beef on
skewers surrounded by small carrots, green beans and rice; and then
a green salad of lettuce and basil, very fresh, and so to a cream cake,
for example St Honoré, and then the fruit, fresh fruit or macedonia,
you could give them a choice, which could be served with petits-fours
and some nuts on the table, too; then of course the cheese and coffee;
the chocolates you pass round with the liqueur, sambuca, cointreau,
cognac, and the bride cuts the cake which goes round; Betty's eldest
relation should toast the *sposi* in champagne as the champagne glasses
are always kept full throughout the meal, and the *sposo* replies to toast
the relatives of the bride and Betty's eldest uncle toasts the relatives
of the groom; and you give cigars; the waiters should come from
Rome so they would know what to do and serve with white gloves.
The bride should give away flowers from her bouquet, then you must
remember . . .

Lauro looked at his young bride-to-be with panic on his face but she failed to notice. He panicked all the more that she was listening, enthralled, to her aunt, after all the two years' association with Lauro, and then becoming engaged to him and all the times he had described the sort of life he led, with Michael and Mary, with Maggie and Berto, and their friends in Sardinia, at Ischia, in the Veneto, at Mary's house at Nemi, with its well-served meals of which nobody ate very much so that it was all sent back to the kitchen for the servants to guzzle and drink, and the funny, quite outrageous, chatter and gossip with always little bits of laughter but never a real rowdy laugh. In the world Lauro knew, there was silence in between the talk, and afterwards music and space, and nobody talked of the food at all; they took the good food for granted and if the men discussed wines or the women certain dishes, it was all like a subject that you study in a university like art history or wildlife. For two years Lauro had distilled all this into Betty's ear, but now, it seemed, to no avail, for she was chattering away about the wedding-feast, as loudly and eagerly and rapidly as everyone else, breaking into the half-finished sentences of the others as indeed they were all doing. It was a big food-babble, rising louder and louder and dinning around Lauro's ears, he being only half able to isolate the source of his unhappiness since certainly the family looked very good and up-to-date and prosperous and distinguished. Lauro wanted to run, but he thought of Agata in the Radcliffes' kitchen with one hand on her hip and the other pointing at him, and her screaming accusations and all those tears threatening the vengeance of her father and brothers. He had nowhere to run to; once he was married to Betty it would be too late and Agata would become a muttering bundle of impotent umbrage, violated for life.

The food affair died down and now they were discussing the money and the marriage portion and the financial arrangements for the couple and their house. Betty should keep her job in the boutique in Rome and she had her car. Betty's mother was about to open a new boutique in Rome, at which point Lauro could give up his job as secretary to the Radcliffes and get the money due to him for liquidation of the contract with a good bit besides; those people had plenty of money.

There came a moment when they let Betty's eldest uncle speak. It

was a moment of gravity. Betty's mother filled the liqueur glasses
with a sweet syrupy drink and handed them round accompanied each
by a lace-edged napkin with a little lacey circlet to rest the glass on.
The uncle spoke.

'Betty,' he said, 'is entitled to her share of the land. We have a bit
of land.' And he pulled the black, smart brief-case that rested on the
arm of the sofa beside him on to his knee, opened it, and extracted a
folder. From this he brought a much-folded large document and a
map which he spread out on the marble-topped dining-table.

Lauro began to take some notice, and the thought of Agata and his
fury against her subsided, together with the memory of her accusations and the slightly older memory of the occasion when, just at the
magic moment he had wanted to withdraw, the calculating bitch had
told him she was on the pill, it was all right. These rankling images,
as at the cinema, changed into that of the actual scene before him,
Betty's uncle and her land.

Betty's family comprised her mother's side; the father was
unknown and said to be dead. The grandparents, too, were dead and
there remained only the uncles, co-proprietors of the fields represented in the big map open on the table.

Lauro bent over it with his arm affectionately round plump Betty's
shoulder. He played with her hair and touched her neck as he looked,
for he was excited by the surprising idea that she had so much land
of her own. They traced a line. Betty's portion was about ten acres,
on a plateau among the cliffs of Nemi. 'But it can't be there,' Lauro
said.

The uncle's finger traced the boundaries. 'Of course it's there,' he
said, and patiently he took out of his brief-case the title deeds, tracing
their history for five generations right into young Betty's hands.

'This is good land,' said the younger uncle. 'Better a few *ettari* of
good land than a hundred kilometres of waste.'

'But some of that land has been sold. There's a house there.
The Marchesa bought it and a Mr Mallindaine, an eccentric
Englishman, lives there. I used to work for him.'

Betty's mother started to laugh and so did the uncle. 'She bought
it, yes, but not from us,' said Betty's well-groomed mother. 'Some
lawyer came along and sold it to her. He said he represented the
Church and it was Church property. She got false deeds. We didn't

protest, naturally, when she put up the house. It's just as well to bide one's time.'

'It isn't hers,' Betty said, 'and the house is illegal. It's *abusivo*. We can make them take it down.'

'Any time we like. If we like. We can denounce them.'

'Send the police along to that house,' said Betty's skinny aunt.

'Why should we? Better let them pay us than pay a fine to the State,' the elder uncle said. 'We can sue. But she won't take it to court; she'll pay.'

'Once you leave the job, Lauro,' Betty's mother said, 'you can give the Marchesa a piece of news: she's got an illegal house and is trespassing on your land.'

Betty's mother took Lauro's ash-tray, almost empty as it was, into the kitchen and brought it back clean.

'The title deeds of the land,' said Hubert, 'were transferred to Maggie on 8 February 1968, a date I can never forget; and at the end of April this house was started on cleared land where no house previously had stood. The house took three years and two months to construct.'

'The building permit?' said Massimo de Vita. 'Was that a fake, too, or didn't you have one?'

'Maggie had a building permit, of course,' Hubert said. 'I don't know what she's done with it. She probably has it in her company offices for safe keeping.'

'A pity she didn't come to me sooner,' said Massimo. He was growing a beard, as yet not long enough to cover the extra chins which would not go away. He looked excited and hastily dressed, as one who had been, as in fact he had, working long hours for several days. In that time he had established beyond doubt that the lawyer who had arranged for Maggie to buy the property at Nemi was not to be found and his name nowhere on the legal records of Italy. He had further discovered that Lauro's impudent claim that the land on which Hubert's house was built belonged to his fiancée was not impudent at all, it was true. The whole of the transaction had been a fake, including the documents, and the land presumed to have been Church property belonged to Lauro's prospective bride at this moment.

'She should have had me for her lawyer in those days,' said Massimo. 'Now I have to write her a letter and see how I can get her out of this mess.'

'She gave me this house,' Hubert said sulkily. 'It is mine. I supervised the building of it for three years and two months; it was agony; getting things done in Italy is agony; when I moved in a few months later Maggie cut off the funds she had promised in order to maintain it. I can sue.'

'It's up to me,' said the lawyer, 'to say whether you can sue or not. Meantime, let us look at the facts. You occupy this house – no?'

'Yes,' said Hubert, meekly.

The library door opened and Pauline Thin put her head round it. 'Coffee?' she said chirpily.

'Get out!' barked Hubert. Pauline withdrew.

'But you had no building permit.'

'There was indeed a building permit,' Hubert said. 'I remember obtaining photo-copies from the lawyer to satisfy the building contractors. Everything was regular.'

'Well, it wasn't regular,' said Massimo, 'and the lawyer least of all. Dante de Lafoucauld, what a name for an Italian lawyer . . . You should have known . . . You should have –'

'What's the matter?' said an aggressive male voice from the door. It belonged to a skinny sun-bronzed chest, shoulders and pair of arms topped by a yellow-haired head: Walter, with his deep yellow moustache, having been called in from his sun-bath and, bored by Nemi and resentful of Hubert, being now only too keen to take up a quarrel on Pauline's behalf. Some other voices, male and female, questioned and commented behind him; Pauline had brought some of the local young people to the house for the day. She did this many, many days now, gradually building up something like a commune under the protective wings of the Brotherhood of Diana and Apollo; so far, Hubert had felt it wise to refrain from expressing all the alarm that he felt, even although these young people had seemed to take over the house, left a mess behind them all over the place and never did any work.

Hubert shouted at Walter, 'Get out! I'm discussing serious business with my lawyer.' He rose and lumbered over to the door, gave the young man a hefty push, slammed the door shut and locked it. A clamour of protest arose from the other side of the door, subsiding after a few minutes as the footsteps of the lithe and sandalled young set flip-flopped down the staircase into the overgrown garden where these people were wont to lie and watch the intertwining of the weeds and get their bodies ever browner by the good offices of Apollo.

'Now,' said Hubert when he had simmered down at bit, 'one problem at a time, if you please. *Una cosa alla volta.*'

'Precisely,' said the lawyer, on the defensive. 'It's hardly my fault that –'

'Down to business,' said Hubert. 'Presumably, when Lauro gets married, he will start putting me out of the house.'

'I don't know about that,' said Massimo.

'Or they will want some money. A lot of money,' Hubert said, 'to keep their mouths shut.'

'There could be several legal opinions,' said Massimo. 'The law is very contradictory. Certainly they will want some money. Certainly. But can they claim it? The house does not exist.'

'I mean this house.'

'It does not exist. How can it exist? It is not on the records. In Italy if a house is not on the records, it has been constructed illegally and we call it *abusivo*. An *abusivo* construction does not exist in legal terms. The family who own the land can make the Marchesa pull it down.'

'But will they?'

'It depends on their frame of mind and if they can come to terms. It depends also on whether the land they own is only the top soil. In Italy, sometimes the sub-soil belongs to somebody else; it could belong to the Church or the State. At any rate the family can make trouble for the Marchesa.'

'She will have to pay,' Hubert said. 'Maggie will have to pay them off.'

'Even then,' said the lawyer, 'the police or the town council might discover that it is *abusivo* and cause the house to be destroyed, but it is unlikely they will know that the house is *abusivo* unless the family reports it.'

'Well, it's my house. Maggie gave it to me.'

'She had no right to do so. It doesn't exist.'

'She will have to make reparation if the house is pulled down,' Hubert said.

'Oh, certainly she would have to do that if she gave it to you. The legal transfer of the house to your name unfortunately did not take place. Technically the house is still hers. Although of course I believe you, it is obvious that verbally she gave you the house. But now it is certain, anyway, that she can't put you out. There are many tenants in *abusivo* houses who cannot be put out and who need not pay rent either. Because the house does not exist.'

'And the contents of the house?' Hubert said.

'It would be difficult,' said Massimo, moving his plump hands in the air as he spoke, 'to say anything about the contents of a house that does not exist. How can a non-existent house contain contents? How can it have a tenant? You don't exist when you inhabit a house that is *abusivo*.'

'Under Italian law?' said Hubert.

'It could be argued,' the lawyer said. 'It could be argued for a very long time and the longer you stay in a house the more difficult it is to get you out.'

'Italian law,' said Hubert, 'is very exciting. Positively mystical. I approve strongly of Italian law.'

Massimo laughed merrily and looked at his watch, very flat, very gold with its golden band encircling his plump wrist. He said something about lunch-time, but Hubert was musing on a private dream of his own from which he presently emerged to say, 'The house seems to me to be perfectly safe as headquarters of the Brother-Sisterhood of Diana and Apollo. We can ignore Maggie's protests about the use the house is being put to; that's my opinion.'

'And mine,' said Maggie's lawyer. 'I tear up the letter now which the Marchesa sent me to that effect. I never received it.'

He took a letter from his brief-case and tore it in small pieces.

'It doesn't exist,' Hubert observed.

'I never received it,' said Massimo. 'She did not register it and so it is easy never to receive a letter with the postal situation in our country being what it is.'

The door opened and Pauline stood on the threshold of the library. 'Why have you unplugged the telephone?' she said. 'Someone is wanting to use it.'

'I don't want to be disturbed,' Hubert said. 'Miss Thin, are you my secretary or are you not?'

'I'm hungry. We're all hungry,' she said, 'and the lunch is ready and the cook is getting angry.'

'How much pleasanter it was,' said Hubert to the lawyer, 'before we had our good fortune.' He rose with the lawyer and swept past Pauline, declaring that the blessings deriving from his ancestor the goddess Diana were mixed ones indeed.

As he descended the stairs Massimo loitered to grasp Pauline and press her against the wall of the landing; then he kissed her heavily whether she liked it or not.

THIRTEEN

'Have you read the papers?' Berto said, his eyes reposing on an abyss of horror.

Maggie was in Switzerland intently but vainly hunting Coco de Renault through the woods and thickets of the Zürich banks, of the Genevan financial advisory companies, the investment counselling services of Berne, and through the wildwoods of Zug where the computers whirred and winked unsleepingly in their walls, where the office furniture was cream leather in the tall buildings, and the dummy directors of elaborately-titled corporations entered the glass front-doors set into the marbled façades, walked up the stair-cases lined with the cedars of Lebanon, to take their places at their large desks at ten in the morning, after a massage and a swim in the pool.

Mary and Michael had gone to the Greek islands on a yacht, to get away from it all, to get to know each other again and for a number of other purposes described in similar phrases which Mary had written down on a list. They were gone and the house at Nemi was closed up, the pretty maid having left their service with her aunt who, in view of the girl's condition, had carried the suitcases, refusing all help from Michael and Mary, but serving them with polite but pregnant assurances that justice would be done on the girl's behalf and Michael would be hearing from their lawyer. Mary had stood beside Michael in a very positive way, cool and blonde, rich and loyal. She had said the right thing; 'My husband is innocent.' Then she had said the wrong thing: 'We're not afraid of your Communist lawyer.' This had brought a duet of retorts from the niece and aunt, to the effect that Mary would pay for those words, the politics of their lawyer were not her business; she had committed an outrage against the Republic of Italy by speaking disrespectfully of their lawyer and his politics; she was a whore who slept with everybody including

Lauro and she had also been seen in bed with her mother-in-law. Mary had stood on, her arm in Michael's, cold-lipped, till the women got into the car and drove off.

Lauro, too, was away. He was on his honeymoon, having first spent a morning with Maggie, at Michael's house, breaking gently to her the news that none of her three houses at Nemi was really hers and that Hubert's in particular was built on the dowry of Lauro's bride. Maggie had assumed at first that Lauro was weaving a fantasy in some obscure desire to rouse her passions and end up with a love-making scene. She had been indulgent about his stories, assuring him sweetly that she held the title-deeds of all her properties everywhere, or at least Coco de Renault did; Maggie took her cheque book out of its charming little drawer and wrote out a very large cheque to Lauro for a wedding present, which he received graciously and lovingly. When they got up from the sofa, pulling their clothes straight, however, Lauro again came round to his incredible story. 'Really, Maggie, that lawyer was a crook. He can't be found in Italy. He's sold you land and houses that didn't belong to him. He chose a couple of abandoned houses and a piece of vacant land and falsified the papers, that's all.'

'The real owners would have come forward by now,' Maggie said.

'In the case of this house of Michael's,' Lauro said, 'it belongs to a large family, twelve, fourteen, cousins, all of them in America. That crook was clever. But when one of these cousins comes home for a visit you'll have trouble. In the case of the Bernardini house, it once belonged to a cousin of my fiancée who died, but his son is the heir; he has a job in England, a very important job in a chemical factory. He won't like to see someone occupying his house if he returns to look for it in Italy.'

'The Bernardini house was a total ruin,' Maggie said, 'a complete wreck, and I spent a fortune on the reconstruction; I put in the tennis court and the pool; I put in the lily-pond and I laid the lawns; then the Bernardinis started all over again making big changes. The same with this house here; Michael had it before he was married; we flew one of the best architects in Los Angeles over here to restore this house; it was a wreck when I bought it.'

'You didn't buy it, Maggie,' said Lauro, quietly. 'You only thought you did. Take Hubert's house which you put on Betty's land, for instance, well, it just doesn't exist officially.'

He comforted Maggie greatly that morning as she telephoned one after the other office in Rome to try and trace that lawyer Dante de Lafoucauld whom it now appeared nobody had ever heard of, and whom Maggie herself had met only twice, in Rome, in the Grand Hotel in the winter of 1968. Nobody had heard of him at all. Maggie rang the office of Massimo de Vita, who was out. She left her name with an answering service, and then went into hysterics, blaming Massimo for everything and saying how awfully suspicious it was that he didn't have a secretary any more, only an answering service attached to his phone. 'Only crook lawyers have answering services,' Maggie moaned, while Lauro poured her out a brandy and said, 'Maggie, Maggie, drink this, Maggie dear. I love you, Maggie. You didn't have Massimo de Vita for a lawyer in 1968, did you? You only went to de Vita for the first time a year ago, didn't you? How can he be to blame?'

'They're all in it together,' Maggie screamed. 'Why hasn't he got a proper office with a secretary? It was the seediest office I ever saw. Now he hasn't even got a secretary. I hate to deal with answering services.' The telephone rang just then, from Massimo de Vita in response to her message on the answering service. He was just about to write to her, he said.

'I have to talk to you,' said Maggie. 'Have you ever heard of an Italian lawyer called Dante de Lafoucauld?'

'Yes,' he said. 'I heard that name last week. He isn't any sort of Italian lawyer. I don't know who he is. He's a crook. Apparently, you see, Marchesa, you were badly advised, and this man, whoever he is, forged some documents for some houses which don't belong to you –'

'You know him?' Maggie said. 'Then you know the man?'

'I never heard of him till a week ago, when I was looking into the matter of the eviction of Mr Mallindaine. Then it all –'

'He had a beard,' wailed Maggie. 'He had a dark beard.'

'So have I,' said Massimo. 'Marchesa, since last we met, I have grown a beard. I will do what I can for you in this affair, although you realize, Marchesa, that when the houses are not yours –'

'Crooks, all of you!' Maggie yelled, whereupon her voice was immediately overlaid by that of Lauro who had taken the telephone from her hand. 'Doctor de Vita,' said Lauro, 'you must excuse the Marchesa. She's very upset. I will be in touch with you and arrange a meeting.'

The lawyer said a few words in Italian for Lauro's ears only, partly legal in substance, partly sexual.

'*Si, si, Dottore,*' said Lauro, and hanging up the receiver continued his work of calming Maggie down. He was somewhat successful until she got it into her head to ring Coco de Renault. The lines were engaged for every number she tried where Coco might be: Nemi-Paris, Nemi-Geneva, Nemi-Zürich. 'It's lunch time; it's one o'clock,' said Lauro. 'Everyone will be out. I'll fix you some lunch, Maggie. Leave the telephone and I'll tell you all you need to do in the case of Betty's land. It's simple and, after all, you can afford it.'

Maggie rang Berto and gave him the story, which he didn't believe. He replied quietly, thinking her to be temporarily deranged, and said he would join her shortly at Nemi. He sounded reluctant to do so; he said he was occupied with problems to do with the safety from robbers of his house in the Veneto.

'We can't stay here. There are no servants,' Maggie said. 'Lauro's getting married on Saturday and Agata's left. I have all these houses and nowhere to stay.'

'We can stay in Rome. Or we could stay with the Bernardinis,' said Berto. Maggie hung up, and rang the Bernardinis. Emilio would not be home till six. The young people were out. Maggie collapsed into tears and presently let Lauro bring her a delicate lunch-tray.

That stormy morning over, Maggie set off the next day with Berto's car and driver for Rome where she had a full-scale massage treatment, then onwards, glowing and resolute, for Switzerland in pursuit of Coco de Renault. She was anxious to see him in any case about the lack of funds. Something was happening to her monthly cheques which were not arriving at the Rome bank as usual, so that she had been unable to pay her bodyguard. She said nothing to Berto. The bodyguard had left. That was embarrassing enough. And now it was imperative to get from Coco the title-deeds of the houses and so prove them hers.

Berto was staying with the Bernardinis meanwhile and had wearily realized the truth about the houses at Nemi. 'If I had met Maggie earlier,' Berto told Emilio, 'she would never have done anything so foolish. There's nothing for it but for Maggie to pay reparations or else surrender the properties; she can manage that all right. I wish she would try to see things in proportion.'

'It would be hard on us,' said Emilio Bernardini, 'to have to leave here after all the work we've put into the house.'

'I dare say something can be arranged,' Berto said.

'I dare say,' said Emilio, smiling to reassure his friend.

'Do you trust Coco de Renault?' said Berto, gazing across the trees towards the tower of the castle and the rows of little houses built into the cliff below it, huddled in half-circular terraces round the castle like the keys of an antiquated type-writer. He looked away from the view and into Emilio's face, suddenly realizing that the man was not quite his usual cool self.

'I did trust him, of course,' said Emilio. 'When I introduced him to Maggie of course I trusted him. He handled some affairs of mine, very badly as it turned out. I can't say, honestly, that I trust de Renault now. It's very embarrassing, and I wish I'd never brought him together with you and Maggie. But I had no idea she would hand over so vast a part of her fortune to him to manage. In fact, I think she put everything in his hands, which was a foolish, an unheard of, thing to do. I would never have expected her to hand over *everything*.'

'Has she done that?' said Berto.

'I think so, yes.'

'And you have doubts about de Renault?'

'I do, yes. I have had quite a shock in my own case. There is some-thing shady about him, and I'm very sorry, very embarrassed.'

'Poor Maggie,' Berto said mildly, 'I hope she won't get any more shocks. I think only of Maggie herself, you know. A wonderful woman, a wonderful woman. She doesn't need money to make her a wonderful woman. It's only that she's used to it.' Berto added after a while, 'It's hardly your fault, Emilio. I should myself have taken more interest in Maggie's affairs. Perhaps I could have persuaded her not to put her trust in de Renault. Perhaps. For my part, how could I hold you responsible? After all, I've known you since you were a schoolboy.'

Emilio said, 'Thank you, but, you know very well, you can't trust every man who was at school with your son. These days, whom can you trust?'

'One's friends,' said Berto. 'You know, Emilio, you're too sad by nature. Why are you so sad?' And this question, the asking of which would have seemed quite absurd in another society, was really quite normal at Nemi, on the outskirts of Rome in the middle of June 1975, for Berto and Emilio.

'Why are you so sad by nature?'

'Life is sad.'

It was the next morning, reading the newspaper, that Berto said to Emilio, 'Have you read the papers?' This was an unnecessary question since the news, on that morning and the next, was a national event: the regional elections throughout Italy had confirmed a popular swerve to the political Left. It could fairly be said that Italy had turned half-Communist overnight. Both halves were fairly stunned by the results.

Berto, keening at the wake in those days, detained Emilio from going about his morning's business, with prophecies and lamentations. The Communists became 'They', the Italian '*Loro*'. Berto said, '*Loro, loro, loro* . . . They, they . . .'

'It's the will of the people,' Emilio said, but he spoke into heedless morning air, and Berto continued, 'Look how they write in the newspaper; they say one has the sensation that something is finished for always. And whatever they mean by that, it's the truth. Something is finished. Loro, loro . . . They, they . . . They will come and take away everything from you. They took away everything from us in Dalmatia. They will take, will carry away . . . Loro . . . ti prenderanno, ti porteranno via tutto . . . They will come and take . . . Everything you possess . . .' The gardener's son, passing by and catching these words, wondered how that could be, his possession being a motor-scooter. 'They will kill . . . ti liquideranno . . .' said Berto. 'They will take over, and they will –'

Emilio, who, although not himself a Communist adherent, had none the less voted Communist in these elections to express his exasperation with Italy's government-in-residence, did not have the heart to say so to the older man. After all, he had been at school with Berto's son, and Emilio would not shatter Berto's kindly affection.

Emilio kept his dark, young secret and merely observed, sadly, 'After the capitalists have finished with us I doubt if there will be anything left for the Communists to take over. De Renault, for example –'

'Better her money should go to a swindler than to the Communists,' Berto said.

FOURTEEN

With the elections and the strawberry festival in the air, and Maggie, so far as Hubert had ascertained, on a trip to Switzerland, and with Lauro away on his honeymoon, Hubert felt it wise to call a rally of his followers and prepare for battle with any such apocalyptic events and trials as are bound to befall the leaders of light and enlightened movements, anywhere, in any age.

Maggie, he hoped, had gone to Switzerland to arrange for the surreptitious payment of his claim for the fake Gauguin, and maybe to raise funds to meet the demands of Lauro's bride and the eventual claims of the other owners of the properties she had thought were hers; she would do this, he reckoned wrongly, without breathing a word to her pig of a husband. He was wrong not only in this reckoning, but also in the assumption that Maggie had received her lawyer's letter about his demand to be compensated for the fake Gauguin. The letter had indeed been sent to her by registered post, but the mails from Rome were fairly disordered, and the letter had not in fact reached Maggie at the Veneto before she had left the villa. Guillaume had signed for it and put it aside, on the tray in the hall, where it innocently awaited the most peculiar circumstances of her return. Hubert did not know this, and in fact he had got into a habit of false assumptions by the imperceptible encroachment of his new cult; so ardently had he been preaching the efficacy of prayer that he now, without thinking, silently invoked the name of Diana for every desire that passed through his head, wildly believing that her will not only existed but would certainly come to pass. Thus, like ministers of any other religion, he was estranged from reality in proportion as he mistook the nature of prayer, offering up his words of praise, of gratitude, penitence, intercession and urgent petition in the satisfaction that his god would reply in kind, hear, smile, and wave a wand. So that, merely because he had known in the past that the unforeseen stroke of luck can happen, and that events which are nothing short of a miracle can take place, Hubert had come secretly to take it with a superstitious literalness that the miraculous may happen in front of your eyes; speak the word, Diana, and my wish will be fulfilled. Whereas, in reality, no farmer prays for rain unless the rain is long overdue; and if a miracle of good fortune occurs it is always at the moment of grace unthought-of and when everybody is looking the other way. However, Hubert, largely through his isolation at Nemi and from not having seen Maggie in person for a number of years, believed that Diana of the Woods could somehow enter Maggie's mind, twist a kind of screw there, and force her to do something she would not otherwise have done.

Moreover, he had not allowed for a change in Maggie, a hardening. In the carefree past she had been more or less a docile pushover where money was concerned, and Hubert miscalculated the effect upon her of being married to steady-minded Berto, of having had her suspicions aroused to the point of almost-justified paranoia by various threats to her moneyed peace, and, most of all, by the new economic crisis which Hubert had mentally absorbed in those months from what he read and heard, but which had not closely touched him.

Maggie would come back from Switzerland, he felt sure, and make a settlement for the Gauguin. Indeed, he could hardly think of Maggie without the word settlement coming into his mind.

Lauro and his buxom horror-beauty of a wife would also return and, should it please the gods, Lauro might even join the Fellowship of Diana and Apollo, in the same way that the three other boys had returned to him, those secretaries of the first, beautiful summer at Nemi, when the house was newly built, in 1972, that year of joy and outrage, when Hubert was free to leave his doors unlocked, could come and go as he pleased, but when Maggie began to desert him, searching as she did after strange gods and getting married to Tullio-Friole. As it happened, the return of the secretaries was a mixed blessing, but Hubert thanked Diana for them all the same.

In the meantime he thought it well to declare a special congress of his flock. Pauline Thin, who in kindly moments Hubert called 'Our Mercury', sent messages by telephone and by grape-vine word of mouth to numerous fellow-worshippers who lived within easy travelling distance of Nemi; she also sent out a number of telegrams, cautiously-worded in each case, in order to get together a preliminary meeting of kindred souls, the elect Friends of Diana and Apollo, and so prepare for an even grander gathering which Hubert projected for the following autumn and which he spoke of variously as an 'international synod', a 'world congress' and a 'global convergence'. Hubert was aware that the ecclesiastical authorities as well as the carabinieri already viewed his house with suspicion and that his activities were regarded with a certain amount of local disfavour. 'They can't pin anything on me,' Hubert said, 'not drugs nor orgies nor fraud. We are an honest religious cult. All the same, we have to be careful.' Mostly he feared Lauro and the Radcliffe family, feeling sure they would, if they could, use any eventual excuse to bring trouble on his Fellowship, which was covering expenses by now, very nicely. What Hubert had in mind for his final project was to try and syphon off, in the interests of his ancestors Diana and her twin brother Apollo, some of the great crowds that had converged on Rome as pilgrims for the Holy Year, amongst whom were vast numbers of new adherents to the Charismatic Renewal movement of the Roman Catholic Church. News had also come to Hubert of other Christian movements which described themselves as charismatic, from all parts of Europe and America; a Church of England movement, for instance, and another called the Children of God. Studying their ecstatic forms of worship and their brotherly claims it seemed to him quite plain that the leaders of these multitudes were encroaching on his territory. He felt a burning urge to bring to the notice of these revivalist enthusiasts who proliferated in Italy during the Holy Year that they were nothing but schismatics from the true and original pagan cult of Diana. It infuriated him to think of the crowds of charismatics in St Peter's Square, thumbing their guitars, swinging and singing their frightful hymns while waiting for the Pope to come out on the balcony. Not far from Nemi was the Pope's summer residence in Castelgandolfo. Next month, he fumed, they will crowd into Castelgandolfo, and they should be here with me.

Pauline, meanwhile, was having the time of her life. Men pressed her against the wall and kissed her whether she liked it or not. She found herself at the centre of Hubert's young following, surrounded by attentive people and to spare. She was determined to keep her privileged position of having been in with Hubert from the start, holding on to it partly by a habit she had of reminding Hubert by little hints, privately from time to time, that some of those records she had been obliged to put in order over the past three years still puzzled her. Pauline's allusions to the records inevitably subdued any attempt by Hubert to get rid of her, as he could now afford to do. He, meanwhile, on these occasions, finding himself stuck with her in this uneasy relationship, got himself quickly out of his troubled state of mind by telling himself he was fond of Pauline, very, very fond. When he told himself this for a few minutes continuously, he believed it, and did not appear in the least aware of having capitulated to a piece of blackmail, except that on such occasions he called her Miss Thin for the rest of the day. Perhaps it was his age; at all events he associated his pagan cult with his own very survival and was ready at least to endure Pauline for it; he was prepared to love her as far as he could and to let her fill the house and garden with anyone whomsoever, so long as they didn't bring in forbidden drugs, use up the hot water in the house, and provided they subscribed to the Fellowship. On these conditions he was content with the arrangements that Pauline made and especially with her rule that nobody could approach him except through her; that suited him very well.

Pauline herself had put a number of young people to work for the cult. She had roped in Letizia Bernardini as press office and Pietro Bernardini as public relations officer. There was an older man, Pino Tullio-Friole, Berto's son, who also made regular pilgrimages to the home of Hubert, descendant of Diana, bringing contributions of money and precious objects and some of his wealthy friends who liked to attend the religious services and afterwards sleep with whoever was available. Pino, who was in his early forties, despised Maggie and resented her marriage to his father.

Hubert brooded especially over one of the many press cuttings Letizia had produced for him. It was dated 18 May, and was taken from the English-speaking paper of Italy, *The Daily American.*

'Cardinals, bishops meet, dance in Rome,' was the headline. It said:

Rome, 17 May (AP) – Bishops, archbishops and cardinals, struggling to keep their hats in place, sang and danced in ecstasy, embracing one another and raising their arms to heaven.

The Most Rev. Joseph McKinney, auxiliary bishop of Grand
Rapids, Mich., joined hands with the Most Rev. James Hayes,
archbishop of Halifax, who in turn linked arms with Leo, Cardinal
Suenens of Belgium.

The unlikely chorus yesterday opened the Ninth International
Conference on Charismatic Renewal in the Roman Catholic
Church.

The conference theme of 'renewal and reconciliation' – the
theme of Holy Year – underlines the movement's search for whole-
hearted approval in the official Church.

A crowd of about 8,000, most of them Americans, gathered at
the catacombs of St Callixtus, burial place of the early Christian
martyrs, for the opening ceremony. A young band led the congress
in song, and delegates from Quebec to Bombay testified to the
growth of the movement in all continents.

Cardinal Suenens, archbishop of Malines, urged participants to
use the four-day reunion 'to renew your faith, to renew your hope
in the future, to love each other like you never did before.'

The Charismatic Movement, a predominantly lay movement
claiming more than half a million followers, emerged in main line
Protestant churches in the early 1960s and in Roman Catholicism
in 1967, among students and professors at Duquesne University
in Pittsburg.

It is characterized by fervent prayer meetings, gifts of the spirit
such as 'speaking in tongues' and efforts to breathe new life into
personal religion.

In a recent report, American Catholic bishops credited the
movement with 'many positive signs . . . a new sense of spiritual
values, a heightened consciousness of the action of the Holy
Spirit, the praise of God and a deepening personal commitment to
God.'

But they warned of dangers inherent in the revival – divergence
from the official Church, fundamentalism, exaggeration of the
importance of the gifts of prophecy and speaking in tongues.

'Tongues is not the important thing; the important thing is the
change in your life,' said Bob Cavnar, a retired U.S. Air Force
colonel who came here for the meeting from Dallas, Tex.

Cavnar, introduced to the movement by his son Jim, was one of

70 congress elite renowned for speaking in tongues and selected to
receive messages to the conference from the Holy Spirit.

Hubert kept many such press cuttings, read and re-read them,
with a sense of having been cheated of his birthright. He had sent
Pauline at the beginning of June to one of these meetings and afterwards had locked himself with Pauline into the drawing-room, or
rather, locked out the rest of the drifting acolytes and lovers who at
present made up his household, to hear her story.

'It started off,' said Pauline, 'with a mass.'

'In church?'

'No, no. It was an altar set up in this flat in the Via Giulia. I don't
know whose flat it was. Well, they had a mass, there was a Catholic
priest with his vestments, and the congregation, about thirty people.'

'What sort of people? Rich, poor, how did they strike you? All
English-speaking? What language was the mass?'

'It was in English, but there were lots of Italians and French, all
sorts. All sorts of people and some nuns. Quite a lot of nuns in their
habits; and later I found some were nuns and priests in ordinary
clothes. They seemed all ages, really, but only one or two really old,
and they were nuns.'

'It is from ordinary people that the great revenues come,' said
Hubert. 'They are filching the inheritance of the great Diana of
Nemi, the mother of nature from time immemorial.'

'I did talk about Diana, don't worry,' Pauline said. 'A number of
people were very interested. And do you know who was there? –
Those Jesuits, Cuthbert Plaice and his friend Gerard Harvey the
nature-study man, were there. Father Gerard, in fact, was urging
some of the young men to come to one of our meetings and telling
everyone how wonderful Nemi was, how the environment comes
right up to the back door and so on. Father Cuthbert was asking me
a lot about your personal origins, Hubert, and I told him well, it was
a long story. Then –'

'Miss Thin,' said Hubert. 'I want the whole picture of this charismatic meeting and you can tell me afterwards what the Jesuits said.
At the same time, my dear, I must say it was most commendable of
you to get your word in about the true Fellowship. You're wonderful, Miss Thin, you really are. Tell me about the mass.'

'Well, the mass only preceded the meeting. It was an ordinary mass except for the swinging hymns, and the fact that the Kiss of Peace was real kisses, everyone kissed everyone. That sort of thing. The nuns seemed to like it and there was lots of embracing and singing.'

'We should have nuns in the Fellowship,' Hubert said. 'Diana always had her vestal virgins. We should have vestal virgins watching a flame on the altar day and night.'

'Well, they would have to be part-time,' Pauline said. 'Who is going to come and watch a flame all day?'

'When we have a greater following,' Hubert said, 'all these things will fall into place. Did the Jesuits participate in this orgy?'

'Well, I wouldn't say it was an orgy. The Jesuits were there as observers, anyway. The prayer meeting that followed the mass was more exciting, when they spoke with tongues and made emotional comments on the scriptures. They made a sound like an eastern language, Hebrew, or Persian maybe, or Greek. I don't know what; but that's speaking with tongues. Then they prophesy. There was a woman there, about thirty-five, she prophesied a lot, and would you believe it, she was a doctor. She proclaimed a passage from the Gospels and closed her eyes and threw up her hands. Everyone said "Amen". Then we sang and clapped hands in syncopation, and sort of danced –'

'What passage from the Gospels?' said Hubert.

'Oh, I don't know. Something about St Paul in his travels.'

'That is not the Gospels. It is probably the Acts of the Apostles. What was the text?'

'Oh, I don't remember. Something about the Lord. It was all so noisy, and everybody was excited, you know. It wasn't so important what the words were, I think.'

'It never is,' Hubert said. 'And what were the Jesuits doing?'

'Well, they didn't join in but they seemed to be enjoying it all. Their eyes were all over the place. Cuthbert Plaice saw me. He said "Hi, Pauline, how do you like it?" I said I liked it tremendously, and I really did as a matter of fact, but the feeling wore off afterwards, you know.'

'We must step up our services in the Fellowship,' Hubert said, 'that's clear.'

*

It was a hazy hot afternoon towards the end of June. Beyond the ranges of the Alban hills you had to imagine the sea, for indeed it was there, far away, merging invisibly into the heat-blurred sky-line.

Pauline had been busy over the past ten days, putting such a massive amount of energy into the task she had undertaken that in fact she felt she would never again in the course of her life find it in her to repeat the effort, even although Hubert kept reminding her that this was only a preliminary little gathering to the one planned for the autumn.

At the end of ten days Pauline had arranged a fairly big gathering of Hubert's faithful to be held in the large overgrown garden behind the house stretching to the dark, moist woods. She had announced the event as a 'secret meeting', totally avoiding any written messages. Pauline had spent many hours on the telephone and had travelled around in Hubert's car to notify the Friends of Diana and to exhort attendance. The object of this meeting was to form a nucleus around which the future cells of the Fellowship were to collect.

Pauline had not been able to get much done with the garden, but she had cleared enough to put up an altar and a flowery canopy, and to prepare a covered marquee for the fruit juice and sandwiches.

'What will we do if it rains?' she had asked Hubert snappily on one of those frantic ten days of preparation.

'It will not rain,' thundered Hubert.

On the last day she had been to Rome to get her hair cut and set, and also to buy the remarkable outfit which she now, as the expected throng began to accumulate, triumphantly wore. Too late, Hubert had seen her and exclaimed, 'You can't wear that!' This was a khaki cotton trouser-suit with metal-gold buttons on the coat and its four pockets. Pauline had tucked the trouser-legs into a pair of high canvas boots, so that the whole dress looked like a safari suit. The hunting effect was increased by a pale straw cocked hat which perched on her short curled hair.

'What do you mean?' Pauline said when Hubert, already waiting in his leafy bower, bedecked in his silver-green priestly vestments, had exclaimed, 'You can't wear that!'

'It's entirely out of keeping, and irreverent. You look like the commandant of a concentration camp or something out of a London brothel.'

'It signifies the hunt,' Pauline said. 'Diana is a huntress, isn't she?'

'She's always portrayed wearing a tunic,' Hubert said, 'and a quiver full of arrows.' It was a hot day, and his vestments were heavy, which made him feel sicker than ever.

'Well, I can't wear a tunic,' Pauline said, 'I haven't the figure.'

'The figure!' shouted Hubert from under his greenery and his robes. 'The figure . . .' he shouted across the garden. 'If you think your figure fits into that outfit, with your haunches like a buffalo's –'

Pauline started to cry, pulling from her satchel-bag a large red handkerchief with white spots which it would seem was designed, even the handkerchief, to enrage Hubert. Pauline's skinny boy-friend Walter came out of the house, and stopped in some astonishment at the scene. He had not seen Hubert before in his robes nor Pauline in her new outfit, although he had seen her cry at various times.

Hubert, who had taken care to pose himself under the bower, was unwilling to disarrange the effect. He stood motionless with his arm raised to receive in benediction the people whom he could already hear arriving at the front of the house. Motionless as he was, he screamed in his heat and fury. 'That woman has no sense of stage management. Tell her to go and remove those objectionable clothes. She's supposed to be the chief of Diana's vestals and she looks like Puss-in-Boots at the pantomime. Don't forget I've had experience with the theatre, I've had a lot of success, and when I ran my play in Paris, *Ce Soir Mon Frère*, I took responsibility for all the costumes.'

Walter, unable to make sense of the quarrel, said to Pauline, 'What's the matter with him?'

'I have to wear something to symbolize my authority in the Fellowship,' Pauline wailed from behind her red handkerchief. 'Otherwise I'll just be taken for one of the rest. I know what I'm doing and I've worked myself to death for ten days. The running about, the phoning, the fruit juice, the hairdresser, the sandwiches, and choosing my suit and getting it altered, and making the list and typing the order of business for the meeting.'

'Why don't you take off the boots and the hat?' said Walter against the background of more explosive sounds from Hubert at the other end of the garden. 'You'll be too hot in all that stuff. It looks fine, but –'

'Here they come,' said Pauline, as a group of people walked up the side-path, chattering, to reach the back of the house. 'I'm on duty.' She strode to the little gate that divided the pathway from the garden, threw it open and began to receive.

Some had come from enthusiasm, some from curiosity, and a few peasants and trade-workers of the district who had already been initiated into the cult had come because they liked the international and egalitarian atmosphere.

Pauline had put out benches in front of the throne under the leafy bower where Hubert stood. She scrutinized each person, greeting them with an aloof, red-eyed smile, as she waved them to their seats.

'Why, Pauline,' said Father Cuthbert, 'you look very sporty.' Pauline waved him on, while Walter, beside her, in his blue jeans and open-necked shirt, smiled nervously. The priest passed on, accompanied by his fellow-Jesuit Gerard Harvey.

One local woman whispered to another. 'Those Jesuits always come, both of them.'

'The Jesuits always go two together, never alone,' said her friend.

'Like carabinieri,' said the other, 'because one can read and the other can write,' and her laughter crackled in the air like a fire in the grass until Pauline's frown quenched it.

By four o'clock they were all assembled and the gate was locked. Pauline had confiscated a motion-picture camera from Letizia Bernardini who had brought her brother Pietro to take a film of the proceedings. Letizia looked sour but did not challenge the booted leader. Berto's son Pino was also of the party, he having been especially attracted to this meeting because of Maggie's feud with Hubert.

Not long ago, Letizia's friend, the psychiatrist Marino Vesperelli, whom she had brought to dinner to meet Maggie that night at her father's house two years before, had discovered in the big general mental hospital in Rome a Swedish patient who had no relations who bothered with him, no friends, but who was apparently cured of the drug addiction which had landed him in that place two summers ago. In conversation with the patient Marino learned that he had been at Nemi with Hubert, working, he said, as a secretarial aide; and in this way, with Letizia's help, Kurt had been safely restored to Hubert who was horrified but impotent to protest; besides, Pauline had taken the boy's part. Kurt was now an acolyte in the Fellowship. He got up late and went out often in a little *cinque cento* car that Letizia had lent him: Hubert prowled around Kurt's room and searched his pockets while he lay asleep, hoping to find traces of narcotic drugs or a hypodermic needle, and so an excuse for getting rid of him. However, Kurt was so far blameless, only somewhat lazy, and here he was as part of the household to help with the meeting in the wild-grown leafy garden.

Pauline's energies had brought back two other lost sheep, named Damian Runciwell and Ian Mackay, only a little changed in appearance and very happy to come and spend another summer with Hubert as in the idyllic past of 1972 when they had all lazed and lain around together, wearing fantastic jewellery and cooking fantastic food. Pauline had often heard Hubert talk nostalgically of those days before she had come to work for him, and before Maggie's marriage had spoiled everything. Like a good sheep-dog Pauline had rounded up three of those four secretaries, and brought them happily before Hubert. Hubert had much to bear in these days of his new prosperity. 'I would have brought you Lauro, too, if I could have done,' Pauline assured him.

'I'm sure you would,' Hubert said.

'Well, all I want to do is to make you happy, Hubert,' said Pauline.

'It's the thought that matters, Miss Thin,' Hubert said. 'Diana be praised.'

'Oh, aren't you glad to see these old friends? You know how you always talk about that summer before I came to help you out. Now you can relive it all over again. Except, of course, for Lauro. I'm sorry about Lauro. Only, you know, he's absolutely over there on the Radcliffe side and making a fortune. And getting married, too.'

Hubert would have thrown Pauline out that very evening, the three young men with her, had it not been that she knew too much. And here they were among the crowd of selected followers in the garden.

Hubert smiled on them all benevolently when they were seated. About thirty people, he thought. Pauline Thin must be out of her mind, he thought, to call a secret meeting of thirty-odd people. What sort of secret is that?

He decided to change his plan somewhat, and to refrain from

discussing anything that might be deemed illicit by the Italian or ecclesiastical authorities, such as the raising of funds and the missionary work necessary to internationalize the Fellowship. A service of worship and a testimony of faith might equally serve this purpose, together with a deliberate accent on the charismatic features of the old, old religion of nature.

'I am the direct descendant of the goddess Diana,' he announced, 'Diana of Nemi, Diana of the Woods and so, indirectly, of her brother the god Apollo.'

Sitting apart from the congregation the two Jesuit observers gave out charismatic smiles in all directions and made way for a late arrival whom Pauline had sent to sit with them. Another observer, Hubert thought. How many observers do you have at a secret meeting? He glared at Pauline who looked angrily back, with fury on her face under her ridiculous hat. Evidently she was still dwelling on Hubert's insults. As well she might, Hubert thought with desperate resentment of the woman as he looked at her, ordering people around, placing them here, guiding them there, with those boots on her awful legs. Hubert, under the leafy trellis, breathed deeply. He noticed that Pauline now held a black-bound book in the hand that indicated the seats; Hubert thought it looked like his Bible but then he put the thought aside, not seeing what she could possibly want to do with it. As she also held the confiscated camera at this moment, Hubert assumed she had also, probably quite needlessly, taken charge of someone's book: bossy little nobody.

Walter, the weak fool, was beside her, holding a list and ticking off names. Who were all these people? Pauline had told Hubert from time to time of new people who could be trusted. But he had no idea they amounted to so many. Two American art historians, very cultured, very rich, Pauline had said. A girl from Rome, 'my best friend there', Pauline had said. Then she had said on one occasion, 'a girl-friend of my friend and she happens to be Michael Radcliffe's mistress'. Hubert had felt satisfaction at this. Yes, but how did they add up to so many? Hubert did not know most of these people who sat before him.

From the house stepped another robed figure. He was dressed in a toga-like garment which bunched and bundled about his tubby body. It was the lawyer Massimo de Vita; he had come to stand by Hubert's throne and give a simultaneous translation for the benefit of the Italians present. 'Friends,' said Hubert, holding out his arms in benediction, while Massimo announced, '*Amici*'.

'Friends,' Hubert said. 'Brothers and Sisters of Nature. As I have said, I am the descendant of Diana and Apollo, the gods of the old religion that goes back beyond the dawn of history, into the far and timeless regions of mythology where centuries and aeons do not count.'

Massimo de Vita kept even pace behind Hubert, who spoke slowly, somehow without his usual energetic conviction; he was still ruffled by Pauline Thin; she had put him off his stroke. 'Diana,' he went on, 'Goddess of Wildlife, is older than man. She fought on the field of Troy and was humiliated by her jealous step-mother who, as it is written in Homer, took the quiver of arrows from Diana's shoulders and whacked her with it. But such was the charisma of Diana, the virgin goddess, protectress of nature, that she took no revenge, but rather decided to come to Italy, change her name, and dwell amongst us at Nemi. You must know that her name in Greece was Artemis and not far away from the hill upon which we are gathered here in this garden is Monte Artemisio; and down below us lies the sanctuary of Diana, my ancestress, ravished and pillaged . . .' And with worthy self-effacement Massimo de Vita recited, '*Diana, la mia antenata, rapita e saccheggiata . . .*'

Meanwhile the sudden voice of a woman cried out the determined statement, 'I'm going to testify.' Hubert, startled, looked towards the voice, while the toga'd advocate, also surprised, instantly pulled himself together, and, believing this to be part of the show, since the voice was Pauline's, continued his dutiful translation '. . . *adesso vengo testimoniare . . .*'

'What is this interruption?' said Hubert, as everyone turned to look at Pauline.

'*Cos'è questo disturbo?*' translated Massimo into his loudspeaker, although his eyes looked desperately about him for some guidance. He got none whatsoever. He looked towards Pauline, seeing her for the first time that day in her strange sporty outfit and immediately presumed that this interruption was a prearranged affair: a sort of dialogue, all part of that sense of theatre Hubert had so often said was necessary for the success of the Fellowship.

'Miss Thin,' Hubert bellowed into his amplifier, 'do you realize you are in Church in every important sense?'

Massimo continued translating.

Pauline bounded up to the leafy bower and stood beside Hubert, grabbing the loudspeaker. 'I have a right to testify and prophesy,' she proclaimed, 'and I want to testify from the New Testament.'

Father Cuthbert jumped up and down in his seat while his companion, Gerard, smiled eagerly. The rest of the congregation stirred and asked of each other what it was all about, and then fell silent as Pauline's voice boomed out, 'The First Epistle to Timothy, Chapter 1, verses 3 and 4:

As I besought thee to abide still at Ephesus, when I went into Macedonia, that thou mightest charge some that they teach no other doctrine.

Neither give heed to fables and endless genealogies, which minister questions, rather than godly edifying which is in faith . . .'

The congregation remained silent, waiting for further enlightenment which it was clear Pauline, adjusting the loudspeaker, was preparing to give. Only Cuthbert Plaice moved to whisper something with gleaming eyes into his fellow-Jesuit's ear. Hubert, immediately sensing sabotage, attempted first to possess himself of the microphone. But Pauline hung on to it. Hubert therefore, in terror of what she might say next, all in one gesture made as if he were adjusting the instrument for her better to speak and then stretched his left arm at right angles to his body so that it rested across her shoulders in a protective attitude. Thus he made it appear that Pauline's interruption was part of the service, and even his first exclamation – 'What is this interruption?' – might have been part of a dramatic litany. Pauline looked amazed, and turned to Hubert as if to ask if he really meant it.

Massimo, meanwhile, was still catching up with the Italian translation of Pauline's text, which he found difficult.

'Proceed,' said Hubert, grandly.

Two young men in the congregation who had been drawn to the meeting by the rumour that Maggie, whom they both knew slightly, was to be present, sat near the front. One was a former chauffeur of Maggie's and the other was that portrait-painter who had been recommended by Coco de Renault, and for whom she and Mary had somewhat disastrously and very expensively sat. Before setting out for Nemi they had pepped themselves up with trial injections of a new amphetamine drug. The scene before them gave the two young men to believe that the new drug was a very great advance on any previous drug they had sampled, and, as Massimo's garbled version wobbled over his loudspeaker, the two young men began to clap their hands in rhythm.

Pauline pulled herself together to proceed with her testimony under the surprise of Hubert's bidding. With Hubert's arm fondly resting on her shoulders she changed her tone of fury to one of breathless timidity. 'I only wanted to point out,' she told the congregation, 'that the words of the Apostle Paul refer to Diana of Ephesus, where there was a cult of Diana, and that's what inspired me. If you remember in The Acts, and I could find the place, I think –' She started to look through the Bible in her hand, while the loud rhythmic clapping increased, others of the congregation being encouraged to join in. As she floundered, Father Gerard, perceiving her difficulty, charismatically rose and called out, 'Chapter 19.'

'The Acts, Chapter 19,' said Pauline, turning to the place, while Hubert stood loathing her, imprisoned with his arm in its draped and silvery-green sleeve resting consolingly on her shoulder. 'Read,' he commanded his jailer; whereupon the Jesuits exchanged joy-laden glances. 'He's being very broad-minded, isn't he?' whispered Cuthbert Plaice. The hand-clapping increased and some of the congregation began to sway. Pauline visibly cheered up and now read aloud to this rhythm, with her finger on the place.

'For a certain man named Demetrius, a silversmith, which made silver shrines for Diana, brought no small gain unto the craftsmen;
    Whom he called together with the workmen of like occupation, and said, Sirs, ye know that by this craft we have our wealth . . .'

'*Piano, piano,*' pleaded Massimo. 'Read slowly, Miss, I can't keep up.' Pauline began to change her rhythm, stumbling along until she was reading in a kind of syncopated time to the loud hand-clapping, allowing two beats of theirs to one of hers. 'Courage!' bawled Hubert grimly. 'Read to the end.'

'. . . Moreover ye see and hear, that none alone at Ephesus, but almost throughout all Asia, this Paul hath persuaded and turned away much people, saying that they be no gods, which are made with hands:

So that not only this our craft is in danger to be set at nought; but also that the temple of the great goddess Diana should be despised, and her magnificence should be destroyed, whom all Asia and the world worshippeth.

And when they heard these sayings, they were full of wrath, and cried out, saying, Great is Diana of the Ephesians.'

'Enough, enough,' said Hubert, drawing the microphone away from her. Massimo had by no means caught up, but he skipped a good part, few people present being any the wiser, and ended up, *'Basta basta! Evviva la Diana d'Efeso.'*

Hubert turned to Pauline, who was now thoroughly bewildered by his actions, and embraced her on both cheeks, with the ritualistic gesture of the kiss of peace. He then made a sweeping indication that she was dismissed and, to the ever-louder clapping of the crowd she descended amongst them. They were making other noises too, now, and standing on the benches.

'And I say unto you,' crooned Hubert into the microphone, 'that Diana of Ephesus was brought to Nemi to become the great earth mother. Great is Diana of Nemi!'

'Diana of Nemi!' yelled someone in the crowd, which inspired Pauline's boy-friend Walter to strike up his guitar. Soon everyone was chanting, 'Diana of Nemi! Diana of Nemi!' The seats were empty, the congregation in raptures all over the place, dancing, clapping, shouting. Hubert gazed on the scene with benevolent satisfaction, relieved that nobody seemed to have taken in the true meaning of the passage. He smiled indulgently, there under the leaves. Then he sat down on his throne, gathering his robes about him, smiling even upon Pauline who was dancing and singing ecstatically with the others and looking such an absolute mess, believing herself once more in Hubert's favour and not caring in the least that he had turned her treachery to his own account.

'I want to testify!'

Hubert turned from his musing, annoyed to find a thin girl standing before the microphone at his side. He recognized Nancy Cowan, the former English tutor to Letizia and Pietro Bernardini who was now simply part of their household, waiting for Bernardini to marry her in the course of time. Hubert rose, uncertain what to do, since the people who were jumping about the garden had come to a standstill at the sound of her voice, and Walter, the damned fool, stopped strumming his guitar.

'I want to say,' said Nancy, 'that the biblical passage you have heard is a condemnation of the pagan goddess Diana. It implies that the cult of Diana was only a silversmith's lobby and pure commercialism. Christianity was supposed to put an end to all that, but it hasn't. It –'

'Well said,' Hubert boomed into the microphone. He had taken over, edging her out of place, and he now put a hand on her shoulder as he continued. 'Our Sister Nancy tells us that Diana of Ephesus was betrayed. Christianity was betrayed, and now we have the great mother of nature again, Diana of the Woods, Diana of Nemi. Great is Diana of Nemi!'

Massimo, who had joined the crowd, returned to his place in time to translate a portion of this speech, but meanwhile something was going wrong with the ritualistic side under Hubert's leafy bower, for, as he had spoken, Nancy had thrown his hand off her shoulder and was now tugging and tearing violently at his robes.

The clapping recommenced, everyone crowding round to see the new event taking place before Hubert's throne. It looked like a fight, and the bemused congregation turned into an audience. Walter, assuming that this affair, too, was part of a previous plan, strummed up once more. 'Great is Diana of Nemi! Long live Diana of Nemi!' Nancy was fairly strong, but Hubert now had her by the hair. His sleeve was half torn off. Presently Letizia excitedly came to help Nancy in whatever role it was she was playing; she was probably drawn to the girl's assistance by the fact that she felt in conflict about Hubert, disliking him personally but fascinated by his nature cult. The sound of hand-clapping mounted again, all round the fighters; Letizia was fairly carried away, so that, in passing, having drawn blood from Hubert's cheeks with her nails she frenziedly tore of her own blouse under which she wore nothing. She fought on, topless, while Nancy concentrated on tearing the green and shining robes piece by piece from Hubert's back.

The noise in the garden was louder than ever. The two priests stood some way from the throne and scene of battle, exhorting frantically. Cuthbert came a little too close and received a casual swipe from Hubert which sent him to the ground. Soon the clothes were torn from the Jesuits, and in fact everyone in the garden was involved in the riot within a very short time.

Mr Stuyvesant and his young friend George Falk did a tour of the house, meantime, to see if there was anything worthwhile. They puzzled for a long time over the good fake Gauguin, then passed on, touching nothing and apparently just breathing as they walked. They noted several valuable objects and the lack of any burglar alarm, unaware as they were that the house would very shortly be emptied of its contents even before they had time to inform their friends what the contents were.

In their self-contained way, they walked back through the ecstatically distressed crowd in the garden, got into their car and drove off.

The party in the garden did not end abruptly, but piece by piece, stagger by stagger. Marino Vesperelli, the psychiatrist who had steadily wooed Letizia for the past three years, lay naked and very fat under a mulberry tree, repeating fragmentary phrases with his eyes staring at the twinkly-blue of the sky between the leaves. 'Exhausted. Group therapy,' he said. 'Letizia. The group.' She, meanwhile, lay on her back across him, gazing up likewise at the branches wherefrom was hanging, for some reason, the twisted and bashed-in skeleton of Walter's guitar. Letizia looked down at her breasts and turned over to comfort her plump suitor.

Pauline wandered in the overgrown and now overwrought garden, looking vainly for her hat while Walter waited for her in the road, his car already packed with some of their possessions. Hubert had in fact thrown her out. He gave her twenty minutes in which to leave, refusing absolutely her offer to bathe a wound on his hand. 'I'll kill you,' Hubert said.

'I thought you were charismatic,' said Pauline. 'At the reading of my testimony from the Bible you showed charisma.'

'Look at my head, Miss Thin,' said Hubert.

'I didn't do it,' Pauline shrieked.

'To all intents and purposes,' Hubert said, 'you did.'

Massimo de Vita came to Pauline's room shortly afterwards and told her she was in trouble, she must pack and go. 'Italian prisons are not very nice. You brought drugs to this house. You created an orgy. People have been hurt and disturbed greatly. Soon it will be all over the countryside and the carabinieri will inquire.' She packed a few things, but not all, unwilling to make such a clean break. To give Hubert a last chance she returned to look for her hat in the garden, as she explained to the waiting Walter. Under Hubert's window Pauline called up, 'Hubert!'

His bloody head appeared. 'I'll wish you good afternoon,' he said. This was followed by one of the heavy metal taps that had been wrenched from every bathroom and washbasin in the house. It hit her on the head and blood spurted down her face. She ran, then, out to Walter and the car, and set off with him towards Paris.

The young portrait-painter had lost a tooth but he felt that the trip which his new amphetamine-based drug had induced was well worth it; and he said as much to his friend, Maggie's former chauffeur, as they sat indoors, squeezed together on the draining-board of the kitchen sink with their feet dabbling in the basin which was filled with cold water.

'It's all over,' Hubert moaned. 'My hopes . . . my . . . I'll kill that woman Pauline Thin if I see her again. I shall have to leave Nemi, but I'll see Miss Thin shall die.'

He was lying on his bed with Massimo hovering over him. His cheeks and hands were scarred and swollen with scratches from the fight, but the most visible wound, a cut on his forehead stretching from the eyebrow to his fairly receded hairline, had come about from his precipitate flight into the house, when he simply banged his head on the lintel of the door.

Massimo, who had early taken refuge from the riot in the garden, was trembling but unharmed. He wrung out a towel in a basin of water beside Hubert's bed, and applied it to the wounded head. He said, 'What do we say when come the journalists? If arrive the police . . . ?'

'I will kill her. She has to die,' Hubert said. 'I shall make her die wherever she is, because I will it. I will send emissaries to kill her.'

The door opened then, and Hubert's three restored secretaries appeared. Kurt Hakens, his red hair now short-cut, with his arms looking like legs and his legs all uncontrolled, Ian Mackay, squat and tough, looking far more like a swarthy Sicilian than a Scotsman, and Damian Runciwell, the big-boned Armenian who had once been the best of the secretaries as secretary. This Damian looked at Massimo and said, 'Get out.'

There was something in the secretaries' attitude that made Massimo place the bowl of water on the floor, drop the damp towel into it and stand up, ready to go.

'Boys, boys!' said Hubert. 'This is no time to be rude. Go and kill Pauline Thin. She must be hovering around somewhere. She'll never leave.'

'Out,' said Damian to Massimo, who went.

'Boys, I've been wounded severely,' said Hubert. 'Look at my head.'

'We've come to kill you,' said Ian, producing an ugly, long and old-fashioned revolver from his trouser pocket.

'Put that silly toy away and bathe my head,' Hubert said. 'Do you want me to have to go to hospital. As it is, I wouldn't be surprised if the carabinieri arrived at any moment.'

Kurt had taken out a revolver, too. His was shiny and modern-looking. 'For God's sake, what are you doing? It might go off,' Hubert said.

Damian now turned nervously to the others and said something that Hubert couldn't hear. He jerked his head towards the door, perhaps indicating that they should leave, or perhaps referring in some way to Massimo, who had been the last to depart.

Ian, with his revolver pointed at Hubert said, 'Who was he?'

'Who? Massimo de Vita? He's my lawyer,' Hubert said, sitting up in some alarm, with his hand to his wounded head.

Damian walked to the door, opened it and stood half in and half out of the bedroom. He said to the other two men, 'Come here a second.' They followed, Ian still keeping a watch on Hubert, and started arguing in whispers which presently began to sound like the spits and hisses of recrimination.

Hubert screamed, 'What the hell's going on?' and started to get out of bed. Whereupon the three surrounded him and pressed him back. Damian was crying all over his broad face.

'Hubert,' he said, 'can you give us a drink? It's all too unnerving, my dearie. It's all too much.'

Ian put his revolver back into his trousers pocket where it bulged unbecomingly. Kurt rather coyly went over to the bed and placed his smart little gun upon it.

'Have you boys been taking drugs?' said Hubert.

'My word of honour,' said Kurt. 'I'm cured. My psychiatrist will tell you.'

'Drugs,' said Ian. 'All he can think of is drugs when there's a threat on his life. He doesn't think that certain people might have a certain reason to pay us to kill him.'

'We never meant to do it, Hubert,' said Damian, weeping still. 'Not really.'

'Bathe my wound,' said Hubert, 'and tell me who sent you to scare me.'

Damian started washing Hubert's wound at the point that Massimo had left off. 'We need a drink,' said Ian.

'Well, go and fetch a drink. Fetch some disinfectant and a dressing of some sort,' Hubert said. 'I don't want to get stitches in my head. I shall bear the scar of Pauline Thin all my life. When you've had a drink you can go and find her, shoot her, and hide her body in the woods.'

'Hubert, the Marchesa de Tullio-Friole sent us to kill you. Really she did,' said Damian.

'Maggie? She offered you money?'

They were silent then, and obviously embarrassed. Hubert said, 'Then you'd have done so if you hadn't bungled it, if you hadn't come in when my friend Massimo was here?'

'No, Hubert, it was all a pretence. We would have hid you and shared the money with you.'

'Would you go to court and swear that Maggie bribed you to murder me?' Hubert said.

'No,' said Ian.

'No,' said Damian, 'I wouldn't like to go into the horrible criminal atmosphere of a law court, Hubert.'

'No, I wouldn't go near the police ever again,' said Kurt.

'I might force you to testify,' said Hubert. Ian's hand went to his bulgy pocket. 'But I won't,' said Hubert. 'Descendant as I am of the great Diana of Nemi, I have been struck by disaster after disaster all in one afternoon. Such is the fate of the gods. Have you ever read Homer? Has any one of you read Homer? Worse things than this occurred to the gods and their descendants in those days, and so it isn't surprising if they happen to me in times like these. In fact, it proves my rights and titles, *Rex Nemorensis*, the King of Nemi, king of the woods, favoured son of Diana the mother of nature.'

Ian came back with a bottle of brandy, four glasses, a bottle of kitchen alcohol and a wad of cotton wool. 'It's all I could find,' he said. 'This house is not at all as well equipped as it was in the old days when we were running it.'

'Tell me,' said Hubert, 'did you really come here to kill me?'

'Of course not,' said Damian, crying again. 'Don't remind me,' he said.

'Ian, I want that revolver, please. Give it to me.'

Ian handed it over. Hubert examined it well. Then he examined the gun that Kurt had placed on his bed. 'Who gave you these?' he said.

'Maggie. She got them out of her husband's armoury. Mary was with her,' Ian said.

'Yes, Mary was there,' said Kurt.

'How much did she offer you?'

'She didn't specify. She said she'd pay a fortune but month by month in instalments, in case we talked. She said Mary was her witness as an alibi that she was somewhere else with Mary that day, so if we got into trouble it was useless to try to incriminate them. She meant it, Hubert.'

'You tell me you had nothing in advance? She paid you nothing?'

'Not a dollar, not one little dime,' said Ian, very quickly and definitely, and the other two murmured agreement.

'Then you are imbeciles,' Hubert said. 'I know that woman. She once said to me, "Faggots are things that you put on the fire." Very amusing. She thinks you're expendable. I will never know for sure whether you three boys meant it, either.' He locked the two guns and, placing them under the sheet beside him, lay back. 'Give me some brandy,' he said. 'I don't think you would have had the nerve to go through with it, anyway. Maggie has always been utterly foolish. She never consults the experts.'

*

Early next morning, Massimo returned to the house ostentatiously with a removal van, waving a file of documents that might have contained anything. To establish himself well as an outsider he stopped at the post office to ask the way to Hubert's house, volubly explaining that he had come on behalf of his client, the Marchesa Tullio-Friole to order the house to be vacated.

One by one the contents were stacked into the van and taken away to a safe place. Hubert was left with a bed, a stove, his everyday clothes, the television, the refrigerator, four kitchen chairs and four deck chairs. His tattered green robes as well as the good ones went with the van. His documents, so neatly arranged by Pauline in their boxes, went too. The pictures, fake and real, were stacked carefully and so was the furniture, expertly packed in the movers' cartons. Off went all these goods under the tutelage of Massimo de Vita, and Hubert sat in the kitchen with his boys. 'It's like that previous summer before Maggie got married,' he said. 'Darlings, find something to cook.'

After lunch Hubert telephoned to Massimo de Vita 'Just to check,' he said, 'that the goods are in a safe place.'

'They are safe, don't worry,' said Massimo.

'When will they be leaving the country?'

'Be careful on the telephone,' said Massimo softly and then, in a louder voice, he said, 'With the valuable stuff you have to be careful of thieves listening in, you know. Your possessions, Mr Mallindaine, will be leaving Italy within a few days. I have an export permit and all the documents. As a foreigner, you are easier to export than many other clients.'

FIFTEEN

Maggie was being driven by car from Geneva to Lausanne when she remembered the hired assassins she had sent to Hubert. Seen in the light of the greater outrage perpetrated upon her by Coco de Renault, the arrangements she had made with these frightful people now seemed foolish. She hoped they had been too weak or had lacked the opportunity to carry out her orders. She had made no advance payments, only a gold watch apiece, each one slightly different to show good taste; and Mary would have to stand by her if there were any accusations. When she reached Lausanne Maggie put a call through to Mary from her hotel.

'Mary,' said Maggie, lying on the bed wrapped in towels, for the call had come through while she was in her bath, 'I've drawn the ace of spades in the game of life.'

'Excuse me?' said Mary.

'I say I've met with disaster.'

'Oh, have you had an accident?'

'Coco de Renault has completely disappeared with all my money.'

'That's impossible,' Mary said.

'I have to find him,' said Maggie, 'and I have to get back home. My cheques here are bouncing and my bank managers are not in the office when I want to see them; they are all otherwise occupied to a theatrical degree. I've never felt so humiliated in my life. Tell Berto to send me some money.'

'All right, Maggie. But there must be something wrong.'

'Don't tell Berto about Coco's disappearance. I don't want to give him a shock. He'd be furious.'

'Berto's in trouble,' said Mary. 'He had a burglary.'

'But I thought he warned the police about those two men who came to case the joint.'

'I know. Two detectives went along, and they said the burglar alarm was O.K., then the next day, it was only on Tuesday, Guillaume let in a couple of carabinieri, only they weren't carabinieri, they were people dressed up like carabinieri. They tied up the servants and they took the Veronese and all the silver, and they also took that portrait, school of Titian. Berto says they will hold the paintings for ransom as they're no use on the market, but Berto won't pay ransom. He says his hairs have gone grey overnight, but he already had grey hair. I like Berto so much, Maggie.'

'What about my jewellery?' Maggie said.

'They took that too, Maggie.'

'Guillaume!' shrieked Maggie. 'I don't trust that Guillaume. He must have been in with it. It was an inside job. Guillaume has to go. I'll tell Berto. It's either Guillaume or me. Berto must choose.'

'Maggie, the police questioned all the servants and the police believe the servants. Guillaume got hurt in the struggle, too. Didn't you read the papers? It happened Tuesday and it was all in the papers yesterday. Berto says –'

'My jewellery,' Maggie said, 'is the important thing to me at this moment, and Guillaume has it.'

'Maggie, there's an echo on the line; it's an awfully bad line.'

'It wasn't in the papers here,' Maggie said.

'It was in the Italian newspapers. Maybe it isn't a big enough robbery to make the international headlines,' said Mary. 'There have been an awful lot of robberies.'

'A Veronese is an international robbery,' Maggie shouted frantically.

'Well, some art thieves took a Rembrandt from Vienna the same day. Did you read about that?'

'No, I didn't. The press is hushing it all up,' said Maggie.

'I guess there are too many to report,' Mary said.

'Look,' said Maggie, 'I'm coming home. Tell Berto to get me some money here by tomorrow morning. I have to get out my best jewellery from the bank and sell it, and Berto has to sell some of his land. We're paupers. Guillaume has to go to jail and I have to get the contents of my house from Hubert. I hope nothing has happened to him, Mary; it was silly of us to –'

'Not on the phone,' Mary said. 'I told Michael what we'd done. He was so furious. He said not to mention it on the phone. Anyway those boys are staying over there in that house with Hubert and all the furniture's been taken away by your lawyer. They had an orgy couple of weeks ago, but I wasn't there, myself. Everyone else was.'

'Which lawyer took my stuff?' Maggie said.

'Massimo something. The one in Rome.'

'He's a crook,' said Maggie. 'He's a Communist and he's working for Hubert. I gave Hubert's boys each a gold watch and all they can do is have an orgy. Did the police break it up? Why didn't you call the police?'

'I wasn't there. Nobody denounced them to the police. Everyone was afraid and they got away. The police went round last week to have a look but all they found was Hubert and the boys in the empty house.'

'Berto will never believe it,' Maggie said, 'and I'm going to fight every inch of –'

'Berto doesn't know a thing,' Mary said. 'We can't hurt Berto. He's too nice.'

'And what about me?' Maggie said. 'Doesn't anyone have any feelings for me?'

'Oh, yes, we do, Maggie,' Mary said. 'Oh, yes, we do. We love you and we care for you a lot.'

The first thing Maggie did when she put down the telephone was to order as many Italian newspapers as possible. Maggie was still, so far as was known, one of the hotel's wealthiest clients, but the best the night porter could do at that hour, well after midnight, was to send to the station for the early edition of *Il Tempo* which he delivered to Maggie at about one-thirty. She was still awake, putting her disasters in order of priority. There was no word of the robbery at Berto's villa; it had evidently become old news. But the headline in the Roman crime section caused her to put another call through to Mary.

'Oh, can't you sleep, Maggie?' said Mary anxiously. 'Michael said I shouldn't have told you all those things, I should have waited. Berto is going to call his bank in Geneva tomorrow morning. He tried to call you but he couldn't get through. It's terribly difficult from the villa. Can't you sleep? Berto says I shouldn't have told you about your jewellery because he should have liked to be with you when you heard.'

'Well, I want to know about your jewellery,' Maggie said. 'You said you were putting it in an out-of-the-way bank for safety.'

'Oh, goodness, yes. It's all in a bank, I don't know, Michael's trying to get to sleep. It's on the Via Appia.'

'Banco di Santo Spirito?' said Maggie.

'Yes, that's it. If you need money that bad, Maggie, I can get you a loan without pawning my jewellery. You just talk to Michael when you come home; I can talk to Daddy and –'

'Number 836 Via Appia?' said Maggie.

'Well, I don't know. I guess there's only one Santo Spirito on the Via Appia.'

'Get up and look,' Maggie said. 'I must know the exact bank and the exact number of the exact street. There has been a robbery at the Santo Spirito. It says here in this morning's *Tempo*, Wednesday, 16 July, that there was a robbery over the week-end and they found on Monday that the gang ransacked the strong-boxes. Get up and see if that's your bank.'

'Oh, no! Oh, no!' Mary said. 'It can't be. I haven't heard anything. Maybe they tried to get me. We just got back this morning from the villa . . .' Maggie then heard her say, 'Michael, wake up, my jewellery's been robbed. What is the address of my bank?'

It was indeed Mary's bank which the belated report referred to. Mary also informed Maggie that she hadn't insured this jewellery, believing it to be safe in its vault. Her voice was strange; she spoke with awe as if she was in church. 'What an experience for you!' Maggie said. 'You poor child, what an ordeal to have to wait till the bank opens in the morning before you can find out whether your box was one of the unlucky ones or not.' She spoke with genuine concern, thinking mainly of a special diamond brooch and an emerald ring of great value that she herself had given to Mary. But Michael came on the telephone, unreasonable with anxiety and short-tempered. 'What sort of a woman,' he said, 'would ring us up in the middle of the night, twice, with the very worst news? You could have let us sleep till the morning. Now Mary's crying. She wants me to call the bank manager. How can I call him in the middle of the night, what good will it do? I don't know him. Mary isn't a bit materialistic, that's what you don't realize, Mother. There's an economic crisis and you've got to face it. It's what –'

'We're ruined!' Maggie shrieked back. 'We've all become paupers overnight, and the first thing that happens when a family is ruined is always a quarrel unless they are very rare people, very exceptional. And I'm just so sorry to see that you are very, very ordinary, and also common from the Radcliffe side. The whole family quarrelled over their trusts and their wills, and what's more, it was only an hour ago that Mary told me you all cared for me and loved me. It isn't my fault if Mary's lost her jewellery. Maybe she hasn't. I hope not. I'm going to speak to Berto.' Maggie hung up at this point, looked at herself in the glass and was amazed to find herself still glowing and handsome. She took a bath, telephoned for a bottle of champagne, asked to be wakened at eight, and went to bed where she slowly sipped three glasses before she went to sleep.

It made Lauro very happy indeed to be summoned from his honeymoon cruise by Maggie, although he was putting on a great air to the effect that she had done something outrageous in putting through a call to the captain of the *Panorama di Nozze*, that cruise ship with twenty-one newly-wedded couples on board on which he and Betty had been spending their honeymoon. Lauro had already, in times past, visited the Greek islands with Maggie's entourage, he had seen the labyrinthine home of the Minotaur and he had been to the Acropolis. The tone of the honeymoon company appalled him. Twenty-one pairs of newly-weds; every morning a round of sniggery remarks; dancing until three in the morning with uproarious jokes about exchanging partners and which is the way to *your* cabin? The awful brides whispering together over cocktails, and Betty no better than the rest.

He sat with Betty now in the comfortable lobby of the hotel in Lausanne, while Maggie, reassuringly radiant, heard out his outraged complaints with an obligingly penitent expression that meant only that she had more important things on her mind than to waste words defending herself.

'You're so right, Lauro,' she said. 'I should have realized . . . I should have been more thoughtful . . . Your honeymoon. It happens once in a lifetime, doesn't it?' She turned to plump, bridal Betty who had clearly been to the hairdresser and had dressed very carefully for this meeting. 'I do apologize,' Maggie said, 'if I may call you Betty?'

Betty drooped her lids and shrugged, as if not prepared to show any lack of support for her husband's complaint. 'We nearly didn't come,' she said. 'But then the captain made out it was so urgent, and the transport being all arranged, Lauro thought maybe you were ill and so we came ashore that day.'

'Lauro could easily have come alone,' said Maggie, 'and left you to finish the cruise.'

'What a suggestion,' said Lauro. 'How could I leave my wife alone on a honeymoon cruise, Maggie, are you crazy?'

'Well, now that you're here, Lauro, may I have a word with you?' Maggie said.

'Go ahead,' said Lauro, refilling all three glasses with the champagne that Maggie had ordered for the party.

'Well, it's business, Lauro. Betty must, of course, get used to business practice, and as you are my confidant and secretary I must speak to you alone. If Betty will give us half an hour. I'm sure there's some shopping she wants to do. The boutiques of Lausanne are charming; she can get some ideas for her boutique in Rome, don't you think?'

Betty said, 'Just what I was thinking myself,' and put down her glass with a sharp tinkle.

Lauro considered the matter importantly, with his lips pouted together. Then he said, 'Yes, I think Maggie is in the right. Come back in half an hour, Betty, all right?'

'Fine,' she said brightly, 'lovely.'

They watched her as she passed through the lane of little tables to the vestibule, and out of the swing doors, in her cream and brown linen suit.

'Are you happy?' said Maggie to Lauro.

'Of course,' said Lauro. 'Betty is a wonderful wife. She's beautiful and also intelligent. We Italians, you know, like women to be women, and to be shapely.'

'I often think Italian girls are very mature in their appearance,' Maggie said, 'a little over-full, but it's a matter of taste.'

'I won't hear a word against Italian girls,' said Lauro, 'and especially my wife.'

'You're perfectly right,' Maggie said in hasty conciliation. 'I only meant that maybe the trouble is that they have their Confirmation too early. In the Anglo-Saxon countries they aren't confirmed till they're fourteen.' She waved the subject vaguely aside. 'It's a matter of national custom, that's all. I'm sure I'm not bigoted. Well, Lauro, I've got something really serious to discuss with you. It's serious and it's private, and I can't thank you enough for breaking off your mass-honeymoon for me, Lauro.'

'It was a very lovely and very expensive, exclusive honeymoon cruise,' said Lauro. 'Today we were to go on donkey-back into the mountains.'

'All on donkeys, together, twenty-one *sposi!*' marvelled Maggie. Lauro looked sour.

'But Lauro, I'm in trouble, darling,' Maggie said. 'I really am.'

Lauro cheered up. 'What's your problem?' he said.

'I see in the newspapers,' said Maggie, 'that a lot of people are getting kidnapped. In Italy it's becoming a national sport. Every day there's someone new. Where are all the millions going to?'

'It's a criminal affair,' Lauro said, 'mainly run by the Mafia but there are independent gangs, maybe political. I don't know. Why don't you keep your bodyguard? What happened to your gorilla?'

'I can't afford a bodyguard. I'm broke,' said Maggie.

Lauro laughed. 'If that were true why would you be afraid of being kidnapped?'

'When it's known that Coco de Renault has disappeared com-pletely with all my holdings, all my real estate, all my trusts, all my capital, I won't have to fear being kidnapped.'

'What are you taking about, Maggie?' Lauro said. 'You ask about kidnaps, then you tell me this story of Renault. I think you try to make out you're poor because you're afraid. But no one will believe you, Maggie. You have to take care. It's not nice to be kidnapped. Sometimes the victim never comes home. Remember how they cut off young Getty's ear. They keep you in a dungeon for weeks.'

'Coco has disappeared. I've tried to trace him. I've had private detectives and my lawyers trying to trace him. They say he's some-where in the Argentine; that's all the news I can get. I'm not sure if they're right or wrong. Maybe the investigators can't be bothered any more. In the meantime, the detectives have to be paid, lawyers' fees have to be paid.'

'And the police?'

'Which police? He belongs to no country. Then if I make a

scandal, the tax people will start nosing into my affairs, that's all. I want to kidnap Coco, that's what I want to do. I want to extort my money out of him. At least I might get a part of it, something. I want to kidnap Coco de Renault.'

Lauro said, 'It's a criminal offence, kidnapping.'

'Oh, I know,' Maggie said. 'I know. Why shouldn't I be a criminal? Everyone else is.'

'Maggie, your husband —'

'He'll never know,' said Maggie.

Lauro sat back in a worldly way with an unworldly expression. 'You're a wonderful woman, Maggie. What's in it for me?'

'Ten per cent,' said Maggie.

'Twenty,' said Lauro.

'Including the expenses and the pay-offs, though,' Maggie said.

'No, no,' said Lauro. 'There's a big risk for those poor people who do the actual work. They risk a life's imprisonment if they don't get shot by the police. Then they have to find the people to do the first part, take the prisoner; then they have to find the good hiding places; they have to find the family and make the telephone calls, and they have to feed the man.'

'All right, thirty per cent inclusive,' Maggie said.

'Who is the family?'

'An American wife, rather ancient-looking, living here in Lausanne. I've seen her at a distance, poor dreary soul. The investigators say she swears she hasn't seen him for five months, but they don't believe her; neither do I.'

'You think he'll visit her one day?'

'I don't know. I think he's probably changed his appearance by plastic surgery. The reason I think so is that he's done it twice before.'

'He'll never come back to Switzerland,' Lauro said. 'If he's now a millionaire in the Argentine, why should he want to see an old wife?'

'There's a daughter at college in America,' said Maggie. 'She'll be at home with her mother this summer. I think he might want to see the daughter.'

'You would have to demand a very large ransom,' said Lauro, 'to make it worth your while.'

'I'll demand a large ransom,' Maggie said. 'After all, it's my money, isn't it?'

'My contacts don't run to the Mafia,' Lauro said. 'I'm not in touch with the underworld at all.'

'Oh, come,' said Maggie, 'don't exaggerate, Lauro.'

'I know very few,' Lauro said.

'If I sell my big ruby pendant,' said Maggie, 'I can offer to those very few rich friends of yours a good sum in advance. My ruby is one of the few things that haven't yet been stolen. I've had some jewellery stolen from the villa and I think Mary has probably lost hers in that job at the Banco di Santo Spirito the other day.' She was crying now.

'I don't know what to believe,' said Lauro, 'but somehow I believe you, or you wouldn't have torn me away from my bride and my honeymoon.' He, too, had tears in his eyes at the thought of his lost paradise as it now existed in his head, if not in fact.

'Betty will be back soon. Can you get rid of her for the afternoon? She can use my car,' Maggie said.

'I suppose so,' Lauro said. 'I get rid of her and I take you up to bed. Isn't that your idea?'

'It's usually your idea,' said Maggie, 'isn't it?'

'I suppose so,' Lauro said.

Dusk had fallen when Maggie arrived two days later at the Villa Tullio. Berto was not expecting her; he had heard no word from her and had been unable to find her at any of the Swiss hotels she usually stayed at. Berto was worried; he could not quite understand why she had needed money. He made arrangements for the money to reach her, but afterwards, when he had tried to reach her by telephone at Lausanne, she had just left the hotel.

Mary also had tried to reach her, overjoyed that her safety-box, being one of those set high in the wall of the bank-vault, had escaped the gang's frenzied operation. Mary had telephoned to Berto in the Veneto. 'I'm worried about Maggie. Where is she?'

'I don't know,' Berto said. 'She's left Lausanne, and I can't find her anywhere else. I'm worried, too. Have you seen this morning's paper? Another kidnapping.'

'Oh, Berto, darling, don't worry,' Mary said. 'Would you like me to come and keep you company?'

'No, my dear, don't think of it.'

The chauffeur who drove Maggie home to the Villa Tullio that

night was thoroughly puzzled. The Marchesa had dressed herself up
so peculiarly. She had gone to a flea-market in a small town on the
way home, all on impulse while he waited in the car-park. This
chauffeur had long been in Berto's service and had very few original
thoughts about Maggie. He respected her considerably because she
was Berto's wife and hence the Marchesa, and he felt it natural that
she should have illogical impulses. He had taken her all over
Switzerland on a mystifying route, not consequentially, not econom-
ically planned; first the Zürich area, then the Geneva area, then Zug,
then Lausanne. To him, it was all a great *non sequitur* but Maggie was
always careful to see that he had good rooms and ate well and was
comfortable, as a lady should. It had not caused him to quibble in his
thoughts when Lauro and his bride turned up at Lausanne, that
Lauro at Maggie's request had then sent him on a trip around the
valleys and up the mountains on a sight-seeing tour with Betty for
the whole afternoon, from twelve-thirty to six-thirty. The chauffeur
had lunched at pretty little Caux, high up on a mountain path, Betty
sitting at one table, he at another, despite the girl's invitation to sit at
the table with her. Betty had marvelled at the little chalets, and the
chauffeur had agreed with a totally unscientific will to please. 'My
husband, my poor husband,' Betty had said, 'is busy with that
Marchesa all the afternoon and he's on his honeymoon.' The chauffeur merely said that such was life. 'Her houses at Nemi are built on
my land,' said Betty. 'They're *abusivo*; she has to pull down the
houses or else pay us. That's what they have to discuss, and believe
me –'

As she spoke the chauffeur pulled up at a cottage-weave shop and
asked Betty if she would like to look round it. Betty spent some time
there, buying embroidered placemats and a shawl, then re-entered
the car, into the back seat, daintily, with the door held open for her
by Berto's chauffeur.

The next day Maggie had gone to Geneva and dropped Betty at
the airport to catch a plane for Rome. Then, with Lauro, she had
gone to a newly constructed block of flats where there was no
concierge but a press-button phone at the entrance. Lauro pressed a
button but there was no answer. The big glass-fronted doors were
locked. Maggie got back into the car and waited. Lauro walked up
and down the little pathway with its tidy new plants on either side;

he pressed the button again from time to time; he looked up at the windows; he looked at his watch.

Maggie, who seldom explained anything, had evidently felt it necessary to explain to the chauffeur that they were waiting for a dressmaker, very brilliant and not yet famous, whom she simply had to see. They had an appointment, she explained.

It was too bad, said the chauffeur, to keep the Marchesa waiting. They waited twenty more minutes before a Peugeot drew up. Three youngish men got out, very quickly, and made for the entrance where Lauro was waiting. The chauffeur had not been able to see their faces because they kept them quite averted from him. One of the men, saying something to Lauro, indicated vulgarly with his thumb the car where Maggie sat with the chauffeur and said something in French, which the chauffeur didn't understand, but which sounded disapproving. Maybe the man had not wanted to be seen. At any rate one of the men had opened the door with a key, and Lauro was answering back, looking at his watch. Maggie then got out of the car with her charming smile and followed the four men into the building. That took up the rest of the morning. Maggie emerged without Lauro, and they were off, back to the Veneto, stopping for meals on the way, and then, unaccountably, at a little market-town where Maggie had spent an hour while the chauffeur waited in the car-park.

He had waited, which is to say he had taken an occasional walk around. From what he saw and what he heard, Maggie had no rendezvous with anyone this time. A rendezvous, although its purpose might escape Berto's good chauffeur, might at least have been explicable. What was thoroughly inconsistent was that Maggie had stood there at a stall, innocently buying a heap of dreadful clothes; and they were plainly intended for herself for she held up these rags against her body to get a rough idea if they would fit. A worn-out long skirt of black cotton, a pair of soiled tennis shoes which she actually tried on there in the street, a once-pink head scarf, a cotton blouse, not second-hand but cheap, piped with white, and terrible. The chauffeur wandered back to the car and waited. Maggie appeared before long, with her sunniness intact, and her light-hearted walk, holding in her arms the bundle of these frightful garments, not even wrapped in a piece of paper.

The chauffeur took them from her and placed them carefully in the boot. All he said was, 'The Marchesa should leave her handbag with

me when she goes shopping. There are bad people about.'
Whereupon Maggie searched her handbag, quite alarmed; but everything was all right. They drove on.

Towards dusk next day Maggie wanted to stop in Venice for a rest
and a drink. She left the chauffeur at the quay and, hiring a water-
taxi, directed it to a smart bar. Later she returned in a water-taxi and
kept it waiting while she demanded of the chauffeur the old clothes
from the back of the car. Wrapping them, for very shame, in a tartan
car-rug, the chauffeur handed them over. Maggie redirected the taxi
to the bar.

She returned looking so like a tramp that the chauffeur failed to
recognize her at first. 'Marchesa!' he then exclaimed.

'I changed in the ladies' room,' Maggie had said. 'Did I give you
a fright? I want to play a joke on my husband.'

Onward to the villa. It was dark as they approached. 'The back
entrance,' Maggie ordered. 'I have the key.'

The chauffeur, still puzzled, drove round the villa to the firmly
locked and heavy back gate in the wall which led into the paddock,
the orchard, the kitchen garden, and finally to the great back door.

'Let me accompany the Marchesa,' he said, fetching out his big
electric torch. He had in mind those masked balls he had heard of,
and felt a little guilty and low-class, lacking that sense of humour of
the sophisticated. He decided to try to enter the spirit of the thing.

Maggie attacked the big gate with her key while the chauffeur's
torch shone on it. With the first touch, a furious din broke loose.
Barking of dogs, the screams of women, male voices roaring out the
worst possible obscenities, and above all the words, 'Ladri! ladri!
polizia!' – Thieves, police . . . Maggie screamed, but bells were
ringing now, searchlights beamed from the rooftop of the villa and
Berto's dalmatian, Pavoncino, came streaking towards the gate,
barking only less loudly than the barking in the air.

The pandemonium continued while the chauffeur pulled Maggie
back into the car, bundling her into the front seat beside him. He
drove up a full speed round to the front of the house and got out to
ring the bell.

Here, Pavoncino awaited them, barking. But soon, having recognized Maggie, he was wagging his tail. Maggie sat on and waited. A
police car drew up, then another.

In the midst of the turmoil Berto appeared with Guillaume, both armed with guns.

The police had taken Maggie into custody and were holding the chauffeur with his hands behind his back.

'Berto, it's me,' Maggie called out.

'Where are you, Maggie? I can't see you,' Berto called. 'Are you all right?'

'No, I'm not,' Maggie said.

The police could not understand the English and had already bundled her, in her rags, into a police car, around which the dog pranced joyfully, barking loudly.

The noises in the air ceased abruptly. Guillaume slowly opened the front gate, still with his gun poised. Then, perceiving the dog's demonstrations of welcome, cautiously approached the police car where Maggie sat meekly, handcuffed to two burly carabinieri.

At first he didn't recognize her, and could hardly believe her voice when she called 'Berto!'

'That's my wife,' Berto said. 'Maggie, what are you doing? You've set off my new burglar alarm and all the loudspeakers and the electronic communication with the police station. What's wrong?'

Maggie was released in due course of time, and brandy administered to the chauffeur. The policemen were invited inside and apologized to, refusing, however, to drink while on duty; they seemed happy enough to have a nice glance round the drawing-room.

'I dressed up as a pauper,' Maggie explained in the best Italian she could manage. 'Because I am a pauper. I'm ruined. I just wanted everyone to know.'

Berto, placing to one side for the moment his bewilderment, translated this with considerable modifications. He explained, in fact, that the Marchesa had only meant it as a joke; she had not known of the burglar alarm.

Many more apologies from Berto. Sincere and profound apologies. The police went away and Berto stood looking at his bedraggled wife, still handsome and gleaming through it all as she was.

SIXTEEN

Dear Hubert,

On my return from a business trip to Switzerland I found a letter from my lawyer, Avvocato Massimo de Vita, in which he tells me you are claiming that I gave you my Gauguin, and that moreover my Gauguin is a fake.

As it happens, I did not give you my Gauguin and my Gauguin is not a fake.

I plan, in fact, to sell my Gauguin. In these days of tight money one has to plan one's budget, and Berto plans to take my Gauguin to London to sell it. I plan also to dispose of my Louis XIV furniture. I heard an absurd report that my furniture and pictures had already been taken away from the house, but naturally you would have informed me had they been stolen. There are so many rumors!! However, I plan the move for Wednesday. As you know I'm not so very keen on Louis XIV and I don't need it anyway really. I don't use it, do I? We are planning to collect it next week Wednesday August 27. It is such a long time since we met. We are planning to pay you a visit, Hubert, to discuss your future plans as we are selling the villa to Lauro as it appears the land on which it is built belongs to Lauro's beautiful new bride. Isn't it fortunate that Lauro has been our friend all these years? Would you believe it, but he even cut short his honeymoon to come and discuss my plans with me! What good fortune that the land does not belong to a stranger! In the meantime of course I am taking action against Mr de Lafoucauld who arranged for the purchase of my properties at Nemi as it seems he was most untrustworthy. That is not his real name, of course, but Berto has talked to the police, they have found him in Milan and certainly he will go to prison. Berto has said he no longer cares if his name gets into the papers in connection with a criminal action as we are the innocent party, always have been and always will be.

I hope you can find some other spot in Nemi to continue your plans for your new religion. It sounds very exciting and I would have loved to have been there, too, but I was in Switzerland and besides, Berto is so conventional, he would hate it if I got mixed up with drugs, orgies, etc. etc. Isn't it good that Lauro is willing to make a little arrangement with me for the house, as it is really an illegal house although I didn't know it at the time, of course. I plan to move in as soon as possible. Berto, of course, was angry about the orgy but he would naturally prefer you to go quietly. I mean, we don't want to complain to the authorities as that would be unpleasant. It has been good of you to keep my pictures and my furniture in good condition. I have tried to get in touch with Massimo de Vita to tell him personally what my plans are, but his office telephone number doesn't answer. A few weeks ago I read in the papers that the Lake of Nemi is 'biologically dead' which means it is polluted, but they are building a new sewage system for that clinic, so it doesn't all go into the lake. I am sure your ancestors would turn in their graves and I do feel for you, after those beautiful ships of antiquity sailed so proudly on its tranquil surface. Of course, Nemi is beautiful and Mary will be sorry to leave, but their house is also illegal and I don't know if they can make arrangements with the owners of the land, and in any case Michael says we shouldn't have to pay twice for a house. It is a worry for the Bernardinis also, especially as his wedding to Nancy is to take place soon. She is a very fine young woman and will be a very good housekeeper for him I am quite sure.

If you see Avvocato Massimo de Vita please tell him he has got it all wrong about my Gauguin. I really feel that lawyers these days are very slipshod in their work. Hardly any of them care about their clients any more. I plan to go to another lawyer.

Don't forget Wednesday, 27, the van will be coming, naturally with an armed escort as one can't be too careful these days.

Arriverderci and all my love,

Maggie.

P.S. It is terrible the times we are living in. I just read in the *Herald Tribune* about a dear friend of mine, a financier from the Argentine, Coco de Renault, being kidnapped. Apparently they are asking a fantastic ransom and the poor wife and daughter in

Switzerland are absolutely frantic. I put a call through to them immediately but they didn't want to talk so as to keep the line free for the kidnappers to negotiate. The family say they haven't seen Coco for months and they don't know where he is, which is terrible, but the newspapers say he has to send them a power of attorney to release all his money for the kidnappers, and it's possible the banks will not accept his word in which case he could be killed. It is terrible to read about these events and even more frightening when it is someone you know and it reaches your own door. Personally, I think the wife has already got all his money tucked away somewhere in Switzerland, though the talk of powers of attorney is her way of trying to drive a bargain. They usually put their money in the wife's name or in a numbered account so I hope my friend will be released unharmed, but how dreadful to pay it all to criminals!

Hubert read the letter slowly to Pauline Thin who had returned the day after Hubert's three former secretaries had left.

Since the furniture had been taken away there had been quarrels every day amongst them all; the boys simply didn't have the stamina to sit it out for a month all sleeping on camp-beds and eating in the kitchen. A month was all Hubert had asked of them, just for the sake of appearances.

Maggie's furniture and her pictures had already been sold in London. Even those pictures which had been copies, and the set of Louis XIV furniture which had been reconstructed, with an original leg here, an arm there, had fetched quite a fat sum, while those original paintings and articles of furniture which remained had fetched a fortune. After Massimo's half-share had been deducted there still remained a fortune for Hubert, that fortune which he had felt all along that Maggie should have settled on him. It was now only a matter of keeping up an appearance of poverty for a month or maybe a little longer, so there should be no question that he had made off with Maggie's property. Massimo had left for some unknown destination; he had said California, which meant, certainly, elsewhere; evidently he was used to departing speedily for elsewhere from time to time. Hubert's half-share of the sale was safely in that nursery-garden of planted money, Switzerland.

'Miss Thin,' said Hubert when Pauline arrived at the house the day after the departure of his three discontented friends, 'if you have come to collect your remaining goods and chattels you have come in vain. The bailiffs have been. They have taken everything, including your knickers. All they have left me are the bare necessities and I, descendant of the gods, am a pauper. What is more, Miss Thin, you have much to account for.'

Pauline said, 'So have you. Five months' pay for a start.'

'Don't be vulgar,' he said. All the same, he opened the kitchen cupboard and took a bundle of notes out of a tin. He counted out her pay. 'Women,' he said, 'are incredibly materialistic.'

She sat down on a kitchen chair and checked the money. 'Your boy-friends have gone,' she said. 'I dare say they left for idealistic, not materialistic, reasons. That's why they left you all alone here, without any comfortable furniture. Where did you get this money from, Hubert?'

'It's no business of yours and you're no longer my secretary. You wrecked my Fellowship and you wrecked my reputation. I have had an anonymous letter from somebody in the village comparing me to some false Catholic prelate who set himself up at Nemi with his gang of acolytes two years ago in a villa, with all his holy pictures and his crucifixes and his apostolic papers in order. He claimed to have a commission from the Holy See to purchase vast stocks of merchandise, and when the police finally surrounded the villa he committed suicide. I have all the details here. The author of the letter enclosed the press cutting.'

He had passed it over to Pauline. 'See what the bloody fool killed himself with,' he said, 'a glass of *vino al topicida*! It sounds like some speciality in a restaurant, but it's rat-poison in wine. A very low-class suicide, and I wouldn't care to know the author of this anonymous letter who suggests I do the same.'

'The hand-writing's pretty awful,' said Pauline.

'So is the spelling. Some village woman. What does it matter?'

'Oh, Hubert! You would never think of suicide, would you?' Pauline said. 'I don't want this money, really. Take it back. Here it is.'

'Suicide is not remotely in my mind,' Hubert said. 'But I'll put my money back in the tin for safe-keeping. I hope you've learnt your lesson, Miss Thin.'

'I'll go shopping and I'll cook for you,' Pauline said.

'I had another letter,' Hubert had said, and he then had proceeded to read aloud to her Maggie's letter.

'That woman is dangerous,' Pauline said. 'Where's her furniture at the moment?'

'How do I know? Her lawyer took it away.'

'And your manuscripts, Hubert, where are your documents?'

'In Rome,' Hubert said. 'Transferred to Rome, as was the cult of Diana which, for political and very democratic reasons, spread to Rome in the fourth century B.C.'

'I saw Father Cuthbert in Rome,' Pauline said.

'I dare say you spoke about me. What else would you have to talk about, my dear?'

'Well, Hubert, I think he's got a good idea that you should take up the Charismatic Movement in the Church and run the prayer meetings. You do the murmuring rite so well and Cuthbert said it wouldn't be in conflict with Diana as the preserver of nature, not at all.'

'It is a long time,' Hubert said, 'since Homer sang the wonders of Artemis who came to be Diana. He called her the Lady of Wildlife. There's much to be said for charisma and wildlife.'

'They're the new idea,' Pauline said, meekly. 'You have to make a living somehow, Hubert. You can't stay here with these kitchen chairs.'

'One way and another, Miss Thin,' Hubert said, 'I haven't done so badly.'

'We leave tonight at midnight,' Hubert informed Pauline. It was Tuesday, 26 August, thirteen days after the Feast of Diana and one day before the date fixed by Maggie for the removal of her furniture which wasn't there. That morning, when Pauline returned from her trip to the village to buy provisions, he had taken the newspapers out of her hand, as usual, waiting for her to serve the coffee. 'We leave at midnight,' he said.

Over coffee he handed her a newspaper, folded back to reveal a picture of a decapitated statue. 'This is a sign,' said Hubert. Two statues flanking a fountain in Palermo had been mutilated by vandals; the newspaper had printed the one which had suffered most. The headline read, 'Diana Decapitated', and the picture showed a sturdy and headless nude Diana with her hound and her stag. 'It's a definite sign,' Hubert said, 'for us, don't you think so, Miss Thin?'

'One good thing,' said Hubert, 'about having nothing left to protect is that I can go for a walk.'

He left before sunset, while Pauline set about putting their few household possessions in the back of the station-wagon ready for their transfer to Rome. Bobby Lester, her previous employer so long ago, and a friend of Father Cuthbert, had lent them his flat overlooking the Piazza del Popolo. She placed the tin box with Hubert's money on the kitchen table to keep an eye on it and sat down beside it dutifully and happily doing nothing but reading small paragraphs in the newspaper and listening to the transistor radio. She wore a black cotton blouse and a red skirt that made her hips seem wider than ever; they spilt over the kitchen chair in a proprietary way, and she knew she was indispensable to Hubert's future.

Hubert, meantime, had decided to take his last look at beautiful Nemi, where from every point appeared a different view, every view a picture postcard except that it was real. Down the old Roman road he went, past the old town-council building and into the village. All during July and August Nemi had been crowded with holidaymakers; even a few foreign tourists and some of the pilgrim crowds of Holy Year, lately coveted by Hubert, had brimmed over from nearby Castelgandolfo where the Pope held court in his summer residence. But now, as the road grew darker, there were few newcomers to be seen; most of them had returned to the lodgings which had been provided with great efficiency by the neighbouring convents. After dark, a few local people grouped around the bars and various courting couples leaned over the wall beside the castle, looking at the moon.

Outside the church a mosaic plaque had been put up to commemorate the Pope's visit to Nemi in 1969. Hubert paused on his way to look at it and saw by the road lamp how it bore on the left the crest of Nemi, blue, white, yellow, rich red and gold, surrounded by the motto *Diane Nemus*: the Woods of Diana; on the right was a gleaming emblem of a local Christian order of monks, and above them the Montini papal coat of arms, that of Paul VI, crossed by the gold and silver keys of St Peter. Hubert's walks in Nemi had been few. 'Nemi is mine,' he murmured, 'but I must move on to Rome.' In fact, he felt carefree and rather glad to be leaving, seeing that he was now in funds and how his future prospects, in collaboration with the Jesuits, seemed full of hope and drama, the two things Hubert valued most in life, all things being equal on the material side.

Down he went to the garden walk on the steep cliffs by the lake, across the bridge, towards Diana's temple. The moon was almost three-quarters full and on the wane. 'Always cut wood when the moon is on the wane,' an old countryman had told him during his first years at Nemi when he had gone out to gather firewood. He smiled at the moon, with no one to see him, and felt very deeply that he was descended from Diana the moon goddess.

The spot where Diana's temple had been located was not accessible to the public, and even the local people never went to the thickly overgrown alcoves that remained of her cult. But Hubert knew the way to that area which had been named, in more historic times, the Devil's Grottoes. Not only were the relics of antiquity to be found there, but also numerous caves leading deep into the heart of the cliff under the castle, where vagrants, in the days of lesser prosperity, could take refuge. These caves were now abandoned and overgrown, some of them totally concealed by dense greenery. He plodded through the thick undergrowth, over uneven ground, stopping to hack off a stout branch to help him to beat his path. 'Always cut wood when the moon is on the wane.' The branch broke easily from the low tree.

Suddenly Hubert saw a shape approaching, an old woman it seemed, probably a gipsy, picking her way towards him. She lit her steps with the aid of a flashlamp. Behind her, but much further into the dark thickness of the wooded cliff, he thought he heard an exchange of voices, but then, stopping still, he heard nothing. The crone, dressed drably with a scarf round her head, came closer and was about to pass him with the usual 'Buona sera' of the countryside. 'Maggie!' said Hubert. She stopped and shone the torch on him, and started to laugh.

They sat together looking at the lake and the bashed-in circle of the moon for only a little space. Maggie, of course, had taken up almost from where she had left off, and, without any explanation for her appearance or her presence in that deserted spot, said first that she was fine thank you, how was he? 'Fine,' said Hubert.

So they found a place to sit and Maggie said, 'You would never believe it, Hubert, but my daughter-in-law, Mary, has fallen desperately in love with Berto and he's awfully embarrassed because he loves me exclusively, as you can imagine. He's trying to pass her off to a journalist friend of his, rather elderly, as he feels that Mary really wants an older man, a sort of father figure. It's rather pathetic, but it's all Michael's fault; although he's my own son I know he's neglected Mary and is altogether inadequate, between you and me.'

'It will sort itself out,' Hubert said. 'You look wonderful, Maggie, in spite of all these clothes and things.'

'Hubert, you are always so charming! My clothes are a symbol of my new poverty, of course. And then, dressed like this, one hopes to avoid being kidnapped. It's such a danger, these days. One is in peril.'

'Oh, I know. You told me in your letter about poor Coco de Renault. Any news of him?'

'Well, I wouldn't say *poor* Coco. But maybe he's going to be poor after he pays the ransom. What about you, Hubert? Are you prospering?'

'Mildly,' said Hubert.

'Of course,' said Maggie. 'I happen to know that you've sold all my furniture and pictures. My letter was just to satisfy Berto, and be above-board, you know. Where is Massimo de Vita?'

'Honestly, I don't know, Maggie. There isn't a thing you can do about it.'

'I know,' she said, cheerfully.

'I'm sorry to hear that de Renault made off with all your fortune,' Hubert said.

'I'm getting it back. In fact it has already been arranged,' Maggie said. 'Less thirty per cent.'

'That would be the kidnappers' share,' Hubert said.

'That's right,' said Maggie.

'Where have they got him?' Hubert said. 'The papers seem to have dropped the story, so I suppose he isn't in Italy.'

'Well, some say California and some say Brazil,' Maggie said. 'But in fact he's right here in a cave in this cliff, well guarded. I've just been to visit. Hubert, I simply had to go and gloat.'

'I can well understand that,' said Hubert. 'Is he to be released soon?'

'Some time tonight or early tomorrow morning. The wife delayed a lot and that made Coco very angry. But in the end she had to make over everything to me in Switzerland, all of it. I wouldn't settle for less.'

'Can he be trusted not to report you?' Hubert said.

'Well, naturally, he couldn't indict me. He's too indictable himself. There are times when one can trust a crook.'

'There's something in that,' Hubert said.

She said good night very sweetly and, lifting her dingy skirts, picked her way along the leafy path, hardly needing her flashlamp, so bright was the moon, three-quarters full, illuminating the lush lakeside and, in the fields beyond, the kindly fruits of the earth.

NOT TO DISTURB

ONE

The other servants fall silent as Lister enters the room.

'Their life,' says Lister, 'a general mist of error. Their death, a hideous storm of terror. – I quote from *The Duchess of Malfi* by John Webster, an English dramatist of old.'

'When you say a thing is not impossible, that isn't quite as if to say it's possible,' says Eleanor who, although younger than Lister, is his aunt. She is taking off her outdoor clothes. 'Only technically is the not impossible, possible.'

'We are not discussing possibilities today,' Lister says. 'Today we speak of facts. This is not the time for inconsequential talk.'

'Of facts accomplished,' says Pablo the handyman.

Eleanor hangs her winter coat on a hanger.

'The whole of Geneva will be talking,' she says.

'What about him in the attic?' says Heloise, the youngest maid whose hands fold over her round stomach as she speaks. The stomach moves of its own accord and she pats it. 'What about him in the attic?' she says. 'Shall we let him loose?'

Eleanor looks at the girl's stomach. 'You better get out of the way when the journalists come,' she says. 'Never mind him in the attic. They'll be making inquiries of you. Wanting to know.'

'Oh,' says Heloise, holding her stomach. 'It's the quickening. I could faint.' But she stands tall, placid and unfainting, gazing out of the window of the servants' sitting-room.

'He was a very fine man in his way. The whole of Geneva got a great surprise.'

'Will get a surprise,' Eleanor says.

'Let us not split hairs,' says Lister, 'between the past, present and future tenses. I am agog for word from the porter's lodge. They should be arriving. Watch from the window.' And to the pregnant maid he says, 'Have you got out all the luggage?'

'Pablo has packed his bags already,' says Heloise, swivelling her big eyes over to the handyman with a slight turn of her body.

'Sensible,' says Lister.

'Pablo is the father,' Heloise declares, patting her stomach which quivers under her apron.

'I wouldn't be so sure of that,' Lister says. 'And neither would you.'

'Well it isn't the Baron,' says Heloise.

'No, it isn't the Baron,' says Lister.

'It isn't the Baron, that's for sure,' says Eleanor.

'The poor late Baron,' says Heloise.

'Precisely,' says Lister. 'He'll be turning up soon. In the Buick, I should imagine.'

Eleanor is putting on an apron. 'Where's my carrot juice? Go and ask Monsieur Clovis for my carrot juice. My eyes have improved since I went on carrot juice.'

'Clovis is busy with his contract,' Lister says. 'He left it rather late. I made mine with *Stern* and *Paris-Match* over a month ago. Now of course there's still the movie deal to consider, but you want to play it cool. Don't forget. Play it cool and sell to the highest bidder.'

Clovis looks up, irritably, from his papers. 'France, Germany, Italy, bid high. But don't forget in the long run that English is the higher-income language. We ought to co-ordinate on that point.' He continues his scrutiny of documents.

'Surely Monsieur Clovis is going to prepare a meal tonight isn't he?' says Eleanor. She goes through the door to the kitchen. 'Clovis!' she calls. 'Don't forget my carrot juice, will you?'

'Quiet!' says Clovis. 'I'm reading the small print. The small print in a contract is the important part. You can get you own damn carrot juice. There's carrots in the vegetable store and there's the blender in front of you. You all get your own supper tonight.'

'What about them?'

'They won't be needing supper.'

Lister stands in the doorway, now, watching his young aunt routing among the vegetables for a few carrots which she presses between her fingers disapprovingly.

'Supper, never again,' says Lister. 'For them, supper no more.'

'These carrots are soft,' says Eleanor. 'Heloise doesn't know how to market. She's out of place in a house this style.'

'The poor Baroness used to like her,' says Clovis, looking up from the table where he is sitting studying the fine print. 'The poor Baroness could see no wrong in Heloise.'

'I see no wrong in her, either,' Eleanor says. 'I only say she doesn't know how to buy carrots.'

Heloise comes to join them at the kitchen door.

'It's quickening,' she informs Clovis.

'Well it isn't my fault,' says the chef.

'Nor me neither, Heloise,' says Lister severely. 'I always took precautions the times I went with you.'

'It's Pablo,' says the girl, 'I could swear to it. Pablo's the father.'

'It could have been one of the visitors,' Lister says.

Clovis looks up from his papers, spread out as they are on the kitchen table. 'The visitors never got Heloise, never.'

'There were one or two,' says Heloise, reflectively. 'But it's day and night with Pablo when he's in the mood. After breakfast, even.' She looks at her stomach as if to discern by a kind of X-ray eye who the father truly might be. 'There was a visitor or two,' she says. 'I must say, there did happen to be a visitor or two about the time I caught on. Either a visitor of the Baroness or a visitor of the Baron.'

'We have serious business on hand tonight, my girl, so shut up,' says the chef. 'We have business to discuss and plenty to do. Quite a vigil. Has anybody arrived yet?'

'Eleanor, I say keep a look out of the window,' Lister orders his aunt. 'You never know when someone might leave their car out on the road and slip up. They're careless down at the lodge.'

Eleanor cranes her neck towards the window, still feeling the soft carrots with a contemptuous touch. 'Here comes Hadrian; it's only Hadrian coming up the drive. These carrots are past it. Terrible carrots.'

The footsteps crunch to the back of the house. Hadrian the assistant chef comes in with a briefcase under his arm.

'Did you get out my cabin trunk?' he asks Heloise.

'It's too big, in my condition.'

'Well get Pablo to fetch it, quick. I'm going to start my packing.'

'What about him in the attic?' says Heloise. 'We better take him up his supper or he might create or take one of his turns.'

'Of course he'll get his supper. It's early yet.'

'Suppose the Baron wants his dinner?'

'Of course he expected his dinner,' Lister says. 'But as things turned out he didn't live to eat it. He'll be arriving soon.'

'There might be an unexpected turn of events,' says Eleanor.

'There was sure to be something unexpected,' says Lister. 'But what's done is about to be done and the future has come to pass. My memoirs up to the funeral are as a matter of fact more or less complete. At all events, it's out of our hands. I place the event at about 3 a.m. so prepare to stay awake.'

'I would say 6 o'clock tomorrow morning. Right on the squeak of dawn,' says Heloise.

'You might well be right,' says Lister. 'Women in your condition are unusually intuitive.'

'How it kicks!' says Heloise with her hand on her stomach. 'Do you know something? I have a craving for grapes. Do we have any grapes? A great craving. Should I get a tray ready for him in the attic?'

'Rather early,' says Lister looking at the big moon-faced kitchen clock. 'It's only ten past six. Get your clothes packed.'

The large windowed wall of the servants' hall looks out on a gravelled courtyard and beyond that, the cold mountains, already lost in the early darkening of autumn.

A dark green, small car has parked here by the side entrance. The servants watch. Two women sit inside, one at the wheel and one in the back seat. They do not speak. A tall person has just left the other front seat and has come round to the front door.

Lister waits for the bell to ring and when it does he goes to open the door.

A long-locked young man, fair, wearing a remarkable white fur coat which makes his pink skin somewhat radiant. The coat reaches to his boots.

Lister acknowledges by a slight smile, in which he uses his mouth only, that he recognizes the caller well from previous visits. 'Sir?' says Lister.

'The Baroness,' says the young man, in the quiet voice of one who does not wish to spend much of it.

'She is not at home. Will you wait, sir?' Lister stands aside to make way at the door.

'Yes, she's expecting me. Is the Baron in?' sounds the low voice of the young man.

'We expect him back for dinner, sir. He should be in shortly.'

Lister takes the white fur coat glancing at the quality and kind of mink, and at its lining and label as he does so. Lister, with the coat over his arm, turns to the left, crosses the oval hall, followed by the young man. Lister treads across the *trompe-l'œil* chequered paving of the hall and the young man follows. He wears a coat of deep blue satin with darker blue watered silk lapels, trousers of dark blue velvet, a pale mauve satin shirt with a very large high collar and a white cravat fixed with an amethyst pin. Lister opens a door and stands aside. The young man, as he enters, says politely to Lister, 'In the left-hand outer pocket, this time, Lister.'

'Thank you, sir,' says Lister, as he withdraws. He closes the door again and crosses the oval hall to another door. He opens it, hangs the white mink coat gently on one of a long line of coat-hangers which are placed expectantly in order on a carved rack. Lister then feels in the outer left-hand pocket of the coat, withdraws a fat, squat, brown envelope, opens it with a forefinger, half-pulls out a bundle of bank-notes, calculates them with his eyes, stuffs them back into the envelope, and places the envelope in one of his own pockets, somewhere beneath his white jacket, at heart-level. Lister looks at himself in the glass above the wash-basin and looks away. He arranges the neat unused hand-towels with the crested 'K' even more neatly, and leaves the cloak-room.

The other servants fall silent as Lister returns.

'Number One,' says Lister. 'He walked to his death most gingerly.'

'Sex,' muses Heloise.

Lister shudders, 'The forbidden word,' he says. 'Let me not hear you say it again.'

'It's Victor Passerat, waiting there in the library,' says Heloise.

'Mister Fair-locks,' says Eleanor, looking at the carrot juice which she has prepared with the blender.

'I never went with him,' says Heloise. 'I had the chance, though.'

'Didn't we all?' says Pablo.

'Speak for yourself,' says Clovis.

'Less talk,' says Lister.

'Victor Passerat isn't the dad,' says Heloise.

'He'd never have had it in him,' says Pablo.

'Are you aware,' says Eleanor to her nephew, 'that two ladies are waiting outside in the car that brought the visitor?'

Lister glances towards the window but next he goes to a large cupboard and, drawing up a chair, mounts it. He carefully, one by one, removes the neat jars of preserved fruit that are stacked there, ginger in gin, cherries in cognac, apple and pineapple, marmalades of several types, some of them capped and bottled with a home-made look, others, according to their shapes and labels, fetched in from as far as Fortnum and Mason in London and Charles's in New York. All these Lister carefully places on a side-table, assisted by Eleanor and watched by the others in a grave silence evidently due to the occasion. Lister removes a plank shelf, now bare of bottles. At the back of the cupboard is a wall-safe, the lock of which Lister slowly and respectfully opens, although not yet the door. He demands a pen, and while waiting for Hadrian the assistant cook to fetch it, he takes the envelope from his inner pocket, and counts the bank-notes in full view of the rest.

'Small change,' he says, 'compared with what is to come, or has already come, according as one's philosophy is temporal or eternal. To all intents and purposes, they're already dead although as a matter of banal fact, the night's business has still to accomplish itself.'

'Lister's in good vein tonight,' says Clovis, who has left the perusal of his contract to join the group. Meanwhile Hadrian returns, handing up the simple ballpoint pen to Lister.

Upstairs the shutters bang.

'The wind is high tonight,' Lister says. 'We might not hear the shots.' He takes the pen and marks a sum on the envelope, followed by the date. He then opens wide the safe which is neatly stacked with various envelopes and boxes, some of metal, some of leather. He places the new package among the rest, closes the safe, replaces the wooden shelf, and, assisted by Eleanor and Heloise, puts the preserve-bottles back in their places. He descends from his chair, hands the chair to Hadrian, closes the cupboard door, and goes to the window. 'Yes,' he says, 'two ladies waiting in the car, as well they might. Good night, ladies. Good night, sweet, sweet, ladies.'

'Why did they pull up round the side instead of waiting in the drive?' says Heloise.

'The answer,' says Lister, 'is that they know their place. They had the courage to accompany their kinsman on his errand, but at the last little moment, lacked the style which alone was necessary to save him. The Baron will arrive, and not see them, not inquire. Likewise the Baroness. No sense, for all their millions.'

'With all that in there alone,' says Heloise, still contemplating the closed cupboard wherein lies the wall-safe of treasure, 'we could buy the Montreux Palace Hotel.'

'Who needs the Montreux Palace?' says Hadrian.

'Think big,' says Pablo the handyman, patting her around the belly.

'How it kick's! she says.

'How like,' says Lister, 'the death wish is to the life-urge! How urgently does an overwhelming obsession with life lead to suicide! Really, it's best to be half-awake and half-aware. That is the happiest stage.'

'The Baron Klopstocks were obsessed with sex,' says Eleanor. She is setting places at the long servants' table.

'Sex is not to be mentioned,' Lister says. 'To do so would be to belittle their activities. On their sphere sex is nothing but an overdose of life. They will die of it, or rather, to all intents and purposes, have died. We treat of spontaneous combustion. One remove from sex, as in Henry James, an English American who travelled.'

'They die of violence,' says Clovis who has transferred to the butler's desk his papers and the contract and documents he has been studying closely for the past three-quarters of an hour. He sits with his back to the others, looks half over his shoulders. 'To be precise, it is of violence that they shortly die.'

'Clovis,' says Eleanor, 'would you mind giving an eye to the oven?'

'Where's my assistant?' says Clovis.

'Hadrian has gone down to the lodge,' says Eleanor. 'Gone to borrow a couple of eggs. Him in the attic hasn't had his supper yet.'

'No eggs in the house?' says Clovis.

'There was too much else to arrange today,' says Eleanor as she places five tiny silver bowls of salt at regular intervals along the table, carefully measuring the distance with her eye. 'No marketing done.'

'Things have gone to rack and ruin,' says Lister, 'now that the crisis has arrived. This house hitherto was run like the solar system.'

'Cook your own damn dinner,' says Clovis, bending closely over his documents.

'Don't you want any?' says Heloise. 'I'll eat your share if you like, Clovis. I'm eating for two.'

Clovis bangs down his fist, drops his pen, goes across to the large white complicated cooking stove, studies the regulator, turns the dial, opens the stove door, and while looking inside, with the other hand snaps his finger. Heloise runs with a cloth and a spoon and places them in Clovis's hand. Protecting his hand with the cloth Clovis partly pulls out a casserole dish. He hooks up the lid with the handle of the spoon, peers in, sniffs, replaces the lid, shoves the dish back and closes the oven door. Again, he turns the dial of the regulator. Then with the spoon-handle, he lifts the lids from the two pots which are simmering on top of the stove. He glances inside each and replaces the lids.

'Fifteen minutes more for the casserole. In seven minutes you move the pots aside. We sit down at half past seven if we're lucky and they don't decide to dine before they die.'

'No they won't eat,' says Lister. 'We can have our dinner in peace, while they get on with the job.'

From somewhere far away at the top of the house comes a howl and a clatter.

'I'll have a vodka and tonic,' says Clovis, as he passes through the big kitchen and returns to his papers at the butler's desk.

'Very good,' says Lister, looking round. 'Any more orders?'

'Nothing for me. I had my carrot juice. I couldn't stomach a sherry, not tonight,' says Eleanor.

'Nerves,' says Lister, and has started to leave the kitchen when the house-telephone rings. He returns to answer it.

'Lister here,' he says, and listens briefly while something in the telephone crackles into the room. 'Very good,' he then says into the telephone and hangs up. 'The Baron,' says he, 'has arrived.'

The Baron's great car moves away from the porter's lodge while the porter closes the gates behind it. It slightly swerves to avoid Hadrian who is walking up the drive.

The porter, returning to the lodge, finds his wife hanging up the house-telephone in the cold hall. 'Lister sounds like himself,' she tells her husband.

'What the hell do you expect him to sound like?' says the porter. 'How should he sound?'

'He was no different from usual,' she says. 'Oh, I feel terrible.'

'Nothing's going to happen, dear,' he says, suddenly hugging her. 'Nothing at all.'

'I can feel it in the air, like electricity,' she says. He takes her arm, urging her into the warm sitting-room. She is young and small. She looks as if she were steady of mind but she says, 'I think I am going mad.'

'Clara!' says the porter. 'Clara!'

She says, 'Last night I had a terrible dream.'

Cecil Klopstock, the Baron, has arrived at his door, thin and wavering. The door is open and Lister stands by it.

'The Baroness?' says the Baron, passively departing from his coat which slides over Lister's arm.

'No, sir, she hasn't arrived. Mr Passerat is waiting.'

'When did he come?'

'About half-past six, sir.'

'Anyone with him?'

'Two women in the car. They're waiting outside.'

'Let them wait,' says the Baron and goes towards the library, across the black and white paving of the hall. He hesitates, half-turns, then says, 'I'll wash in here,' evidently referring to a wash-room adjoining the library.

'I thought it best,' Lister says as he enters the servants' sitting-room, 'to tell him about those two women waiting outside, perceiving as I did from his manner that he had already noticed them. – "Anyone with Mr Passerat?" he said with his eye to me. "Yes, sir," I said, "two ladies. They are waiting in the car." Why he asked me that redundant question I'll never know.'

'He was testing you out,' says Hadrian who is whisking two eggs in a bowl.

'Yes, that's what I think, too,' says Lister. 'I feel wounded. I opened the door of the library. Passerat got up. The Baron said "Good evening, Victor" and Passerat said "Good evening." Whereupon, being unwanted, I respectfully withdrew. *Sic transit gloria mundi.*'

'They will be sitting down having a drink,' says Pablo who has cleaned himself up and is now regarding his hair from a distance in the oval looking-glass. This way and that he turns his head, with its hair shiny-black.

'Didn't he ask for more ice?' says Eleanor. 'They never have enough ice.'

'They have plenty of ice in the drinks cupboard. I filled the ice-box, myself, and put more on refrigeration this afternoon when you were all busy with your telephoning and personal arrangements,' Lister says. 'They have ice. All they need now is the Baroness.'

'Oh, she'll come, don't worry,' says Clovis, stacking his papers neatly.

'I wish she'd hurry,' says Heloise, as she slumps in a puffy cretonned armchair. 'I want to eat my dinner in peace.'

Hadrian has prepared a tray on which he has placed a dish of scrambled eggs, a plate of thin toasted buttered bread, a large cup and saucer and a silver thermos-container of some beverage. Eleanor, with vague movements, leaves her table-setting to place on the tray a knife, a fork and a spoon; then she covers the toast and the eggs with silver plate-covers.

'What are you doing?' says Hadrian, grabbing the knife and fork off the tray. 'What's come over you?'

'Oh, I forgot,' says Eleanor. 'I've been in a state all day.' She replaces the knife and fork with one large spoon.

Lister goes to the house-telephone, lifts the receiver and presses a button. Presently the instrument wheezes. 'Supper on its way up to him in the attic,' says Lister. 'Yours will follow later.'

The instrument wheezes again.

'We'll keep you informed,' says Lister. 'All you have to do is stay there till we tell you not to.' He hangs up. 'Sister Barton is worried,' he says. 'Him in the attic is full of style this evening and likely to worsen as the night draws on. Another case of intuition.'

Hadrian takes the tray in his hands and as he leaves the room he asks, 'Shall I tell Sister Barton to call the doctor?'

'Leave it to Sister Barton,' says Lister, gloomily, with his eyes on other thoughts. 'Leave it to her.'

Heloise says, 'I can manage him in the attic myself, if it comes to that. I've always been good to him in the attic.'

'You better get some sleep after you've had your supper, my girl,' says Clovis. 'You've got a big night ahead. The reporters will be here in the morning if not before.'

'It might not take place till six-ish in the morning,' says Heloise. 'Once they start arguing it could drag on all night. I'm intuitive, as Mr Lister says, and –'

'Only as regards your condition,' says Lister. 'Normally, you are not a bit intuitive. You're thick, normally. It's merely that in your condition the Id tends to predominate over the Ego.'

'I have to be humoured,' says Heloise, shutting her eyes. 'Why can't I have some grapes?'

'Give her some grapes,' says Pablo.

'Not before dinner,' says Clovis.

'Clara!' says Theo the porter. 'Clara!'

'It's only that I'm burning with desire to ask them what's going on up at the house tonight,' she says.

'Come back here. Come right back, darling,' he says, drawing her into the sitting-room where the fire glows and flares behind the fender. 'Desire,' he says.

'Theo!' she says.

'You and your nightmares,' Theo says. He shuts the door of the sitting-room and sits beside her on the sofa, absentmindedly pluck-ing her thigh while he stares at the dancing fire. 'You and your dreams.'

Clara says, 'There's nothing in it for us. We were better off at the Ritz in Madrid.'

'Now, now. We're doing better here. We're doing much better here. Lister is very generous. Lister is very, very generous.' Theo picks up the poker and turns a coal on the fire, making it flare, while Clara swings her legs up on to the sofa. 'Theo,' she says, 'did I tell you Hadrian came down here to borrow a couple of eggs?'

'And what else, Clara,' says Theo. 'What else?'

'Nothing,' she says. 'Just the eggs.'

'I can't turn my back but he's down here,' says Theo. 'I'll report him to the Baron tomorrow morning.' He goes to draw the window-curtains. 'And Clovis,' he says, 'for not keeping an eye on him.' Theo returns to the sofa.

Clara screams 'No, no, I've changed my mind,' and pushes him away. She ties up her cord-trimmed dressing-gown.

'Not so much of it, Clara,' says Theo. 'All this yes-no. I could have the Baroness if I want. Any minute of the hour. Any hour of the day.'

'Oh, it's you that makes me dream these terrible things, Theo,' she says. 'When you talk like that, on and on about the Baroness, with her grey hair. You should be ashamed.'

'She's got grey hair all places,' Theo says, 'from all accounts.'

'If I was a man,' says Clara, 'I'd be sick at the thought.'

'Well, from all accounts, I'd sooner sleep with her than a dead policeman,' says Theo.

'Hark, there's a car on the road. It must be her,' says Clara. But Theo is not harking. She plucks at his elastic braces and says, 'A disgrace that they didn't have an egg in the house for the idiot-boy's supper. Something must be happening up there. I've felt it all week, haven't you Theo?'

Theo has no words, his breath being concentrated by now on Clara alone. She says, 'And there's the car drawing up, Theo – it's stopped at the gate. Theo, you'd better go.'

He draws back from his wife for the split second which it takes him to say, 'Shut up.'

'I can hear the honking at the gate,' she says in a loud voice – 'Don't you hear her sounding her horn? All week in my dreams I've heard the honking at the gate.' Theo grunts.

The car honks twice and Theo now puts on his coat and pulls himself together with the dignity of a man who does one thing at a time in due order. He goes to the hall, takes the keys from the table drawer and walks forth into the damp air to open the gate beyond which a modest cream coupé is honking still.

It pulls up at the porter's lodge after it has been admitted. The square-faced woman at the wheel is the only occupant. She lets down the window and says, cheerfully, 'How are your, Theo?'

'Very well, thanks, Madam. Sorry to keep you waiting, Madam.

There was a question of eggs for the poor gentleman in the attic, his supper.'

She smiles charmingly from under her great fur hat.

'Everything goes wrong when I'm away, doesn't it? And how is Clara, is she enjoying this little house?'

'Oh yes, Madam, we're very happy in this job,' says Theo. 'We're settling in nicely.'

'You'll get used to our ways, Theo.'

'Well, Madam, we've had plenty of experience behind us, Clara and me. So we've shaken down here nicely.' He shivers, standing in the cold night, bareheaded in his porter's uniform.

'Your *rapport* with the servants – is that all right?' gently inquires the Baroness.

Theo hesitates, then opens his mouth to speak. But the Baroness puts in, 'Your relationship with them? You get on all right with them?'

'Oh yes, Madam. Perfectly, Madam. Thanks.' He steps back a little pace, as if only too ready to withdraw quickly into the warm cottage.

The Baroness makes no move to put her thick-gloved hand on the wheel. She says, 'I'm so very glad. Among servants of such mixed nationalities, it's very difficult sometimes to achieve harmony. Indeed, we're one of the few places in the country that has a decent-sized staff. I don't know what the Baron and I would do without you all.'

Theo crosses his arms and clutches each opposite sleeve of his coat just below the shoulders, like an isolated body quivering in its own icy sphere. He says, 'You'll be glad to get in the house tonight, Madam. Wind coming across the lake.'

'You must be feeling the cold,' she says, and starts up the car.

'Good night, Madam.'

'Good night.'

He backs into the porchway of the cottage, then quickly turns to push open the door. In the hall he lifts the house-telephone and waits for a few seconds, still shivering, till it comes alive. 'The Baroness,' he says, then. 'Just arrived. Anybody else expected?'

The speaker from the kitchen at the big house says something briefly and clicks off. 'What?' says Theo to the dead instrument. Then he hangs up, runs out of the front door and closes the big gates.

He returns as rapidly to the warm sitting-room where Clara is lying
dreamily on the sofa, one arm draped along its back and another
drooping over the edge. 'You waiting for the photographer?' says
Theo.

'What was all that talk?' Clara says.

'Shivering out there. She was in her car, of course, didn't feel it.
On and on. Asked after you. She says, are we happy here?'

Pablo has got into the little cream coupé and driven it away from
the front of the house as soon as Lister has helped the Baroness out
of it, taken her parcels, banged shut the car door, and followed her
up the steps and into the hall.

'Here,' she says, pulling off her big fur hat in front of the hall
mirror. Lister takes it while she roughs up her curly grey hair. She
slips off her tweed coat, picks up her handbag and says, 'Where's
everyone?'

'The Baron is in the library, Madam, with Mr Passerat.'

'Good,' she says, and gives another hand to her hair. Then she
pulls at her skirt, thick at the waist and hips, and says, 'Tell Irene
I'll be up to change in half-an-hour.'

'Irene's off tonight, Madam.'

'Heloise, is she here?'

'Yes, Madam.'

'Still working? Is she fit and well?'

'Oh, she's all right, Madam. I'll tell her to go and prepare for you.'

'Only if she's feeling up to it,' says the Baroness. 'I think the world
of Heloise,' she says, stumping heavily to the library door which she
opens before Lister can reach it, pausing before she enters to turn to
Lister while the voices within suddenly stop. 'Lister,' she says, standing in the doorway. 'Theo and Clara – they have to go. I'm so very
sorry but I need the little house for one of my cousins. We don't
really need a porter. I leave it to you, Lister.'

'Well, Madam, it's a delicate matter at the moment. They won't be
expecting this.'

'I know, I know. Arrange something to make it easy, Lister. The
Baron and I would be so grateful.' Then she throws open the door
somewhat dramatically and walks in, while the two men get up from
the grey leather armchairs. Lister waits in the room, by the door.

'Nothing, thanks, Lister,' says the Baron. 'We have everything here for the moment.' He waves towards the drinks cupboard in a preoccupied way. The Baroness flops into a sofa while Lister, about to leave the room, is halted by the Baron's afterthought – 'Lister, if anyone calls, we aren't on any account to be disturbed.' The Baron looks at the ormolu and blue enamelled clock, and then at his own wristwatch. 'We don't want to be disturbed by anyone whomsoever.' Lister moves his lips and head compliantly and leaves.

'They haunt the house,' says Lister, 'like insubstantial bodies, while still alive. I think we have a long wait in front of us.' He takes his place at the head of the table. 'He said on no account to disturb them. "Not to be disturbed, Lister." You should have seen the look on her face. My mind floats about, catching at phantoms and I think of the look on her face. I am bound to ventilate this impression or I won't digest my supper.'

'Not a bad woman,' says Pablo.

'She likes to keep grace and favour in her own hands,' Lister says, 'and leave disagreeable matters to others. "The couple at the lodge has to go, Lister," she said, "I rely on you to tell them. I need the lodge for my cousins," or was it "my cousin"? – one, two, three, I don't know. The point is she wants the lodge for them.'

'How many cousins can she possibly have?' says Eleanor, looking at the clean prongs of her fork, for some reason, before making them coincide with a morsel of veal. 'And all the secretaries besides.'

'Cousins uncountable, secretaries perhaps fewer,' says Lister, 'if only she had survived to enjoy them. As it is the lodge will proba-bly be vacated anyhow. No need for me to speak to the poor silly couple.'

'You never know,' says Heloise.

'Listen! – I hear a noise,' says Pablo.

'The shutters banging upstairs,' says Hadrian.

'No, it's him in the attic, throwing his supper plates around,' Heloise says.

'It wasn't plates, it was a banging,' Pablo says. 'There it goes. Listen.'

'Eat on,' says Clovis. 'It's only the couple of ladies in the car again. They're getting impatient.'

'Why don't they ring?' says Lister as he listens to the thumping on the back door.

'I disconnected the back door bell,' Clovis says. 'We need our meal in peace. Since I was goaded to do most of the cooking it's my say that goes. Nobody leaves the table before their supper's over.'

'Suppose one of them in the library rings for us?' Eleanor says.

Lister reaches out for his wine-glass and sips from it. The banging at the door continues. Clovis says, 'It's doubtful if they will call us, now. However, we must no longer respond, it would be out of the question. To put it squarely, as I say in my memoir, the eternal triangle has come full circle.'

'They've as good as gone to Kingdom Come,' says Lister. 'However, it is I who decide whether or not we answer any summons, hypothetical or otherwise.'

'It's Lister who decides,' says his aunt Eleanor.

TWO

It is ten-thirty at night. Lister has changed his clothes and so has his young aunt, Eleanor. They walk hand-in-hand up the swirling great staircase with its filigree of Regency wrought-iron banisters, imported in their time as were so many other appointments of the house. Lister flicks on the light and opens the folding doors of the Klopstocks' long drawing-room, allowing Eleanor to pass before him into the vastness with its curtains looped along the row of French windows. Outside is a balustrade and beyond that the night. The parquet glitters obliquely, not having been trodden on today. The blue and shrimp-pink of the carpet, the pinks and browns of the tapestried chairs, the little tables, the scrolled flat desk and the porcelain vases are spread around Lister and Eleanor, as they enter the room, like standing waiters on the arrival of the first guests at an official reception. A porcelain snow-white lamb, artfully woolly, sleeps peacefully on the mantelpiece where the Baron placed it eleven years ago when the house was built and his precious goods brought in. The Adam mantelpiece at one end of the room came through the Swiss customs along with the rest as did the twin mantelpiece in the anteroom at the other end. Eleanor, wearing a grey woollen dress and carrying a black bag, sits down gracefully on a wide, upholstered chair and leans her arms on a small table, toying with the pink-blond carnations she herself arranged freshly this morning.

She looks about thirty-four. Her nephew, Lister, well advanced into his mid-forties. He wears a dark business suit with a white shirt and a dull red tie. They could be anybody, and more conceivably could be the master and mistress of the house just returned at this time of night from a trip to a city – Paris or even Geneva – or just about to leave for an airport, a night flight. Eleanor's hair is short, curled and dull. Lister's gleams with dark life. Their faces are long and similar. Lister sits opposite Eleanor and looks at a part of the wall

that is covered with miniature portraits. Many objects in this large
room are on a miniature scale. There are no large pictures, such as
would fit it. The Monet is one of the smaller scale, and so is the Goya.
So too are a group of what appear to be family portraits, so that it
seems as if the inclination towards the miniature is either a trait
descending throughout a few generations to their present owner, or
else these little portraits have been cleverly copied, more recently,
from some more probable larger originals. Ornamental keys, enamelled snuff-boxes and bright coins stand by on the small tables.

Lister looks away from the wall, and straight at Eleanor. 'My dear,'
he says.

She says, 'I hear their voices.'

'They are still alive,' says Lister. 'I'm sure of that. It hasn't happened yet.'

'It's going to happen,' she says.

'Oh, my dear, it's inevitable.' He takes a cigarette from the long
silver box and lights it with the table lighter. Then he raises a finger
for silence, as if Eleanor had been making a noise, which she had not.
'Listen!' he says. 'They're arguing in high tone, Eleanor, you're
right!'

Eleanor takes from her bag a long steel nail-file, gets up, goes to a
corner of the carpet, raises it, kneels, then with the file dislodges a
loose piece of parquet.

'Softly and swiftly, my love.'

She looks up. 'Don't be so smart. This isn't the time to lark about.'
She bends to dislodge another, and moving backward a little, knee by
knee, leans forward on her elbows and places her ear to the planks of
dusty common wood beneath the parquet.

'Eleanor, it isn't worthy of you,' he says. 'You look like a parlour
maid. A minute ago you didn't.'

She listens hard, looking upward through space to the high ceiling
as if in a trance. Every little while a wave of indistinct voices from
below reaches the drawing-room, one shrill, another shrill, then all
together, excited. From a floor above, somebody bangs and the sound
is repeated, with voices and a scuffle. Eleanor raises her head and
says, exasperated, 'With him in the attic barking again and banging,
and you carrying on, it's impossible to hear properly what's being
said below. Why didn't Sister Barton give him his injection?'

'I don't know,' he says, leaning back with his cigarette. 'I'm sure I advised her to. This parquet flooring once belonged to a foreign king. He had to flee his throne. He took the parquet of his palace with him, also the door-knobs. Royalty always do, when they have to leave. They take everything, like stage-companies who need their props. With royalty, of course, it all is largely a matter of stage production. And lighting. Royalty are very careful about their setting and their lighting. As is the Pope. The Baron resembled royalty and the Pope in that respect at least. Parquet flooring and door-handles. The Baron bought them all in a lot with the house when the old king passed away. They definitely came from the royal palace.'

'All I heard from down there,' says Eleanor, putting the oblongs of palace parquet back in place and rising, while she folds back the carpet over them, 'was something like "You said . . ." – "No you did not. I said . . ." – "No, you did say . . ." – "When in hell did I say . . ." That means they're going over it all, Lister. It could take all night.'

'Heloise said it could be around six in the morning,' Lister remarks as Eleanor stands flicking her skirt against the strange event that it has gathered fluff or dust. 'Not,' he says, 'that I normally take any interest in Heloise's words. But she's in an interesting condition. They get good at guessing when they're in that state.'

Eleanor is back in her chair again. Down at the back door there is a noise loud enough to reach this quiet room. A banging. A demand. At the same time, at the front door the bell shrills.

'I hope someone answers that door before the Baroness gets it in her head to go and answer it herself,' says Eleanor. 'Any break in the meeting might distract them from the quarrel and side-track the climax, wouldn't you think?'

'The Baron said not to disturb,' says Lister, 'as if to say, nobody leaves the room till we've had a clarification, let the tension mount as it may. And that's final. She'll never leave the library.'

'Well, they must be getting hungry. They've had nothing to eat.'

'Let them eat cake,' says Lister, and he adds,

> 'Think, in this battered Caravanserai
>   Whose doorways are alternate Night and Day,
> How Sultan after Sultan with his Pomp
>   Abode his Hour or two, and went his way.'

Eleanor says, 'It's true they've had some important visitors.'

'The adjective "battered",' Lister says, looking round the quiet expanse of drawing-room, 'I apply in the elastic sense. Also "caravan-serai" I use loosely. The house is more like a Swiss hotel, which you may be sure it will become. But endless caravans, so to speak, have most certainly come and gone here, they have come, they have stopped over, they have gone. I'm fairly to the point. It will make a fine hotel. Put different furniture into it, and you have a hotel.'

'Lister,' she says, 'you're always so wonderful. There could never be anyone else in my life.'

He says, rising to approach her, 'Aunt to me though you are, would you marry me outside the Book of Common Prayer?'

She says, 'I have my scruples and I'm proud of them.'

He says, 'In France an aunt may marry a nephew.'

'No, Lister, I stand by the Table of Kindred and Affinity. I don't want to get heated at this moment, on this night, Lister. You're start-ing me off. The press and the police are coming, and there are only sixty-four shopping days to Christmas.'

'I was only suggesting,' he says. 'I'm only giving you a little thought for when all this is over.'

'It's going too far. You have to keep your unreasonable demands within bounds. I'm old-fashioned beyond my years. One thought at a time is what I like.'

'Let's go down,' says Lister, 'and see what the servants are up to.'

As they come down the staircase voices rebound from the library. Lister and Eleanor continue silently and, turning into the servants' hall, Lister stops and looks at the library door. 'What were they doing anyway, amongst us, on the crust of this tender earth?' he says. 'What were they doing here?'

The other servants fall silent. 'What are they doing here, anyway in this world?'

Heloise, pink and white of skin, fresh from her little sleep, says, 'Doing their own thing.'

'They haven't finished it yet,' says Clovis. 'I'm getting anxious. Listen to their voices.'

'There must have been some good in them,' Eleanor says. 'They couldn't have been all bad.'

'Oh, I agree. They did wrong well. And they were good for a purpose so long as they lasted,' Lister says. 'As paper cups are suitable for occasions, you use them and throw them away. Who brought that fur coat in here?' He points to a white mink coat draped over a chair.

'It looks a dream on me,' Heloise says. 'It doesn't meet at the front, but afterwards it will.'

'You'd better put it back. Victor Passerat's been seen in it,' Lister says. 'The police will inquire.'

Heloise takes away the coat and says, as she goes, 'I'll get it in the end. Somehow I feel I'll get it in the end.'

'She might well be right,' Lister says. 'Her foresight runs high at this moment. Who were those people banging at the back door and ringing at the front?'

'The girls in the car, demanding what's happened to their friend, Passerat,' Hadrian says. 'I told them that he was with the Baron and Baroness and they were not to be disturbed. They said they had an appointment. One of them's a masseuse that I haven't seen before.'

'And the other?' says Lister.

'The other didn't say. I didn't ask.'

'You did right,' Lister says. 'They don't come into the story.'

Outside are the sounds of the lake-water lapping on the jetty and of the mountain-wind in the grandiose trees. The couple in the car are separated, one in the front, one in the back seat, each lolling under a rug. They seem to be sleeping but every now and then one of them moves, one of them speaks, and again their heads bend and the blankets move over their crouched uneasy shoulders. The lights from the house and from the distant drive touch on their movements.

They both start upright as another car, dark and large, pulls up. A lithe, leather-coated young man sprints out and approaches the couple. They are scrambling out of their car now.

'We can't get in the house,' says the one from the front seat. 'They won't open the door, even. We've been here over three hours, waiting for our friend.'

'What friend? What do you want?' says the lithe young man, impatiently jangling a bunch of keys. 'I'm the secretary, Mr Samuel. Tell me what you want.'

The other friend of Victor Passerat replies, 'Victor Passerat. We're waiting for him. It's serious. He had an appointment with the Baroness and with the Baron, and –'

'Just a minute,' says Mr Samuel, looking closely at the second friend, 'just a minute. You sound like a man.'

'I am a man.'

'All right. I thought you were a girl.'

'That's only my clothes. My friend here's a woman. I'm Alex – she's a masseuse.'

'My name's Anne,' states the masseuse, stockily regarding Mr Samuel's bunch of keys. 'Do you have the keys to the house?'

'I certainly do,' says Mr Samuel.

'Well, we want to know what's going on,' says the woman.

'We're worried, quite frankly,' says her young friend.

Mr Samuel places a gentle hand on the shoulders of each. 'Don't you think,' he says, 'that it would be more advisable for you to go away and let nature take its course? Go away, quietly and without fuss; just go away and play the piano, or something. Take a soothing nightcap, both of you, and forget about Passerat.'

From an upper room comes a sound like a human bark followed by an owl-screech.

Anne the masseuse adds a further cry to the night. 'Open that door,' she screams and running to the back door beats her heavy shoulder against it, banging with her fists as well.

Mr Samuel winds his way to her with pleasant-mannered authority. 'That was only the invalid,' he says. 'The nurse has probably bitten his finger again. You would do the same, I'm sure, if one of your patients attempted to place his hand over your mouth for some reason.'

Anne's friend, Alex, calls out, 'Come on back in the car, Anne. It might be dangerous.'

Mr Samuel is touching her elbow, urging her back to their small car. 'There's nothing in it for you,' he is saying. 'Go home and forget it.'

The masseuse is large but she appears to have very little moral resistance. She starts to cry, with huge baby-sobs, while her companion, Alex, his square bony face framed in a silk head-scarf and his eyes pleadingly laden with make-up under finely shaped eyebrows, puts out a bony hand to touch her face. 'Come back in the car, Anne,' he says, giving Mr Samuel a look of hurt umbrage.

Anne turns on Mr Samuel. 'Who made you the secretary?' she says. 'Victor Passerat has been secretary since June.'

'Please,' says Mr Samuel. 'I didn't say he wasn't secretary. I only say I'm the secretary in residence. There are I don't know how many secretaries. Victor is only one of the many and it's only just unfortunate that this appointment between him and the Baron Klopstock should keep you hanging around outside the house on a cold night. Just go home. Put on a record.'

'Is everything going to be all right?' Anne says. Alex has got into the car waiting for her. Anne gets in and puts her hands on the wheel without certainty. She looks at Alex as if for guidance. Meanwhile Mr Samuel has flicked himself in a graceful and preoccupied way to the back door of the house and now selects a key.

The couple in the car stare after him and he gives them one more glance; he lets himself in and quietly closes the door upon them. They drive off, then, up the long avenue, round the winding drive, past the lawns which in summer lie luminously green and spread on the one hand towards the swimming-pool in its very blue basin, and on the other towards the lily-pond, the animal-shaped yews, the fountains and the sunken rose garden. Behind them, and beyond the darkness, twinkles the back of the house – a few slits of light peppering its whole length – and behind that again, in the further darkness, the sloping terraces leading to the Lake of Geneva where the boats are moored and the water stretches across to the mountain shore. The little dark green car, leaving it all behind, reaches the lodge. Anne sounds the horn. Theo, wrapped up, now, in a heavy coat, stands evidently forewarned; he unlocks the gate and swings it wide.

When they have reached the main road and are off, he goes indoors; there he writes down the number of their car on a scribbling block which he has set out ready in the hall.

His wife stands by in her cord-trimmed dressing-gown. 'Why are you doing that?' she says.

'I don't know, Clara. But seeing I've been told to expect an all-night spell of duty without any relief-man, I've been taking a note of all numbers. I don't know, Clara, I really don't know why.' He tears off the sheet and crumples it, tossing it on the sitting-room fire.

'What's wrong with the relief-men tonight?' Clara says. 'Where's Conrad, where's Bernard, where's Jean-Albert, where's Stephen? Why don't they send Pablo, what's he doing with them up there at the house? My sleep is terrible, how can I sleep?'

'I'm a simple man,' says Theo, 'and your dreams give me the jitters, but setting all that aside I smell a crisis. The Baroness hasn't been playing the game, and that's about it. Why did she let herself go to rack and ruin? They say she was a fine-looking woman a year ago. Lovely specimen.'

'She used to keep her hair frosted or blond-streaked,' Clara whispers. 'She shouldn't have let go her shape. Why did she suddenly start to go natural? She must have started to be sincere with someone.'

'Don't be frightened, Clara. Don't be afraid.'

'It's true what I say, Theo. She changed all of a sudden. I showed you her in the magazines in her ski-outfit. Wasn't she magnificent?'

'Go to bed, Clara. I say, go up to bed, dear.'

'Can't I have the wireless on for company?'

'All right. Keep it low. We aren't supposed to be here to enjoy ourselves, you know.'

Theo steps forth from his doorway as another car approaches the gate, flicking its large headlights.

The chauffeur puts his head out while Theo opens the gate, but Theo speaks first, apparently recognizing the occupant of the back seat.

'His Excellency, Prince Eugene,' Theo says, respectfully.

The chauffeur's mouth smiles a little, his eyes drooping, perhaps with boredom, perhaps with tiredness.

'I'm pretty sure they're not at home. Were they expecting his Excellency?' Theo says.

'Yes,' says the visitor from the depths of the back seat.

'I'll just call the house,' says Theo and returns to the lodge.

'Drive on,' says Prince Eugene to his driver. 'Don't wait for him and all that rot. I said to Klopstock I'd look in after dinner and I'm looking in after dinner. He should have told his porter to expect me.' As he speaks, the car is already off on its meander towards the house.

Lister is waiting at the door. He runs down the steps towards the big car as the driver gets out to open the door for the prince.

'The Baron and Baroness are not at home,' Lister says.

Prince Eugene has got out and looks at Lister. 'Who are you?' he says.

'Excuse me, your Excellency, that I'm in my off-duty clothes,' Lister says. 'I'm Lister, the butler.'

'You look like a Secretary of State.'

'Thank you, sir,' says Lister.

'It isn't a compliment,' says the prince. 'What do you mean, they're not at home? I saw the Baron this morning and he asked me to drop in after dinner. They're expecting me.' He mounts the steps, Lister following him, and enters the house.

In the hall he nods towards the library door from where the sound of voices come. 'Go and tell them I'm here.' He starts to unbutton his coat.

'Your Excellency, I have orders that they are not to be disturbed.' Lister edges round so that his back is turned to the library door, as if protecting it. He adds, 'The door is locked from the inside.'

'What's going on?'

'A meeting, sir, with one of the secretaries. It has already lasted some hours and is likely to continue far into the night.'

The prince, plump, with pale cheeks, refrains from taking off his coat as he says, 'Whose secretary is it, his or hers?'

'The gentleman in question is the one who's been secretary to both, sir, for the past five months, nearly.'

'Almighty God, I'd better get out of here!' says Prince Eugene.

'I would do that, sir,' Lister says, leading the way to the front door.

'The Baron seemed all right this morning,' says the Prince on the threshold. 'He'd just got back from Paris.'

'I imagine there have been telephone conversations throughout the afternoon, sir.'

'He didn't seem to be expecting any trouble.'

'None of them did, your Excellency. They were not prepared for it. They have placed themselves, unfortunately, within the realm of predestination.'

'You talk like a Secretary of State to the Vatican.'

'Thank you, sir.'

'It isn't a compliment.' The Prince, buttoning up his coat, passes out into the night air through the door which Lister is holding open for him. Before descending the steps to his car, he says, 'Lister, do you expect something to happen?'

'We do, sir. The domestic staff is prepared.'

'Lister, in case of investigations no need, you understand, to mention my visit tonight. It is quite a casual neighbourly visit. Not relevant.'

'Of course, your Excellency.'

'By the way, I'm not an Excellency, I'm a Highness.'

'Your Highness.'

'A domestic staff as large and efficient as yourselves is hard to come by. Quite exceptional in Switzerland. How did the Baron do it?'

'Money,' says Lister.

The voices, indistinguishable but excited, wave over to them from the library.

'I need a butler,' says his Highness. He takes out a card and gives it to Lister. Jerking his head towards the library door he says, 'When it's all over, if you need a place, come to me. I would be glad of some of the other servants, too.'

'I doubt if we shall be looking for further employment, sir, but I thank you deeply for your offer.' Lister puts the card in a note-case which he has brought out of his vest pocket.

'And his cook? That excellent chef? Will he be free?'

'He, too, has his plans, your Excellency.'

'There will of course be a scandal. He must have paid you all very well for your services.'

'For our silence, sir.'

Upstairs a voice growls and the shutters bang.

'That's him in the attic,' says Prince Eugene.

'A sad case, sir.'

'He inherits everything.'

'How, sir? He's a connection of the Baroness through her first marriage. A cousin of the first husband. I think the Baron could hardly bequeath a vast estate to him, poor thing in the attic. The Baron is succeeded by a brother in Brazil.'

'The one in Brazil is the youngest. The one in the attic is next in line – no relation to her at all.'

'That,' said Lister, 'I did not know.'

'Few people know it. Don't tell anyone I said so. Klopstock would kill me. Would have killed me.'

'Well, it makes no difference to us, sir, who gets the fortune. Our fortunes lie in other directions.'

'A great pity. I would have taken on the cook. An excellent cook. What's his name?'

'Clovis, sir.'

'Oh, yes, Clovis.'

'But he will be giving up his profession, I dare say.'

'A waste of talent.' The prince gets into his car and is driven away from the scene.

Mr Samuel has taken off his leather coat and is sitting in the large pantry office which gives off from the servants' hall, looking through a file of papers. He leans back in his chair, dressed in a black turtle-necked sweater and black corduroy trousers. The door is open behind him and the large window in front of him is black and shiny with blurs of light from the courtyard, like a faulty television screen. A car draws up to the back door. Mr Samuel says over his shoulder to the servants in the room beyond, 'Here's Mr McGuire, let him in.'

'He has the keys,' says Heloise.

'Show a little courtesy,' says Mr Samuel.

'I hear Lister coming,' says Eleanor.

Mr Samuel then gets up and comes into the servants' sitting-room. From the passage leading to the front of the house comes Lister, while from the back door a key is successfully playing with the lock.

Lister stops to listen. 'Who is this?'

'Mr McGuire,' says Mr Samuel. 'I asked him to come and join us. I might need a hand with the data. I hope that's all right.'

'You should have mentioned it to me first,' says Lister. 'You should have phoned me, Mr Samuel. However, I have no objection. As it happens I need Mr McGuire's services.'

A man now appears from the back door. He seems slightly older than Mr Samuel, with a weathered and freckled face. 'How's everything? How's everybody?' he says.

'Good evening, Mr McGuire,' says Lister.

'Make yourself at home,' says Clovis.

'Good evening, thanks. I'm a bit hungry,' says Mr McGuire.

'Secretaries get their own meals,' says Clovis.

'I've come flat out direct from Paris.'

'Heat him up something, Clovis,' Lister says.

'Leave it to me,' says Eleanor, rising from her chair with ostentatious meekness.

'Mr Samuel, Mr McGuire,' says Lister, 'are you here for a limited time, or do you intend to wait?'

Mr McGuire says, 'I'd like to see the Baron, actually.'

'Out of the question,' says Mr Samuel.

'Not to be disturbed,' says Lister.

'Then what have I come all this way for?' says Mr McGuire, pulling off his sheepskin coat in a resigned way.

'To hold Mr Samuel's hand,' says Pablo.

'I'll see the Baron in the morning. I have to talk to him,' says Mr McGuire.

'Too late,' says Lister. 'The Baron is no more.'

'I can hear his voice. What d'you mean?'

'Let us not strain after vulgar chronology,' says Lister. 'I have work for you.'

'There's veal stew,' Eleanor calls out from the kitchen.

'Blanquette,' says Clovis, 'de veau.' He puts a hand to his head and closes his eyes as one tormented by a long and fruitless effort to instruct.

'Do you have a cigarette handy?' says Heloise.

'There's a lot of noise,' says Mr McGuire, jerking his head to indicate the front part of the house. 'It fairly penetrates. Who's the company tonight?'

'Hadrian,' says Lister, taking a chair, 'give a hand to Eleanor. Tell her I'd be obliged for a cup of coffee.'

'When I was a boy of fourteen,' says Lister, 'I decided to leave England.'

Mr McGuire reaches down and stops the tape-recorder. 'Start again,' he says. 'Make it more colloquial, Lister. Don't say "a boy of fourteen", say "a boy, fourteen", like that, Lister.'

They sit alone in Lister's large bedroom. They each occupy an armchair of deep, olive-green soft leather which, ageless and unworn, seems almost certainly to have come from another part of the house, probably the library, in the course of some complete refurnishing. A thick grey carpet covers the whole floor. Lister's bed is narrow but spectacular with a well-preserved bushy bear-like fur cover which he might have acquired independently or which might have once covered the knees of an earlier Klopstock while crossing a winter landscape by car, and which, anyway, looks as if importance is attached to it; indeed, it is certain that everything in the room, including Mr McGuire, is there by the approval of Lister only.

Between the two men, on the floor, is a heavily built tape-recorder in an open case with a handle. It is attached by a long snaky cord to an electric plug beside the bed. The two magnetic bobbins, of the 18-centimetre size, have come to a standstill at Mr McGuire's touch of the stop-switch; the bobbins not being entirely equal in their content of tape it can be assessed that half-an-hour of something has already been recorded at some previous time.

Lister says, 'Style can be left to the journalists, Mr McGuire. This is only a preliminary press handout. The inside story is something else – it's an exclusive, and we've made our plans for the exclusive. All we need now is something for the general press to go on when they start to question us, you see.'

'Take my advice, Lister,' says Mr McGuire, 'and give it a conversational touch.'

'Whose conversational touch – mine or the journalists'?'

'Their,' says Mr McGuire.

'Turn on the machine,' says Lister.

Mr McGuire does so, and the bobbins go spinning.

'When I was a boy, fourteen,' says Lister, 'I decided to leave England. There was a bit of trouble over me having to do with Eleanor under the grand piano, she being my aunt and only nine. Dating from that traumatic experience, Eleanor conceived an inverted avuncular fixation, which is to say that she followed me up when she turned fourteen and –'

'It isn't right,' says Mr McGuire, turning off the machine.

'It isn't true, but that's not to say it isn't right,' Lister says. 'Now, Mr McGuire, my boy, we haven't got all night to waste. I want you to take a short statement of similar tone from Eleanor and one from Heloise. The others can take care of themselves. After that we have to pose for the photographs.' Lister bends down, turns on the machine, and continues. 'My father,' he says, 'was a valet in that house, a good position. It was Watham Grange, Leicestershire, under the grand piano. I worked in France. When Eleanor joined me I worked in a restaurant that was owned by a Greek in Amsterdam. Then we started in private families and now I've been butler with the Klopstocks here in Switzerland for over five years. But to sum up I really left England because of the climate – wet.' Lister turns off the switch and stares at the tape-recorder.

Mr McGuire says, 'Won't they want something about the Klopstocks?'

Lister says, impatiently. 'I am thinking.' Presently he turns on the recorder again, meanwhile glancing at his watch. 'The death of the Baron and Baroness has been a very great shock to us all. It was the last thing we expected. We heard no shots, naturally, since our quarters are quite isolated from the residential domain. And of course, in these large houses, the wind does make a lot of noise. The shutters upstairs are somewhat loose and in fact we were to have them seen to tomorrow afternoon.'

Mr McGuire halts the machine. 'I thought you were going to say that him in the attic makes so much noise that you mistook one of his fits for the shots being fired.'

'I've changed my mind,' Lister says.

'Why?' says Mr McGuire.

Lister closes his eyes with impatience while Mr McGuire switches on again. The bobbins whirl. 'The Baron gave orders that they were not to be disturbed,' Lister says.

'What's next?' says Mr McGuire.

'Play it back, Mr McGuire, please.'

Mr McGuire sets the reels in reverse, concentratedly stopping their motion a short distance from the beginning. 'It would be about here,' he says, 'that your bit begins.' He turns it on. The machine emits two long, dramatic sighs followed by a woman's voice – 'I climbed Mount Atlas alone every year on May Day and sacrificed a garland of bay leaves to Apollo. At last, one year he descended from his fiery chariot –'

Mr McGuire has turned off, and has manipulated the machine to run further forward silently.

'That must be the last of your Klopstock sound-tracks,' Lister says.

'Yes, it is the last.'

'You should have used fresh reels for us. We don't want to be mixed up with what Apollo did.'

'I'll remove that bit of the tape before we start making copies. Leave it to me,' says Mr McGuire, getting up to unplug the machine.

'What is to emerge must emerge,' says Lister, standing, watching, while Mr McGuire packs the wire into place and fastens the lid on the tape-recorder. He lifts it and follows Lister out of the room. 'It's a heavy machine,' he says, 'to carry from place to place.'

They descend the stairs to the first landing of the servants' wing. Here, Lister leads the way to the grand staircase, followed after a little hesitation by Mr McGuire who has first seemed inclined to continue down the back stairs.

'I hear no voices,' Lister says as he descends, looking down the well of the great staircase to the black and white paving below. 'The books are silent.'

They have reached the ground floor. Mr McGuire stands with his heavy load while Lister approaches the library door. He waits, turns the handle, pressing gently; the door does not give.

'Locked,' says Lister, turning away, 'and silent. Let's proceed,' he says, leading the way to the servants' quarters. 'There remain a good many things to be accomplished and still more chaos effectively to organize.'

THREE

'It must have happened quick. I wonder if they felt anything?' says Heloise. 'Maybe they still feel something. One of them could linger.'

Lister says, 'I can't forbear to ask, does a flame feel pain?'

'Lister and young Pablo,' says Mr Samuel who is moving round the servants' room with his camera, 'stand closer together. Lister, put your hand on the chair.'

Lister puts his hand on Pablo's shoulder.

'Why are you doing that? It doesn't look good,' says Mr Samuel.

'Leave it to Lister,' says Eleanor at the same time that Lister says, 'I'm consoling him.'

'Then Pablo must look inconsolable,' says Mr Samuel. 'It's a good idea in itself.'

'Look inconsolable, Pablo,' says Lister. 'Think of some disconsolate idea such as your being in Victor Passerat's shoes.'

The camera clicks quietly, like a well-reared machine. Mr Samuel moves a few steps then clicks from another angle. He then moves a lamp and says, 'Look this way,' pointing a finger to a place in the air.

'Pablo smiled the second time,' says Eleanor. 'You want to be careful.'

'Mr Samuel knows that the negatives are mine,' Lister says, 'don't you, Mr Samuel.'

'Yes,' says Mr Samuel.

'Where is that wreath?' Lister says. 'Where's our floral tribute?'

'On the floor in my room,' says Heloise.

'Go and fetch it.'

'I'm too tired.'

'I'll go,' says Hadrian, going. As he opens the door a long howl comes from above.

'Sister Barton failed to give him his injection tonight,' says Lister, 'and I wonder why.'

'Sister Barton is upset. She didn't touch her supper,' says Clovis.

'She's suffering from fear, quite a thrilling emotion,' says Lister. 'People love it.'

'I sent up cold chicken breast and lettuce cut into shreds the Swiss way, which she imagines in her inexperienced little heart to be the right way,' Clovis murmurs. He is standing with one hand on the belt that encircles his narrow hips. Several gold medallions hang from chains on his chest. Mr Samuel's camera trains upon him, as he seems to expect it to do. He lowers his lids. 'Good,' says Mr Samuel, moving round to Heloise.

'Head and shoulders only,' says Lister at the same time as he answers a buzz on the house-telephone. 'Him?' says Lister into the telephone. 'Why?' The answer fairly prolonged and intelligible apparently to Lister, is otherwise that of a bronchial and aged raven, penetrating the room, until Lister says, 'All right, all right,' and hangs up. Then he turns and says, 'We've got the Reverend on our hands. He's come on his motor-bike from Geneva. Sister Barton has summoned him to soothe her patient.'

'I smell treason,' says Eleanor.

'How do you mean?' Lister says. 'She always has been an outsider, so treason isn't the word.'

'Well, she's a bitch,' says Heloise.

'Here he is,' says Lister, as the sound of a motor approaches. 'Pablo, open the door.'

Pablo goes to the back door but the sound of the motor recedes round the house towards the front. 'He's gone to the front door,' Lister says. 'I'd better go myself.'

He passes Pablo, saying, 'Front door, front door, leave it to me,' and, crossing the black and white squares of the hall, admits the Reverend.

'Good evening, Lister. I thought you'd be in bed,' says the white-haired Reverend who carries a woollen cap in his hand.

'No, Reverend,' says Lister, 'none of us is in bed.'

'Oh well, I came to the front thinking you were in bed. The light's on in the library, I thought the Baron might let me in.' He looks up the staircase. 'He sounds quiet, now. Has he gone to sleep? Sister Barton called me urgently.'

'Sister Barton did wrong to bring you out, Reverend, but I must say I'm relieved to see you, and it just occurs to me after all, she may have done right.'

'Your riddles, Lister.' The Reverend is tall, skinny and wavering. He takes off his thick sheepskin coat. He wears a clerical collar and dark grey suit. He is quite aged, seeming to give out a certain life-force which perhaps only derives from the frailty of his appearance combined with his clear ability to come out on a windy night on a motor-bicycle.

He nods towards the library door. 'Is the Baron alone? – I know it's late but I'd like to pop in and have a word with him before going on upstairs. I've many times sat up later talking to the Baron.' The Reverend is already at the library door, waiting for Lister merely to knock and announce him.

'They are a party of three,' says Lister. 'I have orders from the Baron, I'm sorry, Reverend, that they are not to be disturbed. Not on any account.'

The Reverend, happily breathing the centrally heated air of the hall, sighs and then cocks his head slightly with sudden intelligence, his eyes bird-like. 'I don't hear anybody. Are you sure that he has company?'

'Quite sure,' says Lister moving away, sideways, backwards, indicating decisively the pathway that the Reverend must take. 'Come in with us, Reverend, and warm up. A hot drink. Whisky and water. Something warm. I would like to talk to you personally, Reverend, before you see Sister Barton.'

'Where? Oh, yes.' The Reverend's eyes are losing their previous thread of reasoning and lead him in the precise footsteps of Lister's polished shoes.

'Good evening, I have something here,' the Reverend says to the assembled room, putting his hand in his pocket, as Lister leads him in. 'Before I forget.' He brings out a small press-cutting and puts it on a ledge of the television table, sitting down near it. He feels in his inside coat pocket and pulls out his spectacles.

'Good evening, Reverend,' and, 'Nice to see you, Reverend,' say Heloise and Pablo respectively while Hadrian comes in bearing, platterwise under an airy cloud of cellophane, a large round flower-arrangement that looks as if it began as a wreath of laurel-leaves and was filled in according to taste with various rings of colour – red roses, double daffodils, white lilies, an inner ring of orange roses, and finally, at the bull's eye, a tight bunch of violets.

The sight seems to recall something to the Reverend. He moves his long bones to the process of getting up and says, 'He hasn't died has he?'

'The Reverend means him in the attic,' says Heloise.

Eleanor says, 'I'll put them under the shower and give them a slight spray. Keep them fresh.'

Lister, while assisting the Reverend to relax back into the seat, says, 'We're having our photographs taken, Reverend.'

'Oh!' says the Reverend. 'Oh, I see,' and, plainly, he is practised at habituating himself swiftly and without fuss to newer and younger notions however odd or untimely. He seems to be considering this as he warms to the room. Mr Samuel brings his camera round and clicks at the pensive head, the loose and helpless hands of the Reverend. 'Good,' says Lister, bringing an elegant silver-cupped glass of softly steaming whisky on a tray from the kitchen, and stirring it with a long spoon. 'Do another,' he says to Mr Samuel, standing back meantime, withholding the glass from the Reverend who has begun to stretch out his hand to receive it. The camera clicks smoothly upon the gesture of benediction. Then the Reverend gets his hot toddy.

'Good evening – or rather it's good morning, isn't it, Reverend?' says Mr McGuire who comes in from the pantry office with his heavy tape-machine. 'This is a pleasure,' says Mr McGuire.

'Mr McGuire – good evening. I was in bed and the phone rings. Sister Barton is asking for me. It's urgent, she says, he's screaming. So here I am. Now I don't hear a sound. Everyone's gone to sleep. What are the Klopstocks up to, there in the library?'

Mr McGuire says, 'I really don't know. They're not to be disturbed.'

'The Klopstocks and Victor Passerat,' says Heloise.

'Heloise, it is not relevant who the guest is,' says Lister. 'It might be anybody.'

Pablo has returned with Eleanor from the bathroom quarters where they have left the funeral flowers. He sits on the arm of Heloise's chair. The Reverend looks at the couple and reaches out for the newspaper cutting. He puts on his glasses. 'I brought this along,' he says. And again looks at the couple. He looks at the scrap of paper and looks hard at Pablo. 'I cut it out of the *Daily American* for the Baron to read. It is quite relevant to the practices that go on in this house, and now I'm here and I see the Baron is busy, it seems to me that I can read it to whom it may concern.' He looks at Pablo.

'Let's have it,' says Pablo, leaning nearer to Heloise. She strokes her belly which moves involuntarily from time to time. Lister, seated at the table, silently points to the tape-machine and looks at Mr McGuire.

Mr McGuire heaves the machine on to the table while Lister says, 'I don't quite gather all this, Reverend. Would you mind explaining again?'

Mr McGuire is plugging his wire into the wall.

The Reverend now looks over his glasses at the tape-recorder. 'What's that?' he says.

'It's the new electronic food-blender,' says Lister. 'We're all computerized these days, Reverend. The personal touch is gone. We simply programme the meals.'

'Yes, oh yes.' The Reverend suddenly looks sleepy. His head droops with his eyelids, and his hands with the newspaper cutting held in them move jerkily a fragment lower.

'Reverend, you were explaining about the newspaper item,' Lister says, drawing on a cigarette. 'Naturally, we are all receptive to any precepts you may have to cast before us, real swine that we are, we have gone astray like sheep. Every one his own way, numbered among the goats. Normally –'

'Yes, sex,' says the Reverend, wakeful again. He looks at Pablo, then at Heloise, then back to the cutting.

Lister says, 'Normally it isn't a topic that we discuss between these four walls.'

'You have to be frank about it. No point concealing the facts,' says the Reverend severely.

Lister raises a finger and the discs of the machine begin to spin.

The Reverend says, 'I brought this for Cecil and Cathy Klopstock to see. I think it might have something in it to help them with their problems. I hope it will help you with yours, every one of you.' Then he reads, '"New anti-sex drug" – that's the headline. "Edinburgh, Scotland – Medical science has come up with a drug that keeps sex offenders under control, a doctor has reported to the Royal Medico-

Psychological Association. The head of Edinburgh trials of the German drug told association members of the case of the 40-year-old man who had sexually assaulted a number of girls. The man had a history of indecent exposure, homosexual activity and a need for sex daily. But, three weeks on the new drug, cyproterone acetate, damped down his urges, the expert said. Three other subjects were given the drug. All the men reported being happier." And so on, and so on. – Well,' says the Reverend.

Lister raises a finger and the machine stops. 'You have given out an interesting statement, Reverend,' says Lister. 'It should be heard and seen by all as a comment on many things that have been going on under this roof.'

'That's what I thought,' says the Reverend gloomily, putting away the press-cutting in his pocket. 'I'd better go home,' he says, then.

'The wind has died down,' says Hadrian.

'He should spend the night here,' says Eleanor. 'He can't go all the way back to Geneva on that bike.'

'Quite frankly, I got out of bed,' says the Reverend. 'Go and tell Klopstock I'm here.'

'They are not to be disturbed. I had strict orders.'

'I hope they aren't carrying on in the library. In the library. What time is it?'

'Just past quarter to three,' says Lister.

'I should be in bed. You should all be in bed. Why did you bring me all this way?'

Lister goes to the house-phone, lifts the receiver, and presses a button. He waits. He presses again, leaving his finger on it for some minutes. At last comes a windy answer.

'Sister Barton,' says Lister into the phone. 'Why did you bring the Reverend all this way?'

The Reverend says immediately, 'Oh, yes, of course, my poor boy upstairs,' while Lister listens patiently.

The Reverend is creaking himself out of his chair. Clovis, who has been sitting with his arms folded and his little mouth shut tight, jumps to help him.

Lister is heard to say, 'There was no need,' and replaces the phone.

Lister says to the Reverend, 'Sister Barton says that him in the attic needed you, but now he's gone to sleep.'

At that moment a long wail comes from the top of the house, winding its way down the well of the stairs, followed then by another, winding through all the banisters and seeping into the servants' hall. 'She's woken him up,' says Hadrian. 'That's what she's done.'

'It's deliberate,' says Eleanor. 'She wants to bother the Reverend, that's all.'

'I wonder why?' says Clovis. 'What's her trend?'

'Take me up,' says the Reverend.

Heloise has gone to bed. She is propped up with pillows, drinking tea. At the foot of her bed, sitting on either side, are Pablo the handy-man and Hadrian the assistant cook, both of them as absolutely young as Heloise.

'I really could sleep,' she says. 'I really feel like another nap.'

'No,' says Pablo. 'Lister wants us all to be suffering from shock when the police arrive. Lack of sleep has the same effect, Lister says.'

'I could act a state of shock at any time, and besides there's my condition.' She yawns, balancing her cup of tea in her left hand while covering her mouth with her right. 'Lister's wonderful,' she says.

'Terrific,' says Hadrian.

'Marvellous,' says Pablo. 'I never saw such a sense of timing.'

From the floor above comes the noise of a sharp clap, followed by another and another.

'It sounds like guns going off,' says Heloise.

'Well it isn't,' says Pablo. 'It's shutters. The wind must be rising again. I loosed those shutters really good, didn't I?'

'Let's put on a record,' says Hadrian. He slides off the bed and goes to the gramophone, to choose a record, first turning them this way and that, his sharp eyesight quickly discerning the details printed on either side of the disc, even though that part of the room is dim, the only light being that by Heloise's bed.

From above the shutters make further reports, followed by a more subdued clatter from a window below. Hadrian puts on a record and sets it going. The noise fills the room for an instant until Hadrian turns down the volume.

Then, while Heloise lights a cigarette, the two boys dance to the rock music. Heloise puts her tea-cup on the table by her bed. She takes a comb from a fringed satchel which is lying on the bed and a hand-mirror from her bedside table. She lays them on the bed while she loosens her hair which has been pulled back, pony-tail style. Then she holds up the glass and begins to comb, swinging her shoulders a little in time to the rock vibrations, her tongue tapping the beat against her teeth. The boys dance, facing each other and swinging, their feet moving always in the same small area of shiny pinewood flooring.

Heloise's room is furnished much like that of a young daughter of the house. Posters, slogans and pin-up photographs cover part of the walls. The furniture is low-built with straight lines, and upholstered with dark red, black and yellow stuff. A white woolly rug lies askew before a desk piled with coloured magazines and crayons and some boxes of various medicines. The boys' feet just miss the rug as they continue to dance.

Heloise says, 'She didn't drink much, I'll say that for her.' She stubs out her cigarette.

Pablo stops dancing. He says, 'You're thinking thoughts, Heloise.'

Hadrian, who continues dancing by himself, says, 'Heloise, relate.'

'What do you mean, I don't relate?' she says.

'When you relate you don't ask what you mean. There's such a thing as a trend.'

'Who do you think you are, you – Chairman Mao?'

Pablo starts dancing again. The record ends. He turns it over and puts on the other side.

'Clovis is all right, too,' Heloise says. 'I'll miss Clovis.'

Pablo says, 'He could stay with us. Why shouldn't he stay with us?'

'Clovis can stay with us,' says Hadrian.

'The Baroness was natural,' says Heloise. 'I'll say that. Why shouldn't she be photographed and filmed in the nude?'

Hadrian stops dancing. 'You know what?' he says. 'Sorry for Victor Passerat I am not. Neither alive nor dead.'

'Nor me,' says Heloise.

'He had a kind of something,' Pablo says, jerking his arms as he rocks.

'I know,' says Hadrian. 'But it didn't correspond.'

'Funny that it had to be him,' says Heloise.

Pablo says, 'It could have been one of the others.'

Hadrian says, 'But she decided on him. She got hooked on him.'

'It was inevitable,' says Heloise.

'It could have been someone else,' Pablo says. 'Anyone could have made his mistake.'

'There's such a thing as a trend,' Hadrian says. 'If he was hooked on the Baron he should have coordinated.'

'Well he didn't coordinate,' says Heloise, putting her looking-glass back on the table, then lighting a cigarette.

They stop talking for a while. Heloise smokes her cigarette, languidly regarding the dance. When the music ends, the young men together silently choose another record and put it on. First Hadrian, then Pablo, start once more to dance, bobbing and swaying as if blown by a current which fuses out from the beat of the music.

After a while, Heloise says, 'I like Mr McGuire.'

'The finest sound-track man in the business. He coordinates,' says Hadrian.

'Very professional, though,' says Pablo. 'That kind of puts a division, doesn't it?'

'Mr McGuire and Mr Samuel,' says Hadrian, 'are in a class by themselves. You can't judge against them just because they made a success. They're a great team.'

'They went to prison for it,' Hadrian says.

'Is that true?' Pablo says, and simultaneously Heloise says, 'Did they? When was that?'

'Yes, when they started the business six, seven years ago. Mr Samuel told me a lot about it,' Hadrian says, stopping his long spell of dancing without any sign of having spent energy. 'Mr Samuel told me,' he says, 'that they were doing it for small money. If you do a thing for peanuts you get caught for a crime. You have to do it privately for big money like everything else.'

Pablo stops dancing and sits on the bed.

'How did they do it before?' he says.

'It was the same technique. Mr Samuel did the photography and Mr McGuire did the sound-track. They put code ads in the papers. They got a lot of responses.'

'A lovely technique, they have,' Heloise says. 'I must say I liked it when they did me with Irene and Lister. Mr McGuire kept saying,

"Speak out your fantasies", like that. I didn't know what the hell to say, I thought he meant a fairy story, so I started with Little Red Riding Hood and Mr McGuire said "That's great, Heloise! You're great!" So I went on with Little Red Riding Hood and Lister and Irene changed sides. They joined in with Red Riding Hood. Lister was terrific as the grandmother when he ate me up. You can see in the film that I had a good time. Then Irene got eaten up by Lister's understudy. Mr Samuel is an artist, I'll say that, his perspectives coalesce.'

Hadrian says, 'Eleanor always does her Princess bit. You can't get her to do anything else.'

'Too old to change,' Pablo says. 'But she does it good. I like the Princess and the Pea where she can't sleep on her bed. You should always do your own thing in a simulation. It all works in. The Baroness shows up good doing the nun in the Congo with Eleanor doing the Princess bit. Puss in Boots is a big bore.'

'I can do the nun in the Congo,' says Heloise.

'So can I,' says Pablo. 'I like it.'

'Goldilocks and the three bears is best,' says Heloise. 'They got the idea of fairy stories from me. It was my idea, or anyway, it just came to me.'

'Are your health and security cards stamped up to date?' Pablo says.

'I don't think so,' says Hadrian.

'Mine aren't,' says Heloise. 'I meant to remind the Baroness.'

'Lister would have seen to it if it had mattered,' Hadrian says. 'Obviously, it doesn't matter.' He takes up another record, looks at it, says, 'The Far Fetchers. Not bad,' and puts it on while Heloise says, 'Anything goes for me.' The boys are dancing now. Heloise says, 'She went to finishing school in Lausanne and learnt to eat an orange with a little knife and fork without ever touching the orange.'

'Who?' says Pablo.

'The Baroness.'

The young men dance on.

'There must be fog coming up on the lake,' says Heloise. 'I can see it in the room already. It gets through the double windows, even, doesn't it?'

Pablo begins to sing to the music. He sings: ' "Pablo, the Baroness wishes to see you." – Knock, knock, "Come in, Pablo." – "Good morning, Madam, anything I can do, Madam?" – "Pablo, the shutters upstairs they bang so much. I think they must be loose." – "Right away, Madam." – "See you later, then." – "See you at the party, Baroness."'

'See you at the party,' sings Hadrian.

'Don't make so much noise,' says Heloise. 'Lister's busy upstairs with the Reverend and Miss Barton.'

'There's something going on up there,' Hadrian says, stopping still as the music ends.

'Lister can adjust whatever it is. Lister never disparates, he symmetrizes,' Heloise says and lights a cigarette.

Pablo goes to the window and looks out at the fog. 'Lister's got equibalance,' he says, 'and what's more, he pertains.'

'Definitely,' says Hadrian.

Mr Samuel is sitting in a big chair looking through a bound typescript and Mr McGuire is looking over his shoulder.

Clovis sits at a round table which is covered with blue velvet. His elbows are on the table and his chin rests gloomily on his hands.

'It's a winner,' says Mr Samuel. 'Congratulations, Clovis.'

'It has a great deal of scope,' says Mr McGuire.

Clovis raises then lowers his eyebrows. His look of gloom does not change, his elbows remain still.

'A first-rate movie script,' says Mr Samuel. 'Some of the scenes are beyond belief. Only an authority on the subject could have pieced it together.'

'The lines are terrific,' says Mr McGuire, running his fingers fondly over his tape-recorder which lies closed on the table. 'You edited those tapes perfectly, Clovis.'

Clovis remains mute.

Mr Samuel says, 'That's a good idea to open with, where you build up the Baroness like an identikit, when the police are looking for the motive and they put an eye here and a nose there. Very visual, Clovis.'

'I'm waiting to hear,' Clovis says. 'We should have heard. Yesterday was the deadline.'

'We'll hear,' says Mr Samuel. 'Don't worry. The motion picture industry is a very funny thing.'

'The serialization's come through,' says Clovis, moving his right elbow from his chin in order to tap his hand on a bulky file which lies on the table. 'That contract's safe.'

'The film's in our pocket,' says Mr McGuire. 'Our only problem is the casting. You have to have everyone younger than they really are. If Hadrian plays Lister, Pablo could play Hadrian.'

'It's just that I wonder if they'll give Pablo the part.'

'They'll have to,' says Mr McGuire.

'Eleanor can play the Baroness. The same shots as I've got, she only needs to follow the original film and dialogue,' says Mr Samuel.

'I'm worried about Pablo,' says Clovis.

'He's very photogenic,' says Mr Samuel.

They fall silent as Lister enters the room followed by the Reverend.

'Where is Eleanor?' says Lister.

'Not here,' says Clovis.

'Give the Reverend a nice drink,' says Lister, going over to the house-phone.

'No, I should be in bed,' says the Reverend. 'I have to get up in the morning to see about the wedding.'

'I'm sorry, Reverend, but we shall probably have an urgent mission for you in this house tonight arising out of Sister Barton's request. You really must stay.'

'You must stay, Reverend,' says Mr McGuire. 'We'll make you comfortable.'

Lister has lifted the receiver and has pressed a button. He stands waiting for a reply which does not come. He presses another button, speaking meanwhile over his shoulder to those in the room. 'Sister Barton,' he says, 'has asked the Reverend to perform a marriage service. She wants to marry him in the attic, who apparently assents so far as one can gather.' Having got no answer from the phone he presses another button and meanwhile says to the others, 'I've managed to dissuade the Reverend from such an irregular action at the present moment.'

'She's out of her mind,' says Mr Samuel. 'Off her head,' says Mr McGuire. And now Lister has got an answer on the phone. 'Eleanor,' he says into the speaker. 'Any news? Any luck?'

The answer whistles briefly. From outside the house comes a clap of thunder. Lister says into the speaker, 'Be thorough, my dear,' and hangs up.

'A storm in the distance coming over,' says Mr McGuire.

Clovis brings a glass of hot whisky to the Reverend who is sitting dazedly on the sofa. The Reverend takes the drink, and places it on the table by his side, with his fingers playing gently on the glass. He begins to hum a hymn-tune, then he nods with sleep, opening his eyes suddenly when a crackle of thunder passes the house, and letting them drop again when the noise is past.

The house-telephone rings. Lister answers it and it hisses back through its wind-pipe.

'Irene?' Lister says. 'Yes, of course let her in. Use your common sense.' He hangs up. 'That porter,' he says to all in the room, 'is a humbug.'

The house-phone rings again. Lister takes the instrument off the hook very slowly, says into the speaker, 'Lister here,' and trains his ear on the garrulous sirocco that forces its way down the narrow flue of the phone. Meanwhile a car draws up at the back. A window can be heard opening above and Heloise's voice calls 'Hi, Irene' into the stormy night. Mr Samuel, who is peering out of the window, turns back to the room and says, 'Irene in the Mini-Morris.'

The house-phone in Lister's hand gives a brief gusty sigh. Lister says, 'Darling, did you find the files locked or unlocked?'

The phone crackles amok while a double crash of thunder beats the sky above the roof. A long wail comes from the top of the house and from another level upstairs comes an intermittent beat of music. The back door rattles, admits footsteps and clicks shut. Lister at the phone listens on.

'Then be careful,' he says at last, 'not to lock them again. Leave everything as you found it. Take the copies and put the papers back. And hurry, my love. There is no cause for alarm –

> But at my back I always hear
> Time's wingèd chariot hurrying near –'

A tall skinny chinless girl with bright black eyes has come into the servants' room meanwhile.

Lister puts down the phone and says to her,

> 'And yonder all before us lie
> Deserts of vast eternity. –

Where have you been all night, Irene?'

'It was my evening off,' says Irene, removing her leather, lamb-skin-lined driving gloves.

'Evening off,' says Lister. 'What kind of an hour is this to return to the Château Klopstock?'

'I got caught in the storm,' she says. 'Good evening, Reverend. What a pleasure!'

The Reverend opens his eyes, sits up, lets his eyes wander round the room, then, seeing his drink he takes it up and sips it.

'Too strong,' he says. 'I'd like a cup of tea before I go.'

'Listern to the storm, Reverend. You can't go all that way back to Geneva on your motor-bike tonight,' says Lister.

'Out of the question,' says Irene.

The outside telephone rings, piercing the warm room.

Lister says to Clovis, 'Answer it. If it's a cousin wanting to talk to the Baron Klopstocks they are not to be disturbed. Who else could it be at this hour except a cousin?'

Clovis is at the switchboard of the outside telephone, in the pantry office. The Geneva exchange is speaking audibly in French. Mr Samuel and Mr McGuire stand behind Clovis.

Clovis responds, then putting his hand over the speaker he says to them. 'It's for me, from the United States.'

'It's no doubt about the film,' Lister says. 'They should have telephoned yesterday. But it's still yesterday over there. They always ring in the middle of the night from the United States of America. They think that because they are five hours back we also are five hours back. Irene, go up and fetch Heloise and the boys. Bring them down here, we have things to discuss.'

Irene goes and Lister once more takes up the house-phone, presses a button and waits for the hum. 'Eleanor, are you coming?' he says. The house-phone gives vent as before, while thunder smacks at the windows and Clovis can be heard from the pantry office chatting joyfully to the United States. Lister says at length into the house-phone speaker, 'Good, it's just what we need. Bring it down, love, bring it down at once. Put back the originals, and leave unlocked what you found unlocked and locked what was locked.'

Clovis has come to the room again, followed by Messrs McGuire and Samuel. The Reverend sleeps. Clovis smiles. 'It's all tied up,' he says, 'and Pablo's getting the part of Hadrian, too.'

FOUR

'At a quarter past seven, while the sky whitens,' says Lister, 'we all, with the exception of Mr Samuel and Mr McGuire, shall go up to our rooms, change into our smart working-day uniforms, and at eight or there-abouts we blunder downstairs to call the police and inter-view the journalists who will already have arrived, or be arriving. Mr Samuel and Mr McGuire will be in bed, but in the course of the breaking open of the library door by the police, they too will float down the staircase, surprised, and wearing their bath-robes or some-thing seemly. We will by then have put the Reverend to bed and he can sleep on through the fuss until, and if, wakened by the police. He in the attic and Sister Barton will be back in their quarters. They –'

'Why should they be out of their quarters during the night?' Heloise says.

'Let me prophesy,' Lister says. 'My forecasts are only approxi-mate, as are Heloise's intuitions.'

'Let Lister speak,' says Eleanor.

The storm has moved away from the vicinity and can be heard in the distance batting among the mountain-tops like African drums.

Clovis says, 'We've got nothing to hide. We're innocent.'

'Well, we are crimeless,' Lister says. 'To continue with the plans. Heloise, you are pregnant.'

The house-telephone rings. Eleanor lifts it up and bends an ear to its bronchial story. Heloise laughs.

'All right, let them come inside the gates. But don't let them out again,' Eleanor says, and puts down the phone. She says to Lister, 'That's Victor Passerat's two friends. They are threatening to call the police if we won't produce Passerat.'

'Here they come,' says Hadrian, at the window, and presently a car bumps up the drive. Presently again, a banging at the back door.

'Let them in,' says Lister. 'Bring them in here.'

'That's right,' says Clovis. 'Better straighten things out.'

Mr Samuel goes out to the back door and returns followed by Anne the masseuse and her friend, Alex. They stand staring at the assembled household. They look from Eleanor to the dozing Reverend, they look at laughing Heloise, at Pablo and at long-legged Irene and Lister.

'I understand you want to use the telephone,' Lister says. He waves towards the pantry office. 'Well there it is.'

'We want Victor,' says Anne.

'He is in the library with the Baron and the Baroness. They're not to be disturbed. Strict orders.'

'I feel afraid for Victor,' says Alex.

'Why not ring the police as you've suggested?' says Lister waving again towards the pantry office. 'The telephone's in there. We are having a busy night waiting up for the Baron and the Baroness.'

'I'd rather keep the police out of it,' Anne says.

'Yes, I dare say. What sort of reward are you hoping for, large or small?'

'Victor's our friend. We know Cathy Klopstock, too,' says Anne.

Heloise says, 'Why don't you call the police and tell them you've got those tape-recordings and films ready in your car, so that Victor and the Baroness can do a deal with the Baron, and then clear out? – Threats of exposure.'

Eleanor says, 'Don't be crude and literal, Heloise. This has been a tiring night. I wish you had bought some decent carrots for my juice.'

'You have to be frank with these types,' Heloise says.

'They don't connect,' says Pablo.

'Come on, let's go,' says Anne to Alex, whose eyes brim with tears.

They follow Mr Samuel to the back door and leave the house.

'Heloise,' says Lister, 'as I was saying, you're pregnant.'

Mr Samuel comes back into the room as Heloise gives out her laughter.

Mr Samuel says, 'They've locked the doors of the car. Evidently they're going on a trip round the grounds.'

Mr McGuire goes to the window in the dark pantry office. 'They've gone round to the front of the house,' he says.

'Let them prowl,' says Lister. 'About your condition, Heloise. There's a solution to your problem.'

'It's no problem,' says Heloise.

'You marry the Baron,' says Lister, 'and become the Baroness.'

Pablo says, 'He's gone to meet his Maker. He shoots the wife and secretary when they talk too fast. Then he shoots himself, according to the script. He sorts out the mix-up the only way he knows.'

'Eleanor has found some new evidence,' Lister says. 'It was quite unforeseen, but one foresees the unforeseen. He in the attic is the Baron's younger brother. Heir to the title and, under the terms of the Trust, most of the fortune.'

'I thought he was related to her, not him,' says Hadrian.

'He's a nephew or something, isn't he?' Clovis says. 'If not, I have to amend the script.'

'A younger brother of the Baron.'

'He turns my milk,' says Heloise.

'Mine too,' says Lister. 'But he's the heir.'

'There's the young brother Rudolph in Brazil,' says Mr Samuel. 'He was always thought to be the heir. All that money.'

'The one in Brazil is younger than him in the attic,' Eleanor says. 'Him in the attic is next in line. He inherits. Sister Barton knew what she was doing when she sent for the Reverend tonight and offered to marry her patient out of pity.'

The Reverend has opened his eyes on hearing himself referred to. He has sat up, rather refreshed from his nap.

'My poor boy in the attic,' he says. 'Sister Barton is a fine woman. I think it should be done.'

'He in the attic has prior responsibilities,' says Lister. 'Does anyone know his Christian name?'

'I never heard it mentioned,' says Heloise.

'Sister Barton calls him Tony,' says the Reverend.

'His name,' says Lister, 'is Gustav Anthony Klopstock. It's on his birth certificate, his medical certificate exempting him from army service, and it's in their father's will.'

'The Registers?' says the Reverend.

'He's also mentioned in a social register for 1949. That's the latest we have in the house. It occurred to me he must have died, but I was wrong. I admit we were in error,' Lister says. 'But fortunately we left room for error, and having discovered it in time, here we are. There is a vast difference between events that arise from and those that merely follow after each other. Those that arise are preferable. And Clovis amends his script.'

'I wouldn't have married him for choice,' says Heloise. 'He doesn't cognate.'

'You don't have to cognate with him,' says Hadrian. 'You only need get your marriage-lines in black and white.'

'Reverend,' says Lister, 'do you recall that night last June when the Klopstocks were away and him in the attic got loose? Remember we called you in to catch him and calm him down?'

'Poor boy, I remember, of course,' says the Reverend. 'He didn't know what he was doing.'

'He's not officially certified,' says Eleanor. 'The Baron and Baroness wouldn't hear of it.'

'That's true,' Lister says. 'And I wish to draw the Reverend's attention to the result of that rampage last June.' Lister indicates Heloise who smiles at her stomach.

'Good gracious me!' says the Reverend. 'I wouldn't have thought he had it in him.'

'We must lose no time,' says Lister getting up. 'Prepare the drawing-room, Eleanor. It's past five o'clock. I'll go and give orders to Sister Barton.'

'I would need a few days,' says the Reverend firmly. 'You can't marry people like this.'

'It's a special case, Reverend. You can't refuse. In fact, you may not refuse. Look at poor Heloise, her condition.'

The central posy of violets is missing from the funeral wreath which lies under the shower in the scullery bathroom being gently sprinkled to keep it fresh. Heloise in her bedroom holds the posy in her hands. Pablo stands by admiringly. 'I've unpacked all my things again,' he says.

'What a business,' she says. 'Nobody needed to pack their things, after all. All those trunks and suitcases.'

Hadrian appears at the door of her room holding the white mink coat lately left in the cloak-room by Victor Passerat. 'Just right for the occasion,' she says, putting it on.

'Lister says it has to go back in the cloak-room immediately after the ceremony,' Hadrian says. 'The police will want to know what coat he was wearing. Lister is keen that the police should see this coat. It speaks volumes, Lister says.'

'It doesn't meet in the front,' Heloise says.

'You look nice,' Pablo says.

There is a knock at the door and Irene walks in.

'You really going to marry him?' she says.

'Sure,' says Heloise. 'Why not?'

'Then you'll need some music,' Irene says. 'How can you have a wedding without music?'

'Eleanor could play the grand piano,' says Hadrian.

'No,' says Heloise. 'I like Eleanor but she's got a lovely touch on the piano. I can't stand that lovely touch.'

'Mr Samuel plays the piano and also the guitar,' Pablo says. 'Mr Samuel energises.'

'Bring down the gramophone,' says Heloise. 'That's better; because Mr Samuel will be taking the photographs and Mr McGuire has to do the sound-track. This thing's got to go on record. It's got to compass.'

'It's still stormy,' says Hadrian as a flash of lightening stands for a second in the square pane of the window. A clap of thunder follows it. 'There must be trees felled in the park,' he says.

'I shall arrange for them,' says Heloise, 'to be swept up some time tomorrow. Let's go down to the room. They're all waiting.'

Upstairs there is a scuffle and a howl.

'Isn't it usual for the bridegroom to arrive first?' says Irene.

'It's all right if he's late on account of his health,' says Pablo. 'Let's go.'

'Clara,' says the porter, 'your tea, dearest. It's nearly half-past five, and I'm early bringing it up. I've got the jitters, somehow. I've just got orders not to open the gate before eight and after that, let everyone in. "Absolutely everyone." Can you understand it? Why should everyone come at eight in the morning?'

'Oh, my dreams, Theo,' she says, sitting up in bed and reaching for her frilly bed-jacket. She puts it on and takes her tea from Theo's waiting hand.

'He said, "Let everyone in after eight o'clock, not before." This job's beyond me, Clara. We have to move on.'

'Oh, but I love this little house. It was always what I wanted. You know I think the Baroness got sentimental with one of the secretaries. I think she's going to run away with him.'

'Those two strange ones who came in the green car asking for Victor Passerat all the time,' Theo says. 'They came back up here a few minutes ago. They didn't get to see Victor Passerat. Now they're anxious to go home but I've got orders not to let them out. The gates don't open till eight, then everyone, absolutely everyone, can come and go as they please.'

'Where have they gone then, those two?'

'Back to the house to wait there.'

'Do you know, Theo, the one that sat beside the driver doesn't look like a lady. Very hard face. Like a man.'

'Don't dwell on it, Clara dearest.'

The drawing-room is being re-arranged for the wedding. Irene and Eleanor bustle and give orders to Pablo and Hadrian who are moving chairs and tables. The Reverend wanders with a perplexed air from one end of the room to the other, carefully piloting himself around the busy workers, weaving in and out between the minute tables and small sofas, and puzzling his brow absentmindedly at the tiny portraits and litter of small ornaments.

'I really think,' says the Reverend, pulling his press-cutting out of his pocket, 'that Baron Klopstock should take this pill.'

'Too far gone,' says Hadrian, standing back to see if the table he has placed beside another squares off neatly. 'He's past caring.'

Clovis comes in with an embroidered tablecloth which he lays carefully across the two oblong tables which Hadrian has placed end-to-end. 'It makes a very good altar,' says Clovis. He snaps his fingers. 'A large candelabrum from the dining-room!' he shouts. Irene skips out of the room, while Lister with Heloise on his arm appears in the doorway of the ante-room at the far end.

The Reverend puts his press-cutting back in his pocket.

Eleanor says, 'We are to use the Book of Common Prayer appointed to be read in the Church of England.'

The Reverend says, 'I always marry according to the Evangelical Waldensian form, which is very free.'

'Heloise,' calls Eleanor, her voice rising on the last syllable, 'what religion are you?'

'None,' says Heloise. She lets go Lister's arm, comes in from the ante-room and relaxes into a comfortable chair.

'What religion were you brought up in?' says the Reverend.

'None,' says Heloise.

'Where were you born?'

'Lyons,' says Heloise, 'but that was by chance.'

'It should be Evangelical,' says the Reverend.

'In this house it is the Book of Common Prayer,' Eleanor says. 'Do you want her to have that child out of wedlock? We haven't all night to spend arguing, Reverend. The father has assented but he might change his mind.'

'Let me see the English book, then,' says the Reverend. 'I have it within my competence to make exceptions in a case like this. Perhaps I could simplify the English form. I don't read well in English, you know.'

Eleanor points to a flat, leather-bound book lying ready beside the small porcelain statuettes on a wall-table. 'That's it,' she says. 'It can't be simplified, it's impossible.'

Lister advances into the room, stopping to twist a bowl of flowers to better taste. He says, 'Eleanor, the bridegroom is C. of E., I think.'

'No, they're Catholics.'

'Oh, well, he went to Winchester, an English school.'

'No, he never went to school. He was always unable.'

'He went for a week.'

'It isn't enough.'

'Eleanor,' says Lister, 'we can have any little irregularity put straight later.'

'That's right,' says Heloise. 'This coat's heavy.'

Irene comes in with a large branched candlestick in ornamental silver with long white candles set in its sockets. She places it on the covered table.

'Don't light the candles yet,' says Eleanor, raising her eyes to the ceiling, from above which comes the sound of a scuffle and a howl. 'Goodness knows what might happen. We don't want a fire.'

'He's had his injection,' Lister says.

'Well it hasn't taken yet,' says Heloise.

'Come back into the little room and stand with me,' Lister says to Heloise. 'The bride should enter last and enter last she will.'

The scuffle upstairs continues and is accompanied by a repeated banging.

'Is that the wind or is it him?' says Eleanor. 'Is it the shutters?'

'It could be either,' Pablo says listening expertly.

'I'd better go and help,' says robust Hadrian. He bounds out of the drawing-room and up the stairs.

Heloise has again joined Lister at the door between the ante-room and the drawing-room and from there he gives his final instructions. 'Remove the Sèvres vases – take them away, just in case. Irene, your skirt's too short, this is a ceremony.'

Heloise says, 'Irene likes to show her legs. Why not?'

'They're all she's got,' says Clovis.

'He's coming!' says Irene.

The wind now whistles round the house and the remote shutters bang as another latent storm wakes up. Footsteps descend heavily and the occasional howl that accompanies them becomes, as it approaches, more like a trumpet call.

Mr Samuel now enters with his camera. Mr McGuire follows with his tape-recorder which he places on a table in an angle of the room, unplugging a lamp to make way for the plug of his machine. He tests it out, then pulls up a chair and, folding his arms, waits.

As the footsteps and the trumpet-blast tumble their way down, Pablo puts a record on the gramophone with a pleased, but unsmiling expression. It is a new rendering of *Greensleeves*, played very fast even at the beginning, and plainly working up to something complex and speedy.

'Not so loud,' says the Reverend, but his words cannot be heard at the door of the ante-room, where Pablo has settled the gramophone by the side of Heloise and Lister. 'Play it more quietly,' Lister says.

Pablo turns it down.

'It seems unsuitable but one has to go along with them,' says the Reverend as Hadrian and Sister Barton edge into the drawing-room, supporting between them him from the attic. It is immediately noticeable that the patient's howls and trumpetings appear to be expressions of delight rather than pain, for he grins incessantly, his great eyes glittering with ecstatic gladness.

Lister, with Heloise on his arm, advances slowly to meet the bride-groom. 'What a noise he's making,' says Heloise.

'There must be at least eighty-two instruments in that band you've got for your wedding march,' Lister says, 'another can't be amiss.' An instant of quick lightning at the windows followed by a grumble of thunder reinforces his argument.

The zestful cretin's eyes fall first on Irene. He neighs jubilantly through his large teeth and shakes his long white wavy hair. He wears a jump-suit of dark red velvet fastened from crotch to collar-bone with a zip-fastener. This zipper is secured at the neck by a tiny padlock which very likely has been taken, for the purpose, from one of the Baroness Klopstock's Hermes handbags. Beside him, holding him fast with one arm round his shoulders and with the other hand gripping his arm, is a young nurse whose youthfulness does not help. Hadrian, his eyebrows tentatively raised, holds the other arm.

'My boy,' says the Reverend to him from the attic who now stands shaking off his keepers with his powerful shoulders.

The other servants stand back, and Hadrian joins them. Eleanor casts a glance behind her to the open door, and stands a little nearer to it.

'A vivacious husband,' says Lister. 'Miss Barton, try to hold him firm. It's an exciting moment in his life.'

'It's a scandal,' says young Sister Barton. 'It's me he wants to marry.'

At the moment he seems to prefer Irene, and, breaking loose, plunges upon her. Heloise says, 'He doesn't level, you can't really construe with him.'

He is lifted off Irene, who demands a cigarette, and he is then con-signed, still wishfully carolling, to the strong arms of Hadrian and Pablo.

'Make it look like something,' says Mr Samuel, training his camera. Immediately they open their mouths in laughter to combine with his, and group themselves on either side of him so that their restraining arms are concealed, only Hadrian's arm of fellowship and Pablo's con-gratulatory hand in the bridegroom's being revealed. Mr McGuire's bobbins whirl sportively while the scene lasts.

'Just hold him there,' says Lister, 'for a minute.'

But now the captive has caught sight of the bride, tall, pink and plump, and indicates his welcome with a huge fanfare of delight, straining mightily towards her.

'Reverend,' says Miss Barton, 'this is not proper. He's had his injection and these girls are simply nullifying the effect. In his normal state he is very much attached to me.'

'This bit of group-therapy,' Lister tells her, 'is precisely what he needs. Poor man, confined up there all the time with you!'

'I am perplexed,' says the Reverend. 'I have to know which one he wants to marry.' He smiles at the prisoner and says, 'My boy, which of the ladies is your preference, if any?'

The bridegroom gives a cunning heave, triumphantly dragging Pablo and Hadrian in the direction of Heloise who is now taking a light for a cigarette from Irene's. He also spares a glance of beatitude for Eleanor, but continues to make for Heloise with determination.

Lister says, 'It's Heloise, obviously.' The storm beats on the windows and detonates in the park. The music comes to an end, causing him from the attic to crow and romp a little, and to touch the padlock of his zip lovingly.

'He wants to take his clothes off,' says Sister Barton. 'Take care. He's been known to do it.'

'Who is the father of your child?' says the Reverend desperately to Heloise.

'Well,' says Heloise, taking a chair, 'it isn't born yet. Four months and a bit to go. Pablo was busy helping the Baron every evening at the time and Hadrian was off-duty. Mr Samuel and Mr McGuire were in the Baron's team, too, following their respective professions. Then –'

'The Baron?' says the Reverend impatiently. 'Don't tell me he's never attempted to exercise *droits de seigneur*, because Baron Klopstock was well known in his youth.'

Lister says, 'A pornophile, merely. Pornophilia does not make for fatherhood, Reverend. At least, in my experience, it doesn't. Now, if the Baroness could have been the father in the course of nature she might have been, but the Baron, no.'

'Let me see,' says the Reverend, looking round the room. 'Who does that leave?'

'All the rest of them,' says Heloise. 'Let's have some music.'

'Someone from outside,' says the Reverend.

'Do you mean one of the guests at one of the banquets, Reverend?'

'No, one of their private affairs, perhaps.'

'Heloise was strictly on duty at the time,' says Lister. 'Very busy. The secretaries were fully occupied and there were no visiting cousins. You saw for yourself how it was the month of June. You were a constant visitor at large.'

'Then it rests between Clovis, the poor boy Klopstock here, and you, Lister,' says the Reverend, ticking them off again on his fingers while mentally going through the roll-call.

Lister whispers in the Reverend's ear.

'Oh,' says the Reverend. 'Well it isn't Clovis. That leaves you and the poor boy.'

'I am enamoured to the brim with Eleanor,' says Lister, 'and her prayer-book carry-on.'

'Lister,' says Eleanor.

'Eleanor,' he says.

'It's got to be him in the attic,' says Heloise. 'I'm waiting.'

'It could only be him or the Reverend,' Lister says.

'Lets us begin,' says the Reverend. 'Bring him over – carefully, carefully. He must stand here with the girl.'

'The music,' says Heloise.

'Sister Barton,' says Pablo. 'If you don't come and help I can't go and put on the wedding record for Heloise.'

'It's atrocious,' says Sister Barton, weeping but not helping. 'To take him away from me now, after all I've done.'

The Reverend looks for a moment at Sister Barton then looks away as if finding her unsavoury. 'Have you got a Protestant Bible?' he says. 'If not, we'll do without.'

'The English Prayer book,' says Eleanor, but she cannot be heard above the noise of the storm and the ecstasy of the man from the attic, whom Clovis is now assisting Hadrian to hold. Standing beside Heloise the patient is apparently dumbstruck and gazes at her with only his grin. *Greensleeves* starts up again.

'It's getting late,' says Lister.

'The Book of Common Prayer,' says Eleanor.

'It's within my competence as a pastor to perform a legal marriage in this country according to my own simple formula,' says the Reverend looking at his watch then at him from the attic, while pointing to Heloise. 'Gustav Anthony Klopstock, do you take this woman to be your wedded wife?' he says.

The bridegroom escapes, once more, to tumble upon Heloise.

'That means "I do",' says Pablo, helping with the others, to rescue the bride.

'Nobody can now say he wasn't in his right mind at the time of the marriage,' says Lister. 'He knows perfectly well what he's doing.'

'In my condition,' says Heloise.

When the couple are set in place again the Reverend says to Heloise, 'What is your father's name?'

'Klopstock,' says Heloise.

'Klopstock?'

A howl of delight is emitted by the Klopstock from the attic.

'Kindred and Affinity!' shrieks Eleanor above the boisterous instrumentals of the storm, the music and the groom.

'It is a coincidence,' Lister says, spreading his hands like a conductor of an orchestra pleading a *pianissimo*. 'Her father is a humble Klopstock, a riveter. No connection with the House of Klopstock whose residence this is, where galaxies of generals, ambassadors, and their bespangled consorts mingle with cardinals and exiled Arabians by night when the Baron and Baroness are not privately engaged.'

'Are you of age?' says the Reverend to Heloise.

'I'm twenty-two,' she says, swinging a little to the rock-music as it speeds up, and shaking the white mink coat.

'She's twenty-three!' says Sister Barton, still tearful.

'Well you're a major,' says the Reverend to Heloise. 'Heloise Klopstock,' he says, 'will you take this man to be your wedded husband?'

'I will,' says Heloise.

'They have no ring,' says the Reverend looking round irritably.

Lister produces a ring immediately.

'He'll only put it in his mouth and swallow it,' weeps Sister Barton.

'I shall place the ring on the bride's finger by proxy,' says Lister, doing so.

'I hereby pronounce you man and wife,' says the Reverend placing a hand on each shoulder of Heloise and her new husband who, now overjoyed, once more leaps out of reach, this time gambolling to the far end of the room. Numerous precious vases crash to the floor.

Mr McGuire hastens to protect his bobbins, while Mr Samuel says, clicking his camera, 'Marvellous! His laugh's very like a large-mouthed cry of elation such as any beauty queen might give at the moment of her election.'

'I would never resemble him to that,' says Heloise.

Her husband is sprightly and will not be caught. He rips the whole zip-fastener from the stuff of his suit and exultantly dances out of the garment. Then, capering lustily with carols and further damage to the furniture, he pulls the mink coat off his wife's back, drags her into a corner and falls on top of her.

Pablo rushes to intervene.

'Leave him be. He has every right,' says Lister.

'He has no right at a wedding,' says the Reverend. 'It's not the thing to do.'

Sister Barton sobs and the storm revels, while Heloise shoves with hard athleticism and finally escapes, fleeing to the safety of the sound and film-track area. 'Give me a comb,' she says.

Clovis is blowing out the candles.

Mr Samuel says, 'This will need a lot of editing.'

'In my condition,' says Heloise, 'and I've lost a shoe.'

The bridegroom is being held by Sister Barton, Hadrian and Pablo, and is being clothed with the embroidered table cloth by Eleanor.

'Bite his finger and keep him quiet,' says Clovis to Sister Barton.

'He was only doing his thing,' says Hadrian.

Lister says, 'Kings and queens of olden days used to consummate in public. They had four-poster beds with curtains. The court had to stand by to see the curtains shake when Mary Queen of Scots married the Dauphin of France, compared to whom our friend from the attic, here, is an Einstein. And so, my dear Heloise, nobody can now contest the validity of your nuptials on the grounds that they haven't been consummated.'

'They were not consummated,' say Heloise. 'Only almost.'

'To the eye of the candid camera,' says Lister, 'the marriage was consummated. Isn't that so, Mr Samuel?'

'Yes,' says Mr Samuel. But nobody is listening. Lister is offering a pen and two sheets of typewritten paper to the Reverend. 'The marriage certificate,' he says. 'Will you sign your witness, Reverend? I have already signed. In duplicate.'

The Reverend is looking round him as if wondering where he is.

'Sign?' he says. 'Oh yes, of course, I'll put my name. And the happy couple has to sign, too.' He beams at everyone, takes out his glasses, rests the piece of paper on Eleanor's flat prayer book and signs. 'The bride-groom,' he says, 'then the bride.'

'Bite his finger,' says Clovis to Sister Barton, 'or you're fired.'

Tearfully, she takes the little finger of the trumpeting patient in her mouth and bites. He starts to giggle and, although she lets go, does not stop. Lister places the pen in the giggler's hand and raising the paper and the hard book to a convenient level, moves the limp and helplessly amused hand over the space provided until the name is traced, Gustav A. Klopstock. 'The Anthony would have taken too long,' says Lister, very satisfied in his expression of face. 'You never know when his milder spells will stop. Now, Heloise.' Heloise takes the pen and writes her name above the typed address, in the space reserved for her. 'We register this tomorrow,' says Lister. 'It's a quarter to seven. Time has flown, Sister Barton, Pablo will assist you. Give him a nice warm drink and an injection.'

'I must go home to bed,' says the Reverend. 'Where did I leave my bike?' He looks around the very untidy drawing-room.

'In this storm,' Lister says, 'you can't ride back to Geneva, Reverend. We have a bed for you. We shall always have a bed for you, Reverend. Eleanor, show the Reverend to his room.'

'Nice of you, very kind under the circumstances,' says the Reverend. 'I want to show a press-cutting to Cecil Klopstock. Where is he?'

'The Baron is not to be disturbed.'

'Tell him I want to see him when he wakes up.'

FIVE

'Bear in mind,' says Lister, 'that when dealing with the rich, the journalists are mainly interested in backstairs chatter. The popular glossy magazines have replaced the servants' hall in modern society. Our position of privilege is unparalleled in history. The career of domestic service is the thing of the future. The private secretaries of the famous do well, too. Give me another cup of coffee, please Eleanor. It's almost time to go up and change.'

They are seated round the large table where breakfast seems to be as rapidly begun as nearing its end. The storm has retreated from the near vicinity of the house, but continues to prowl on the lake and the mountain-sides. Every now and again there is a banging of fists, a shouted demand, on the back door. Nobody takes any notice.

'Are there any grapes in the house?' says Heloise.

'No, you had the last of them,' says Clovis.

'Well, you're wrong,' says Irene, 'because I brought her a huge big bunch from Geneva. They're in the pantry. I got them from that boyfriend who's a steward on the first class TWA.'

'Irene, what a treasure the Klopstocks have lost in you by their death!' says Lister.

Irene looks modestly at her crumby plate.

Clovis yawns and leans his elbow on the table and his head on his hands. 'I'm worn out,' he says. 'I'll be glad to get to bed.' He gets up, goes into the pantry and returns with a tray on which are set a plate of large green grapes, a bowl of water in which to dip them and a tiny pair of scissors with which to snip them off their twigs. He places them before Heloise. 'Long live the Baroness!' he says.

Heloise pats her stomach.

Mr Samuel then goes to open the back door. He can be heard saying, 'You'll have to wait, Victor Passerat's not available just yet.'

'We've lost the keys of the car!' says the woman's voice.

'Well, look for them.'

'The ground's all wet. We're soaked through. Can't we come in and telephone to a garage, or something?'

'Sorry, strangers aren't permitted.'

'What can we do? We can't get in the car, and we can't get out of the gate. The porter won't open it for us.'

'Take a stroll in the grounds,' advises Mr Samuel.

'It's wet. We'll get caught in another downpour. This is a terrible place.'

'You should always,' says Mr Samuel, 'avoid terrible places.'

Returning to the servants' dining-room he says, 'Amateurs. Where's my camera? It's just possible I could get a few shots of them to fit in an educational film I've got going. The young have to be taught about the average aberrant in the street.'

He takes his camera to the window and focuses.

Lister, dressed smartly for the day's work, stands at the open front door like a gloomy shopkeeper looking at the dark, rumbling sky as Theo comes up the drive on his bicycle. Theo makes a questioning sign, pointing round to the back of the house. 'No, come here,' says Lister.

Theo tremulously parks his bicycle against the dripping hedge and walks the rest of the way.

'I called for you, Theo, because there is something strange to report,' Lister says. 'Come right in.'

The others are coming downstairs, with sleeplessness in their movements and on their faces. The servants are dressed in their morning overalls. Behind them come Mr Samuel in a knee-length blue bath-robe and Mr McGuire in a black and white striped dressing-gown.

'What's going on?' says Mr Samuel.

Theo says, 'There's something peculiar been going on all night.'

'Do you like the job, Theo?' says Lister.

'Yes, Lister,' he says.

'Well, you can keep it. Only remember that nothing peculiar has been going on, as indeed it hasn't. I want only to inform you here and now that the light is on in the library as it was last night when we went to bed with orders not to disturb the Baron Klopstocks and their guest and, furthermore, this morning the door is locked from the inside and there is no response.'

'What's happened?' says Theo. 'You know, my Clara has had dreams, terrible dreams. Have you knocked hard enough?'

Lister goes to the library door, tries the handle, shakes it, then knocks loudly. 'Sir!' he says, 'Madam!'

'We'd better break it down,' says Theo, looking at the others one by one.

'I have orders not to disturb,' Lister says. 'We shall call the police.'

'Clara will be frightened,' says Theo.

'Tell her to confide in the police about her dreams, and get it off her chest,' says Lister. 'The more she says about her dreams when questioned, the better. As far as you two in the lodge are concerned we have been such stuff as dreams are made on all through the stormy night.'

'There's a couple been wandering the grounds all night,' says Theo. 'They came in the car and I wouldn't let them out, as you ordered. Now they've lost the keys of the car and they're taking shelter under a tree. They look a suspicious pair to me.'

'Forget them,' says Mr Samuel. 'They're only extras.'

'Better go back to Clara,' says Lister. 'It's nearly eight o'clock. See that the gates are opened.'

'All right, Lister,' says Theo in a hushed voice, looking towards the library. Then he departs quickly through the open door, mounts his bicycle and starts off up the drive. He gets drenched almost immediately for at that moment the storm descends with full concentration on the Klopstocks' country seat. Theo pedals vigorously, and rounding a bend he is forced to get off his bicycle and press forward on foot along the loud storm-darkened avenue, streaked every now and then as it is with a dart of lightning. On the way he passes a clump of trees under one of which, shrinking into the bark, are the couple of wandering friends from the car. Theo staggers onwards up the twisting drive and at the porch of his house lets fall the bicycle, bends through the torrent to the gates of the house, unlocks them and throws them open. Then he returns to the lodge and tumbles indoors.

Meanwhile the lightning, which strikes the clump of trees so that the two friends huddled there are killed instantly without pain, zigzags across the lawns, illuminating the lily-pond and the sunken rose garden like a self-stricken flash-photographer, and like a zip-fastener ripped from its garment by a sexual maniac, it is flung slapdash across Lake Leman and back to skim the rooftops of the house, leaving intact, however, the well-insulated telephone wires which Lister, on the telephone to Geneva, has rather feared might break down.

Having alerted the police and quiveringly recommended an ambulance with attendant doctors and nurses, Lister now telephones to the discreet and well-appointed flat in Geneva which he prudently maintains, and extends a welcome to the four journalists who have been waiting up all night for the call, playing poker meanwhile, with the ash-trays piled high.

'Our four friends,' Lister then instructs the household, 'are to have first preference in anything you can say to them. They will, of course, have the scandal exclusives which Mr Samuel and Mr McGuire have prepared in the form of typescript, photographs and sound recordings. The television, Association Press and the local riff-raff are sure to question you wildly: answer likewise – say anything to them, just anything, but keep them happy. Isn't that right, Clovis?'

'Yes, the arrangements between our four special friends, ourselves, and our numbered accounts in the Swiss Trust Corporate can be left to Lister. We don't have any arrangements with the others. Keep them happy, that's all. For the television, throw your heads into your hands and sob, or display a sad disapproval of your late employers.'

'I want to go to bed,' says Heloise.

'I shall see that you are allowed to retire at the earliest possible moment, Heloise.'

'Listen to Lister,' says Eleanor.

Lister then books a telephone call to the residence of Count Rudolph Klopstock in Rio de Janeiro, and having done this, says to the others, 'There's a delay to Brazil and they're five hours back. We should get the Count somewhere between four and five a.m. Rio time, and allowing for human nature on the telephone exchange between here and there the news will get around pretty quickly.'

'The brother ought to know,' says Eleanor.

'Know what?' says Lister.

'About the brother,' says Eleanor.

'At the present moment,' says Lister, 'all we ourselves know is that the library door is locked with the Baron, the Baroness and their young friend unresponsive. We're justifiably apprehensive, that's all. Here comes the crime squad. Group yourselves apprehensively.'

He opens the front door to the sound of sirens in the storm. Two police cars pull up at the door followed by an ambulance. An inspector of police, a police detective, two plain-clothes men, three uniformed policemen and a police photographer troop in the open door. The ambulance crew alight and come in out of the rain.

'This is the door, Inspector,' says Lister, leading the way to the library.

The Inspector turns the handle, rattles it, bangs on the door and listens.

'Are you sure there's somebody inside?'

'We fear so. The light's still on as it was last night. The Baron gave orders they were not to be disturbed,' Lister says. 'I have already put through a call to the Baron's brother, as I felt it was right.'

'Open the door,' says the Inspector. Two hefty policemen break it down. The Inspector and his men crowd into the room. Lister follows while the rest of the household approaches the threshold. Mr Samuel's camera clicks. Mr McGuire has a small, light apparatus dangling from his wrist. The body of the Baroness is lying on the floor by the window in a large dark red stain. That of Victor Passerat lies curled against a bookcase which is well splashed with his blood. The Baron's body is slumped over a round table with a revolver not far from his fingers.

The women scream.

'Take the girls away,' says the Inspector to a plain-clothes man. 'Put them in the kitchen and make them calm down.'

Clovis leads the way to the servants' quarters while the Inspector says to Lister, 'Didn't you hear anything during the night? No shots? No shouting or screaming?'

The wind encircles the house and the shutters bang. From the attic comes a loud clatter. 'No, Inspector. It was a wild night,' says Lister.

Up the drive comes a caravan of cars.

The doctor has scrutinised the bodies, the police have taken their statements, they have examined and photographed the room. They have confiscated a letter written by the Baron, to the effect that he has just shot his wife and his secretary and is about to shoot himself, that this is the only solution and that he has no ill feelings against anyone. The Inspector has permitted Lister to read it but has refused it to the reporters who now swarm in the great hall and make a considerable hubbub.

The women have been released from the kitchen, having given their shaken and brief testimony, and again join the household group at the door of the library.

'I must have a last look,' says Eleanor. Heloise casts a doleful eye at a television camera which does not fail to register it. The noise from the reporters swells as, one by one, the covered bodies on their stretchers are borne out of the room. 'Here they come,' says Lister to his troop, 'Klopstock and barrel.'

The bodies are stowed away in the ambulance. The police seal off the main quarters of the house, pushing the reporters out into the subsiding storm, and requesting the servants to retire to their wing.

The doctor then suggests he takes away the ladies to be treated for shock, but they bravely resist. 'The porter's wife,' says the Inspector, 'could do with a bit of treatment. Better take her.'

'I should take them both, sir,' says Lister.

The reporters now crowd in the back door. 'Inspector,' says Lister, 'I shall deal with them briefly then turn them out. We're all rather shaken. If you want any further information we are here.'

'Very helpful,' says the Inspector. 'I'll leave a couple of my men to guard the house. Don't let anyone into the library or upstairs, any of you.'

Heloise says, 'They won't go upstairs, you can be sure of that. My Monet and my Goya are upstairs. One can't be too careful.'

'I beg your pardon?' says the Inspector.

'She is overwrought,' says Lister and says a word or two in the Inspector's ear.

'Yes, yes,' says the Inspector, eyeing Heloise.

Lister murmurs another few words, gesturing towards the ceiling.

'Oh yes,' says the Inspector, looking up. 'We know about him. Relative of the Baroness.'

'No, the Baron.'

'Really? – Oh, well. An unfortunate family.'

Lister adds a further piece of information in an undertone.

'Yes, well, if he's the father, you did the right thing,' says the

Inspector, anxious to join his men in the police car which is now waiting at the back door. He shoves his way through the crowd, refusing comment, and drives off.

Very soon Lister's four friendly journalists go to their car with their brief-cases under their arms, and drive away.

'Now for the riff-raff,' Lister says to his clan. 'Eleanor and Clovis can take one bunch in the sitting-room. Heloise and I will hold our press conference in the pantry. Hadrian and Irene can sit round the kitchen table with Pablo, representing the young approach. Mr Samuel and Mr McGuire – you can go the rounds.'

They settle themselves accordingly. The cameras flash. Microphones are thrust forward to their mouths like hot-dogs being offered to hungry pilgrims.

The voices drown the hectic howl which descends from the breakfasting bridegroom.

Eleanor is saying, 'Like a runaway horse, not going anywhere and without a rider.'

Hadrian is saying, 'The flight of the homosexuals . . .' to which his questioner, not having caught this comment through the noise, responds, '. . . the flight of the bumble bee?' 'No,' says Hadrian.

Lister is saying, '. . . and at one time in my youth I was a professional claque. I applauded for some of the most famous singers in the world. It was quite well paid, but of course, hand-clapping is an art, it's a question of timing. . . .'

'Togetherness . . .' says Irene.

Hadrian is saying, 'Death is that sort of thing that you can't sleep off. . . .'

Pablo's voice cuts in, '. . . putting things in boxes. Squares, open cubes. It's a mentality. Framing them. . . .'

Eleanor says, 'Like children playing at weddings and funerals. I have piped and ye have not danced, I have mourned and ye have not wept.'

Lister, turning in his chair to a prober behind him, is saying, 'He didn't do his own cooking or press his own trousers. Why should he have consorted, excuse my language, with his own wife?'

Clovis says, '. . . not on the typewriter – you wake the whole household, don't you? What I call midnight oil literature is only done by hand. It's an art. Yes, oh no, thanks, I intend to make other arrangements for publication.'

Irene is saying, 'No, he wanted it that way, I guess, until she did a Lady Chatterley on him . . . A Victorian novel, don't you know it? She was really quite typical at heart when it came to Victor.'

Lister is heard to recite, 'For the thing which I greatly feared is come upon me, and that which I was afraid of is come upon me. I was out in safety, neither had I rest, neither was I quiet.'

Eleanor is saying, 'No. No living relatives on her side.'

Pablo says, 'Ghosts and fantasies rising from sex-repression.'

Clovis says, 'Descendant of the Crusaders.'

'. . . somewhat like the war horse,' says Lister, 'in the Book of Job: He saith among the trumpets Ha! Ha! and he smelleth the battle afar off, the thunder of the captains and the shouting. . . .'

'. . . hardly ever seen,' Eleanor is saying. 'He wears a one-piece suit zipped and locked. The Swiss invented the zip-fastener. . . .'

'Well it's like this,' says Pablo, 'if you put friendship out to usury and draw the interest. . . .'

The Reverend has now come down for his breakfast and stands bewildered in the doorway of the servants' sitting-room where Eleanor and Clovis are holding their crowded conference. He has his press-cutting in his hand.

'Reverend!' says Eleanor, pushing over to him.

'There's a man on the landing outside my room. He made me come down the back stairs. Where's Cecil Klopstock? I want to show him this.'

Eleanor is swept away and replaced by five reporters. 'Reverend would you care to elaborate on your statement about the sex-drug . . .? Did the Baron . . .?'

Eleanor, herself surrounded once more, is saying, '. . . frothing and churning inside like a washing machine in full programme.'

Lister, beside her, addresses another microphone, 'The glories,' he says, 'of our blood and state

     Are shadows, not substantial things;
     There is no armour against fate;
     Death lays his icy hand on kings:
       Sceptre and crown

Must tumble down,
And in the dust be equal made
With the poor crooked scyth and spade.'

'Could you repeat that, sir?' says a voice. Clovis pushes his way through the mass of shoulders and reaches Lister. 'Phone call from Brazil,' he says. 'The butler won't fetch Count Klopstock to the phone. Absolutely refuses. He's locked in the study with some friends and he's on no account to be disturbed.'

'Leave word with the butler,' says Lister, 'that we have grave news and that we hope against hope to hear from the Count when morning dawns in Rio.'

Hadrian is saying, 'When my brother had the flower-stall at the Piazza del Popolo and Iolanda had a little pitch for the newspapers a few steps away . . . It was a windy corner.'

The Reverend, though trembling, is eating his breakfast in bed. The storm has passed and the sun begins to show itself on the wet bushes, the wide green lawns and the sodden rose-garden. The reporters with their microphones and cameras have trickled away. Lister is looking at the cigarette-stubs on the floor. Clovis opens the kitchen window. A homely howl comes down from the attic.

A car approaches up the drive.

'No more,' says Lister. 'Send them away.'

'It's Prince Eugene,' says Eleanor. 'He's gone round the front.'

'Well, he'll be sent round the back,' says Lister, kicking a few cigarette stubs under the sideboard. 'Let us all go to bed.'

Footsteps can be heard squelching round the back of the house, and the top half of Prince Eugene's face appears at the open window.

'Have they all gone?' he says.

'It's our rest-hour, your Excellency.'

'I'm a Highness.'

Eleanor says, 'Was there something we can do for you, your Highness?'

'A word. Let me in.'

'Let his Highness in,' says Lister.

Prince Eugene enters timidly. He says, 'The neighbours have been parked out on the road all morning. They didn't have the courage to come. Admiral Meleager, the Baronne de Ventadour, Mrs Dix Silver, Emil de Vega, and all the rest. Anyway, I got here first. Can I have one word with you, Lister, my good man?'

'Come into the office,' says Lister, leading the way into the pantry office. Mr Samuel's camera flicks imperceptibly, just in case.

Prince Eugene takes the chair indicated by Lister. 'Any of you like to come over to my place? Have you thought it over? It's very comfortable. I can offer –'

'At the moment, sir,' says Lister, 'we want to go to sleep and we don't want to be disturbed.'

'Oh, quite,' says the Prince, rising. 'It's only that I wanted to get here before the others.'

'It's very understandable,' says Lister, rising, too. 'But in fact we've made our plans.'

'Miss Barton? – Would she consider a few light household dutires? Surely the poor fellow can't go on living here?'

'Miss Barton will be needed. Heloise desires her to stay. Heloise was a parlour maid but she married the new Baron early this morning.'

'You don't say! They got married.'

Lister whispers in his ear.

'Oh, I understand. Quite drastic, though, isn't it?'

'They can marry or not marry, as they please, these days, sir,' says Lister. 'Times have changed. Take Irene, for instance.'

'Which one is Irene?'

'The very charming one. Quite the most attractive. A very good little cook, too.'

'I can offer her a very good wage.'

'These days,' says Lister, 'they want more.' He again murmurs a few words in the Prince's ear.

'I'm not the marrying type,' whispers the Prince shyly.

'It's the best I can offer, your Highness. She's happy enough with her evening off at the airport.'

'Well, I'd better be going,' says the Prince.

'Thank you for calling, sir.'

Lister leads the way to the back door, where Prince Eugene hesitates and says, 'Are you sure we can't make some alternative arrangements with Irene?'

'Yes,' says Lister. 'I have others in mind for her in this part of the world who would be grateful to have her seated at their table. She's a very capable young housekeeper. The Marquis of –'

'Very well, Lister. Arrange the details as soon as possible. Accept no other offers.'

The Prince tramples round once more to the front of the house, gets into his car and is seen to be driven off, sunk in the back seat, pondering.

The plain-clothes man in the hall is dozing on a chair, waiting for the relief man to come, as is also the plain-clothes man on the upstairs landing. The household is straggling up the back stairs to their beds. By noon they will be covered in the profound sleep of those who have kept faithful vigil all night, while outside the house the sunlight is laughing on the walls.

THE MANDELBAUM GATE

CONTENTS

PART ONE

1. FREDDY'S WALK

Sometimes, instead of a letter to thank his hostess, Freddy Hamilton would compose a set of formal verses – rondeaux, redoubles, villanelles, rondels or Sicilian octaves – to express his thanks neatly. It was part of his modest nature to do this. He always felt he had perhaps been boring during his stay, and it was one's duty in life to be agreeable. Not so much at the time as afterwards, he felt it keenly on his conscience that he had said no word between the soup and the fish when the bright talk began; he felt at fault in retrospect of the cocktail hours when he had contributed nothing but the smile for which he had been renowned in his pram and, in the following fifty years, elsewhere.

'Oh of course, Freddy Hamilton. Everyone loves old Freddy my dear; Freddy's sweet.'

Freddy, of so many British consulates throughout his subdued, obedient career, would have been touched to hear it; he would have smiled. He did not really want to excite any sort of passion in his friends, or linger in their minds under some inflammable aspect. A very boring guest or a very entertaining one could provoke all sorts of undesirable feelings in people – revulsion, heart-quickenings, murderous attachments, the sort of emotions that had always led to trouble at school and university, and they led to international incidents as well.

He liked to get his verses off quickly so that there should be no apparent sign of effort on his part. As he walked through the amazing alleys of the Orthodox Quarter of Israel's Jerusalem which teemed so dangerously close to the Mandelbaum Gate, he started thinking of a triolet in his long-practised manner to catch the next day's Foreign Office bag into Jordan. Freddy had just come through the Gate. He had diplomatic immunity and so was permitted to pass through the Gate every week-end from Israel into Jordan and back again; from Jerusalem to Jerusalem. Few people passed from Israel into Jordan;

there were difficulties, and for Europeans a certificate of baptism was
required. Foreign diplomats were not allowed to pass by motor-car,
which was understandable, as papers and bombs might be concealed
in a car.

Freddy carried his week-end luggage – a zipper-bag – and took his
usual route into the New City. It was the hottest day so far of 1961.
He had refused the taxi-cab that waited at the Gate; he hated taking
taxi-cabs anywhere in the world; he felt morally against the tips, as
all his uncles before him had felt. Excepting, of course, one uncle, the
one who had messed up the money in the thirties and absolutely
ruined the family, and who had not felt strongly against giving away
tips to cabbies and so on. As Freddy turned a corner he came into
collision with a tiny dark-eyed boy with fluffy side-hair falling down
his cheeks, too fine as yet to be formed into shining ringlets like those
of his male elders among the Orthodox sect. The child's nose
bumped into Freddy's knee, and Freddy took him by the hand to
steady him out of his bewilderment. A bearded, befrocked old man
with a very large face muttered in Hebrew to the infant, who had
already regained his bearings and was busy studying Freddy from
head to feet. A woman of unguessable age, wearing lots of black
clothes, snatched the child away, and he trotted off, his legs in their
long woollen stockings moving like swift shuttles to keep up with his
mother, but he still craned his head round wonderingly at Freddy.
The woman scolded the child meantime, evidently trying to impress
on him the undesirable nature of Freddy. Freddy walked on behind
the heavily garbed pair, feeling decidedly in the wrong for having
touched the child's hand; they had probably taken him for a modern
Jew, one of the regular Israelis of whom this sect disapproved
perhaps more heavily than they did of the honest unclean foreigner.
Well, thought Freddy, to continue . . .

> . . . would have preferred
> To make my grateful feelings heard,
> But every time articulate
> Scarcely a word.

It was not a triolet after all. Joanna, his hostess on the other side, had
been extremely agreeable to him since his posting to Israel. He had

spent three week-ends in her cool villa, and she loved to have these bread-and-butter verses. There would have to be an additional stanza, perhaps two. Joanna was to visit him over here in Israel; she had not yet been to Israel. He would have to remind her about her visa, and tell her how best to make the crossing. It was not a triolet after all, but a form of rondeau. There was the business of Joanna's getting a visa, and he would meet her on this side of the Mandelbaum Gate. The intensity at the Gate was quite absurd. One could understand the border incidents where soldiers would flare up an incident suddenly and unaccountably. But there at the Gate the precautions and suspicions of the guards were quite absurd. No Israeli money allowed into Jordan, no Israeli postcards, the Jordanian police almost biologically unable to utter the word 'Israel'. The Israeli police were inordinately dramatic: 'Safe crossing,' they would say as one left the emigration hut. The Israeli porter would run and dump one's baggage half-way and run for the life of him back to his post. The Jordanian porter would wait till the path was clear; he would run the few seconds' space to pick up the bags and run for the life of him back to his post. They dramatized everything. Why did people have to go to extremes, why couldn't they be moderate? Freddy bumped into a man in European dress, rushing out of a shop as they all did. The man said something in Arabic. Freddy had thought he was a Jew. You couldn't tell the difference sometimes. Some of them had extremely dark skins, almost jetters. Why couldn't people be moderate?

It was not a triolet after all, but a sort of rondeau, Freddy turned up an alley. Another child, a girl, bumped into him in the narrow, crowded street. This time he did not put out a guiding hand, and she slipped away with the subdued expression of the children of this quarter, quite unlike the vivacious young of the regular Israelis. Freddy was rather sorry for the boys with their sausage side-curls and black knickerbocker rig-out, especially those adolescent boys who walked in a goody-goody way, by twos and threes. It must be hell for them, he thought, to be so different from the rest of the country, especially if they ever want to break away. He had felt sorry for the Arab boys on the other side – underfed, driving their mangy donkeys, thin, and in rags. He was moved to pity for all young boys, on the whole, recalling the term-times of his youth. He was convinced that the boys with ringlets were going through the same sort

of hell, which was the only sort Freddy knew. The ringlets, like the
Gate, were quite absurd.

'Quite absurd!' On the strength of this phrase he had struck up
friendships all over the place. He was accustomed to exotic sights and
squalid smells, narrow oriental streets, and people who went to
extremes, it was all part of the Foreign Service. But outside of the
Embassy, and even inside it, he never really felt at ease with chaps
until sooner or later they remarked that the place was quite absurd.

> . . . feelings heard,
> But every time articulate
>   Scarcely a word.
> But you have far too long deferred
> Your visit to the Modern State,
> So choose and name the cheerful date.
> Joanna, I can hardly wait
> To meet you at the quite absurd
>   Mandelbaum Gate.

He was approaching the end of the Orthodox Jewish quarter, and
had turned into a street at the end of which rattled the modern state.
There, small shops burst their sides with business, large cars streaked
along the highway, and everywhere the radio sets told the news in
several tongues ranging from Hebrew to that of the B.B.C., or
attacked the hot air with oriental jazz. Up there at the end of this
orthodox street, it was said, the Orthodox Jews would gather on a
Saturday morning, piously to stone the passing motor-cars, breakers
of the Sabbath. And across the street, streamers stretched from building to building, bearing an injunction in Hebrew, French and English:

DAUGHTERS OF ISRAEL, OBSERVE MODESTY IN THESE
STREETS!

This, Freddy assumed to be for the benefit of any tourist-woman
who might, for some mad reason, wish to walk in this Orthodox
Jewish quarter wearing shorts or a low-cut sun dress; the local
women themselves needed no such warning, being clad and covered,
one way and another, all over.

For the time being Freddy had been placed in rooms in a Jerusalem hotel while waiting for an Embassy flat to fall vacant. He was in no great hurry for the flat, preferring hotel life where one need not mix, need not entertain one's colleagues, and could generally escape. His colleagues at this posting seemed a bit intense and know-all; they were on the young side and had not yet settled down. Freddy noticed, crossing the street, a young woman who was at present staying at his hotel, a Miss Vaughan. She was accompanied by a tall, intellectual-looking Jew. Freddy put down his bag in the hot street. He wanted to be specially civil to Miss Vaughan, having struck up her acquaintance in the cool leafy courtyard of the hotel one evening over two long drinks, and having then, on another occasion, inadvertently said the wrong thing; whereupon Miss Vaughan had felt for his embarrassment.

They crossed over to him where he waited on the kerb, and inquired if he had enjoyed his week-end. He had once before, very briefly, met her companion, a teacher of archaeology, Dr Saul Ephraim of the Hebrew University, who was acting as Miss Vaughan's guide. He had turned out to be amiable in the surprising way of the Israeli intellectuals; it took one by surprise because one did not expect a violin with its strings taut and tuned for immediate performance to be suddenly amiable. Dr Ephraim spoke a slightly American tone of English, suddenly amiable and easy as if from some resource that had been waiting under his skin for an encounter with Freddy. He wore an open-necked shirt and flannels, his neck lean and long-muscled. Freddy chatted as he observed these things, telling of his week-end in Jordan: 'I've got some charming friends over there.' Ephraim would be in his young thirties. He was anxious to hear news of Jordan.

'Haven't you ever been there?' said Freddy.

'Not since the war.'

'Of course, not since the war.' To Ephraim 'the war' was the war of 1948.

'It's absurd,' said young Dr Ephraim.

An unloading of water melons began to take place close to them. Freddy had once been hit by the corner of a crate while passing an unloading operation at Covent Garden. He was nervous, and moved the couple aside along with himself.

'Both of you come and join me for a drink when you've finished,' said Freddy then, lifting up his bag.

Miss Vaughan was about to say something when an old bearded man out of the many, with small ancient eyes, approached them and spoke to Dr Ephraim in guttural Yiddish. Ephraim answered some brief thing, using his hands and shoulders to throw off the subject to the air. The old man spoke a few more words and moved away, muttering and glancing backward at Miss Vaughan.

'What did he say?' said Miss Vaughan.

'He said, "Tell your lady-friend to dress herself properly in these sacred streets as they have always done before."'

Freddy looked at Miss Vaughan to see how she was dressed. She was wearing a harmless blouse, sleeveless, and a dark skirt. He looked up at the admonishing banners and smiled his smile. He smiled again at Miss Vaughan, who stood with her sharp features and prim grey and black hair drawn back, looking less intense than Freddy feared she really was. It occurred to him that by contrast with Ephraim she would be in her late thirties. She was still questioning Dr Ephraim about his conversation with the old man. 'And what did you say to that?'

'I said, "Well, it's a hot day." And he replied, "Well, it was a hot day two thousand years ago."'

Freddy was glad he had met the couple, for he was always lonely after his week-ends on the other side. He pushed his way up the streets among the loitering mystics and beggars whom the Israelis in general abhorred, being bumped into quite often by the women who inevitably darted out of the shop doors with their purchases and their children, without looking first to right or left. He thought he might ask young Saul Ephraim to recommend him a Hebrew teacher if Miss Vaughan remembered to bring him back to the hotel for a drink. One ought to learn some modern Hebrew to get along in this country. Ephraim might take on the job himself, but Freddy, reflecting that this was highly improbable, was instantly annoyed with himself for thinking it in the first place. One did not meet many Israelis, only the officials and so on, but of course one had not much time. The weekly visits to the other side took up his free days. Dr Ephraim would be thirty-one or thirty-two. Abdul Ramdez, the life-insurance agent who kept trying, without success, to sell Freddy a policy, but who was amusing, had undertaken to give him lessons in Arabic. Ramdez would be in his middle twenties. One had to be careful about one's teachers of Hebrew and Arabic; here on the spot they were all apt to get intense. Ramdez was an Armenian Arab, or so he claimed.

A chanting of children's voices came from an upper-storey window as Freddy pushed up the street towards modernity and his hotel. This upper storey was a school; it was always in full chant when he passed, for the children of this sect learned their lessons, all subjects alike, by plaintive rote, singing them out in Hebrew. This always fascinated him, at the same time as it put him off his stroke, for usually, when he passed the spot, he was thinking of his thank-you verses. At present his mind was already on the third stanza of his current piece, so that Joanna could be suitably and gracefully reminded to get a visa and make sure that she stated she was coming on a pilgrimage to the Christian shrines.

But he could not get his rhythm right against the chanting of these children of the Orient, even after he could hear it no longer and was out among the speedy wide streets of people and motor traffic in the modern city. All the way back to his hotel, when he was really too hot to bother and his thoughts were mere heatwaves, the chant went on at the back of his head, accompanied, as always on these return journeys, by an assertive counter-chant rising spontaneously from something indomitable in Freddy; and so, pitting culture against culture, the metrical precepts of Samuel Taylor Coleridge chanted themselves lovingly round his brain:

> Trochee trips from long to short;
> From long to long in solemn sort,
> Slow Spondee stalks; strong foot! yet ill able
> Ever to come up with Dactyl trisyllable.
> Iambics march from short to long: –
> With a leap and a bound the swift Anapaests throng;
> One syllable long, with one short at each side,
> Amphibrachys hastes with a stately stride: –
> First and last being long, middle short, Amphimacer
> Strikes his thundering hoofs, like a proud high-bred racer.

Even in his bath, when he was thinking of other things,
Coleridge's lines continued to churn in the background – even
when they had chased away the Hebrew plain-chant; and even,
although he was scarcely aware of it, when he sat out in the small
green courtyard of the hotel to await Miss Vaughan and Dr
Ephraim. He wanted to be specially agreeable to Miss Vaughan,
having put his foot in it last week on their third or fourth meeting.
Freddy hated more than anything the thought that he had hurt
someone's feelings in a direct encounter. He hoped she would
bring the archaeologist with the lean brown neck. The afternoon
was fading, and he tapped silently with his fingers on the wicker
arm of his chair and gazed up through the lofty trellis at the
cooling light.

> Trochee trips from long to short;

The waiter brought his drink and Freddy dwelt for a gay and not
indelicate moment on the young Israeli, and he felt like Horace in the
Ode, demanding simple service under his lattice vine. *Persicos odi,
puer.* . . .

From where he sat he saw Miss Vaughan come into the hotel
entrance, alone. She moved towards the staircase but glanced
towards the terrace. Freddy rose and raised an arm in a welcoming
way, and she turned and joined him.

'Dr Ephraim couldn't manage as it was rather late and his family
were expecting him. I ought to go and change.'

'What will you drink?' said Freddy. His first meeting with Miss
Vaughan now came back to him, fused with subsequent meetings
here in the green courtyard. He saw them all with that total per-
ceptivity of his which might have made a poet of him, given the
missing element. His first impression had been of a pleasant
English spinster; she was a teacher of English at a girls' school; she
was on a tour of the Holy Land; Freddy had discussed with her the
dear subject of formal English lyrical verse; he had, on another
occasion, confided in her that he was compiling an anthology in his
spare time, and had before the war published a volume of his own
occasional verses. She had responded in a detached sort of way,

which was what one liked. She was edgy; she wore on her engagement finger a ring of antique design embedded with a dark-blue stone; but for some reason Freddy had not felt that the ring referred to an engagement to marry anyone; such things were not unaccountable in an English spinster; it was probably somebody killed in the war.

Now, sitting with her near the same spot as when they had first spoken three weeks ago, he was filled with a sense of her dangerousness; he was obscurely afraid. He wished the young archaeologist had come with her.

But he was obliged to be particularly civil to Miss Vaughan. He fingered the wicker chair.

With a leap and a bound the swift Anapaests throng . . .

Last week he had joined her out here after dinner. The State of Israel had that day sent up its first guided rocket. He remarked that there seemed to be a lot of rejoicing going on in the streets, and one of them suggested going out later on to watch the children dancing. The children danced in the public gardens until late every night in any case. They fell to talking about politicians and the Bomb.

She had said, in a lazy casual way – for by this time they were fairly at ease with each other – 'Sometimes I think we ought to chuck out the politicians from world government and put in the Pope, the Chief Rabbi, the Archbishop of Canterbury and the Dalai Lama instead. They couldn't do worse and they might do better.'

Freddy had reflected on this without undue seriousness. 'There would have to be a Greek Patriach as well,' he said, 'and then the Buddhists and the Hindus would want their say. There would be no end to it. But it's a good idea. I imagine there would be objections from the Jews to the Chief Rabbi. Most of these Jews here are unbelievers, so far as I can gather.'

'Not quite,' said Miss Vaughan. 'I think they believe in a different way from what you mean. They believe with their blood. Being a Jew isn't something they consider in their minds, weigh up, and give assent to as one does in the Western Christian tradition. Being a Jew is inherent.'

'Yes, I'm afraid so.' Freddy gave a little laugh.

As if he had not spoken at all, she continued, 'As a half-Jew myself, I think I understand how –'

'Oh, I didn't mean to say . . . I mean . . . One says things without thinking, you know.'

She said, 'You might have said worse.'

Freddy felt terrible. He groped for the idea that, being a half-Jew, she might be only half-offended. After all, one might speak in that manner of the Wogs or the Commies, and everyone knew what one meant.

He now noticed the Jewishness of her appearance, something dark and intense beyond her actual shape and colouring. Freddy felt worse. It was a diplomatic as well as a social error, here in this country. This was the first year of the Eichmann trial. Freddy felt like a wanted man who had been found hiding in a dark cupboard. He felt an urge to explain that he was not a mass-butcher and that he had never desired to become a *Sturmbannführer, Obersturmbann-führer, Superobersturmbannführer*. He said, 'I like your young guide. How did you come by him?'

She said, 'He's a friend of a friend of mine, another archaeologist who's working on the stuff at Qumran just now.' Plainly, she was embarrassed by his embarrassment.

Freddy clutched at the subject of the Dead Sea scrolls as at a slice of melon in the Sahara. He said: 'That must be enormously exciting. I want to visit the place myself some time soon.'

But she was occupied with her reaction to Freddy's distress. She began to speak, with furious exasperation, about the Israeli, a former Czech, who had been allotted to her as a guide to the holy places. He had been overbearing. He had been obstructive. He had taken her on a trip to Nazareth and had wanted her to whizz through the whole scene in half an hour, whereas she had insisted on spending the day there. He was a fanatical Christian-hater who had wanted to show her the cement factories and pipelines of Israel instead of the shrines, and had been reluctant to drive her to the top of Mount Tabor, the probable scene of the Transfiguration, and she had not insisted because this insufferable man . . . It emerged that she herself was a Roman Catholic.

Anxious about the extremity and urgency of her tone, Freddy looked round for the waiter. He said to her: 'Let's try the white wine.' He ordered two glasses, and called after the waiter, 'But it should be chilled.' He said to Miss Vaughan, 'They are inclined to serve it warm.'

The waiter appeared with two glasses of local white wine. In them were floating two chips of ice, rapidly melting from their original cubic form. Freddy and Miss Vaughan were silent until the waiter had gone. The ice melted entirely in the hot evening air. Freddy smiled at the two glasses on the table. Eventually, they even sipped the lukewarm mixture. 'They simply don't understand about wine at most of these hotels,' Freddy said. Well, it was a relief, at least, that they could have an English giggle about something.

Freddy now wondered if it was his long walk through the Orthodox quarter in the afternoon heat that had put him on edge. He felt decidedly afraid of Miss Vaughan. She fidgeted with the ring on her engagement finger. She looked very strained. Perhaps she, too, was feeling the heat. However, he was resolved to be agreeable in view of his blunder last week.

She said, 'Your geraniums are flourishing.'

He had given her two of his pots of geraniums before leaving for Jordan last week. They were special geraniums. He had smuggled them across from Joanna's prize collection.

He said, 'Good. I was hoping Dr Ephraim would look in. I want to consult him about a Hebrew teacher.'

'He had to return to his wife and family.'

'Oh yes, quite.'

'He might give you Hebrew lessons himself. They don't get well paid at the University here.'

'Well, I was sort of hoping that.'

She said: 'Before I go to Jordan we must arrange a meeting.'

'When are you going?' he said.

'I don't know yet.'

It was a puzzle to him that she had not already gone to Jordan. She kept saying she was 'waiting to go to Jordan.' He wondered if she waited for a visa. If they suspected her Jewish blood she would not get a visa. But, on the other hand, if she had a certificate of baptism and kept quiet it should be easy.

He saw that she was pulling at a fraying piece of wicker on the arm of her chair.

Iambics march from short to long . . .

She said, 'I'm glad to have the geraniums. I water them every morning when the post arrives. It takes my mind off things. I'm waiting for a letter to arrive before I can go off to Jordan.'

'If it's a question of a visa, perhaps I could help,' said Freddy.

'Thank you, but you can't help,' she said.

'The Christian shrines over there are far more interesting than here,' he said. 'At least, there are more of them.'

'I know,' she said, 'I hope to be able to see them soon. In fact, I'm hoping to get married quite soon to an archaeologist who's working over there. The one who's at the Dead Sea area.'

'I'm sure I could help if it's only a matter of a visa.'

'I'm waiting for news from Rome,' she said. 'He has been married and is divorced. It's a question of whether his marriage can be annulled or whether it can't be annulled. I mean annulled by the Church. If it isn't annulled by the Church then the marriage is off. There's a fifty-fifty chance.'

'Oh dear,' said Freddy. He said, 'Is it as serious as that?'

She said, 'Yes.'

'Won't you be going to join him in Jordan?' Freddy said. He noticed she was pulling at the fraying wicker, and felt a panic about where this conversation might lead; he could see she was feeling strongly about something or other. He was afraid she had some tiresome deep conviction.

She said she would not go to Jordan at all if the news from Rome was against the nullity of his previous marriage. She said she would never see the man again in that case.

'Oh dear,' said Freddy. He said, 'What does your fiancé feel about this?'

'Well, of course, he feels it's a bit unfair. He isn't a Catholic himself.'

'It does seem a bit unfair,' said Freddy mildly. 'It seems a bit extreme, when a couple of grown-up people –'

'Do you know,' said this passionate spinster in a cold and terrifying voice, 'a passage in the Book of the Apocalypse that applies to your point of view?'

'I'm afraid the Apocalypse is beyond me,' Freddy said. 'I've never had the faintest clue what it's all about. I can cope with the Gospels, at least some parts, but –'

'It goes like this,' she said, enunciating her words slowly, almost like a chant:

I know of thy doings, and find thee neither cold nor hot; cold or hot, I would thou wert one or the other. Being what thou art, luke-warm, neither cold nor hot, thou wilt make me vomit thee out of my mouth.

Freddy did not reply. People should definitely not quote the Scriptures at one. It was quite absurd.

Miss Vaughan leaned back in her chair and drew her hand over her prim hair in a relaxed way. Freddy remained silent.

First and last being long, middle short, Amphimacer
Strikes his thundering hoofs, like a proud high-bred racer . . .

Then Freddy rose as one who had quietly closed a door and said, 'I must go and get off a bread-and-butter letter to my hostess before dinner.'

2. BARBARA VAUGHAN'S IDENTITY

People should definitely not quote the Scriptures at each other, thought Barbara Vaughan, regretting her attack on Freddy – or rather, it had been a delayed counter-attack, but he would probably not have recognized this devious fact.

People who quoted the Scriptures in criticism of others were terrible bores and usually they misapplied the text. One could prove anything against anyone from the Bible. She regretted to the smallest detail her denunciation, from the Apocalypse, of the cool Foreign Office man. In reality she greatly enjoyed the regretting, because it excluded from her thoughts the other problems – the vital ones which were, for the present, insoluble. To these her mind always came round at length, as in a concerto when the formal recapitulation, the real thing, wins through. But meantime she fiddled up and down the scales with the ridiculous scene with Freddy last night in the courtyard.

She sat on a low wall, regretting on and on and generally gathering strength, beside the Basilica of the Transfiguration on the summit plateau of Mount Tabor. She had hired a car for herself that morning, for she was tired of the travel agency guides. They had plenty of good information to offer, but they offered it incessantly. Through the length and breadth of the country the Israelis treated facts like antibiotic shots, injecting them into the visitor like diligent medical officers. Well, they were proud of their country, and she had no fault to find with the facts as such. The tiring aspect of every journey she had made throughout the past three weeks was the hard work involved in separating the facts relevant to her point of view from those relevant to theirs.

The facts relevant to her point of view: Barbara Vaughan's intelligence had come to maturity in the post-graduate tradition of a great university's English department. She had then applied herself to music, but too late to meet her own exacting standards: she now no longer played the cello. By constitution of mind she was inclined to think of 'a Catholic point of view' to which not all facts were relevant, just as, in her thesis-writing days, she had selected the points of a poem which were related only to the thesis. This did not mean that she had failed to grasp the Christian religion with a total sense of its universal application, or that she was unable to recognize, in one simple process, the virtue of a poem. All it meant was that her habits of mind were inadequate to cope with the whole of her experience, and thus Barbara Vaughan was in a state of conflict, like practically everyone else, in some mode or another.

Like practically everyone else – and she was one of those afflicted by her gifts. For she was gifted with an honest, analytical intelligence, a sense of fidelity in the observing of observable things, and, at the same time, with the beautiful and dangerous gift of faith which, by definition of the Scriptures, is the sum of things hoped for and the evidence of things unseen.

'We approach Beersheba,' a guide had said on her first tour, shortly after her arrival in the country. 'Look, all this has sprung up in thirteen years.'

The guides of Israel irritated Barbara largely for the reason, not altogether obscure to her, that they were extremely virile men and yet were not the one virile man whose proximity she wanted; they were not Harry Clegg, the archaeologist at present working on the site of the Dead Sea excavations in Jordan. She was disposed to resist the guides' pronouncements from this cause alone, even if she had not the plain excuse to object continually, 'I've really only come on a pilgrimage. I really only want to see the ancient sites. I'm really not interested in Scotch-tape factories.'

'We approach Beersheba.'

Suddenly, as it seemed, from behind a few palm-trees Beersheba had appeared in a white dazzle of modern blocks reaching down to the great desert waves of the Negev. The desert lapped like a sea on the glittering strips of concrete that defined Beersheba's outlying blocks of flats.

Barbara Vaughan said, 'I'm really only interested in the Beersheba of Genesis.'

'This is the Beersheba of Genesis.'

They drove slowly through the streets. Barbara looked from the houses to the desert, and from the desert to the houses. Beersheba was the place where the patriarch Isaac, blind in his old age, mistakenly gave his blessing to Jacob, who had posed as his elder brother Esau. The old man, uneasy, felt the son's hands and arms, which were gloved in the hairy skin of a goat, and was taken in by the disguise. 'The voice is the voice of Jacob,' said the old man. He felt the arms and hands – 'but the hands –' The mighty blessing, once bestowed, was irrevocable. Smooth Jacob, not tough, hairy Esau, got the spiritual inheritance and took the place that the Lord had reserved for him among the Fathers of Israel, such being the ways of the Lord in the Middle East. Barbara reflected that God had not been to Eton. Jacob would have made a marvellous Jesuit . . . She said, 'Well, only the desert and sky look in character, but I suppose it's the authentic site. I feel sleepy.'

'This is Beersheba, the birthplace of Jacob, the Father of the Twelve Tribes of Israel. We have a new school for immigrants. To teach them trades and Hebrew. I show you.'

The modern town indeed had its own beauty. As they were driving back through the streets Barbara caught sight of a brass plate outside a dark glazed shop doorway. It read Detective Agency.

'What do they want with a detective agency in a new town?'

'Many things. The last three, four years there have been maybe some divorces. Population, thirty-two thousand. See, we have here a clinic with also an extension.'

That was how it had been since her arrival.

'I'm really interested essentially in the Holy Land.'

'This is the Holy Land.'

Saul Ephraim, of course, had been the most sympathetic. He knew Harry Clegg. One could relax with Saul. And once, when he advised her, 'Be tough with these official guides. Don't let them bully you. Tell them you only want to see places of antiquity. You can see modern housing estates and shopping centres anywhere in the world,' – for some reason she then replied, 'It's all antiquity in the long run.' The archaeologist had shrugged in his casual, Jewish way. 'In the long run!' he said. 'The modern flats won't last as long as Herod's water-pipes have lasted.'

People should definitely not quote the Scriptures at each other, thought Barbara, as she sat on the wall up there at Mount Tabor. She looked down on the green and blue of Galilee, while her mind gazed equally at the problems of years ago, of last year, last week, yesterday, tomorrow.

Saul Ephraim, her only real friend in this country, frequently brought to mind one of her cousins in their student days, when they had lingered over the supper table on long argumentative Sunday evenings at Golders Green, while the tall flowers outside the french windows seemed to grow silent and more silent. She was conscious of Saul Ephraim in this aspect as he spoke of Herod's network of sewers and water-pipes and told her how these had recently been turned to use again by the new State. He was an unbeliever, well and accurately versed in the Old and New Testaments, with a conscientious indifference to their relevance outside the field of an antiquarian's interest. This was a type of mind Barbara could understand and cope with.

On the occasion of his telling her to be tough with the guides, they had been at Jaffa, where they leaned over the sea-wall, contemplating, as they talked, the old harbour, which was too shallow to accommodate modern shipping. Some way behind them stood the reputed house of Simon the Tanner, where the apostle Peter lodged when he was fetched from Lod to come and raise Dorcas from the dead. It seemed the occupant nuns would not allow visitors on that day. Barbara again experienced a feeling that had overcome her in the recent weeks, when she had actually reached the site she was seeking: it was a feeling of abrupt indifference, as when at Nazareth she had taken great pains to find a shrine entitled the 'Mensa Christi' – reputedly a slab of rock once used by Christ as a table. She had climbed a long, hot hill from curiosity to see the object and to find out what legend attached to it. But on arriving at the small building, she had found it locked. Near by, a gnarled old Franciscan monk, the custodian, sat dozing on a stone, the key in his hands. She did not trouble to approach him. She did not by then possess sufficient interest in the 'Mensa Christi' to do so.

So it was at the house of Simon the Tanner at Jaffa. Saul had gone round to the back door to try to gain admittance. She said, 'Don't bother, I'm not all that interested;' he gave up the attempt, with only one series of unanswered bangs on the door.

They had leaned over the sea-wall, surveying the ancient sea. Beside them was a paved courtyard leading into some low-built dark doorways. A woman from the interior screamed, then wailed, and finally emerged into the courtyard sobbing loudly. She was an Arab girl wearing a tight, short Western dress, very unkempt. She was upheld by two other women. Her dress was torn from her shoulders. She had obviously been roughly treated. She was hurried by her two women friends into another dark doorway. They were followed by two men, Arabs in European clothes. One of the men stopped to look at Barbara. He seemed to recognize her. His gaze caused her to take a special note of his face. He was blue-eyed. Where had she seen him before? Was he the guide at Joseph's Workshop at Nazareth? The woman was wailing still from within the house.

'I think one of those men is a guide,' she said to Saul when the blue-eyed Arab followed the others.

'You've got guides on the brain. No, they aren't guides,' he said.

She said, 'Oh, of course, I remember. He's the man who comes to see Mr Hamilton at the hotel – a life-insurance agent.'

'A what?' said Saul.

She then remarked, without relevance, that the Scriptures were specially important to the half-Jew turned Catholic. The Old Testament and the New, she said, were to her – as near as she could apply to her own experience the phrase of Dante's vision – 'bound by love into one volume'. Then, perceiving that Saul Ephraim was giving serious thought to what she had said, she gave a timid English laugh, and added that of course she realized one could make a fetish of the Scriptures.

She had hired a car early that morning and had driven northward through the Judaean hills to Galilee. The scene with Freddy Hamilton resembled an alcoholic hang-over. On the way, she began to feel a sense of her own identity, and realized that this was in fact what she had begun to lose amongst the answers she had been obliged to devise to the questions of Israelis since her arrival in the country. She recalled that day she had been driven by a guide along the road to Caesarea . . . It was eleven in the morning:

'A half-Jew?'

'Yes.'

'Which half?'

'Through my mother.'

'Then you are a whole Jew. The Jew inherits through the mother by Jewish Law.'

'I know that. But one says half-Jew to mean that one of the parents is a Gentile and the other –'

'But the Jew inherits through the mother. You are then a full Jew by the Law.'

'Yes, but not according to the Gentile parent's law.'

'What was your father's Law?'

That was a question indeed.

'I'm afraid he was a law unto himself,' Barbara had said to this questioner, a large blond Pole. He laughed at that.

She told him of her father in the wild upsurge of his middle age and downfall. 'He broke his neck while fox-hunting. The horse threw him. He landed in a ditch and died instantly.'

'My father died also in a ditch. Shot by the S.S. Why have you made yourself a Catholic to deny your Jewish blood?'

'I don't deny it. I've just been telling you about it.'

'You are brought up as a Gentile or a Jew?'

'Neither. No religion.'

'And your mother's relations and your father's relations, what religion?'

Barbara had felt displaced, she felt her personal identity beginning to escape like smoke from among her bones. 'What a lot of questions,' she said. So they drove along the road to Caesarea through the fertile plain of Sharon, cultivated to the verge of the road on each side. They had found the car to be cooler with windows shut than open to the hot breeze. But not much cooler. 'A lot of questions,' she had said, twice, with the resigned dying-fall of a victim deprived of fresh air and civil rights.

'I ask her a question, she makes a big thing of it that I am Gestapo,' said the guide to some invisible witness.

Barbara said, 'Well, it's hot.'

He said, 'I ask you, because you say you are half-Jew, you say you are a Catholic, and I ask you only what is the religion of your mother's relations and the religion of your father's relations. It is a natural discussion, if you would say to me, who are you, who is your mother, who is your father and how do you come to be an Israeli guide, and I would answer those questions. Then I should ask who are you, what is the family, your brothers and your sisters –'

Barbara thought, 'Who am I?' She felt she had known who she was till this moment. She said, 'I am who I am.' The guide spoke some short Hebrew phrase which, although she did not know the language, quite plainly signified that this didn't get them any further in the discussion. Barbara had already begun to reflect that 'I am who I am' was a bit large seeing it was the answer that Moses got from the burning bush on Mount Sinai when he asked God to describe himself. The Catechism, it was true, stated that man was made in God's image chiefly as to the soul. She decided, therefore, essentially 'I am who I am' was indeed the final definition for her. But the thesis-exponent in Barbara would not leave it at that. They entered Caesarea, home of ancient disputations, while she attempted to acquaint the guide with the Golders Green Jewishness of her mother's relations and the rural Anglicanism of her father's, the Passover gatherings on the one hand and the bell-summoned Evensongs on the other, the talkative intellectuals of the one part and the kennel-keeping blood sportsmen of the other. The Polish Israeli was bewildered. Barbara added that her parents themselves were, of course, exceptional, having broken away from their respective traditions to marry each other. And she herself was of course something else again. The guide persisted in his point: Why had she turned Catholic? If she wanted a religion she was already a Jewess through her mother. Barbara knew then that the essential thing about herself remained unspoken, uncategorized and unlocated. She was agitated, and felt a compelling need to find some definition that would accurately explain herself to this man.

He was demanding a definition. By the long habit of her life, and by temperament, she held as a vital principle that the human mind was bound in duty to continuous acts of definition. Mystery was acceptable to her, but only under the aspect of a crown of thorns. She found no rest in mysterious truths like 'I am who I am'; they were all right for deathbed definitions, when one's mental obligations were at an end. 'I am who I am', yes, ultimately, as a piece of music might be what it is; but then, one wants to analyse the thing. Meantime, she thought, the man wants to know who I am, that is, what category of

person. I should explain to him the Gentile-Jewish situation in the
West, and next, the independence of British education, and the peculiar independence of the Gentile Jew whose very existence occurs
through a nonconforming alliance. And next, the probabilities of the
Catholic claim, she thought. The fierce heat of noon penetrated her
sun-glasses. She thought, later on I must make an attempt to explain:
I'll explain after lunch.

But why? At Caesarea they had looked at the historic ruins and the
recently excavated ramparts of Herod's city; they looked at the pre-
historic Mediterranean Sea and were refreshed by it. The man was
dogmatizing about dates and events at Caesarea, the most important
of which was, to him, the recent moment when excavations by a team
of archaeologists had begun. They ate lunch at an outside table under
an awning. The guide said: 'In Poland the Catholic priests used to
lead the pogroms.'

'Well, they shouldn't have,' she said.

'Why are you Catholic?'

Why? Why did she trouble about these questions? The man was
a hired guide. She was paying for his services. Anywhere else
one would take up a properly resentful attitude. But here in Israel
it was unthinkable; one paid their travel agency, they were hired, but
these facts appeared irrelevant to the relationship. Here on this
territory the Israeli guides were far more autonomous in their attitudes than any French citizen on home ground, or any English
guide in England. The Israelis generally did not merely show one
round, they guided, whether they were official guides or not. It
occurred to Barbara that all in some degree rather resembled the
Irish and the Welsh in their territorial consciousness, and she was
reminded, too, of the games of her childhood where one's own
chalked-out area, once won, contained whatever features one said it
did, neither more nor less. She kept remarking to the guide that the
country was beautiful, since this was easy to say, being true. It duly
pleased him. He said, 'I swam for it,' and explained that he had
arrived as an illegal immigrant on a ship in 1947, and had swum
ashore by night.

She had returned to the hotel after the trip to Caesarea in a state
of exhaustion and nervous panic that reminded her of the sensations she had experienced as a result of anaemia, for a few months,

some years ago. She was now in good physical health; it was spiritual anaemia, she ruthlessly decided, that she was suffering from. Instead of saying goodbye at the door and tipping him like a tourist she acted on a desperate placatory impulse and asked him in for a drink. Then, immediately realizing that she was yielding to a familiar weakness, that of humouring the constitutional tyrant, she now recalled having parked the fellow on Freddy Hamilton, who was reading a newspaper in the quiet green courtyard, and had said she would be back presently. She had taken a long time to come down from her room, and when she did she found the huge guide had begun to expand on the adventures of the past day. Courteous Mr Hamilton had seemed more than merely courteous, he was listening with deep interest. The guide was checking off the fingers of his left hand, one by one, as he said, or nearly sang, 'I gave her Abu Gosh, I gave her Ramle where is Arimathea for the Christians, I have given her Lod as you call Lydda, traditional birthplace of St George –'

'Patron Saint of England,' said pleasant Mr Hamilton.

'Correct. I gave her Haifa, I have given her Mount Carmel –'

'Ah, here's Miss Vaughan,' said Freddy Hamilton. 'Ah, Miss Vaughan, I've been hearing an account – let me . . .' He rose to help her to pull up a chair from another table. The guide continued, on his right hand, 'I gave her the grotto of the Prophet Elijah, I gave her, then, the Persian Gardens and the Temple of the Bahai Faith.'

'Ah yes, I've heard of the Bahai Faith. Very interesting. Very decent people, I hear. Founded after the last war. Money to burn.'

'In this the lady was not interested. She did not wish to visit the Bahai Temple.'

'I think we did enough for one day,' Barbara said.

'A very full day,' said Freddy.

When the Israeli had gone, Freddy said, 'Nice fellow. Seems to know his job.'

'I found him insufferably overbearing.'

'Did you? Oh well, you know, we're foreigners here now. One inclines to forget that. British to them means something different from British to us, I'm afraid.'

Saul Ephraim, to whom she had recounted that day's excursion in

detail, said, 'You seem to be unlucky with our guides. Not surprising. You're British. Well, that's all right, more or less. You're a
Catholic convert – O.K. But you're a half-Jew as well. The three
together are a lot.'

'I should have thought being a half-Jew would be held in mitiga-
tion of the rest.'

'You ought to know better.'

She did know better. The family on her mother's side at Golders
Green, with whom she spent half of the vacations of her youth, had
proved as innocently obtuse about her true identity as had the family
at Bells Sands, Worcestershire, with whom she spent the other half.

Barbara, on the summit of Mount Tabor, conscious of the Holy
Land stretching to its boundaries on every side, reflected wearily
upon her reflections. She thought, my mind is impatient to escape
from its constitution and reach its point somewhere else. But that is
in eternity at the point of transfiguration. In the meantime, what is
to be borne is to be praised. In the meantime, memory circulates like
the bloodstream. May mine circulate well, may it bring dead facts to
life, may it bring health to whatever is to be borne.

At Bells Sands – it was the Easter vacation, just after her sixteenth
birthday – her energetic tennis-playing grandmother, with hair dis-
creetly dyed the colour of steel, sat on the arm of a chair in her white
pleated dress, swinging one of her long sinewy legs, brown summery
legs in good condition; the party was gathered in the dining-room
after tennis; it was tea-time. Her grandmother took a teacup from the
tray offered by the young, round-shouldered parlour maid. Barbara
had been saying she must go and pack. Her cousin Arthur, then at
Sandhurst, later killed in North Africa, was to drive her to the
station.

'Must you go tonight, darling?' said her Vaughan grandmother.
Barbara passed round the cucumber sandwiches. 'Why not go up
with Arthur in the morning? Stay and be comfy.'

'No, I'm expected. It's the Passover. An important festival.'

The warmth of the spring oozed in through the french windows
as if the glass were porous. The silver teapot danced with light and
shade as a breeze stirred the curtains. The air was elusively threaded
with the evidence of unseen hyacinths. So it must have been before

she was born, when the family understood that her father was going
to marry the Jewess, and there was nothing left to say.

'Well, I admire you for it,' said her grandmother.

The young men were eating the cucumber sandwiches two at a
time.

'For what?'

'Your loyalty to your mother's people. But honestly, darling, it isn't
necessary. No one could possibly blame you for skipping it. After all,
you don't look as if you had a drop of Jewish blood. And after all
you're only half. I assure you no one minds.'

'I'm awfully fond of them, you know. I don't feel the least temptation to give them up. Why on earth –?'

'Yes, I know you're fond of them, it's only natural that you should
be. Only I want you to know that I admire you for being so loyal,
darling. I think I'm right in saying that we all of us admire you.'

'Grandmother!' said Barbara's other cousin, Miles. 'Grandmother, shut up.'

'There's nothing to admire, no effort,' Barbara said. 'The
Aaronsons don't call it loyalty when I stay here. They take it for
granted.'

'Well, I should hope so, Barbara dear. This was your father's home
and it's yours, too.'

Barbara perceived that she had courage, this lithe grandmother of
hers. It took courage for her to speak steadily of her son, her
favourite, her disappointment in life, now dead from a fall while
hunting. It had been an indigenous sort of death, but the mother
would have preferred him alive with his unfortunate marriage, all the
same.

'Well, there's time for another set before you change and pack,
Barbara,' said Uncle Eddy, gazing out at the sky as if he could tell the
time by it. The lawn lay beautiful as eternity. A servant was calling
in Eddy's two children from an upper window; presently their high
voices came quarrelling from the shrubbery and faded round the
back of the house. There was a stir in the beech leaves like papers
being gently shuffled into order. The drawing-in of an English afternoon took place, with its fugitive sorrow.

'See here, Barbara,' said her grandfather at Golders Green a few
hours later, 'these are the bitter herbs which signify our affliction in

Egypt. . . .' He enumerated the items on the Seder table, the eggs, the cake, the paschal lamb.

She was familiar with the scene from previous Seder nights, but her grandfather, knowing she had not been formally instructed and had no Hebrew, was careful each year to explain everything. There was always a great deal she was ignorant of, which the other grand-children, her cousins, took for granted. But she recognized the excitement of this Feast when, as a child, she and the other children had sat up late with their elders at the exotic table, every face shining with candlelight, every morsel of food giving a special sensation to her mouth, not only because it tasted different from ordinary food, but because on this night every morsel stood for something else, and was food as well. The children drank wine and deliverance with it. . . . The unleavened bread, crisp *matzho* that made crumbs everywhere, was uncovered. 'This is the poor bread which our fathers ate in the land of Egypt.' Barbara had understood from her fifth year that it was not actually the same wafery substance, here on the table at Golders Green, that had been baked by the Israelites on the first Passover night, and yet, in a mysterious sense, it was: 'This is the bread which our fathers ate . . .'

'This is the night,' said her grandfather, an unageing man, to Barbara, now so conscious of having turned sixteen, 'when we give thanks to God for our ancestors' redemption. He split the sea for us and we passed over on dry land.' She listened, as if she had not heard it before, while her cousins, now grown old, between eighteen and twenty-one years of age, took their places. Like herself, they had been recognizably intellectuals, with an additional bent for music, before they had turned fifteen.

The cousins, undergraduates in philosophy, law and medicine, were gathered in purposeful concentration round the Seder table, where usually, on summer evenings after supper when the table had been cleared, they leaned over the shiny wood surface far into the night, loquacious on the subjects of Nietzsche, Freud, Marx, Mussolini, Hitler, and the war impending. Now they were about to intone in due order the responses on the subject of the Exodus from Egypt into the Promised Land.

A small dark girl of eight was present, a refugee orphan from Germany who had been allotted to this family in the emergency parcelling-out of rescued children in those late nineteen-thirties. Her eyes were wonderful pebbles in the candlelight.

The young men pushed back their skull-caps, for the room was warm with mesmeric ritual as much as with actual heat.

It was only a few months ago, in the Christmas holidays, that Barbara and these alert young men, her cousins on the Jewish side, had reached the conclusion one evening that agnoticism was the only answer, their atheist mentors having erred on the dogmatic side. But here and now they were suddenly children of Israel again, Barbara always included, because, after all, blood was blood, and you inherit from your mother's side.

In former times, Barbara, being the youngest member of the Feast, yet knowing no Hebrew, had repeated after her grandfather the euphonics of the question reserved to the youngest of the company. But tonight the German child was repeating in Hebrew the question:

Why is this night different from all other nights?

It is different, Barbara had thought. The elder Aaronsons hoped she would one day marry a Jew, a doctor or a lawyer, somebody brilliant. They did not believe that her Gentile relations could be particularly well-disposed towards her. As for love, how could you expect it? The elder Aaronsons said, Barbara, bless her, she'll make a nice match in five, six years' time. They felt she would compensate for her intractable mother, who now never came to the family gatherings but only wrote letters from Paris.

Her grandfather intoned joyfully. He was in good voice. The very old Auntie Bea's rings twinkled on her moveless hand as the candles flickered in a little draught. Michael, her closest friend among the cousins, for Barbara's benefit, murmured an English rendering of the versicle liturgy to the accompaniment of his grandfather's deep patriarchal boom, and the young men's gruff responses:

> If He had brought us out of Egypt,
>   and not sent judgement upon them,
>   It would suffice us.
>   If He had sent judgement upon them, and
>   not upon their gods,
>   It would suffice us.

> If He had sent judgement on their gods and
> not killed their first born,
> It would suffice us.

The German child was following the Hebrew in her book with her forefinger, smiling with recognition. Barbara felt proud of the child in a Jewish way, and exchanged a glance to this effect with her young Aunt Sadie, who also glowed as Jewish women do, with approval of intelligent and happy children.

> If He had parted the waters for us, and
> not let us pass through it on dry ground,
> It would suffice us.

The previous Sunday, at Bells Sands, Barbara had gone with Uncle Eddy's two children after church to roll their bright dyed Easter eggs in a dell at the end of their woods, where she and her cousin Arthur had always rolled their eggs as children. Was it only last Sunday? The scene pictured itself without warning in Barbara's mind, light-years away, and rapidly disappeared. Only last Sunday, the end of Lent 1939? She had a sense of temporal displacement. The Passover Feast was coming to an end. She heard the familiar lilt of the riddle song, 'One Kid', from the lips of her lolling cousins. They were supposed to loll. It was part of the ritual. Now, that was a thing her Vaughan grandmother, who complained of backache each Sunday after church, she being one who made a point of sitting up well, would never understand.

Afterwards in the kitchen, the small child helped with the washing-up. Nobody would let Barbara do a thing. All the women were anxious to spare her a job. It was always the same here, at Golders Green. None of her aunts, or even the old servant, would let her wash up. Now, seeing the pile of dishes, Barbara seized a clean dishtowel from a rack where it was hanging.

Her young Aunt Sadie attempted to take the cloth from her in a good-humoured way but very firmly, and vaguely Barbara was aware of a lip-silence among the women working and clattering among the plates and cutlery at the sink.

'Hee-ee, you're not kosher.' This was her youngest Aaronson

cousin, Michael, standing at the doorway of the kitchen, with his owl-like face, horn-rimmed glasses, wide smile, red cheeks and Jewish nose.

His young Aunt Sadie said, 'Michael!'

Michael spread his hands and hunched his shoulders, pretending to be very foreign. 'Vot you vont in my keetchin . . .'

Young Aunt Sadie said to Barbara, 'We use different dishcloths for drying the plates. Milk and meat are kept separate. We don't eat both together, that you know. But we don't wash them up together, either. We keep the towels separate.'

'Vot you expect?' said Michael. 'She is neither Yeed nor Goy ees mein cousin Barbara.' He put his arm round her shoulder. 'She ees a bit milk and meat in the same dish, vot you expect?'

'Stop it, Michael. He's a clown, that boy,' said young Aunt Sadie, busy with the women. They kept pushing him tolerantly out of the way. Barbara, too, felt cheerful about his presence in the kitchen. The younger generation in this household were slightly more indulged than they were at Bells Sands, where all affection was casual, unstated, understood more or less. Barbara, who at Golders Green came in for a share of the unequivocal benevolence towards the young and their capers, their demands, and their wild theories, was automatically soothed by the tolerant atmosphere in the kitchen. But still, she was not permitted to stack the dishes away, lest she stack them in the wrong places.

'We've got special dishes for the Passover. Everything separate. The usual plates and things are not used during the Passover,' said young Aunt Sadie, instructively, to Barbara. Young Aunt Sadie tried to take the place of her mother, who, since her father had broken his neck in a ditch, had married again, this time to a Japanese embassy official, and lived in Paris; she was a very lost limb to the Aaronsons.

Barbara surrendered the washing-up to her relations, feeling her ignorance in these matters to be an abyss of details. She was aware, too, that she would never make an attempt to acquire the missing knowledge; there were too many other things that she had resolved to learn. She looked at Sadie and said resentfully, 'I'll never learn your ways, I'm afraid.'

'Well, you might learn some manners,' said quick-tongued Aunt Sadie.

'Sadie! Sadie! She is, bless her, a child only,' said the very old Auntie Bea.

Michael said, 'And she's been eating ham sandwiches at her tennis party this afternoon. Not kosher, that girl.'

'Cucumber sandwiches,' said Barbara.

Old Auntie Bea, who was always anxious to make the peace, and the syntax of whose utterances was the joy of the younger generation, dried her plump fingers, and nodding her head towards Barbara, said 'Cucumbers! I have made yesterday cucumbers in pickle, twenty. Thirty-six last week in the jars I have with vinegar made, cucumbers.'

At Joppa, then, when Barbara came to be leaning over the sea-wall, she said to Saul Ephraim, who reminded her much of the Aaronson cousins of her youth: 'My Gentile relations tried too hard to forget I was a half-Jew. My Jewish relations couldn't forget I was a half-Gentile. Actually, I didn't let them forget, either way.'

'Quite right. Why should you forget what you are?' said Saul. 'You were right.'

'I know that. But one doesn't altogether know what one is. There's always more to it than Jew, Gentile, half-Jew, half-Gentile. There's the human soul, the individual. Not "Jew, Gentile" as one might say "autumn, winter". Something unique and unrepeatable.'

He smiled as if he had heard it all before.

'Then why did you choose the Gentile side in the end?'

'I didn't choose any side at any time.'

'You became a Catholic.'

'Yes, but I didn't become a Gentile. It wouldn't be possible, entirely, seeing that I'm a half-Jew by natural birth.'

'Well, but look, Christianity's a Gentile religion. It's all the same to me, but it's a question of fact.'

'Not essentially. After all, it started off as a new ordering of the Jewish religion.'

'Well, it's changed a lot since then.'

'Only accidentally. It's still a new order of an older firm.'

'Did you get your Catholic instruction from the Jesuits, by any chance?' he said.

She giggled. 'Yes, in fact I did.'

'I thought so.'

'You can discredit the Jesuits but you can't refute the truth.'

'Well, you can't expect our population to make these distinctions. Catholic is Gentile to them.'

'Perhaps I should hush it up while in Israel, that I'm a half-Jew by birth,' she said.

'You'd be wiser to hush it up when you go over to Jordan. Here, you only risk an argument, but there you might get shot.'

The wall on which she now sat on the summit of Mount Tabor was part of an ancient fortress, the foundations of which lay about five feet on the far side. Looking behind her she could see the weedy floor of this excavated plot. In the self-absorption of the hour, even this small rectangle of archaeology related itself to her life. She recalled the dig at St Albans in Hertfordshire last summer. A Roman villa was being excavated. Her cousin, Miles Vaughan, now married and living at St Albans, took an active interest in the old Roman area of the city and always entertained the archaeologists when they came in the summer to work on the ruins. Barbara was intending to spend only a week with her cousin. She prolonged her stay. She went down to the dig as a volunteer. Miles said one day, 'You're causing a scandal, Barbara – you and Harry Clegg.' He said it in an entirely jocular way, as one might say to a small boy, 'My, you're a big man!' and Barbara was shaken by this. Miles had not for a moment realized how near the truth he had struck. Neither he nor his wife, Kathy, apparently, had noticed how close her friendship with the archaeologist Harry Clegg had grown in the past three weeks. They had simply ignored the evidence. 'You're causing a scandal, Barbara – you and Harry Clegg.' Barbara was stabbed by his tone of voice. It affected her with a shock of self-recognition. She felt as if she had caught sight of a strange face in the mirror, and presently realized that the face was her own. Barbara understood then, that her self-image was at variance with the image she presented to the world. She understood that, to them, she was a settled spinster of thirty-seven, by definition a woman, but sexually-differentiated only by a narrow margin, sharp, clever, set in her ways, a definite spinster, one who had embraced the Catholic Church instead of a husband, one who had taken up relig-ion instead of cats. It was this concept that entitled Miles to tease her.

'You're causing a scandal, Barbara . . .' But Miles, a grown man . . .
he was too innocent for words. She had looked at him. Yes, he was
joking. He gave her a little pat on the shoulder and went out to the
car.

Barbara went and looked at herself in the mirror, full-length, in
her room. Her hair was drawn back tight, her face was thin and
smooth, her blouse and skirt were neat. Everything was quite neat,
prim and unnoticeable. She had not guessed she looked quite like
that, but now that she saw herself almost through the eyes of others,
she was amazed. She wondered if she was a hypocrite; but that
appearance in the glass, she thought, comes of long habit. Having
restrained the expression of my feelings over the years I look as if I
had none. It comes from a long habit of approaching the world with
caution, this appearance of being too cautious to live a life of normal
danger.

The figure in the looking-glass fascinated her. No wonder Miles
did not really know her.

She had thought then, but who am I?

I am who I am.

Yes, but who am I?

Because, in fact, she was already deeply involved in a love-affair
with Harry Clegg, the archaeologist. The local country people had
taken note of them during the first week of their meeting. But her
cousins would never do so. They would simply ignore the evidence.
She looked in the mirror and understood why. And understood why
she attracted the man. It was the very quality that deceived her
friends. It was this deceptive, ascetic, virginal look that Harry found
intriguing. It was not her mind alone, she told herself as she sized up
her appearance.

All the summer weeks of their first meeting she had felt in a state
of complete liberation from guilt. Moral or social censure were
meaningless. The hours and days were barricaded with enchant-
ment. She prolonged her stay on the simple excuse to Miles and
Kathy that she was enjoying it. They accepted this, they were
delighted. She did not mind baby-sitting in the evenings with Harry
Clegg to keep her company. Harry Clegg was a scholar, of course, but
not their type socially; he was a mild joke to them, a small, dark,
scowling creature with too much untidy hair. A scowling creature

except when he smiled. He was brilliant, the Vaughans admitted, a
dedicated scholar. That he was regarded in every informed society
but theirs as a distinguished man, the Vaughans did not know. They
conveyed, with innocent remarks, in their diffident way, their amusement at the points where his lower-class origins were evident. Harry
would never have entered Kathy's drawing-room or Miles's
consciousness, nor would have wanted to do so, had he not been dabbling in the local excavations. Miles and Kathy merrily departed for
dinner parties, leaving the professor baby-sitting with Barbara and
presumably discussing archaeology with her for all he was worth.

But Barbara and Harry Clegg were in the spare bedroom, making
love, just like the nannie and the butler in the absence of master and
mistress in the old days. Sometimes one of the children would wake
and call. Barbara would swear and get up. Just like the old-time
nannie.

Sometimes they settled down in the rough hut on the site of the
excavations, like teenagers stormed by the sensual presences of the
summer night. At any other time Barbara would have thought it ludicrous. A few weeks before she would have thought it absurd. But this
was no time for sophisticated thoughts. She felt herself to be in love
with Harry Clegg in an entirely exclusive form as yet unrealized in
human experience. It made nonsense of the rules. There were no
moral laws to fit it. The form of their love seemed to her to derive from
a faculty of inner knowledge which they both possessed, a passionate
mutual insight so unique in her experience that she felt it to be unique
in human experience. Harry Clegg – shock-haired, unhandsome –
who would have guessed he would be her type? Miles referred to him
as 'the red-brick genius'. But that was to reckon without Harry Clegg,
who loved her. He loved her disguise as an English spinster, not
merely as disguise but as part of her inexplicable identity. She was not
an English spinster merely, but also a half-Jew, and was drawn to the
equivalent quality in him that quite escaped both the unspoken definition 'Englishman of lower-class origin', and the spoken one 'red-brick
genius'.

It happened one day that Barbara's cousin, Michael Aaronson,
came down for the week-end with his wife. He was a recognized
expert in International Law, with a subsidiary interest in a firm of
solicitors who had dealt with the Vaughans' family business for the

past ten years, such being one of the odd and latter results of that Vaughan-Aaronson marriage which had caused so much alarm at the time. Business apart, other Vaughans and Aaronsons of their generation were now on visiting terms, this having happened gradually from some point after the war, when wedding invitations and acceptances had started to flutter between the two families; while Barbara, who was now the only visible link between them, tended to be regarded as something practically invisible by both sides. She now saw them infrequently, her life being centred in the girls' school where she taught. Michael was the only one she corresponded with, he was still her best-friend of the Aaronsons.

He was surprised to find Barbara at St Albans on a long stay. More perceptive than Miles, he noticed her absorption with Harry Clegg.

He said, when he was alone with her, 'Are you getting attached to that archaeologist? He seems keen on you.'

'Yes.'

'Good luck, then.'

'Thank you, Michael.'

'He's a distinguished fellow. Looks terrible. They always attract women, somehow, when they look like that. Are you thinking of marriage? Because if you're going to get married the family won't like it.'

'Which family?'

'Oh, the Vaughans, of course. He's the wrong background.'

'The Aaronsons would have said the wrong blood.'

'Yes, the old people were upset by Spencer's marriage.' Spencer was one of the cousins, who had recently married a Gentile.

'They wouldn't worry about who I married, now,' Barbara said. 'They always knew I wasn't quite the right blood for them. Only half right. The other half was wrong.'

'Oh, well, the old people –'

The Aaronson grandparents were dead, but numerous aunts and uncles had reached their sixties and seventies since the Golders Green days before the war.

'And the Vaughans,' said Barbara cheerfully, 'always knew I hadn't quite the right background. They felt I was too fond of the Aaronsons. My environment was half wrong.'

'Then you've got something in common with Clegg,' Michael said. 'The outcast status.'

'Yes, quite, but we also have common intellectual interests. We've got a lot to talk about.' She had turned sharp and defensive, like Aunt Sadie.

'That sounds more like sense, I'll admit. You're the most sensible woman I know.'

'I'm not. He's a married man.'

'Any chance of a divorce?'

'He's got a divorce,' Barbara said.

'Oh, Christ, yes, you're a Catholic. What are you going to do?'

'I haven't begun to think.'

'Keep me informed,' Michael said, 'when you do begin to think. Anyhow, I'm glad this has happened. I thought you'd given men up.'

'Well, evidently not.'

'I know. Silly of me.'

Down at The Fighting Cocks, the public house that stood on the verge of the Roman area of St Albans, small murmurs passed round concerning the midnight movements of a couple of the current archaeologists (for the patrons thought Barbara was one of the team). 'You're causing a scandal, Barbara – you and Harry Clegg.' Yes, but Miles and his social circle never got to hear of the small scandal at The Fighting Cocks; nobody there knew the archaeologists by name, or cared. The local people grinned as the lovers left the pub. 'Free love on the old Roman road,' commented a man, and it was left at that. Meanwhile, Barbara and Harry walked along the ramparts of Watling Street by moonlight and bedded down in the hut.

A year later, on the summit of Mount Tabor, where the warrior poet, Deborah, once mustered her troops against an enemy of the Lord named Sisera, Barbara turned and gazed out towards the Dead Sea, where her lover now was working on the site of Qumran. She recalled, the day she left St Albans, saying good-bye to Miles, Kathy, and the children. Miles took her to the station, talking of his married plans as married people do – the holiday abroad and the new garage – suspecting her of no other passion than her recent one for botany and no deeper regret than that she had given up playing the cello. She had felt then, how much more of a sexual person she was than he. She could not remember when first she had associated her Jewishness with her sexual instincts and distinguished herself from her Gentile relatives by a half-guilty feeling that she was more afflicted by sex than they were; so that, when she fell in love with Harry Clegg, she felt more blessed by sex than they were, by virtue of her Jewish blood. This basic error with an elusive vapour of truth in it persisted so far as she continued to associate, without even questioning the proposition, her Jewishness with sex, and to feel that she partook of the sexual virility of the world in consequence. Miles had said, as he kissed her on the platform at St Albans, 'It's been lovely having you.'

She smiled at this in the train. She was fond of Miles and his thin, but so innocent, imagination. He would use that correct phrase, 'It's been lovely having you,' to departing visitors on platforms, without variation, till he was too infirm to see people off at all. Kathy, at the door of the house, had said the same thing. Kathy always had a full day, full of social activities and routine. It took this sort of English couple, Barbara thought, to let a love-affair ripen and come to flower under their roof without suspecting anything. They would have been horrified to know about the spare bedroom episodes. Barbara, who on later reflection was herself mildly shocked, was at this moment amused. She was in love. A trite late-flowering. A very late one. She didn't care. She would not have cared if Miles or Kathy had discovered her in the spare bed with Harry Clegg. What could they have said? 'Oh! sorry –' and withdrawn. And later: 'Look here, Barbara –' And what would they have said? That would have depended on the inspiration of the hour. She was merely amused at the notion, when it occurred to her that she had taken some sort of revenge on them, in return for the evening when she had listened to Kathy and Miles, for a few moments, gaily mimicking Harry's Coventry vowels. They were as good as foreigners, herself and Harry Clegg. And they made love like foreigners, which was all right, too.

The train carried her away to London, and all things considered, she decided she would never be able to convey to Miles the exceptional event, her love, that finally justified her abuse of his hospitality. Miles would have been afraid to listen, lest it upset the brotherly arrangement he had come to with his wife.

I know of thy doings, and find thee
neither cold nor hot.

It was after her return, in the new term, to the school where she had been teaching for six years, that her normal process of reasoning set in, and as her love took greater hold of her, so did she take hold of it. There was a deadlock. Their love letters became a vehicle for arguments that gruelled her in the new term and infuriated her, with their revelation of something absolutely undisplaceable in her nature, her Catholic faith.

They wrote the love letters of academic intellectuals, that is to say, they were not much as love letters. Her references to their love were light and frivolous, as if it were something that didn't matter basically but was a mere luxury of civilization. She partly believed this. His were funnily crude. On the question of what was to be done about it she was serious and practical, assembling and setting forth arguments in sober order. The nature of their love-affair underwent a change in the course of this correspondence. Barbara's letters at times resembled essays in theology. She gripped her fountain-pen with tight, tense fingers.

For in the first month of the new term, as she uneasily took up her old teaching life, she felt the relevance to the situation of her being a Catholic. As matters stood, she could not marry a divorced man and remain within the Church, unless his marriage was in fact invalidated by the Church. All this she wrote to Harry Clegg, with supporting theology, in the excessively rational terms employed by people with a secret panic or religious doubt. 'The Church,' she wrote, 'is nothing if not logical. You, above all people, will understand, even if you cannot . . .'

He turned up at the school to see what the hell she was playing at. He, above all people, the third Saturday of term. She was standing at her sitting-room window using it as a looking-glass while she tied a scarf round her head. She was about to go down to the post office to send off a fat envelope, a letter to him, bulging with pregnant hopes and theological debate. She heard a scrape on the gravel as of a wild old motor-car, and saw, beyond her reflection, his quite tame Consul, a shining two-year-old, which he always drove so hard.

She ran down to meet him. She now realized quite clearly that she did not want Ricky to meet him; Ricky had become, over the past six years her closest woman friend. Ricky was Miss Rickward, the head-mistress. They had frequently been abroad together. It had even been suggested by Ricky, and vaguely assented to by Barbara, that they would share a flat together on their retirement. Ricky was forty-two, a knowledgeable spinster. Somehow, at some time, an unspoken agreement had been arrived at, to the effect that they shared the same sense of humour and disregard of men. It was, in a way, understood that when they retired . . . How? Why had all this been understood? At what point in their talkative and confidential relationship had it become a difficult thing for Barbara to speak of a prospective husband, a lover? – leave out the question of a love-affair?

She ran down to meet Harry. They stood on the gravel path and kissed each other. She got into the car and made him drive out of school bounds, miles away, into a woodland clearing in the heart of Gloucestershire.

From her wall on Mount Tabor, she looked over to the kingdom of Jordan, in the hazy blue direction of the Dead Sea, where Harry, in his shabby old clothes, was probably peering at, and pronouncing a fake, a square inch of papyrus placed on a table. 'They've already started to write new Dead Sea Scrolls,' he had told her in a recent letter to England. Here, of course, the only letters she got from him were notes smuggled by friends. But since that Saturday afternoon, they had stopped arguing in their letters. It was he who had recognized the fact that the arguments, however unacceptable, stood for an immovable conviction, something similar to his dedication to his field of scholar-ship. He would not, for the love of Barbara or anyone else, attribute a date which he believed to be false to a manuscript or object of antiq-uity; not to fit any theory dear to his own heart, he wouldn't. He rec-ognized the same seam of hard rock in Barbara. He submitted to her idea of having the validity of his marriage examined by the ecclesias-tical lawyers of Rome. There was a chance that the marriage could be invalidated, although it seemed to him on ludicrous grounds, by the fact that he had not, so far as he knew, been baptized. But he was obliged to prove this negative fact, and it was not so easy as it sounded. And even it was considered slim evidence towards an annulment.

Meanwhile, Barbara, searching her own motives like a murder squad, suspected that her refusal to marry him had been argued less from her fear of separation from the Church than from a fear of revealing to Ricky the existence of a man in her life. How? Why was

Ricky's astonishment to be feared? Ricky's disappointment in her? It was too absurd. It was real.

Barbara dropped hints to Ricky throughout the rest of the year. 'Dr Clegg,' she said, 'a brilliant archaeologist, a friend of mine –' 'Extremely interesting,' said Ricky, 'but I wouldn't,' she said, 'let it become a burden, this letter-writing. A correspondence like this is bound to interfere with your work in term time. Is he handsome?' 'No,' said Barbara, 'not a bit.' 'Perhaps he can't find a woman,' Ricky said, with an expression of genuine academic consideration of the matter. 'Not handsome by vulgar standards,' Barbara said.

Meanwhile she had been reconciled to the Church, in a frigid sort of way, as one might acknowledge, unsmiling, the victor in battle, in whose presence one is signing a peace treaty. She was obliged to repent. What of – the love-affair? No, adultery, to be precise. Yes, but to be precise, it was impossible to distinguish the formal expression of her love from the emotion. 'Go and repent,' said the priest, worn-out with this involved honesty. 'It was a love-affair,' Barbara explained. 'Yes, well, don't pretend it was the Beatific Vision.' Barbara went so far as to repent that she could not repent of the forbidden love-making, and as is the plain expectation of all Christians she got the benefit of the doubt on the understanding that she put an end to the sex part of it.

By summer-time she was standing on Mount Tabor and looked out towards the Dead Sea where Harry Clegg was working. That morning, a letter from him had been thrust under her door, having been smuggled through the Gate in the American embassy-bag from Amman.

Latest bulletin from the Holy Romans – they'll take at least another month to decide. But for goodness' sake, come over. You can't spend your whole summer holidays over there without seeing what's going on here, let alone seeing me. I shall not attempt any of that rotten nasty sex stuff, in fact I wouldn't touch you with a barge pole, if I had one. Hurry up, Barbara, there's some interesting stuff to see here.

She looked towards the Dead Sea and thought of his thick-featured, dark face utterly intent on the work in front of it, and forgot, in her tenderness, that she was a spinster of no fixed identity. She was aware only of the vulnerability peculiar to his detachment, and of a desire to protect him in the practical aspects of his life where he was too absorbed to protect himself. She suddenly felt to be insignificant the business of being a Gentile and a Jewess, both and neither, and that of being a wolf in spinster's clothing, and the business of the letter she would have to write to Ricky. She was thinking of the red-brick genius whose accent her cousin Miles had mimicked with such perfect exaggeration, Harry Clegg, the sweet scholar from an address, now extinguished by the war, in Coventry. He would have been, to her grandmother at Bells Sands, 'a rather common little man' for her to take up with, to her grandfather at Golders Green a non-Jewish disappointment for her to take up with. To the Jews a stumbling-block, a folly to the Greeks. But it did not matter. Even the fact that the academic world recognized his true value and standing was irrelevant. The point was, he was entirely lovable to her, this lover from last summer's Roman remains.

'Go and repent. . . .'

> Goe and catch a falling starre,
> Get with child a mandrake roote.

It is impossible to repent of love. The sin of love does not exist. Over at the Dead Sea, she thought, just over there, he is ferreting about in the sand or maybe he has discovered an inkwell used by the Essene scribes, or something.

To the east, from the top of Tabor, was the valley of Jordan and the very blue waters of Galilee with the mountains of Syria, a different blue, on the far side. On the west, far across Palestine, the Carmel range rose from the Mediterranean. There seemed no mental difficulty about the miracles, here on the spot. They seemed to be very historic and factual, considered from this standpoint. This feeling might be due to the mountain-top sensation. But was it any less valid than the sea-level sensation? Scientifically speaking?

A coach-load of organized pilgrims arrived at the Basilica. Barbara returned to her tree-shadowed wall. They were led by a Catholic priest. One of the Franciscan custodians of the shrine came out to meet them. The priest-guide assembled his flock outside the church and explained to them that this was the place where Christ was trans-figured.

Only probably, said Barbara's mind; there's a rival claim for Mount Hermon, over in the distance.

In the presence of his disciples, Peter, James, and John, said the priest. His garments white and dazzling.

Wherever it did take place, she thought, I believe it did take place all right. Transfigured, and in a radiant time of metamorphosis, was seen white and dazzling, to converse with Moses and Elias.

'Do you remember what he was conversing about?' said the priest to his twenty-odd faithful.

The death he was to die.

'His forthcoming death in Jerusalem,' said the priest. 'It's described in Mark and Luke.'

He read the chapters, while the Franciscan monk waited with folded hands to escort them into the shrine.

> . . . There came a cloud and overshadowed
> them. And they were afraid when they entered
> into the cloud.
> And a voice came out of the cloud, saying,
> 'This is my beloved Son. Hear him.'

'This is also the place,' said the priest, closing his book, 'where Deborah of the Old Testament collected an army against Sisera. You get it in the Book of Judges, and her song of triumph, remember. Mount Tabor is the place mentioned. A good spot, strategically, as you can see. They all camped up here. It's only 843 feet. Looks higher from below.'

The crowd disappeared into the church. Barbara walked out of hiding and breathed the miraculous air. It was after receiving Harry's letter that she had hired the car that morning. Harry was . . . Her mind once more took refuge in the anxious memory of the scene she had made with Freddy Hamilton the previous evening. She duly felt bad about it. People should definitely not quote the Scriptures at one.

If the Ecclesiastical Courts were going to take at least another month to give their verdict on the validity of his marriage, by then she would have returned to school and started a new term. She had almost decided that morning, in the same mental gesture as she had decided to hire a car, not to return to school at all. She must write to Ricky soon. She would write to Michael first.

But why don't I go down to Jerusalem, Barbara thought, and pass through the Mandelbaum Gate? Why is it that I'm not on my way, now, from Jerusalem, across the plains of Sodom and Gomorrah to the Dead Sea? Why don't I go over and see him?

Because I'm a pilgrim to the Holy Land and one shouldn't abuse hospitality.

Because I've got to have time to think.

Because I don't really want to sleep with him in the present state of affairs.

But why don't I go?

Because it's dangerous there for someone of Jewish blood.

But no one could possibly find out.

Barbara had a separate passport issued by the Foreign Office in London, for the purpose of entering Jordan from Israel. She had the required certificate of baptism signed by a priest:

I declare that Miss Barbara Vaughan is a member of the Roman Catholic Church and has been known to me for some years.

No one could possibly guess that I'm a half-Jew.

Then why?

Because I'm a spinster that's taken a religious turn. A Gentile Jewess, neither one thing nor another, caught up in a crackpot mystique. I declare that Miss Barbara Vaughan is a member of the Roman Catholic Church and has been known to me for some years. Life is passing.

Then why do I not go down to the Dead Sea?

Because the time hasn't yet come for me to go down to the Dead Sea. When the time comes, I'll go down to the Dead Sea.

I go on, she thought, with questions and answers in the old Hebraic mode, chanting away to myself.

She thought, then, that it might be a pleasant gesture on her part to ask Freddy Hamilton, as a favour, if he would get a letter across to Harry Clegg in Jordan for her. It would save the delay of sending it by post through Cyprus. Freddy Hamilton was the sort of person who would take it as a good gesture, the asking of a favour.

> I know of thy doings, and find thee
> neither cold nor hot . . .

Well, it makes me hot and cold to think of what I said, she thought. People should definitely not quote the Scriptures at each other.

And she recalled, without reason, that Freddy had said to her only last week, 'Most of the Christian shrines are over in Jordan, of course. You really must go over and meet these friends of mine. They love having visitors, and there's a delightful English atmosphere.'

She smiled cheerfully and got back into her hired car.

3 . A DELIGHTFUL ENGLISH ATMOSPHERE

Freddy was over in Jordan for the week-end. He sat on a wooden bench, writing a letter, in a part of the garden that Joanna Cartwright had planted with numerous wild flowers and herbs of the Holy Land that she picked up on her rambles. Most of them were recognizable to Freddy as belonging to the same botanical tribes as the wild flowers of the English fields and hedgerows of his schooldays before everything had been changed. Indeed, some of Joanna's finds were no different at all, so far as he could see, from those pointed out to him, on walks, before he was sent to school, by that governess whose name Freddy had understandably forgotten. Joanna's flowers were not even a larger species.

Freddy's writing-pad rested on his knee. 'Dearest Ma . . .

. . . but I hope you are not serious. Surely Benny intends to remain with you at Harrogate! Dearest Ma, there must be very little for her to do. I quite fail to see how it *can* be too much for her. The hotel staff seems to do most of the *doing*, and all Benny has to do is *be*. I think, quite honestly, she has too little to occupy her time, and that is mainly what is making her irritable. I wish I could be more helpful, dearest Ma, but you must realize that things have changed and one has to put up with much, nowadays, that would have been unthinkable in the past. Indeed, you are fortunate in having Benny. She would not be easy – perhaps impossible – to replace!

Only a few of Joanna's wild plants were still in bloom. A young Arab boy in his teens, with skinny, deformed legs, wearing only shorts, had come out of the house with a watering-can and was drenching the precious clumps in their dark, shady corner; he had an air of special concentration, plainly having been instructed in the seriousness of the job. A few yards away, on the long green that led to the house, the lawn-spray made a whispering splash under the sun while the Arab's watering-can in Freddy's cool corner splashed intermittently. The small tickets that Joanna had stuck into the ground to mark her plants showed up in their black capital letters under the wash of water. Joanna had categorized them by their place of origin. Partly from familiar memory and partly by his immediate eyesight Freddy could read the tickets from where he sat; Gethsemane, Mount of Olives, Valley of Jehosophat, Siloam, Jericho, Bethlehem.

Last spring, when he had begun to visit the Cartwrights at week-ends, these garden beds had been in full bloom. To Freddy, although he was no botanist, they had always looked very English, set here in the garden above Jerusalem; they looked decidedly different, at all events, from what they had looked all over Palestine in the prolific spring. And now, ambling about in the far associations of his thoughts, Freddy contemplated the neatly printed labels of each clump blossoming under the watering-can, and recalled another bold, amateur-handed script, poker-worked into the wood by his great-aunt herself, and how the letters had started up from her little skew-wired tickets. She had been a wild-flower gatherer who had planted a patch of her garden in clumps, labelled according to country names: Bird's-foot Trefoil, Lady's Finger, Tufted Vetch, Hair Tare, Viper's Bugloss, Forget-me-not, Ling, Small-Flowered Crowfoot. . . .

'I think, dearest Ma –' Freddy's fountain-pen moved like an energetic snail over the letter-pad resting on his knee. He used a broad nib that left a trail of familiar patterns, his words; it was always a matter of filling in a lot of pages for Ma, she liked him to send long letters. The pen scratched noisily against the splash of the watering-can in the hot afternoon, and Freddy functioned on with his letter, as he had done for thirty years of his natural history, a letter a week.

> . . . both try to forget the garnet brooch incident. I shall drop a note to Benny. It is true there was no reason for her to 'blow up' about it. But do remember how touchy Benny has always been. Of course, one should be careful to ascertain the *facts* before one

speaks in haste, although, goodness knows, as you say, Benny has known us long enough, and really ought to exercise a little understanding, as you are good to her. At the same time, dearest Ma, don't *please* go giving away your stuff so readily. I feel Benny is quite well off without 'extras', and indeed, the garnet brooch must have become quite valuable by now. (You say it is *only* a semi-precious stone, but these semi-precious stones in old settings are becoming very rare.) However, I am glad that Benny is recovering her good sense and does not continue to feel aggrieved. As I say, it would be hard to replace Benny in times like these, and to be accused to her face of 'borrowing' the brooch was no doubt, to Benny, a source of . . .

Freddy looked up. I mustn't appear to carp at her, he thought. On the other hand she looked in his letters for a certain amount of response to provocation. In a manner, it kept her going, to have a sort of unreal running bicker with him, serialized into his long weekly letters and her longer weekly replies.

The Arab odd-job boy finished his watering and silently returned to the house. Like that young Hardcastle, Freddy thought. Like Hardcastle, the gardener's boy of Freddy's youth, who had moved back and forth, remotely attending to things, unloquacious, unsmiling, totally unwilling to conspire in Freddy's games. 'Still waters run deep,' Freddy's mother had said, and true enough, young Hardcastle, when he attained the age of fifteen, had disappeared from the job, from the village, from his home, last seen by the bus driver who had borne him away never to be heard of again. Many young Arab boys in Palestine reminded Freddy of Hardcastle. They slightly disturbed him. He preferred the vivacious type in the alley bazaars, arguing, cheating, flashing Arabic code-words at each other in the presence of a stranger, or shouting cheerful abuse at their fellow-youngsters who led the mangy over-laden donkeys up the narrow pathways of Jordan's Jerusalem continually.

Freddy saw the morose boy approach once more from the house. Freddy, in his shaded arbour, wished to break the silence, if only to make concrete his mournful sense of its being ultimately unbreakable. But his Arabic lessons had not progressed so far as to enable him to say, as he desired to do: 'You fellows are lucky being able to stand the sun direct on your skin in the heat of the afternoon. We English have to keep in the shade.' Freddy looked down at the letter and thought he must work round to write something on the question of the Arabic lessons he was taking from Abdul Ramdez, since his mother had replied to his first mere mention of the lessons: 'I hope you are not getting too thick with that Arab teacher. When your Uncle Hamish was stationed in Egypt, *his* Arab teacher was quite scandalous.' Yes, and so was Uncle Hamish.

The odd-job boy had moved the lawn-spray to another part of the lawn, and had returned to the house. Freddy listened for voices; Joanna had evidently not returned, for he heard none.

Usually, on his week-end visits to the Cartwrights, Freddy left his office on the Israeli side of Jerusalem early on Friday afternoon, plodding through the Mandelbaum Gate with his diplomatic pass in one hand and his zipper-bag in the other, always blinking in the glare, since he hated wearing sun-glasses, which made one look so much like a rotten gigolo or spy. He came in the heat of the afternoon so as to reach the cool bungalow sooner. Both Cartwrights were usually out till five, busy with their work. But Freddy would make himself at home. Lemon tea, then a seat in the arbour, writing letters.

'Dearest Ma . . .' Freddy stared at the bungalow to gain thought. It was a slightly crooked house. He had heard that the Arab build-ers simply built a house, they did not use any instruments, not even a set-square. The walls and windows were slightly crooked. But the bungalow had a decidedly English appearance, probably due to the chintz curtains flapping in the breeze, and to the garden that seemed to support it. Joanna's geraniums were marvellous, massed by the back porch. And the lawn really was green. Most of all did he feel at home with the wild-flower clumps. He had, in fact, contributed a few plant roots from the Israeli side of the border, some of which had flourished. Joanna's labels bore witness to Freddy's contribu-tions from the Israeli side: Mount Zion, Galilee, Nazareth, Mount Tabor . . . Bulbous Buttercup, Speedwell, Yellow Cow-wheat, Hound's Tongue. Freddy supposed he was wrong, he knew little about wild flowers, really, but he had a theory that these plants that he had pulled from the soil for Joanna, and those she had gathered for herself, were not indigenous at all. Their seeds had been brought to Palestine and sown, he suspected, by a conspiracy of the English

Spinster under the Mandate. A second cousin of his had done the same service for India, where she had returned after every home leave with a shoe-box full of wild flowers gone to seed. This virgin cousin had expressed the sentiment that when she scattered these flowers abroad in the fields and sidewalks of India, she was doing something to unite East and West. Her father had shouted her down, in his fierce manner, denouncing the practice. 'Never the twain shall meet –' he reminded her, as if the words were Holy Writ. The old brigadier had gone on to tell Cousin Beryl that she was only making a lot of damn difficulties for the botanists; he added – irrelevantly as it had seemed at the time – that he himself had once forbidden an Indian servant to marry a girl from Bhutan, because it would only lead to a damn muddle in the offspring. But every third summer, Cousin Beryl, dressed always in loose, white shantung garments, packed her seed box and bore it away to Lahore. So it must have been, thought Freddy, with the spinster ladies of General Allenby's time out here. He had not yet propounded his theory to Joanna. She would be sceptically interested in it. He was waiting for a moment when it was absolutely necessary for him to say something interesting.

To arrive here, a mile from the outskirts of Jerusalem on the Jordan side, Freddy had jostled his way from the guardhouse at the Mandelbaum Gate, through the Old City's network of alleys, past the Damascus Gate. It had been too hot to take a crowded bus, and not for one moment was he tempted by a taxi. Sometimes Joanna could manage to meet him with her car, but Freddy was just as well pleased when she couldn't. Past the Damascus Gate, towards the Holy Sepulchre and down to the Via Dolorosa, plodded Freddy, dodging the loaded donkeys and stick-wielding boys, who in turn were constantly dodging the vast wide motor-cars that hooted with rage and frustration down the lanes; these cars were filled with hooded Arabs of substance and their emancipated wives. Freddy and numerous tourists had to flatten themselves hastily against a wall or a tangy-breathed donkey whenever the fanfare of a motor horn heralded one of these feudal-minded carloads. At the Via Dolorosa he ran into the huge Friday pilgrimage headed by the praying Franciscans, who moved from station to station, on the route from the Pillar of the Flagellation to Calvary. Freddy, with a number of the English Colony, had followed a much larger procession than this, last Easter, along the Way of the Cross; he had found it religiously moving, but it had exhausted his capacity for any further experience of the sort.

This Friday he dodged down a side-turning into the shop of an Arab dealer called Alexandros, whom he knew, to wait there till the procession had passed. Alexandros had been conducting a business courtship with Freddy for the past five months over an icon that Freddy had his eye on. The dealer was an Orthodox-Catholic from the Lebanon. Most of the Moslem Arab shops were shut on Fridays, and Alexandros therefore did some extra trade on that day of the week. He was serving a tourist, an Englishwoman, when Freddy arrived, but he immediately sent a young assistant out to fetch Freddy some Turkish coffee. Freddy relaxed in the large cool shop and, as he waited for the deal to be done and the coffee to arrive, he thought of the hours to come, on the shady bench in Joanna's garden, getting his letter off – Yes, you are right . . . no, I think you wrong . . . anything you like, dearest Ma. . . . and felt this hot effort to reach the house was worth it by virtue of the cool contrast ahead of him.

Alexandros, whose wares were superior to those of most of the other traders in the area, was attempting to persuade the customer of this fact. She seemed rather stupid and sceptical, as Alexandros implored her credence, using his arms to do so, a little more in the French merchant manner than the Arab. Freddy's feelings expanded towards the salesman and contracted against the woman. Heavy Alexandros, dark, middle-aged, went on to explain that the little wooden crib-figures, for which he was asking five pounds the set, were by no means comparable to the mass-produced figures obtainable from the surrounding shops, on all days but Fridays, for a pound the set or eighteen shillings after the argument. Freddy, newly relaxed after the glare, smells and sticky heat of his plod from the border station, was prompted by a nervous reflex to intervene in the argument, and, much as the timid spinsters of the old days, while abroad, would be moved to violence against the maltreater of the donkey, Freddie now stood up. 'Madam,' he said, to his own astonishment, 'I can vouch for the fact that those articles are what Mr

Alexandros says they are, that is to say, hand-carved from pinewood. This shop, as he says, stocks only superior curios.' He sat down again. His Turkish coffee arrived and was placed before him.

The woman looked at Freddy in a reserved way; she could see that he was at home in the shop. Freddy realized she was more suspicious than ever. His irritation by her doubts of his Alexandros was increased by the fact that this fat Englishwoman was only a passing tourist and he was more or less a resident; and there had been nothing more annoying to Freddy throughout all his postings in the Foreign Service than the sight of his compatriots making mistakes while passing through.

Alexandros, delighted by Freddy's remark, was saying in a tri-umphant wail, 'You hear what this gentleman tells you, Madam. This gentleman is Mr Hamilton, a very high officer of the British Government. He is my customer. He comes to Alexandros regular.'

Freddy murmured, 'Perhaps the lady really wishes to think it over, Alexandros.'

The woman indicated, by picking up her gloves, that she was about to take advantage of this offer. But Alexandros spread out his hands and said, 'Madam, this crib – look at the three Kings, how beautiful, and the camels, they are alive, and Saint Joseph here. The workman-ship. You have it for the sake of your family, Madam. They will say, in the next generation, "This was when the Mama went to the Holy Land! She bought this set for the Epiphany crib!"'

The woman seemed to waver at this. Then she said: 'I'll think it over and let you know in the morning.'

'It is the last. It will go by morning. When the procession is fin-ished the people come in to Alexandros. Alexandros does not close his shop on a Friday, like the Moslems.'

'I'll ask my travel agent here. He advises me what to buy and where to go. Thank you.'

Alexandros followed her to the door. 'Who is the travel agent?'

'Ramdez. I'll ask him.'

Alexandros let her go, then. He came and sat beside Freddy. 'We can have a talk now.' He seemed to have forgotten the woman. Freddy said, 'I mustn't stop. I've got some correspondence to attend to when I get to the Cartwrights'. I expect your customer will come back for that crib-set. It's handsome.'

'Not if she follows advice from Ramdez. Travel agent, yes, he is agent for all the curio-shops, he gets his share from them all. But he is not agent for Alexandros.'

'I know Ramdez,' Freddy said. 'And I know his son Abdul over in Israel, he's teaching me Arabic.'

'The son is political for his living,' said Alexandros quietly.

'Oh, really? I thought young Abdul represented a life-insurance company.'

'Yes, like the father. The father is agent for everything.'

'Ramdez wants me to take out a policy. At least that's what they say that they're after me for.'

'Which Ramdez? The father or the son?'

'Well, both together, actually. They manage to communicate, I don't know how. Anyway, whenever I come over here, old Ramdez turns up with news of Abdul. And when I get back there, Abdul turns up with the latest information from his father. I understand they don't get on very well together.'

Alexandros laughed with Freddy. He took a bunch of keys from his pocket and opened a drawer, from which he took another key. With this he opened a glass cabinet and brought out the icon picture that Freddy admired. Alexandros smiled fondly at the flat, impassive Madonna and Child done in blue and faded gold. Neither man was quite sure of its date. They hoped it was twelfth-century. Freddy was consulting experts and generally looking into the subject in the meantime. 'It isn't normally the sort of thing I go in for,' he said, as he always did. Alexandros replied, 'It is early, not late, this icon.'

'Yes, it's early, but the tradition varies so little, it's difficult even for the experts to judge how early.'

'I see an expert soon,' said Alexandros. 'He is coming from Italy. Next month.'

'It appeals to me in any event,' said Freddy.

'It is yours. I keep it for you.' The dealer put it back in the glass case and locked the door.

'I can't afford it,' Freddy said.

'It's not a question of what you can afford. It is a question that you take home something from the Holy Land that is worth taking home.' Alexandros started packing the crib-figures into a small box

padded with cotton wool. 'I am taking these to the lady at her hotel.
I see her this evening.'

'Why bother to go after her, Alexandros, for goodness' sake?'
Freddy said. 'It's only a fiver.' Alexandros was a substantial dealer.

'I make a sale,' Alexandros said.

Freddy lifted his zipper-bag. 'I'll look in some time tomorrow,
perhaps.'

'I make a sale to the lady,' Alexandros said, and anxious to explain
himself more clearly, he added, 'Why do you walk all the way from
the Mandelbaum Gate to the Bungalow Cartwright? – Mr Hamilton,
a Chevrolet with driver is ten shillings only for this journey.'

'I never take taxis and I never hire cars,' Freddy stated, 'not if I
can help it. My father never did.'

'So I never let slip a tourist customer. So I go to the hotel after
dinner and bargain with the lady and she gets the fine crib-set for
four-fifteen, four-ten. It is my upbringing.'

'How do you know her hotel?' Freddy said.

Alexandros thought this question too amusing to need an answer.
He said good-bye to Freddy in the French of the Lebanon, and
Freddy responded, in his French of the Home Counties, to the effect
that he, also, had been very greatly enchanted.

The hot walk from the Gate was well worth it, Freddy thought, if
only because of the relief one felt when one turned in the familiar
doorway of the bungalow. On the last lap of his walk, uphill, he was
tempted to start composing a set of verses to send on his return to
Israel, thanking Joanna for the week-end which had not yet come to
pass. A villanelle perhaps . . . It is so very different here / In modern
Israel from your / Delightful English atmosphere . . . Freddy realized he was cheating. The bread-and-butter verses could not in
honesty be started until he had actually set foot on the other side of
the Mandelbaum Gate on Sunday afternoon. He put temptation
behind him and plodded up the hill to the week-end before him.

The bungalow was set in a clump of trees not far from a steeper
hill that led to a tumbledown Orthodox church and the Potter's
Field, where some way off, lived a marvellously feeble old monk,
much liked by Freddy, and whose eyes alone seemed to keep his
brittle limbs alive in one body, so spiritually did they burn in his

skull. Freddy caught sight of the monk's blue robe moving up there among the shrubbery as the old man came out to feed his chickens; whereupon Freddy had felt at home already, and had plodded the few steps onward to the silent bungalow, the garden bench awaiting him beside Joanna's wild-flower arrangement, and the letter-pad on his knee. 'Dearest Ma . . .'

You see, dearest Ma, the trouble is . . .

The trouble, in fact, was . . . Freddy's thoughts dropped to a whisper in his brain. JERICHO, MOUNT OF OLIVES, GETHSEMANE. Hair Tare, Tufted Vetch, Hawk-bit, Corn Bluebottle. The trouble, in fact, was . . . Freddy's thoughts whispered on, refusing to be shouted down by any other voice that might arise in his brain to hush them up. The trouble was that Ma was a peculiar type of tyrant-liar whose lies could only with difficulty be denounced because of her long-sustained tyranny, and whose tyranny could hardly now be overthrown because of her long-condoned lies. It was not only these days in her old age, but by very constitution, that Ma was like this. Consequently, it had taken most of their lifetime for her four children to realize that they were part of an unspoklen conspiracy to concede that Ma's falsehoods were truth. It was curious how, to this day, none of her children – although Freddy's three sisters were married women – had it in them to look any of the others in the eye and suggest that dearest Ma was not really a very nice person, let alone to aver that she had cheated them all quite openly, as if by divine right, of various inheritances, denouncing the two sons-in-law as her enemies merely on the basis of their rational questioning.

Freddy pondered his letter, with its hypocritical advice. 'At the same time, dearest Ma, don't *please* go giving away your stuff so readily . . .' It was the best Freddy could do, at this late stage in his career as Ma's son. Knowing Ma, it was doubtful whether the garnet brooch belonged to Ma in the first place. It had probably been coaxed from some other, more feeble, resident in the hotel, or even stolen from Benny, and then handed over, or handed back, at some point, to Benny. At all events, it would be a confusing affair, that being Ma's way of operating. The whole idea, anyway, was that Benny should be accused of something . . . SILOAM, JERICHO, Clary or Wild Sage.

The young Arab boy had been in the garden again, and had now slipped like a lantern-slide into the house, leaving the picture as before. Ma was seventy-nine, of course, one should make allowances for that. Nonsense, Ma had always done this sort of thing. Benny would be nearly seventy, now. Poor Benny. Poor Benny, she, too, was far involved in the family secret. It was like a blood-pact. She had started to respond to Ma's moral blackmail long years ago when she was Freddy's nurse, and now Benny, a religious crackpot at the best of times, fully accepted that she was always suspect, always liable to crafty dealings, invariably in the wrong. Freddy thought, for a wistful moment, that he might in normal circumstances write to one of his elder sisters, Elsie: 'Do see what new trick Ma's up to. Apparently, she's bullying Benny about a brooch.' That is alliterative, noted Freddy, in his panic to note something. Because it was impossible to write to his sister as if circumstances were normal. She would only reply: 'Whatever do you mean by your reference to dearest Ma's new trick? Benny has been very irritable lately, I believe. She has too little to occupy her time, and dearest Ma can't be expected to . . .' They were all in it together, and it was too late. He bent over his letter, to fill in a harmless page about the housing situation in Israel.

You see, dearest Ma, the trouble is . . .

The trouble was, she should have been an actress, as she had wanted to be in her youth. She might have worked off her self-dramatizing energies in that way.

> The trouble is, that the Israelis have not nearly enough houses for their own people, let alone for foreigners. The days of grand mansions are over, and the Consulates and Embassies all over the world, I'm afraid, are . . .

Joanna and Matt Cartwright had arrived, their voices came from the house, mingled with other voices and many footsteps. Joanna came out, waving to Freddy. She was a vitamin capsule to Freddy, who carried small red vitamin capsules about with him to swallow after meals taken outside the British Isles. The sight of little Joanna shooting across the lawn in her red linen dress raised Freddy's spirits.

Matt was still a dark shape in the shadow of the doorway, beyond the porch. He emerged, another comforting sight. Matt was a large man, without being tall; he was perpetually untidy, with a lot of grey hair. He was bringing some other people out to the garden whom Freddy did not see at first, since he had risen to greet Joanna and was kissing her. She said: 'We've brought a friend of yours in for a drink,' and she added, casting up helpless eyes and mouthing her words silently, 'and – we – had to – bring – his – awful – wife – and – daughters – as – well.' And here they were, already coming up. As Joanna turned to them brightly, Freddy recognized the elder blue-eyed Ramdez, who was accompanied by a dumpy middle-aged woman and two girls, one plump and one thin, all in European clothes. Matt Cartwright went to help with the setting out of garden chairs. A servant moved the tables to their cool corner. Freddy moved his letter-pad from the bench and the thin girl settled there beside him. Joanna was amiably introducing everybody.

Freddy, his letter-pad useless in his hand, sat suffering indistinctly. His heart, that had lifted at the sight of Joanna, had become suddenly heavy at the sight of old Ramdez thumping after her with his women. He experienced the sensation of one who has had a disturbing dream, the culmination of which was the ringing of a telephone, and wakes with relief to discover the telephone is in fact ringing beside his bed, and answers it, only to hear disturbing news. For old Ramdez, the wealthy Arab whom everyone called 'the Agent', since his business interests covered a travel agency, a life-insurance agency, a detective agency (and no doubt he was a political agent, too) – old Joe Ramdez had already impressed himself on Freddy as a terrifying liar.

Freddy had first encountered him because of the son, young Abdul, over in Israel, who came to teach him Arabic and every time remained to press him to take out a life-insurance policy. This policy, which was now some months pending, was a subject of conflict within Freddy. The Middle East Visitors' Union Life Trust was the name of the company represented by young Abdul Ramdez in Israel and by old Joe Ramdez on the Jordan side. Freddy was in very serious doubt about the standing, the existence even, of this insurance company, a policy in which, according to Abdul, would lead to the payment of five thousand pounds on Freddy's death.

'But I haven't got anyone to leave five thousand pounds to,' Freddy had said. 'I haven't got a wife.'

'You got children?'

'No.'

'You got nephews or a nice lady? You got a friend, you definitely got a friend.'

'I can't think of any relative or friend of mine,' Freddy said, 'who isn't far richer than me.'

This was precisely the truth. But he liked young Ramdez, the eager boy, and was good-humoured. This had been early in the spring, shortly after Freddy's posting to Israel.

Young Abdul said, 'You go to see my father, Joe Ramdez, when you go across to Jordan. My father's the leader of the Middle East Visitors' Union Life Trust agency in Palestine. I work for him. This is a confidence to you alone.'

'You'll get yourself into trouble,' Freddy said. Business connexions between Israel and Jordan were illegal in both countries.

'I will now explain to you the endowment scheme for the Visitors' Union that will bring you a lump sum at the age of sixty-five and you save your British income-tax with the premiums that you pay each month. It is a scheme for Englishmen. You must first join the Visitors' Union itself which my father has formed of his own idea. You see him in Jordan, he will explain. We work together.'

'He'll land in trouble with his government for dealing with an Israeli Arab, even his own son. There was a case of a melon dealer the other day –'

'My father's never in trouble with the government. He's a friend always to the government. You see Joe Ramdez.'

Freddy had folded away his Arabic lesson-books. 'Be careful,' he said to the blue-eyed, dark young man. 'You won't be able to carry on this insurance business for long without the Israelis finding out.'

'There's nothing for them to find out, Mr Hamilton. I keep all the names and records in my head. My father keeps the documents, like what you will sign.'

This had been early in April. Presently, the name of Joe Ramdez had cropped up in Freddy's office. He was apparently the owner of a travel and tourist agency in Jordan. 'God knows what he's up to,' Freddy's colleague said, 'not that it concerns us much.'

'I'll have a look at him,' Freddy said. 'One likes to know who's who.' He filed a confidential report about the insurance business carried on between young Abdul and his father. He reflected wearily on the difficulty of making any real friends among the inhabitants of countries where one was posted. He had only taken three lessons in Arabic from young Abdul at that time. Freddy decided to discontinue the lessons with Abdul. He made up his mind to appoint a new teacher. A pity, because Abdul was a pleasant fellow in his eager recklessness. Freddy had felt he could understand Abdul. But after all one could never understand these people. This young man was involved in too many things for Freddy's liking.

'Arabic's a terrible bore,' Freddy said to his colleague.

'Frightful. I don't see the point in learning it, really. At least, not unless one is going to stay here for ever.'

'Young Ramdez is all right,' Freddy said, 'but he seems to be involved in too many things for my liking. Life insurance. Terribly persistent about a policy. I'm getting another teacher.' As he spoke, Freddy felt greatly relieved to have arrived at this decision, he even felt a satisfactory sense of having accomplished the object of it.

And so it was not necessary, after that, actually to get rid of Abdul Ramdez by discontinuing the lessons in Arabic. And, after all, Abdul continued to call at the hotel three times a week to instruct Freddy, who had progressed sufficiently to be able to exchange formal phrases with Arab officials at official gatherings, but not as yet advanced enough to make much headway with the Arabs in the Arab quarters. Young Abdul spent one hour on each of the lessons, and lingered, usually, another hour to depict himself and his early life in romantically exaggerated scenes which delighted Freddy but did not altogether deceive him. Abdul had also boringly continued to press Freddy on the question of the insurance policy, each time exaggerating the mild interest Freddy had expressed on the previous occasion.

'As you have said you have definitely decided –'

'No, no, I haven't decided anything. I only said . . .'

It seemed that the tendency to exaggerate ran in the family. But what one could take from an attractive young fellow like Abdul in Israel was a different matter when it came to the preposterous Joe Ramdez over here in Jordan. Freddy had sat in Joanna's garden, appalled and altogether beset by an inarticulate dread while Ramdez approached, followed by his womenfolk.

'It's a question of sincerity,' Joanna said in her quick, chattery voice, as she passed the teacups. She was interrupting her husband to assist him in making the point of his story. Matt Cartwright, accustomed to these interruptions, went on in his slow way to describe a qualm occasioned by his having newly got false teeth. He was explaining in detail that, when a spontaneous smile occurred on his face in response to his usual feelings, something now happened in his mouth to prevent the smile taking the same form as it used to do.

'They don't fit yet,' Joanna said. 'He's got to be patient with them, till they settle down.'

Matt went on his slow way. This story was to be their standby for some months to come. He said, 'Then, when I find myself giving a slightly different sort of smile, d'you see, so help me God, I find myself feeling a slightly different sort of emotion. I feel a bit false.'

'He feels a bit false,' Joanna chattered, 'and it makes you wonder what sincerity is. I mean to say it's a question whether the movements of one's facial muscles are adapted to one's feelings or the feelings to – Mrs Ramdez, don't you have anything *in* your tomato juice?'

Matt fell silent. Joe Ramdez beamed at Freddy, uninhibited by any relation between his feelings and his facial expression. The Arab family all declined alcoholic drinks. The younger daughter had a haunted look. The elder girl was, like her mother, fat and stupid-looking, but the younger daughter was like her brother Abdul, lean and blue-eyed, and she looked haunted. There is a history, Freddy thought, behind that blue-eyed young pair.

Freddy had seen the mother and girls before. They worked in the travel agency. Joe Ramdez had introduced them as 'my little team'.

Joe Ramdez now said to Freddy, 'It's better to smile without the heart behind it than not to smile at all.'

'Oh, he won't agree with that – not Freddy,' said Joanna, while Freddy realized he was looking as depressed as he felt.

'Have my wild flowers been watered this afternoon?' Joanna said. 'Freddy, did you see them being watered at all?'

'I did,' Freddy said, as if it was a duty he had performed; he longed for that earlier departed hour in the afternoon before this crowd had appeared.

He said, 'I always feel this garden has such a delightful English atmosphere.'

The younger girl looked apprehensive. The father smiled with a curious histrionic glitter of the eye, by which many modern Arabs intended to express proud loathing; they had got the trick from the cinema, over the years. At any rate, Freddy realized he had said the wrong thing.

Not that Joe Ramdez really cared one way or another. Freddy was aware, however, that Joe had taken the opportunity of umbrage to put him in the wrong. Freddy said, 'I only mean, of course, that these wild flowers of Joanna's are nothing more or less than English wild flowers, planted in the countryside by silly women during the Mandate.'

'Freddy!' said Joanna.

'Early tomorrow morning,' said the wounded Arab, 'I'm taking my little team on a trip to Amman. It's our only chance before the tourist season, of really getting into our delightful Jordanian atmosphere.'

The younger girl looked desperately at Freddy. Evidently she was longing to behave in a Westernized mode to suit her clothes, and, no doubt, her feelings. There was no guessing the variety of feelings amongst the very young in these parts.

'So we must go now,' said Joe. His little team got up with him. He said to Freddy, 'By the way, I've got to send you a medical form and proposal form. A boy will bring it. I know the doctor whom you can go to. He's good for deferred endowments even when appearance is unhealthy. I had a client last week that went to Dr Russeifa with his form. Appearance was older than age given. There was impairment of sight and hearing. Pupillary and patellar reflexes were abnormal. Plenty of abdominal varicosities – well, Dr Russeifa has told me all this trouble, but he fixed the client's medical. Russeifa will make you all right. I'll make the arrangement.'

When they had gone, Joanna said to her husband, 'Did you hear what he said about Russeifa? I don't believe a word of it. Russeifa's one of the most conscientious men in the medical team.' They were both deep in local welfare work and were in a position to know what they were talking about.

'Ramdez is a liar,' Freddy said, 'the biggest I've ever met. Like an alcoholic. He lies as he breathes.'

'Well, Freddy . . .' said Joanna. She was relaxing on the bench with her drink, relieved at the departure of the Ramdez guests, and now she seemed uncertain how to chatter on, since it was unusual for Freddy to denounce anyone like this.

'They think in symbols,' Matt said.

'That's it,' said Joanna. 'It's the Arab mentality. They think in symbols. Everything stands for something else. And when they speak in symbols it sounds like lies.'

'It is lies,' said Freddy.

'Oh, Freddy, come! Why are you taking out this insurance policy with Ramdez, dear? It's asking for trouble.'

'I'm not taking out any policy,' Freddy said. 'His son, who teaches me Arabic over in Israel, has been trying to talk me into it, but I've made no definite decision.'

'You should have said definitely no,' Matt said. 'If you don't say no, they take it you mean yes. That's symbolic thought.'

'Not to me,' Freddy said.

'Is young Ramdez a nice fellow?' Joanna said.

'A remarkably pleasant young man.'

'Freddy, you mustn't let him get round you for any insurance policy out here.'

'I don't think they're really interested in insurance, anyway,' Freddy said.

'Nor do I,' said Matt.

'Nor do I,' said Joanna.

'They're interested in you, Freddy,' Matt said.

'You're a symbol, Freddy.'

'Yes, but of what?'

'Something useful in the Foreign Service —'

'God help me,' Freddy said, 'I thought that's what I really am.'

'What did you mean by saying that my wild flowers of the Holy Land are English flowers?'

Freddy felt the moment was not ripe to explain his theory to Joanna. Indeed, it might undermine her at this tired moment, which was the last thing . . . He said instead, 'Miss Vaughan, the school-teacher lady, is very pleased with the geraniums you sent, very touched, you know. I believe she's coming over next week. As I say, she's a bit tense, but you'll do her good, Joanna dear.'

'Oh, do you know,' Joanna said, 'I was talking to Joe Ramdez about Miss Vaughan. He's promised to send one of his drivers to the Gate to pick her up. Isn't it nice of him? Now really, you must admit that's good of him. If one of the Ramdez men is there to meet her she won't have any trouble with the officials.'

'Is he doing it for free?' Matt said.

'Oh yes, and he'll lay on a guide and everything to take her round.'

'He must have a reason,' Matt said.

'We are the reason,' Joanna said.

She was darting between her husband's chair and Freddy's seat on the bench, in her red dress, collecting their empty glasses and handing them back filled with good strong drinks. 'Joe Ramdez,' she said, 'would do anything for us.'

'You didn't,' said Matt, 'tell Ramdez that this woman had Jewish blood?'

'Of course not,' Joanna said. 'I only told him there might be trouble with her visa, seeing that it's unusual for Christian pilgrims to go to the Israel side first.'

'They mustn't know anything about her Jewish blood,' Matt said. 'She'd be in trouble. We'd all be in trouble. The government here is looking for a bit of trouble with the Jews at the moment.'

'She's only half,' Freddy said.

'Half is enough,' Matt said. 'They think in symbols over here. The Jewish half is the symbolic half.'

'Which half is the most important to her?' Joanna said.

'Don't ask me. Miss Vaughan's only a recent acquaintance, you know. Very pleasant woman, of course. And with a British passport. After all, she —'

'Most of the people arrested as Israeli spies have got British passports,' Matt said. 'She'd be taken for an Israeli spy if they knew of any Jewish blood or background and arrived here by way of Israel. Does she realize that?'

'I really don't know,' Freddy said. 'Is that true? It sounds quite absurd.'

Joanna, in her inexhaustible enthusiasm for seeing to the welfare of others, said, 'Freddy, you aren't taking Miss Vaughan's difficulty seriously enough.'

'I don't see what can be done, Joanna dear,' said Freddy, so deeply conscious of his fault that he leant forward and rested his chin on his hand to try and be serious about Miss Vaughan's difficulty. 'She's a devout R.C. and she naturally wants to visit all the shrines of the Holy Land. There's really no difficulty.'

'What about the man?' Matt said.

'Yes, what about the man?' Joanna said.

Matt said, 'I take it that's the whole point of her coming here.'

'Oh no, she wants to visit the holy places.'

'I'll take her up to the Potter's Field,' Joanna said. 'The guides won't go near the Potter's Field, they're terrified.'

'You keep away from the Potter's Field,' Matt said.

'I shouldn't go there too often, Joanna,' Freddy said. The hill road to the Potter's Field bordered on disputed territory, and wanderers in the area were likely to be shot at by the patrolmen of either country.

Matt said, 'This man that's digging at the Dead Sea – why doesn't he come up and look after her? He should go across to Israel and see her, instead of her coming here to see him.'

'The scholars aren't allowed to go back and forth. The Jordanian government won't allow it,' Freddy said. 'Of course, the Israeli scholars get to know everything in time.'

'He could leave Jordan by air and enter Israel by sea. He could easily get there if he wanted to,' Matt said.

'Well, she wants to come here for religious reasons.'

'Let her come,' Joanna said.

Then Freddy, dismayed by a disastrous thought that had occurred to him, but proud since it proved he was taking Miss Vaughan's difficulty seriously, said, 'But look, young Ramdez over in Israel probably knows about her Jewish blood.'

'Are you sure?' Joanna said.

'Well, she's been talking about it. Young Ramdez hears everything about everyone,' Freddy said. 'It's part of his business.'

'If young Ramdez knows, then old Ramdez will know,' Matt said. 'And what he knows the government get to know. Tell her not to come.'

They moved indoors since it had fallen dark. At dinner, Joanna said to Freddy, 'You could make difficulties in Israel for young

Ramdez, couldn't you, if he made difficulties for your Miss
Vaughan?'

'Joanna!' said Matt.

'Well, I was only thinking in symbols. What would the Israelis do
to him, Freddy, if they knew he spied for the Jordanians? Shoot him?
Put him in prison?'

'Mislead him,' Freddy said.

'You could threaten him,' Joanna said.

'Joanna!' said Matt.

'I'm thinking in symbols. I'm thinking of Freddy's poor Miss
Vaughan.'

'She isn't really, you know, *my* Miss Vaughan,' Freddy said. 'She's
only –'

'Now Freddy, you know you're involved whether you like it or –'

'Joanna!' said Matt. 'Stop teasing Freddy.'

'A very intense person,' Freddy said.

'Who? Me or Miss –?'

'*Joanna!*'

. . . at my friends the Cartwrights. Then after dinner this evening
we had some amusement from Joanna Cartwright's puppet
theatre. (Do you recall, dearest Ma, that house in Lewes we used
to visit, where they had some very grand puppets? – Joanna's
puppets are not quite so grand.) She is extremely agile at managing
their movements. There is also an extraordinary series of gramophone records which, by clever timing, accompany the puppets'
movements perfectly. They seem to speak.

By the way earlier in the evening we were discussing Miss
Vaughan about whom I have already told you – she is staying at my
hotel. She may be coming over to Jordan, but much depends on
whether we can assist her to resolve some difficulties that have
arisen over her entry into the country. I think this will interest you,
dearest Ma, since you inquire in your letter about 'a teacher at
Miss Rickward's school in Gloucestershire, very near Elsie's'. –
Yes, that *is* Miss Vaughan! – Remember you asked me this question before. Benny will remember, I'm sure. I am glad to hear Elsie
brought Miss Rickward to see you. She is decidedly the same Miss
Rickward who is a close friend of Miss Vaughan out here. You

were right in assuming that Miss Vaughan's fiancé is an archaeologist who is working at present in the Dead Sea area where the
Scrolls were discovered. Apparently there is some hitch about the
proposed marriage, since he is divorced and she is R.C. Of course,
it is quite absurd, in my opinion, when a couple of grown-up
people . . .

Freddy had filled most of the pages he had to fill, and it was time
for bed.

At eleven o'clock on Saturday morning Freddy took Joanna and Matt
to Alexandros's shop to show them the icon. Joanna, sitting at the
back of the car with quantities of shopping, waved to everyone whom
she recognized, including Joe Ramdez, who stood in the street
outside his business premises, wearing a red fez, talking to another
Arab.

'He hasn't set off for Amman yet,' Freddy said.

'They're going to Amman in the symbolic sense,' said Matt.

'He's waiting to pounce on Miss Vaughan,' Joanna said, for the
subject of Miss Vaughan and her difficulties had by now taken a fantastic turn among them, from so much talking it over. First thing in
the morning Joanna had declared she had thought about Miss
Vaughan far into the night. She regretted talking to Ramdez about
Miss Vaughan's impending visit. But she was used to dealing with
other people's predicaments, even when she had helped to induce
them, and in fact could not easily adapt herself to the idea that
anyone outside her immediate acquaintance had no problems to be
sorted out. Her imagination clung to the intricate danger attached to
Miss Vaughan's story, and she had managed, in the course of the
morning, by batting the shuttlecock of Miss Vaughan's name back
and forth between herself and the two men, to infect even them with
a kind of irrational excitement over the ways and means by which
Miss Vaughan could be trapped by her Jewish blood, could be
arrested as an Israeli spy far beyond the assistance of the British
Foreign Office, on her arrival in Jordan.

Freddy had begun to feel a little frightened. He certainly did not
want to be involved in an international incident. And for Miss
Vaughan's own sake, he really must, he had decided, somehow

prevent her from visiting Jordan. He had a strange difficulty now, in remembering what she looked like; he had in his mind only the outline of a frail, sharp, nervy, dark woman, fearfully indiscreet.

Matt himself said to Freddy, as they drove into the Old City: 'Can't you do something at the office to prevent her from coming over – take away her passport, or something?'

'Oh, no,' Freddy said. 'Anyway, she's nothing to do with us.' He did not like the sound of his words as they were the sort of words that always, to the outsider, suggested Pontius Pilate washing his hands of a potential source of embarrassment; none the less, Freddy felt sympathy for Pontius Pilate, a government officer, and for all those subordinates of Pilate who, like himself, no doubt, had been officially dim, dutiful, and absolutely against intervention between individuals and their doom. Freddy said, 'If she gets into trouble we can make a protest afterwards.' His reflections had been unusual in the form they had taken, and he felt they were quite absurd; it was only because Matt had now parked the car and they were emerging from it to face the narrow Via Dolorosa within sight of the Ecce Homo Arch, the place from where, by erroneous tradition, Pontius Pilate had addressed the crowd. The real Judgement Palace of Pilate had newly been excavated, and was some yards distant from the Via Dolorosa, and some feet deeper. Miss Vaughan herself, of course, was the sort of person who somehow induced one to think in terms of religion if one thought about her at all.

Most of the way to Alexandros's shop Joanna kept referring with genuine concern to Miss Vaughan's predicament, hushing her voice considerably in due acknowledgement that any mention of Jewish blood was inflammatory in these parts. The Arabs generally, when they were obliged to talk about Jews, did not permit themselves to utter the word Jew; instead, they quaintly spoke of 'ex-Jews' and of Israel as 'Israel, so-called'.

Matt said, 'It could happen by accident,' in reply to Joanna's inquiry as to what means of execution was used against Israeli spies.

'It could happen by accident.' Freddy believed the liquidation of spies and suspects had nearly always taken place, as it were, by accident, unless there was some political reason for holding a trial. And now Freddy was grateful for the company of his friends. Joanna's serious sense of Miss Vaughan's impending danger and Matt's urgent appeals to Freddy as to what should be done, gave him a sense of being with responsible people, whose safe conduct he could rely on. For it had begun to gnaw at Freddy's mind that, for all he knew, Miss Vaughan might be an Israeli spy; he knew nothing of Miss Vaughan's identity but what she had told him. Of course, he could not mention this suspicion to the Cartwrights; he would have to make official inquiries first.

At Alexandros's shop, the first person Freddy saw was Barbara Vaughan. She said, 'Oh, hallo, Mr Hamilton.' He stared at her stupidly, as if at a complete stranger. Then, just as she began to look puzzled Freddy pulled himself together and said, 'Miss Vaughan! What are you doing here?'

'I'm looking at some stuff,' she said. The crib-figures, which Alexandros had evidently failed to sell to his customer of yesterday, were spread about on the glass top of a display cabinet. Alexandros said, 'This lady likes the crib. She knows it's good. Mr Hamilton, tell your friend to take this crib and not let it go.' And he said to Barbara Vaughan, 'It is for the family – they will say in the future, "This crib was when the Mama went to the Holy Land," and that is why you should take it.'

Barbara Vaughan laughed. Joanna had murmured to Freddy, 'Is that her?' and Freddy had nodded. He introduced Miss Vaughan to the Cartwrights. She looked plumper than the image he had held in his mind, and it was part of the unexpectedness of the encounter that he noticed she spoke in a natural tone pitch and moved without furtiveness or strain.

Freddy had recovered his senses so far as to remember what he had brought the Cartwrights here for. They, in their well-mannered way, gave no indication that Miss Vaughan had been the subject of their speculations all morning and most of the night before. Everyone looked at, and admired, the icon. Barbara Vaughan gave out, as a guess, that it was done in the early sixteenth century, not earlier, because the Madonna was not done full length. She thought it unlikely that any departure from the formal Byzantine mode, such as this half-figure depiction of the Madonna, would have occurred at an earlier date.

Plainly, the jeopardized Miss Vaughan they had been discussing was a different person from the Miss Vaughan who stood, pointing

out, in an ordinary English way, her judgement of the date of a painting, and who then listened with untroubled interest while
Alexandros debated the question, citing a few rare icons of an earlier
date that had passed through his hands.

In the end, Miss Vaughan declined the crib, but bought an antique
silver fish on a chain, which she put round her neck there and then.
Joanna, who had immediately adapted herself to the real Miss
Vaughan, expressed admiration, Matt aiso added some words of
approval. Alexandros explained that the fish, to which three small
curious coins were attached, was of Turkish origin. 'It's a Christian
symbol,' said Miss Vaughan. 'That is correct,' Alexandros said, 'and
the coins are Turkish charms, attached by the Turkish convert in
case Christianity should not be true. He was fully covered, as they
say in regard to policies for the insurance of life.'

They left the shop in a united wavelet of amusement, and Freddy
said immediately to Miss Vaughan, 'When did you come?'

'Yesterday,' she said.

'How did you come?'

'Through the Mandelbaum Gate.'

'Any difficulty? Speak low.'

'No. I've got an extra passport, you know, that doesn't show the
Israeli visa. And my baptismal certificate. A guard came and met me
and said, "Welcome to Jordan!"'

'Did they ask any questions? Speak low.'

'Yes, they asked where I'd come from. It was awfully funny,
because they could see perfectly well where I'd come from. But as
long as you don't mention Israel, it's all right. The formal answer in
my case is "From England", and that's what I said. Then they asked
what I'd come for. I said, a pilgrimage to the Holy Land. They had
a look at my passport and said, "Enjoy your visit". That was all.'

'Well, well,' said Freddy.

'Jolly good,' said Matt.

'Where are you staying?' Joanna said. They had started winding
up the narrow crowded street, Joanna walking ahead with Barbara
and the two men more or less behind them.

'The guest-house at St Helena's Convent. It's quite comfortable.'

'You'll be safe there,' Joanna said.

'Oh goodness, yes. I'm the safe type.'

Joanna laughed, and Matt, who had taken both women by the arm to guide them through the crowds, laughed too. The Cartwrights responded to any excuse for laughter. Freddy felt very relieved. The whole question of Miss Vaughan was suddenly normal, as if it had never been otherwise.

They took her home to lunch, treating her as rather more than a new acquaintance, not only because she was Freddy's friend, but because one always did, in foreign parts, become friendly with one's fellow-countrymen more quickly than one did at home.

They had coffee brought out into the garden after lunch. As swiftly as water finds its own level, they had already formed a small island of mutual Englishness; their intimacy had ripened under the alien sun to the extent that the two women were addressing each other by their first names; and when Joanna said to Barbara Vaughan, 'I expect you're looking forward to seeing your fiancé again?' it was possible for Barbara to reply in a confiding manner which, at home, ought to have taken some years to mature: 'Well, d'you know, I don't at all want to see him. I've been waiting and waiting to hear about an annulment verdict from Rome – for as a Catholic I can't marry him unless his previous marriage is anulled. Then I've been in a state of conflict for weeks, whether or not to come over to Jordan and see him. One way and another, my emotions are exhausted. I simply don't feel anything for him any more. In fact, I've gone off him.'

'It's perfectly understandable in the circumstances,' Joanna said in her practised way, 'that you should go numb. But it's only temporary. Your feelings will come back.'

Freddy found himself hoping not. This Miss Vaughan who claimed so emphatically to have gone off her fiancé was decidedly more agreeable and relaxed than the febrile Miss Vaughan in love.

'He's probably the wrong chap for you,' he said in an avuncular manner which came easily to him at that moment, seeing that Miss Vaughan had just declared herself unattached.

Matt, anxious to take some sort of possession too, said, 'Get him up to Jerusalem. Bring him along here. Maybe we can sort things out.'

Barbara smiled. 'But I've gone off him,' she said. She seemed to be amused at herself in a sophisticated way, and was pretty-looking as she leaned back in the garden chair, holding her coffee cup.

'Who is the fellow, anyway?' Freddy said. He knew the man's name, Harry Clegg, and also that he was a distinguished archaeologist.

Barbara said, 'Harry Clegg's his name. He's well known in archaeology.'

'I've heard of Clegg,' Matt said.

'Yes, but who are the Cleggs?' Freddy said. 'That's all I mean.'

Joanna said, 'Freddy, if you're trying to undermine him with Barbara, she'll get her feelings back, and go and marry him tomorrow. That's what I'd do.'

Freddy said apologetically to Barbara, 'I only wondered if you knew anything much about his family.'

'Well, he doesn't seem to know much, himself, about the family,' Barbara said, 'and he doesn't care. He can't even trace his birth certificate. Really, he's a charming person; it's only that I don't feel –'

'Good God!' Freddy said. 'You should be careful who you take up with.'

An Arab servant had appeared with a fresh pot of coffee, and they kept silence until he had receded like a wave of the sea that had lapped against the garden wall. Barbara got up, meanwhile, to examine the labels on Joanna's wild flowers of the Holy Land, and to deflect attention from herself, as the social moment offered and required.

'*Cotyledon*,' Barbara murmured, examining a plant which grew about ten inches high. It was not in flower, but it had, near its base, a group of curious circular leaves, sunk in their centres, like flowers themselves. Freddy had frequently tried to place this plant from memory, for he had seen it before. It stood in the clump marked Bethlehem. 'I got it on a hillside near the Shepherds' Field,' Joanna said. 'I daresay the same plant has been growing there since the time of Christ. What's the name of it, did you say?'

'It's called pennywort, commonly. The botanical name is *Cotyledon umbilicus*. I wonder how it got to this country.'

Joanna took this in good part. 'I thought it was indigenous,' she said.

'It's possible,' said Barbara. But she did not sound convinced. She said, 'I'd have to look it up.'

'Some sort of flowers must have been blooming here at the time of Christ,' Joanna said. 'They can't all be British imports.'

'That's true.'

'I had a cousin used to take wild-flower seeds to India and scatter them there,' Freddy said.

Barbara said, 'I do that from time to time when I go abroad. To tell the truth, I smuggled a few *Anthyllis* seeds – that's Lady's Fingers – into Israel and scattered them on Mount Carmel on the sea verge. They grow well by the sea. Lovely yellow flowers. It was wildly against the regulations, but I couldn't resist it. I never can. It's a habit.'

Freddy felt happy, and was struck by the thought that Miss Vaughan was remarkably well informed. He felt it proper that she should have scattered Lady's Fingers in some corner of a foreign field.

'You could have been arrested by the Israelis,' Matt said. 'They're extremely strict about what goes into their soil.'

Barbara got ready to leave. She said she had an appointment with a guide.

'Which guide?'

'I went to a travel agent called Ramdez. They've got –'

'You mustn't use Ramdez,' Freddy said.

'Don't take on a guide,' Matt said. 'We'll take you round. Don't waste your money.'

'I've engaged one, though. This afternoon he's going to take me to see what he calls "the tomb of Solomon, son of David, the ex-Jewish king".'

Joanna said, 'Matt will go and pay him off. Stay and look at my puppets instead, then when it's cool we'll go for a drive round.'

'You see, you mustn't,' Matt said quietly, 'go round here alone. It's a question of your Jewish blood.'

'Nobody will know anything about my Jewish blood unless you talk about it.'

Freddy said, 'Actually we've discussed your position in Jordan quite a bit. Because, you see, it's more dangerous for you here than I thought it was. I intended to beg you not to come. Anyone with Jewish blood is automatically arrested as an Israeli spy.'

'My passport's all right,' Barbara said. 'I'd call for the British consul if there was any trouble.'

Their island was beginning to disintegrate. Having said his piece, Freddy felt, in reality, that Miss Vaughan was not in such danger as she had seemed to be in their imagination. Here she stood, calmly, in flesh and blood. As for her being, in fact, a spy . . .

'I think it would be a bit unfair,' Joanna said, 'to involve the British consulate in an incident of that kind.'

'Why?' said Freddy. Perhaps it was the heat, or his age – he could not fathom it afterwards, although he had no regrets – but Freddy felt much the same irate urge to declare something at this moment as he had felt the day before in the shop when the woman customer was being tiresome with Alexandros. 'Why, Joanna?' he said. 'Why shouldn't she appeal to the consulate in the event of her being molested in a foreign country?'

'It's so much a matter between Arabs and Jews,' Joanna said. 'We can't officially take sides, can we?'

'It's a blood-feud between Semites,' Matt said, 'that's all it is.'

Joanna said, reproachfully, as if both men were at fault, 'I'm sure this must be a very embarrassing conversation for Barbara.'

'It doesn't seem to be about me,' Barbara said. 'You are talking about a situation that's outside the scope of the consulate.'

'Won't you sit down, Barbara, while we're talking?' Joanna said. 'What I mean,' she said to Freddy, 'is that Barbara's Jewish blood is outside official range in a sense.'

'Jewish blood or not,' Freddy said, 'the point is, it's hers, and it has got to be protected by her country.'

'Yes, well, to get back to the individual case,' Matt said, 'we know Ramdez. He's a snooper for his government. He probably knows already about the Jewish part of Barbara's origins, through his son in Israel.'

'The son is a hostage, then,' Barbara said.

'Now I think that's a bit unfair,' Matt said.

'There is too much talk,' Barbara said. 'Everything would be easy if people didn't talk so much.'

'Why is it unfair?' Freddy said to Matt. 'I think it's a very good point, that Ramdez can't very well move against Miss Vaughan while his son is in Israel. Young Abdul is a hostage.'

'Because, mad as it sounds, Jewish blood is illegal here. I – Joanna and I – we think it's a lunatic situation. But it seems a bit unfair of Barbara to tempt the law and risk involving a young Arab in Israel.'

'The trouble with you,' Freddy said, fully conscious and rather astonished that he was wrecking the delightful atmosphere, 'is that you blow neither hot nor cold, but lukewarm – What was that passage in the Bible, Miss Vaughan? Can you recall it? – It goes something like, you blow neither hot nor cold and I will spew thee out of my mouth. Something like that. Very apt.'

4. ABDUL'S ORANGE GROVES

'I'm a man of passions and enthusiasms, Mr Hamilton,' said young Abdul Ramdez. 'That is to say, I'm passionate in general, but I don't get worked up about any particular thing for long. In this way I avoid the great Arab mistake, as we have obsessions that leave us exhausted and incapable of action when the time for action comes. Do you know what I say to my Arab friends and also to the friends of my father when they tell me too much, do this, do that, Abdul, in the name of freedom, revenge, unity? I say, okay, okay. But do you know what I say when they ask me again, too much? Do you know what I say then to freedom and revenge, and to Nasser and to Hussein and to the national spirit? Like I've told you before, I –'

'Yes, yes,' said Hamilton, who was plainly enchanted, 'but don't say it here, Abdul. There are some terms we English don't use a great deal of.'

'In childhood I hear many terms by the English army,' Abdul said.

'Well, of course, the army.'

'Is it me teach you Arabic or you teach me English?' Abdul inquired.

Abdul took for granted the fact that he enchanted Frederick Hamilton, because he enchanted everyone, even those who were suspicious of him, except for the high-minded Israelis and Arabs who disapproved of anyone like him on principle, or the police forces of both allegiances. He observed the man who sat in the other arm-chair in this hotel sitting-room. 'Say me some poetry,' Abdul said.

Mr Hamilton sat a little more upright in his chair and recited across the space between them, lit as it was by sunlight dustily filtered through the mosquito-wire window:

> As I ride, as I ride,
> With a full heart for my guide,

So its tide rocks my side,
As I ride, as I ride,
That, as I were double-eyed,
He, in whom our Tribes confide,
Is descried, ways untried
As I ride, as I ride.

Abdul was amused by this. Earlier in the afternoon he had been going over with Hamilton the rudiments of Arabic versification, which, as Abdul put it, had been handed down unchanged from the eighth century: '. . . only we could begin to make changes now like we could make changes in government, and later on we could change the desert wastes and the sky even, if we could first make changes in ourselves.'

Hamilton more or less belonged, in Abdul's view, to that total category of the human race known to Abdul and his companions as the System. It included their fathers, the Pope, President Nasser, King Hussein, Mr Ben-Gurion, the Grand Mufti, the Patriarch of Jerusalem, the English sovereign, the civil servants and upper militia throughout the world and all the other representatives of the police forces of life who, however beneficent, had absent-mindedly put his generation as a whole in difficulties. Abdul spoke often of his 'generation'. As he was a good deal older than he claimed to be, he meant by this to measure his state of mind rather than his years. He had come early to the conclusion that the easiest method of dealing with the situation, and the one that best suited his personal constitution, was to act with inscrutable folly, to mix up his elders as to his motives, to defeat and exasperate them by transparent guile and hypocrisy, to have no motives at all, but to be enchanting throughout his days. It was not a lonely course, he had many like-minded friends. It had been found and declared by an analytical witchcraftsman that Abdul's character contained intelligence among other ingredients, he knew largely what he was doing. He had reflected upon himself as an Arab, and decided upon a course. His friend, Frederick Hamilton, who sat with Abdul in the sitting-room of his hotel in Israel, was part of the System. Nevertheless, Abdul liked him, as he was easy to manage and did not make demands for his full money's worth of Arabic lessons, but rather seemed pleased to sit and talk in English

to Abdul, at his appointed hours, for himself alone. In a way, it
seemed to Abdul, Hamilton was not aware that he was part of the
System.

'Say that poem again.'

As I ride, as I ride –

'It is a fine poem, Mr Hamilton,' Abdul said when Hamilton had
finished.

'It isn't considered to be so. But it's interesting because there are
forty lines with the same rhyme. It's by Browning, a famous
Victorian poet.'

'I have seen "The Barretts of Wimpole Street" about Robert
Browning. It was popular with the Arabs as we have many stories in
Arabic like that, where the father forbids the marriage to the daugh-
ter and the lovers escape.'

Mr Hamilton looked at his Arab grammar and said, 'I suppose we
should get on with our work.'

Abdul did not see any need to reply for a moment or two. He was
smelling the room and Mr Hamilton. There were Miss Vaughan's
geraniums, now, in addition to those which Hamilton had always had.
Abdul could never smell anything from Hamilton himself, which was
just as typical of the man as certain odours were typical of other
people. Abdul's father had always deplored his son's highly developed sense of smell from his youth up. Joe Ramdez had considered
it to be an atavistic trait in Abdul, and thought it was uncivilized of
him to cultivate this habit of smelling people in rooms. Abdul
claimed that he could 'smell an enemy', but his father discovered that
Abdul's enemies were not his enemies, and denied Abdul's claim to
any smelling talent in this direction.

'You could try the next exercises on page fifty-three,' Abdul said
to scentless Mr Hamilton. But he smelt again, and suddenly, holding
up his index finger, said 'Oh!'

'What's the matter?' said the Englishman, looking up from page
fifty-three.

'I smell your new suit, the fabric.'

'No, it's an old suit.' Mr Hamilton opened the jacket and squinted
inside the inside pocket. '1934,' he said. 'It's marked 1934, so that

means I've had it for twenty-seven years. It's older than you, Abdul.'

'It smells,' Abdul said, groping for the association of the smell, not remotely reflecting that he was, in fact, older than the suit.

'I've had it in moth-balls during the summer. I've just got it out as the nights seem to be getting chilly.'

'I like moth-ball scent,' Abdul said. 'When I served at the altar in Cairo, the Coptic priests smelled of moth-balls as they kept moth-balls among their fine resplendent vestments.'

'I thought you belonged to the Armenian Church.'

'No, the Coptic Church.' Abdul did not see any need to explain why, a few weeks ago, he had given Hamilton a long account of how he had broken with the Moslem faith to run away with an Armenian girl, to further the wooing of whom he had adopted Armenian Christianity. He did not see any need to refrain from so enjoyably muddling up his friend and he continued to talk of the Coptic Church in Egypt: 'You see, my father sent me to school in Cairo when he saw that I was too far advanced for any of the schools in Palestine. Many of my friends were sent to school in Beirut but I was sent to Cairo, where I was baptized a Christian in the Coptic Church.'

'What I am not sure about –' said Mr Hamilton. He was flicking through the notebook on which he had been writing his Arabic exercises for four months since April last.

It occurred to Abdul that Hamilton was not well. He had already perceived this when he had come into the room, but had immediately veiled the idea from his thoughts, since Hamilton had behaved normally, had said, 'Well, Abdul, how are you?', had got up, smiled in his usual way and sat down, partly distrustful, as usual, and partly enchanted. In the meantime Abdul had sat down, too, and then started to talk about himself, so that the sense of Mr Hamilton's being not well had passed from him. Abdul noticed now that the man's hair was not combed well, as it usually was. Otherwise, he looked the same.

'What I'm uncertain about,' said Hamilton, flicking through his notebook, 'is whether I'm getting anywhere. It took me a month to learn the Arabic characters. By the end of May I could read and write "The house is small," "The king is angry with the doctor" and "Is the bride ready? No!"'

Abdul laughed and Hamilton smiled eagerly, as if surprised at the success of what he had said.

'"News about the experiments reached the upright princes yesterday,"' said Hamilton, reading aloud from the textbook. 'That was last month. Since then I've done "Mohammed (may God pray for him!) was a good man," "Your speech was delightful but you did not mention the blood which flowed in the Arabs' battles" and so on.' Abdul laughed again, which Hamilton seemed to appreciate. 'But I never have occasion to use phrases like that,' said Hamilton, putting on a sad air; 'I ought to learn some vocubulary and understand what the Arabs around me are saying, and talk to them, perhaps.'

Abdul said, 'The Arabic for the street you learn later, Mr Hamilton. I'm laughing at these exercises as you read them in English, as you make them sound like poetry that means much. Read some more.'

Hamilton said, 'What does it mean, that phrase "May God pray for him!"? Do the Moslems ask God to pray? Who does God pray to?'

'It's only a saying,' Abdul said, 'of the elderly people. They say "May God pray for him and save him!" all day, as they speak of their dead relations all the day long.'

He was watching the Englishman to see how unwell he was, and in what precise way he was afflicted. Hamilton read another exercise: '"The students of Damascus University have arrived in Cairo for an important meeting with their Egyptian brethren." Of course,' he said, 'it isn't true to say I've made no progress, but I can't say that I'm learning enough to mix with ordinary Arabs. I don't want to master the language like a scholar, I only want to be able to make myself understood while I'm out here, during the next few years. Now I managed to pick up enough Hungarian to get along with when I was posted to Hungary, and I did that by means of conversational lessons rather than schoolroom stuff, and I'm wondering if our best plan isn't to adopt that method, and –'

'You wish to spy among the Arabs of Israel to report their pro-Israel activities in Jordan,' stated Abdul, 'or else you report them to the Israelis for anti-Israel talk.'

Hamilton said, 'Good gracious me!'

Abdul said, 'I don't think you are a spy.'

'I should hope not,' the man replied.

'Then you shouldn't entertain suspicions of me.'

'Why, Abdul! Why, of course I simply never –'

'I'm difficult for you to understand,' Abdul said. 'And we should be turning to page fifty-four.'

Hamilton translated, 'Despite what the unbelievers say, the righteous are under the protection of Allah.'

'It's boring,' Abdul said. 'We should make our own exercises, and you could talk better with the Arabs in the street.'

'Entirely what I've been thinking,' said Hamilton. He looked so unwell that Abdul wanted to give him some kindness or make him laugh as one would do a sick child.

'Let us try, for the next lesson, before we come on to particles and conjunctions, some exercises with new words in them. Bad words.'

This sort of suggestion usually cheered Hamilton up although he always refused to let Abdul go further than that. Once, Hamilton had said, 'Where did you learn English?'

'Some from my father, some from my mother, but most from a beautiful English schoolmistress that I had when I was fifteen. Her father was a colonel in the British army.'

Mr Hamilton had said, 'Did she plant English wild-flower seeds in the countryside, by any chance?'

'I don't know,' Abdul said. 'But I planted Arab wild-flower seeds in her. She was my first woman.'

Hamilton had said, 'Now, now, now,' but nebulously smiling meanwhile, as if at some reflection of his own which Abdul could not share. Hamilton had then seemed to realize with sudden alarm that Abdul's words had been uttered in the presence of the geraniums, for he looked at them in a guilty way and said, 'I ought not really to permit such things to be said about an English girl.' But Hamilton was not making any big issue out of it and seemed to be cheered up, on the whole.

'Bad words,' Abdul now said. Hamilton smiled faintly. Plainly, he was not well. Abdul was neither glad nor sorry, partly because he had become unaccustomed to having any emotions during the hours of daylight. For that, he needed his company of friends at Acre, and some dancing with a little howling maybe, with the long chants going on in the background.

In the meantime he said with a giggle. 'Bad words next week. You could throw away your grammar book if it bores you.'

'I don't want bad words,' said Hamilton, looking round the room in a disorganized way. 'What I must do, obviously, is master a larger vocabulary.'

'True,' said Abdul. 'Take a set of conversational sentences, then, like for instance, "I am an honest man, but you are a deceiver." "Why do you call me a deceiver?" "Because you have promised me to take out a life-insurance policy through my father's agency, and you have said to your English friends in Jordan that you do not intend to do so." "How do you know of this?" "Because the servants of your English friends are spies for my father." Of course,' Abdul said, 'this group of sentences would be better expressed in conversational Arabic, but you might as well try to put them together in the formal style.'

Hamilton said, 'I have not promised to take out any life-insurance policy.' But his voice was tired.

'My father,' said Abdul, 'sends messages to me at risk to his life to persevere with you about the policy. So I fulfil a pious duty to my father, and finish. I do not care personally about insurance policies, they're crazy things.'

Hamilton's head rested on the back of his chair, since he was slumped low in it this afternoon, not, as usual, sitting alertly. He let his head rest back, as if about to close his eyes which, however, remained half-open, focused on Abdul between their lids.

Abdul sat in silence, experiencing the torpor and boredom of afternoon life, much as he had very often done in the presence of his elders during his childhood. It seemed reasonable, after a while, to suppose that Mr Hamilton had fallen into a kind of doze, for although his eyes were not entirely closed, his breathing became more rhythmical and loud, as one in sleep. Abdul's eyes slid to the round table beside him, where Hamilton had been writing letters. Two were sealed in envelopes, ready stamped for posting, they lay one on top of another at an angle, the top envelope concealing the address on the lower. The top envelope was addressed to Professor M. S. Dexter, All Souls College, Oxford, England. Beside these sealed envelopes lay some pages of unfinished letters which Abdul had already noticed in a contributory way to his sense of Hamilton's being out of sorts; usually Hamilton was a man who finished doing one thing before starting another.

The man was now nearly asleep. Abdul sat in a deliberate, breath-held stillness, looking at his Englishman. He found himself wondering if Hamilton was going to die, tomorrow or next week, or now, his soul wafting away from him, preserved in a faint moth-ball atmosphere. Abdul turned his head silently so that he could read, by squinting obliquely, the nearest of the three unfinished pages on the table, evidently a continuation on the back of the first sheet.

have just written to a friend at All Souls, a Fellow, to tell him I've discovered a rhyme for 'Capricorn'. My friend, Sam Dexter, probably knows more about rhyme than anyone in the country, although of course, his subject's Old French. Goodness knows what he'll think of this rhyme for 'Capricorn' – I saw it in an American picture magazine, in an advertisement for a breakfast food called 'Apricorn'. (I understand Apricorn is, as its name implies, a kind of packed cereal food flavoured, by some process, with apricot essence.) Whether Dexter will allow 'Apricorn' as a *word* at all, I very much doubt.

But you see, dearest Joanna, I must keep my mind occupied with something. To be suddenly confronted with a doctor's order of two weeks' rest is not, in itself, conducive to peace of mind. As you say, I could have gone to Greece. But I'm unused to moving about without previous plans. I could think of nothing to do on the spur of the moment but wait here. Besides, there is always a chance that if any news of Miss Vaughan should reach us I may be of some assistance. Until the mystery of her disappearance has been cleared up, one is bound to experience some anxiety, merely from having recently been acquainted with her, however little actual connexion one has had with the person. The newspapers seem to have dropped it in the last few days, I expect by special compliance with the investigating authorities and our Embassy in Amman – I have had no further trouble from the reporters, as I trust you have not. I expect at least some news will emerge before long. One must hope for the best but it is impossible not to fear the worst.

I have been making every attempt to regain my powers of concentration even to the extent of attempting (in vain, alas!) a verse or two in *terza rima* to say some pleasant things to you, dearest Joanna, who have been so good since my stupid collapse. To lose one's entire memory, even for a couple of days, is disconcerting to reflect upon *afterwards*. One's confidence is greatly undermined. I still have no recollections of how those two days passed. I am advised against mental effort for the time being but of course, it is impossible to resist attempting to solve the mystery. I must have slept – I must have shaved, and so on. When I got to the hotel I felt tired and hot as usual after my walk from the Mandelbaum Gate on Sunday afternoons. But it was Tuesday, and they had been looking for me. I am convinced that I had an attack of sunstroke and it must have affected my memory. But where did I sleep? Where is Barbara Vaughan? Please, by the way, thank Matt for his note. But I do *not* think I would wish to consult the psychiatrist although I am sure, as Matt says, he is brilliant. Psychiatry is too abstract for me to take up at my age, I'm afraid. When I go to a doctor I like to come away with a bottle of medicine or some pills, or a prescription to be made up. However, the suggestion has

The letter had been left off half-way down the second page. Abdul looked over to Hamilton, who had now fully closed his eyes in sleep. He began to read again, carefully, the first part of the letter only – 'Apricorn' . . . 'Capricorn'. . . . He dwelt on the glamour of the name 'All Souls' which he knew to be that of an Oxford college. For he was less interested in the rest of the letter and the evident personal crisis that had occurred to Hamilton than he was fascinated by the entire vision of that state of heart in which one wrote to a Fellow of All Souls about a rhyme for Capricorn. It could not result in any large benefit to Hamilton or his friends, nor could this piece of information damage Hamilton's enemies. It was disinterested and therefore beautiful, even if it was useless to the immediate world. And this was something Abdul could never make his middle class Arab acquaintance understand – how it was possible to do things for their own sake, not only possible but sometimes necessary for the affirmation of one's personal identity. The ideal reposed in their religion, but somewhere in the long trail of Islam, the knack of disinterestedness had been lost, and with it a large portion of the joy of life. His father would never accept that Hamilton's activities were as meaningless as they looked. What is his motive? Is it political? Why does he write those verses to send to the Cartwright house? Are they in code? Why does he spend so much time in Jordan? Have you found out why he is learning Arabic? Have you read any of his private correspondence? Has he agreed to take out a policy yet, will he come to see me and complete the form? Why does he want to know street Arabic? Why does he stay on at a hotel, this Hamilton? This Hamilton, why does he walk everywhere instead of taking a taxi? There must be a reason, everything means something. Is it political? Does he practise a vice? But me, Abdul thought – if my father, cousins, uncles, had any knowledge about me, it would be the same thing. Have you joined the nationalists then? Are you in with the Sufis? Have you turned in with the Jews, after all, like the Sheik of the Negev? What do you do at Acre? What have you done, did you do, are doing, might, will do at Acre with those youths of mixed blood, mixed sexes, those young Jewesses, those Arabs, those Jews, those Arab girls, those Yemenites, Syrians, those Israelites, Samaritans, those boys, girls, boys. . . . Are you a nationalist?

'Nationalist of what, Father? What territory, what people?'

'I don't understand you. Don't forget you're an Arab. Are you a monarchist?'

'Which monarch do you refer to, Father?'

Such conversations were few, for Abdul's meetings with Joe Ramdez, on the other side of the Gate, were arranged with dangerous difficulty. Abdul felt now, as he frequently did, a sense of being mentally closer to Hamilton than to his own father. Even so, that was not saying much, for Abdul's affinities with his own generation, and within that category, with the secret mixed-blood conclaves at Acre, placed on him and his companions the necessity of a double life; the gulf that separated him both from Hamilton and his father was wide; it was deeper and darker than had usually existed between generations. Perhaps not since the times of the Prophet . . .

Hamilton was stirring in his chair.

'Are you asleep, Mr Hamilton?' Abdul said softly.

Hamilton settled his head back again and breathed deeply.

'Are you awake, Mr Hamilton?' Abdul said.

The brief twilight had fallen and was fading into night. Abdul felt tenderly towards Hamilton. He squinted to see if he could read the other unfinished scrap of a letter that was lying on the table, but it was too far away. He reached out his arm and picked it up.

> . . . is not, dearest Ma, and cannot possibly be, the person whom you went to hear playing the piano (or the violin – in your next paragraph you refer to 'this famous German who played the violin' but first you have mentioned *piano*) at Auntie Bella's before the Great War. The Eichmann who is on trial here in Jerusalem is an inferior sort of person with no connexions whatsoever. I believe his antecedents are quite obscure. I do not think he plays the piano or the violin. You must be thinking of some other German. The Germans are a musical nation, of course, and so it is conceivable that this fellow used to play the fiddle, as indeed used Nero, you remember.

Hamilton stirred, with opening eyes. 'Poems,' he mused. 'Poems.'

Abdul the letter still in his hand, said, 'Speak more of those lines, Mr Hamilton, the rider's song. "As I ride, as I ride."'

'You know, Abdul,' said Hamilton, who had now fully woken up, 'it is wrong to read other people's letters.' But he did not seem much concerned on this point, and while Abdul returned the sheet of paper to the table, Hamilton recited, keeping time with his right hand:

> Could I loose what Fate has tied,
> Ere I pried, she should hide
> (As I ride, as I ride)
> All that's meant me – satisfied
> When the Prophet and the Bride
> Stops veins I'd have subside
> As I ride, as I ride!

'I don't know in my head what it means,' Abdul said, 'but it means something in the blood-veins.'

'Yes, a little something. You know, Abdul, I think I've had a touch of sunstroke. But I must pull myself together. I have been advised to rest. But I begin to think I would be better advised to occupy my mind with something difficult. I want to take Hebrew lessons. Do you know Dr Saul Ephraim of the Hebrew University? He was a

friend of poor Miss Vaughan – have I told you that Miss Vaughan
has disappeared, over in Jordan? We are very anxious about her. Well,
I must get in touch with Ephraim. Do you know him?'

'I know his youngest brother better. I know him well, Mendel
Ephraim. The brother Saul has no dealings with him, though. He's
out of the family.'

'Really? What does he do?'

'He's a smuggler. This is a secret that I am passing on to you for
your spy records. He smuggles leather goods, shoes and so on, across
the border by night. I trust you with a secret, Mr Hamilton. I am in
smuggling with him also.'

'Oh, Abdul, I don't know where I stand with you. Now, before you
go, there is something I very much want to ask you. It's important
and serious, Abdul, and I want a serious answer if you can give it.'

'Why didn't you ask before?' Abdul said.

'Because it's important, you see, and I don't want you to treat my
question frivolously. I want to impress on you the seriousness –'

'You are asking me what has happened to Miss Vaughan?'

'Yes. Do you know?'

'No, but I'll find out.'

At Acre, the stronghold of the Crusaders on the Mediterranean, west
of Galilee, the fortifications stand in golden ruins, piled on the
foundations of earlier ruins. It seemed to Abdul Ramdez that the
laborious construction of ruins had been the principal means by
which the forebears of the whole human race, stretching back into
history, had passed the time of day. Arabs lived in the shelter of the
eighteenth-century ruined fortresses, and even now in the years of
the establishment of Israel, burning with its mixture of religion,
hygiene and applied sociology, the poor Arabs still hung out their
washing on the battlements, so that it fluttered all along the antique
sea-front, innocent of the offence it was committing in the eyes of
the seekers of beautiful sights and spiritual sensations, who had come
all the way from the twentieth century, due west of Acre. Indeed, the
washing draped out on the historic walls was a sign of progress,
enlightenment, and industry, as it had been from time immemorial;
it betokened a settlement and a society with a sense of tomorrow,
even if it was only tomorrow's clean shirt, as against the shifty tent-

dwelling communities of the wilderness; and however murky the cave-like homes along the shore, and however indolent the occupants, they were one up on the Bedouin, at least in their own eyes if not in the sight of the tourist cameras which photographed the Bedouin shepherds continually but deplored the hung-out washing at Acre.

Acre had many years ago become the spiritual home of Abdul Ramdez, although he nominally resided in Jerusalem. His real age was thirty-four. He had found, by experience, that nobody questioned that he was twenty-five when he gave this age as his; he was youthful-looking and had cultivated and kept in good repair the mannerisms of his youth; and Abdul had found, too, that most people took a man, in all respects, for what he said he was.

It will have been seen that it would be a waste of time to rely on any statement about himself and his life spoken from the lips of Abdul Ramdez. The facts are as follows. He was born in 1927 at the small and ancient town of Madaba in the Transjordan, east of the Dead Sea. He had three sisters, four half-sisters, and one brother. At that time the family consisted of his father, an unmarried uncle, Joe Ramdez's first wife, who acted as general manager of domestic life, a second wife (Abdul's mother), who looked after all the younger children regardless of whether she or the other wife had borne them; then, also, Abdul's elder brother and five of the seven Ramdez girls, who were still children, the other two being married. In addition, there lived in the house a female constitutional victim, heavily garbed in black, of indefinite age and origin, who did the bulk of the housework from early morning till late at night. At Abdul's birth in 1927 there were fourteen persons in the household.

It was a middle-class urban family such as the British Mandatory officials liked to deal with, since they understood them better than the more tribal and nomadic Arabs, on the one hand, and the elusive rich ruling families with sons at English schools, on the other.

In the year of Abdul's birth, when the Transjordan became an independent state, the entire family, accompanied by, and, as it were, borne on the back of, the veiled servant woman, moved across the Jordan River into Palestine, where the British Mandate remained in force. The reason for this move was that Joe Ramdez, until then a schoolteacher, had found the British army and civil service officials to be both agreeable and profitable. He had taught them Arabic, had taken them to see the sights they ought to see and kept them away from a few things they ought not to see, and obligingly upheld their axiom that the Arabs think in symbols, this being a more workable view for them to hold than that they did not think at all. So he followed the Administration to Jerusalem, where Abdul grew up in the new small suburban house, following the servant woman everywhere every day from the opening to the closing of his eyes, until he was eight years old. She was called Kyra and, unlike the other women of the household, had never brought herself to any point of emancipation. She wore her black veil to the market, with her basket in one hand and Abdul's hand in the other.

Joe Ramdez prospered and formed his travel agency, employing a few Arabs from Nazareth as guides to Christian pilgrims throughout Palestine. Abdul remembered a few of the British men, and sometimes their wives, driving up to the door for their Arabic lessons on occasions when his father did not go to them. Quickly, the women and girls of the Ramdez establishment would scuttle out of the way, leaving the main room, where they had been lying full length on settees, to loll somewhere else or to make tea. A continual lolling of lazy women about the house, perpetual sunlight and heat, and red plush upholstery, formed the distorted impressions that Abdul retained from his childhood, although in reality the women of the Ramdez house were moderately active and did all that was necessary to the general comfort, and the winters were cold, and actually only one room had been furnished with red plush upholstery. It was true that the other rooms were full of untidy beds and were hung with female clothing all over the walls and that the women did not have much chance to participate in the visits of the Europeans. Abdul's younger sister, blue-eyed like himself, was exceptional among the females, in that she felt it keenly when she was hushed out of the way with the other girls while Abdul was proudly introduced to the strangers.

The red plush had covered the long settles; these lined three of the walls of the square room that led straight in from the road. Here the visitors were received and here Abdul sat noiseless, in a trance of red plush, while the English got their Arabic lessons from his father. The walls bore three enlarged photographs, one of General Gordon, one of Abdul's grandfather on his mother's side – a Syrian of mixed Arab and Norman stock, the progenitor of the blue-eyed children – and one of a crowded pilgrimage to Mecca, moving up to the Great Mosque. After the lessons the Ramdez women would slink in with cups of mint tea and swiftly merge back into the gloom of elsewhere.

That was life in the old days. At the age of eight Abdul went to school in Jerusalem. His father prospered. Presently, the house had two refrigerators. The first and elder wife, whose children by Joe Ramdez were now married, returned, perhaps by inducement from Joe, to Jericho whence she came; whereupon Abdul's mother started calling herself Mme Ramdez, and, with clothes more modern than ever before, assisted in the travel business, walking forth from the front door daily.

Abdul went to the University of Cairo at the age of sixteen. There he belonged first to one, and then to another, cell of Arab politics. With eighty-odd of his fellow students he one day marched behind a banner marked 'We Want Freedom', past the British Headquarters, was fired upon, and escaped with a fright only, three of his fellow-students being slightly wounded. This was in 1944. The demonstration, Abdul learned later that day, was against King Farouk, although some of the participants claimed it had been against the British. Abdul had thought it was probably against the proprietor of Shepheard's Hotel, who had been attempting to ban the students of late; but he did not worry very much. It made him feel good to belong to an Arab movement. He liked to feel that it was something to be an Arab, although he disliked the Lebanese and wished all the Arabs were Palestinian or Transjordanian and less alien in their ways. Abdul's teacher in history, a Syrian, was pro-Hitler. Another of the teachers, an English communist, was the guiding spirit of another student faction. The cells split open from time to time, forming themselves anew, after some shouting, fighting, and expulsions of students, into regional structures, so that the Lebanese, the Egyptians, the Tunisians, Arabians and Syrians were plotters in separate fields of political allegiance. Every man among the Arab students proclaimed himself a nationalist, this word being their only common denominator. 'Islam', another word of rousing properties, was at first rousing only to the Moslem believers. The atheists among the students were at that time greater in number than at any time before or since; agnosticism, or any form of recognized doubt, was unknown to all but Abdul, who presently discovered it by chance. In the meantime he had joined practically every movement in the university, demonstrating with them sometimes but meeting in secret as often as possible for seditious discussions, since he liked them, they roused him up.

When he had turned seventeen he took on the teaching of Arabic to an Englishwoman who was an officer in the Women's Auxiliary. She lived at the big hotel, where Abdul called three times a week. She was twenty-seven years old. She had the use of a friend's empty flat where, after a few weeks, she slept with Abdul. It was as near a love-affair on both sides as could be. On her side, it was a desperate reaction to grief; her husband had not long since been killed in battle. On his side, it was an impact with self-knowledge in many forms. He had already had sexual relations with young Arab girls in Cairo. But even physically he realized himself more acutely as a man with this Western woman, discerning at the same time, by a process of reflection acquired from her, that he had hitherto regarded all Westerners, both male and female, as a masculine type of race.

Every time he slept with this girl he found himself with a problem which for want of a more precise definition, he termed 'spiritual'; he was afraid of her. When he spent days and nights at the flat without sexual relations with her, as he frequently did, he found himself with a physical problem; for he wanted very much the physical contact with this bold foreigner. That she herself was taking some sort of risk in carrying on this relationship did not occur to him, until she was suddenly unavailable, detained and being questioned pending a court-martial; Abdul lay low. He started attending to his studies, he did not go near the flat or any busy part of Cairo. He remained in the college precincts, attending lectures and reading his books from early morning to early evening, when he went to bed and lay listening for the footsteps of the police. Within three weeks he heard that the English girl had been recalled to headquarters in Britain pending her release from the forces, on the recommendation of one of those psychiatrists whose main job in war-time was to smooth over such events as this, and Abdul realized, with relief, that her lover's identity was unknown.

Meanwhile, Abdul had acquired from the woman something

ineradicable, and which was so much part of her nature that she had been herself totally unaware of it: self-humour. It was a form of endowment at the same time that it was a form of corruption. It undid him as a middle-class Arab enemy-hater with a career in the army or a position in business.

'I am an Arab Nationalist,' he had announced to her. 'I despise the British.'

'Nationalist of what nation?' she had said, quite innocently. 'What place, what territory?' He made these responses his own and used them for years afterwards.

'Islam is united.' But he knew it was not.

This was not the only innocent remark the girl had made which affected him. From the histrionic or dramatic point of view he was henceforth a spoiled Arab. He could not take any propaganda seriously. And she had unwittingly instilled scepticism into him, had taught him to be a doubter and, at the same time, a faint-hearted hater. He was by no means the only Arab of his generation to react in this way to the fervour of the resistance movements at Cairo while the big war was going on outside. Many were influenced by the Lebanese who mostly considered themselves to be a different cultivation altogether from the rest of Middle-Eastern humanity. Many joined the Allied forces.

Abdul, then, joined all the student factions, merrily uncommitted at heart and, in the same spirit, out of the sheer desire for discovery and scope, would have joined the British army had they accepted him. He was found to have tuberculosis, was sent back to Palestine and, within a few weeks, to a sanatorium in Lebanon. There, his sister Suzi, the blue-eyed one, came to visit him at various intervals, sometimes accompanied by Mme Ramdez and sometimes by black-veiled Kyra, smelling like her usual self with the addition of eau-de-cologne which she had applied to her forehead in consideration of foreign travel.

It was at this time that the secret affinity ripened between Abdul and Suzi. She was then fifteen, Abdul nineteen. He talked of new ways of life and outlook, undreamt of even by their modernized parents. His imagination went wild in most particulars, but Abdul conveyed to her, as only tubercular patients can, the excitement of what was in his mind. He said that the modernization of Joe Ramdez was simply a new form of the old exploiting mentality. In this way Suzi discovered the future as an idea, and together the brother and sister merged in a pact of personal anarchism; they started to fool everyone; they conformed to outward demands and resisted in spirit, the Arabic mysticism in their nature easily adapting itself to this course. Suzi, on one of her visits with Kyra, had a love-affair with a French officer and managed to convince her suspicious chaperone, and later her mother, that she was merely cultivating his acquaintance in her role as a spy. To be a spy of some sort was the respectable thing for any literate Arab, even if it only involved spying on each other. To spy on a Westerner was a matter of special commendation. The girl noticeably handed a note to Abdul in his hospital bed, every time she visited him. These were really love-notes from herself to Abdul; and they were partly sincere, for the temperamental sympathy between the brother and sister was not unlike an erotic passion, so new to their Palestinian lives was their liberation of spirit; Abdul's attitude to her as a woman was not to be found in any other Arab of her acquaintance, and only superficially in the French officer, who very soon left with his regiment for other parts. Abdul treated her as a girl-friend, and she was bold and merry with him; it delighted him, even more than had his encounter with the Englishwoman in Egypt.

He read her notes, when they began to reach him by messenger three or four times a day, with enormous secret amusement, returning similar messages even before old Kyra's eyes. He explained to all Arab personnel at the hospital who might be concerned, that these notes were in aid of 'the Arab struggle'. This was highly acceptable, and nobody inquired what sort of struggle to what precise end.

After the end of the war, Abdul, partially cured in both lungs, returned to Palestine where the huge Jewish immigration had turned the old Arab hostility to the Jews into hysterical hatred. The British military were active everywhere, unable to cope with the illegal immigrant shiploads that managed to come ashore, week by week, in spite of the vigilant army and air force in Palestine and their ships off the coast. The British were hated by the Arabs for not killing all the Jews.

Joe Ramdez had opened at Haifa a small branch of his travel agency which was one of the main British sources of secret intelligence concerning the illegal immigrant ships. Abdul was now placed in charge of this establishment, where he gaily accepted payment by both British and Jewish agencies in the matter of illegal immigrants. One way and another he had a bright time of it, distrusted on all sides, yet frequently confided in on the mere hypnotic strength of his attractive personality, and was eventually retained by various intelligence agencies more from fear of what he could divulge than from his usefulness as a spy. Joe Ramdez took his son's duplicity for granted, the only difference between the two processes of thought, father's and son's, was that, whereas Abdul knew and joyfully recognized his double-dealings for what they were, the father took a double course of life to be a single, natural line of human proceeding and would have been wild with anger if anyone had openly called a lie of his a lie, or suggested some moral defection on his part; and he expected the same treatment from everyone outside his own family. But when a British officer said to Abdul, leaning over the desk at the travel bureau in Haifa, 'Ramdez, what a frightful, bloody young liar you are!' Abdul replied, 'I know,' with his quick, young smile. In any case, he was not quite twenty-one at the time, which alone was very disarming. Abdul adored life, the Mediterranean waters, the sun, and his sister Suzi.

Bullets were flying from all quarters. Abdul closed down the agency in Haifa. He took off his smart-cut suit of clothes and put on a white shirt and khaki shorts. Bullets from the small black window apertures of the Arab quarters sang about his ears; the bullets pelted down from the mountains of Carmel. Abdul did not return to his lodgings. He waited in an upper store-room of the travel agency until this local rising had been put down, then he emerged one night, thin from lack of food, and closed the doors of the travel agency at Haifa for ever. He got to friends at Acre, where he obtained a birth certificate dated 1931, which made him a plausible sixteen years of age. There, too, on the strength of some knowledge of the Catholic religion that he had picked up while in hospital in Lebanon, he persuaded a simple and ancient Franciscan monk to baptize him before witnesses and sign a baptismal certificate. Abdul did all these things without any distinct notion of their subsequent usefulness, but merely on the prompting of an instinct for self-preservation. By no means did he wish to fight in an Arabs' war with the Jews or anyone else. A careful copy of the baptismal certificate was made for him by his friends, with the substitution of Suzi's name, and this copy was conveyed in secret to his sister in Jerusalem. Certificates of baptism were useful for crossing borders in this pilgrim territory, they were useful for many things. He began to love Acre, with its band of friends and its crowds of poor.

Presently he set off for Nazareth where Christian Arabs were mostly congregated. He begged lifts all the way from the British military, explaining that he desired to get to the hospital at Nazareth as he had been spitting blood and was afraid of being sniped at by the Jews. How old was he? Sixteen. He had, in fact, developed a short, recurrent cough. The British soldiers searched him for bombs, found five pounds in his pocket, his birth certificate and baptismal certificate; that was all. He had not changed his name. Abdul Ramdez, a fairly common name, was as good as any. He coughed frequently. 'Hop in,' said the Englishmen. On the second lift that he got in a military jeep, which took him all the way to Nazareth, he found himself coughing less controllably than before, and towards evening he did indeed spit up blood.

At the tubercular sanatorium in Nazareth, after he perceived how the war was going, he took lessons in modern Hebrew. He now had assurances that his lung disease, in spite of long neglect, could be quite cured. He got modern Hebew lessons from a Baptist missionary woman who visited the hospital, and explained to the suspicious Arab patients that a knowledge of Hebrew would enable him to continue his profession of spying on the Jews when he should be discharged. Once or twice his textbooks were destroyed in hostile rage by one or another Arab, but on the whole he managed to convince almost everyone of his nationalistic loyalty, by almost daily renewals of vows of hatred against the Jews. He felt no hatred on so large a scale, since all his energies went into his will to live well in the world, to get the best he could out of Palestine and to be free to say any frivolous thing that came into his head regardless of the impression it might make. At night, when he lay among the row of sleepers, he felt the security and comfort of being together with his own people. By day, he surged with individuality again.

The state of Israel was three years old and was warily at peace, separated by an armistice line from Jordan, when Abdul left the

sanatorium. Jerusalem was now divided; his father's home and business establishment were in the Jordanian sector. Infrequent messages,
mostly verbal, had passed between Abdul and his family while he was
in hospital, carried in secret by various individuals – a foreigner, a Red
Cross officer, an Arab spy, a Church of Scotland minister.

Abdul was aware that none of the family except Suzi had any
conception of his mind and how deeply bored he was by the mentality that now presented to every Arab in Palestine the blood-duty of
becoming a professional victim. Abdul saw years of futile service
ahead in this uninteresting cause. He knew of the homeless
Palestinian refugees massed along the frontier, and he discerned then
what a foreigner could not so accurately foresee, that there was a
living to be made out of the world by preserving a refugee problem.
Abdul guessed, and was presently proved right, that his father, for
one, was doing his big bit on the refugee question and would in time
make a fortune out of it. Joe Ramdez was in fact already active in
newly established agencies for negotiating contracts with merchants
for supplies bought by foreign relief funds.

Just before he had left hospital, Abdul had got a brief note in
Suzi's handwriting. 'How are Abdul's orange groves thriving?' He
puzzled for a few moments, then smiled. The displaced poor were
already being urged to recall the extent of the lands and possessions
from which they had fled before the Israelis' onslaught. More and
more, the bewildered homeless souls, in thousands and tens of thousands, agreed and then convinced themselves, and were to hold for
long years to come, that they had, every man of them, been driven
from vast holdings in their bit of Palestine, from green hilly pastures
and so many acres of lush orange groves as would have covered
Arabia.

Abdul had earned some money by teaching the children while in
the sanatorium. On his discharge he bought a car on the instalment
plan and drove to Acre, passing through the green hills and battered
villages of Judea. He said to himself, at times when he sped past some
fruitful plantation, 'There go Abdul's orange groves.' He was bored
far beyond the point of fury with his elders, he was bored with the
fervent industrious Jews bursting with their new patriotism. It had
been necessary for him, a Palestinian Arab, to obtain a permit before
he could leave Nazareth. He was an inferior citizen still; the Jews had

only replaced the British. The officious Israeli policeman who issued
the permit, a man younger than himself, made Abdul feel sick. He
was beyond fury. He laughed. The Israeli guard called a fellow-
officer to his side and then asked Abdul what there was to laugh at.
Abdul explained that he was newly out of hospital and it was a nice
day. He was allowed to go. He did not want to grow older than he was
then, in 1950. At that time he was twenty-three.

At Acre the people he had known were gone, but as happens, the
place itself, by some invisible influence or tradition, had drawn the
same sort of people, the young or the young at heart who belonged
to nothing but themselves, for whose temperament no scope existed
in any society open to them, and who by day enacted the requirements of their society. These were lapsed Jews, lapsed Arabs, lapsed
citizens, runaway Englishmen, dancing prostitutes, international
messes, failed painters, intellectuals, homosexuals. Some were silent,
some voluble. Some were mentally ill, or would become so.

But others were not. Others were not, and never would become so;
and would have been the flower and pride of the Middle East, given
the sun and air of the mind not yet to be available. They met in a
cellar at Acre, lined with wooden benches, lit with oil lamps and
cleared for dancing. Abdul would have preferred the beaches or the
cafés, and the open sky, but at least in the cellar an Arab could laugh
at the Arabs or mimic the solemn Israeli guard without being knifed
or shot. Three knifings were to occur within this little community
over the next ten years, but they were not political; they were to do
with sex or drugs, and in two cases the wounds were slight; in the
third the body was successfully disposed of from a fishing-boat.

Nothing much had changed by 1961, the year of the Eichmann
trial, when Abdul Ramdez drove to Acre, the golden city of the
Crusaders on the Mediterranean. At Christian festivals, Easter and
Christmas, he was able to pass over to Jordan openly with mass
pilgrimages to visit the Christian shrines, on the strength of his baptismal certificate, acquired with that good foresight before the war
with Israel. Suzi, with the certificate he had obtained for her, got past
the officials to meet him at the churches. She was still unmarried at
thirty-one. She was unhappy, and only Abdul knew it. Sometimes he
crossed the border illegally, but he did not always see Suzi on these
occasions. He had contrived to meet his father several times since the

partition of Palestine. 'Are you a nationalist? . . . A Nasserite? . . . What party? . . .' But messages between Joe Ramdez and Abdul passed frequently. They were comparatively easy to smuggle back and forth across the border.

Nothing much had changed at Acre over the years except the place of rendezvous and Abdul's real age. He was now thirty-four, but he kept himself lean, was strict with himself and looked no more than the age he had decided on. He did not trouble about the future. Twenty-five. Foreigners like Hamilton were puzzled at times by Abdul's maturity of knowledge.

'But surely, Abdul, you must have been a young infant at that time. How could you remember King Farouk before he grew fat?'

Abdul piled lies upon truth, without attempting to convince. He felt he was making an almost poetic effort. He derived huge pleasure from mixing everyone up so much that they saw through it in the end.

'Sometimes, Abdul, I wonder if you're just treating me to a big leg-pull.'

Hamilton had said this one day. Abdul thought it intelligent of him. He said, 'Well, what have I got to lose, Mr Hamilton? You know that all the Arabs in Palestine are dispossessed. There's nothing to lose, now that Abdul has lost his orange groves.'

'Did you possess orange groves?'

'Vast groves.'

'I don't believe it. Come, Abdul!'

'I am an Arab,' said Abdul, looking fierce, 'and you may not accuse me of a lie. Anyway, I have lost a good travel agency business in Haifa. The Jews have got it.'

Hamilton had laughed and regarded him fondly.

Abdul drove to Acre on the following Sunday and thought for a while of the Hamilton he had seen a few days before, unwell, bewildered. Someone at Acre would know, or find out, what had happened to the Englishman over in Jordan and what had happened with Miss Vaughan. It would be a pity if Hamilton started to make trouble, and stopped being friendly.

The new meeting-place at Acre was more spacious and comfortable than any previous one. New young people came in from time to time.

The building stood in the great muddle of the poor Arab quarter. It was equipped as a laundry, and in the daytime the lower ground floor functioned as a cheap washing establishment where, in one room, an unpunctual and inefficient supply of warm water was available, with wash tubs and soap, at a cheap rate, to the poor women who had to do their washing themselves, and who were slightly advanced beyond the river-washing set.

The club-rooms could not really be called club-rooms, since the traditions and organizations of any sort of club-life did not belong to them. These meeting-rooms were in the cellars and on the floor above the laundry. Windows from all sides kept watch on any possible police approach from the sea or from the street. Some of the upper rooms were always hung with washing, hauled high on pulleys, which, at night when the lights were on, could be glimpsed above the half-curtains from the alleys outside.

Two Pakistanis, students from the Hebrew University of Jerusalem, came to open the door for Abdul. They were temporary caretakers, since the laundryman who looked after the house at Acre was away to the north on business.

Abdul had two rooms of his own on the upper floor, but everyone else used them. The rooms had some rush matting on the floors and brightly-covered low divans, with a bare wood table in each, and, in one room, a wireless set. He went there sometimes to sleep, and read, or talk. He went to talk about nothing or everything, and, quite often, about business.

Soon Abdul and his friends would move their premises. It had always been like this, and there could be no question of their applying for a night-club licence to make their meeting-ground legitimate so far as that would have gone; the part of their activities which was illegal could have been protected by a night-club pretence, but the Israeli police surveillance would have been intolerable. The law could not altogether prevent, but it could harass, those few young Jews and Jewesses who came to the house at Acre because there was no other place acceptable to the reality of their feelings in the world around them. The group was seldom more than twenty-five in number at any one time.

'What have you been doing?' Abdul said in English, as the students knew no Arabic or Hebrew.

One of the Pakistanis, a very small man, replied, 'Considering the lilies.' This was a well-worn remark in that house, but it was new to the Pakistanis, who did not know its origin and merely liked it.

An Arab girl in khaki shorts and shirt brought in some coffee. She spoke to Abdul in English seeing that the Pakistanis were present: 'Mendel came back safe. Hassan is returned. Mendel saw your sister.'

Abdul put down his coffee, he hugged and kissed her for all this news.

The taller Pakistani said, 'Your sister Suzi has been very involved. She sent a message, she is very involved.'

'Very involved,' said the girl. 'Mendel will tell you, he's coming soon, he's on his way.'

'What is she involved about?'

'The tourist agency. Very interesting.'

'She must be up to something,' Abdul said, and went to the window to smell Acre. Night had fallen and he heard the splash of oars.

It was ten at night, in the cellar of the laundry at Acre. Here the Crusader foundations could be seen, quite clearly, rising unevenly up to two feet above the flagged floor, until the Crusader stones met the stones that had been set upon them, probably by the next conquerors – the Turks, perhaps.

The light from the oil lamps was thinly misted from their smoke. About a dozen people, young, not of local origin, were gathered, or were drifting in and out of this room. It would have been impossible to tell from their appearance only which of these young men and women were Jews and which were Arabs. The difference was discernible in their accent of speech, although colloquial Arabic was mostly spoken. The two students from Pakistan and a handsome large-limbed western girl with a mass of long brown hair, who was the daughter of a Church of Scotland clergyman resident at Tel Aviv, were the only non-Semites. The rest were Arabs and Jews, most of whom were maturely sixteen years of age and upward to the reaches of their late twenties or early thirties. Abdul, if anyone had considered it worth finding out, was the eldest. They were dressed in jeans, dresses or shorts, and corporately they had the coffee-bar look of the young, everywhere.

A girl was plucking the strings of a guitar, making soft aimless Arabic music with few notes. Nobody was dancing at the moment. Abdul had fetched a tin of beer from a scarred, lop-sided oil refriger- ator which stood in the passage outside, from which anyone who wanted beer took it, depositing the money in the ice-tray. Abdul sat drinking alone, watching the door until Mendel Ephraim appeared.

Mendel Ephraim was one of his closest friends. He was the young- est brother of that Saul Ephraim, the teacher of archaeology at the Hebrew University, who knew Barbara Vaughan and had sometimes acted as her guide in Israel. Ephraim resembled his brother in his taut sinewy look, but he had a slight shoulder-blade stoop; he looked like an intellectual eagle. He was twenty-six. The family had given him up because of his failure as a son, a Jew and an Israeli; they held him in suspicion, but did not know what to suspect him of. He had a job in a tobacconist kiosk at the foot of Mount Zion. Mendel's failure to respond to the State of Israel was their greatest puzzle and embarrassment. Many of the Ephraim family were unbelievers, and it would not have mattered if he had refused only the religion; but many non-religious Israelis were accustomed to speak in historical terms of Israel's destiny; the Old Testament was to them a sacred book because it was the history of the Jews rather than a spiritual record; and it was quite common for those who did not accept any religious or divine element in life, to maintain that the Messianic prophecies had in fact been fulfilled in the establishment of the State of Israel. 'The country, Israel, is the Messiah,' they said frequently. Young Mendel Ephraim was as indifferent to this social mystique as he was to religion. He had worked on a border *kibbutz* and been caught, nearly shot, while attempting to cross into no-man's-land, heaving a spare-part of a tractor, which he explained was urgently needed by the Arab farmer on the other side. He had been closely interrogated about these communications with the farmer which had led up to the jaunt, but all he would admit was, 'I could see he was in trouble with his tractor. You could see. Anyone could see.'

The family had given him up. It was known he was friendly with Abdul Ramdez the Arab, and he had to spend a lot of time shaking off the private detectives and secret-service agents who followed him from time to time. He was never certain whether these spies were employed by his family or by the state. He did not care. He shook them off when he travelled out of town, being well acquainted with the terrain of the country-side and its devious hill routes, and having accustomed himself to cave life. He was not entirely alone among his generation in his truculence; there were other Jews like him scattered about.

Abdul, however, seemed to him even more akin in mentality, being far more humorous than most, and more articulate. Besides, he was in a way of business with Abdul. Whether Arab or Jew, it was part of life for Semites who, like themselves, were of long merchant origin to be occupied in some business.

Mendel had got himself a tin of beer. He came and sat down at Abdul's shadowy table. They kept silence for a few moments. Then Abdul said, in Arabic, 'You're back safe.'

'I've got news for you.'

'Yes, later. You're back safe, that comes first. Hassan's safe, too.'

The courteous contours of the old language half-imposed themselves on these preludes to their conversation, sentence by sentence, as if tradition itself were fumbling its way among the aberrant communications of the two men. Mendel said, 'I have news for you about your sister. The business can wait.'

'The business can wait, but tell me immediately how much danger there was, this trip. Did you have difficulties?'

'Only when your sister Suzi recognized me. I thought she would call out when she saw me at the Holy Sepulchre this morning.'

'You didn't go to the city in broad daylight? Mendel, you're mad. What did you do that for?'

'Well, I was dressed-up the Arab part.'

'Somebody might have spoken to you. The voice, Mendel. It's dangerous. Anyone can tell by the intonation that you're no Arab.'

Mendel spoke in a harsh whisper. 'If I had been forced to speak, I would have had laryngitis. Lost my voice. It was exciting, though. I'll never forget it.'

Abdul said, 'There is a reason that you found Suzi.'

'Yes, I'll tell you the news. Just before dawn I got to the Potter's Field, and we were wrapping up the sacks in the cave, ready to return. I saw Suzi coming out of a car. She went into that old house just past the church.'

Abdul laughed. 'Suzi must be up to some game.'

Mendel said, with a sardonic Jewish spread of his hands, 'Helping her father in the travel business, like a good girl. Like you help him with the insurance.'

Abdul said, 'Get on with the story. Was it connected with Miss Vaughan? The police are looking for her all over Jordan. There's a big fuss.'

'Yes, well I questioned the old monk, but you know, he doesn't answer, he just gives you a blessing, Father, Son, Holy Ghost. So I keep a look-out. After all, finding her up there in the Potter's Field, I thought she might be in some trouble. She wouldn't be the only one in trouble that you find up there. In the middle of the morning she comes out with two tourists. One is a man. The other is veiled and dressed like an old Arab woman, like your servant.'

'Kyra,' said Abdul.

'I look and I think it is Kyra. It looks like Kyra. But no, it is an English tourist woman called Barbara Vaughan who wants to pray at the Christian shrines. I am to find this out later. But when I see Suzi and I see Kyra at the Potter's Field, I see them drive off with the man, down to the city – so I walk to the city and I find the car at the Holy Sepulchre. By this time it's eleven in the morning, you know, so I have to look like a Christian Arab, genuflecting and kneeling wherever they go. I'm just behind them. I end up at the Catholic Mass at the place of the crucifixion of Jesus, or maybe the place of one of the thieves, better still, for my part. There are a lot of people, tourists and some Arab women. I move in and stand next to Suzi, and she sees me, and she looks startled. It is at this point I feel afraid, since an Arab woman looks hard at me as if I'm up to no good with a woman, as if I'm trying to make friends with Suzi at the church service. But Suzi pulled herself together and looked away, and the suspicious woman began to pray, and the service went on. Then, when the Orthodox service began at the next altar, and the chanting began, I was able to whisper to Suzi. Guess what I said?'

'Shalom,' said Abdul, putting on the Hebrew inflection.

Mendel said, 'I said, "I've got laryngitis, Suzi, you understand, so I can only whisper. What's going on with you?"' Then she told me about the tourist who's going all over Jordan with her, disguised as the old servant. Suzi told me this, but understood she had to fit in her talk with the chanting of the Orthodox people standing beside us. So she chanted, they chanted, we all chanted. But they were very close by, these chanters, and she's a clever woman, your sister Suzi. The tourist is a half-Jew. No wonder she looked like old Kyra clutching the edge of her veil and very weak on her feet. It appears the police might be looking for her and she thought, maybe, I must be the police. It's a bewildering place, the Holy Sepulchre. Suzi said to tell you she's all right and she'll be seeing you soon.'

Abdul said, 'I've been to the Holy Sepulchre. I was there once.'

Mendel said, 'The tourist is returning to Israel.'

'How?'

'Somehow. She's called Barbara.'

'I hope Suzi won't attempt to cross over.'

'She said she's all right and she'll be seeing you soon. Leave her alone. She needs a bit of pleasure. A little bit of danger, a bit of pleasure, what's the difference?'

'When did you get back?' Abdul said.

'This evening. I walked back up to the Field as if I owned the place, and all the orange groves beyond it as well. Very slowly, striding like an Arab. I'll show you –'

Mendel got up and walked with a leisurely swing of the arms, like an Arab. Abdul laughed and so did some others who had been dancing on a flagged space on the other side of the room.

Mendel sat down. 'I lie up in the caves until sunset begins. I look for Hassan and he comes. He's a bit hungry. So am I. The bones, you know all those bones, are hard to lie on. Anyway we haul off at sunset and get across. No incident. We've got five gross of sandals, some dozens I think, leather purses, also a few more things.'

Abdul took from his pocket a rubber stamp, breathed deeply on it and brought it down sharply on the scrubbed wood table before him. It left a clear blue mark: MADE IN ISRAEL. Then they both laughed very loud together for a long time, as if they were boys in their teens like many in the room, instead of men of twenty-six and thirty-four.

Mendel went upstairs to sleep on one of Abdul's divans. Abdul went to start rubber-stamping the soles of smuggled sandals. These goods had been hauled up to the Potter's Field, day by day, on mules, and dumped at the back of the bone-littered caves that surrounded the field. It was their third successful haul. Abdul had gone on one of these trips and next time it would be his turn again. These goods sold in Israel for a huge profit, and even so, Abdul reflected, they sold cheap in the shops, and it was a public service. After a while Abdul, too, lay down and slept. The noise from the cellar was like a faint rhythmic lullaby, for the doors of the meeting-place had been made nearly sound-proof.

About midnight the men stirred. Abdul rose and heated up some spicy lamb stew on an oil stove. He took some to Mendel. They ate without speaking, sitting side by side on the divan. Then they washed at the tap outside the rooms and descended once more to the party. The outlaws were in full swing.

Abdul said to Mendel, in English, 'Do you know, I've discovered a new rhyme for "Capricorn".'

Mendel replied, 'Abou Ben Adhem (may his tribe increase!)'

'Well, you're crazy,' Abdul said, 'but it's a good life. You may have one of my orange groves when I get them back, you may have two.'

A young Jewess came to join them, playing with her guitar meantime. She was playing a popular jazz tune from Jordan to which accompaniment a slim Arab girl was doing a mimic version of an obscene dance performance that was current in the nightclubs of Amman. The tune was called 'I Love Hussein', which was sung with variations by the guitar player. The dancer wore only a filmy scarf wound round her body in a comic fashion that seemed to all, in the excitement and heat of the night, far more funny than it was. Then Mendel danced with a girl while Abdul squatted on the floor beside the guitar player.

Drugs of various kinds, kef, marijuana, and various experimental mixtures were now being passed round. Some of the younger people started howling and dancing convulsively before the excitants had time to take effect. They were stopped by the more practised smokers and drug-eaters, and told to wait till their reactions were involuntary, at which time the significance of their experience would be more completely revealed. Besides, too much noise might invite a police raid. In the deep hours, Mendel and Abdul, narcotically exalted, began to chant their Song of Freedom which never failed to hypnotize the audience by its depth of meaning, although the words of the song varied every time, being a spontaneous composition. But the notes of their chant were familiar, they were those of the mosques, the synagogues, and the churches of the Coptic, Syrian and Greek rites; the same set of notes would break into the air of Acre, presently, at three in the morning, when the muezzin would rise to call from the minaret nearby, and the same arrangement of notes could be heard from the windows of Rabbinical and Moslem schools all over Israel.

The two men chanted, sitting cross-legged with their audience encircling them, in the heat of the party-cellar until one after another became drowsy and either curled to sleep on the spot or stretched and departed into the sharp dark air of early morning. The cellar was aired merely by vents in the upper walls, and by cracks in the ceiling which let in some small whispers of the fresh night from the open windows above. The young Jewess strummed on the guitar, her cheeks bright with the heat and her black curly hair falling over them. Abdul and Mendel, fiery-eyed with a sense of portentous utterance, their voices merging each with the other as one verse ended and the next began, in true style, chanted on to the end and beyond the end, when, with full and satisfied hearts, followed by the few who remained wakeful enough, they fell upstairs to sleep. And even as they climbed, they chanted in colloquial Arabic jargon mixed often with Hebrew:

'My father goes blah O blah O blah for the love of Allah,' chanted Abdul.

'My father goes chime chime chime O mine, hard luck, chime,' sang Mendel.

'My mother goes quack all day, she goes quack, clack-clack.'

'My sister goes tittle-ittle ittle tittle-ill-tee tee goes my sister.'

'Eichmann went to battle and killed the children of Israel.'

'Mahommed put all the children of Israel to death also, for the love of Allah. There was blood.'

'The children of Israel had dispossessed the holy ones of Mohammed. They are refugees. They weep.'

'It was a long time ago, my friend. Even yesterday was before our time, it's dead too.'

'The past has got nothing to do with you my friend, and nothing to do with me. It's all dead history.'

'Behold what Deborah did to the children of the Canaanites. She slaughtered them with her army.'

'Look what the wealthy shepherd did to the *kibbutzim* in 1946. He shot and killed, the wealthy Sheik and his men. Blah, chime, amen.'

'Look what the Stern Gang did at Dir Yassan, they massacred the lot. Blood, blood.'

'My father, blah, blah. Long live Ben Gurion! Long live Nasser! Long live Islam! Long live all fat men! Israel! My mother goes quack-quack all day.'

'Recall Judith the beautiful, who killed the captain asleep. My son, my son. Tittle-tee.'

'It's all a long time ago. Great is the God of Israel! Mighty is Allah! We dance and sing and make love with each other, it is better than all that religion and hatred all the day long.'

'The Arabs have been neglected by history.'

'The Jews have been rejected by history. Write it down. You might forget it.'

'We want Freedom.'

'Self-government is better than good government. Write that down too.'

'Hussein went to school in Harrow which is in England.'

'Everything is different now. Please all come to the party. My mother makes a party for the girls to do the Twist.'

'Yes, everything is changed. I speak French and English. We all make love together.'

'Come and live in Abdul's orange groves, and pick as many oranges as you like all the afternoon.'

'Come along to Abdul's orange groves.'

5. THE VIA DOLOROSA

On Saturday the 12th of August 1961 when Barbara Vaughan had last been seen, Freddy had accompanied her from the Cartwrights' front door to Matt's car outside in the roadway. Freddy remembered the afternoon that Barbara had spent with them, he remembered it vividly. Matt was going to drive Barbara back to the convent. Joanna had come out to the car, with a parcel in her arms, and had bundled into the back; she wanted to be dropped somewhere. Freddy had waved them good-bye. He had returned to the house. It was empty.

This was the last thing he remembered until he was walking along his usual route from the Mandelbaum Gate to his hotel on the following Tuesday, which was the 15th of August. Only he had thought it was Sunday the 13th of August. Tuesday at 4 o'clock instead of Sunday at 4 o'clock, his usual time for returning to Israel after staying with the Cartwrights in Jordan. Freddy went over and over the facts in his mind. He had come out to wave good-bye . . . he was bareheaded under the hot sun . . . he had returned to the house . . . it was Saturday the 12th of August . . . the house was empty . . . then Freddy was following his usual route to the hotel . . . he was tired and hot. He had gone to bed. The manager had come up to his room and inquired if Freddy was all right . . . the ambassadors had been looking for him. 'Which ambassadors,' said Freddy from his sleepy pillow, 'what do you mean?' It turned out that he meant Freddy's colleagues from the legation. It had turned out that this day was not Sunday the 13th but Tuesday the 15th.

'A touch of the sun,' Freddy said.

Amnesia, was the doctor's conclusion. Some mental disturbance.

Nonsense, I'm suffering from sunstroke.

Had he been drugged by the Arabs? Had he been robbed? There was no evidence of either. In any case, Freddy said, I would be sure to remember if I'd been drugged or robbed.

It was very confusing. Begin again. The manager appeared. 'Are you all right, Mr Hamilton?'

Freddy said he was, and closed his eyes.

The manager said that the ambassadors had been on the telephone two or three times.

Freddy opened his eyes. 'Ambassadors?'

It appeared that the manager was referring to Freddy's colleagues at the legation.

'The ambassadors . . . Are you all right . . . the legation.'

'What do they want?' Freddy said, lifting his head off the pillow.

'They want to know where you are. All day yesterday, and all this morning, you didn't come. They say your friends where you stay in the Jordan Embassy don't know where you have gone since Saturday. They look also for Miss Vaughan, who was a guest in this hotel, and went to Jordan.'

'I don't stay with anyone in any Embassy,' Freddy said. 'The Jordanian Embassy is in Amman. I stay with friends in Jerusalem who are part of a welfare relief mission. Everyone knows them.'

The manager said, 'Now I phone your office and tell them you are safe. Do you like some tea, coffee?'

'There won't be anyone there,' Freddy said. To the Israelis Sunday was a week-day; they always forgot that the Legation offices closed on Sundays.

Freddy said, 'It's Sunday. There's no one there.'

'Sunday?' said the manager.

Freddy leaned up on his elbow.

'What day of the week is it?' he said.

'Today is Tuesday the 15th of August. They look for you in the office two days. Where you have been is not my business, Mr Hamilton, all right? As I say to him, we can put you through to his room. He says, I been put through to his room but there's no answer from his room. Then another gentleman calls me to speak —'

'It can't be Tuesday. It's Sunday. I always come back on Sunday evening,' Freddy said, and lay back among the pillows. The manager departed. Freddy decided to compose a very special set of bread-and-butter verses for Joanna, to compensate for his boorishness.

There had been a slight fuss about Barbara Vaughan in the garden. You blow neither hot nor cold. He decided to have a rest first, and get up for dinner, by which time he would have accumulated some executive energy to apply to the verses.

His younger colleague, Rupert Gardnor, anxiously disposed to laugh it all off as a lark, arrived that evening with Dr Jarvis. Freddy sat up, fresh from sleep, and began again. From what Gardnor told him, it appeared today was Tuesday indeed. Freddy believed Gardnor. 'I must have lost my memory,' Freddy said. 'I couldn't tell you where I've been. Hand me my wallet, like a good chap. I hope I haven't been robbed.'

They decided Freddy had not been robbed. He said, 'I must have had a touch of sunstroke.' Gardnor said, 'I'll wait downstairs.' It was uncertain whether he meant he would wait to see Jarvis or Freddy. Jarvis gave no response; he was busy with Freddy.

Jarvis said he would look back tomorrow and make a more thorough examination; the pulse was a bit unsteady; the temperature was normal.

'I'll be at the office tomorrow,' Freddy said.

'On no account.'

Freddy didn't like to think of them discussing him down there. He got up and dressed quickly.

He expected to find Gardnor still in conference with Jarvis when he came down. Instead he found Gardnor drinking in the courtyard.

'The vet gone?' Gardnor said.

'Yes, he's coming back tomorrow. But I'll be in the office tomorrow.'

'I'd follow his advice,' Gardnor said. 'You might have a relapse.'

How does he know what his advice was? Freddy thought. He said, 'It must have been sunstroke.' He ordered a drink and tried to be fair to Gardnor.

They dined together. Gardnor said, after dinner they must find some quiet spot where he could tell Freddy the latest. 'The latest is rather amusing.' By the latest he meant some secret matter in the office.

Freddy expressed himself keen to hear the latest. He said he didn't feel very hungry. 'And the point is,' Freddy said, 'where did I stay? I must have slept. I must have shaved.'

'Well, you didn't sleep and shave on this side of Mandelbaum,' Gardnor said. 'It must have been on that side. We've checked at the Gate, and you came through at 5.18 p.m. today.'

'It passes my understanding,' Freddy said.

'Could you have been drugged? How do you feel?'

'A bit upset,' Freddy said, 'but I haven't been drugged. Jarvis had a look at my eyes with his torch and said, "Well, at least you haven't been drugged" – I suppose he'd know.'

'Oh, yes.'

'Sunstroke,' Freddy said, and accompanied his friend to a quiet corner of the public lounge where Gardnor, in a quiet but gleeful voice, described the latest. This was an involved story about an Israeli counter-intelligence ruse. Freddy felt very drowsy and wished Gardnor would go home.

'The Israelis,' Gardnor breezed on, 'are anxious about an intelligence leakage that they've traced to Beersheba . . .' Freddy felt his eyelids droop, and propped them open as it were with invisible matchsticks. Gardnor's story was connected with the water-pipe-line project, planned by Israel to stretch from Galilee to the Negev, and, branching beneath the desert scrub, to blossom there. This plan had already aroused wild hostility from the Arab States, as much by its symbolism as by its practical advantage to their enemy, Israel. The Arab Press and radio presented the plan as one designed mainly to deprive their people of their own rivers and so kill them off. It was no secret either, in this year of the Eichmann trial, that the pipes were already being laid. In the Israeli press the exact diameter of these huge water-pipes, 108 inches, had been published, but many Arab agencies, prompted both by the accepted rules of propaganda and by genuine suspicion, had reported these monstrous sucklings of Arab life-blood to be the largest known, although, they said, the exact dimensions were as yet withheld by the Israelis.

Gardnor now described to Freddy how the Israeli Intelligence, keen to track down the spy who they knew was operating from Beersheba, had arranged to spill from a rail truck two sections of the metal pipes. For several weeks they had lain by the side of the track gleaming in the sun for all to see who passed on the parallel motor road, and they were explained by government press officers as having fallen accidentally from one of the goods wagons which bore these pipe sections regularly to their destination. The pieces of pipe-line were even pointed out to tourists by the guides, to show off the great engineering plan by which the wilderness of the Negev would open like the rose in a few years' time. Those pipes over there, the guides would say as they drove slowly past the spot – our water-pipes, to bring water from the north to cultivate the desert; they are 108 inches in diameter; look at them!

Gardnor said to Freddy, who sat round-eyed with the effort to keep awake, '. . . and in fact, I happened to see them myself when I was down there last Sunday week, and I *thought* at the time that they looked rather *big*, you know. Of course, one can't actually judge these measurements if one isn't an expert, and, of course, I only saw them from the road, which was about two hundred yards from the place where the pipes were lying. But anyhow, it *did* cross my mind at the time that those sections of the pipe-line *did* look a bit bigger than I'd expected, from the official description. And of course 108 inches in diameter is a *lot*, anyway. Well, anyway, what the Israelis had done –'

Oh go home, Freddy thought, sitting with his eyes forced wide. He began to close in on his ordeal, and to consider his own dumb sufferings, a course of mind which Freddy normally abhorred. Gardnor's hushed confidence continued to scorch Freddy's eardrums, and he sat and put up with it, not caring whether he followed the story or not.

'. . . The Israelis, you see, were after the spy chap operating in the area. And what the Israelis had done,' Gardnor assured Freddy, 'was to build a special couple of pipe-line sections far bigger than those they're actually going to use, and to plant them beside the track. Great huge fellows they were – as I say, I saw them myself and they looked enormous, as I say. And of course, they kept a watch on the spot. Well, last Sunday night –'

'Last Sunday, the 13th?' Freddy said. His eyes moved to Rupert Gardnor's face, which had faintly checked its expression at this interruption. Freddy's mind was fixed on last Sunday and its adjacent days as on an aching tooth and its touchy neighbours. Freddy said again, 'Last Sunday, Rupert, did you say?'

But Gardnor was mercilessly intent on cheering up a colleague in his misfortunes. 'Last Sunday,' Gardnor said more clearly, moving closer in the evident assumption that Freddy had not heard his lowered tone. 'Yes, last Sunday night, apparently. Well, they kept a watch . . .' Freddy was touched and soothed by the man's polite implication that there was nothing really the matter with him, and that nothing really had happened. The man was behaving exactly as he himself would have done, of course; that was to say, one would naturally take the line that a few days' lapse of memory suffered by a chap in one's own department was different from what it would be if it happened to anyone else. He allowed his eyes to relax from there propped-open fixedness.

'. . . kept a watch on those pipe sections. Eventually, after a couple of weeks – as I say, last Sunday night – they spotted a man hanging round the place. He got over to the rail track and started measuring the diameter of the pipes. Well you see, these were the specially planted ones, not the real ones, which are *in fact* 108 inches in diameter. These were much bigger. And as expected the Arabs got the information within the course of the night. It was also received by an Israeli agent over in Jordan, who signalled back the news over no-man's-land at dawn. The size of the fake pipes was, I think, something like 195 inches, but that isn't the point. The point is, the Israelis have got their spy over here – the man who was measuring it. He's an Israeli employed by a quite innocent detective agency in Beersheba – and the Arab Intelligence, of course, are now in a stew as to whether the diameter of the fake pipes, I think 195 inches, really is the size, or whether the official size –'

'The size of those fake water-pipes,' Freddy said suddenly, for no reason that he himself could think of at present, 'is 185 inches, not 195. The size is 185 inches, that I know.'

Gardnor's immediate reply was a long silence, which was the first of the silences in conversation that Freddy was to encounter, and which now woke Freddy out of his half-doze. Then Gardnor said, 'How do you know?'

'What?' said Freddy.

'Oh, nothing,' Gardnor said. 'Only the information didn't reach Jordan until Sunday night, and there was nothing about it in our office until after they'd arrested their spy. We got a memo, Monday morning, from the Israeli Intelligence, and I suppose the Americans are in the know as well, in case we took the ruse seriously and started

making inquiries and representations and so on. But you weren't
there in the office, Monday morning. That's why I'm wondering how
you know anything about the affair.'

'I don't know anything about it. At least, only what you've told
me,' Freddy said, in distress. 'But you're right . . . my dear Rupert,
I honestly don't know where I've been since last Saturday afternoon.
It will come back. A touch of sunstroke –'

Gardnor smiled in an embarrassed way and said, 'Oh yes, I know,
but you do seem to have heard something about the fake water-pipes,
and you seem to be informed about the exact size. And all this stuff,
you see, came to us as Top Secret, of course.'

'I've heard of Topper Secrets,' Freddy said.

'That's true. It isn't so very sigificant. But one wonders . . . it's
rather as if you'd picked it up somewhere, and one wonders . . . well,
Freddy, do you mind if I mention this at the office? I mean, if I don't,
it wouldn't be quite the thing, you see, Freddy. What would you do?'

'I'd put in a report,' Freddy said. 'You'll have to do so.'

'I know.'

Freddy said, 'I think if I could get some sleep it would all come
back.' Gardnor was really in rather a hurry to observe his duty.

'Of course,' Gardnor said, sitting upright now, very tense and
anxious, 'it would be better if you put in a statement yourself. I prefer
it, quite honestly. Could you write it tonight?'

'No,' Freddy said. 'It's your job, if you feel it's so terribly pressing. You know you'd be questioned, anyway.'

'Well, I'll say it's done with your approval, and I'll send you a copy.
Do you mind if I have another drink? Makes you feel like the bloody
Gestapo when you've got to do a thing like this and report an ordi-
nary conversation with one of your own chaps.'

Freddy said, 'Oh, come!' He sat back with closed eyes while
Gardnor ordered his drink, and shook his head when Gardnor asked
him if he wanted one.

When Gardnor's whisky arrived with a tinkle of glasses and loose
change Freddy opened his eyes again. Gardnor said, 'There's
another point, Freddy, that may have escaped you. It isn't so much a
question of what you've heard in the missing days, as a question of
what you might have said, presuming you've been in the way of
hearing things of a security nature.'

'The point hasn't escaped me,' Freddy said.

Gardnor's face, which was normally placid and healthy from a recent sun-tan, looked pasty, as if he had eaten something that disagreed with him.

'I'm sure I said nothing out of place,' Freddy said. 'Sure of it.'

'So am I.'

'But I agree, that's a question that is bound to arise. Well, it'll all come back, anyway. A good night's sleep –'

Gardnor now took the hint, swallowed down his drink and left.

Freddy, on that first night of his return from oblivion, pondered for some hours, lying awake in his exhaustion. He had a sense of having exerted himself a great deal, of having been to a number of different places. But what had he done and where? His memory gave no answer. Freddy gave up for the night; he let his mind murmur ironically to itself the boast: 'I can call spirits from the vasty deep,' and he fell asleep, turning his mind's tongue on Hotspur's reply: 'But will they come when you do call for them?'

'I am told very privately,' Freddy said, 'that she is hiding somewhere in Jordan, and is safe so far. Where exactly she is, or whether she will remain safe is another question. I don't know. My informant could say nothing about that. I intend to mention nothing to the authorities until she's out of the country, and I know of course, Joanna, that you won't either.'

'We won't breathe a word,' said Matt. 'Who told you she's still in the country?'

'I'm not in a position to say who my informant is.'

Abdul Ramdez had in fact come to Freddy at the hotel, the day after his visit to Acre, to give him the information that Freddy had asked for. 'She's still in Jordan, she's in hiding. She's safe so far. But you will not inform the authorities, Mr Hamilton, or she will no longer be safe, and moreover, someone very close to me will be in danger also. I can say no more.'

'You can trust me, Abdul,' Freddy said. 'If there's something I can do to help her, anything that you may hear of, let me know. When will she be leaving Jordan? How will she manage it unobserved?'

'I think soon. She will get away. I don't know how it is to be arranged. I tell you all that I am able, as you are so anxious.'

'I won't forget this kindness, Abdul.'

Freddy said to Joanna, once more, 'Not a word. It might lead to bloodshed.'

'Oh, Freddy, I wish you wouldn't keep talking about bloodshed.'

'It's a dangerous part of the world,' Freddy said. 'So I beg you, not a word to a soul.'

'Of course not. They would only start searching –'

'Now, Joanna, don't blame yourself,' said her husband. 'You were perfectly all right to her.'

'It was I who was at fault,' said Freddy. 'It was –'

'Now, Freddy, we've had all that. Do put your feet up and rest. It's you we're worried about.'

'It was the beginning of my sunstroke,' Freddy said.

'You've got to rest. Sit on the sofa, Freddy. That chair's uncomfortable.'

'I can't rest,' Freddy said.

He called the partial collapse from which he was still suffering his 'sunstroke' for want of any better explanation of its cause. Dr Jarvis, on his second visit to Freddy at the hotel, had thought it was probably an attack of 'coast memory', which he said was a type of amnesia that affected white men in the tropics, especially Africa.

'That would be caused by sunstroke,' Freddy had said.

It was difficult to know the point at which one was justified in being affronted by a doctor's remark. This particular quack, Freddy considered, had gone a bit far when he had replied, in an off-hand sort of way, that he believed this type of amnesia was sometimes hysteric in origin but that of course he did not know what type of amnesia it was – he wasn't a specialist in that subject.

'Well,' Freddy had said, aloofly, 'I hope – I *hope* – that it *isn't* hysteric in origin.'

'Hysteria in the medical sense doesn't mean, necessarily, a wild outbreak of emotion, screaming and so on,' the doctor said. 'It's a term we use.'

'Oh, I know all that,' said Freddy.

This doctor said, 'We may use the word "hysteric" to describe any symptom – it may only be a headache or a stomach disorder, caused by some form of mental disturbance.'

'Yes, but I've got no mental disturbance,' Freddy said firmly. 'So if you are thinking of recommending me to see a psychiatrist, my answer is no. Not while I've got my wits about me, and remain officially sane, do I consult any psychiatrist.'

'Your sanity isn't in question,' the doctor said, as one appealing to reason. Freddy felt deeply resentful of this doctor, who was an English Jew, now an Israeli practising in Jerusalem. His name was Jarvis. Many Foreign Service personnel, including the British, used him for their regular doctor. He had already attended Freddy, some months ago, when Freddy had arrived in the country with an arm swollen and inflamed from a new vaccination. Dr Jarvis had seemed a very agreeable and efficient fellow at that time, but now Freddy found himself in unaccustomed distress; he felt a choking resentment and could hardly recognize himself in the sensation. Why, he thought, is this Jew called Jarvis? It's an old English name, how does he come by Jarvis? His father must have been Jarvinsky or something; I should just like to ask him which of the Jarvises he is, which of the two branches, the Kent Jarvises or the others in Wales. I should just like to see how he'd answer that question. Jarvis, indeed, with his talk of mental disturbances. But Freddy, in his distress, was still graced with those habits of good behaviour which restrain wild-running excesses of thought; he was endowed also with that gift which some men keep furtively out of sight like a family skeleton, an inward court of appeal with powers to reverse all varieties of mental verdicts. And in the space of time that it took Dr Jarvis to sit down at the table in Freddy's hotel sitting-room and write out a prescription, Freddy reflected, I suppose the man is performing his job according to his lights.

Bewildered as Freddy was, and gripped intermittently by waves of panic about his forgotten days, he said, 'My father had a favourite joke about psychiatrists. He used to say, "Anyone who consults a psychiatrist wants his head examined."'

Dr Jarvis smiled as one who tries to do so. 'Look,' he said, 'I haven't said a word to you about a psychiatrist. In fact, I haven't got a great deal of time for them, myself. They all hold different theories. There's hardly two who would treat a patient in the same way. You don't know where you are with them. They're a lot of bloody robbers as well. I've known people, sick people, remain in the hands of psychiatrists, two sessions a week, for twenty years, and nothing to show for it.'

'You don't say so!' Freddy said, cheering up a little. 'Twenty years . . .' A few days' temporary absence of mind due to sunstroke was really nothing to worry about.

'All I was going to suggest,' said Jarvis, 'was that we get a diagnosis, as far as that's possible, to see what caused your loss of memory and perhaps prevent it happening again.'

'What sort of diagnosis? Who from?' Freddy said. 'I don't want to be unreasonable, but these mental specialists – as you say yourself, they aren't agreed, they've got no proof, no unassailable theory. Whereas if you settle for sunstroke, well, that's an old-established thing, and you know where you are.'

'Let's make it sunstroke,' said Jarvis.

'Oh, all right, I'm willing to be diagnosed,' Freddy said. 'I'll go as far as that. But I won't necessarily accept their diagnosis, or act on it, or answer their probing questions. Probing questions are plain bad manners to me, and that's the long and the short of it.'

'Oh, well, bad manners, good manners – they don't exist in the Unconscious.'

'I don't believe there's such a thing as the Unconscious,' Freddy said. 'How could there be a certainty about something unconscious? If something is unconscious then it's unknown. So the Unconscious is only a hypothesis at the best.'

'Hypnosis is sometimes employed in cases of amnesia,' said the doctor, his face abstracted from Freddy's protests, 'to establish association with whatever has caused it. There's also a recent drug that releases memory, but I'd have to look into it.'

'I would never agree to be hypnotized. Out of the question. No one should submit their mind to another mind:

> He that complies against his will
> Is of his own opinion still.

– that's *my* motto. I won't be brain-washed, thank you.'

Jarvis was unmoved. 'I don't advise further consultation at the moment. Seeing how you feel about it, there wouldn't be any point.

It would only tend to make you feel worse. I'm going to insist that you take some leave. Get these pills: three a day, half an hour before meals.'

'Are these the memory drugs?' Freddy inquired, scrutinizing the prescription.

'No, that isn't the drug I referred to. Those are just old-fashioned sedatives.'

'I feel perfectly all right, actually,' Freddy said. 'Perfectly normal.'

He felt terrible, actually, and when the doctor had left, he sat with his head in his hands, while currents of horror, unidentifiable, unknown to experience, charged through his mind and body continually. Mind or body, it was impossible to distinguish one from the other, they were both and neither. The telephone rang. It was Gardnor, wanting to come round for a little chat, as he put it. Freddy said he would see him at five-thirty. He shivered although the day was warm. He poured lots of water on his neglected geraniums. He shivered again. Then he got his winter suit out of his cabin-trunk where it hung among the moth-balls. If he still shivered by evening, Freddy decided, he would then put it on. What day of the week was it? Time was apt to become confusing.

Before lunch that day, some letters were brought up to him. One from Ma, one from his sister Elsie and one from Joanna. Freddy decided to spend the afternoon writing letters. He took his letters down to lunch with him, but read only Joanna's:

Thank God you've been found, Freddy dear, we were off our heads with anxiety. And whatever *can* you have done with Barbara Vaughan? – Of course, it's only a coincidence, your disappearing together, but really Freddy, we did seriously wonder if you'd eloped with her! ! I'm in constant touch with the people at *your* end, in case there's anything I can do at *this* end. Rupert Gardnor tells us you're in good hands. Follow the doctor's advice, won't you, Freddy dear, and . . .

Freddy decided to start a set of verses in *terza rima* for Joanna. He did, in fact, start them on the way upstairs after lunch, but then he fell asleep. When he woke it was half past three. He wondered what had happened to Miss Vaughan, then lost the thought. He checked the calendar – Wednesday, the 16th of August. It would not do to go wrong again. He opened Ma's letter.

He could not make head nor tail of most of it. She kept referring to her 'last letter' in which she had apparently described some dreadful threat of Benny's following some new dreadful upset about the old garnet brooch. It was plain, Freddy thought, that she had forgotten to post, or perhaps had not even written, this last letter. At all events, Freddy did not know what she was talking about, and could only guess that the two old women were being tiresome as usual. He decided to ignore the bit about Benny, her threats, and the garnet brooch, and reply only to Ma's query about Eichmann, who she fancied was a famous pianist she had met in the old days.

His sister's letter was a brief intimation that her friend, Miss Rickward, was to arrive in Jordan next week-end and that she believed Freddy knew a Barbara Vaughan, who taught at Miss Rickward's school. 'Between ourselves,' Elsie had written, 'it was a shock for Miss Rickward to learn that Barbara Vaughan was engaged. Poor Miss Rickward is making a trip out there to see what Miss Vaughan is up to and so on, and any assistance you can give . . .'

Freddy put them aside. He would answer all the letters tomorrow. Perhaps in the morning. Abdul was coming tomorrow. Freddy fell asleep again till Gardnor arrived at five-thirty.

By the end of that week Freddy realized that he was more than ordinarily a subject of concern at the Legation. Gardnor came on four successive evenings, and on Friday took Freddy to his flat for dinner. Freddy was touched beyond the ordinary. There was a look of private strain about Gardnor that Freddy had not noticed before.

It appeared that Gardnor's report had set off an agitation in the office. Freddy was not quite clear what it was about, but it seemed that most of them felt he should be in hospital, receiving treatment for his lost memory.

'It will come back in its own time,' Freddy said.

Rupert Gardnor was now very much on Freddy's side. He was extremely anxious to impress on Freddy that any form of treatment, especially hypnosis, would constitute, in his view, a weak course of action.

On Friday they sat drinking in the leafy courtyard of Freddy's hotel.

'I feel,' Freddy said, 'that if I concentrate on other things, the memory will return in due time.' And he thought desperately of some other thing to talk about to Gardnor, there and then. He could only think of a successful bet he had once laid with his fellow officers at sea during the war, already having tried it successfully in a forfeit game with his nephews and nieces at a Christmas gathering. 'I bet you a round of drinks,' Freddy now said, 'that you can't spell desiccated.'

Gardnor took him on, and spelt it 'd-e-s-s-i-c-a-t-e-d'.

'Wrong,' said Freddy.

Gardnor tried again, for another round, spelling it 'd-e-s-i-c-a-t-e-d'.

'There are two c's,' said Freddy.

'Well, I never knew that before.'

'No one does,' Freddy said.

'You could make a living out of it.'

'So I shall, if I lose my job.'

'Well, I hope it won't come to that.' Gardnor spoke with such a trace of seriousness that Freddy looked to see what expression he wore. But he seemed cheerful enough.

'We've got a new man coming from London next week,' Gardnor said. 'I've no idea who he is.'

'Really? What's his job?'

'I don't know. I only heard about him late this afternoon. But I suppose he's from "Q".' "Q" was the Foreign Office Internal Security department. Gardnor spoke softly. Two or three other tables on the terrace were occupied.

'Why d'you suppose that? Has anything new been going on?'

Gardnor looked round casually and beckoned to a waiter who was hovering in the vine-framed doorway that led from the terrace to the hall. He ordered some drinks to be served indoors. When they had moved indoors and got their whiskies-and-soda in a quiet corner of the big room, Gardnor said, 'There's been a leakage about the agreement with Kuwait. The Jews don't think it comes from any of their men, they think it's us.'

'Well, that's the Embassy's affair,' Freddy said. 'It's nothing to do with us here in Jerusalem. Whitehall should send its snooper to Tel Aviv, that's where he should go.'

'Oh, we can't pretend to know nothing of Kuwait,' Gardnor said.

'No, that's true. Well, we'll discuss it another time.'

'Everyone feels you should have treatment, Freddy. But I disagree – I mean, for your own sake. You look jolly fit to me.'

'When Barbara Vaughan turns up, if she does turn up safely, she may throw some light on the mystery. I don't know, of course; but she did disappear from the convent on the same day that I disappeared from myself, so to speak.'

'We're more or less certain she's gone away. Her boy-friend left Jordan about that time. They've gone off together.'

'I hope so,' Freddy said.

The following week Joanna met him at the Jordan end of the Gate and drove him to the house. She said, 'I've made inquiries of anyone who might have recognized you on those days last week-end, Freddy, but no one saw a sign of you. I've asked Ramdez, I've asked Alexandros and all the shops, even the barber. No one saw you at all. Of course, they always deny everything, on principle. Where can you have been?'

'I must go over everything carefully from the beginning. Perhaps here in Jordan it will come back to me.'

It was now ten days since Barbara Vaughan's disappearance. She had not been seen since she left the Cartwrights' house on that Saturday afternoon of her visit, when Freddy had unaccountably turned on the Cartwrights: 'The whole trouble with you is, you blow neither hot nor cold. . . .' Of course, the row had blown over. The Cartwrights had apologized effusively for their tactlessness and for blowing neither hot nor cold. 'Yes, it *is* true, Matt,' Joanna had said to her husband. 'There are some things too serious . . . poor Freddy is right. Poor Barbara . . .' All that fuss had blown over. Barbara had returned to the convent-hostel where she was staying; at least she had been driven to the door by Matt and Joanna; at least that was what Joanna and Matt said. Freddy found himself in an uncomfortable state of suspecting absolutely everybody's testimony and this, in turn, made him feel guilty. But he was certain, now, where at first he had only begun to notice, that small silences occurred in the course of conversations with visitors and friends from the legation. They were keeping something back from him, he was sure. When at last he had agreed to come across to Jordan to stay for a while with the Cartwrights, there again he noticed the hesitation, the silences.

'Has Barbara Vaughan been found?'

'No, Freddy, you know we'd tell you if she had. Personally, I think she's left the country.'

'If you hear that she's been found, be sure to tell me. I was privately informed that she is safe so far. I can't tell you more than that, and I can only tell you that much in confidence. But if you should hear that she is dead, killed, by whatever means, be sure to tell me.'

A little silence. Then, 'Freddy, dear, you're being morbid.'

'I know, Joanna, but one must face the –'

'Freddy, you know that Clegg had gone on leave just before she disappeared. It's only reasonable to suppose they've eloped.'

'I don't believe it, Matt.'

'But he went away, just as she did, without telling anyone where he was going. She must have got out of the country somehow. There's a Dutch line from Amman. Goodness, it would be easy. She was just another tourist with a passport; how could they remember her face? It's such an ordinary face.'

'Well, Joanna, there's no record of the name Vaughan on any of the airlines. I don't –'

'Oh, it's easy to move about and pass these border posts, Freddy. A little money goes a long way out here. Everyone's bribable.'

'Well, I'm not convinced, that's all. She had changed towards Clegg, you remember.'

'Well she must have changed back again.'

Freddy said, 'If one wasn't involved, it would be awfully funny. In fact, it is funny. The woman disappears, then it turns out that Clegg has disappeared; and at the same time I disappeared for a few days. It'll make a jolly good story one day if Barbara Vaughan gets out of it alive.'

The small particle of silence flickered in the air between Freddy and the Cartwrights again. Then Joanna said, gaily, 'It will all blow over, Freddy.'

'Time for drinks,' said Matt. 'What will you drink, Freddy?'

'Promise me one thing, Joanna,' Freddy said.

'What?'

'That you'll be careful when you go clambering about the hills up here looking for wild flowers. That short-cut to the Potter's Field, you know it's dangerous. It borders on Israel. In fact, it's disputable whose territory it is.'

'Oh, Freddy, I've done it dozens of times. Why do you say this?'

'I've got a premonition of bloodshed,' Freddy said. 'Which isn't like me at all. But somebody – I can't help feeling – is in danger of bloodshed.' He was thinking, wildly, as he had done all week, it might be Abdul on his smuggling trip, if he's to be believed . . . It might be Barbara . . . Joanna, gathering wild flowers . . . Somebody I know.

'Freddy, that's an odd thing for you to say,' said Matt, suspiciously.

'He's not in the brightest of spirits, dear,' Joanna said, angry at her husband's tone.

'Not in character,' Matt said. 'Freddy, tell us honestly. Have you really lost your memory? Is it true? Or is it a matter of expediency? I think you'll be frank with us.'

'We're on your side, either way,' Joanna said.

'Then is that what the Foreign Office suspects?' Freddy said. 'Is that what they're thinking?'

'In fact, I did hear a rumour that they're anxious about something,' Matt said. 'Something in the security line.'

'I lost my memory all right,' Freddy said. 'I haven't a clue what happened to me. Matt, you old humbug, what a question to ask me.'

Joanna hugged Freddy. 'We're on your side, anyway,' she said. 'You should let the doctors question you and try to bring back the events. They do it by a process of association.'

'I can wait a while,' Freddy said. 'What actually happened is bound to come back.'

What actually happened to Freddy between the late Saturday afternoon when he lost his memory in Jordan and the early Tuesday afternoon when he regained it in Israel was to come back to him a little later – the outlines of his movements forcing themselves back to him, at first, in a series of meaningless threads. The details followed gradually, throughout the days and into the years ahead and occurred, then, in those fragments, more or less distorted, which are the normal formations and decor of human memory.

The little heated fuss in the garden had blown over. That was definitely one of the things he remembered on his return to Israel.

'The trouble with you,' Freddy had heard himself tell his friends, 'is you blow neither hot nor cold.' Blow cold, blow hot, it had all blown over. Matt drove Barbara back to the convent, and Joanna, cheerfully breezing-down the recently inflamed atmosphere, left the house with them, a bulky parcel of groceries in her arms. She was holding it like a baby. The parcel was not tied with string; it was loosely bundled together in brown paper; one could see portions of a sugar-package, a bag of flour, and a tin of something sticking out of the upper end of the bundle, like an infant's head. Joanna had said that, while the car was out, it would be a chance to take that stuff to someone or other, one of her poor Arab families. Freddy had seen many such bundles of groceries being borne out of houses, at home and abroad, by many such busy Englishwomen, killers of two birds to the stone, all through his life. At home, the Welfare State had done nothing to change their habits. The scene was all the more typical in that Matt had already gone out to the car, thrusting past her, without any attempt to relieve his wife of the bundle; there was no hint of expectation on her part that he should do so. Freddy's aunts and sisters, all their school friends and the wives of Freddy's school friends had been for ever dashing out of the house to get a place in the car, with breathless parcels of groceries entwined in their arms, while the husbands pushed past them to the driver's seat.

This had been the last scene to impress itself on Freddy's mind before he mislaid the records. He was on the road, his head bare under the hot sun. He waved good-bye as the car drove off, with Barbara beside Matt in the front and Joanna in the back.

After that his actions and thoughts were as follows: He returned to the house and felt it to be suddenly empty. He thought he had better go up and rest. As he went towards the staircase he passed the letter tray. Two letters had arrived for him by air mail from England. This was not unusual. Quite often his mail, having arrived at his office in Israel after he had left on Friday afternoon, would be put in the diplomatic bag and sent through the Gate to the Consulate in Jordan; one of the consuls would then have it sent over to the Cartwrights where they knew Freddy was staying. And so it was quite to be expected that Freddy should find a letter or two lying on the tray addressed to him, at any odd hour of the week-end.

He took the two letters upstairs, glancing at the envelopes. He saw that one came from his mother and the other from Benny, and when he reached his room he was tempted to put them away out of sight, unopened. This feeling, too, was usual, his habitual reaction to letters from Harrogate where his mother and Benny resided at great expense, mistress and servant grown old together and living on that vital substance of mutual reproaches and complaints against the hotel, which formed the main themes of his mother's letters to Freddy. Benny's less-frequent letters were equally tedious; her religious feeling, so jolly in the hymn-singing nursery days, had become a mania and a great bore to Freddy: 'Mr Freddy, the Lord knows and only He knows what it is to live with her. I have tried to bring home the Word of Jesus to her heart, but the Devil and his Minions have got her in their bloody claws. Mr Desmond gave a sermon last week that was your living Mother to a T. I have spoken to the girls, Mr Freddy, but it is up to you –'

The 'girls' were Freddy's elder sisters. They were quite capable of solving any of their mother's problems, and took some trouble to do so. But Freddy was aware that his mother did not want a solution to her problems, she wanted a solver of problems, and no one would suffice but Freddy himself. Benny was to some extent a participant in the unspoken plot to get unattached Freddy to resign his job and come and live with them. It was an old story to Freddy, who had no intention of laying himself, a human sacrifice, on the altar at Harrogate. In the course of the years he had sometimes become alarmed at Benny's religiosity. Her letters bore more and more graphic references to the Devil and his sulphurous regions, and more and more exhortations to Freddy himself to come home from his heathen posts to Christian Harrogate, and serve Christ rather than the Foreign Secretary. And Freddy had duly sent off his weekly letters to his mother, and to Benny from time to time, adapting their tone according to his judgement. It was largely a matter of keeping them quiet.

Freddy, then, looked at these two letters and felt, as he commonly did, that he wanted to shove them out of sight. But as usual he decided to open them and answer them right away so that the job would not be hanging over him. He was annoyed with his mother for having written a second letter in one week, without waiting for a reply to the first; he was afraid she was getting very forgetful.

Freddy sighed. He hung his coat on a chair and sat down in his shirt sleeves, feeling cooler and more as one getting down to business. He put on his reading-glasses. Benny first: he smoothed the thin sheets and began reading. The old story, only worse. He skimmed over it.

Dear Mr Freddy, the time has come at last to tell you my Temptations are getting beyond human endurance. . . . Yesterday your Mother said . . . and on Tuesday, do you know what she did when I went over to the chest of drawers? She . . . Your mother is . . . I hear those Voices again in my dreams and in the early morning . . . Blood . . . Mr Freddy and those temptations come back to me that I told you of last month . . . You had better come, Mr Freddy . . . Mr Desmond says to pray . . . I dare not tell him all my mind as he is so good . . . but I have prayed . . . I started to speak of my fears to your sister Elsie. But you know how bossy she is, she would have me in a Home, so I shut up after that. Your Mother goads me on, she is a true friend of the Devil . . . She . . . She . . . She . . . I am afraid . . . afraid . . . There will be Bloodshed come out of it. . . .

Really, Benny is letting her imagination run wild, Freddy thought. As if the heat and humidity of Jerusalem isn't enough to try one's reason, without those letters. . . . Elsie is probably quite right to suggest Benny's going into a Home, but that would leave Ma without a companion. Let them both go into a Home, Benny and Ma, too. Ma, of course, Freddy thought, is behind all this religious excess of Benny's. She would goad anyone to strangle her or slit her throat, and in a way one quite sees how poor Benny feels. Freddy, looking up from Benny's letter to reach out for the other one, caught a glimpse of himself, smiling, in the little looking-glass on the dressing table. The smile disappeared. He opened his mother's letter.

I fear that Benny is . . . isn't quite . . . Benny, I'm afraid, is definitely . . . She has, of course, pilfered my garnet brooch again. Three pounds were missing from my purse and nobody but Benny had access; literally nobody. Elsie is, I'm afraid, most unsympathetic. She has a heart of iron although I write of my own daughter. I see no alternative for you but to come . . . Benny . . . Benny . . .

Freddy took his letter-pad and wrote:

DEAR BENNY,

I have your letter and am sorry to hear you are feeling unwell just now. I hope Mr Desmond has advised you to see the doctor. You should tell Mr Desmond all your troubles you know, Benny, and if he is a good man, as I know he is, he will understand. These Ministers of Religion know that very good Christians have troubled minds from time to time.

You must bear with my mother. She is getting old, you know, like all of us.

I am extremely occupied just now on some important Government business, but as soon as I can get leave I shall come to join you for a few weeks at Harrogate, and we shall have a merry time.

You know how much we all appreciate you. You must look upon me, and upon my sisters, as your friends. We depend upon you. Don't let us down after all these years.

Your devoted,
FREDDY

He wrote to his mother's doctor:

DEAR DR ARLINGTON,

I understand – by the tone of letters received from my mother and our old servant Miss Bennett – that the latter is in a somewhat troubled frame of mind. I shall be grateful if you will have a look into her general health the next time you call in to see my mother. I'm afraid these old people are apt to let their imaginations run away with them.

You know my sisters' addresses of course, in case anything serious should be found wrong with Miss Bennett. But unless she is suffering from a serious ailment, I, for one, would prefer to keep her as active as possible. The idea of going into a 'home' seems to upset her; and as, of course, she has been with our family since her girlhood, I would like her to end her days in the comfort provided by the hotel, and with the feeling of being useful to us, as indeed she is.

Your sincerely,
FREDERICK HAMILTON

Next, he wrote to his mother:

. . . be patient, dearest Ma. You know that Benny will give you back the brooch eventually. Are you quite *sure* you did not make Benny a present of this brooch? You are always so marvellous. Remember, only a few weeks ago, there was a question of the garnet brooch. I do not recall how it was resolved (if indeed you informed me) but you see Ma, Benny is . . . You are, of *course*, Ma dearest, the *only* one who . . .

Freddy put these letters in envelopes, one by one, and addressed and stamped them. He then put them in his pocket. He went out for a walk intending to post them.

It was nearly half past five, and a great sunset had begun to blaze across the hills of Jerusalem, darkening the valley of Gehenna that ran beneath him to join the valley of Jehosophat in the East. Freddy crossed the sandy motor track which led to the Cartwrights' front door and picked his way to the footpath, the short-cut from the city, up which he had trudged on all his visits. He stood there, on the stony path on a ridge of the Hill of Evil Counsel which rose behind him to its summit at Haceldama, the Potter's Field, bought, by repute, with the unwanted blood-money of Judas and serving, throughout subsequent generations, both the dead and the living, as a graveyard for itinerant paupers and a hide-out for smugglers. The all-over properties and associations of this spot were hallowed by a small, musty Greek Orthodox shrine and that ancient, frail monk who was sublimely unaware of anything in the world around him except his hen-coop and God; within the latter category were included all of the human race who crossed his territory on their sightseeing tours or smuggling business, for he seemed to look right through them into God, and treated all accordingly with mesmerized awe, having very few words actually to say to them. Freddy had always found his old monk extremely satisfying company. One could talk to him without the effort of conversation; the monk would express all that was necessary in the pose of his shrivelled body under its loose blue robe, and in the light of his dark eyes, enormous in their deep bony sockets. Freddy had once said, looking round him, 'This is called the Hill of Evil Counsel but it should be called the Hill of Good Counsel.' Not that the monk had ever given him any counsel, but that was how Freddy felt about the man's responsive silence. The time Freddy had stood in the doorway of the dark Orthodox chapel and, regarding the heavy-laden altar and the exotic clusters of coloured lamps hung round it, said, 'It's not really my cup of tea, you know,' the old man had conveyed his complete endorsement of that idea by some emanative gesture that Freddy could not locate in any particular movement the monk had made. Freddy, in this first hour of his absence, turned and looked up towards the field; he could see from where he stood on the footpath a projecting angle of the monk's quarters, and caught a glimpse of the blue cassock as it seemed to potter about the yard, bearing the old man's spiritual bones and constitution inside it. He is rounding up his hens for the night, thought Freddy, and at that moment the thought also went through his head that, if necessary, he could spend the night up there. He was quite sure the monk would give him a bed and would not mind being woken up at however late an hour, since everyone was the sweet Lord to him.

It did not occur to Freddy that there was something irrational in this notion. But as if he recalled a decision already reached by a form of reasoning, he returned to the Cartwrights' house and packed his clothes into his zipper-bag. Next he took his writing-pad to write a note of excuse to Joanna. None of the house servants was evident, but they were probably hanging around, and would witness his two departures from the house, one without his bag and the other with it. He took a little thought, then wrote:

JOANNA DEAR,
    I've decided to return earlier than expected to attend to some

private business that's cropped up. I'll write next week. Forgive haste. Bless you, Joanna dear.

FREDDY

That would not mystify. Joanna must have seen his letters on the tray before she left. He put his writing-pad into the zipper-bag and zipped it up, leaving out the letters he had received from his mother and Benny, now replaced in their envelopes. These he put in his pocket, stuffing them in with a rustle of air-mail paper, beside the three unposted letters he had written.

Freddy went to the lavatory, not from need, but in case there should be a long journey ahead of him without access to a lavatory. Then he took up his zipper-bag and went down, leaving his note to Joanna on the letter tray. As he walked out of the door he could still hear the gurgle of the lavatory drain behind him; it was a newly installed system, but even so, Joanna had been complaining that it was too noisy and not really very reliable; one had to yank the chain in a certain way or it wouldn't work; one had to acquire the knack.

He crossed the motor road and saw below, where the evening had deepened, the lights of a car; it was most probably the Cartwrights', since the road only existed to serve a few residents in the area. They were returning and he would be gone. He picked his way cautiously over a few feet of scrub-land to the rocky footpath which branched away from the main road, winding down the Hill of Evil Counsel. The sunset was at its climax, touching the spires and hills of Jerusalem so that they seemed to rise from vague darkness; in the east the Mount of Olives with its three summits, the Hill of Offence, the Hill of Olivet, and the Hill known as the Viri Galilaei; to the west, Mount Gareb; and in the north, the Scopus range. Freddy went down as it were to meet them, for in the illusory light the mountains had seemed to mingle with the domes and minarets of Old Jerusalem. He suddenly knew what he was looking for, he knew his first task, but he began to puzzle about where he could find it without going too far, or encountering any difficulty, or having to go to an hotel and waste money on a drink. Then an idea occurred to him: Alexandros. Freddy experienced a great sense of relief that puzzled and amused him; he entered the windy streets of the Old City feeling very young and happy – more wideawake than he had felt for years.

The letters were in his pocket, those to his mother, Benny, and his mother's doctor, together with those from his mother and Benny. To dispose of them quickly was his first object.

It was twenty minutes to seven when he reached Alexandros. Most curio shops in the area were still open, but Alexandros seemed to have shut early. A light was on in the shop window and at the back of the premises. Freddy peered inside the doorway and knocked. No one seemed to be in the shop. He rattled the letter box. A few passing tourists stared at him and at the shop, and loitered, as if wondering what sort of bargain this man was after, and whether they themselves were missing something. A voice from above his head called something in Arabic. Freddy stepped back on to the street and looked up.

'My friend!' said Alexandros.

'Am I disturbing you?' Freddy said.

'I come.'

As he let Freddy in, a middle-aged European couple with an Arab guide tried to follow. Alexandros spoke to the guide in Arabic, the drift of which Freddy was able to understand. As Alexandros was apparently about to refuse these late customers, Freddy said, 'I would like to speak to you privately, Alexandros. Attend to them first.' Freddy retreated towards the dark far end of the shop, as one not wishing to be observed.

The man and woman, conversing with each other in German, pressed into the shop, sensing resistance.

'I will deal with them quickly,' Alexandros murmured. 'They are not a serious type of customer, but perhaps they buy.'

'May I use your lavatory?' Freddy said.

'Of course.' Alexandros then spoke to the guide, instructing him in Arabic to wait with his tourists inside the shop and see that they did not touch anything. He led the way to the small closet behind the shop and Freddy followed.

'It is the western style as you see,' Alexandros said, and Freddy realized that this was indeed an unusual feature for an Arab establishment, where one would normally expect the system of sanitation set into the floor. 'The last tenant of the shop was a Jew,' said Alexandros with his French-Arab gesture of the hands and shoulders that so much conveyed his impartiality to the humours and chances of war, fate and life.

Freddy tore up first the letters from his mother and Benny. Down they went. He waited for the cistern to refill, rightly judging it to be a slow one. He did not want to block up Alexandros's lavatory, or force the cistern to work by repeatedly yanking the chain. While he waited, he realized that the contents of the three sealed envelopes he had in his hand would probably not go down so easily as had the air-mail paper from Harrogate that he had just got rid of, since his own writing-paper was heavier stuff. So he took out his cigarette lighter and, thankful to find it was in working condition, burned up the three letters he had written that afternoon, holding them over the lavatory pan, and dropping in the charred remains one by one, first Benny's, then the doctor's and lastly Ma's. He pulled the chain. Down they went. But not quite. A few charred fragments – those last corners of paper that he had held between finger and thumb – remained float-ing. Freddy waited for a further four minutes until the gurgle faded to a whisper, pulled sharply and hoped. His total effort was doomed to success. The last of the Harrogate relics disappeared. He emerged from the tiny cabinet to find Alexandros hovering anxiously outside the door.

'Are you all right, Mr Hamilton?'

'Perfectly all right,' Freddy said. 'I was just disposing of some tire-some correspondence.' As he followed Alexandros into the front shop, settling on a sofa in the large space reserved for special custom-ers, Freddy assured his host that he had been careful as regards the drains.

'Mr Hamilton,' said Alexandros, 'you're a wise man. If a corre-spondence is tiresome, what can a man do? He tries his best, he tries to say one thing, he tries to say another thing. Then after a few months, a year, two years, if there is no satisfaction, then pouff? – he should put the entire affair down the drain. Finish.'

Freddy said, 'It lasted longer than two years. It has gone on all my life. Family trouble.'

'Oh well, your family; I thought it might be a lady. In the case of the family, Mr Hamilton, a man must do the same as with a woman. If they make troubles without end, troubles all the time, there is a point where a man must put the business down the drain. Let the family go their way. Finish. I see you have delayed long enough.'

'I should have done it years ago,' Freddy said. He could feel Alexandros looking at him with approving wonder, and realized that some new thing about his appearance was conveying an unaccustomed liberated impression. 'Do you know,' Freddy said, 'I feel quite young, Alexandros.'

'You're not an old man. Myself, I tell you in confidence, I don't live in an old man's way. I'm fifty-seven.'

'I'm fifty-five.'

'Middle age,' said Alexandros, sinking into a chair opposite Freddy. 'If a man has lived older than his years till middle age, then he should start to live younger.'

'One can make a fool of oneself,' Freddy said. This apparently touched a talking-point in Alexandros. He stood up and said, 'One may do this, always. Agreed. But this depends also on the company. In the consideration of this or that company – this person, that person – one is foolish, one is wise. I also make a fool of myself in the consideration of my wife that I have left my business at Beirut in the hands of my second son, to come here among the Moslems. My wife is a good woman and a fine Mama of the family. But she does not trust my second son's wife, a woman who is a Catholic also like ourselves. My wife is telling me I am a fool to leave the business in Beirut where this wife of my son can make changes. My wife is also against the Moslem religion. Here in Jerusalem she won't speak to our neighbours, she weeps that in Beirut we have all Christian neighbours. So, to my wife I look like a fool. But to my sons I am not foolish. They say, the Papa goes to Jerusalem, he makes a specialized business of fine goods, he sends his first son to the university and his second son he permits to have a life for himself in Lebanon. Another thing, Mr Hamilton – myself, also, I like the Moslem religion all right. I am an Arab. The Christian religion agrees with the religion of Islam in many particulars. But women do not know of this.' He sat down.

Freddy said, 'I often think all religions have something in common when you take away the damn nonsense. How do you feel about the Jews? I've got a special reason for asking you, Alexandros.'

'The Jews,' said Alexandros, in the quieter tone of voice demanded by the subject, 'are good for trade. There is no business here in Jordan since the Jews have departed. The prices are too low. They understand the markets and the variety of quality merchandise for the visitors of one quality or another quality. The country is poor because the Jewish economy is absent. You must not say Alexandros told you this. Not to anyone, please.'

'As persons? How do you feel about the Jews individually? I want to ask your advice about a friend who's got Jewish blood. I've got to attend to it right away, in fact.'

Alexandros spread his hands and cast up his eyes. 'I have known good and bad. People – they are people.' He looked then at Freddy's zipper-bag and said, 'But you do not intend to return to Israel tonight? The Gate is closed. It's too late.'

'I know,' Freddy said.

Alexandros waved a hand towards the curtain which hung across the narrow staircase. 'You must dine with me, please. I then drive you back to the Cartwright house in my car.'

'I won't be returning to the Cartwrights. My friends think I've gone. But to tell you the truth, Alexandros, I mean to stay in Jordan until I've helped a friend of mine out of difficulty. In fact, now that I've got rid of those tiresome letters I've got an overwhelming desire to do so.'

Alexandros folded his arms.

'I suppose,' said Freddy, 'you think I've gone off my head. And if so, I can only –'

'Mr Hamilton! I am far from thinking such a thing. To my mind you are an extra sane man. Is it a man or a lady, this Jew?'

'A young woman of my acquaintance,' Freddy said. 'That lady who bought the silver fish from you. She –'

'Zobeida! . . .' Alexandros was over by the staircase, pulling the curtain aside, linking himself still to Freddy's presence by an arm outstretched in his direction – 'Zobeida! Make a place at my table for a guest. Lela! Tell Zobeida I have a friend –'

'Look,' Freddy said. 'I don't want it known that I'm still in Jordan. I don't want the Cartwrights to hear. I have a reason.'

'Then nobody shall hear,' said Alexandros, and disappeared upstairs.

Saturday night to Tuesday afternoon: the events were to come back to Freddy in the course of time; first, like an electric shock of fatal voltage, but not fatal, and so, after that, like a cloud of unknowing, heavy with the molecules of accumulated impressions and finally when he had come to consider the whole mosaic of evidence, when he had gathered the many-coloured fragments of what actually happened, and had put the missing parts in place, then he came to discern, too late for action but more and more clearly as the years sifted past, that he had been neither a monster nor a fool, but had behaved rather well, and at least with style and courage. Looking back at the experience in later years Freddy was amazed. It had seemed to transfigure his life, without any disastrous change in the appearance of things; pleasantly and essentially he came to feel it had made a free man of him where before he had been the subdued, obedient servant of a mere disorderly sensation, that of impersonal guilt. And whether this feeling of Freddy's subsequent years was justified or not, it did him good to harbour it.

Now, on the first evening of those missing days, Freddy began to see himself, as he sat at Alexandros's table, in a physical way under such an aspect as he had seen himself in his Cambridge days when he had been a boxing half-blue. It may have been that Alexandros was now regarding him with the special interest called for by the occasion; Freddy was not sure of this, for Alexandros was offering his special reserves of hospitality, as he would his rare pieces, which were generally kept from display in the shop. However that may have been, Freddy felt as the conversation proceeded, a sense of his appearance which he had not thought about for years; and although his thoughts and speech were given to the eager matter of discussion, a left-hand accompaniment, as it might be played on the piano, went on in his brain concerning his own physical presence; 'well preserved', thought Freddy, would describe the effect, and certainly I'm in good shape due to walking and exercise; hair turning grey, but plenty of it; five foot ten, no stoop; rather short neck. It's a pleasing appearance – how astonishing – but that's merely a fact I simply haven't thought of since I left Cambridge – or, at least since. . . .

Alexandros had sent the women of the household away before Freddy joined him upstairs. It was a charming room, containing a few very good objects that apparently Alexandros could not bear to part with; there was no suggestion of an antique dealer's residence, it was that of an uncomplicated, tasteful Arab, and it might have been a room in the house of any western man of Freddy's past acquaintance who had a leaning towards Oriental rarities if he cared to have rarities at all. The ceiling was low and white, as were the walls. The floor was newly laid with plain polished wood, partly covered by two modern and remarkably handsome Persian rugs. On one wall was hung a carpet of great age and mellowness, the most beautiful Freddy had seen. Its colours glowed forth throughout the evening in a process of slow revelation. A pair of mosaic jars that Freddy could not closely examine, forming table-lamps, were placed at either end of the room, and glimmered quietly in pale blue, green, and russet under the shaded lights. Freddy also noticed a Dutch landscape painting on the more shadowed of the walls, and on the largest wall, a dazzling Russian icon in a large, wrought-silver frame. The rest of the room was furnished casually – a good, small table, a dining-table covered in a white lace-edged cloth and laid for the meal in shiny silver and china which was discernibly Mme Alexandros's best, some rush-seated chairs and a narrow soft couch with damask-covered cushions. It had seemed to Freddy, as he entered this room, that his perceptions must have been getting terribly dull over the years, and now that they had begun to return, he was more enthusiastic than ever about the rightness of his tearing up the letters and disposing of them down the lavatory.

He said to Alexandros, 'I hope Mme Alexandros is not put out by our dining alone.'

Alexandros said, 'Another time, you will meet my wife here in my home. There are many days before us. I told her it is a matter of my business. As you don't wish to be seen, Mr Hamilton, it is important that I serve the dinner to you myself.'

It was a dish of rice, chicken, and olives. Alexandros had fetched it and had again disappeared, returning with an unlabelled bottle. 'Wine from Palestine,' he said. 'It comes from over the border, but not through the Mandelbaum Gate.' Freddy recalled an Embassy row in Jordan because one of the consuls had brought over a bottle of Israeli wine, with the label on it, which his servant had reported to the authorities.

They ate, and Freddy felt Alexandros's eyes upon him and experienced that sense of his own physical qualities, and the qualities of the room, and, most of all, the carpet glowing on the far wall. And he, in turn, perceived large Alexandros in his physical presence, sitting opposite him, fleshy, brown-skinned, thick-jowled with curly black hair, semitic nose, and vital dark eyes. But the heavy man, by a spread of the fingers or a gesture of neck and shoulders, gave out a weightless courtesy. Freddy felt he could lift Alexandros on one finger, and was perfectly at ease with his own self-awareness harmonized at the back of his mind with the immediate subject of their conversation, Barbara Vaughan's predicament.

'She's nothing to me,' Freddy said, 'in the usual sense. And I'm nothing to her. She's engaged to an archaeologist who's working on the Dead Sea material. She says she's gone off him, but –'

'Off him? That is to mean she's changed her mind and doesn't love him now?'

'That's what she said. But I rather doubt that she means it. The point is, whether she's in danger, roaming about Jordan. A half-Jew . . . I think she is in danger.'

'You have had sleep with her? Excuse me that I ask out of curiosity. One desires to understand all sides of a business.'

Freddy thought this intelligent of Alexandros. 'As a matter of fact,' he said, 'I haven't slept with her. I don't know if she's the sort of woman that one would want to sleep with. I'm afraid I hadn't thought of it.'

Alexandros raised his brows, gave a shrug that might have signified anything, and, in the same gesture, put a large portion of his dinner into his mouth.

'Too nervy,' Freddy said. 'It would be a lot of hard work to sleep with a woman like that, I should imagine.'

'I imagine very different,' Alexandros said. 'It is of course one of the things of interest that one asks oneself in secret thought when a lady comes to the shop to buy – how is she like in the bed? – and I have thought this morning when she came to the shop, that she is a sexual woman.'

'Would you say so?' Freddy realized, with envy, that Alexandros never permitted himself a moment's boredom.

'To the fingertips.'

'How astonishing.'

Alexandros nodded slowly. He was evidently delighted to be established as the expert that he was.

The evening warmed around them. 'She's in danger if it is known that she is a Jew by blood,' Alexandros said.

'Even though a Christian?'

'She has been first to Israel, so she would be thought a spy.'

'I'm not sure how seriously my friends, the Cartwrights, realize it. I'm afraid we discussed the question rather a lot –'

'Yes, I know,' said Alexandros. 'The servants of the Cartwrights have reported. My shop boy has told me already this evening that we have a Jewish tourist in Jerusalem, and she was the one who bought the silver fish from our shop. One cannot help this news spreading. They fear Israeli spies.'

'She's a half-Jew.'

'This makes more suspicion. You should know this, as you are in a foreign service.'

'Indeed, I understand.'

Alexandros said, 'Perhaps you must see the British consul and arrange for her to leave the country. Keep her in the convent for the meantime. It is a pity, but –'

'A pity!' Freddy said. 'It's a damn disgrace that a girl can't go on a pilgrimage of the Holy Land, a Christian convert visiting the shrines, without fear of arrest.'

Alexandros radiated response. 'You are right! Perhaps you let her take the risk. Perhaps the danger is not so much. The government spies will follow her but perhaps they will hesitate to make an arrest.'

'Ramdez is her travel agent,' Freddy said. 'I can't think what possessed her to go to Ramdez. Obnoxious fellow.'

'If Ramdez is the agent, then she could meet danger from private retribution. Ramdez is dangerous.'

'Private retribution?'

'An accident may befall her on her travels. Between the police posts are many miles of desert. She may suffer an accident. This, too, you know of.'

'I do understand,' Freddy said, struck now by his recollection of political deaths by accident. He jumped to his feet. 'Alexandros, we must do something.'

'Be seated, Mr Hamilton.' Alexandros, in his usual manner,

prolonged the last syllable to synchronize with the action that accompanied it. His gesture now was to place his two large hands on Freddy's shoulders and press him back into his chair. He then left the room, but without seeming to withdraw any of his presence, for Freddy could hear his footsteps, heavy with long-accepted proprietorship, beating towards the back of the house, and from there, his voice domestically urging his requirements in Arabic, above a kitchen clatter.

Freddy had an urge to make himself useful by piling the used plates together. It was a habit he had acquired since the war when visiting servantless friends. But he forbore. Alexandros would prefer to do everything himself. He was a marvellous host.

Alexandros could be heard on his return, treading more quietly in caution of the stuff he was carrying, which nevertheless rattled a little as he entered. It was a dish of fruit, coffee and a decanter of brandy with cups and glasses. 'I make a good waiter at the table,' roared Alexandros, setting down the tray with the last word, 'tabe-oool'. And when he had shut the door he sat, clasped his hands as if congratulating himself and said, 'My wife and her servant are thinking I am making big business with a representative from a great museum, as I have told the household. I have said the negotiations are very secret as you are in rivalry from another collector who follows you to gain knowledge of your expert discoveries. We have many such dealings here in Jerusalem. There was much secret business with great collectors and great museums and their spies, and also with many governments when we came first to Jerusalem, as those were the years of the discovery of the Dead Sea scrolls. There were many fragments in many hands. As also with other items of antiquity in Jerusalem. So Alexandros can make a story to silence his household of this meeting tonight, and Alexandros is a good waiter at the table.' He unclasped his hands and poured coffee, pushing the used plates and cutlery out of the way. 'And we make a plan for Barbara.'

'Alexandros, you're a good fellow.'

'I'm not too old to enjoy this rescue of a woman,' said Alexandros.

'Neither am I, come to think of it. I'm prepared for anything. But I don't want to involve you in any danger, Alexandros.'

'Danger is pleasure. What else is pleasure when a man has been married to one wife thirty-two years? You are married with a wife in England?'

'No. Few people know it but I was married once.'

'She has died?'

'No. It was when I was very young. The marriage didn't last a year. She turned out to be no good. Incurably no good. What we call a bad lot.'

'It was bad luck.'

'Oh, I've forgotten about the whole thing. It was a misfortune that can happen to a family like any other misfortune.'

'I had a cousin who was like this. In Beirut. She was with many men of different nationalities. I don't know if she's dead, living. We refused her in the end from the family. What could we do? We gave her money, but this failed. Nothing sufficed. She is perhaps in prison. Have you divorced this wife?'

'Oh, yes, and made a settlement on condition of her not marrying again.'

'This is honourable.'

'It's like buying a horse. If it turns out to be a bad horse, one should keep it off the market in case some other chap should get hold of it.'

'Exactly. I do not disagree.'

'Not everyone,' Freddy said, 'would agree with us. In Europe, these days, it's considered unfair to stipulate a condition that might deter anyone from marrying again. But in my view I did the only possible thing. It's a question of one's point of view. It was the only conceivable thing to do. Anyway, it was a long time ago. Nobody mentions the affair in our family, except my old mother from time to time, when she wants to be tiresome. It was a long time ago. My goodness, it must be getting late!'

'Only eleven o'clock,' Alexandros said. 'There are ahead all the hours of the night. And we have only to plan everything.'

They had not drunk a great deal; it was more the stimulus of their evening, wrenched as it was from the line of habit, that gave them heart to leave the house together at half past two in the morning, burning with an imperative sense of duty towards Barbara Vaughan.

Freddy's had been the idea of getting her up in Arab disguise, while Alexandros, his hand clapped suddenly to his brow to hold intact the brimming tide of inspiration, had contributed the Ramdez daughter as her best possible escort.

'Which daughter?' Freddy had said. 'Aren't there two?'

'The unnatural one,' Alexandros said.

'With the blue eyes, like young Abdul?'

'That's the woman. She is not so bad. It's only that she should have been a man. There was a mistake in the making of her. She holds opinions different from her parents. So here they say she's the unnatural one.' Alexandros sprang to his feet. 'We go,' he said. 'It's a matter that can permit only of arrangements in the dark of the night.'

He advised Freddy to keep well into the shadow of the houses, but himself walked with a sort of arm-swinging march in the middle of the street where the moonlight lay. He seemed to be exercising some of Freddy's new resources of freedom as well as his own natural supply. Freddy kept pace with him from the shadows, not for one wild moment doubting the success of their plan, conceived as it had been in an hour of genius and of brotherhood; all was perfectly feasible, or as good as done, and he walked in that dispensation of mind in which impossible works are in fact accomplished and mountains are moved.

They turned into the Via Dolorosa, and there Alexandros strode on in the light of lamps and moon like the Archangel Michael leading his legions to storm the gates of Hell which should not prevail against them, as was written. Freddy moved in to keep pace beside him in the narrow street. They now walked shoulder to shoulder.

They came at last to the convent where Barbara Vaughan was staying. It looked very much closed for the night.

'I speak personally to the janitor,' said Alexandros, moving into the lamplight to verify the amount of paper money that he had produced from his pocket to harmonize with his intention.

'This is on me,' Freddy said, getting out his wallet.

'The janitor is inexpensive. Keep your money to speak to the officers behind the desks if inquiries should arise concerning Barbara in the course of the holy pilgrimage.'

Freddy waited. The night now began to give out the chanting of the minarets, from Israel across the border to the west of the convent, then nearer, to the north, from the direction of the Holy Sepulchre. It was three o'clock. The chanting voices echoed each other from height to height like the mating cries of sublime eagles. This waiting for the return of Alexandros in the morning hours of Jerusalem was one of the things Freddy was to remember most vividly later on, when he did at last remember the nights and days of his fugue. From the east, beyond the Wailing Wall, a white-clad figure raised his arms in the moonlight and now began his call to prayer, and soon, from far in the south, then in the south-east, and from everywhere, the cry was raised.

6. JERUSALEM, MY HAPPY HOME

'Who's there?'

The voice answered, very close to her but on the other side of the door, with hushed urgency, 'Freddy Hamilton. Don't make a noise. Let me in.'

It impinged on Barbara that this was highly improbable, that she was in a convent bedroom, and that there was no lock to the door. She hesitated in a woken daze long enough for the voice to announce itself again. This time it said, 'Is that Barbara Vaughan?'

'Yes.'

'Well, it's only me. Please open the door and I'll explain.'

This sounded authentic. She slid one arm into her dressing-gown and was about to open the door when the handle turned and Freddy's face appeared.

He said quickly, 'Don't make a noise. This is a convent, you know.'

She said, while sticking her other arm into the sleeve, 'What's the matter?'

He came in then, and silently closed the door behind him. He said, 'Forgive me for intruding like this. An emergency. I've come to get you out. You're in danger, but I've got everything planned and you'll be quite safe with me.'

She was still unclear about the reality of Freddy in the room. She had set the front of her hair in two rollers, which she now removed and put into the pocket of her dressing-gown as she said, 'It's terribly late. This is a convent, you know. What's happened?' But now she giggled, partly with relief that the quiet, repetitious tap-tap at the door which had eventually wakened her, was only Freddy's.

Freddy said, 'I'm afraid it's all very informal. But I just want you to pack your things and come with me. There's a car coming round to pick us up and we're going up to the Potter's Field to spend the night. Everything is planned, so don't worry. Just pack quickly and quietly, and come with me.'

She felt a returning wave of the fear she had gone to sleep with. 'Am I to come like this?' she said, plucking at her dressing-gown.

'There's nobody about outside. You won't be seen. There's only me and Alexandros from the curiosity shop, a man I could trust with my life. Alexandros will drive us to the Potter's Field. Hurry, Barbara. In an emergency, one can't be Victorian about things, you know.'

She started to pack her bags and laughed softly to herself again, for Freddy's word 'Victorian' brought comfortably to mind a private family joke – how one of the deep-voiced Vaughan aunts had declared when her son had been ignominiously expelled from school: 'I refuse to be Victorian about it. Of course, the boy is a little *oriental* in his ways, I'm afraid, but then his father is a little oriental and so was his grandfather. And in point of fact, no one in the family, right back to William the Conqueror, has ever been Victorian about it.' Barbara said to Freddy: 'How did you get in? Have I got to bring everything? I haven't paid for the room. It's ten past three.'

Freddy said, absent-mindedly, while looking round. 'This is no time to be Victorian . . . Is there anything I can do? Don't forget your sponge-bag.'

She packed on. 'If any of the nuns : . .'

Freddy fastened the locks of her suitcase while she put the final objects in her small case. She told herself that Freddy Hamilton was behaving unexpectedly and that it was an odd situation. Meanwhile she looked at the bed. 'I'd better –'

'Oh, leave the bed. Hurry.'

She fumbled with her hair, feeling it strange to be going out with her hair straggling loose, and wearing her slippers and dressing-gown as if being taken suddenly to hospital or prison. But it never occurred to her to object to this departure.

Freddy looked out of the window, peering sideways towards the front of the convent. 'It's there,' he said. 'Good old Alexandros. He's waiting with his car.' He lifted the suitcase and said, 'I'll go first. You follow when I get down the first flight. Not a sound, remember. This is a convent.'

She pulled the bed straight as he spoke, and tucked in the

loose blanket to give it a made look. She put three pounds on the dressing-table. 'It's too much,' Freddy said. 'Three would be exorbitant.' She took one back. 'Quite enough,' he said. 'The Catholics are rolling in money.' It was as if he had said 'the foreigners' in one of those private exchanges between Britons.

He lifted the case, whispered 'We're off!' and opened the door. He whispered again, 'Not a whisper,' and stopped to listen lest anyone in the house had been aroused. The oldest nun, a scholarly antiquarian who was reputed to know more about Jerusalem, more of its unrecorded secrets, than anyone else, was snoring at the top of the house; she had told Barbara that she had been given a room at the top of the house because she snored, and had mentioned the fact quite casually, in the course of remarking on the difficulty to old bones of climbing the stairs; the ordinary social vanities did not enter the lives of these nuns.

Freddy, with the suitcase, had reached the landing below; he had one more flight to descend. Barbara followed, gripping her hand-luggage and, quite unnecessarily, the edges of her Liberty dressing-gown which were already held in place by its tie. Freddy was now on his way down the last flight of stairs, to the ground floor. She found herself palpitating with the thought of being discovered leaving this place in her night-clothes with a man and her luggage; the other residents were five middle-aged pious Catholic women from Stuttgart, and the nuns were nuns, and moreover had particularly fussed over Barbara as being Englishly cool, spinster-like and, as she supposed, a bit more nun-like than the five loquacious matrons from Stuttgart. This breathless fear of Barbara's as she began to follow Freddy down the stairs then bore upon her common sense as being so excessive as to weigh the balance of probability in favour of its being groundless; the nuns, she reflected, were hard workers and hard sleepers, while the Stuttgart pilgrims no doubt slept so very much like logs. By the time she had turned the bend on the staircase towards the lower landing she had become confident of an easy exit, and crept down the remaining steps in synchronized time to the snores of the attic nun. She paused on the landing and looked along the corridor to where the Mother Superior, a woman of about Barbara's age, had her quarters.

From the floor above, where she had come from, a noise of running water and padding footsteps came in muffled spasms between the overwhelming attic snores; this was probably caused by one of the German women moving around in the night, having awakened either by habit or by the sound of Barbara's packing and departure. A tinted glass window above the staircase she had just come down let in the moonlight, but the next flight down to the front hall was in blackness by contrast to that dusty amber windowlight above. Barbara lingered on this landing, between the half-light and the pure dark, as if waiting for something. Along the corridor, where the Mother Superior slept, nothing stirred. Barbara did not know why it should. Almost disappointed, she moved to follow Freddy cautiously down the very dark staircase.

Freddy, half-way, came to a curve in the stairs and bumped the suitcase loudly into the wall. Barbara halted on the third step and whispered down to him, 'Are you all right?' He did not reply, but she could hear him continue to pick his step by muted step. She glanced behind and upward, and could not place her sense of something unaccomplished in the silence. The front door was unlocked and Freddy now held it open so that the moonlight flooded her last footsteps from the sleeping convent. They had got away.

Immediately on passing into the night air she realized that she had almost hoped to be caught, it would have been a relief and a kind of triumph and justification. For there had been a decided element of false assumption in her reception at the convent the previous day, after they had inquired politely and estimated her type. Of course she was an English Catholic convert. She was indeed the quiet type. But there was a lot more than met the eye, at least she hoped so. She had thought, as the Mother Superior made her benign speech of welcome, and the old novice-mistress hovered with an admiring smile, if only they knew. And she was inwardly exasperated, as she had been with her cousins last summer, when she had carried on a love-affair with Harry Clegg, there in the house, and they, in their smug insolence, had failed to discover it. And why? She thought now, with the old exasperation, what right have they to take me at my face value? Every spinster should be assumed guilty before she is proved innocent, it is only common civility. People, she thought, believe what they want to believe; anything rather than shake up their ideas. And if a nun had in fact put in an appearance on the landing when Freddy had bumped her suitcase at the bend of the stairs – a startled nun switching on all the lights, the Mother Superior perhaps – what would she have said?

Freddy was opening the door of a large car, at the wheel of which sat a man whom she recognized as the Arab shopkeeper from whom she had bought the ornamental fish that morning. Freddy had pushed her suitcase in the back of the car, and turning to her he said, 'Hurry!' She had never seen Freddy Hamilton looking so happy. She had not thought he had it in him.

And what would she have said if one of the nuns had caught them, if one of them came to the door even now that she was getting into the car, lifting the Liberty dressing-gown as if it were a long evening dress and she departing from a late night party? 'My dear good woman, things are not what they seem, as you in the religious life ought to know. Foolish virgin, hasn't experience taught you to expect the unexpected?'

She said to Freddy, 'What on earth would we have said if we'd been caught?'

Freddy said, 'If they're decent women, as I'm sure they are, you could have explained about your Jewish side.'

The faint sound of the bolt being slid into place behind the heavy studded convent door reached them through the car windows. Whoever had let Freddy in was locking up again.

She said, 'They're decent women but I don't think I would have got much sympathy as a Jew, even if they'd believed the story. It would have embarrassed them, in this environment.'

'What d'you think, Alexandros?' Freddy said as the car started. He was in the front while Barbara sat behind with her suitcase. She looked back. Not so much as one belated inquiring light had gone on in any of the windows.

Alexandros said, 'Madam, they would think something else to see you come with a man and your baggage. Maybe they shall say in the morning that you are a wolf in the raiment of a sheep.'

'So I am,' Barbara said.

'What a jolly good idea this is,' Freddy said, and they all laughed at each other's words with an overflow of relief, success, and the moonlit morning air; meanwhile, the car wound and swirled unhindered to the south, across Jerusalem, in the direction of the Potter's Field.

*

Ten days before she had left Israel Barbara had received two unexpected letters from England and failed to receive an expected letter
from Harry Clegg in Jordan, smuggled to her in the American bag
from Amman. When returning to her room she always looked for the
envelope lying on the carpet by the door. The absence of any word
from Harry Clegg had made the presence of the two English
envelopes, which arrived together on the same morning, rather irri-
tating. One was from Ricky, her old friend, the head of the school
where she taught. The other was from her cousin, Michael Aaronson.

She first opened Miss Rickward's letter. In a way she had been
missing Ricky, whose faults were many but amorphous, and whose
virtues were well defined, among them being an exceptional capacity
for retaining knowledge, shrewd intelligence of a scholarly order, and
a scrupulous, almost obsessive literal honesty; all of which virtues,
apparently in the nature of things, precluded humour. Ricky was a
good talker, in that she could converse seriously for hours on a
subject, the absence of any wit in her talk having the compensatory
value of keeping the main topic in line, without any of the far-flung
diversions that humour leads to. Ricky could discourse for hours on
the history and development of the existentialist philosophy. It had
been pleasant for Barbara, it had given her a remote sense that she
was doing something in life, if only mentally, to sit and listen, with
an occasional comment, while Ricky expounded the doctrine that
existence precedes essence.

But could Ricky apply this notion to the world she existed in? To
Barbara? Herself? Barbara had looked round the room of her hotel
in Israel that morning, and was irritated by the unmade bed. She
decided to take her letters downstairs and read them in the courtyard; then forgetting her decision, sat on. Ricky could discuss the
psychological and biological differentiations of the male in all their
subtleties past and present. She could speculate on their future. But
did she recognize an attraction between a man and a woman before
her eyes? When one of the girls at her school, a large-built matron of
fifteen, was found to be pregnant by the local cinema owner, Ricky
said, 'The poor child was only proving the theory of reproduction
for herself. She's a natural empiricist, an intelligent child,' and might
have written as much, as solemnly, in a letter to the parents of a girl
who had burnt her fingers on a hot test-tube.

Barbara had glanced at the crack beneath the door, not quite aware of what she was still hoping for; the stir and thrust of a white envelope from Jordan.

Ricky once had an admirer, the shy widowed father of one of the girls. He had sent her the enviable present of a bunch of roses, fourteen, each one of a different species. 'I wonder,' Ricky said, 'where he got the impression that I'm a student of horticulture. Someone must have given him that impression, Barbara.'

But there was no end to Ricky and the various ways in which Barbara genuinely missed her. Barbara was, moreover, aware of various ways in which Ricky resembled Harry. The main difference was that Harry was a man. The next difference was his actual achievement in life, which was already recognized everywhere; whereas Ricky, of South African origin, having come to England on a scholarship, had gone far, but achieved little. Both, however, had done what they had done through their own efforts without family advantages. And Harry seemed to resemble Ricky in appearance, more in Barbara's memory than in the presence of either. Barbara had never seen them together, and she partly knew that the resemblance she discerned was, after all, a matter of the lights and shadows cast on their features by some lonely lamplight of affection within herself.

Ricky was a keen promoter of Scripture-reading at school; she was herself a lapsed Congregationalist with a puritanical bias. Once, after last summer's holidays when Barbara had fallen in love with Harry Clegg, Ricky was setting the senior girls an essay on the subject of the Second Coming to be illustrated by scriptural texts; she demonstrated this procedure by quoting a passage on the return of Christ to judge the world: 'Then shall two be in the field; the one shall be taken and the other left. Two women shall be grinding at the mill; the one shall be taken and the other left. Watch therefore . . .' Barbara, standing by, listened distantly to Ricky's moral implications, but heard closely the literal ones. It's certainly a point, thought Barbara, that two engaged in a common pursuit do not consequently share personal identity, and absurd though it is to affirm this evident fact, Ricky feels towards me as if the opposite were true. Sooner or later she'll have to find out that my destiny is different from hers.

She had opened Ricky's letter first. The one from her cousin

Michael was not likely to be a personal stimulus one way or the other. The letter from Harry was what she had wanted, and with that instinct for any sensational distraction, any quarrel, any irritant, of one who has endured a near-miss, she opened Ricky's letter first. Disappointingly at first, and then astoundingly, it read:

MY DEAR BARBARA,

Thank you for your two postcards which both arrived last week, on Tuesday and Friday, respectively. I am pleased to hear you are having a not uncomfortable trip. The experience should be a profitable one – in the spirit if not in the letter!

I hope the food (if I am not treading on holy ground by mentioning that mundane but essential factor) is not unwholesome. How well I remember those weeks following your return from Spain . . . 'Nuff said!

You will be surprised to learn that I have been through a very strange experience during the past fortnight. It is an experience that can only be described as a troubled if not a shattering one. Indeed, I was undecided, or, as one might say, torn in mind, with regard to the advisability or otherwise of mentioning the matter to you. Suffice it to say that my nights, for the past week, have been both anguished and sleepless. Yesterday I arrived at the decision to inform you of my distress, giving you the full account of its cause, and . . .

Bewildered, amazed at the emotion and mounting tone, Barbara sent her eyes flowing down and across the next few pages in frantic grasp of their gist. Ricky had learnt of her engagement to Harry Clegg, that was all. Elsie Connington, a mother of one of the pupils who had become more closely connected with Ricky than with herself, and whom Barbara now recalled having once met, had entertained Ricky for the week-end, in the course of which they had visited Elsie's mother at Harrogate, a Mrs Hamilton. Elsie was Freddy Hamilton's sister, it appeared . . . Freddy had written to his mother that he had made the acquaintance of a Miss Vaughan, who hoped, the Catholic Church permitting, to marry a Harry Clegg, an archaeologist. And the old woman had passed this on to Ricky. So it appeared, and so it was. Barbara felt furious, first with Freddy for his

gossip. She wondered why he had failed to tell her that his niece was
at her school: then, realizing he was probably unaware of this fact,
she turned on herself for confiding so much in Freddy. At last, she
read through the letter again, and began to feel a wholesale sense of
nausea:

> Words cannot express my astonishment, my dear Barbara, let
> alone my horror. I said that I, as your most intimate friend, most
> emphatically deny any such idea on your part. I said that your
> acquaintanceship with Mr Clegg had been brief, casual and quite
> innocent of any romantic nonsense, since you were, to my certain
> knowledge, not in a remote degree inclined towards matrimony. It
> would be disastrous if you made a mess of your life.
>
> It was naturally disconcerting to me to be informed by a third
> party that Clegg was in your part of the world. The fact that you
> had spoken of him to Mr Hamilton would appear to me, pending
> further evidence, to indicate . . .

Barbara said aloud, '*Pending further evidence* – Oh, my God! Oh,
Jesus Christ!' What has it come to, she thought, between Ricky and
me? Ricky's letters were usually written with difficulty, woodenly.
But this uncharacteristic outpouring, this confession, almost – what
had it come to? It's like a letter, she thought, from an insufferable
man to his unfaithful mistress, or a wife to a wandering husband, or
a possessive mother to a teenage daughter, or a neurotic Mother
Superior to a nun with a craving to get out. Who am I to Ricky and
who is she to me? She's only a friend. I've taken no vows.

Barbara let up the venetian blinds of her room, hot as the Israeli
morning already was. She sat down and brought Ricky's image to
mind, her dark, short-cut, curly hair, the plump, apple-coloured
tomboy face. Small and sturdy, Ricky took shape before her, wearing
her tweed skirt and wool jumper with flat brogues in winter, a cotton
dress and sandals in summer; dark hairs showed through her stockings on school days and, on summer holidays, shaggily coated her
bare legs. On many summer evenings before school broke up,
Barbara had sat on the small veranda outside Ricky's sitting-room,
drinking after-dinner coffee, listening to the gramophone record in
the background, her eyes fixed absently on Ricky's dark hairy legs.

Barbara was aware of them now, as she recalled her own fascinated stare, as she thought, how has an ordinary friendship between two women reached this point? How? Ricky must be a latent Lesbian; and I? I'm in her clutches, but she's in mine. Yes, why, Barbara thought, haven't I told her about Harry? Why? Or why haven't I written as I intended to do, why not? It was only right if she was my closest friend, as I thought she was. It is only natural that Ricky should expect me to confide what's going on.

Only the night before, Barbara had returned to the excessively difficult attempt which had hung over the past three weeks, to write an honest letter to Ricky. Again, it had been unsuccessful. Barbara could see, from where she sat, on the writing-table close by, abandoned sheet after sheet of paper, not yet torn up and tidied away for the morning, where she had left them on the frustrated night before:

DEAR RICKY,
I have been meaning to tell you –

DEAR RICKY,
I know you will be surprised, but I feel I must –

MY DEAR RICKY,
I have been touring strenuously so haven't had time to write properly. But now I want to write a decent letter and tell you, first of all –

VERY DEAR RICKY,
You will be happy to know I am hoping to marry Harry Clegg – the archaeologist whom I met last summer. We are very much in love. Much depends on the decision of the Church as to the annulment of his previous marriage, bu –

DEAR RICKY,
The heat, combined with strenuous –

I didn't tell her, Barbara thought, because I intended to write. And I haven't written because I was afraid, and that's the truth. It's as if I were married to Ricky, only worse.

She thought, it's the male element in Ricky that has attracted me. Then she imagined herself in bed with Ricky, in physical contact, shuddered a lot, and thought, I must get married, I really must. This is no good. She recalled the freedom of last summer, and longed for her humorous lover.

At all events, she thought, I must leave the school. Ricky has become over-familiar and I must leave the school. Immediately; not even a term's notice; I must write and do that. This decision brought her immense relief. Barbara could not understand why she had not thought of anything so simple before. She had small private means and was not pressed to find another job immediately.

She sat up to the table and wrote:

DEAR RICKY,

There are many things I cannot explain at the moment, but I shall do so in time. I do beg you to have patience with me, both for failing to discuss my plans with you and for now reaching a decision I feel must pain and know must inconvenience you.

I can't return to school, and regret very much that I can't give you a term's notice. I can only hope you will be able to replace me at this short notice, and it won't upset your trip to Brittany. Please, dear Ricky, go to Brittany for my sake, or I shall feel bad about it.

My plans for the future are so far unsettled, but I truly *can't* return to school.

I'll let you know later about collecting my things, and will ring you myself, as soon as I get back to England. I'm going to Jordan next week to visit the shrines – can't say how long I'll stay there.

Don't worry about this, will you? I assure you there's nothing to worry about.

Love,

BARBARA

She saw, without stopping to bother about it, that her handwriting was slightly larger and heavier than usual. She sealed and stamped the letter, took it down to the letter-box, thrust it through the slit, went and had a look out of doors at the shining street and returned to her room, where she pulled down the cool blinds and slumped, heavy with relief and the recent weight of what she had been carrying. She felt very much one of the Vaughans at that moment. Whatever the points of inward debate or the pinchings of self-accusation, none of the family would have hesitated to act otherwise; intrusive people must be put down, and that was the long and the short of it. She now remembered saying to Harry, when they had discussed their marriage:

'I don't know how I shall break it to Miss Rickward.'

'How do you mean?'

How did she mean? It was only possible to answer, 'Well, she'll miss me. We've become very attached after six years, and she doesn't think of me as marrying.'

'Oh, bugger *her*,' said Harry.

Recalling this, Barbara laughed to herself and opened the letter from her favourite cousin, Michael Aaronson. She had not expected to hear from him as they did not correspond regularly, but she reflected that Michael always seemed to turn up, by mail, or in person, at a welcome time. And his news was, in fact, an announcement of his arrival in Israel the next day. He had been 'sent or called, depending on how you look at it' to 'confer or be conferred with' on the Eichmann trial.

Michael was diffident about his career. He had taken his degree in international law before the war, and had been called in for the Nuremberg Trials. He had since been occupied in practice as a solicitor, but Barbara perceived his pleasure at being once more involved in an expert's field. He expected to be in Jerusalem for two weeks. He would be fairly occupied, but 'Be sure to be there,' he wrote.

She realized how lonely she must have been, and felt so good about the prospect of seeing Michael that the thought of Ricky's lonely distress came back guiltily upon her, but even so she did not regret her letter. She went out for a walk, called in at the travel agent and rearranged her dates; today was a Monday, and she had planned to cross into Jordan on the Wednesday of that week. It was necessary to give advance notice to the travel people, since they were obliged to make advance arrangements for a crossing of the Mandelbaum Gate, and only certain days were available to individual travellers. She obtained a permit for Friday of the following week, which would probably precede Michael's departure, but she was unwilling to linger in the country much longer.

For it had become imperative for her to continue the pilgrimage. She sat in a café, trifling with her coffee spoon. The relief of leaving her job and learning of Michael's arrival enabled her to summon peacefully to her attention the image of Ricky, still mutedly importuning. Ricky would, of course, ascribe hypocrisy to her motives in coming to the Holy Land 'on a pilgrimage'. Barbara was content to be thought deceitful, hypocritical. It consoled her guilt towards Ricky. And yet her own ruthlessness and swift action continued to surprise and please her. She thought, I'm satisfied with that letter. But Ricky's a kind woman, she'll be hit by my leaving her. In a sense Ricky gave me a home.

She sagged with relief. It felt marvellous to be homeless. Ricky would think of the motives that had drawn her here to the Holy Land. A religious pilgrimage! A lover. A man. Barbara was already a Catholic when she had met Ricky; they had carefully avoided religious discussions; and only once or twice had she discerned Ricky's irritation with some observance of her religion, and felt irritation when Ricky let fall a remark about some Catholic dogma which revealed not only her disapproval, but a muddled notion of what the dogma was. Ricky was all for doing the right thing for the right reason; she was fierce-principled about motives. To Barbara, one of the first attractions of her religion's moral philosophy had been its recognition of the helpless complexity of motives that prompted an action, and its consequent emphasis on actual words, thoughts and deeds; there was seldom one motive only in the grown person; the main thing was that motives should harmonize. Ricky did not understand harmony as an ideal in this sense. She assumed that it was both right that people should tear themselves to bits about their motives and possible for them to make up their minds what their motives were. Herein, Barbara reflected, lies the difficulty in dealing with Ricky if I should ever be drawn to have it out with her. For she has settled with herself that her motives are sound, and she opposes my marriage in good conscience.

She decided, in any case, never to have it out with Ricky. Having it out with people was not in her nature, all the Vaughan in her upbringing went against it. She longed for Harry, the only man she had known who conducted his courtship with few words and without any demands for heart-sought declarations and the wear and tear of mutual disclosures from the interior.

She thought of Ricky, sitting in her room on a winter evening, leaning back, relaxing among the effervescence of school life, the tumble of books and papers, with her legs dark-shadowed under her stockings. Ricky's own books, clean and bright, lined the walls to the ceiling. Ricky had no doubt read most of them, closed them, and put them away, unchanged by them as they were by the passage of the years. Titles that she had not been conscious of taking special note of appeared before Barbara's inward eye: *The World of Zen*, *Antic Hay*, *The Notebooks of Sigmund Freud*, *A Skeleton Key to Finnegan's Wake*, *Neurosis and Human Growth*, *Thus Spake* . . . One way and another, she felt she knew Ricky through and through, and firmly closed her mind to its whispering intelligence that Ricky, having now, in that letter, surprised her, might do so again. Coleridge's *Table Talk*, Aristotle's *Poetics* . . . Oh well, thought Barbara, paying her bill. And, feeling specially strong, healthy and Vaughan-like she returned to her hotel to see if any word had come from Harry Clegg. At the front door she met Freddy Hamilton emerging with a zipper-bag in his hand and a suitcase at his feet. A Legation car drew up.

'I'm just off to Tel Aviv; got a job to do there,' he said. 'Hot, isn't it? I'll be glad to be back with my friends in Jordan, weekend after next. It's cooler there. When are you going over?'

She was involuntarily reserved. 'Next week, probably. It depends.' But she told him of her cousin's promised arrival the next day. 'Something to do with the Eichmann trial.'

This seemed to remind Freddy Hamilton of something. He said, 'I'm not sure that it's safe for you to go over, really. Let me make some serious inquiries first. I'm sure they don't welcome Jews or part-Jews, especially coming by way of Israel. At the worst you'd probably be deported. Probably – but one never knows – they get hot-headed. Is your fiancé meeting you in Jerusalem?'

'I don't know. I don't think so.'

'It might be better if he could. Those Dead Sea scholars might get better protection for you than the British Government could. That's what things have come to. How well you're looking! The climate must suit you.'

Thereupon she forgave him for gossiping about her to his mother. All the same, she would be careful what she told him in the future, now that Ricky had met the old lady. And so, on that Saturday of the following week, when she next saw Freddy with his friends, unexpectedly, in the curiosity shop in Jordan, she decided to answer, if he should inquire about her fiancé, 'I've gone off him.' That would put an end to the gossip. It was not Freddy Hamilton's business, certainly not his mother's, nor Ricky's. 'I've gone off him' – light and airy. She decided to stick to that, and they could think as they pleased.

The best piece of furniture in the room was the camp-bed, and Barbara lay upon it, awake, gazing straight through the small window at the night sky, which, by contact with her emotional eyesight, was elated with stars and lyrical energy.

The camp-bed was so new that the old monk's domestic man, himself an ancient, but sturdier, benignity, had to untie the cords and wrappings, fresh from the shop. The servant's few teeth caught the light from the paraffin lamp as he gloated over his treasure of a camp-bed: 'One of our ladies, not rich, has given this to keep open the door for strangers. Here the officers are afraid to come at darkness. God is good.' He muttered on, while they set up the bed, stiff at the joints as it was with newness. Through the thin walls Freddy could be heard moving about and creaking his bed as he sat, presumably taking off his shoes since a shoe-like thud on the floor, dropping dead-weight with tiredness, was followed presently by another. Alexandros's car started up below; he was to send early tomorrow a young woman, Suzi Ramdez, who was accustomed to taking English visitors around the country, and who could be trusted.

Now Barbara lay awake, marvelling at her escape from the convent. She was also extremely intrigued by the change that had come over Freddy Hamilton, and by the fact that he had engineered the escape at all. She thought, it's like the enactment of a reluctant nun's dream, and she laughed softly in the darkness, thinking of the absurdity of the phrase 'escape from the convent' that had kept recurring in their conversation in the car, on the way to the Potter's Field, and which didn't really apply to her, a free, travelling Englishwoman, at all.

But it had been an escape of a kind, as witness to which she could cite her present sense of release. She was sure there was a certain amount of physical risk in her venture into Jordan. But try as she might, she did not care. And the urgent sense of apprehension she should be feeling, all facts considered, was lacking, try as she might to reason with herself. If she should be arrested openly there would be some sort of fuss, if she were to come to some secret harm, well that was that. The reality of the hour was her escape from the convent, and there was no room for any sense of a more immediate danger in the face of the familiar and positive dangers of heart and mind that were, in any case, likely to arise anywhere one went, across all borders and through all gates.

She thought, it was really very funny, that escape from the convent. It would make a good story to tell her cousins on the Vaughan side when they asked her about her visit to the Middle East. And the Vaughan side of herself lay on the camp-bed considering the funny aspect of the affair, since this was what they liked best to do; whenever the Vaughans were thrown, provided they managed to pick themselves up, they usually ended by making a good story of it.

For the first time since her arrival in the Middle East she felt all of a piece; Gentile and Jewess, Vaughan and Aaronson; she had caught some of Freddy's madness, having recognized by his manner in the car, as they careered across Jerusalem, that he had regained some lost or forgotten element in his nature and was now, at last, for some reason, flowering in the full irrational norm of the stock she also derived from: unselfquestioning hierarchists, anarchistic imperialists, blood-sporting zoophiles, sceptical believers – the whole paradoxical lark that had secured, among their bones, the sane life for the dead generations of British Islanders. She had caught a bit of Freddy's madness and for the first time in this Holy Land, felt all of a piece, a Gentile Jewess, a private-judging Catholic, a shy adventuress.

'This is more fun,' Freddy had said in the car, 'than I've had for years.'

'It is for me fun that I have sent to Suzi Ramdez a secret message in the middle of the night, to her bed where she sleeps. A very fine woman, Suzi Ramdez. Her father would come to me with a knife –'

'Is there any danger of his finding out?' Freddy said.

'Plenty danger. But Joe Ramdez does not kill. If he comes to me tonight, tomorrow, with the knife, still he does not strike. Alexandros has plenty friends, and those friends are enemies of Ramdez.'

'You never have a dull moment out here,' Freddy said, meanwhile grinning at Barbara, who sat in the back with her suitcases and savoured Freddy's phrase 'out here'. Every place east of Europe or west of the Atlantic Ocean was more or less one of the colonies to Freddy.

'We did that escape from the convent beautifully,' Freddy said. 'Great fun. We did it a treat. Every stair was creaky –'

'*Every* stair,' Barbara said. 'I nearly died.'

'I expect I'd have been lynched by the nuns if I'd been caught. Have they ever had a man in the convent before?'

'Not in the sleeping quarters. Maybe, of course, the doctor.'

'The doctor,' said Alexandros, 'is not a man. The doctor is permitted in the harem after sunset even. "Many doctors come by night to the rich man's harem": Arab proverb by author Alexandros.'

Freddy went on elaborating his version of the escape from the convent, and Barbara added her bits, slumped in her dressing-gown among the suitcases, building up, for Alexandros, the breathless suspense of the descent down the convent staircase. 'I nearly *died!*' It was not any escape from any real convent, it was an unidentified confinement of the soul she had escaped from; she knew it already and was able to indulge in her slight feeling of disappointment that they had not been caught. It was fun to get away but it would also have been fun to get caught and to have had to explain something, and for Freddy to have explained. It would have made a funny story to tell Harry later on.

She could not understand how Freddy, in the course of the few hours since she had last seen him in the Cartwrights' garden, had so come to lose his unbecoming and boring balance, his tepid correctness. He was not at this moment so terribly drunk, and had certainly gathered enough wits to plan the night's escapade and the elaborate course of the bright pilgrimage to come, the details of which he was now explaining with enthusiastic precision. He had thought of everything. 'You, as Suzi's servant, will have to be deaf and dumb, because, of course, you can't speak Arabic. I'll come as far as Jericho with you, then leave you with Suzi, as I ought to be back at the office Tuesday at the latest. . . . Suzi Ramdez apparently is experienced in Catholic pilgrimages . . . Marvellous plan, don't you think?'

Barbara reclined, happily making her responses in the dialect of their tribe: 'Absolutely brilliant . . . terrific idea, Freddy . . . Yes, honestly, I'm thrilled . . .'

'Well, of course, Alexandros thought of it first.'

'No, pardon me, you had the first word.' Alexandros rushed his car into gear as they turned up the Hill of Evil Counsel.

'We both cast the first stone,' Freddy garbled lyrically, and went on to tell Barbara how he'd got some boring letters from home and written some boring replies but had put them all down Alexandros's lavatory.

'What a brilliant idea,' Barbara said, and half-wished she had thought of doing the same with Ricky's letter and her reply to it. Ricky must have received her letter early last week. Barbara had not expected to hear from Ricky, for her plan at the time of writing had been to leave Israel within the next few days. Fortunately, now, it would be ages before she knew, if she ever did know, how badly Ricky had taken it. Barbara had not supplied an address in Jordan. 'Marvellous idea,' Barbara said. 'I had a ridiculous letter from England to answer last week, but I answered it. I should have put it all down the loo, reply and all, that's what I should have done.'

'One always should,' Freddy advised her, as from long experience. 'Any correspondence that's bloody boring, just pull the chain on it. That's my motto.'

With only a small delay after their first battering onslaught at the door, they were handed over by Alexandros to the ancient monk, who peered and smiled behind his lamp, and handed them over to his ancient friend who had turned up, crumpled from sleep in his blue robe. They were then taken over a stony path through the yard to another, more ramshackle house. There Alexandros left them, embracing Freddy on both cheeks, while Freddy, first remarking cheerfully, 'like a couple of French generals', responded.

It was going on towards four in the morning when she was left alone in the little attic room to which she had been taken. It contained a large, sagging horse-hair arm-chair with the stuffing emerging from both arms, two sacks which served for floor mats, a marble-topped table on which stood a basin and a ewer filled with dusty water, a wooden box on which stood a pair of field-glasses in good and shiny condition, a new cake of carbolic soap, a dented celluloid miniature of the Taj Mahal, an English novel, dated 1910, entitled *Diamond Cut Diamond*, a tin of lighter fuel, a broken pottery beaker, a small rough towel marked 'Hotel Dixie', and a pair of elephant-figure book-ends. Another large wooden box, marked 'Fragile', was open and contained, at the bottom, about six pairs of unused sandals; there was a large wicker hamper with the lid half-gaping to reveal a top layer of gold-embroidered ecclesiastical vestments, and the room also contained an icon hung on a nail in the wall, a tarnished silver altar-lamp, a pair of primitive mill-stones such as the country women still used for grinding corn, and, on the flat top of this hand-mill, a well-worn pack of playing cards and a packet of drinking straws. Barbara, her luggage, the new camp-bed and a grey army blanket had now joined the company. She, having taken some note of all this, had turned out the lamp, and now lay in her dressing-gown, with the blanket folded at her feet in view of the warmth of the air that coursed in towards her from the stars, and was moved to praise the sweet Lord's ingenuity, marvelling at her escape from the convent and at Freddy's unexpectedness. Later, when she discovered that Freddy had obliterated these days from his memory, what shocked her most of all was that so much of that carefree and full-hearted Freddy had turned sour with guilt. She herself then reminded him of this or that delightful incident, piecing the days together for him, fragment by fragment. But they were, to him, stolen days, and not for many years could he come to think of them with total pleasure.

But even now, before the pilgrimage had begun, Barbara discerned some temporary quality in Freddy's mood. Not knowing the cause, she formed the theory then, as she lay contemplating the early morning sky above the Potter's Field, that Freddy was given to fluxes of temperament, and, like a man who knows he has played the fool while drunk, might presently regret or might laugh unhappily about all this wild commitment of his. Not that Freddy's new spontaneity and forthcoming spirits resembled a fearful mania. He was decidedly at ease.

A change began to come over him, she thought, in the Cartwrights' garden, when everyone was arguing so absurdly about the rights and wrongs of my Jewish blood: 'Jewish blood or not,' had said Freddy, 'the point is, it's hers. . . . And the trouble with you,' Freddy had said, 'is that you blow neither hot nor cold, you are lukewarm – how does it go, Miss Vaughan? – lukewarm, and I'll vomit thee out of my mouth.' It would make a splendid story to tell her Vaughan cousins. Freddy must meet the Vaughans; his next home leave, she would get her cousin Miles Vaughan to ask Freddy to dinner. Very likely she would be married by then. Very likely. The Vaughans would accept Harry Clegg without a murmur once she was married to him, and they had seen the funny side of everything.

The expected letter from Harry had not arrived, but a note from his friend at the American Embassy in Amman had been enclosed in the envelope, smuggled in by the American bag, which had appeared under the door last Wednesday morning. This friend, whom she had never met, was obviously well informed about their situation; he wrote informally but cautiously, and she understood that she must read beween the lines:

DEAR BARBARA,

Harry asked me to let you know he has left for Rome to see some members of the Congregation of the Rota about some ancient documents. He'll write you from there some time next week. He'll be staying at the Hotel Regina Carlton.

He doesn't feel, by the way, that you'd be vitally interested in the excavations at Qumran at the moment, and he isn't there to show you around. I've been to that area myself, of course, but, not being an archaeologist, I get more fun out of the many books that have been written about the findings of the scrolls and the excavated Essene community offices. There's some talk of a documentary film of it though. Some of the unit (though not the producer, of course . . .) who are working in the Transjordan at the moment, on the Lawrence of Arabia movie, toured the site and think there's good material for a documentary.

Well, Harry looked fine and sends his love. But you'll be seeing him yourself quite soon, I hope.

Sincerely yours,

MARTIN J. FONTEYN

From this, she gathered that Harry had gone to be interviewed about his plea for annulment at the Congregation of the Rota in Rome, where all the documents had been sent. And also that he did not want her to go to Jordan, not only because he was no longer there but also because he now thought it unsafe. The whole rigmarole about the film unit visiting Qumran was plainly an occasion for citing the case of the producer, a Jew who was prominently reported to have been conceded permission to work on Jordanian location only on the strength of the film's economic benefit to the country, but was obliged, so people said, to sleep on a yacht each night, three miles away from Arab soil. Barbara rightly deduced that what Mr Fonteyn was trying to convey was that Harry now considered it risky for her to travel into Jordan on account of her Jewish blood.

She had almost decided then not to go on with the pilgrimage but to remain in Israel until at least she heard from Harry in Rome. Her cousin Michael was due to arrive in Israel that afternoon, nine days before the small hours of this Sunday morning, when the stars were flickering out in the early light while the many-shaped furnishings round the camp-bed on which she lay gradually cropped up again, pale blue, and while from all quarters live sounds of cockcrow had come to pass, and of monastery cats supremely celebrating.

Michael had arrived in Israel in the late afternoon of that Wednesday, his welcome, full-faced bespectacled self. He was immediately immersed in his legal business, and would not be free until dinner. Barbara filled in the hours by driving round Jerusalem, as she had so often done in the past weeks. She now went everywhere without a guide in a hired car, and had revisited most of the ancient sites up and down the small narrow country where layers of Rome and Byzantium reclined a few feet beneath the soil. She was brown from the sun of Tiberias on the shores of Galilee and the sea-walk at Acre. She had sat in the cool shade of the ruined synagogue at Capharnaum and waded among the pebbles. Most of all she had sat in the cool churches of Israel, where sometimes a priest, one of the Franciscan custodians of the Catholic shrines in the Holy Land, would come and sit beside her and talk about the only sphere he knew, the Christian Incarnation whose physical centre, for the time being, was that particular spot. Nazareth: this is where it really began, the mission of Jesus to the world. Cana: this is where Jesus turned the water into wine for the wedding, his first miracle, and everything begins with that. Capharnaum: all the important teaching and miracles of Jesus took place here, in the synagogue and round

about; it was here St Matthew worked in the customs house, a pub-
lican, and was called to follow Jesus; Peter and Andrew came from
Capharnaum; here in the synagogue that must have been here before
these ruins were built, Jesus gave the New Testament, here in the
synagogue, pledging himself to be the Bread of Life to the people of
the world, and that was the new Covenant; and he walked on the
water at Capharnaum, stilled the storm, raised Jairus's daughter
from the dead, and the centurion's steward, Peter's mother-in-law,
the man with the withered hand, the man possessed by an unclean
spirit . . . Barbara looked out beyond the ruins to where the antique
sea sparkled, and fully assented that here precisely at Capharnaum,
as at Nazareth, as at Cana, the spiritual liberation of the human race
had begun. And here at Capharnaum, said the Franciscan friar . . .
the man sick of the palsy, and numerous other sick and possessed
. . . just behind the sea-road, the Sermon of the Beatitudes . . . the
multiplication of the loaves and fishes; all at Capharnaum; and here
is a curious thing that you find in the Gospels of Matthew and Luke:
Jesus said of it, 'Thou, Capharnaum, which art exalted unto heaven,
thou shalt be thrust down to hell.' A little way up, at Bethsaida, was
where James and John lived, and Peter, Philip and Andrew were
born. Mary Magdalen came from Magdala, along the lake.

At the place of Mary Magdalen Barbara had found locked gates
and a high wire-net fence; peering through she saw a black car with
the white diplomatic number plate. This site was in the hands of the
Russian Orthodox; at that time the Russians in Israel were particularly suspicious and it was quite common for the Russian-held
shrines to be closed to the public. Barbara waited a while in the sun
to see if there was any sign of life in the small conventual house. Not
a curtain stirred. Here, too, at this birthplace of doubtful authenticity there had undoubtedly been a beginning. She had driven along
the coast to Tiberias and had gone for a swim in Galilee, and afterwards eaten one of its fish, sitting in her bathing-dress at a shoreside
café; there she was joined by a young woman, also wearing a swim-
ming-suit, whom she had known casually years before in London,
and had met again briefly a few days ago in Jerusalem, Ruth Gardnor,
now the wife of someone in the British Foreign Service; she was
spending a few days at Tiberias. Barbara sat and talked to her about
their only mutual acquaintance in this country, Freddy Hamilton,

and after they had agreed several times that he was sweet, and Ruth Gardnor had sighed, said 'Poor Freddy!' and explained that the man had been crushed, ruined, by a dominant mother, they parted with amiable insignificant promises to meet again soon.

In the last few days before Michael's arrival Barbara had concentrated her driving in the area round Jerusalem, partly to have access to her hotel while awaiting the smuggled news from Harry Clegg, and partly because she was anxious to get away across the border into new territory, the other part of the Holy Land, and enjoyed gazing over to Bethlehem or to the Mount of Olives, and, on a clear day, the domes and walls and rooftops of Old Jerusalem. She would stop the car at various points, day after day, as she discovered the best angles for sighting her target.

> Jerusalem, my happy home,
> When shall I come to thee?

The lines sped to mind, and simultaneously seeing in her mind's eye the medieval text to which she was accustomed and, with her outward eye, an actual Gethsemane passively laid out on the Mount of Olives across the border, she sensed their figurative meaning piled upon the literal – 'O my sweete home, Hierusalem' – and yearned for that magnetic field, Jerusalem, Old and New in one.

> When shall I look into thy face,
> Thy joys when shall I see?

Saul Ephraim, finding her hired car parked one day near the Hebrew University, drew up his own battered vehicle beside it and sounded his horn till she appeared from among the thick-leaved bushes where she had been standing, some yards off the road, to get a better view. Saul said, 'If you stand there long enough you'll get shot. It's practically on the border.'

'Has anyone been shot standing there?'

'Maybe not exactly on that spot, but shooting incidents occur from time to time. Someone gets shot, then we retaliate, and someone else gets shot, maybe two, three. Keep away from the border.'

She had asked Saul Ephraim to look in after dinner on the night of

Michael's arrival, hoping to arrange a small guided tour of the country-side during Michael's visit. Her memory now played on Michael's arrival as she lay on the camp-bed, yielding her present excitement to a passive in-gathering of past facts as did the stars their bright pointedness to the first blue light of dawn.

'I've given up my job.'

Michael said, 'Tired of it?'

She had explained or tried to explain the very involved and subtle affair of Ricky, and how it had crept on her, become intolerable, Ricky's personality . . . Ricky's incredible letter finally . . . finally . . . She gestured the inarticulate end of her sentences – 'It's difficult, Michael, to explain; Ricky's been a good friend, but it's just –'

Michael took the words out of her hands.

'She was too possessive,' he said, as if there were no subtle, unique, inexplicable quality about the relationship. And of course, when he said it, she knew this was the ultimate definition and felt relieved. Michael resembled Harry in his habit of making obvious rational comments about difficulties he did not feel were worth the trouble of analysing. Harry, who would give years to a problem of archaeology, would dismiss most personal complications with a brief, banal, but altogether reassuring phrase or two; Barbara never failed to feel consoled by his common sense, so very like Michael's now, when she was beset by some interior burden that didn't really matter: 'She was too possessive.' Barbara laughed.

'Well, I've left the job. I'm not even giving a term's notice; just not going back.'

'Are you still thinking of getting married?'

'I hope . . . the Church . . . this annulment . . . the documents . . . Harry's in Rome . . . the . . .' The jagged edges of the celluloid Taj Mahal, seen from the side, took shape in the pale first light over the Potter's Field and looked like the half-profile of a face she had never seen before; all around her, conical, circular and angular bulges began to appear; she distinguished the field-glasses that she had seen by the light of the paraffin lamp an hour ago. It would soon be bright morning. Michael had said, 'You really must stop messing the poor fellow about, you know, Barbara. If you want to marry him, marry him. He's free and you're free to be married according to the laws of the land.'

'You know that to me marriage is a sacrament. If I marry outside the Church I'll have to remain outside the Church. That's going to be difficult for me. Year after year – it will be difficult.'

'Yes but what else are you going to do?'

'He's gone to Rome . . . annulment . . . questions . . . his marriage; it's just possible that it could be found invalid . . . his wife's married again, she's quite cooperative about everything. It's a legal question, you know, like any other legal question.' Michael quite saw that. He was never obtuse about the legal formations of the Catholic Church.

Someone shuffled in the house below, and she knew it was five in the morning. She was to be ready by ten. Suzi Ramdez would arrive at ten. Barbara thought she might sleep now, but it didn't matter if she missed a night's sleep, it was worth it. She had taken her last look at Jerusalem from the other side of the Mandelbaum Gate that afternoon of Michael's arrival when, before returning to the hotel to meet him, she had gone to the top of Mount Zion where David's Tomb was preserved, and had seen, in the Abbey of the Dormition the reputed room of the Last Supper and the crypt where by tradition the Blessed Virgin lay before her death or, as some said, her falling asleep before her assumption into heaven, whatever that taking up might be, to wherever heaven was. It was from this site of the Dormition in Israel that Barbara had seen Old Jerusalem, distant yet not far, where she now lay waiting in the early morning for her new guide on the pilgrimage.

'I wouldn't go to Jordan if I were you,' Michael said. 'All things considered, I wouldn't go.' Saul Ephraim had joined them with his Israel-born wife, who spoke only Hebrew. Saul said, 'They're bound to know by now that you've got Jewish relations. The Arabs have their messengers, you know.' He looked round, and Barbara caught sight of an Arab porter, far away in the entrance hall. Their own party was now sitting in the open, under the leafy trellis, and one could see through to the adjoining room, and through again to the hall. The Arab porter was talking to someone, a familiar outline; it was Freddy Hamilton's Arabic teacher, the blue-eyed young man called Abdul. Saul said, 'They could make a lot of trouble for you. There is a definite danger from police officials, they are armed, they act in hot blood and explain afterwards. People who come here do not realize that. Particularly, you have come from England first to Israel, then you go to Jordan. The normal route is from Jordan to Israel. They suspect Israeli spies. Why didn't you go to Jordan first?'

'Oh, personal reasons, you know.'

It was through Harry Clegg that she had come to know Saul Ephraim, his former colleague. Saul looked at his wife and said something evidently witty in Hebrew, for she laughed. Saul explained, 'I'm telling her that your fiancé's over in Jordan, and that's why you came here first.'

Michael had turned thoughtful since Saul had urged the probable danger of her appearance in Jordan, and lawyer that he was, he protested. 'But look here, you know, there *are* internal laws and international laws. Even if Barbara was a full Jew she couldn't be touched if she possessed a British passport. It's the Israelis they're against, it's a political matter, not a religious or racial one. The Arab States don't recognize Israel, they claim that the Jews in Israel are usurpers of their territory. The worst that could happen to Barbara, by law, is deportation as a spy, and only then on the combined evidence of her Jewish blood and her entrance into the country via Israel – that might create reasonable grounds for suspicion. But otherwise she couldn't be touched. Not legally.'

'Not legally,' said Saul, spreading his fingers in irony; he explained the argument to his wife, who replied vivaciously. 'She says,' said Saul, 'that they carried off a couple of men from the *kibbutz* she worked on before we were married. They raided and captured the men. One was a Britisher. They didn't do it legally, of course.'

There was talk, talk, talk. It became an academic subject, absorbing them for over an hour. Barbara said, 'It's difficult to separate the apocryphal from the true in this part of the world. It always has been.'

'Anyway, all things considered, don't go,' Michael said.

'And you say Harry's in Rome. So what's the point?' said Saul.

'Yes, what's the point? But I'm on a pilgrimage. The other Christian shrines are over there –' On, on, on. 'But we have Nazareth. We have a Christian shrine up on Mount Zion,' Saul said, and repeated this to his wife, who showed interest. Barbara said, 'It's the crypt of the Dormition,' and explained to Michael the legend of the Virgin's Falling Asleep. 'Some say she actually died, some say she only fell asleep. The Church has left it open. I was up there today, in fact . . .' She had been to pray at the crypt of the Falling Asleep. The noises of the first light over the Potter's Field had halted now, pausing for the authentic dawn. The shuffling in the house had stopped. The recumbent statue of the Virgin at the crypt was an unusual representation. The two suitcases, one small, one large, stood beside a much larger, open box with her clothes spilling out of them; then she perceived they were not her clothes, but those vestments bulging from the hamper that she had noted by the light of the oil lamp.

Saul had said, 'For a stage of the pilgrimage you might go to the Eichmann trial.'

'I haven't been,' she said.

'I know. That's what I'm saying.'

'I don't see that she wants to go there,' Michael said. 'I think the whole thing's a mistake, myself.'

They turned out for a walk in the teeming streets that were only now cooling down, and Saul argued fiercely about the necessity of the Eichmann trial. Michael said, in the end, that since it was on, Barbara should go, should come with him for an hour or two tomorrow.

'Why?'

'Why? Because it's got to do with you.'

'And a subject for a Christian pilgrim,' Saul said.

She had thought of the trial as something apart from her purpose; it was political and temporary. In the same way she had placed the *kibbutzim* of the country in the category of sociology, and had resisted attempts to be shown over one of them. She had seen over a model *kibbutz* in Surrey.

She said, 'Look, I've got a tidy mind. Everything's a subject for a Christian pilgrimage if you widen the scope enough. I only want to cover a specific ground without unnecessary diversions. I can follow the Eichmann trial in the papers.'

Sharp-witted Saul said, 'You can follow the history of the Jews in the Bible without visiting the historical spots. This trial is part of the history of the Jews'; and Michael was saying, 'You should come.'

'I don't want any advice. Thanks all the same.'

'Quite right,' said Michael. 'Only take my advice about not going into Jordan. You might cause us a lot of worry.'

'All right.'

But in the end she did the opposite on both counts. 'All right.' She heard her own voice again in that dawn and retrospect at the Potter's Field, in that attic where to the left of her camp-bed she now noticed, at eye-level, a shining rifle laid parallel to herself; it rested on a dark, oblong object; it had a small clump of dry furze, broom or withered flowers protruding from the barrel; she had not seen this thing in her first survey of the room by lamplight in the earlier darkness, and was most of all mystified by the fuzzy plant stuck into the gun's gleaming barrel. She shifted her head slightly and saw two unequal slivers of light along the recognizable arms of the horse-hair arm-chair from which the stuffing escaped at the ends, no rifle at all, no clump of shrivelled flowers, only the two arms of the old chair at the perspective of eye-level, one protruding slightly about and to the left of the other, and both catching the morning light to resemble the barrel and butt of a gun. 'All right,' she had said to Michael and Saul, conceding their point that she might cause her friends a lot of worry by going into Jordan from Israel, however lawfully. She recalled, now, her sense of uneasy reprieve. She planned in her mind to return to England with Michael in two days' time. Tomorrow, she had thought, while he's at the Eichmann trial or conferring with the lawyers, I can go and pray at Nazareth, at Capharnaum, Galilee, or perhaps only to Mount Zion again, the Tomb of David and the place of the Dormition of Our Lady. But next day she went to the Eichmann trial instead; the next day for no reason at all, for some reason she could not remember, it was something Michael said abstractedly at breakfast when he was in a hurry and ready for the day's business, it was some clear thing she would never now remember, probably some word of Michael's, innocently reinforcing some decision she had already made, overnight, in sleep.

Lying on the camp-bed she wondered whether to try to sleep or whether she had better make an effort to stay awake. She was too interested to sleep. Michael got her a public ticket for the trial, a ticket for visitors or maybe the Press; her handbag was searched and her person examined for the bulges of a possible revolver, camera, or tape-recorder by a policewoman in a small sentry box. She was allowed to pass through to the gallery, to the Press seats as it might be; and there she had listened by earphone to the translations of Eichmann's defence, as in a familiar, recurrent but always incomprehensible dream. The prisoner in his bullet-proof glass enclosure was already an implanted image in the public mind; he had been photographed and filmed from every angle, as had the three judges, the defending and prosecuting counsel, and the public. Saul Ephraim had said, 'It isn't the most interesting part of the trial,' meaning that the impassioned evidence from survivors of the death-camps was over; after that, it had been generally agreed that court proceedings had entered a boring phase; Eichmann was being examined day by day by his own counsel, in a long-drawn routine, document by patient document. Many journalists had gone home. Barbara was not prepared to be taken by the certainty, immediately irresistible, that this dull phase was in reality the desperate heart of the trial. Minute by minute throughout the hours the prisoner discoursed on the massacre without mentioning the word, covering all aspects of every question addressed to him with the meticulous undiscrimating reflex of a computing machine. Barbara turned the switch of her earphones to other simultaneous translations – French, Italian, then back to English. What was he talking about? The effect was the same in any language, and the terrible paradox remained, and the actual discourse was a dead mechanical tick, while its subject, the massacre, was living. She thought, it all feels like a familiar dream, and presently located the sensation as one that the anti-novelists induce. Or it is like, she thought, one of the new irrational films which people can't understand the point of, but continue to see; one can neither cope with them nor leave them alone. At school she usually took the novels and plays of the new French writers with the sixth form. She thought, repetition, boredom, despair, going nowhere for nothing, all of which conditions are enclosed in a tight, unbreakable statement of the times at hand. She had changed her mind, without awareness, at that moment, of any disruption in the logic of personal decisions, but merely allowing herself to recognize, in passing, that she would inevitably complete her pilgrimage to the Holy Land in Jordan. This mental fact was the only one that seemed able to throw light on the ritualistic lines which the man in the glass box was repeating, or to give meaning to her mesmerized presence on the scene.

Bureau IV–B–4. Four–B–four

I was not in charge of the operation itself, only with transportation . . .

Müller needed Himmler's consent.

I was not in a position to make any suggestions, only to obey orders.

And technical transport problems.

Strictly with time-tables and technical transport problems.

I was concerned strictly with time-tables and technical transport problems.

Bureau IV–B–4. Four–B–four–IV–B–4.

High on the tribunal platform the three judges sat attentive to what was said, their faces distinct from each other, but each bearing the recognizable scars of the western intellectual. The large black-robed counsel for the defence stood facing them, every now and then raising both arms as if bestowing a benediction upon the signs and tokens of his proper business in life, those carefully numbered documents on a lectern before him, but in reality simply jerking his arms free of the overlapping sleeves of his gown. Women reporters in casual dress and sandals, some of advanced age, came and went, the new-comers halting with their identification cards before the armed guards at each doorway. The Israeli citizens were mostly men, shirt-sleeved, arms folded. Sometimes derision, short and spontaneous, pelted forth from the public seats, intruding upon one of Eichmann's monologues. The presiding judge would then look alertly across the hall – but the people were already silent and the lips in the glass-bound dock continued to move.

This had been a stage in the trial where individual and small groups of victims were being dealt with, in one sense easier to grasp than the hundreds of thousands of dead that had so far formed the daily theme of the trial, and in the same sense, more horrifying. A little later, in the recess, she heard a man say, 'Thirty children yesterday, today a Mr Wilner.'

The counsel for the defence consulted his document and drew his client's attention to specific names, Misters this and that and their sons, locked in reality. And his client, a character from the pages of a long *anti-roman*, went on repeating his lines which were punctuated only by the refrain, *Bureau IV–B–4*. Barbara felt she was caught in a conspiracy to prevent her brain from functioning.

At first glance the impression is created that in fact from the order of the documents as they are clipped together here, *Bureau IV–B–4* . . .

The man was plainly not testifying for himself, but for his pre-written destiny. He was not answering for himself or his own life at all, but for an imperative deity named Bureau IV–B–4, of whom he was the High Priest.

A searchlight from the city of Jerusalem in Israel, 1961: the voice of the presiding judge was uttering a question:

You mean, that the remark that the man is dead, in spite of all the tonics administered to the man, was also part of the information received by you from the General Government?

The witness, having sprung to attention, gave formal ear to this speech from an alien cult concerning a man being dead. He then sat down and patiently expounded, once more, the complex theology in which not his own actions, nor even Hitler's, were the theme of his defence, but the honour of the Supreme Being, the system, and its least tributary, Bureau IV–B–4.

According to office routine, a question was addressed by Bureau IV–B–4 to the Government General area and after a reply was received from there. After a reply was received. Reply was received. Here, Bureau IV–B–4 of Head Office of Reich Security. Here IV–B–4 for the first time enters the correspondence after the matter was channelled through the department, and it informs the Foreign Ministry, referring to that letter of the Foreign Ministry from the 16th of June 1942, that the above-mentioned Jew of Argentinian nationality died on the 12th April of that year in spite of aid and all the matters listed there. Listed there. All the matters.

And here is once again one of these cases where Bureau IV–B–4 only served as a kind of through station, transit station.

This must have been written in the report received from the Government General area, because. Because otherwise . . .

Presently, a slight hesitation occurred in the court proceedings, a pause. The counsel for the defence looked courteously towards the tribunal, as if waiting for one of the judges to say something, while they, in turn, were under the impression that he was about to speak. The presiding judge then leaned forward and accompanied a sign for the lawyer to proceed with a brief remark in German. 'What are we waiting for?' duly said the English translator's voice in the ear-phones.

> – What are we waiting for?
> –We're waiting for Godot.

The lawyer proceeded: 'I come now to the matter of the Jewess Cozzi –'

It was a highly religious trial.

To get through by telephone that night to Harry Clegg's hotel in Rome, she had kept Michael waiting for three-quarters of an hour; they were to go out to dine at a restaurant. When she had finally made her telephone call she found him sitting in the courtyard with Saul Ephraim, a white-haired wiry woman who turned out to be a reporter from an Israeli newspaper, and a young rabbi who was learned in the archaeology of the Dead Sea, and who had met Harry Clegg several times. When he had introduced Barbara, Michael said to her:

'You won't be going to Jordan?'

'Yes, of course, it's all settled.'

'What did *he* think of the idea?'

'Well, he knows I want to go, and he sees the point.'

The lady-reporter, whom Saul had brought to interview Michael, said she did not see the point, that a Jew should go to an enemy country in a time of war, 'and we have war conditions right now.' She had come to Palestine in 1936, she said, and did not know of any time when there was not a state of war with the Arabs. The young rabbi said he understood she was a Catholic with a British passport;

there would be no difficulty for her in Jordan. Saul and Michael had obviously spoken generally about her position, while she had been upstairs getting through to Harry in Rome. The young rabbi said, if she was going on a pilgrimage, she was going on a pilgrimage.

Which was exactly what she had said to Harry a few moments before when eventually she had got through to the Regina Carlton Hotel in Rome and he had been brought to the telephone. He said he was in the middle of dining with a priest.

'What priest?'

'How do I know what priest? They all look the same.'

She did not pursue the question, but inquired how things were going.

He said, 'Fine. But I don't think you'll get your divorce.'

She said, 'I'm not trying to get a divorce, I'm not even married. It's you who are divorced and you are trying to get the Church to recognize it by annulling the marriage, Harry dear.'

'Yes, that's what I mean. It's you that wants it, that's what I mean.'

She said, 'I'm going to marry you anyway.'

He said, 'I know.'

She said, 'How do you know?'

He said, 'Well, I just haven't any doubt about it. It's all on the cards.'

She started to laugh, but stopped as soon as possible because of the expense by long-distance telephone. It was so much part of his charm that he was very innocent of chivalrous attitudes, and also, she thought it funny that he had reached this conclusion by ordinary deduction while she, delicate probing instrument that she was, had taken a year to settle on the fact that she would marry him anyway. She said, 'The only point at issue is whether we can get married by the Church or not, that's to say, whether I'm going to have peace of mind for the rest of my life or not.'

He said, 'I know. That's what I'm here for. I went along at nine this morning and I've got another appointment for tomorrow.'

'Along where?'

'To see the officials, they're all high-up priests, at the Congregation of the Rota. It's all supposed to be secret, I had to give a promise of secrecy about the proceedings. But they were very civil. "If you please, Signor", and "Yes, Signor". They asked a lot of questions. I was there for four hours, then a break, then two hours, and I've got to go tomorrow.'

'I think you're a hero.'

'Oh, it's all right. This priest I'm dining with says there isn't a hope. He's got nothing to do with it, of course, only he's a Belgian staying at this hotel, and I've been telling him the case. He says there's always a long delay unless the divorced party was a Catholic married in another Church. That's the only occasion when it's easy.'

She said, 'I know.'

He said, 'Did you get a message from me through Fonteyn at the American Embassy in Amman?'

She said, 'Yes, but I'm going on to Jordan next week. I'm going to finish the pilgrimage.'

He said, 'I don't think you should. Something might blow up and you might find yourself in trouble.'

She said, 'Not with a British passport'; and she said, 'I went to the Eichmann trial today. Michael's here, and –'

He said, 'Michael who?'

She said, 'My cousin Michael. He's here as a consultant on the Eichmann trial. It made me feel rather sick. It's more appalling than you'd think from the papers.'

'It makes everyone sick. Why don't you go home to England?'

'I've given up my job. I'll tell you about it when I see you, maybe in Jordan.'

'I'll be here for two or three weeks. I've got some manuscript business to see to besides this game at the Rota.'

'Well, I'm going to Jordan, anyway. I feel a terrible need to do something positive, and if I'm going on a pilgrimage, I'm going on a pilgrimage, that's all.'

'I understand,' he said, 'only take care of yourself, dear girl.'

'I'll write to you tonight,' she said.

Saul Ephraim's friend, the young rabbi, said, 'If she's going on a pilgrimage, she's going on a pilgrimage,' and shrugged, smiling. She smiled back. The woman reporter's hand rested on a notebook that lay on the broad wicker arm of her chair. She said to Michael, 'Will you see something of our country? Israel is for a Jew also the Holy Land, not only for your Catholic cousin.'

It passed through Barbara's mind that this woman might put

something about herself in the report she was going to write about
Michael. She did not want to be reported in the Israeli newspaper as
Aaronson's convert cousin who was about to continue her pilgrimage
in Jordan, but she was too much afraid of the woman's irony to
mention this thought, and felt certain that any plea for discretion
would be distorted to mean that she was denying her Jewish relations. Instead, she asked the rabbi about his work in archaeology, and
they talked of Harry, and the rabbi said he had got much private
information from Harry about the latest discoveries at Qumran; all
the men on the spot, he said, were against the conditions of keeping
the Jewish scholars out of it, but they were forced to comply.

The woman reporter departed and they went to eat. Barbara
walked along with Saul Ephraim, and said, 'I hope that reporter
won't mention me in connexion with Michael. There's no point in
drawing attention to oneself.'

'Why should she mention you?' Saul said. 'Your cousin is the one
she's interested in, he's the legal expert, and they make something of
his visit in the paper in connexion with the trial. But who are you,
Miss Vaughan?'

Barbara was silent. She had always found Saul Ephraim to be
friendly and confiding, but there was now a touch of quick-fire
resentment in his tone and words. She could not find the cause of it,
and in the newly bright morning at the Potter's Field, remembering
what Saul had said, she rested in that question, as she knew one must
from time to time.

She was getting hungry as the noises of the morning clattered in
the house below; she could hear evidence of the chickens being fed
in the old monk's house at the other end of the yard. She remembered the names of the various sorts of food on the menu the last
night she had spent in Israel with Michael and Saul Ephraim. Since
her arrival in Jordan less than two days ago she had eaten very little,
largely because of the heat and the exhaustion of the preceding days.
Her only square meal had been lunch on Saturday at the Cartwrights,
those desperately well-meaning friends of Freddy Hamilton. She felt
very hungry and wondered if they would be offered anything to eat
before departing from this hide-out. Philaphel, Chamous, Eggplant
in Sesame-seed, Sanich, Kebab, Pila, Tchina: the names had been
spelt in Roman characters beside the Hebrew on the menu of the last

meal she had eaten in Israel, with Saul Ephraim and Michael. Michael was to leave the next day, by night flight. She left before him; he had accompanied her, with Saul, as far as the Israeli customs shed at the Mandelbaum Gate. Saul said to her, 'Touch the Wailing Wall on my behalf, and pray. When we have cause for grief, all the old people among us, and many of the young, grieve still more that we are separated from our Wall of Lamentation.' She had been to touch the Wailing Wall on Saturday morning, alone. The nuns in the convent had been surprised when she asked to be directed there; they had said that the guides were not often requested to take pilgrims to this spot, but it was a holy place of the Jews and very ancient, and they would send a guide with her who would show her the Wall and the Temple area as well. Barbara declined a guide, and she said she would see everything properly next week. She had walked round the Old City, alone, marking her route by a tourist map she had obtained from a travel agent, Ramdez, recommended by various Catholic organizations in England as well as by the convent nuns here, as specializing in the provision of guides who understood the Christian shrines. A woman at the Ramdez office had given her the map, and she had wandered round alone, planning a more detailed tour of the city; she had touched the Wailing Wall for Saul Ephraim and prayed, but unobtrusively, since she was watched by numerous loafing Arabs, in various stages of undernourishment and deformity, who slowly sidled up, apparently to befriend her; she had been at first astonished that their attitude was not at all hostile, considering their plight; then she had felt very nervous. So she had wandered up the Via Dolorosa until she had come to Alexandros's shop, and there had been found by Freddy, in the process of buying a silver fish on a chain . . . by Freddy and the Cartwrights, and had been taken home by them, and entertained, and finally been involved in that absurd discussion in the garden. The change in Freddy, she thought, occurred there in the garden, where that clump of wild flowers, carefully tended wild flowers, frequently watered wild flowers . . . she couldn't remember what they had been exactly but she had recognized them at the time; silvery dimpled leaves, *Umbilicus rupestris*, Navelwort; spiky pink flowers, *Epilobium angustifolium* of the Willow-herb family. . . . Freddy said, 'Jewish blood or Gentile blood, the point is it's hers.' That was unexpected. Barbara had thought she had recognized his type, and knew him through and through; but no. And the Cartwrights, who had known him far longer, were decidedly taken aback. 'Your trouble,' Freddy had said to them, 'is this. You blow neither cold nor hot. How does it go, Miss Vaughan? – Neither hot nor cold. You're lukewarm. Lukewarm, and I will vomit thee out of my mouth.' It had been an embarrassing moment, exhilarating moment, an interesting . . . Barbara closed her eyes against the glare of the risen sun beating its rays through the window. I'd better get up now and see what's going on, she thought. Freddy's trouble was obviously his overbearing mother. It was truly exhilarating to think of his tearing up all those letters and putting them down Alexandros's lavatory, it made one's pulse beat cheers for Freddy. His mother, like Ricky. Only Ricky had not got away with much from her; not for long, Ricky hadn't. Freddy had been weak for too long. 'Crushed,' Ruth Gardnor had said, crossing her long brown legs under the open beach-robe at Tiberias on the shores of Galilee. 'Poor Freddy has let himself be crushed by her.' She might, herself, have been crushed by Ricky, if she had not had so much of her stubborn, hard-riding father in her. Ricky was altogether too masculine and too feminine; both and neither. Poor Ricky would have had her letter by now. Babara opened her eyes and moved to rise from the camp-bed. . . .

She woke, blinking in the sunlight, upon the opening of the attic door and moved to rise from the bed. A young woman, a blue-eyed, brown-skinned Israeli, came in. No, a blue-eyed Arab woman, dressed in a blue shirt and dark skirt, like a lithe Israeli. She was carrying, over her arms, some cloth that looked like the black-out curtains of war-time England. 'What's the time?' Barbara said, feeling down into the pocket of her dressing-gown for her watch, and realizing, then, that the young woman was Suzi Ramdez.

Suzi dumped the black stuff and sat down on the horse-hair armchair. 'Ten minutes past ten o'clock. We arrive at the Holy Sepulchre at eleven for the Mass. That's first stop. Have you slept good? It's a beautiful day, Barbara. I call you Kyra for the rest of the trip. Kyra is my servant. I have sent her to far away on request from Alexandros. In Jerusalem everyone knows Kyra, but we will not remain long in Jerusalem. I do this by arrangement with Alexandros because I am the secret lover of Alexandros. Alexandros is beautiful. My father would kill me to know what we do, but Alexandros would prevent him. Do you bring news of my brother Abdul? You must wear these black clothes. I laugh to think of this, like playing children again. You are my Arab servantwoman and you must be deaf and dumb so you do not understand Arabic when addressed to you by Arabs. Kyra is not deaf and dumb, but I say to any friend that speaks to you, stand back, she has a sick throat and chest. I shall be always by your side. Alexandros has given all this instruction, to be at your side. So don't speak. What is the news from my brother? Are you the lover of Freddy? He is quite a great beauty, a real man. I read many English books, German and Italian also, poetry particular in original language. Alexandros has told my mother I am the most intelligent woman in the kingdom of Jordan; he does not say to my mother the best lover, believe me. I am too proud to marry a man of fine family but no education. Freddy has said to tell you we are under starter's orders: what is starter's orders?'

'A horse-racing term,' Barbara said. 'He means –'

'Yes, true, I guess the meaning, we better hurry up.'

'I'm only half-awake,' said Barbara, getting off the bed and tentatively picking at the black garments she was to wear. 'But I'll thank you properly when I wake up properly.'

'You are to be a deaf-mute anyway,' Suzi said. 'So we talk only in private, in the car, where your lips are hid by the thick veil. You must be like a servant to me always, you keep by me like you are humble. I hope your God Jesus is going to be sincerely grateful for all this business you make for him. We pack your silken dressing-gown in the bag and you put all of your clothes off first. It is right to be an Arab woman from the body outwards. This next to your skin is from Kyra's box, almost new from the shop but these two garments, the robe and the veil, are dusty like for Kyra. Myself, I would not wear those black, old-fashioned clothes if I had a million pounds for it, but you are a woman of great principle and determination like Alexandros has informed me at our meeting in the night.'

Barbara dressed in the black garments, which were bulky but not as heavy as they seemed. 'How can I see through the black veil?' she said.

'In the light, the veil will be no more difficult than sun-glasses, you will discover.'

'I ought to have practised the part.' The robe was shorter than that worn by most Arab women of the old order. 'Is it too short?'

'It is like a poor woman's dress that has been given it for alms by another lady. It's all right.'

'I caught a glimpse of your brother the other day, but I didn't see him to speak to,' Barbara said, feeling that this was the first piece of information due.

'That is a pity.'

'I didn't know I was going to see you.'

'Abdul must have been doubtful of you for a friend, or else he would have sent a message. He's my favourite man like Alexandros. Now you come and eat some breakfast. Do you drink coffee or tea? There is tea but it is not like English tea. Come, follow.'

There was no time to think; it was a lovely feeling, and Barbara was still sleepy. It was good to be in other peoples' hands, responsible only for a plausible wearing of the servant's clothes and the representation of a deaf-mute Arab woman. There was no time, as she dressed up and listened to Suzi's talk, to reflect on what was happening; her thoughts merely fluttered, like a moth approaching and retreating from a bright light. She dipped her face-cloth below the surface of the dusty film on the water in the jug and wiped it over her face, saying, 'Where can I wash?' while Suzi said, 'There's a water-tap downstairs, but you get a big wash tonight, it's not so necessary for you to be washed just now.' And indeed, it mattered so little that Barbara laughed with Suzi, put on the veil, then lifted it so that she could see better to pack the dressing-gown in her suitcase.

'Give me the passport and the money. The luggage and belongings we leave here; they are safe,' Suzi said. 'Freddy is ready. Come, follow.' Suzi arranged the veil over Barbara's eyes once more.

She was afraid to descend the dark wooden staircase with this veil covering her face, and she lifted it again as she followed Suzi downstairs. Freddy was there, drinking coffee at a table in a large white-washed room. Before he could see her she covered her face again, to make an effect. Freddy looked up. 'Is she coming?' he said. Suzi's laughter rippled; it was the laugh of a cultivated woman. Barbara thought then, it's going to be all right, and astonished herself by her confidence in this unknown Arab girl; and it seemed the tone and quality of Suzi's laughter was the reason.

Freddy said, 'Oh, of course, there you are, it's you, Barbara.' She threw back the veil and said, 'Does it work?' He said, 'You look absolutely splendid. I wish Alexandros could see you.' He said something about her being hot in all that stuff. Suzi began explaining that it was quite light in weight, and moreover very well designed for hot weather as the folds could billow and catch the breeze: 'The Arab women of this old type are no fools.'

Barbara was looking at the food on the table – bread, watermelon, olives and cream cheese. She took coffee and said, 'Can we get some food after Mass?' and explained that she intended to take Holy Communion and was obliged to abstain from solid food for three hours beforehand. Suzi began cheerfully to issue voluble caution not to reveal her eyes while taking Communion, 'but lift the veil so – I am accustomed to taking Catholics to the Holy Sepulchre, but for you it will be necessary to take the Holy Wafer with the eyes covered, as this is necessary for you, to make sure you are not seen by others. The priest will –' Barbara meanwhile was assailed by a consideration from the distant reality of her private life; she thought, if I do intend to marry him, whether the Church allows it or not, does the intention alone constitute a mortal sin? She thought, then, if there's a doubt in one's mind, then it's all right. Rather wearily she felt her old identity returning in spite of this new disguise and the elation of the fantastic moment she had plunged into. It's too much for me, she thought, all this bothering myself and questioning all the time; I've had enough of it.

She said, 'Oh, I won't risk it.'

Suzi said, 'You are very wise. It's best that you should not move from the crowd to the Communion rail, but you will stay by my side and nobody will notice you if you keep quiet and humble. If anyone who knows Kyra well shall approach us in Jerusalem, maybe I shall say you are Aliyah, the niece of my servant Kyra. I shall say something, believe me. You say nothing.'

'I thought she was to *be* Kyra,' Freddy said. He was reading a local English-language newspaper, which was several days old, just as if he were breakfasting late at home with this morning's Sunday paper.

Suzi cut a slice of the crumbly bread and passed it carefully to Barbara. 'There's no need to fast then,' said Suzi. Barbara ate her breakfast with a sense of reprieve which seemed to extend over the

three of them, and over the whitewashed room with its plain wood
furnishings and the surprising telephone hung on the wall. Suzi's
dark, thin face had a touch in it of western anxiety, the mark of the
emancipated; Freddy's face, too, gave the map of his life. But for the
moment, they were both relaxed; she thought, there's something in
this undertaking that lifts a burden of nerves from us all; by every
reasoning the physical experiment alone should be nerve-wracking
to contemplate, but it isn't. Suzi said, 'Finish up your coffee.'
Barbara did this, glancing at that page of Freddy's paper which was
turned towards her. 'Eichmann's Quality Truthfulness' stated these
local headlines, 'Marilyn Monroe Gall-bladder Operation'. Barbara
said, 'I think it's going to be fun.' Freddy did not reply for a moment,
busily finishing what he was reading on his side of the paper. 'Hero's
Welcome to Major Gagarin in London', stated Barbara's side.
Freddy cast down the paper and jumped to his feet, taking a deep,
contented breath as if the air were full of blessings. 'Yes, hurry up,
girls. We start in five minutes. Under starter's orders! Get ready. The
car's outside.'

Barbara said to Suzi, 'Might this lead you into trouble?'

Suzi laughed. 'Everything I do might lead me into trouble. One day
I shall run away. Now there is no danger for me except that my father,
Joe Ramdez, shall suspect that I play a trick. If we fall in with the
police we say you are an eccentric English lady, as they understand
this. Or I say something to the police and to some I can give money.
You say to them you are English if the police arrest you, and that you
always wear the national costume of the countries you visit. I do not
think this will happen with the police, as I am never stopped at the
police posts with my tourists, and Freddy looks like my tourist.'

'It's good of you,' Barbara said, and followed her to the car.

'That is not all the opinions of me,' said Suzi as she went ahead.
'But you speak like Kyra.'

It was a large blue American car of the type generally provided for
hire by the travel agencies. 'You get in the back,' Suzi said to Barbara,
adding, as Barbara gathered up the folds of her clothes to do so,
'Never mind that you have difficulty to get in and out of the car as
this looks O.K. for an Arab village woman.'

Freddy started up the car, and looked round the empty yard.
'Shouldn't we say good-bye?'

'They are all gone farther down the hill to the monastery to be busy with the Masses in the church,' Suzi said. 'And we are sightseers and tourists now, so we don't say good-bye.'

'We're off!' Freddy said. 'The pilgrimage is begun. First stop, the Holy Sepulchre.'

Suzi said, 'Now I tell you the places of interest that we see. We leave Haceldama and we approach the ancient Jerusalem. Over there is Mount Scopus and we come to the valley of Jehosophat, which is the scene of the Last Judgement. I have read your Bible and Christian books besides the Koran, and the Bible also is a great book.'

'But rather obscure,' Freddy said. He added, 'mystifying', in case Suzi had not caught his meaning.

She said, 'That is not so much a fault when you can read two or three times, and you can find different opinions as to meaning. Incidentally, over there, as we turn, is Israel, where you came from; the people here do not use this name for that territory, you must not speak this name, it's better to avoid. Is it true that the Jews have imprisoned Martin Buber in the Hebrew University, and will not permit anyone to go visit with him because he speaks in favour of the Arabs?'

PART TWO

7. THE PASSIONATE PILGRIMS

Freddy Hamilton, Barbara Vaughan, Suzi Ramdez – each, in later years, when they looked back on that time, remembered one particular event before all others. It was different in each case. Alexandros, too, had his special recollection that was to gleam suddenly. Michael Aaronson remembered only the worry and waiting, as he sat in his office looking out over London Wall, when it was certain that Barbara had disappeared.

'What I remember most vividly of all,' Barbara told her cousins later on, '– and I'll never forget it – was when I went into the wrong room at the house at Jericho and found Ricky in bed with Joe Ramdez. I nearly died.' For Freddy it did not come easy to talk of those days, lost in comedy and found again in tragedy: as if switching the dial of the wireless from confused station to station, he would rapidly send the pointer of his mind through a range of recollections until he came upon the clear moment of waiting outside the convent where Barbara was lodging, while Alexandros bargained with the porter for the unlocking of the door. But he would not speak of it. Instead, he would dwell on another more concrete moment – and by that time it was common knowledge that he had stood in the hot sandy courtyard of the house at Jericho and recognized, before he himself could be observed, Gardnor's wife walking towards a palm-tree, and casually extracting a small folded paper from a deep slit in the ragged bark. 'It simply came to me immediately there and then,' Freddy said to a small group of colleagues, one Saturday afternoon two years later, when they had returned to the house where they were guests, after watching village cricket. 'It just came to me that this was Nasser's Post Office, as we called it. We'd been looking for the spot high and low since the leaks began some months before. When I saw Gardnor's wife I simply knew it. And then I went and got the damned sunstroke and forgot it for two or three weeks. However, it all came back. Just in time for us to get Gardnor. Unforgettable. Gardnor's wife, at Nasser's Post Office, getting her orders and passing on our stuff.' Freddy took his fountain-pen from his inside pocket, and from his outside pocket he brought the cricket score-card, on the back of which he drew for his friends a diagram of Nasser's Post Office – the road, the house, and the palm-tree, marking with a cross the spot where he had first stood and then crouched, concealing himself behind his car, while Mrs Gardnor went to the tree and collected the message from the tufted bark. 'Of course,' he said, 'I put in some more investigation on the spot. And I proved right. I wasn't mistaken. Unconsciously, I must already have suspected Gardnor. We all did, as it turned out. But as he himself admitted in court, he knew we couldn't act without real proof. . . . It was only a stroke of chance . . . quite absurd. . . .'

But to take the events as they happened, so far as is human: Freddy went first, an unobtrusive foreign visitor among a crowd in the forecourt of the Church of the Holy Sepulchre, and was followed by Suzi and Barbara, unnoticeable among another crowd, on that first Sunday morning of the pilgrimage. Some of the people had come for sightseeing purposes; these blocked the way until they had done gazing at the many-shaped structure, clicking cameras, craning up to the domes and terraced rooftops that expressed the divine ideas of those zealots and their conquerors who made them, and staring also at the heavy wooden props and scaffolding which modern times had contributed to the edifice in order to prop it up. When the people at last surged into the huge, cool, and altogether sepulchral interior, they separated into several groups, each clustering round its own guide or pastor for further directions. Freddy, who had been to the church before, began to make his way to the flight of stairs leading to the Choir of the Greeks at Golgotha, where the Anglicans and Catholics worshipped at their respective Orthodox and Latin altars. As he broke away from the crowds, Freddy failed to notice a procession moving towards him from the chapel which stood over the Holy Sepulchre itself, in the centre of the huge rotunda where the crowds were gathered. The people had made a pathway for the procession, which comprised a Coptic priest followed by his incense-swinging acolytes, newly emerged from a Mass. Freddy, vaguely assuming this procession to be only one of the little bands of variously garbed visitors among the others congregated in the area, sacrilegiously barged into one of the acolytes, and extricated himself with an apology which was not understood, so that he was abused by the thin, pale acolyte with something between a hiss and a spit.

From their part of the hall Suzi and Barbara could see the encounter. Barbara said, 'Oh, goodness,' and was immediately seized by Suzi, who gripped her arm to remind her to be deaf and dumb. An English female voice not far from Barbara said, 'Oh, look at that terrible man –' obviously referring to Freddy. Barbara had turned to look in the direction of the voice, and then, when she quickly realized she was not supposed to have heard it, she fixed her veiled eyes, very unhearingly, very unspeakingly, in front of her. But the voice had been disquieting; for a moment Barbara had thought she recognized it.

Presently, they were up in the Greek Choir where two Masses, one Orthodox, one Latin, were in progress, assisted by two congregations haphazardly thronged, kneeling or standing on the bare pavements before each altar, only a few feet from each other. The Greek Orthodox service at the main altar of Calvary that stood above a round earth-hole, the traditional site of the Cross, was mainly attended by an English mass-pilgrimage numbering about sixty and an American group of about twenty-five, mostly women with a few ageing men, and several clergymen, who were evidently leading the pilgrimages. Among them were also some individual pilgrims of unguessable nationalities and numerous local Arab worshippers, the fruits of the missions to Palestine from generation to generation. Only two Arab women over in the Greek congregation were veiled and dressed as Barbara was, but she was thankful even for them, for in fact at the Roman Catholic altar where she now stood with Suzi she was the only veiled woman.

And in fact, the three Franciscans who stood aside throughout the Mass, custodians of their altar, sent each other a communal glance at the sight of Barbara. The glance was a familiar question: when would these Arab convert-women throw off their old traditions and understand that Catholic Arabs were not obliged to cover their faces but only their heads? – they were as bad, in their way, as the young tourist girls who came, not only to visit the holy places, but to the Mass, without any covering on their heads at all, and with dresses without sleeves.

But the venerable brothers had more than Barbara to bother them that day. It was a memorable Sunday that lasted them all their old age, one of the worst of the increasingly bad memorable Sundays when the modern foreign priests, chiefly English and American, came to the Holy Sepulchre with their pilgrimages to say a Mass at the Altar of the Nailing of the Cross. That would have been very good, but instead of saying their Mass and going away, these upstart clergy very often insisted on giving a sermon. Sermons were not encouraged, as the demand on the use of the famous altar by visitant priests and their pilgrims was heavy on Sunday mornings, and even a short sermon held up the next Mass on the list.

But it was not so much the fact of the sermon on this particular Sunday, but its substance that made the occasion a prototype, for the three honest custodians on duty, of things to be deplored during times of recreation; and thus it contributed to bind together their staunch years to come.

The visiting priest of that hour was an Englishman in his middle thirties. He was one of the priests accompanying a pilgrimage of about forty English Catholics; they now mingled with the local congregation and with the other foreign pilgrims among whom was a close-knit body of Japanese nuns. As the nuns somewhat established the variegated quality of the scene, Suzi had worked Barbara through the crowd to a point near them, whose long black robes provided a protective colouring for her outfit. The eyes of the Franciscans had automatically moved to the young priest on the altar, and they kept a special watch on the assisting acolyte, a local Arab boy; for it was their duty, to which they devoted extreme diligence, to see that the ritual was correctly observed at this Altar of the Nailing of the Cross. At the other altar in the chapel the Greek rite proceeded under the equally jealous eyes of its custodians, and the chanting murmur of the Orthodox responses droned busily about the ears of the Latin persuasion, so that the blessed mutter of the Roman Mass could scarcely be heard by the faithful; the Franciscans were accustomed to this and were aware that nothing could be done about it. It was true that from time to time feelings came to a boil, and a quarrel would take place between the subordinate brothers of either communion, not to mention the words that had been known to arise when the Copts, Syrians, or even the Gregorian Armenians overstepped the mark on the sacred site of the death, burial, and resurrection of the Saviour. Doctrinal arguments, these simple servants of the Orders left to their superiors; but the question of who had the privilege of sweeping whose paving stone was their province; not many years since, it had come to a fist-fight at Bethlehem on a Feast of the Nativity because a young novice brother of the Orthodox had presumed to clean a certain painted-glass window, this task being properly within the province of a newly arrived Franciscan brother who, simple peasant boy as he was, nevertheless perceived that the prestige of the One True Church was upon his shoulders, and started a fight.

Sometimes there had been errors of protocol on the Franciscan side, as they humbly conceded amongst themselves. Not long ago, when the Archbishop of Canterbury visited the Holy Land, a few good Franciscans, carried away by the event, had kissed his ring on his arrival at the great Sepulchre. On being told later by their superior that they ought not to have done so, their spokesman offered the reason: 'We thought it might move Her Majesty to do something for us.' It was indeed difficult to realize that the British Mandate was at an end.

The English priest at present saying Mass on the altar had nearly reached the moment for his sermon; he had no right to give a sermon, no matter how many English pilgrims he had brought, when time was pressing for the next Mass on the list. As if to aid and abet him, the Orthodox Mass had only a few seconds before come to a quiet end. He had not even asked permission; had merely said as he brushed from the vestry, 'I'm going to say a few words to the pilgrims, very few.' The friars' eyes were upon him as he concluded the Ordinary of the Mass and turned to the congregation.

'I will say a few words,' he said, 'on the text of St Paul's Epistle to the Hebrews, chapter 13, verse 14: "We have an everlasting city, but not here; our goal is the city that is one day to be."

'In the Name of the Father, the Son, and the Holy Ghost. Most of us have come a long way to Jerusalem. It has been the instinct of Christians since the time of the Early Church to see Jerusalem before they died. Jerusalem was a place of pilgrimage for the Jews, centuries before the time of Christ. The act of pilgrimage is an instinct of mankind. It is an act of devotion which, like a work of art, is meaning enough in itself. The questions, "What useful purpose does a pilgrimage serve? What good does it do?" are by the way. People put themselves out to visit places sacred to their religion, or the graves of poets and statesmen, or of their ancestors, or the house they themselves were born in. Why? Because that is what people do.

'We usually expect to receive for our trouble the experience of a strong emotion. We expect to be moved, when we reach our destination, by awe or nostalgia; or we hope for a shade of sadness or in some way to be spiritually exalted. But so far as feelings are concerned, our feelings when we get to the place are usually a matter of good or bad fortune, as the case may be. A lot may depend on the weather. And this is more particularly the case where a pilgrimage of religion is concerned. A religious pilgrimage has always been associated with difficulty, danger, heat and bother and general human wear and tear. We who have come by air from the West have so far had an easier journey than the devout Moslems do, who surge in their thousands to Mecca by cheap transport, any transport, to pray at the shrine of Mohammed. We have it easier than Mary and Joseph did when they came up to Jerusalem for the feast and, in the course of all the jostle and bother and commerce of the pilgrimage, lost their child and only missed him when they were on the way home, so that they had to trail all the way back, a day's journey. I say that we –'

The friars had already summed up their man and they conveyed their verdict to each other by the flicker of a glance. One of the new upstarts; comparing the Moslems to good Catholics in the same breath. . . . So far, so bad. They discerned that worse was to come.

'We had a streamlined journey to Jerusalem,' went on this firebrand. 'But we have come in the hottest and least comfortable season because it's the only time we could manage to come at all. Otherwise, quite rightly, we would have chosen to come in the spring or autumn. However, we know that Our Lord Jesus Christ was here in the summer time, when life was less comfortable than it is today, when the smells were smellier and the sick and the poor were more numerous and less hopeful of cure. Don't let yourselves be bothered by the commercialism that goes on around the sacred places. There was commercialism in the courts of the Temple in the time of Christ. Don't be put off because the shrines that commemorate what was once the simple life of Jesus are overwhelmed with glittering ornaments, silver lamps, jewelled inlays and the like. They are nothing like the Temple was that Our Lord frequented himself, healing the ordinary sick among all the grandeur. And we have come to be reminded of Our Lord. It does not count what feelings are, if our feelings can be conditioned by the weather or the artistic tastes of the people around us. A good disposition is more precious to God than fine feelings. In Jerusalem, our Blessed Lord suffered, died, and rose again to life. It is enough that we are here.

'So it seems to me that you shouldn't expect to feel exalted by awe and reverence on days like, for instance, today, among the crowds in the narrow streets and the temperature rising. In the next few weeks don't wear yourselves out rushing round the shrines just for the sake of having said a "Hail Mary" and touched every altar with your rosary, like a child who invents for himself a sense of impending doom unless he steps over every crack in the pavement. There is no need to visit every shrine in the place. There are far too many shrines. Some of them are sheer fake, others are doubtful. That's not to say that the important sites that mark the life of Jesus, such as the spot we stand on at this moment, are not sacred places. They have been sanctified by centuries of the great Dead who have come –'

The three friars gazed at the priest as with one gaze. They had known it. The incipient *défroqué* was undermining the Holy Land, and as he went on to enumerate for practical purposes the shrines which his pilgrimage might well skip and the dubiety of their origins, their thoughts went to their brethren, the custodians of the Holy Land to whom these places were their whole heart and life; tears came to the eyes of the eldest friar as he thought of the venerable Franciscan, well past ninety, who kept the house where Our Lady was conceived by St Joachim and St Anne, and who had wanted nothing for himself all his life but to show it to the pilgrims and pray with them as they came, and collect alms for the poor of the place, and die there on that spot. Now this enemy of the Faith on the altar was openly preaching what other young foreign priests had only so far hinted. Moreover, he was saying more than a few words, he was preaching at length, and he should not be preaching at all. The youngest friar, a lay-brother, murmured fiercely that he would tell this priest after the Mass that he had transgressed by setting back the time of the next Mass. Already a fresh batch of pilgrims was waiting at the entrance. But the aged friar made a gesture of restraint towards the young brother. The other friar, also an old man, then whispered his support of the young brother, but he too was silenced by the elder

one: 'Observe meekness,' he said softly, 'it is our calling. Moreover –'
He paused to give full ear to the voice from the altar, to hear what next
outrage was being uttered. When he had heard enough he continued,
'Let us not provoke this man lest the bishop should say to us, "You
have knelt to kiss the ring of the Schismatic of Canterbury, but one
of our own good Fathers you have treated with reproof."' At this they
folded their hands and waited to hear what the Judas and intellectual
standing at the Altar of the Nailing of the Cross would say next.

He was saying, 'It is not absolutely certain, for instance, that the
Holy Sepulchre stands on the site of Golgotha. There are strong
arguments of archaeology in favour of this place where we stand
being the place of the Crucifixion, and for a Catholic these arguments
are strengthened above all by the fact that this place was traditionally
revered as Golgotha before the Emperor Constantine, in the fourth
century, built the original church on this site. Archaeology is continually enriching our knowledge of the holy places. Where doubts of
historic authenticity exist, they are as thrilling in their potentialities
for quest and discovery as a certainty would be. The weight of probability leads most of the experts to believe that this is the site of
Calvary. But other learned people have argued against it. Whether
true or not, our religion does not depend on it. We know for a certainty that Our Lord was crucified, that he died and was buried, and
rose again from the dead, at a place outside the walls of Jerusalem; if
not at the spot where we stand, then at some other spot near by. If
you are looking for physical exactitude in Jerusalem it is a good quest,
but it belongs to archaeology, not faith. In the time of Christ the
people built up the tombs of the Prophets, as he reminded them with
a bit of irony. I am sure some were authentic, some doubtful.
Jerusalem has been in many hands. Then, as now, soldiers patrolled
the Holy Land. Jerusalem has been destroyed, rebuilt, fought over,
conquered, and now is divided again. The historical evidence of our
faith is scattered about under the ground; nothing is neat. And what
would be the point of our professing faith if it were? There's no need
for faith if everything is plain to the eye. We cannot know anything
perfectly, because we ourselves are not perfect. When we have come
to perfection in time, then faith, like time, will be done away. "We
have an everlasting city," St Paul has said, "but not here; our goal is
the city that is one day to be." For there is a supernatural process

going on under the surface and within the substance of all things. In the Jerusalem of history we see the type and shadow of that Jerusalem of Heaven that St John of Patmos tells of in the Apocalypse. "I, John," he says, "saw in my vision that holy city which is the new Jerusalem, being sent down by God from Heaven, like a bride who has adorned herself to meet her husband." This is the spiritual city that is involved eternally with the historical one. It is the city of David, the city of God's people in exile: "If I forget thee, O Jerusalem, let my tongue cleave to the roof of my mouth; if I prefer not Jerusalem above my chief joy." It is the city of Jesus, not only of his death, but of his rising again alive. It is the New Jerusalem which we seek with our faith, and which is the goal of our pilgrimage to this old Jerusalem of history. "What is faith?" said St Paul. "It is that which gives substance to our hopes, which convinces us of things we cannot see."'

The priest glanced at his watch and the friars at each other. He made a slight gesture of pulling himself off a subject that was leading far, and said, 'I don't mean you to be afraid of saying your prayers at the wrong shrine. It's always the right place if you pray there.

'We know the creed of our faith and what we believe. Outside of that it is better to know what is doubtful than to place faith in uncertainties. Doubt is the prerogative of the believer; the unbeliever cannot know doubt. And in what is doubtful we should doubt well. But in whatever touches the human spirit, it is better to believe everything than nothing. Have faith. In the Name of the Father, the Son, and the Holy Ghost. *Amen.*'

They felt he had done his worst. The friars stood moveless, watching him return to the altar and begin the second part of the Mass.

'*Credo in unum Deum, Patrem omnipotentem, factorem coeli et terrae, visibilium omnium, et invisibilium –* '

Suddenly he had broken off and had turned once again to the people. This alone was irregular. . . . But he was about to speak, with an advisory finger pointed. . . . 'I forgot to mention the Milk Grotto, near Bethlehem. Don't go near the Milk Grotto. It's a pure fake. They claim there's a legend that milk from Mary's breast fell in this grotto where for some reason she happened to be nursing the infant Jesus, in consequence of which the walls of the grotto turned white. They make up packets of white stuff from the walls for pilgrims to take away. The stuff is supposed to be a comfort to nursing mothers or some such hocus-pocus. Keep away from the Milk Grotto, it's only a chalk cave.'

The communist agent returned to the altar and began again. '*Credo in unum Deum* . . .'

When the Mass was ended and he moved from the altar towards the friars, the youngest again made a move as if to say a few wild words. But both elders restrained him; and when the Englishman brushed past them, muttering the prayers appointed to be said after Mass, the friars stood mute, with downcast eyes, content to wait for their justification in Heaven, which, being all Italian territory, would be so ordered that foreign firebrands like this one would be kept firmly in their place.

Freddy already thought highly of Suzi, who had told him what a lovely smile he had. This was something he vaguely recalled having heard before at an earlier time of his life; it was a pleasant reminder – '. . . Freddy's attractive smile', or '. . . your nice smile, Freddy' – something like that. Suzi was very outspoken but that was the Ramdez touch; Abdul was the same. By the time he came to stand outside the Holy Sepulchre after the service, waiting for the girls to emerge, he had forgotten Suzi's compliment about his smile but only thought highly of Suzi. The girls had gone to look round the Holy Sepulchre and visit the other shrines. Suzi had told him to wait for them outside, had pushed confidently through the crowd, followed mutely by Barbara. Things seemed to be going well. Freddy had thought the sermon rather long but quite practical in its way. He had been to a Roman Catholic Mass once or twice before, for funeral services, and considered there was too much of it. He was not, anyway, a very religious man. He entertained a patriotic belief in God, but since his youth he had been to church about as seldom as he had been to Buckingham Palace. However, he disapproved of letting young chaps into the Foreign Service who openly professed to have no religion at all. A security risk, Freddy felt decidedly. He looked up at the scaffold props of the Holy Sepulchre and wondered if Joanna and Matt would hear of his lingering presence in Jordan. He didn't really care one way or another; and when his mind turned on those tedious letters from Ma and Benny, his anxious replies, and the all-responsible letter to the doctor which had gone swirling down the lavatory at Alexandros's place, he felt respectably at one with the world. Things were going well. It was like being at the races when one had started off with a pound each way and the horse had come in, perhaps second, at a good price; then, if one did quite nicely in the second race, even at a modest price, one knew one's luck was in for the day.

One's luck was in at last, and the enterprise of Barbara Vaughan's pilgrimage had got off on a good start. He thought highly of Suzi Ramdez. Somewhere along the road to Bethlehem, their next goal, a pink gin before lunch would be a good idea.

Barbara, meanwhile, existed in numb misery. The clothes she was draped in, although they were loose, seemed to form a kind of oven for her burning body. The crowds pressed as if deliberately all round her, pushing crude faces close to her veil. Her eyes prickled and she felt their roots were red hot. Everything in her life was remotely in the past, Harry Clegg was a few feet of over-exposed film. Nothing worse, she thought, can happen; it was the only thing she could think, but if she had tried she could not have placed what exactly that happening was, than which nothing could be worse. At a point during the sermon, she had wanted to say something to Suzi like 'I want to go out and be sick', but being in any case uncertain whether she actually wanted to be sick or not, she had remembered she was a mute. From the sermon she had got the erroneous impression of a sanctimonious voice pounding upon her physical distress. Now she followed Suzi, who was treating the crowds like those waves of the Red Sea between which the Israelites passed dryshod; the people made way for Suzi, but on Barbara they pressed with enlarged noses and twisted mouths on the other side of her veil. She was beyond feeling ill, it was merely that nothing worse could happen.

She stood beside Suzi before a stone slab and wanted only to lie on it full length, without the black shrouds she was wearing; she yearned for its coolness and for a long sleep, a sleep of death. Through her fever she heard the voice of an English-speaking Arab guide addressing the group which Suzi had joined. He was saying that this was the Holy Sepulchre itself, the tomb that had belonged to Joseph of Arimathea, where Christ was laid on that first Good Friday when his body was taken down from the cross. The body of Christ was embalmed with spices and herbs and wrapped in a linen shroud as the cool night was falling. Suzi took Barbara's arm to draw her closer to the front of the group where the guide was pointing to this and that memorial of the burial of Christ. Barbara's head was drumming; her ears had begun to ache. She held back and clung only to the one thought that nothing worse could now happen.

They were going down some cool dark steps. The guide had gone ahead and waited below for another group of people to move away before he collected his brood about him. The brood was talking softly, menacing Barbara. She heard that this was St Helena's Chapel, where the true Cross had been found in the fourth century. Barbara wanted to return to the slab and lie on its cool surface; an image of Tess of the d'Urbervilles in the last scene at Stonehenge passed her mind and was gone indiscernibly, so that she did not know what caused her to start and give a little shudder, as if touched by a bat that had somehow got into the crypt. She had stopped on the dark stair-way, and the people behind her wanted to pass down. Suzi reached up and took her arm. Nothing worse can happen now. A woman who did not seem to belong either to the group that was about to leave the chapel or to the approaching group, was standing apart looking round her, sturdily clutching with one thumb the shoulder strap of her sling-bag; in the other hand she held a slip of paper about which she evidently wished to consult someone. Barbara and Suzi had reached the ground of the crypt. The woman approached their guide, but he had turned to consult with the departing guide about some guide-business. The lone woman then approached a man among the crowd that Barbara and Suzi had joined. She was within breathing distance of Barbara's veil. She was Ricky. She was Miss Rickward. She said to the man, offering the slip of paper, 'Excuse me, but can you read Arabic?' The man said, no, he was afraid he couldn't, but perhaps the guide . . . He looked round for their guide, who was nowhere visible at that moment. 'You see,' Ricky was saying, 'it's an address that I've been directed to. I'm looking for a friend.' The man then caught sight of Barbara at the same time as Ricky did, and he started to say, 'There's an Arab woman there, she'd be able to –' Ricky approached Barbara with her piece of paper: 'Excuse me, but can you tell me –'

Suzi's arm shot forth like the arm of one holding back yet another Red Sea. 'My poor servant is dumb,' declared Suzi. 'Very dumb, also holy. Praise be to Allah! She can utter no word, neither falsehood nor blasphemy. Do not approach my holy mute, I command you, but stand at a distance, and if there's anything you want, ask *me*.'

'Oh, I beg your pardon,' Ricky said, stepping backward, as did the other people in their near vicinity. Suzi was reading the words on the piece of paper. She read out, 'The Crusaders' Inn. Ask for Jaber Khalil, from Amin Mahgoub, St Helena's Convent.' Suzi explained how to get to the Crusaders' Inn while Barbara looked at Ricky through her veil without feeling a thing, since nothing worse could happen than had already happened behind her throbbing head. She heard Suzi tell Ricky to ask for the proprietor, Mr Khalil, while Ricky informed her gratefully that she had got the address from the doorman at St Helena's Convent; she had not been allowed to enter the doors of the convent as an outbreak of an infectious disease had occurred there that morning. 'And,' said Ricky, 'I'm trying to catch up with an English friend. I thought she might have come here for a church service.'

'Good luck, then,' Suzi said, shaking off the intruder as firmly as if she had not been in total ignorance of any connexion between Ricky and Barbara. Suzi moved with the group towards the Altar of the Finding of the Cross, where the guide was now standing ready for them. Holding fast to Barbara, she thrust far into the stifling crowd, who now made a little space for this woman of Jerusalem and her picturesque servant.

'She has seen all the Holy Sepulchre,' Suzi said, when they found Freddy in the courtyard. 'But Barbara must come again on the return journey.'

'I'm ill,' Barbara said. 'My throat's closing up. I've got a fever.'

Suzi said, looking straight ahead, 'Don't speak. Say nothing. Even now, you might be noticed. Wait till we get to the car. You must keep it up.'

'It must be those clothes,' Freddy said. 'She'll be all right when we're on the road to Bethlehem. I think if we can get a drink somewhere before lunch it would be a good idea. Let's get moving.'

But there was no mistaking the fact, when they got a look at Barbara's unveiled face on the way to Bethlehem – the hectic flush and the dead-white ring round her mouth – that she was ill beyond what could be accounted for by the heat and the clothes she was wearing. They turned back to Jerusalem and once more Freddy banged on Alexandros's shop door, while Suzi stood on the pavement supporting Barbara, looking up at Alexandros's face in the window.

'The lady wishes to contribute to your Arab Refugee Fund,' Freddy said, falling back on his past experience of Hong Kong and so forth. He said, 'The lady wishes to remain anonymous.' He handed over ten English five-pound notes out of Barbara's newly-acquired supply – 'and is honoured by your acceptance of this donation for so great a cause.'

Dr Russeifa stuffed his payment into the inside pocket of his coat, thanking both Freddy and the lady on the refugees' behalf. Freddy, careful to mind his manners, then asked the doctor to state his fee for his professional services. 'No fee,' said Dr Russeifa, 'I am perfectly honoured to be of assistance to the unfortunate lady. This outbreak of scarlet fever has of course made her a victim, and is without doubt the fault of our enemy, so-called Israel, who sends such germ-warfare to our country daily.'

The disease had not spread far; Freddy's information was that there was one case, a Swedish pilgrim, in the convent where Barbara had stayed. Barbara was now lying on a sofa in a small room in Alexandros's living-quarters.

At first she had said she didn't care what happened. She had murmured that nothing worse could happen, and closed her eyes. After taking two aspirins and a glass of water, she opened them. She had partially recovered her senses and had become talkative by fits and starts. She had insisted on writing out a large cheque on her English bank which Alexandros said he could cash.

A doctor, Freddy had insisted. He said it was probably some local bug she had caught, a temporary thing, but still one must have a doctor.

Alexandros knew of three English doctors in Jerusalem. Freddy had met one of them at the Cartwrights. He hesitated. Alexandros said, 'Would these English doctors make an official report of it?'

'Yes, I'm afraid they would have to. Especially if she's got something infectious. They'd have to put her in hospital of course, and, of course, inform the British consulate and the Jordanian authorities.'

'Suzi!' called Alexandros, and went to fetch her before she answered his call. She had been with Mme Alexandros explaining things in such a way that the woman could not possibly understand yet could not decently admit to being puzzled. Alexandros had brought Suzi into the little room, conferring with her in Arabic. He then threw wide his arms and announced, 'We have Russeifa. Dr Russeifa is the doctor for the Joe Ramdez Insurance Company. You give him quite a little cash and he will attend to Barbara very quiet.'

'A mild case of the scarlet fever,' Dr Russeifa said. 'The temperature is not too high, one hundred degrees is nothing.'

'Well really,' Freddy had said, 'ought you not to report all cases of the disease?'

'I shall report the case. You must assure me she will be kept in isolation two weeks. The treatment is simple. Only tell me she will be kept in isolation and looked after in bed. Then I report that the case is all right and has left the country. I give all the instructions necessary to the young woman Ramdez, who will, in turn, give them –' Alexandros's hand was in the doctor's and they were suddenly exchanging profuse smiling words in Arabic while the doctor was being propelled by Alexandros to the door. Alexandros escorted Russeifa heavily downstairs, he could be heard decisively locking the shop door and marching up again. He rubbed his hands together once and said, 'Now we know what to do. Goodbye to Dr Russeifa.'

Barbara, on the sofa, said, 'There's a woman in Jerusalem who's chasing me. The headmistress –'

'Just lie quiet, my dear,' Freddy said, thinking her delirious.

'We leave for Jericho as soon as we are ready,' Suzi said.

'Jericho?' Freddy said. Everything had been out of his hands since Suzi and Alexandros had conferred together. 'My father's first wife lives there,' Suzi said. 'She is in seclusion, and if we pay her a little she will keep Barbara, as she has kept other friends so often.'

'Do you know,' Freddy said. 'I think Barbara ought to go to hospital.'

Alexandros went to a table beside the sofa on which lay a heavily gilt leather-bound book. 'The Koran,' he remarked, as he took from between its pages a folded half-sheet of newspaper. He said, 'I received the newspaper of Israel early today. I get it on all Sundays and burn when it is read. But this piece I have kept.' He handed it to Freddy, who saw the photograph of a bespectacled man under a heading: 'London Consultant for Eichmann Trial.' Under the photograph was the title 'Mr Michael Aaronson'. And beneath that again he read, while Suzi came and looked at it too:

Mr Michael Aaronson of London, an international law expert who took part in the Nuremberg trials, has been in Israel on a short visit for consultation on the Eichmann trial. Mr Aaronson, who declined to reveal the precise legal points of the discussions with the authorities, said he was greatly impressed by the conduct of the trial from the point of view of International Law. He said he was not in agreement with that section of the British press which continues to question the right of Israel to hold such a trial on her own territory.

Mr Aaronson, who is in general law practice in London, also said that what little he had seen of the country had proved a strong incentive to return at leisure, which he hopes to do one day with his wife and three children.

While in Jerusalem, Mr Aaronson was able to spend some time with his cousin, Miss Barbara Vaughan, who has been spending a vacation in Israel. Miss Vaughan, who teaches school in England, is a Roman Catholic convert. She claims that her new religion is not in conflict with her Jewish blood and background, and is enthusiastic about Israel and the Israelis. Miss Vaughan left on Friday for a tour of Jordan.

'Does this paper get round, here?' Freddy said.

'It comes to the authorities, of course, and you may be sure the Army Intelligence,' Alexandros said. 'By now they are on the watch for her. You know, this rumour will reach the people that there is a Jew from Israel in Jordan, and there could be a hue and cry among the people. The government has made the people think in a certain way of a Jew, and so whatever is the law for a British subject is neither here nor there when they have to contend with their own people's voices. Many Arabs here have voices that they will use to their own advantage. So now you take her away to Jericho where she can remain till she is able to leave the country.' Alexandros sat down, so dejected that Suzi said, 'I would come over to console you in my arms, Alexandros, but I might carry to you the scarlet fever.'

Alexandros got up and went to the silver-framed icon in the wall, from behind which he produced a bulky envelope. He then unscrewed the base of the mosaic lampstand, from which he took a small cardboard box. 'I give you the rest of the money,' he said.

'Are you sure you can cash a large English cheque?'

'Oh yes, I can cash through London. It is illegal.'

Alexandros opened the envelope and brought out a batch of English five-pound notes, which he counted. Then he opened the small box and extracted four fifty-dollar notes. Suzi said, 'What a lot of money, but Barbara says she couldn't care less. I hold her travellers' cheques also.'

'If it comes to the point where she does need money, then money will be the answer,' Freddy observed. 'Travellers' cheques are less useful in certain cases.'

Alexandros thought this funny, and began to throw off the weight of the affair. He said, 'She may yet finish the pilgrimage. What is two, three weeks in bed? Then,' he said, his voice rising in a chant of triumph and hope, 'the police are no longer looking for her, and we see she will go to Bethlehem, she will go to see the Shepherd's Field and the Milk Grotto perhaps; she will go to the Mount of Olives, the Garden of Gethsemane, and the Basilica of the Agony; she will visit the palace of the High Priest Caiaphas and the church of St Peter in Gallicantu, also Absalom's Pillar, also the Tombs of Zacharias and James, along the Kidron Valley and the Valley of Jehosophat, by the Tombs of Kings, and she will go to Bethany and the Tomb of Lazarus.' Now Alexandros was standing large, seeming to occupy most of the room, like an Arab lord of ancient times calling over the sites of past victories, or a prophet the titles of the Lord's decreed grounds of abode: 'She will see the house of Martha and Mary, also Jericho and the River Jordan at the spot where Christ was baptized by John the Baptist, the dove descending; and the Dead Sea and the Wilderness of Temptation.'

Suzi Ramdez always said that the main thing about herself was that she was ambitious. Her strength lay in her vagueness about the limitations of her life; and her weakness derived from its actual limitations which she stood ready to demolish at any time. Beyond any rational expectation she enjoyed the respect of her father, Joe Ramdez. His character twisted around him, spreading and clinging like a vine, while hers was a solitary palm-tree outlined sharp against the sky. Her acceptance of him was total. She knew he was in business for political purposes, that he was in political things to enable him to score off personal vendettas; she knew he was also in business for business purposes, and was a political informer for the Jordanian Secret Service, that he passed intelligence to the United Arab Republic concerning the Jordanian Government; and that these activities were all balanced to a fine point which so depended on instinct that he could no more have put them down on paper than he could actually see his own face. They all revolved around blackmail of sorts, the arranging for forged visas and other papers, and, when dealing with foreigners, a plausible technique of feigned misunderstandings. Suzi did not think of her father as a crook or a traitor, but she knew that he was. He thought of himself as a patriot, an Arab, and overwhelmingly as a man who, in all his actions, did justice to himself. In a world of officials and businessmen who continually and piously did themselves justice he was at home. His indulgence towards Suzi was a secret weakness. He put her in charge of the travel agency over the heads of her mother and her elder sister Lia, who was married to a poor hotel clerk. Suzi was the manager of the Joe Ramdez Company, travel agents. Joe had put her at the top because she never asked the sort of questions that betrayed civic fear, as did his wife. He tolerated her outspoken ways because she took the place of his son Abdul, and he felt he might eventually lean on her, as on a son, in his old age. When she had refused to marry any of the men he had procured for her, he had not insisted. When she had turned twenty-eight he had given up urging her to marry. She was now thirty-three. Privately, she bossed her mother and sister as if she were a man, but with everyone else Suzi was at pains to be accommodating. When she went out with the family she was the most demure of them all, so that it was difficult for their friends to place an actual finger on Suzi's difference from other daughters. Alexandros told her he knew of a rich Lebanese, a widower, who would want her for a wife even though she was not a virgin. She said, 'I don't need to marry an old widower. I could marry a young man, and if he was looking for a virgin, that's all right, because Abdul has told me of a clever surgeon in Cairo who could stitch me up. But I don't want to marry a man who wants a virgin; maybe I'll go to Tangiers and marry a European or an American who looks for a woman, not a virgin.' Alexandros had been her lover for more than four years. She made him laugh and feel strong like no other woman. He respected the women of Islam generally, and Christian Arab women, like his wife, were good women. But they did not have the power of provoking laughter as Suzi did; and they made a man feel strong only because they were weak, not because they were free. The nearest thing to Suzi he had ever seen had been a lovely Indian princess who had done business with him in Beirut. She had been educated abroad, was freely-spoken, and had made her husband laugh as he stood, in turbaned elegance, watching business being done.

Suzi had told her father that morning that she was taking Freddy on a sightseeing tour. She did not mention Barbara, having been warned by Alexandros not to mention Barbara. Joe Ramdez had been excited to hear of Freddy's tour of the country-side. He told Suzi to remember Freddy's position, by which he meant her to see what she could get out of him by way of information. 'Naturally I am keeping his position in mind. Otherwise, why do you think I am doing this job myself rather than give him a hired guide?' He was proud of Suzi. He said, 'No matter if it does not appear to be secret, or if it is not secret, any information is valuable.' It was difficult for the government officials, all of whom were spies of some sort, to know what was secret or not, in any case. They would frequently be dazzled by a report already available in publications which had not reached them, or which lay forgotten in their files. He said to Suzi, 'Don't be too friendly with him. Remember you are an Arab. He will communicate more if you make him feel an intruder in our land; that's always the way of the British.' When she left the house he said, 'Take a proposal form for the life insurance.' She said she already had a proposal form, and bounced off.

The life-insurance agency served many purposes, as did the travel agency. Mainly, it gave basic information about visiting and resident foreigners, from which could be traced, through the Ramdez network of Arabs who had fled for politics or crime to other parts of the world, even more personal and professional information. Information was always good. It could be turned into money more often than not. Every government bureau throughout the world prized information; however irrelevant it might seem today, it might be relevant one day. To know of a Foreign Service man's private habits, for instance, his friends, his parents and his blood-pressure, could be very rewarding, very useful.

Suzi had driven off to the Potter's Field in independent spirits. She was the manager and fairly rich. She had met Alexandros in the night, which was good. She liked to do something for Alexandros. She remembered meeting Mr Hamilton and Miss Vaughan before, on the day the family had visited the Cartwrights. They had drunk fruit juice in the garden. Mr Hamilton was called Freddy and had a lovely smile.

Barbara said from the back of the car, 'If you're going to catch it, I'll feel awful.' At present she felt less awful than she had felt earlier in the day. Suzi at the wheel was making a cheerful tumble of talk. She said, 'It will be the blame of your religious high principles.'

'I'll try to live them down.'

'I think I've already had the scarlet fever. I know I had a rash and was to be kept in bed with aspirins one time when I was seven. Latifa, my father's first wife, will know.'

Freddy said, 'I haven't had it.'

'Oh dear!' Barbara said.

'But I don't feel I'm going to catch it, somehow or other,' he said.

'It would be the penultimate straw,' Suzi said. 'The worst straw would be for Barbara to be captured.' She had made Barbara curl up with her head down when she passed the first sentry post on the road to Jericho. Her conversation was like the turning wheels of a fast car. Freddy began to sing 'The Eton Boating Song' in a tuneful, unpractised voice.

'What is this?' Suzi said.

'"The Eton Boating Song."'

'You went to Eton when a little boy?'

'No, Lancing. But I sang in the choir.' Freddy looked round at Barbara and inquired with only his facial expression how she was getting on. Barbara raised her veil and winked back. Freddy sat up straight again and was silent for a while, staring at the desert hills. Then he said, 'The last time I sang it was in my cabin with a few fellow officers one night outside Montevideo harbour. We sang others songs as well, my dear. We were celebrating the scuttling of the *Graf Spee* on 18 December 1939.' This had to be explained in detail to Suzi, who was, Barbara thought, as splendid a listener as Freddy was a waffler. She was feverishly delighted with them. 'We refer to it as the Battle of the River Plate,' Freddy was saying, 'but there was very little battle, really. We just made it too hot for her, so she couldn't stay in and she couldn't come out.' Suzi said, 'Who was *she?*' 'The *Admiral Graf Spee*, my dear,' Freddy said.

And it was plain to Barbara that he hadn't lost his carefree mood on account of her scarlet fever. She felt weak and hot, but was no longer in misery. She kept realizing, with a shudder of gladness, the fact that she had a real sickness; it was a respite from responsibility for herself, and that felt good.

'We come to another police post,' Suzi said. Barbara curled up, with her head down, an old sleeping bundle.

'Now look up,' said Suzi at last, 'they are all gone by. I raise my brown arm and wave at these police. We are coming now to the terrible plains, the pressure is terrible, they are the lowest spot on earth, thirteen hundred feet below sea level where were the wicked cities of Sodom and Gomorrah which God destroyed.'

Within a few minutes they were in the desert plains. For some reason never explained, in the middle of the wilderness by the road-side, an advertisement board was set up, stating 'Boutay for Pianos' and nothing else. 'Whether or not this is the plain of Sodom and Gomorrah,' Freddy said, 'by God, it feels like it. Are you all right, Barbara?'

'I feel drowsy and heavy. I may expire,' she murmured. She closed her eyes and felt she could just about cope.

'We stop to get a drink at the Dead Sea Hotel,' Suzi said. 'We shall buy drinks and take them to the car.'

Freddy was rustling something, the road-map, muttering something. Barbara opened her eyes. Freddy said, 'We don't need to go all this way to Jericho. The road —'

'A police truck is coming. Keep down, Barbara,' she said, and when the rattle of the motor had passed into the distance behind them, Suzi said, 'I need to be seen on this route with my tourist in case they check up already for Barbara. We need to drink something from the Dead Sea Hotel, but we buy it quick.'

Freddy said to Barbara, 'Did Alexandros show you that piece in the Israeli newspaper?'

'No. I don't think so. What piece?'

'About your meeting your cousin in Israel; and it published the fact that you were coming to Jordan.'

'I knew it,' said Barbara. 'I just knew that would happen. A frightfully resentful woman came to interview my cousin Michael, and I got mixed up with her. What did she say?'

'This piece said you were a Jewish convert Catholic very keen on Israel – something like that; anyhow, enough to set off an alarm over here. I thought it was as well to tell you, so you'll know where you stand just now. But don't worry. I'll get something else put in the Israeli paper tomorrow when I get back – something about you deciding not to go to Jordan after all, but spending the rest of your time in Israel instead. We'll have to cook up some story to hang it on, but don't worry. I know the editor of one of the papers. A very decent old chap, we're on good terms with them at the office. I'll see to it the moment I get back. I'll be there before the next bag goes. Don't worry.'

Barbara was outside the context of worry. She sighed and said, 'Freddy, dear, you're sweet.' Whereupon he beamed round at her.

'You have such trouble for your religion,' Suzi said, 'but you were clever to become a Catholic rather than remain a Jew, as the Jews get in trouble from the Christians as well as the Arabs. It is no life to be a Jew. I would do like you if I was to be in your place.'

'Oh, but she believes in it,' Freddy said. 'It's a matter of conviction, isn't it, Barbara?'

'I suppose it is,' she said, 'but at the moment I don't feel conviction about anything.' The air was breathless.

'Oh, at the moment, naturally – That's one of the things the sermon was about, you remember. He said, "Don't trust your feelings," or "Don't judge by your feelings when you're out here in this heat" – something like that – remember?'

'No, I don't remember a thing.'

'Did you convert to be a Catholic on account of a feeling?' Suzi said.

'No, I took a long time to make up my mind.'

'You did right and clever. I would do the same if –'

'Her religion's sincere, I'm sure,' Freddy said.

'I do not say insincere. I say she did right and she did clever. I am most sincere, believing myself in religion, but I also do correctly and a clever thing to remain a Moslem in any country where Moslem is O.K.'

Freddy began, 'But look –'

'Leave us alone, Freddy,' Barbara said.

'It's too bad that you have to suffer for your pilgrimage,' Suzi rattled on. 'The Moslems, too, suffer for pilgrimages maybe and maybe not, some have a jolly good time on these journeys. But you believe, that I know, you have Jesus to be God and he was crucified and suffered for your sins; isn't it so?'

'That's right.'

'Well you say he took your sins upon him. The Christians say he took all this blame and suffered for it in their place. So if you have these misfortunes now, it is not your blame at all. You have no sins whatsoever to suffer for, as your God Jesus has taken these sins. Therefore all your suffering and inconvenience of scarlet fever is God's blame.'

Her logical premise at an end, she said, 'Keep down, we come to the Dead Sea Hotel.' Barbara glimpsed through her veil and the quivering heat of the air, the great expanse of the steel-blue salt lake and a lonely structure, the hotel, and saw before she curled up, a white-shirted young man on a veranda, idly peeling the paint off green wooden supports. The car slowed down but did not stop. It cruised along while Suzi said, 'I take my tourist for a view of the Dead Sea only, as there is a Secret Service boy on the veranda at a table and there must be men inside. Look only at the spots across the lake that I am pointing to, Freddy. Keep down, Barbara. We see what we see.' In a few minutes the car had begun to put on speed and soon Suzi said, 'You can sit up again now. I shall tell you if any car follows or passes.'

Barbara longed for a drink. Freddy said, 'I'm thirsty – I don't know about you girls. It was madness of me not to bring something.'

'It's God's blame, as I said. But never mind; we go to Jericho very quick,' Suzi said. 'In Jericho is the most ravishing beautiful water. I will get you to Jericho as I have promised Alexandros.'

Freddy started to sing again. It was one of the things that puzzled him most, and shocked him, when these incidents came back to mind after his lapse of memory, that he sang quite a lot on the way to Jericho. He was to remember it clearly with a sense of special irresponsibility: 'But why was I *singing?*'

The house at Jericho was some distance from the town. Nobody came out to welcome them, as if, Freddy thought, by special arrangement, or by habitual practice. Suzi hurried Barbara indoors and disappeared at the back of the house. Freddy followed with his zipper-bag and stood waiting in the large room into which the front door opened. The floor was tiled with a chipped but attractive bird design, which suggested that the clay-like fabric of the house had been set on ancient foundations. A round dining-table stood in the middle of the floor, surrounded by chairs. Freddy presently pulled one chair out and sat down with his zipper-bag on the floor beside him, gazing out of the open door into the sandy forecourt where a palm-tree, Suzi's car, and a primitive well were the only visible objects.

There were three other doors in this room, one in each wall, leading, as Freddy correctly assumed, to three different wings of the house. The old foundations had probably been laid in the form of a cross by some Crusader mission or a later Christian community, and the house was no doubt built on the site of a church or a chapel within a larger place of worship. The door through which Suzi had hustled Barbara was the one opposite the front entrance. A small sound of voices came from this direction, as if they were quite a long way off, behind another closed door. Freddy was extremely thirsty. It occurred to him that Suzi might have intended him to follow her into the part of the house where she had taken Barbara, so he took his bag and went over to the door. It had been locked from the inside. He tried the two side doors, but these, too, were locked. From each door there came a sound of quiet, distant voices, too far away from him to distinguish whether the speakers were men or women. He put down his bag and went out into the forecourt to see if it gave access to the back of the house.

It was then that he saw Ruth Gardnor. Long-legged in blue slacks and a white blouse, she walked out of an alley that lay between a high, ragged wooden fence and the side of the house, in the breathless gold afternoon, and, like a fashion model, without looking one way or the other, made straight towards the palm-tree. Freddy was near Suzi's car. He did not think of concealing himself until he had seen her take from the tufted bark of the tree a brown envelope and slip it into the pocket of her slacks. Then he crouched, while she returned across the forecourt, pacing steadily as she always did. Gardnor's wife. Her hand left her pocket and swung empty with her moving arm as she walked. She did not trouble to look round her, and Freddy was again struck by the impression that this was a performance of prearrangement and habit, in the same way that he had felt the absence of anyone about the house to welcome them when Suzi's car had drawn up outside.

He got back into the room, sat down and waited; meanwhile he thought over the amazing notion that had entered his mind. This is Nasser's Post Office, he thought, and Gardnor is the man we're looking for. Gardnor is our man. The more he thought of it the less amazing it appeared; in fact, everything pointed to Gardnor. Intelligence was not Freddy's present job, but he was informed enough about what was going on in the office in Israel to know of the recent intelligence leaks, and, although no theory had been formed as yet, questions had been more or less asking themselves, and had not been answered. And where was Nasser's Post Office? This is it, Freddy thought. And Gardnor is our man. Yes, thought Freddy, but one doesn't reach conclusions this way. Let's start again; start from nothing: I know nothing but what I've seen. I shall simply have to see more, and get some definite idea what's going on. If this is Nasser's Post Office then our people in the field ought to have got it first shot, they really ought.

He had been half-conscious of the well in the forecourt as if it was nudging him. Soon he was fully conscious of his great thirst. His thirst asserted itself. The door through which Suzi had disappeared was now opened as quietly as if it had never been locked. Suzi looked in: 'Oh there you are! Where have you been hiding? Barbara is in bed now and going to sleep. She has had mint tea. Come to my sitting-room and my wash-place. Do you like mint tea?' Freddy followed her into a long passage with skylight windows. There were doors on each side of the passage. He started to say that he hadn't been hiding, but Suzi continued: 'We better discuss the plans for the future two weeks, because I am absolutely at sea what to do for the best, except I know that in the case of very bad fortune for Barbara the British Embassy in Amman must help her, but thus she gets no more pilgrimage in Jordan; or else my friends, one or two, can help, but thus she has to give great lots of money. So it is best that we have good fortune. . . .' She opened a door into a sitting-room furnished in western cretonne comfort, and ended her speech '. . . like I have pledged to Alexandros. So we plan for good fortune.'

Freddy put down his bag and smiled at her. 'Show me this wash-place of yours, there's a good girl.' She had looked at him when they got into the room, with her very deep-blue eyes set in her brown face, looking extraordinarily like Abdul. When he came back she was pouring out tea, and he kissed her. He thought, this is quite absurd; he had intended to lead the conversation somewhere in the direction of Ruth Gardnor, and her presence in the house. Suzi said, 'You have a lovely kiss as well as smile.' He thought, then, that his kissing her was not incompatible with investigation into Ruth Gardnor and what went on in this house; on the contrary. And he thought, I might even have planned it but I didn't, it's quite absurd. He kissed her again.

Later on that evening she said to Barbara, 'Freddy likes me, and I think it is because he likes Abdul. Never mind why, it's fine.'

It occurred to Freddy that he was a different sort of man from most men in all important respects. He did not mean morally, but essentially. He was astonished that he had never realized this before, and wondered if other men felt the same. He was increasingly at ease with Suzi without being aware that this was mainly due to relief at finding her part of the house well appointed, in western style. The day had been a strain. He drank his tea, took more, kissed Suzi again, and, as she nuzzled up to him, he told himself that of course he would not think of using her as a mere means to some external purpose. He said, 'This is a large house. Very fine.'

'It's an old Crusader church in the foundation.'

'I thought it must be, from its shape. Who lives here besides your stepmother?' He suddenly did not want to let her know that he had seen Ruth Gardnor, now that things had become personal.

'Friends, contacts, clients of my father,' she said, 'also employees for his night-clubs, also at times, sub-agents for travel, insurance, et cetera, et cetera. Are you married to a wife?'

'No,' Freddy said.

'Have you been married?'

On imperceptible second thoughts Freddy said he hadn't.

'I thought at first, you must be the lover of Barbara. But when I see you together I know you are not lovers, I mean bed-lovers.'

'We're getting into deep waters,' Freddy said, reclining among the chintzes.

'I can swim,' she said.

'I dare say.' She was beside him on a large flowered and frilled divan which was presumably her bed, but he was only partly aware of the girl's outline since he was looking particularly at her blue eyes and their setting between her brow and cheek-bone. He said, 'Abdul's giving me lessons in Arabic, you know.'

She laughed, short, clear, with a touch of general mockery. She was very like Abdul. 'I can give you lessons in Arabic,' she said.

'I dare say.'

She said, 'Speak in Arabic what Abdul has taught you.'

He repeated, in slow formal syllables, one of the exercises from the Arabic grammar, 'The affairs of our nation became secure after the murder of the author of that harmful book.'

'Abdul is wasting your time. You do not need to speak these words except in Egypt and Syria. Here we have not murdered the authors of books, I don't think. We don't have authors of books much, though. Poets, a few. Sometimes the assistant in the store can be a poet. The Prophet Mohammed was not favourable of poetry. I think he was in the wrong for that, but I can't say anything against the Prophet out loud, naturally. The Arabs love poetry, and they ignore that the Prophet was against it. When I say this, that, this, that, against the Prophet and the religion, the people say it's the reason no one has married me. Also because I have lovers; they don't know this exactly, but they know enough, and they say, "No one will marry Suzi Ramdez. Why buy a goat when you can get two pennies' worth of milk."'

'I shouldn't worry about *them*,' Freddy said. 'You should have your poetry and your boy-friends.'

'They are lovers, not boys.'

'I write poetry,' Freddy said.

'Make me a poem.'

'All right. When I go away I'll write a poem to say thank you.'

'Maybe you wait and see how much you want to say thanks to me. What is your job for the British Government besides poetry?'

'Oh, it's nothing much,' Freddy said.

'You handle all the intelligence and the top secrets of these treaties with the Arab countries? Do you get wind of all the intrigues between Syria, Lebanon, Egypt, Kuwait and so forth?'

Freddy marvelled at this direct interrogation. 'No, I'm not much more than a sort of filing-clerk, actually.'

'Filing-clerk is best job for getting the secrets. When we seek for spies in our government we look first for the filing-clerk. They know all.'

'Well, I don't know all. None of us knows all, in fact. We're a jolly incompetent bunch. Always getting caught on the hop. It's well known.'

'But what is not well known is the top secrets.'

He was not sure how naïve she was. She was remarkably like Abdul. He said, 'Where is Barbara's room?'

'In this wing of the house. Two doors to the left. Now I'm going to look at her. If she sleeps, that's good. By tomorrow there is no more infection, but she just stays in bed.'

'I'd be *most* interested to see over the house before I leave.'

'Oh, no. The other parts are not mine. It's forbidden to enter. Latifa, my father's first wife, is very old-fashioned.'

She left the room and must have been away about half an hour, for Freddy dozed off for a while, and she was still absent when he woke. He had at first intended to spend the night in Jordan, crossing through the Gate on Monday morning. But now, since he had seen Ruth Gardnor he was determined to wait an extra day, if necessary to find what she was doing here and see if his suspicion about the place had grounds. He could put up at a hotel in Jericho, no doubt. He wondered if Suzi knew of Mrs Gardnor's presence in the house, and if Suzi herself intended to remain with Barbara in this house during her two weeks' incarceration.

Among all the factors that filled Freddy with an exaggerated sense of his irresponsibility, when he came to remember these forgotten days, was his treatment of Barbara. He was amazed, when it all came back to him. That he could have contrived the scheme at all, dressing her up like that, and so exposing her to far more suspicion, had she been caught, than if she had been going round undisguised – permitting her to travel with scarlet fever – allowing it to go probably unreported – then leaving her in the hands of total strangers in Jordan, with a promise, never fulfilled, to arrange for an announcement in the Israeli papers that she was still in Israel – and then, the subsequent upset, with Barbara's relations pressing for news, and the embassies and Arab authorities all at odds. . . . When he tried to convey this to Barbara later on, she replied, genuinely surprised, 'Irresponsible? No, you were splendid, Freddy. You were never responsible for me; I'm responsible for myself. I knew what I was doing. I'm grown-up.'

In Suzi's sitting-room he had faith in his plan, he was beyond questioning the success of Barbara's pilgrimage. One who can move mountains does not stop to doubt the success of Barbara's pilgrimage, and the scarlet fever was to him only a slight set-back which, by happy chance, had led him to Nasser's Post Office here. Suzi had not yet returned; he withdrew again into a half-doze and was once more on that afternoon's journey from Jerusalem, through the steep craggy wilderness of Judaea and the oppressive plains, to the heavy Dead Sea with its saline content bearing no breath of life.

He was still in his second doze when Suzi returned. She sat and watched him, amused and quiet, as later her brother Abdul would watch him, that day in the following week when he would call at Freddy's hotel in Israel to give him his Arabic lessons, smell the moth-balls of Freddy's winter suit, and wait, idly reading Freddy's letters, till Freddy should wake from his tired sleep.

Suzi watched him and decided to put him up overnight and take him back to Jerusalem the next morning. She had spoken to Barbara, who was now cool and lucid. Barbara was very happy about her scarlet fever since it would keep her out of the way of her English enemy, Ricky. Suzi had very quickly understood, when Barbara told her about the headmistress of the school who was pursuing her out of love and hatred, and who would like to stop Barbara's marriage to her lover, Harry. It seemed perfectly understandable to Suzi, and she had only interrupted Barbara's explanation to say 'We have also these things of oppression among our Arab women,' and 'I wouldn't have thought that the English have also these affairs where the woman pursues the woman to stop the business of lovers, and makes hell.'

'Oh, you'd be surprised,' Barbara had said. 'And what's more . . .'
And when Barbara next explained that the headmistress was that very
one who had tried to speak to her at the Holy Sepulchre, they had
both laughed with very much hysteria; Suzi had fallen limp upon
Barbara in her laughter, and Barbara had said, 'Don't. You'll catch
my scarlet fever.'

'I've had it already. My stepmother just told me.'

Then they started all over again until the laughing was spent
out and Barbara closed her eyes with a weak, final, convulsive
gasp.

Presently Suzi had said, 'Freddy will put that piece in the newspaper of the Jews, and then I shall see that it is made known to this
English mistress. If she goes round asking, "Where is my friend?"
and, "Has Miss Vaughan been here?" – this will be easy to get done.
Soon she gets the reply that you never came.'

'I'd rather be taken into custody by the Jordanian police,' Barbara
said, 'than be caught by her.'

'This I can well understand. The police want always the body but
not the soul.'

'Not in every country.'

'No. This is an Arab virtue. The Arabs don't intend to interfere
with a person's soul except when women are jealous, or a father is
furious, and then they're crazy of course.'

'The western people do it all the time. They do it more and more.'

'There's an Englishwoman staying in this house. She'll be here for
ten days or so; very kind. So when I must go tomorrow to Jerusalem,
she'll take care of you. I have to come back here, Wednesday, and I
can come again at the week-end.'

'You're taking a lot of trouble. . . .'

'I do this anyway. I come here very frequent. Alexandros has asked
me to take care of you. So I do a couple of extra journeys maybe back
and forth, for Alexandros and for you, until you're well.'

'Who's the Englishwoman?'

'Very nice girl; very kind. She can be trusted; she won't ask questions if you do not ask questions of her.'

'What's she doing here?'

'You should not ask this question; then she won't say of you,
"What does she do here?"'

'Where's Freddy?' said Barbara.

'In my sitting-room. Perhaps I keep him here for tonight and take him back tomorrow morning. Do you think he'll propose to sleep with me?'

'Six to one against,' Barbara said.

Freddy opened his eyes, and saw Suzi lolling on the divan, watching him. He said, 'Oh, hallo, what's going on?'

'Barbara is much better. Like Dr Russeifa prescribed, it is a mild attack.'

'You mean, as he diagnosed.'

'Yes.'

'What he prescribed was the treatment.'

'She'll be through with the treatment tomorrow. Afterwards, it's only stay in bed.'

'Was I asleep?' said Freddy.

'Yes, I was watching you.'

'What were you thinking?'

'I was thinking that life is love.'

'Very profound. And love is life.'

'Very true and very apt,' she said.

Their dinner was conducted in intimate style, a candlelight affair. Freddy found himself envying Alexandros, the usual guest of honour who, Suzi told him, stopped here frequently on his way to Madaba where he purchased coins and other antiquities from a coin-dealer there. The coin-dealer, she explained, employed a team of small boys over a large area round Jericho, where excavators were busy; and these boys were permitted by the diggers to pick up a few small odd-ments, such as coins, and even when they were not permitted to do so, the boys got a lot of findings. These were turned over to the central dealer at Madaba, an Orthodox priest, who often came by quite rare things that way. Alexandros was one of his best customers, Suzi said, and this made for many trips, many occasions to stop the night at Jericho, where she herself was obliged to come also to the house on business.

Freddy envied rich-voiced Alexandros in this room. He reflected that life was love, and that he had been living all his life in a half-dream, as if he had been a somnambulist or an amnesiac. One had rehearsed the motions, not minding what they were all about. Clough, dead and famously lamented a hundred years ago, had located the virus:

> One has bowed and talked, till
> > little by little,
> All the natural heat has escaped of the
> > chivalrous spirit.

Only one small skip of flame, Freddy thought, and I see by its light all the other ashes cooling off in the fireplace.

'Don't be sad,' Suzi said. 'I wish Abdul was here. What are you miserable for, Freddy? You sit and look down through the meat on your plate, right through the plate, and through the tablecloth. . . .'

It was lamb on a skewer. The tablecloth had a lace edge. 'I'm not miserable, my dear,' Freddy said, with a smile.

'Nor happy neither.'

Neither hot nor cold. 'Make me happy, then,' he said. 'You're the hostess.'

She plunged into the job. 'You have a lovely smile. Abdul should be here. I'm sad for Abdul that he's nothing and I have all the position with my father. He could be here, we could have got papers for him, but he won't be the son of his father and be in his influence. When we were children Abdul used to discover finds in the ruins when the archaeologists came to dig at Jericho and Jerash and Madaba. My father was not rich, only a teacher, at that time when we were little. But Abdul didn't give his little things of the ruins to his father to sell to the dealer and help for his education. Some, Abdul gave to me, and others he gave away to the most wealthy of the foreign tourists who came to the place. They said, "What a sweet little boy!" and Abdul would laugh so much at that. Because he would take no money for his presents. Sometimes I see them try to give it back and I hear them say to him, "Sorry – no baksheesh" and he would run away leaving them with the ancient coins, ornaments, whatever, in their hands. He plays tricks today, the same. My older sister, who is helping now in our travel bureau, says Abdul has a mad devil inside him. But my father's first wife, Latifa, who lives in this house, always took Abdul's part. She said he was a good child to give presents to the rich visitors as that's what our Arab tent-men did in the old days. She said a speech to Abdul's defence: Everyone gives to the poor; they try to save their souls by it. But if a poor man gives to the rich, his soul is already with God, and the souls of the rich are mysteriously moved and relieved of a burden.'

Freddy gave himself up to the pleasure of talking about Abdul, as far as he could. He felt it was just bad luck that he could not derive the total experience of Suzi that was available to him, so like she was to Abdul and so vivid. He thought it was just bad luck that this one excitement should be surrounded and vitiated by another: the question of Gardnor's wife. And although he told himself, there at Suzi's table, that his duty in life came first, pleasure second, and that he would not wish it any other way, and that he would keep his wits about him, in reality there was not much to choose between the excitement of possibly exposing Gardnor and the excitement of Suzi's potentialities; and as the evening proceeded these combined possibilities were highly erotic in their effect. Gardnor, he thought, is our wanted man. Gardnor, in his glittering confidence, a dispenser of sympathy and understanding to absolutely everyone; Gardnor, living it high with an attitude to debt that belongs to the eighteenth century; Gardnor in that very smart and expensive workman's cottage in Chelsea, with a Bonnard lit up over the mantelpiece and a Picasso in the lavatory; Gardnor and his wife and other superior women; Gardnor, Freddy thought, is our man. Gardnor, Freddy reflected, has too frequently made a point of his atheism; if a man can't hold religious convictions, well he can't, but it's a private and secret thing, and if a man can't keep his own top secrets how can he be expected to keep his country's? The unmarried fellows, Gardnor had said, half-jokingly in Freddy's presence, are our big security risk. And he had given Freddy an emancipated smile, then glanced at his wife before glancing at the clock; the Gardnors, in London, always had to go on somewhere else. Gardnor, Freddy thought, is the man we've been looking for; and this is Nasser's Post Office. The pieces fitted together as he watched Suzi's blue eyes and brown hands; and the disquietude that came over him at Gardnor's subsequent trial, the pity for Gardnor which he expressed when sentence had been passed and it was all over, were perfectly sincere since he could not help recalling with shame the sensual joy that had gone into the discovery. He told Suzi she was the most extraordinary woman he had ever met, and told himself it was just his hard luck that he could not be wholeheartedly her man, but needs must probe for Ruth Gardnor. He said, 'Who else is in this house at the moment besides Latifa and ourselves?'

'Perhaps a tourist or a paying guest. Nobody permanent but Latifa and the servants. A few girls perhaps; my father brings them to train for the night-club, they come from Aden, Tangiers, sometimes Europe. This is a big secret I'm telling you, about these girls. Can you keep a secret?'

'Of course.'

'Can you keep secrets if it would help your country to know them?'

'Those sorts of secrets never come my way,' Freddy said. It was just hard luck finding himself on duty like this. He added, 'But I would always keep a beautiful woman's secrets.'

She said, 'I wouldn't trust you if I had any secrets.'

He said, 'Abdul trusts me. I know about his trips across the border. You see, Abdul trusts me more than you do.'

She said, 'What a stupid boy he is to trust you, and you've done nothing for him, not even have you given him your life insurance. You know, Freddy, I like your lovely smile. When Abdul was in hospital in the Lebanon, I visited that place to see him and I met with a French officer. . . .'

Suzi's clock struck midnight. So ended Sunday the 13th of August. She showed him to a small room largely filled with a broad divan bed and hung with fine rugs; Freddy sensed the hand and style of Alexandros. Suzi, in her speech-making way, made the following announcement: 'I have to go and attend to duties and many other dutiful affairs, including Barbara and her great safety in this house. Then, one hour's time or more, I wait a message from Alexandros as we don't talk this business by telephone which is unsafe from the government eavesdroppers and press officers. So we do all business by night messengers, and all this business takes maybe two hours. Now you sleep. Maybe I wake you up later on to say good night.'

She left abruptly with a business-like something on her mind. Freddy was suddenly and blindly enraged. Wild-bloodedly he was convinced he had been deliberately tricked by her; and that she had

known far more about him than he had himself; and that she had realized, where he had not, the lack of hope and fun in his life up to this
evening, and had held out hope and snatched it away. Freddy cursed
her in his mind for the miserable unspeakable Arab girl that she was.
Then he sat on his bed for about ten minutes, and started to reflect
that she probably couldn't help going about her business, and that she
probably could not guess how fugitive his sexual feelings were and
how hopeless, to him, was a lingering lapse of two hours between the
idea and the execution. He thought, I'll be damned if I'll sleep with
her now. And this way of putting it consoled him. He decided to find
out, if he could, what Suzi was up to, and out of his mind faded the
cloudy drama that must have begun to form earlier in the evening: the
notion that he would gain her confidence, through making love to her,
on the question of Ruth Gardnor's presence in the house.

He opened his door into stillness. Very soon he heard some movements from a far wing of the building; whether these sounds were
voices he could not tell. He decided to go out for a walk in the night
air, and well-mannered emotions returned to his heart.

He went out for a normal walk in the night air. Three weeks later,
when his lost memory crushed back upon him, the most elusive part
of all was that night and the two days that followed.

'Take it easy, Freddy.'

'Gardnor's wife was in that house.'

'Yes, we've got all that, Freddy. We've got Gardnor, too.'

'You've got Gardnor?' Freddy said to his questioner; but he had
already been told this several times.

'Yes, thanks to you, Freddy, we've picked up the lot.'

'It was Nasser's Post Office,' Freddy said. 'I knew it the moment I
saw . . . You're sure of the place? I could draw a sketch.'

'Yes, we got it this morning, half an hour after you told me. Take
it easy, Freddy. You ought to be in bed, you know.'

'I knew there was going to be bloodshed,' Freddy said. 'I've had a
feeling of bloodshed ever since I lost my memory. But I thought it
would be here, out here in Palestine. I didn't think it was going to
happen in Harrogate.'

'Freddy, you *must* rest.'

'If I'd posted the letters I wrote,' Freddy said, quite lucidly, 'this wouldn't have happened. But I didn't post the letters. I put them down the lavatory.'

'There's absolutely nothing you can do about it, Freddy. Believe me, absolutely nothing you could have done.'

'I'll have to get back to England and see about Benny. If she's tried for murder –'

'She's going to be found unfit to plead. They'll put her away somewhere safe. Now, Freddy, the point is that you've got to take it easy. Don't try to think about everything, and when anything occurs to you, jot it down. The whole business will come back to you eventually. No hurry. We want you to get a rest.'

'You've got Gardnor?'

'Yes, we've got Gardnor. They're getting a statement.'

'One thing you can do,' Freddy said. 'You can get me a booking on a plane tomorrow –'

'Not tomorrow, Freddy. Honestly, doctors' orders. In a few days . . . Joanna and Matt can take care of you, and anything you want, we're here, you know.'

'Poor Gardnor,' Freddy said. 'I'm sorry for Gardnor, you know.'

'Well we all feel that, Freddy. But he hadn't any pity for you, remember.'

'He tried to pin it on me,' Freddy said.

'Oh yes, but we had our own ideas about that. You know what we knew.'

'I wish I could remember exactly what happened after I went out for a walk after dinner that night.'

'It'll come back, Freddy. You've done enough talking for today. Very useful talking, believe me.'

Freddy looked at the two telegrams on the table and at the three memorandum papers which placed the long-distance calls on record. Had they been lying there since early morning? 'I knew there would be bloodshed,' he said, 'but I thought it would be here in this dangerous place, not Harrogate.' The telegrams, and the records of long-distance calls between Jerusalem and Harrogate had, he was sure, been on the table since early morning. Joanna had not moved them. The doctor had left. Freddy had refused to go to bed. He sat with the others to eat lunch on the veranda, while the chap from Whitehall kept jumping up to answer the telephone.

The doctor had said he would return later. 'I don't need him,' Freddy said.

'Eat something, Freddy,' Joanna was crying very desperately, unable to stop. She wasn't wearing her red dress today.

'Freddy, eat something. Oh, there's the telephone. . . .' The chap from the office went to answer it.

'Didn't I say there would be bloodshed?' Freddy said.

'Yes, Freddy, you have been saying so. Don't talk of it any more.'

Freddy said, 'I once heard a story of a man who went on a holiday and forgot that he'd left his dog chained up. When he'd been away a fortnight he remembered the dog and was afraid to go back in case of what he'd find. If I hadn't destroyed those letters –'

'Here's Matt,' said Joanna. 'Matt, come and sit by Freddy and don't let him talk too much.'

'What did that damned doctor give me?'

'A sedative – nothing – something like aspirin.'

'Did my mother linger? She must have lain a long time before –'

'No, it was instantaneous, Freddy.'

'How do you know? That's what they always say.'

'It's absolutely plain,' Matt said in a firm voice, 'that death was instantaneous.'

Freddy's colleague returned.

'I didn't think it would be Harrogate.'

'Everyone from the office sends no end of good wishes and we all want you to rest, Freddy.'

'You've got Gardnor?'

'Yes, we've got Gardnor.'

Miss Rickward, when it thankfully dawned on her that the travel agency in Jerusalem to which she had been recommended would be open on Sunday like other Arab places of business, had walked into the Ramdez place and found the proprietor, Joe Ramdez, alone and in charge.

Joe Ramdez was at that moment totalling up last quarter's sum of insults and injuries received from his enemies, and it so happened that the balance outweighed the injuries and other deeds of justice inflicted. This sometimes occurred within one quarter's accounting, but never before to so large an extent that the balance could not foreseeably right itself in Joe's favour within a short time. But at this moment of a Sunday in the summer of 1961, Joe sat with his elbows resting on his desk and his head on his hands, attempting to assemble into a process of thought the cracking explosions of anger that were going off in his brain-particles; this was difficult, because the only thought that could possibly emerge from his calculations was that he was losing ground on all sides; business, government, home, he was losing. It was then that a tourist, whom he did not immediately consider to be a woman of moral force, great courage, beautiful strength, substantial means and stout sympathy, entered the door; he was to perceive Miss Rickward in this light within a short time. Meanwhile he looked up and saw only a tourist, and did not know what to do with his exasperation since the tourist trade was a mere apparatus for his affairs, and being a genius within the limits of his environment, Joe Ramdez held the superficial in contempt. He inwardly placed on his wife and Suzi the respective curses of husband and father for not being on duty, and the curses of a brother-Arab on his three worst enemies, Sadok Abboud, Abdullah el Sabah and Ismah-Azhari for putting him into a mood of anger and grief; then he turned his attention to boring Miss Rickward.

She made herself interesting before long. A Miss Vaughan, she said. She had come to look for a Miss Vaughan. The convent was closed to visitors on account of an epidemic, and the address she had been directed to was not really suitable; it did not look clean. 'I must find somewhere to stay,' Miss Rickward informed Joe Ramdez, 'and I must find Barbara Vaughan.'

That morning when Joe had received from his government contact that information was required concerning a British Jewess, under the name of Barbara Vaughan, who had arrived in Jordan from Israel last Friday, he had questioned his family as to whether they knew of her. His wife had no recollection of the name. Suzi, in a hurry to leave on some profitable trip with a British Embassy man, a friend of Alexandros, treated the question with impatience. 'How should she come to our agency if she's an Israeli spy?' Joe Ramdez was initimidated by his daughter's vigorous reactions to most of his suggestions, and had inquired only in a casual manner if she had come across a Miss Vaughan. He had found no record of her name when he looked for it on his arrival at the office; this, of course, meant very little, since the putting down of anything in black and white, except when absolutely necessary, was discouraged by Joe.

Before leaving the house he had called his wife a dumb animal, whereupon she had lit a cigarette and blown smoke contemptuously across the teacups. He had come to a point where he longed for a new wife and regretted having committed himself so far to modern progress. He repeated to himself, while opening up the office:

Let him who believes in God and in the supreme Day harm his neighbour; let him treat women well. She was made from Adam's rib; and it is the upper part of the rib that is the most curved. If you try to straighten it you will break it, and if you let it alone, it will stay bent. Let man therefore treat women well.

Joe's father had been adept in applying these words to every situation that concerned a woman, and Joe was now thinking of them with a stress on the curved rib: his second wife was a bent creature in her heart, and would never be straight. He was in a mood to place his curse upon the emancipation from the old tradition and, in general, the course he had permitted his family life to take with the result that now he had only old enemies and no old comforts.

Then had walked in that sturdy portion of English rib, Miss Rickward, presenting him with her exceedingly interesting inquiry for the whereabouts of Miss Vaughan.

'Be seated, Madam,' said Joe, 'and I shall send for coffee.' Immediately a rustle in the back quarters preceded a young boy who passed through the front office and out of the door as silent as a beam of light. By the time he returned, Joe had gone a long way to measuring Miss Rickward's substance, and with the experience he had long acquired of the Englishwoman on her travels, calculated that her cheap, shapeless, pink-and-red cotton dress, broad brown sandals, large old dark-brown leather shoulder bag, unvarnished fingernails, short dark curly hair, weather-pink face, a touch of lipstick, eyes the colour, near-grey, of western spiritual compromise, and her yellowish, much-filled teeth, added up to a woman of some authority and wealth.

Sipping the thick coffee, she let fall the words 'Oh, how distressed I am!' and also a tear. Joe Ramdez was moved, he was delighted to find that she was as vulnerable about her friend as any high-class Arab woman would be about her most important friend or enemy in the harem. Joe was delighted to find Miss Rickward was vulnerable at all. Moreover, she did not look like a ferret, as so many Englishwomen did. She said, 'I mustn't trouble you with my personal difficulties. But I would so much appreciate any help you can give me in tracing this lady.'

'You have my help,' Joe said. 'We'll get her.'

Ricky said, 'She can't be far off. Possibly she has gone to the Dead Sea, and if so, I must follow her there. She has got herself entangled with a man who is one of the Dead Sea Scrolls team, and she threatens to marry him. Only Miss Vaughan doesn't know, as I know, the type of person he is, the type of background and so on. I've found out a lot about his personal history –'

'Those scholars at the Dead Sea are a gang of ruffians,' Joe said, thinking of the one he had fallen foul of over a deal, the first year that the scrolls were discovered and the forgeries began.

'You're extremely sympathetic,' Miss Rickward said. Her voice was still shaky with distress. 'You Arabs are gifted with sympathy and a sense of brotherhood. I've read quite a lot about Islam.'

Joe said, 'I work for the renewal of the people's hopes and the completion of their happiness.'

'I admire Islam,' she said. 'Barbara Vaughan is a Catholic. Catholicism, I'm sorry, I can't admire.'

Joe Ramdez laid his large hand on hers and inquired closely about Barbara Vaughan.

After she had taken Freddy to his room and left him there Suzi went on a tour of the house. She was sorry to have to leave Freddy to cool off just when he had warmed up, but there were certain duties to be performed before she could settle down for the night with the easy mind she needed for that purpose.

First, she went to Barbara's room and opened the door to hear if the patient was sleeping. Barbara stirred, 'Suzi?'

'All right? Don't wake up if you're all right.'

Barbara put on the bed-light and leaned up on her elbow. 'What's the time?' Her face was still flushed.

'Do you want water?'

'Yes, a good idea.' Barbara poured a glass of water from the jug at her side.

Suzi came in and closed the door.

'How do you feel?'

Barbara was taking her own temperature. Eventually she said, 'A hundred. That's not bad.'

'A mild attack,' Suzi said, sitting on the edge of her bed. 'Speak quiet. I wish you could have been well enough to sleep with Freddy.'

'I don't want to sleep with Freddy.'

'Don't you think Freddy's attractive?'

'Yes, more than he was when I met him in Israel. There's a curious change come over Freddy.'

'You wouldn't sleep with him?'

'No, I've got the other man.'

'I'm the secret lover of Alexandros, but the more I sleep with Alexandros the more I can sleep with another man. I love Alexandros so much. He gives me the idea of love.'

'Have you ever defrosted an old refrigerator?' Barbara said.

'Yes, we have old refrigerators.'

'Well, you know how it goes drip, drip, drip, very slowly. I'm like that; only just beginning to defrost, drip, drip, drip.'

'Have you ever opened someone else's combination safe?'

'No.'

'Me neither, but I know how it's done. Sleeping with Freddy would be like that. One must find the right combination and one has to play around, try this way, try that way, gentle, and listen with the careful ear.'

Barbara smiled. She took a small mirror from her handbag and looked at herself in it. 'I'm the scarlet woman,' she said. She giggled feebly and settled down to sleep.

'It's God's blame. Ring the little bell by your side if you feel ill at all, but don't go out of your room, as the servants are inquisitive about you.'

Suzi next visited the girls' quarters in the north-east wing of the house; this was joined by a corridor to the south-west wing which Latifa occupied so that it should be easy for her to supervise the girls.

The girls had been brought in to train for night-club life and its lenient ramifications; they were one of Joe Ramdez's business enterprises; they came from Morocco, Marseilles, Lebanon, Syria, and other surrounding countries, although once a girl was brought in who had somehow originated in Vladivostok and two others who had been from Liverpool. There were usually four or five girls in the house at any one time. Joe Ramdez found them useful for his special tourists. Foreign civil servants and diplomats who had become more than usually involved with one of Joe's pretty prostitutes instead of taking a more sensible interest in his stable of Arab horses at Amman, were usually persuaded, after a while, to join his Middle East Visitors' Union Life Trust, from which, one way or another, Joe had derived a good annual income for many years.

No sounds came from the girls' wing except heavy breathing from behind the doors; Suzi despised females who breathed noisily in sleep, she felt it was indelicate and a sign of carelessness, for women should blow their noses and sleep in seemly tranquillity. In general Suzi loathed the girls, not troubling to separate them fairly from the deeper object of her antipathy, the whole business operation in which they were involved. She had tried to persuade her father to give them up for a more profitable and more tasteful, possibly more subtle, form of corruption. There were many ways of tempting foreigners into a vulnerable situation, besides these insufferable girls. Joe had replied that he was well aware of the alternatives to girls; one of them was boys, and as far as he was concerned he was not going to encourage the vile foreigner in his despicable habit of coming to the Arab countries for boys. It was his duty to the honour of his country to provide girls. Suzi said, very often, that the girls were not even good performers in the night-clubs. But Joe barked back at her, louder than his bite, that they were too good for the foreigners. Suzi had realized she was up against the amorphous mixture of honour and revenge that brewed within her father's heart, and continued to exhale vapours of resentment towards the girls from her own obscure heart's brew. Her aim at the moment was to prevent the girls from contact with Freddy and to preserve him from any hint of contact with them. She went to find her stepmother, Latifa.

She found her playing gin rummy with Ruth Gardnor, who lit up at the sight of Suzi. She was evidently bored, for Latifa was slow. Latifa said, 'Yusif is coming.' Her eyes remained on the cards. Latifa always called Joe by his Arab name, Yusif. Suzi was uncertain whether Latifa was making one of her mysterious prophecies or whether she had received definite word from her father that he was coming to the house.

She said, 'When? How soon?'

Latifa did not reply. Suzi concluded that Latifa was indulging her gift for second sight. At some time in her middle age this first wife of Joe Ramdez had been struck by an illness which left her with a facial twitch, a diminished pace of thought, and some extra intuition. Latifa's prophecies were not infallible, but they often came alarmingly true.

Suzi did not want her father in the house at this moment; not by any means.

She said to Ruth, 'Listen, I don't want my father to have anything to do with the sick girl.'

'That's all right. Leave it to me,' Ruth said, warmly. Suzi was very attached to Ruth Gardnor. She had found her to have a good heart, and to be particularly understanding and helpful in her affair with Alexandros. She admired Ruth's elegant figure, and felt she brought tone to the house.

Ruth said, 'I doubt if your father will be coming here if you're not expecting him. Latifa said earlier that she felt he was on his way to the house; he hasn't come yet.'

Latifa waited for the game to proceed. She never intruded on Suzi's affairs, but did merely what was required by her husband, and obliged Suzi if paid to do it.

Suzi said, 'Ruth, there is my other guest. I think you shouldn't let him see you, as you are maybe known to him.'

'Who? Alexandros?'

'No, its not Alexandros. It's an Englishman.'

'Oh!'

'Just keep yourself concealed. He'll be leaving tomorrow.'

Ruth looked very worried. She said, 'Well, I'm going to bed. Good night, Latifa. Good night.'

Latifa, a large woman, sat in her fine draperies staring at the cards. Suzi kissed her, and followed Ruth to her room.

'What's his name?' Ruth said. 'Anyone I know?'

'Mr Hamilton of the British Government office in Israel.'

'Freddy Hamilton!'

'Yes. You know him?'

'My God! Why did you bring him here?'

'It's all right,' said Suzi. 'It's all right, my dear.' She was sure it was all right. She said, 'He's not here on any business.'

'I'll have to leave right away.' Ruth walked round the room, looking carefully. 'Has he seen me? Does he know where my room is?'

'No, no, of course not. Anyway, I tell you, Ruth, he has no brains for this job. He's not much in your government.'

'They don't need too much. They only need to be in the office.' She went to the wardrobe and looked inside. She said, 'Has he had any opportunity to snoop?'

Suzi laughed, and Ruth tried to laugh with her. Presently it emerged that Suzi thought 'snoop' was a sex term and that Ruth had been referring to the possibility of Freddy's meeting the girls. Ruth continued to laugh harshly at this mistake, and explained in a strange tone of voice that she had meant 'pry'. She displayed a special anxiety to be patient and calm with Suzi, and was obviously concealing a deeper anxiety about her business. This made Suzi feel like a stupid little Arab girl in the other's estimation, and she wanted to explain her personal view, unorthodox as it was to the Arab spy-trade, that the best way to avoid suspicion was to go about everything as naturally as possible. She had already tried to convince Ruth Gardnor that her business, whatever it was, could best be conducted by hand, by word-of-mouth, and by bribery. 'Let a man come to the door,' Suzi had said. 'Let him repeat his message, or let him hand a letter. Let him take his money and go.' But no, Ruth had devised, among other methods, one by which she collected code-messages from the bark of the palm-tree and deposited messages in the same place. Ruth had argued that the messenger, if he could be bribed to contact her, could be further bribed to describe her appearance. By no means, Ruth said, must she be seen; and anyway, those were her instructions. She would not be brought to understand that Suzi's father had influence with the Arab contacts; it was unthinkable that they could be bribed against Joe's honour and survive. But Ruth showed no confidence in the unspoken laws that had so far kept the Ramdez house inviolable. Suzi had wondered for a moment if her father's enemies were perhaps more powerful than she believed, but she put the tepid thought aside and insisted that Ruth was crazy in making all those intricate arrangements, and in bringing a radio transmitter into the house, when the Arab rumour-system was so much safer.

'I've hardly used it,' Ruth said. She was lifting the transmitter out of her wardrobe. 'Where can I hide this?' She got out a suitcase and started to put things away in it.

Ruth had panicked. Suzi was amazed; she had never seen the kindly woman in this mood before. Presently, Ruth seemed to become aware of Suzi's bewilderment. She said, 'Suzi, if you knew how serious it would be for me if Hamilton got on to anything. . . .'

'You take a cigarette and sit down,' Suzi said. 'There's no need for him to see you if you keep in this end of the house. Why should he suspect? A matter of fact, the last place he would suspect espionage would be this place, since I have brought him here. This throws them off-scent. Now I tell you that Alexandros is a friend of Freddy, and I do all this for Alexandros. Freddy is not looking for spies, he's looking for fun, this trip.'

Ruth said, 'You don't know that type of Englishman as I do.' She went to the door, opened it, peered out and closed it again. Then she sat down and lit a cigarette. She looked at her watch. She said, 'The messenger should be here between half past one and two. It's one now. I wonder if my note's safe till he comes.'

'In the tree?'

'Yes, I'd better go and have a look.'

'That is crazy. You lose your nerve.'

'I'm going to have a look. I wish we'd never got mixed up in this business. But once you're in it, you're in it. I must send word to my husband that Hamilton's here. I'm going to –'

'Freddy might see you. Don't go out.'

'He can't see in the dark. At least, he can't do that.'

'Better you remain indoors,' Suzi said, 'as he might bump into you at the door or something. I'll go and look. How far up the tree is it?'

'About five feet.' Ruth stopped packing. She said, 'I can't leave the house. I've got to wait and meet a contact this week or next at the latest. It's very important. What shall I do? That message in the tree – go and see if it's all right. It's not important in itself, but I can't be too careful. Come back at once and tell me if it's still there.'

Suzi started to go. 'In fact, bring it back to me – Suzi dear – do you mind?'

Suzi left, but Ruth was at the door, whispering her back.

'No – leave it. Don't bring it. The man will get it between one-thirty and two. Just make sure it's still . . . Come back and –'

Suzi was on her way. Outside she walked softly round the house. The light was still on in Freddy's room. She crossed to the tree and began feeling up the bark. Five feet . . . no. Up the bark, and all round it, tuft after tuft, feeling sure she was missing the one small pocket where the folded paper would be. Up the tree and round it again, as far as she could reach. It must be higher, too high for her. Ruth was taller than she was, and probably . . . No, she couldn't reach, couldn't find the thing. The man had probably been to fetch it.

She returned to Ruth, earnest about keeping her friendship. 'It's there,' she said. 'Don't worry.'

Ruth produced a new anxiety. 'What has this sick girl to do with Freddy Hamilton?'

'Oh, nothing. She stayed in the same hotel as him in Israel, and she's on a pilgrimage. I brought them together in the car. Just tourists. You don't ask questions about this woman, Ruth, and we don't ask questions from you, like I told you.'

'Yes, I know. I understand.' Ruth looked strained and shaken. 'I'll keep my side of the bargain.'

'You have a drink. You go to bed.' Suzi wanted to see Freddy again before he went to sleep. She felt jittery, too, and said, 'I'll go to keep Freddy company. You don't think of him any more. He won't go near your tree or nothing.'

Ruth relaxed a little, and said, 'Goodness, are you having an affair with Freddy Hamilton?'

'Of course,' said Suzi.

'Well, I only wish you'd gone somewhere else to have it.'

'It's my father's house,' Suzi said. But she added, like a saleswoman, 'and it's the most discreet house in the kingdom of Jordan.'

'Good night,' Ruth said. 'And keep your eye on Hamilton, for my sake.'

Suzi started to make her way back along the dark corridor to her own part of the house, but turning towards the door that enclosed it, she decided instead to take another puzzled look at the tree.

This time she found the note easily. It was tucked firmly into a tuft of bark well within her reach. She wondered if Freddy was in his room, and if she could be seen in the moonlight.

He was in his room. He was scribbling with his pocket pen on a piece of paper. He had in fact just finished decoding the message which he had copied from the note he had replaced in the tree-bark; the code had been fairly simple, but he was pleased with himself, brisk and expert at cracking a code as he had been on H.M.S. *Achilles* in the war, when he had cracked many a tough code-signal. He was making a final, brief note of the formula, now, committing it to memory with the message it revealed, before destroying the record according to the old routine.

Suzi had entered without knocking. She said, 'What are you writing?'

'A poem,' Freddy said.

'Let me see.' She reached for it and tried hard to snatch it from his hand. He caught her arm playfully, and her gold bracelet became unclasped and fell to the floor. Freddy got it first, and made game with it, holding it out to her, then snatching it away and holding it behind his back, in an effort to distract her attention from the piece of paper in his left hand.

Suzi sat on the bed. 'Let me see the poem and you can keep the bracelet,' she said, holding out her hand for it.

'I'll read you the poem,' he said. He sat down some distance away from her, near a table-lamp which he adjusted to gain the small moment for thought under a good reading light; the necessity of the occasion forced him to act neatly. 'The poem is for you,' he said, 'naturally.' He peered at the paper. He said, 'It's crumpled and –' Then smoothing the crumpled sheet, he read:

> Now is the time for secret pleasantries
> With a girl-friend lurking in her corner ambush,
> The time to steal a token from
> Her arm or unprotesting finger.

'Go on,' Suzi said. Freddy was aware that she had an impression of the quantity of writing on the page he held. He said, 'Well, that's the last verse, in fact. I haven't really worked over the others. I usually finish the last first. Do you like it?'

'I've read something like it before, I seem to think,' said Suzi. 'But not so good, and not quite like written for me. But I remember a poem I read like it.'

Freddy laughed with quite genuine amusement. 'You cunning little thing,' he said. 'Of course you know it's a translation from Horace. I have the Latin here, too. Listen –'

> nunc et latentis proditor intimo
> gratus puella rasus ab angulo
> pignusque dereptum lacertis
> aut digito male pertinaci.

She came towards him for the paper. 'Let me see.' But he raised it high, and getting out his lighter, made a flame, as he had done when burning the Harrogate letters in order to send them easier down the lavatory drain. He said, as she caught his right arm, 'I'm going to follow a custom that we practised at Cambridge University, my dear, when I was young at Cambridge. When we wrote a poem to a beautiful lady we read it to her and burned it.' He set the paper alight and Suzi drew her hand away from the quick flame. As it consumed the page, Freddy moved only enough to drop it on the tiled floor between the rugs where it lay in black, furled ash. 'We burned the poem,' said Freddy, treading the charred flimsy furl to powder, 'as a symbol of consummation of our love for the lady. Even a translation – I offer it to you – it's something better than I could compose myself.' She was looking at the black powder on the floor mingled with tiny remaining shreds of white, unconsumed paper which could reveal nothing of that message, insignificant in itself, but really very important for Freddy's purpose; a mere report of some pipe-lines on the side of the road in Israel, measuring 185 inches. Quite a size; they had probably been planted there. However, that wasn't his business, the point was that this house was undoubtedly, undoubtedly, that one place in the whole vast area of possibility through which far more serious stuff from the office had been leaking to Cairo and beyond. It was Nasser's Post Office and Gardnor was the man.

It was only within a few days that Freddy would be sitting in his hotel, forgetful of this moment, wearily listening to Rupert Gardnor's long, insufferable story about the Israeli pipe-line. 'Those fake pipe-lines, you see . . . I think they were something like 195 inches in diameter, at least –'

'The size of those fake water-pipes is 185 inches, not 195.'

'How do you know?' Yes, how did he know? Gardnor made much of the need for an Intelligence investigation of Freddy during the two weeks that followed this conversation, and as it came out later, used that time to cover up or destroy most of the evidence against himself. But not all. Ruth Gardnor got away to Cairo. Gardnor alone stood trial in the winter to come.

'Are you sure you've got Gardnor?' Freddy said on that day when his memory returned like a high tide, with an undercurrent ebb and flow of details.

'Yes, we've got Gardnor.'

'Got a statement?'

'He's giving it now. Another day or two, and he'd have got away to Cairo.'

'Did they find the house at Jericho all right?'

'Of course. You're not to worry, Freddy. Take a rest and give us any more details when you're O.K. Just as and when. We've got all we need. The Jordan authorities have cooperated.'

'Did you find anything at Jericho?'

'Oh, a transmitter, you know, and cameras, the usual stuff in the usual places – the cellar, the wardrobe. We haven't got his wife, she's hiding somewhere. The Jordan authorities are having a good search. They've been very helpful. Very efficient.'

'I wouldn't count on them getting her,' said Freddy. 'They didn't get Barbara Vaughan.'

'Well, we've got Gardnor. That's the –'

'That's the main thing,' said Freddy, looking at the unbelievable telegrams and memoranda of telephone calls between the office in Israel and Harrogate. He clung to what was believable in those first hours of remembrance. Gardnor was under arrest.

'So you see,' he said to Suzi when he had burned the paper to fragments, 'the love poem is yours for ever.' He genuinely felt it to be so at that moment, as she looked at his triumph in black ash on the floor, with a half-smile and a half-frown, as if puzzled, hesitating to take his word, and yet pleased with his gesture, and in any case, respecting his victory. Freddy thought she was adorable in her sudden loss of con-

fidence after being so sure of herself all day, and he was delighted with
his own accomplishment. He decided that the next urgent move was
to get her to bed, then tomorrow he might compose for her some
verses of his own, in chant royal perhaps, or *haiku*, why not?

He said, 'It's bed-time, isn't it?'

She sifted the powdered ruins of the paper with the toe of her shoe
and looked at him with becoming admiration. 'You telling me,' she
said. 'It's been a busy day, Freddy, more or less. Where is that bracelet that you laid plots with your poem to steal? Did you have busy
days at Cambridge University?' They found the bracelet.

As it turned out, it was she, not Freddy, who was uneasy in love-
making, for she had the distracting suspicion that his very confidence
in bed with her might derive from some secret success in counter-
espionage. She wanted very much to believe in the poem that had
been deftly and symbolically burnt for her, but an accurate translation of her Arabic thoughts in reserve would have been that it was
damned unlikely. So she missed half the fun of sleeping with Freddy
in his access of goodwill and ardour, and enjoyed only the other half.

At about three o'clock, when they had just fallen asleep, Suzi woke
quickly from a sound in the stillness beyond the house and started up,
waking Freddy. The sound became more specific, a car approaching.

'Listen,' she said.

Freddy was less sensitive to the approach of motor-cars outside his
accustomed places of sleep. He said, 'What is it?'

Then, from the direction of Jericho the first of the three-o'clock
cries arose, followed by another high call from another mosque.
Freddy said, 'It sounds very beautiful,' and moved closer to her.

She said, 'It's a car coming to the house.' It was now an unmistak-
able sound. The car pulled up outside, near the front of the house.
Suzi was out of bed, listening at the window. The night air was
flooded with the distant chanting from many mosques, and presently
overflowed with a louder voice from the courtyard, then the sound of
a woman's grateful tones, a shuffle and arrangement of footsteps
outside and the banging of the car door. 'Latifa!' shouted the man's
voice. 'Latifa!'

'My father,' Suzi said. 'He's brought someone and he's shouting to
be let in.'

*

'Do you mean that I am to share this room with you?' said Miss Rickward.

'Of course,' said Joe Ramdez. 'Or it is better to say I share it with you, since you are my honoured guest and I have made you this room at your disposal. It is yours, I share with you.'

'But where will you sleep?'

'With you, in the bed, my fruitful vine.'

It seemed to her that she had always known that this was how it was done. Ricky felt rescued, she felt vindicated, and she longed more than ever to crush Barbara Vaughan.

When Barbara first came to the fact, beyond all reckoning, the amazing fact, that Ricky was having a romantic love-affair with Joe Ramdez, a serious relationship and no mere spinster's holiday fling, she began to work backwards from that point to see where she had begun to miscalculate Ricky. Even doctors, she thought, sometimes do not know why a person does not die. But there was no telling at what point, over the six years she had known Ricky, she had failed to discover a dormant capacity for going to bed with a latent Joe Ramdez. It then occurred to Barbara, and recurred more strongly after she had learned of Ricky's marriage and her sale of the school in England, her eager embrace of Islam, and the total handing over of her lot to Joe Ramdez, that there had been no secret state of mind in Ricky. What had been overlooked was perfectly obvious, and it was, after all, precisely a woman of virile ways and blunt intellect, and yet of unfathomable emotions, who would respond and ramify most sensuously towards a muscular ageing Arab of lordly disposition, should that one chance occur, as it had done. Joe Ramdez was in fact the only type of man that Ricky could understand, and Barbara reflected that, most probably, Ricky imagined all love-affairs started and proceeded as directly as hers did, and that all women who go to bed with a man go to bed with a type of Joe Ramdez.

It was the only way she could explain the fact that Ricky, even after her meeting with Joe Ramdez, pursued the purpose for which she had followed Barbara to the Holy Land, which was to prevent her marriage to Harry Clegg. She had brought with her, of all things, a copy of the records of Harry's birth and baptism, which in desperate zeal she had managed to dig up, where Harry and his lawyers in their methodical defeatism had failed. Ricky's wild intention in doing so had been to prove to Barbara that the man she wanted to marry was illegitimate, a fact that Barbara knew already. And it turned out that the document Ricky produced for Barbara's inspection made it perfectly easy for Harry's previous marriage to be annulled by the Church, and for her to marry him within its communion. This business of the birth record was the joke of their lives.

But what neither Barbara, Harry, nor the Church knew, and were mercifully never to know, was that Ricky, shortly after her meeting with Joe, destroyed the first paper she had brought so carefully with her, substituting a second one, misguidedly devised, though brilliantly forged. This was done at the instigation of Ramdez in his eagerness to avenge Ricky against Barbara Vaughan, her treacherous friend who had grieved her, and his own enemy, the Jewess who passed as it were through his fingers and escaped the country.

'We were told,' said Ricky at that future date when she discovered that something had gone wrong with the scheme, '. . . we were assured, that a certicate which proves Clegg to be a baptized Catholic would prevent him from ever getting an annulment of his previous marriage, since Catholics do not recognize divorce. I simply cannot understand it.'

She was then talking to a Catholic priest. He seemed aware of vexation in her tone, and looked at her, puzzled. 'Well, it's better, this way, isn't it?' he said. 'What a good thing for the couple that you found this certificate.'

Ricky, terrified of having aroused suspicion, agreed that it was.

The priest said that it was a common mistake, of course, to assume that a Catholic could not obtain an annulment of a previous marriage, since in fact if the Catholic had been first married outside the Church, as in the case of Harry Clegg, the Church did not recognize the marriage. But where a non-Catholic applied for annulment in such a case, difficulties arose, since this was outside the province of the Church. It was all perfectly logical, really. . . .

If only, Ricky thought, I had given them the paper I brought over, that first paper . . . Born to Amelia Clegg . . . Father unknown . . . Christened at Tate Street Methodist Chapel . . .

Ramdez laid yet another curse upon his son Abdul for providing the false information about Catholic divorces. Abdul had claimed, when he was in hospital in Beirut, to have gone over to the Catholic

Church. Ramdez did not know whether to believe him, but he cursed him then, even although Abdul explained that he was still a Moslem as well. Abdul had done that, if he had done it at all, to offend and shame his father. And now, when appealed to for the information that surely he, having received the Catholic teaching, was in a position to know, Abdul had answered falsely to spite his father's new, fine, substantial wife, who had come freely to him with all her confidence, her trouble, and her riches. Joe Ramdez laid a father's curse on Abdul again and yet again.

Barbara, in her relief, kept saying to Harry, 'I was going to marry you anyway.'

He said, 'I know. I'm not forgetting it.' The Congregation of the Rota had turned down his application for an annulment only a week before the new evidence, Ricky's bright information, turned up to make everything easy. He said, 'My aunts never told me my mother was a Catholic. Anyway, they were not really my aunts. Perhaps my father was a Catholic, too. An Irish couple, I expect, whoever they were. I know more about the Etruscans than I do about my own parents, and in fact I've got no curiosity about them at all, whereas the Etruscans –'

'It's so funny, Ricky thinking this was going to mess us up.'

'Yes, I know, silly old bitch.'

She said, 'I would have married you, anyway. But it would have taken courage to continue being out of the Church. It's the keeping it up I was afraid of.'

'From the way those clerics spoke,' he said, 'I was sure it would be impossible. Well, now it's possible.'

'With God, everything is possible,' said Barbara.

From time to time for years afterwards, and far into her long widowhood, Ricky would inquire of Catholic priests, as a matter of theoretical interest, what was the position of a Catholic marriage based on evidence which both parties believed to be true, but which, in reality, was faked.

They would all look puzzled, at first, and ask Ricky if she had ever heard of such a case. 'No, no,' Ricky always said. 'Only I read of it in a novel.' The priests all said in effect, 'Well, if both parties remain in ignorance and the Church is satisfied, then it's a valid marriage.'

'According to the logic of the Catholics, that seems impossible.'

No, they mostly said, it was quite logical if one started from the right premise. Others said, well, logic or no logic, that was the case. One of them replied, 'With God, everything is possible.' Another went into the question of the validity of the blessing Jacob received in place of Esau, even under conscious falsity.

If Ricky had been anywhere close to Barbara during those years after Joe Ramdez's death in 1963, she might, sooner or later, have been unable to prevent herself confessing to the forgery, at whatever risk. But she was nowhere near Barbara. She had started a private school for the children of English and American residents and wealthy Jordanians. She was not tempted to commit herself in any letter to Barbara.

All this was yet to be. The first night in the house at Jericho, Barbara on her drowsy bed heard a man's voice in the darkness. She felt cooler, and touched her forehead to make sure she actually was cooler, and the fever had gone. She did not care about the man's voice but let fate blow over her and presently fell asleep.

Suzi had said to Freddy before she rushed from his room, 'You are my tourist. Tomorrow we go to Jerash and see the ruins. My father must see I take this trouble over you as you are a British Government man.' She had gone to her own room, where she opened the window and called out in a sleepy voice, inquiring what was the matter. She could not see her father from the window, but her voice was answered by her father's from the front of the house. She had gone to the door and let him in. Latifa was just coming out of her room, and Suzi could hear her slopping along from the wing she occupied.

Her father had brought a visitor, a woman whom Suzi recognized as the tourist who had approached her that morning when she was with Barbara in the Holy Sepulchre. As they entered, Suzi stood well in the light so that the woman, Barbara's pursuer, could see her; and so she satisfied herself, then and there, that Miss Rickward did not recognize her. Suzi thought, she is a real enemy; and was partly resentful at not being recognized from their short encounter.

Miss Rickward showed herself eager to please Joe Ramdez's daughter. Latifa was not introduced to her but stood by as part of the reception machinery. In Arabic, Suzi explained to her father that a new girl had been sent that day and had immediately gone down with scarlet fever. She had the girl in isolation in the western section of the house, and warned her father not to go near it. The girl was not gravely ill, but highly infectious.

'See that the authorities don't get to hear of it,' Joe said, 'and start pushing their noses into our affairs here. Why have these thieves and whoremongers sent me a girl with disease?'

'It's Allah's blame,' Suzi said.

'Quiet, blasphemous slut!'

He then returned to the English tongue and Miss Rickward, enchanted as she was with everything.

And before long she was in the large dark-tapestried room with Ramdez.

'I share with you.'

'But where will you sleep?'

'With you, in the bed, my fruitful vine, my pillar of cedar, golden minaret.'

She said, 'I have always had a leaning towards Islam.' She looked round for her suitcase. Ramdez had placed it in a corner behind a dark screen that must have been bright at one time. Ricky went behind the screen to undress. She said, 'If these lovely tapestries were cleaned, they would come up exquisitely.'

One way and another the spirit of the Crusaders in their everyday aspect brooded over the house that night. Ricky, when she had got into bed, sat up in it and recited, in her buxom, bough-laden poetry voice, the famous Islamic Throne Verse in the English Translation:

God – there is no god but He, the Living, and Self-subsistent: Slumber seizeth him not, neither sleep. To Him belongeth what-sover is in the Heavens and whatsoever is in the Earth. Who is there that shall intercede with Him save by His Will. He knoweth what is present with men and what shall befall them, and nought of His knowledge do they comprehend save what He willeth. His Throne is wide as the Heavens and the Earth, and the keeping of them wearieth Him not. And He is the High, the Mighty one.

'My rose of Islam!' said Joe in admiration, heaving himself into bed beside her. 'Well of sweet waters!'

Ricky said, 'I am a virgin. Does it signify?'

'It is highly satisfactory,' Joe said, as he used to say, long ago, when he was a young schoolteacher, and was giving a lesson in Arabic to one of the British administrators in his spare time.

Freddy contemplated a meeting with Joe Ramdez without panic, not even that panic he had always felt in his previous encounters, at the Cartwrights, with Joe, when it had been merely a matter of mental association. Normally, of course, he was terrified of blatant liars like Joe and always felt a ruinous urge to conspire with them, as he did with his mother, to the effect that they were honest people. In his youth at Cambridge Freddy had known a liar whom he hated so much that he had given him a solid-gold hunter watch – not his good one, but a very good one.

This Monday morning, however, Freddy felt quite equal to Joe Ramdez, whose daughter was so sweet. He sat and had breakfast with Suzi while the rest of the house was still asleep from its busy night's doings. He said, 'I'm going to miss a day at the office. Oh, well –' The day's newspapers arrived and he sat screened by the local English-language one, while Suzi waited with wifely patience to talk to him seriously. 'Australia Urges Britain Not to Join Common Market,' Freddy read aloud. 'What utter nonsense,' he said. 'Australia should keep her nose out of it. We must have our markets abroad and trade with the foreigners. We always have done and we always will. What's the point of having foreigners on your doorstep if you're going to let them put you out of business?'

'Very wise and true,' Suzi said.

'We simply must decide to join the Common Market.'

'My father has brought the woman called Miss Rickward. They both hunt for Barbara. I want you to know,' Suzi said.

'We'd better get her out of here, then,' Freddy said.

'She should rest in bed.'

'I wonder if her ex-fiancé could help? He's working at Qumran.'

'What ex-fiancé?'

'She was engaged to an archaeologist there, but she broke it off. Went right off him. So she said.'

'Well, she must have gone on him again. She says he's in Rome just now. She's going to marry him, definite.'

'Really? She might have told *me*.'

'She had the scarlet fever too bad to tell you yesterday, Freddy. Were you hoping to be the next fiancé?'

'No,' Freddy said. 'I had no such aspirations.'

'Well, we can't move her anywhere. So it means we stick around till my father goes back to Jerusalem with his woman, in case he finds Barbara. I have told him she is somebody else with scarlet fever, so I think he will keep away from my section of this house.'

'What about the other Englishwoman who's here?'

'She will take care of Barbara when we leave her. But I prefer to wait for my father to leave first. No risks.'

'I ought to be back in Israel tonight,' Freddy said.

'No, you wait tonight,' she said.

He said, 'It's a tempting thought.'

She said, 'If you mean what I think you mean, it's not so easy with my father in the house. He is the only one that's permitted to sleep with anyone he likes.'

'Well, he wouldn't be sleeping with Miss Rickward, if she's the woman Barbara's trying to avoid. Miss Rickward is the head of an English girls' school, if you know what that means.'

'Miss Rickward is in the bed with my father this moment, if you know what that means,' Suzi said.

'How remarkable!' Freddy said, his coffee-cup so moving in his hand, without a pause from the saucer to his lips, that he did not seem to think it very remarkable.

He was listening to the bang of a car door outside, the engine starting up and the sound of its being driven away from the house.

He finished his coffee. He examined the tips of his right index finger and thumb and rubbed them together.

'That was our other English guest that I told you of,' Suzi said. 'She has gone to visit some friends in Amman, but she'll be back tomorrow to look after Barbara. She will be good to her all right, but to tell you the truth this lady is a little bit mad.'

'Oh, really? What lady is that?'

'Remember I told you we have a woman staying here for a rest?'

'Oh yes, of course. Who is she, anyway?'

Suzi said, 'I shouldn't tell you this. It is our secret, poor woman. I shouldn't tell you as it is a lady married to a government officer of the British. Her name is Mrs Gardnor. She –'

'Gardnor!' Freddy said. 'Why I know the Gardnors, of course. He's stationed with me in Israel. Awfully nice chap. I know Ruth too, of course. What's wrong with her?'

He thought Suzi looked relieved. He was sure she had been testing him to find his response; but now she looked relieved, and he hoped he had passed the test. But, he thought, this darling girl knows damn well – must know, ought to know, maybe, though, isn't quite sure – that the paper I burned last night was no damn poem at all. He stopped himself fidgeting with the tips of his fingers and thumb where they had been nipped by the little flame.

She said, 'Yes, you must,' and then his ears caught up with the words she had spoken a split second before: 'You must promise to tell no one what I am going to tell you.' And now she said, 'Yes, you must.'

'Of course,' Freddy said. 'What is it?'

'Why are you looking so much at me?'

'Because you're so charming to look at with your fawn skin and those blue eyes.'

'My skin is not fawn, it is green this morning from never sleeping all the night.'

'It isn't green, it's lovely.'

'No, it's like an ancient scroll is my skin.'

'Nonsense.'

'You don't say "it's lovely" and "nonsense" when you make love talk to a lady in Jericho. This is a place of the true Arabian civiliza-tion and if I say I look like old hell, then it's your place to say a speech about me, that I resemble the winding River Jordan, when I turn from the shoulders to the hips, and that my voice is the bleating of a thousand flocks, and my skin is smooth and perfecter than the udder of the camel.'

'Oh, I can think of more suitable things to say than that. Much more romantic. I'll write another poem for you. In chant royal, which is a romantic verse form, or *haiku* might be more right for you, as it's Oriental.'

'You know *Omar*?'

'Why yes, of course. The translation, I mean. It's –'

'All the English are crazy for Omar. Abdul learned it at school, he could say it all in English, not Persian, which we don't speak. Then Abdul got sick with T.B. and was in hospital, and there he said to me, *Omar Khayyám* is all olive oil poured over the troubled waters. Too much oil, and you don't see the truth. So don't copy *Omar* for a poem for me, I would make you put it on fire and burn your fingers. You have a lovely smile.'

'I would say you were a pomegranate,' Freddy said, 'only you taste sharper and sweeter. Pomegranates look good but they taste insipid.' And all this conversation was soon to be gone from his memory for many months, suddenly returning on a day when the sun was a crimson disc between the bare branches of Kensington Gardens, and the skaters on the Round Pond were all splashed over the heads and arms with red light, as they beat their mittens together and skimmed the dark white ice under the sky. So it was to be throughout the years; it was always unexpectedly, like a thief in the night, that the sweetest experiences of his madness returned; he was amazed at his irresponsibility for a space, then he marvelled that he could have been so light-hearted, and sooner or later he was overwhelmed with an image, here and there, of beauty and delight, as in occasional memories of childhood.

But he did remember almost immediately, when, three weeks later he remembered anything at all, the promise he had made to Suzi Ramdez that Monday morning at breakfast.

'Promise me that you won't speak of Mrs Gardnor's breakdown in your office. We have taken her as our guest, and there would be great distress for us to betray this poor woman's sickness, so that they laugh at her in her husband's office in Israel.'

'We wouldn't dream of laughing at –'

'Promise. Never speak of her. Promise, and I shall explain how she is mad.'

'Yes, of course, I promise. I won't say a word.'

'She imagines that she is being spied upon and is mixed up in political things to spy upon the Arabs, maybe. I don't know. She writes stupid letters in code and hides them places, to find them again and say "Look what I find!" So we make her well again soon and let her rest as we have promised her husband who brought her to us.'

'Doesn't she see a doctor?'

'Oh yes, many doctors. Two times a week she goes to visit a psychi-atrist, very clever, in Amman.'

'Poor woman.'

'She will take great care of Barbara. It will do good for herself to have this job, and she is so kind. Never will she betray Barbara if we tell her so. You say nothing of this to your government friends, please, as you promised. Then we count on her to be good to Barbara and keep her secret.'

Freddy said, 'I see.' At that time he was not sure how much Suzi expected him to believe. He said, 'I see. Oh, well, if she'll keep an eye on Barbara, that's all right.'

'I shall come myself many times while she is sick. Maybe she gets up in ten days. This morning she's O.K. already. No temperature or nothing. And the infection is past, so you could sleep with her, even.'

'I don't want to,' Freddy said. 'I want to sleep with you. But I'll go and see her now, I think. Does she know your father and Miss Rickward are in the house?'

'Oh no. It would only make her a fever perhaps. She knows only that some people are here and she must keep quiet in the room.'

On that day when the two young consuls brought and broke the news to Freddy that his mother was dead, murdered by Benny, knifed by Benny insane, killed in violent blood, and the memory of his absent days in Jordan first flooded upon him and was half-lost again, it was then some hours before detailed scenes, one by one, began to seep back. There was Benny's letter – Bloodshed, Mr Freddy . . . She . . . I hear those voices again . . . There will be Blood come from it. . . .

'I thought it would be here,' Freddy said. 'Somewhere in my mind I knew there was to be bloodshed, but I thought the danger was here, I didn't think it was in Harrogate.'

And he recalled his answers to the letters. There was something urgent he had to remember. He had answered the letters, but hadn't posted them, hadn't posted them. Where had he left them? Yes, but he had set them on fire. That was so. He had burnt his finger and thumb. And presently, the image came to him of that moonlit wait outside Barbara's convent, while Alexandros went to bribe the janitor, and he heard again the chanting voices from minaret to minaret calling the faithful to prayer under the stars.

'Where is Barbara Vaughan?' Freddy said.

'Oh, her? Well, apparently she got back to Israel yesterday. We only heard this morning. We'd assumed, you know, that she'd gone to Rome, but it seems she's been hiding in Jordan. Her family are awfully relieved to know definitely that she's safe and so are we, of course. Silly woman.'

'Did she ask for me?' Freddy said.

'No, she didn't mention you. Look, Freddy, you should lie down, you know.'

'I must get back to London,' Freddy said. There was something urgent to remember. His head was in his hands, and it was then he saw, once more, that walk of Ruth Gardnor's across the forecourt to the palm-tree in Jericho.

The consuls did not leave after that. They stayed on for lunch, which Joanna herself served to them in a room alone, in compliance with their request, withdrawing as silently as their Arab boys when she had done so. One of the young men then left abruptly, returning at half past five in the afternoon. He announced: 'We've got Gardnor.'

And meanwhile Freddy had given every other part of the story he could then heave to mind. 'There was the Arab woman, you see, a daughter of Ramdez. Now, I know for a fact that she suspected I'd got this message from the tree that night, so next morning she went into a long rigmarole about Ruth Gardnor having had a nervous breakdown – a great secret, and Gardnor didn't wish it to be known to us.'

'Understandably,' said Freddy's colleague, with a bit of a smile.

'Yes, according to Miss Ramdez, Gardnor didn't wish anything to be known to us. This Arab girl's yarn was that Ruth was mad as a hatter, and was sending herself messages, believing herself to be a spy. I listened to it all, of course . . . Well, I can only say I'm sorry I didn't get this news to you immediately. I could easily have dropped into our embassy at Amman, but to be quite honest I'm sure I would have been followed and then Gardnor would probably have been alerted. And of course the telephones are all tapped. Spies everywhere over there. I waited over till Tuesday, hoping to get some more evidence, you know, and then, don't you see, it all went. It all went out of my mind. I just lost my memory, that's all. God knows what else I did all that time.'

Then he worked over the story again.

'Freddy, take it easy. I'll get Joanna. She'll –'

'You're sure you've got Gardnor?'

'Oh yes, we've got him. He isn't giving much trouble.'

'He's talking?'

'Well, he's begun.'

'I must get back to London.'

'You must get to bed.'

'Gardnor, of course, has been anxious to implicate me,' Freddy said. He was not sure, but he felt fairly certain he had been under unofficial house arrest at the Cartwrights during the past few days of his amnesia.

'Oh goodness, Freddy. Gardnor's report would never have stood up. One needs evidence, you know.'

Yes, one needed evidence. And while investigating the sources of evidence, suspicion must have lingered. How long had his mother lain dead in a mess of blood? Freddy wanted to know the details. He said, 'Are you sure you've got Gardnor? Really *got* him? Was there any difficulty getting into the house at Jericho?'

'No, they say from Amman that the Jordan police were quite helpful. There were a few things there – cameras and a transmitter – the usual. Ruth Gardnor had gone, of course. She must have got wind of something from the police or someone.'

'Well, if you've got Gardnor, that's the main thing.'

After breakfast with Suzi he had gone to see how Barbara was. He said to her, 'You know, if we put you in the Embassy at Amman – send for them to fetch you – they'll look after you and you'll be quite safe. Don't you think you should do that, and cut out all this pilgrimage lark?'

She said, 'What would *you* do in my place?'

To his later horror, he said, 'I'd be inclined to stick it out, person-ally. I'd hate the idea of these fellows getting the better of me.'

'That's exactly how I feel,' she said. 'Now I'm in it, I'm going to stay in it.'

'Of course,' he said, 'I'm not a half-Jew and I haven't got scarlet fever. So I don't want to encourage you to take these risks. On the other hand, if you do manage to lie low for a couple of weeks, and then get up and put on those widow's weeds again, and get around the country, it would be rather a triumph for *us*.'

'That's what I'll do. The only thing I dread is the boredom. Is there anything to read in this house? Is there a wireless or something?'

'I wouldn't have a wireless on if I were you,' Freddy said. 'You might atract attention. I'll see if I can find you some books, or Suzi will get you something to read. But don't move from this room and don't make a noise. By the way, Joe Ramdez is in the house. He's supposed to be leaving tomorrow, but I'll wait till he leaves, so don't –'

'My God, he may be looking for me! Everyone must be looking for me after that piece in the Israeli paper.'

'Suzi has warned him to keep away from this part of the house. He thinks you're a Moroccan dancer, just arrived from Tangier with scarlet fever. Are you frightened, though? Because –'

'No, I'm not frightened. The danger doesn't seem so very real to me, somehow. It'll make a lovely story to tell afterwards.'

'Yes, that's what I was thinking, too,' Freddy said. He thought Barbara Vaughan was a jolly good sport, and it was the one solid opinion he formed during his lost days in Jordan that he retained ever afterwards.

She said to Harry later, when she was safe, 'I honestly couldn't swear that I went through all that from a determination to pray at the Christian shrines. It's true I'd set my heart on the pilgrimage. But, to be perfectly honest, I might have taken refuge at the Embassy – Freddy did suggest it – only in fact, I could see he really wanted me to be a *good sport*. And Freddy was so very nice, I sort of couldn't let him down.'

'To hell with Freddy,' said Harry.

'Oh no, Freddy's nice. He got me out of the convent. I thought highly of him for that.'

'You thought he was a good sport.'

'Well, yes, that's about it. A jolly good one.'

'He was off his nut, though.'

'Well, I wasn't to know that. And really, he wasn't all that mad. You would like Freddy if you knew him.'

'I know. He sounds all right. Tell me – suppose you'd been killed

– what's the technical Catholic difference between a martyr and a jolly good sport?'

Joe Ramdez was standing patriarchally by the well in the forecourt talking to Suzi in Arabic when Freddy came out into the sunny morning air.

He turned to Freddy with affable arms. 'Welcome to my home. Have you slept well?'

'Delightfully, thank you.'

Suzi had a haunted look. She said, 'I drive Mr Hamilton out for a day to see the general view of Jericho, Elisha's Fountain, the Mount of the Temptation in the Wilderness and the beautiful Greek convent there, also the River Jordan, the Allemby Bridge, and –'

'Alle-n-by,' said Ramdez. 'You always say "Allemby" like a Cockney corporal of the General's army. It is Allenby, may he rest in the Bosom of God.'

'The Allenby Bridge and through the hills of Judaea to the Dead Sea. We go also to Bethany, the Tomb of Lazarus that was raised from the dead, and the Inn of the Good Samaritan. Then we –'

'She does not stop talking once she has started. Suzi is the worst of all my women in my household for talking,' Ramdez said to Freddy. 'Only on the first times of meeting a new person she keeps quiet, but that is her trick, she's a clever one. When she meets a nice gentleman, he thinks she's a quiet good woman, but soon she is talking.'

'Your daughter's a splendid guide,' Freddy said.

Ramdez said, 'She is splendid also, for an insurance agent. Suzi – did you explain Mr Hamilton the proposal forms and the opportunities?'

'Yes, Father, and Mr Hamilton will get the medical test all right.'

Freddy said, 'As I told Abdul, I must wait till I have a reply from my lawyers in London. They look after all that side of things.'

'Lawyers are no good,' Ramdez said. 'Listen to me, lawyers are robbers.'

'Oh, I know that. I quite agree.'

'We have in this insurance scheme many diplomats from Britain and also from America. Mr Scriven is one, Mr Pole is two, Mr Carson is three, Mr Macintyre, who is gone from here and now in West Indies, is four, Mr Gardnor is five, Mr Redding, six – naturally, I do not remember all the names on the record, but these diplomats are all investors in Middle East Visitors' with great benefits.'

'Really? A very impressive list,' Freddy said. Scriven was a filing-clerk in the office at Tel Aviv; Pole was secretary in the Post Office in Amman; Carson he didn't know – probably someone in the American Embassy; Macintyre he remembered as the name of a chap who had been recalled from Israel two years ago for some misdemeanour with a girl; Gardnor, yes, Gardnor; Redding, he couldn't place. So much for the diplomats.

'You've got Gardnor?'

'Yes, Freddy, it's all right. He's coming across with it nicely today. Not that he was much trouble yesterday, but he probably thought it over during the night, and today we're getting the lot. He says he feels liberated, in a way, now that it's all out.'

'Well, you might take a look into Scriven at Tel Aviv and a chap called Pole in Amman.'

'Yes, I believe we're working on Scriven and Pole, and a few others on Ramdez's list.'

'You've got hold of his list?'

'Yes, it cost us an absolute fortune. And I don't believe it's worth a penny to us. No big security risks except Gardnor; only chaps who've made fools of themselves with girls and so on.'

Scriven . . . Pole . . . Macintyre . . . In the forecourt at Jericho Freddy looked out at the Judaean wilderness and said to Ramdez, 'An impressive list.'

'So you must join also.'

'One's salary doesn't amount to much in the Foreign Service,' Freddy said. 'One has to make ends meet, you know. I'm afraid we'd better be on our way if we're to see all those delightful scenes that your daughter described.'

The cars were parked across the forecourt and Suzi started to move. Ramdez said, 'Wait, I have a favour to ask of Mr Hamilton.'

Suzi looked miserable and embarrassed, as she had on that first day that Freddy had seen her, in the Cartwrights' garden. 'You ask so many favours, Father, and Mr Hamilton has paid in advance for the pilgrimage-tour inclusive,' she said.

He had not in fact paid anything in advance, but was to settle the

bill with Alexandros. Three weeks later, when the events came back
to him, he did so, and meantime Alexandros had held his peace, not
believing for one moment the rumour that Freddy was suffering from
a lapse of memory, but rather assuming that Freddy had some good
private reason, perhaps connected with his career or his social reputation, for choosing to regard the episode as non-existent.

'This is one small favour,' said Ramdez, 'which I am sure you will
oblige with, Mr Hamilton, since it concerns a lady of your country.
I have brought with me a very nice tourist who is on a pilgrimage
and also had paid in advance. But I have now business to attend to
in Amman today. So you take this nice woman along with you in the
car today, returning with you this evening, and Suzi will adjust the
small difference for one day's private tour for one, and one day's
private tour for two; it makes a bit cheaper. But this would be a
favour as this lady is so greatly distressed. She has followed from
England to look for a lady-friend and maybe you will find the friend
on your route.'

'Well, that should be all right,' Freddy said. 'Quite all right. Is she
ready to come?'

'I'll go and summon her now from her room. By the way, do you
know Miss Barbara Vaughan?'

'Oh yes, she's saying at my hotel in Israel. But surely she isn't the
lady who's going to accompany us? She –'

'Oh no, she is the lady that my client, Miss Rickward, is looking
for. Do you know where she might be?'

'So far as I know she's still in Israel –' Joe Ramdez clapped his
hands over his ears at the repeated word 'Israel'; he smiled, but not
very sweetly.

'– Occupied Palestine,' Freddy said with deference '. . . I know she
was thinking of coming here but I believe she changed her mind.
Anyway, she's either still in Occupied Palestine or on her way to
Rome to join her fiancé, who is there at the moment. A very nice
person, Miss Vaughan.'

'Ah, thank you. I will tell Miss Rickward what you say. Wait, excuse
me, half a moment.'

Freddy said, then, to Suzi, 'That settles that. And I'll see that a
notice goes into the Israeli paper tomorrow morning.'

'In Amman,' she said, 'it is possible they have a list of every name that has passed through the Mandelbaum Gate from Israel. And my father will find it.'

'Then we must make sure they understand she's left the country – gone to Rome. Let's wait and see how much your father discovers.'

Ricky bustled out with him, very voluble on the subject of Freddy's niece, who was a pupil at her school, and through whose mother Ricky had met Freddy's mother at Harrogate one day. 'It was only when your mother told me of the bits in your letter concerning Barbara Vaughan that I knew she was engaged to the man. Then she –'

'Let us go,' said Suzi, 'and you talk about the friend in the car. But I tell you this, that if you look for an English visitor in our country, you have to look well, since they are under every olive-tree and in every cave of the hills, and there is no stopping their curiosity for adventure everywhere.'

'My friend is on a pilgrimage. A Roman Catholic pilgrimage. That narrows it down, my dear,' Ricky said. She looked yearningly at Joe, who kissed her hand and placed her carefully in the back of the car. He evidently expected Freddy to go in beside her, but Freddy got in the front at the wheel, leaning to open the door beside him for Suzi.

'My daughter should drive,' said Joe, as Suzi got in beside Freddy. 'It is her job, and you should come back here to be comfortable with Miss Rickward.'

Freddy beamed at him. 'Mr Ramdez,' he said, 'a businessman like you should know that when one pays in advance one never gets full value.' He started up the car while Joe Ramdez leaned over the back window to say softly to Miss Rickward that he would be back from Amman, promptly, that evening. As Freddy drove off, Joe went over to his own car, then seemed to change his mind and returned to the house.

Freddy drew up a few yards from the house. 'I'm so very sorry,' he said. 'I'll have to go back for my sun-glasses.' He manoeuvred the car to a turn. His sun-glasses, which he wore only when absolutely necessary, were actually in his pocket, but he wanted to see what Ramdez was up to. He was uneasy about Barbara's being left without friends with that man on the premises. 'Stupid of me,' Freddy said.

Ricky had moved from her position behind Freddy to the position behind Suzi. Now, when they had turned round, she moved to the middle of the seat. 'While you are indoors,' she said, 'I would be so very grateful if you find me a cushion.'

'Are you not comfortable, Miss Rickward?' Suzi said. 'Would you like to change with me?' The car was a well-sprung, fairly new Chevrolet. 'The back seat,' Suzi said, 'is usually the more comfortable place.'

'No, no, a cushion will do. Yes, it is more comfortable at the back, I'm sure. It's only that I have a slight touch of cramp. It's probably due to the strain of travel. A cushion would be very satisfactory.'

The phrase 'very satisfactory' gave Suzi immediately to think of her father, who used it a lot when speaking to the British. And the live wires of her mind gave instantaneous connexion from her father to Ricky's fidgeting in her seat. As Freddy drove up to the door, Suzi, attacked by the complete answer, put her hand to her mouth to suppress the burst of laughter which more or less spluttered forth. She jumped from the car and said, 'I get a cushion. Excuse me that I laugh at Freddy for forgetting his sun-glasses, he is so like all the Englishmen, they never get away from a place but have to return.'

'Stay here, I'll get the cushion,' said Freddy, as he got out. 'Just tell me where –'

'No, I must find a soft one.'

Joe appeared at the door just as they were entering. He looked extremely fierce-eyed at this return, although he smiled and nodded at Freddy's self-deprecating explanation.

'I was just about to depart,' said Ramdez in the tone of a man very distracted by other business. He raised his arm in salute to Miss Rickward, called that he would see her later, went straight to his car and drove off at speed. From this busy display, even before Freddy got to his room and found that his zipper-bag had been left unzipped, although not by himself, he had the sense of their having interrupted Ramdez at some leisurely snooping. There was nothing for Ramdez to find, anyway. He took his sun-glasses from his pocket and put them on. Suzi then appeared, carrying two large cushions, and collapsed into his arms, cushions and all, while she told him of her absolute conviction that her father had 'unflowered and nearly killed' poor Miss Rickward in the course of the previous night. 'A matter of fact,' Suzi said, 'I heard a noise. I thought it was cats. But it wasn't cats, it was Miss Ricky.'

They came soberly to the car and Suzi arranged the cushions for Ricky. 'You must have had a hard time on your travels,' said Suzi.

'I don't usually complain,' Ricky said, 'it's only —'

'Then you must have been tough, all your travels,' said Suzi, 'but you'll be O.K. now.'

'Ready?' said Freddy. 'Right. We're off! Let's try to get back early, and not give Miss Rickward too much travelling.'

It was late on Tuesday morning that Freddy and Suzi finally departed for Jerusalem. Barbara was very conscious now of being left in the house without anyone she knew, although, when she had said good-bye to Freddy and Suzi, she had been almost relieved at their departure, for their continual anxious popping in and out of her room with warnings about this and that had exhausted her. They had given instructions about what she might say or not say to Latifa and the woman who was coming to nurse her; while all Barbara really wanted to do was sleep and, on waking, drink water. Thirst and exhaustion were now the only lingering discomforts of the disease.

Freddy had said, 'I'll be back at the week-end. As soon as I get back to Israel this afternoon I'll see about getting that notice in the paper to put the people here off the scent. And I'll get hold of Dr Clegg in Rome and tell him what's happened. You've nothing to worry about. Only, Barbara, this woman who's going to look after you — be very careful what you say to her, won't you?'

'Yes, Suzi has told me. I'm not to talk and not to ask any questions of Miss White.'

'Miss White isn't her real name, of course. But —'

'Isn't it? What a bloody peculiar set-up this all is.'

'Yes, but you're in a bloody peculiar position. Of course, it's my fault, in a way, for not insisting on your going to the Embassy. If you want —'

'No — oh no. I'm going through with it.'

'You're a good sport, you know.'

'Well, one wants to do what one wants to do, that's all.' She hadn't the slightest notion what she meant by this, but she meant it and it sounded all right. She was sure that Freddy was relieved by her refusal; for some reason he was reluctant to contact the Embassy himself.

'Really a sport,' Freddy was saying. 'Now, I want to tell you about so-called Miss White. If there's anything, Barbara, you can get *out* of her in the meantime – I mean, what she's actually up to here – without, of course, appearing to be inquisitive, I'd be awfully grateful. I can't really explain, but maybe you realize there are a few people roaming round this part of the world whom the F.O. likes to know a little about. Don't take this too seriously, of course, but –'

'My God!' said Barbara. 'Don't tell me there's a British Gestapo keeping track of us all when we go abroad.' She sat up in bed.

'Barbara *dear!*'

She lay down again. 'Well, Freddy, it's bad enough for me to have to hide here in Jordan, and go about in disguise. But one doesn't expect that sort of thing amongst ourselves. Why should I be a government snooper? I detest government snooping.'

'Don't think any more of it,' Freddy said. 'I apologize. I withdraw my request. I beg your pardon. But I trust you to keep your discretion about my request.'

'Oh, Freddy, now you're taking up an attitude. Don't take up attitudes, I can't bear them. What have you got against Miss White, or whoever she is?'

'I couldn't tell you even if I knew. My dear, you're quite right in all you say. I shouldn't have mentioned this matter at all. It was only that, when there's a possibility of the country being damaged in some way –'

'Which country? This country?'

'Of course not. Ours. What do you think I've been talking about?'

'I smell an ideology, that's all.'

Barbara recalled, he had become very amused, he had just about hugged her with joy, and at least he had taken both her hands and looked at her with the affection of one who detested ideologies, too. He said, 'Yes, that's the point. . . .'

They were gone, they were gone, now. Yesterday she had slept most of the five hours when Freddy and Suzi had taken their drive to keep up the appearance of touring. But now Freddy was gone for almost a week and Suzi for some days.

Much earlier that morning, a car had left the house and Suzi had come to Barbara's room to announce the departure of her father with his tourist for Jerusalem. A little later she heard an arrival. Suzi came, with a tray of coffee and biscuits for two, to sit with Barbara and inform her that Miss White had returned and was resting.

Now they were gone. Resting, thought Barbara, and what am I supposed to be doing? She began to think of Freddy and to speculate upon his sex life, whatever it should be. For, plainly, Suzi had greatly taken to him.

But it's none of my business, she thought. Sex is child's play. Jesus Christ was very sophisticated on the subject of sex. And didn't harp on it. Why is it so predominant and serious for us? There are more serious things in the world. And if sex is not child's play, in any case it is worthless. For she was thinking of her own recent experiences of sex, which were the only experiences she knew that were worth thinking about. It was child's play, unselfconscious and so full of fun and therefore of peace, that she had not bothered to analyse or define it. And, she thought, we have invented sex guilt to take our minds off the real thing. She thought finally of Freddy, and quite saw, partly through Suzi's eyes, that he had his attractions, especially here in Jordan.

Suzi, when she had come to say good-bye, promising to be back before the end of the week, was very buoyant. 'You know,' she said, 'I'm a little bit in love with Freddy.'

Jolly good for Freddy.

From being confined with the fever like this, Barbara Vaughan had taken one of her religious turns and was truly given to the love of God, and all things were possible. And, she thought, we must all think in these vague terms: with God, all things are possible; because the only possibilities we ever seem able to envisage in a precise manner are disastrous events; and we fear both vaguely and specifically, and I have myself too long laid plans against eventualities. Against good ones? No, bad ones. It would be interesting, for a change, to prepare and be ready for possibilities of, I don't know what, since all things are possible with God and nothing is inevitable. And then, it is said in the Scriptures: The race is not to the swift nor the battle to the strong. . . . She was trying to remember how it went on when into the room walked Ruth Gardnor. Barbara was sure it was Ruth Gardnor. Then Ruth said, 'Barbara, goodness, it's you!'

'What are you doing here?' Barbara said.

'Now, now!' said Ruth.

Barbara thought this strange. She said, 'What's wrong?'

'You don't ask questions,' Ruth said. 'You're not really ill, are you?'

'Well, yes, I'm down with scarlet fever. But I'm past the infectious stage.'

Only then it occurred to Barbara that Ruth Gardnor was the Miss White she had been told to expect. Suzi had certainly warned her not to ask questions of Miss White. 'Are you the Miss White?' Barbara said.

Ruth crossed her legs and puffed her cigarette, leaning back in the soft chair. She said, 'Yes, of course. And you're not the Barbara I expected to find. But I expect you're used to that. You're not really ill, are you?'

'I've had scarlet fever. To tell you the truth, I'm on the run.'

'Yes, I know. I heard in Amman today that you're being looked for by the local boys.' She laughed then, and said, 'I actually told some people connected with the Jordan Intelligence that I knew you slightly and would look out for you.' She was still laughing. 'How was I to know that the Barbara Vaughan I already knew was the Barbara I've got to look after, here?'

Barbara felt safe in saying little. It was the most plausible course, until she should find out what Ruth was up to. Which was exactly what Freddy had been suggesting. It appeared that Ruth assumed Barbara to be someone importantly on her side, secretly connected with whatever activity she herself was here for, and to be faking illness while lying low.

The fact that Ruth was extremely kind to Barbara throughout the next two weeks was something that Barbara kept repeating when the Foreign Office man came to question her shortly after her escape back to Israel through the narrow Mandelbaum Gate.

'But you know,' said Barbara, 'as soon as she was convinced I really was feeling rather weak she couldn't do enough for me. On the personal level she was terribly sweet.'

The nice young man was amused, because Barbara had just been telling him about her fight with Ruth Gardnor. 'Yes, I do mean a fight,' she said. 'Hands, fists, nails, and feet.' And she said one of the tendons of her neck still hurt from the force of the wrench Ruth gave it, holding Barbara's head in her hands to try to subdue her, while Barbara scratched and bit some part of Ruth. To the Foreign Office man, fascinated beyond the call of duty by the details, Barbara had said, 'I just couldn't stand it any longer. She assumed, of course, that

I was part of her organization. I'm sure of that, because after a day or two she said to me. "Oh, come off it. Suzi's told me you're one of us" – or something to that effect. Then, day after day, I had to pretend to be in sympathy or at least refrain from speaking my mind. So it came to a fight. . . .'

In the retrospect of a few weeks it was curiously more vivid than the reality had been. In her low physical condition at the time Barbara could hardly believe what was going on, and the two weeks passed like an amorphous cloud of cosmic matter interrupted at intervals by specific points of occurrence, small explosions in the spacious night-sky of her boredom. She had no books to read. No one in the house had a book. Freddy had gone away without producing any papers or magazines. Yes, someone in the house had a book. It was in Arabic. Ruth Gardnor told her it was a book of mystical poetry by a Sufi woman mystic of the eighth century. Ruth could read Arabic and translated, 'O Lord, if I worship thee from fear of hell, burn me in hell, and if I worship you in the hope of heaven, reject me from heaven, but if I worship thee for thine own sake then do not withhold thyself from me in thine eternal beauty.'

This was about Thursday, two days after Freddy and Suzi had left. Barbara listened out for Suzi's return. 'Shall I read you some more?' Ruth said.

'No thanks.'

'She's as good as any of the Christian mystics.'

'I know. There's no need to be defensive. All the mystics are much alike to me.'

'So many Catholics won't listen to any other religious writings. It's killing. And the things they swallow themselves. . . .'

This was nothing new to Barbara; ever since her conversion she had met sophisticated women who, on the subject of Catholicism, sneered like French village atheists, and expected to be excused from normal good manners, let alone intelligence, on this one subject. But she thought it worthy of note that Ruth did not doubt she was a Catholic. That Barbara was a half-Jew on a clandestine Christian pilgrimage, Ruth did not for one moment believe. She knew for certain that she had roused the Jordanian authorities' suspicions, and by now she had come to accept that Barbara was genuinely feeling rather weak and by no means feigning her illness.

Ruth was fully convinced that Barbara was part of her spy organization. It was difficult for Barbara, at the time, to piece together exactly what or whom it served, although later, when the episode became a vivid whole in her mind, it was plain that the organization was an Arab nationalist one, communist-affiliated, with headquarters in Cairo.

Now Ruth would say puzzling things as she sat and talked to Barbara. Ruth sat always languidly, with crossed legs and her head leaning back. She had a good, rather raddled, tanned face, long streaked blonde hair and an effortless look of glamour. Somewhere in London Barbara had first met her, years ago, at someone's house, at someone's dinner party – when? where? – just after the war, during the war – no, not during the war or just after, since Barbara did not recall any uniforms at that party. Maybe, though, it just happened there was no one in uniform at that party.

While she listened to Ruth she drank endless grape juice, orange juice, all prepared carefully by hand; by Ruth's kindly hand. 'Rupert and I are fed up with Britain. It's finished. It's become a bloody debating society. Europe is finished. The Jews have finished us off. There's a Jews' world-network, my dear. The American Jews are just plotting to demolish the rest of the world. Even the Kremlin knows that. I met a chap at the Russian Economic Mission the other day, he'd just arrived in Israel. He said he'd yet to find a Jew who was a docker in the Soviet Union. I said, "By God, you'd have to look hard for one who was a docker in the west."'

'What about in Israel?' Suddenly Barbara remembered the party where she had first met Ruth Gardnor with her husband. The night of the dinner party. And the cello: it had been an indifferent performance. Ruth had sat listening. 'The cello,' Ruth had said afterwards, 'is my favourite instrument. It *speaks* to me.' She said to Barbara, 'You know what I mean?' Barbara had said, 'No, I don't.' Now Ruth was speaking again: 'Israel? In Israel they'd have the whole Arab world doing manual labour for them if they could get them. Israel will burn itself out and just become another Levantine state.'

At the time this talk confused Barbara on the point of Ruth's political allegiance. She was accustomed to regard anti-semitism as a note of fascism, not communism. Anyway, it went on day after day, and

Ruth assumed that Barbara was like-minded, as apparently was everyone else connected with the headquarters in Cairo.

In her absence, Barbara fumed and imagined a fight with Ruth, how she would hit and kick her. She jumped from her bed frequently and went into the adjoining wash-room, a small closet with only a shower, no bath. There she would take cold showers and hot showers, many and many times a day, regardless of her weakness.

On no account was she to leave the room. On no account. Freddy had said so. Suzi had said, on no account. Ruth kept saying so. Ruth prepared food of an extremely rare and elaborate order to tempt Barbara. She must have spent all the hours that she did not spend with Barbara on planning, preparing and cooking these meals – chilled exotic soups, veal, chicken or lamb with herb-laden sauces. All for Barbara. They were served on a tray with lace-edged white cloths, for brave Barbara, who, like Ruth, thought Nasser was so marvellous and the nationalist cause so good and so essentially exploitable. 'The Party in Latin America is well aware that the big struggle to come, the final world-struggle, is with the Jews,' said Ruth. Barbara could not eat, her cheeks were sunk when she saw herself in the glass. She wondered if she was going mad, and at times this long thought was indistinguishable from madness.

'How long have you known Freddy Hamilton?' said Ruth.

'Well, I don't really know him at all.'

'He was *here*, you know.'

'Yes. I got a lift from Suzi with him.'

'What was he doing here?'

'Only touring.'

'Are you sure?'

'Yes, quite sure. He's harmless.'

'Don't you think,' said Ruth, 'that Suzi's a bit irresponsible? I mean, bringing him here. It's awfully dangerous.'

'No, I think it's the sort of thing that would put them off the scent if they were at all on the scent.'

'Of course, you realize, we pay those Ramdez people for the use of this house. They're well paid. They ought to protect us.'

Suzi at last returned. Barbara later placed this day as the Saturday of that first week.

'I can't go on like this,' she said to Suzi.

'Only one more week. I'm here for the week-end and Alexandros is here also with me. Sunday night, we return to Jerusalem. But next Saturday, Sunday, I come back to fetch you. Better you should get well and stay in bed the full period that the doctor said. Then the police forget to find you. They already have said you must have left the country.'

Suzi had brought a pile of travel pamphlets, so that Barbara could choose the places she wanted to visit when, a week hence, she would start off with Suzi on the pilgrimage. 'Because,' said Suzi, 'we must have the pilgrimage. This time there is no trouble to anticipate, except you must be dressed still like an Arab woman to prevent trouble.'

'Where are my own clothes?' Barbara said.

'I have them in Jerusalem.'

Barbara was eating quite a lot of cucumber sandwiches. She said, 'I can't eat anything that Ruth Gardnor brings me. I try, but I can't.'

'That woman is crazy. She is now all at once my enemy because I don't join with the nationalist party or this, that, party. We give her the house where she operates, and if they catch her we take the risk for this crime of plot, so what more does she ask of us? She is like a fierce animal to me since I brought here Freddy. Before, she was my friend of the very best. Now she says it's wrong that I bring Alexandros here, and she dislikes that we keep here the girls for the night-clubs. All these things she's afraid of for her secrets which are nothing so very much, according to my father.'

Alexandros paid Barbara a visit, so noisy with greetings and celebration of the long-lost, that various whispers, titters and tripping footsteps at the end of the corridor occurred, whereupon Suzi could be heard chiding in Arabic and French. These were the night-club girls, who were habitually kept out of this side of the house.

Alexandros closed Barbara's door and at Suzi's request kept quieter. He said, 'Mr Hamilton is not so very well.'

'What's the matter?'

'This I can't tell you. But I have heard he is not very well, and perhaps it is sunstroke.'

'Isn't he coming here to Jericho this week-end? He promised to come and see me.'

'No, but I am here with Suzi instead.'

Barbara let herself float on the waves of what was to be. She began to feel stronger on that second Sunday of her illness. She wanted to walk in the cool evening, but Suzi and Alexandros insisted this was dangerous.

'Oh, I don't care about the danger any longer. What have I done? I'm not an Israeli spy.'

'It's dangerous for your health,' said Alexandros. 'For anyone to rise from a bed to walk in the evening is dangerous.'

He seemed to have turned melancholy after talking about Freddy. Later, Suzi came and said to Barbara, 'Freddy is now with his friends the Cartwrights, but he has not sent me a message or nothing. I'm too proud to go there to ask for him. How could I make excuse to call there unless he asks for me?'

'Did he get that piece put in the Israeli newspaper as he promised?'

'Piece?'

'To say I'd changed my mind about coming to Jordan.'

'I haven't heard of it. No, I don't think so.'

'It doesn't matter, of course.' Barbara discerned that Suzi was personally troubled about Freddy's ignoring her since his return to Jordan.

Suzi said, 'I left him at the Via Dolorosa last Tuesday and he walked the rest of the way. He was O.K. then, you know. Alexandros says he's sick, also occupied with affairs; but he could remember to write a note. He can get a letter through the diplomatic courier, easy. He hasn't got the scarlet fever, Alexandros says. Now I don't want Alexandros to see so much why I'm sad about Freddy. Maybe Freddy will leave a message for me at my home in Jerusalem when I return tonight.'

Barbara thought, he's taken fright. Freddy must have decided to withdraw from the tangle. But, she thought, he wouldn't do it this way. He wouldn't do just nothing. Something must be wrong, that's all.

But Suzi, to cheer up the atmosphere, was already recommending the route of their pilgrimage the following week.

They did get away the following week, but not before Barbara amazed herself by throwing at Ruth Gardnor a clock and a vase. Ruth was even more amazed. She was carrying a wireless set with large earphones of the early vintage, which she had managed very cleverly to piece together from two separate sets, one old and one new; this was for Barbara's benefit, for Suzi had not wanted her to draw undue attention to her presence by the sound of a wireless in her room. Barbara threw these objects at Ruth, then in a frenzy leapt upon the woman and battered her head with the disconnected earphones of the wireless. Ruth kept saying, 'My God, please Barbara, quiet! Quiet, Barbara, please – quiet!' Barbara scratched. Every obscene word that she had ever heard and (what was so strange) never heard, Barbara pelted forth at Ruth Gardnor. Ruth took Barbara's head in her hands and wrenched it. It took them seven minutes to wear themselves out. Ruth was wounded with a cut on the forehead and a deep scratch on her chin. Barbara had some bruises that came up later, and her neck ached for weeks. It was something like the rehearsal that had been going on in her mind for ten days. Over and over again, when Ruth in her kindness had brought her some tempting thing and tried to wheedle and coax, very sweetly – over and over again – tried to coax, then sat to talk confidentially about the ideals that she served and those that she felt by instinct only, then Barbara had listened and not argued. Over and over again Barbara had rehearsed the fight, and it had amazingly taken place. Ruth was frightened. She sobbed softly and said, 'How ill you are! Oh, God, and I've no one here to help me.'

Barbara got back to bed, spent out. She said nothing, only listening still in memory to the pounding waves of Ruth's chatter, day after day. Nasser is marvellous. Really, let's face it, Hitler had the right idea. Ten days of Ruth's chatter. It's a network on a world scale. The Jews. They've got us in a net. If you knew how the banking system worked, you'd realize. . . . Would you like to sleep now? Would you like to sit up? I've got to go out for a while, do you mind? But now Ruth was only sobbing in the chair, with blood on her face. Barbara lay and watched her through slit eyes and heard her murmur, 'Oh, I wish I'd someone to help me!' Then Ruth said, 'Have you been told to do this to me?' Barbara said nothing. Ruth said, 'Oh God! Don't they trust me? What have I done? Rupert will have to come over – I can't wait on and on.'

Barbara said, 'Yes, you'll let them down, all right.' She said this out of the dark, but meant it decidedly for a thrust, which it turned out to be. Ruth looked cornered. She said, 'I see.'

Barbara had no idea how they would go on for the rest of the week. This was eight o'clock on Thursday morning. Ruth picked up all the fragments of clock, wireless sets, and vase. Suzi was to come on Saturday or Sunday. Ruth went away after a while, and Barbara fell into a moaning exhaustion, and finally a deep sleep such as she had not enjoyed since her arrival.

She woke in the afternoon when she heard a whistling scrape on the front door of the house, and a car drew up. Shortly afterwards, Ruth came in with tea. Barbara was horrified: Ruth was haggard and patched with small pieces of plaster; she was frantic with worry.

She said to Barbara, 'Listen – don't please, please, make any more fuss, more noise. Joe Ramdez has come again with his tourist woman. If you're caught, I'll be in trouble. H.Q. will blame me. How do you feel?'

Barbara felt like an animal. She wanted to ask, honestly, 'Who are H.Q.?' But she kept silent. Suzi had said on her last visit, 'It's lucky you have none of your own clothes, she has noticed only the garment of Kyra hung up in the press, and this makes her sure that you are a spy with her organization. . . . She was foolish to let you know of her activities for this organization. But she has told, not I.'

'Which organization?'

'I don't know, I don't ask. To tell every Arab organization would take a day, if I should tell you the list. But you must keep quiet about this to your friends, or you make trouble for me. She is only a mad woman.'

'You make trouble for me,' said every face in Barbara's crowded dreams. Later, when the Foreign Office man came to visit her in Israel, there was no point in keeping quiet. Not only had they seen Freddy the day before, but she had seen Abdul that morning. He had come straight up to her room, and she found him at the door, beaming with some extra pleasure.

He took a telegram from his pocket. 'Suzi's safe,' he said. 'Suzi is in Athens.'

'In Athens? I didn't know she was in danger.'

'The police put her under arrest when they broke into the house at Jericho to find Mrs Gardnor. They had to take someone in custody, so they took Suzi.'

'How did she get away? Did they let her go?'

'Suzi is a rich woman.'

'Of course, Miss Vaughan,' said the young man from the Foreign Office, who was her next caller that day, 'we've got Gardnor. But his wife has got away. She's probably in Cairo. Have you any idea –?'

'I'm afraid I can't help you much,' Barbara said in a weak-minded way. 'It was rather a nightmare until, of course, we got off on our pilgrimage at last. The pilgrimage was all right.'

'All these spy renegades lead nightmare lives,' he said. 'Odd people.'

'I'm a bit tired,' Barbara said. 'Do you mind if we leave off now?' She passed her hand up and down the side of her neck. He was a nice young man but he made her feel neurotic.

'Of course, of course. I'm sorry. It must have been an ordeal, that return to Israel. Quite a risk. You might have caused us some trouble, you know.'

'You make trouble for me,' said all the voices still, in her dreams.

'I'm expecting a telephone call from Rome,' Barbara said. To hell with their questions. One had a private life to lead.

The young man was leaving. He said, 'Will you spare me about twenty minutes tomorrow – a few more things.'

'Well, yes. But I'm afraid I won't be able to help you much on your side. Maybe one of your men in Jordan could talk nicely to Suzi Ramdez, the travel agent. She could tell you more than I could.'

'They've got Suzi Ramdez, I'm afraid.'

'Who have got Suzi?'

'The Jordan police have picked her up. They're very zealous when they get moving, but they usually move too late. Anyway, I'm glad they didn't get you.'

She did not give him Abdul's news. She said, 'Have they really got Suzi? Are you sure?'

'Of course. Certainly. We're pretty alert, you know, although we don't look it.' Yes, and Suzi was in Athens.

'Will she go on trial? She wasn't really involved.'

'One never knows what will happen in these political cases. But I'm sure she was involved with everything. Everyone out here's involved with everything.'

Oh, go away, she thought. Keep nice and safe. Take no risks. Look both ways and always brush your teeth.

He said, 'I'll look in tomorrow, then. It's only to check a few things. We want to be on the safe side.'

'One more day shut up in that room,' said Barbara, 'and I would have died of claustrophobia and frustration.' – She was sitting beside Suzi in the car, dressed in her Arab clothes.

'Or perhaps murdered Ruth Gardnor.' And slowly, under her veil, she was rubbing ointment into the strained tendon of her neck. They were driving through the bare Judaean hills, that wilderness of John the Baptist, who was a voice crying there, 'Prepare the way of the Lord.' She thought, it was a voice crying from the hill-top that is meant by a voice crying in the wilderness, for she had previously always thought of that phrase as a piece of delicate rhetoric, signifying a lonely, unprevailing plaint of a wandering prophet. But it looked to Barbara that this voice in the wilderness must have been a high crag-top proclamation, good, loud and frightening, for everyone in the valleys to hear, echoing from peak to peak.

They had left the house at Jericho the day before, Sunday, at nightfall. She had followed Suzi out into the sweet air and walked to the car, two weeks after she had arrived. Their depature had been perfectly simple, for Ruth had again gone to Amman for the week-end and Joe Ramdez had left with Ricky on Friday, that day when Barbara had wandered into his room and found him in bed with Ricky. She had been all that night pacing herself to exhaustion, up and down and round her room. At two in the morning she had taken a warm shower in the small cubicle adjoining her bedroom. If only, she thought, I could lie for a long time in a warm bath, it would soothe away the irritation of Ruth Gardnor. But she turned on the shower which creaked as it sprayed. She had gone back to bed, and tried, as a spiritual exercise, to be grateful for her safety in this room and her recovery to the extent that her energy now seemed nearly to burst her skin open. But she could only tremble with anger; Ruth would come in at seven in the morning with a tray of coffee, meekly terrified of Barbara after the fight, and very anxious to propitiate her against some power she obviously suspected Barbara to hold over her, and against the eventuality of trouble. This was quite clear, although Barbara was in no way informed what sort of power Ruth feared, except that it was to do with the spy business. And Barbara fumed against Ruth's totally

womanly solicitude combined with her totally repugnant human theories, and against the total misunderstanding. She lay and tried to feel
grateful, but even her capacity for gratitude felt gagged; she was the
half-witted mute she had undertaken to be when she first set out with
Suzi in disguise.

And so she had leapt from her bed again, convulsively, and taken
another shower, a cold one. Her neck was painful. Then she had
walked up and down the room till dawn.

Light footsteps outside her window: this was not unusual. Several
times during the two weeks Barbara had heard these morning footsteps and, peering out, had seen a tall girl sidling along the wall of the
house, pausing at every few steps as if to make sure she had not been
heard. The girl had passed Barbara's window and turned the corner
of the house. The first time, she had been wearing a shirt with blue
jeans. She had Asiatic features with dark, lank hair. On the next occasion that Barbara had seen her, she had at first thought this was a
different girl, for she was wearing a short, pink organdie dance-dress
and was barefooted, carrying high-heeled gold sandals, but Barbara
recognized the girl's features as she looked round her before turning
the corner. On subsequent mornings the girl was always dressed in
her pink frills, but once Barbara was puzzled by a matted pile of
blonde hair until the girl turned her face enough to show that she was
the same girl wearing a theatrical wig. Obviously, she was returning
from a secret rendezvous.

Barbara had asked no questions about the occupants of the house,
either of Ruth Gardnor or Suzi. The girl did not look like a political
prisoner. But occasional ripples of talk or a shrill quarrel-burst came
through an open window from the opposite end of the large house,
perhaps when the breeze happened to blow in a certain direction; and
once Suzi had referred to 'the girls' without explanation; and so
Barbara was certain there were a number of girls in the house, and
suspected they were enclosed under some sort of supervision for
some purpose.

All through those weeks at the house in Jericho Barbara had been
weaving plots to run away and take refuge at the British Embassy in
Amman, or with Harry's friend at the American Embassy. But with
only the Arab woman's clothes to wear there was scarcely any chance
of her being able to stop a car for a lift, or of getting near to the town

of Jericho, or of reaching a telephone. It was almost certain that she would have been picked up by the police. A bicycle . . . she longed to steal a bicycle. She could hear bicycle wheels occasionally approaching the house. How did one ride a bicycle in long clothes? It could be done. Cars came and went. She could steal a car. Another week and perhaps this is what she would have done. Who could tell what would have happened if her imprisonment at Jericho had lasted another week, or another day? There would have been no pilgrimage. She would not have been a jolly good sport, but merely someone who made trouble for everybody. Afterwards, she had reason to feel fairly certain that if she had tried to get away she would have fallen into danger or been caused to disappear.

But on that last Friday in the house after the troubled night of creaking shower-baths and frantic thoughts, on that early morning when she once more saw the fly-by-night girl creeping back from her enterprise, the urge pressed on her at least to leave the house and stand for a few moments breathing under the sky. She put on the cotton kimono that Suzi had lent her and left her room. She went on tip-toe along the corridor where she knew a door led to the central area of the house, which in turn led up to the courtyard. There she breathed under the sky and watched the misty pink of dawn on the cliff-tops of the Judaean desert in the distance. Only a well and a palm-tree kept her company in the courtyard. She walked once round the large, spreading house, turning corner after corner, keeping near to the wall, and felt weak from the walk. She heard a sound as she turned into the courtyard and saw an old Arab man with a sack over his shoulder approaching the main door to deliver provisions. He had not seen Barbara. She turned back and tried another door, which was locked. She tried another, which was open and which led to a long corridor similar to that where her room was. She walked to the end, hearing from the various rooms on either side the sound of sleepers and of people stirring themselves to rise from bed. She found a door at the end of the corridor, and in the hope that it would lead to Suzi's part of the house, opened it. The window curtains were drawn and streaks of pink dawn that came through the window at the sides of the curtains and at their points of meeting, enlightened a huge bed. A man and a woman lay sleeping. The woman was Ricky. The man was a dark-skinned, large-faced Semite, an Arab with a mane of grey hair. Barbara peered in the half-light of the room and definitely saw Ricky. It was Ricky with her head thrown back in sleep, a profile on the pillow, her arms outspread so that one of them lay limply across the man's body. Barbara had not yet made another movement since opening the door, but now the man sprang up, wide awake. He seemed enormous, his legs beneath a long white shirt leaping from the bed. Barbara fled back along the corridor and out to the court-yard, pursued by the man, who shouted furiously at her in Arabic, French, English, and some other language. She was not listening. She ran to the front door where Latifa, smelling strongly from her night's sleep, was hauling into the house the sack which the old man had brought. Barbara pushed past her, and as she sped through the entrance chamber and along the passage to her room, she heard behind her a roar and rush of abusive vowels from the doorway against Latifa. Barbara then lay on her bed, worn out. She had lost one of her sandals and her foot had been cut somewhere on the wild run. In about twenty minutes, after she had heard many unusual noises, Ruth Gardnor came in, wearing her dressing-gown. Ruth said, 'Oh, you shouldn't have done that, Barbara. You know I'm responsible for you, I'll be held responsible if anything happens to you. They'll never trust me again.'

'I must be a hell of an important agent,' said Barbara, not caring, at that moment, what happened to her.

'Suzi's told me,' said Ruth. 'So there's no use pretending.'

'Told you what? Told you what? Suzi tells everyone something different.'

'Keep quiet, oh, please do.'

I must be even more of a hell of an important Cairo agent, thought Barbara, than I guessed I was. She was feeling easier, though. The storm was over. She said, 'I've hurt my foot,' and let Ruth Gardnor bathe it and fuss over it with bits of plaster.

Barbara said, 'Who is that man?'

'Joe Ramdez. Fortunately, he thinks you are a whore with scarlet fever.'

Barbara said, 'I'm hungry.'

Ruth disappeared to fetch her some breakfast, and when she returned with a large loaded tray, Barbara said, 'I don't want any-thing. I want to sleep.'

Ruth started to cry and wept for a long time. She said, 'It isn't only that I've got to look after you. I've become so fond of you. I'm genuinely fond of you, I really am. I admire your courage tremendously and what you're doing for us. . . . And you won't even give me a kind look.'

'I need eyebrow tweezers,' said Barbara. 'Find a pair, please.'

'What for? What for?'

'For my eyebrows.'

Suzi had arrived early on Sunday and they were off at last. Suzi's plans for the week to come were well-made in so far as they did not go wrong, although, in the theory of the layout, nothing should have gone right.

'First,' said Suzi, 'you do not pay me for all this touring and all this schemes and trouble to me that you've been. You pay my brother Abdul on the Israeli territory, when you return by means that we have planned for you. Poor Abdul, he needs this money. But one time we have lost big money in sending it across to him. Money is a temptation to kill. Never will I give Abdul money to take over with him. An Arab soldier even might kill and take, and report afterwards.'

'Does he come over here then?'

'Oh, yes, sometimes Abdul comes. He will come next Sunday and return you to Israel with him. He knows you're with me, because I've sent a message by a friend of his, Mendel, a Jew who I spoke to at the Mass in the Holy Sepulchre when you were taken sick. You were by my side that time.'

It was all one to Barbara how a Jew called Mendel had been at Mass in the Holy Sepulchre. She did not think, now, of unpicking knots, for there was some definite purpose in the air about her, liberated as she was under the black clothes with the landscape flying past the car. Knots were not necessarily created to be untied. Questions were things that sufficed in their still beauty, answering themselves. What am I doing here on a pilgrimage, after so much involvement? Because I am what I am. Suzi said, 'You would not have come to Jordan, perhaps, if you knew first what would happen and how it would bring you the fever. Now your relatives are anxious for you, but Abdul very soon tells them news by secret messages that you are safe.'

'If one knew everything that was going to happen one would never do a thing,' Barbara said.

'Abdul will give you a great bill for the pilgrimage. Freddy does not pay nothing so far, and he keeps far from me.'

Suzi was melancholy about Freddy's desertion. Barbara tried not to mention him very much, so greatly had Suzi taken to him, and so unhappy was she about his silence.

They entertained each other with stories from their lives. Barbara described bits of her love-affair with Harry Clegg, and her life before that, how it now seemed that she had been living like a nun without the intensity and reality of a nun's life. 'It was like going about in disguise,' she said. 'Although I didn't know it at the time, I was no more a celibate type of woman than at the moment, under these clothes, I am your servant Kyra.'

'If you didn't fall in love with Harry that time, you would remain a spinster like me,' Suzi said.

'It's better to be a spinster like you and have lovers that you can give some actual love to, than have shadows in your heart of men that you don't know, and hate them.'

'Many women, not spinsters, do like this.'

'Yes, and men too.'

Still, now and then, Suzi fell gloomy about Freddy's desertion. She said, 'Alexandros has guessed that I had love with Freddy, but he's too delicate to judge me for it. He's a Catholic Arab and can have one wife only; he does not possess me. Freddy did not pay me for his lodging, nor nothing.' Whenever Suzi came to the depth of her disappointment with Freddy she always fell back on the question of his failure to pay the bill. It was a way of kicking the piece of furniture into which one had bumped in the dark and hurt one's leg; and it was easier for her to accuse him about money than say nothing. Barbara said, 'I'll pay Freddy's share to Abdul.' 'That's not the point,' said Suzi. Barbara knew it was not the point. Love, love-affairs, men and women and true-life stories formed the daily entertainment and talk of their week's travelling. Barbara said, 'I'm quite sure Freddy isn't well.' And a few days later, when they had chewed it all over again, Barbara said, 'It may be that he wasn't really well that week-end, for he was rather different from his normal self. But I never noticed him so happy before.'

All the nights of the pilgrimage were spent under strange roofs, off

the main tracks, in the desert villages of the Transjordan. The first
night, Suzi drove straight to Madaba and, leaving the car outside the
Orthodox church there, led Barbara in the moonlight among the
poor, low-built houses that formed themselves into streets, part-
streets, and no streets. Three small boys joined them silently. The
paths were stony and steep. The children stared at Barbara from time
to time, as if discerning, without being able to place the cause, that
she was no Arab woman. They came to a house and Suzi stopped. She
spoke to the boys, who disappeared together in another direction.
Suzi murmured, 'They are gone to bring a doctor for you. I know
these people and arrange this last week with them, so you need not
fear. This is Transjordan country, not Palestine, and here they are
more real Arabs that understand arrangements. Here is the house
where Abdul was born. You don't speak, just follow.'

'I feel all right, Suzi. Only tired. I don't really need a doctor.'

'I like a doctor to see you, now, to be O.K. for the pilgrimage.'

'You're kind.'

'Don't speak.'

It was difficult, anyway, to express gratitude to Suzi. She said, 'You
pay to Abdul the expenses. All arrangements with everyone is costing
me money.'

'Yes, but I mean –'

'I do it for Alexandros, not Freddy.' She had opened the door to a
long room lit by an oil lamp at the far end. She stood on the threshold and listened for a moment. 'Also,' she whispered, 'I do these
things for you as you are more worth than fifty of Miss Rickward.'
And she led the way along the room, which now produced three
arches on either side and was paved with dusty, broken mosaic
designs. It was obviously an ancient and priceless hovel, one of many
that stood unselfconsciously haphazard among the dilapidated buildings of the present century in the towns and villages where Barbara
spent the nights of the pilgrimage. And as she followed, she saw,
within alcoves leading off these arches on either side, many sleeping
or merely reclining women, their clothes hung on pegs all round the
walls. No one stirred or spoke. Barbara followed Suzi. At the blank
end of the room a passage now appeared, turning off to the right.
They went along it, descended some of the winding stone stairs, and
were in a lamp-lit cellar furnished with a large bare mattress on a

wooden base, a tall water-jug on a table with a small water-jug. A thin
film of dark sand covered the floor. Suzi said, 'Here we sleep with our
clothes on in case of damp. This was a better house when Abdul was
born. He doesn't remember it, but he remembers often the other
house where they took him the next year, where I was born. It is in
Palestine. My father was only a teacher then.' She took Barbara's arm
and showed her a small door which might lead to a cupboard, but
when opened, it gave off a strong smell of disinfectant. Suzi brought
close the oil lamp and laughed. 'This is lady's toilet.' There was a hole
in the earthy floor. 'You pour water down from the big jug when you
use. This is Arabian Nights' Entertainment,' said Suzi.

It was unforgettable. The whole week was unforgettable, and Suzi
most of all. She wondered, later, how it was that Freddy had forgotten Suzi Ramdez. And, of course, the question answered itself: she
had been too memorable to remember.

'That Suzi Ramdez woman,' said the Foreign Office man, when he
spoke again to Barbara, '. . . I wish we'd had a chance to talk to her.
But of course the Jordan police have got her. There's no news. She's
probably been shot.'

'I doubt it,' was all Barbara said.

'Why?'

'Well, she isn't the type to be shot easily.'

'Oh, you don't know what they're like, Miss Vaughan. This is the
East, you know.'

Well, let him find out that Suzi was in Athens. Let them find out
themselves, if they wanted to track her down for questioning and
make trouble for her in Athens. . . . You make trouble for me.

'Does Freddy Hamilton know she was arrested?'

'Oh, yes. At least, we've told him everything that's happened. He
doesn't recall much about her. Of course, she was only a guide. They
usually don't have women guides, but as you got into these absurd
difficulties, you know, of course, well . . . You were lucky to find a
travel agent who'd take care of you, don't you think?'

'It led to your getting your information.'

'Oh, yes, we're thankful for that. I don't mean . . . but there might
have been trouble.'

*

He was a young tall doctor carrying a smart leather case, newly qualified in Cairo. He was dressed in a black suit with his shirt collar and
cuffs gleaming white as they caught the light from the smoky lamp.
His shoes, shuffling on the sandy floor, were the only parts of his
appearance that caught the dust of the place. His brown face and
glossy dark hair shone with newly qualified immaculateness. He told
her, in good English, that he was newly graduated from the
University of Cairo. He asked no questions but those pertaining to
her fever and the treatment she had received, her past illnesses, and
how she felt now. He told her this was his first job and he was
employed by the Jordanian Government at a clinic. Barbara lay on
the mattress and did not respond to this information, as she had done
at first, with so much as an 'Oh, really?' or a 'That must be very interesting.' Suzi, squatting in the gloom with a cigarette in her hand, said
immediately, 'He isn't a government officer now with you, Barbara.'

Barbara smiled, whereupon the doctor, neatly holding up in
one hand a hypodermic needle to gauge some stuff he was going to
inject into her, and, with a white cloth held in the other, at the same
time stood back, and carefully, in the brightest patch of light that
fell on the floor, made a movement with a toe of his new shoes. It was
a slow movement, with a practised quality. The movement was
plainly intended to draw Barbara's attention to its significance.
Barbara did not know what it signified. The doctor watched her face.
Then he stood further back. She looked at him, then at the floor, and
saw that it was not the movement of his foot but the mark he had
traced in the dust that he wanted her to notice. It was the simple
shape of a fish. When he saw her recognition, he went on with his
business, gave her the injection, wiped the needle, packed it away
carefully in his new case, gave her some pills, and directed her when
to take them. He then told Suzi that Barbara should not travel more
than four hours a day for the next week, but should lie down and
sleep as much as possible, shook hands with Barbara, wished her a
pleasant journey, said in reply to her thanks that it had been a pleasure, and departed.

'What is this dance he does on the floor for you?' said Suzi, who
had not seen the mark he had traced.

Barbara pointed it out. 'It's a Christian symbol. The very early
Christians under the first persecution used to trace the shape of a fish

in the sand as a sign of recognition to each other. Then they would quickly obliterate it.'

'Why couldn't he say? The Arab makes ceremony of every little thing. We must obliterate this mark.'

'No, leave it, it's beautiful.'

'Then, in the morning, we obliterate. For the poor people of this house might be frightened to see it. The poor always remember signs for thousands of years, and they mix all things in their minds with magic and great fear and horrible trouble. It's God's blame.'

'Wipe it out now, then. It was meant to be seen and remembered.'

Suzi shuffled the sand into shapelessness and said, 'I can eat a camel now as I'm feeling empty. How are you?'

'Very hungry.'

'There is chicken, nothing special, but I bring it anyway. There is a little bit whisky also that I ordered for me here; it's hidden in a secret place as these poor people don't understand whisky, and anyway it's against my religion, too.'

The actual sites that they visited could have been covered in three days had they been able to go by direct routes. But each journey was a brief, cross-country run between the places of pilgrimage and Suzi's houses of refuge. The hours of their travels were mostly marked off by the calls to prayer from all corners of the world, so that the noon call corresponded with their return journey, for they set off early to merge, as far as possible, with the morning crowds at the shrines and churches.

It was a new experience to Suzi, so she said, to go with a pilgrim from England or America who was not in a state of religion all the way and who did not talk all the time of 'prayers and self-sacrifices and charity. Or else, when you have two Catholics, they are talking of Our Lady and the Rosary and Mass for St Peter, and the Novena for St Holy Ghost and St Anthony.'

'I think they are probably sincere,' Barbara said. 'But they do seem to make a career of it.'

'Are you sincere in these devotions, when you go to them talking and laughing with me so much about love-affairs and men and sex? Oh, Barbara, I don't meant that you're not sincere, as I like it so much when everything can be said.'

'Well, either religious faith penetrates everything in life or it doesn't. There are some experiences that seem to make nonsense of all separations of sacred from profane – they seem childish. Either the whole of life is unified under God or everything falls apart. Sex is child's play in the argument.' She was thinking of the Eichmann trial, and was aware that there were other events too, which had rolled away the stone that revealed an empty hole in the earth, that led to a bottomless pit. So that people drew back quickly and looked elsewhere for reality, and found it, and made decisions, in the way that she had decided to get married, anyway.

'What is profane?' Suzi said.

'Your sexy conversation.'

'No, yours. I never had such a sexy pilgrim. But I see what you say of the child's play is true. I hate the man in bed who plays at it like he conducts the military band for King Hussein to review the soldiers.'

At Bethlehem, at the Garden of Gethsemane, at the Basilica of the Agony, Barbara knelt for only a few moments and very quickly left, following Suzi up the hewn stairways of caves and crypts.

'What a lot of trouble for such a small moment, here and there,' Suzi said.

'It's an act of presence,' Barbara said, 'as when you visit a bereaved friend and there's nothing to say. The whole point is, that a meeting has materialized.' They stood on the cliff-edge outside the Church of St Peter in Gallicantu and looked across the valley into Israel, where men were working in the fields.

Suzi said, 'We're not being followed, so I know we're safe. Abdul is to take you by the Potter's Field. We should be there by noon on Sunday. You leave with him on Sunday night or Monday before the dawn.'

Barbara was feeling healthier and fuller. She said, 'The fatter I get, the more the thought of crossing the border frightens me. Probably because there's more life to lose in a fat body than a thin one.'

'You talk so silly. Abdul doesn't get caught never.'

That day on the return to the small room in the village near Bethany where they had spent the previous night, and were again to stay, they passed the steep turning off the high road where the Tomb of Lazarus stood open-mouthed by the roadside. They had already visited the place, but Barbara said, 'Let's stop again for a moment.'

She followed Suzi down the rocky path, towards the entrance to the tomb, where two or three Europeans were gathered, and was meanwhile watching a laughing young Arab boy; he was trying to sell something to an American couple who were taking an interest in him. He was offering a simple net sling, and kept repeating, 'The same that David killed Goli-att. Made like the same.' He put a stone in the sling and whizzed it beautifully, far into the air and out across the rooftops. At the passing sound of this rapid-flung object, another woman turned to see what it was. The woman was Ricky. Barbara was less surprised than she might have been, and now realized that she had been expecting, at the back of her mind, to see her, and had been looking out for her across the country as she rode with Suzi; she had even been watching for Ricky on the scrub plains, amongst the shaggy Bedouin and the lean, quivering camels, so obscure had been her watchfulness.

Barbara had been following Suzi to the tomb with automatic steps and now found that she had disappeared. Ricky glanced towards Barbara only as part of the passing scene. Barbara, behind her veil, her lips shut tight against conversation, looked about her and, a short way behind, saw Suzi's head protrude and her eyes beckon from a low house doorway. Barbara went fairly slowly towards the door, stooped, and entered. There, Suzi was handing out money to a large dark woman and a child of tough honey-coloured skin and flaxen hair, one of those chance relics of the late Occupation. Suzi whispered, 'I saw her in time. She must be in the car with those Americans. I think she still looks for you.'

Eventually, the small party left and drove away. Barbara, feeling sick, went and peered down to the musty tomb, descended a few of the steps, breathed the emptiness of earth, but did not follow Suzi, who always thought this particular tomb was fun to go right down into. She liked to frighten herself, she said.

This was the last time Barbara ever saw Ricky. It was the only danger-point of their journey. The police did not trouble them. Tourists and the population passed them on the road, in cars, and occasionally a handsome farming Arab, tall with billowing robes, paced along at the side of the road, his eyes fixed, even by daylight, on the stars.

'They've stopped looking for you here,' Suzi said, 'as I have told so many people you go away to Rome by Saudi Arabia.'

Barbara already knew that Harry had been told she was no longer in Jordan. Barbara had at first objected to this. She had hoped Suzi would get a cable or a telephone call to him through Abdul in Israel, to tell him where she was. But Suzi had said, 'No, he naturally would then come and find you. He might then get in touch with his friend at the American Embassy or with the British Embassy, and it would be an official business to deport you and so forth. Once you have started this you better go on and be that jolly good sport for Freddy. And you have to be a jolly good sport to pay his money for his trip that he owes the firm Ramdez.'

On the way to some Graeco-Roman ruins Suzi told Barbara that the first true love of her life was Abdul, whose story she told, and whose orange groves she explained.

Another time, on the way to see some lovely Arab palaces and Crusader forts far inside the Transjordan, Barbara told Suzi how she recalled her first meeting with Ruth Gardnor and her husband seven years ago in London. There had been nothing special to remember them by, they were guests at a private dinner party in London, and so had Barbara been. She had not spoken much to them. But she remembered the party, indeed she remembered every guest there, because it was at that party she had played the cello for the last time. That was how she remembered having first met Ruth Gardnor. Once or twice after that she had come across her, but that diner party, a good-looking affair, was the meeting she distinctly remembered.

'You play the cello?' said Suzi.

'No, not now. Not any more.'

'You should continue. Music is beautiful. I learned piano but gave up at thirteen. You play good?'

'I was thought to be a promising cellist,' Barbara said.

'Not everyone can be the best. You should continue.'

'No, I went to teach English about that time, at Ricky's school. I had already decided to give up the cello when I played at that party where I first met Ruth Gardnor.'

'That woman is not good in her head,' Suzi said. 'She gets the sack from Cairo, I think. I'm sorry for that. I told her you were their top agent, and I made her messenger swear also to it. She believed it.'

'I know she did. And how did you make her messenger swear?'

'Nothing. His child is needing treatment in hospital, so I sign a document that he's a refugee from Palestine, then his child gets hospital treatment through UNRWA. I do this for many poor Arabs. Only refugees get big treatments free. So I sign, and he swears.'

On the way into Jerusalem, to the Holy Sepulchre, and at last to the Potter's Field, they talked in the car and were silent outside, and talked when they drove on again.

She said, 'I'm afraid. Really frightened.'

Abdul said, 'Why? There is no fear in me, why should you fear? I harness myself to the cart and I take it down a hill and up a hill, and already you are in Israel. Ten, fifteen minutes you are in the cart among the sandals. Then I stamp these sandals with a marker that reads "Made in Israel" and you also I stamp with this, and sell you back to your family for great profit.'

They were to move off in the early morning mist, for there was a dangerous full moon that night. Abdul looked out over the hills and fields of Palestine under the moon. He said, 'It's beautiful but I'm sick of this beauty, as it gives me no admiration in return and no nourishment for my soul in recognition of the worship I give to the land. Very soon I'm going to take a certain one of my friends who is in business with me, and we go together to Tangier and start a café. We have the plan. He is sick, too, of the beauty, although he is a Jew and has some chances in Israel.'

She was too sick with fear to reply. She was wearing her own clothes again and felt vulnerable. She had slept most of the afternoon, since Suzi's departure, in the same upper room near the Potter's Field from which she had set out. Her suitcase was there. Abdul had come to her room at six, smiling, and she thought for a moment she was already back in Israel since she had only seen him there.

Abdul said, 'Take everything small that you value from the suitcase, for you won't see it again. We give your clothes to the poor.'

He said they had better leave the house in a few hours' time and start preparing for the move at dawn, when the mists would fall. He said they could not sleep in the house that night, but must wait in a field.

She said then that she was frightened. He said there would soon be no time for her to feel frightened. They must go and prepare. Meanwhile they ate bread and cheese and drank mint-flavoured tea

in the empty kitchen below, where Freddy had once been to breakfast. Abdul made up some marijuana cigarettes and gave one to
Barbara. 'It will make you feel good and take away fear. Have you
smoked this before?'

'No.'

'It's nothing so much.' He showed her how to smoke it.

She said, after a while, 'I don't feel the slightest effect.'

'First time is never an effect. Two has the effect.'

She smoked another while Abdul talked. He said he would like to
play the guitar and sing, but there was no guitar, and singing or sound
was not wise on this night.

She said she felt sick, either from fear or the marijuana or the tea.

'Smoke to the end and the sickness will go. The reason I would like
to play the guitar and sing a great song is that I have just seen my
father. I see him once, twice a year. The reason I like to sing when I
have just seen him, Miss Vaughan, is that I no longer have to see him
soon. I have seen him and it's in the past tense. You shouldn't think
I hate my father. I say only that I sing when I leave him.'

She said, 'It's having no effect whatsoever.'

'Oh yes. You are red around the eyes. That is the first sign of an
effect. Your friend, Mr Hamilton, is not well. I like Mr Hamilton,
he's my friend, too.'

'What's wrong with him?'

'He has lost a piece of his memory. Some believe this, some don't.
I believe it.'

'Is he at the hotel?'

'No, he's now here in Jordan with his friends, Mr and Mrs
Cartwright. The doctor has made him stay there. Also, his friends of
the British Legation are asking themselves what he has done with his
memory. They are friends to him when he is all right to go punctual
to the job, but when he has lost his way for a time they suspect and
inquire. I hear all these things, Miss Vaughan. And he is also asking
for you. Soon we will tell him all is well. Tomorrow we send by signal
a message that you are found in Israel.'

They were among the cool grass under the moon. Barbara dozed and
woke. Abdul spoke to her when she moved, in case she should cry out
in waking. He said, 'It's all ready. You climb in when I tell you.'

'When?'

'Two more hours. Try to speak to me in case I catch your fear.' He was looking across the field as he spoke, and she now saw, where he was looking, the armed border patrol, two men moving in their direction; they halted at a certain point, and returned along the border-line.

She said, 'Are there any letters at the hotel for me, do you know?'

'I haven't asked this. Soon you will be there. A great comfortable car is waiting for us and soon you will be in your hotel. But now I remember – you know Dr Ephraim the archaeologist?'

'Saul Ephraim? – Yes.'

'He knows of your return and said he would not wire or phone to your husband until you arrive safe, in case of interception by the Arabs.'

'I'm not married yet.'

'Your husband that is to become.' Abdul started to ask many questions about her marriage, and how she could get this marriage that her lover had been to Rome to arrange. She thought, in passing, that he was unusually interested in the affair, but he was not objectionably so; and he explained that as he had once become a Roman Catholic, while a student in Cairo, he was concerned about these things. He said, 'I am not now a believer. I have no faith. I try to do good a little bit, that's all.'

She said, 'I've got a lot of faith. It's all I've got. I don't do good, very much, somehow. I'm not cut out for it.'

He asked again the details of the marriage. She said, 'I doubt if he'll get an annulment. It's very unlikely. I'll marry him outside the Church.'

'That's all right, anyhow.'

'Maybe. It remains to be seen.'

'We go to the cart now. The dawn is coming soon, Monday morning blues. You will climb into the cart and lie still. Keep your head low, low, and never look up till I tell you. Come now.'

The day before the news from Harrogate was brought to the Cartwright's house that Freddy's mother had been stabbed to death by a mad old servant, Miss Bennett, Joanna was up very early and was out looking at her wild-flower garden. It was a warm, misty morning.

The Cartwrights were usually up early on week-days so that they could get in a few busy hours at their hobbies and favourite occupations before going off to their busy clinic. Like most childless couples they were happiest when organized and at it all day. Monday mornings, without their quite realizing it, were specially early-risen and active, as if to atone for their comparatively lazy Sunday.

It was Monday morning, the day before the men from the consulate came with the news for Freddy. Freddy was very much on their hands now, and both Joanna and Matt Cartwright had decided to carry on as far as possible as if nothing had gone wrong with him. However, at five in the morning, Joanna found him already out in the garden, walking up and down with a hand to his head, and his head bent.

'Freddy, darling, aren't you feeling well?'

'Oh, it's you, Joanna.'

'You needn't have got up so early, Freddy. I wish you'd take breakfast in bed.'

'I couldn't sleep, really. I'm afraid that puppet show set me thinking again. Joanna, you know I keep thinking of –'

Joanna knew he would say 'bloodshed', which he did. The previous night she had shown her latest puppet acquisition, newly arrived from England; it was a plain old-fashioned Punch and Judy show, but it was electrically operated. They had turned out the big lights and sat in the dim room watching Punch batter Judy and Judy quarrel and squeak, and Punch with his stick batter Judy again. 'Doesn't it take one back to one's childhood?' Joanna said. 'Remember, at the seaside, the Punch and Judy boxes – don't you remember, Freddy?'

'Oh, my God!' Freddy called out. 'Stop it. I can't stand it. I can't watch this. Excuse me . . . just let me, please . . . I'm going to bed.'

When he had gone, Joanna and Matt turned on the big lights for a few minutes and wondered whether to call the doctor. Then they decided to leave well alone. They turned off the big lights and watched the show again, with less delight, but now with the more rational eyes and comments of puppet connoisseurs.

'I'm sorry it upset you, Freddy,' Joanna said when she found him in the garden next morning.

He said, 'You look very sweet and fresh, Joanna.' She was wearing her red linen dress, with a white cardigan thrown over her shoulders.

She was afraid he was going to say more about blood and bloodshed; this was so often his fear since his lapse of memory – 'I feel there's going to be bloodshed. I wonder if Miss Vaughan . . .' Joanna had earlier recalled that once, when he was in his former good health, Freddy had quietly confided in her his irritation with his mother who, apparently, continually provoked her old companion, Benny. Freddy had not been unduly concerned, but he had said, 'Of course, Benny also takes an odd turn now and then. Religious melancholia. She writes to me that she dreams of murder, bloodshed, and so forth. Oh, these old women.' And she had debated recently with Matt whether Freddy had not meant that his mother, not Benny, was given to this melancholy bloodshed notion, and had inherited the morbidity from her. But Matt had thought this far-fetched. 'If he can be got to a psychiatrist, good and well. But I wouldn't take it upon myself, personally, to diagnose anything off-hand. It will come to a crisis soon, that's certain. Then we'll see.'

'He isn't really morbid,' Joanna had said. 'Not all the time. He's really adorable, is Freddy.'

There was no question of anyone ever disliking Freddy. In most ways he was pleasant for them to have round the house. And as they had become his closest friends in this part of the world it was natural that they should have him round the house when he needed them. Visits from the consulate seemed to upset Freddy. Joanna wanted Matt to discourage them, but Matt was anxious not to interfere with these men, who were only trying to get Freddy's memory back.

But Joanna's mental nerves, which she did not admit to possessing, were being attacked every time Freddy spoke of his premonitions of bloodshed, and he spoke of them on the average of twice a day.

'I can't help feeling it,' he said, that morning. 'It's as if I've already been *told*. It's as if someone had sent me a letter or a message by word of mouth, warning me to prevent this bloodshed that's impending. I wish I could place –'

'Freddy dear, I'm going for one of my flower-hunts. It's just the morning for a find. Matt's gone riding, so go and make yourself comfortable in the study and we'll all have breakfast together. Six-thirty sharp.'

She was away across the misty lawn, with her black hair shining and her white cardigan flashing above the skirt of her red dress. Freddy

felt untold guilt. There was something forgotten, many things forgotten, but one thing overlooked, cast aside. Sometimes he felt he
was drawing near to recalling what it was. Hotter and hotter – as in
a game of blind-man's-buff or . . . Joe Ramdez had called at the
house last Friday while Matt and Joanna were out. He had specifically wanted to speak to Freddy about joining his wretched insurance scheme. 'I'm under medical attention at the moment,' Freddy
said. 'I couldn't think of it.' They had sat in Matt's study. The man
Ramdez had been shown in deferentially by the Cartwrights'
servant, and Freddy did not feel in a position to excuse himself from
the interview. Ramdez had said some disturbing things. 'Mr
Hamilton,' he had said, 'you enjoyed your trip very much, I
believe?'

'Oh, very,' said Freddy, hoping for enlightenment.

'And the young lady? She was satisfactory?'

'What young lady?' Freddy said.

'Mr Hamilton!'

'I honestly don't know who or what you are talking about, Mr
Ramdez.'

'The young lady, Mr Hamilton, from Morocco. Or was it the better
qualified lady who is best liked of all, and yet she is a local product of
the town of Jericho itself? Whichever, Mr Hamilton, is not important. My house is welcome to all.' He got up and bent over Freddy to
whisper, 'and to many of your colleagues. They, too, have poor memories on this point, as it should be with any gentleman. But they sign
my proposal form and join my Trust.'

'I'm afraid,' Freddy said, 'there must be a mistake, Ramdez. I have
no recollection of meeting ladies or of visiting you. I'm sorry, but
that's that.'

'I leave you the proposal form,' Ramdez said. 'In the view of your
present ill health it may be that the annual premium comes a fraction
steeper. But our doctor, Russeifa, examines clients with leniency
always towards the client for insurance, not the company.'

'I don't want a form, thank you.'

'So now I go to see my old friend Mr Hedges at the British
Consulate, I am invited to lunch with him. But I keep discretion of
your private affairs, naturally, when I converse with him.'

Hedges had been posted elsewhere a few weeks ago. Freddy's heart smiled again. He had known it was a bluff. And yet . . . 'Say what you like to Hedges,' he said. 'Anything you care.'

It had been a bluff. And yet there had been moments while Ramdez was talking when Freddy felt himself coming close to forgotten things. He mentioned the visit to Matt and Joanna, casually. 'He was after that ridiculous insurance policy.' Warmer and warmer . . . Joanna said, 'I hope you got rid of him.'

He held his hand to his head and walked with head bent. He saw the stones beneath his feet and realized he had been following Joanna from the garden, and was climbing the hill with Joanna's red dress visible here and there through the misty greenery, as she took the winding path upwards. 'Joanna!' he called. 'Joanna! Come back, my dear.' She had turned. 'Oh, Freddy, do, please –'

He caught up with her. 'Joanna,' he said. 'You know it's dangerous up there.' They were already on the hill-path that bordered so dangerously on Israeli territory that it was often said by sensible local people that there would one day be a shooting incident on that spot. And this was the time of year, in the heat, when border tempers flared.

She said, very patiently, 'I've been here before at this hour. One gets marvellous wild flowers coming from the dew. An hour later, they're withered. But you see, Freddy, if I get them by the root and replant them at once in the shade, and keep them well-watered –'

'I'm thinking of the danger,' Freddy said.

She said, quickly, 'There's going to be no bloodshed. Now do leave me, I like to have a time to myself before breakfast, you know.'

He returned down the path while she continued to climb. He had almost reached the house when he heard a shot resounding on the hillside above him. He turned, and heard another shot. Then he ran back up the path calling Joanna, and gouging up the sand and stones with his shoes as he ran. She didn't reply to his call. He couldn't see her, and he was approaching the flat summit of the hill. She was nowhere. He looked all round. Then he saw by the side of the path a few yards below, a red movement, a crawling. He had run past her and missed her. 'Freddy get down, lie down,' she screamed at him as he came towards her. 'There's something going on.' He bent and walked back from the path, and crouched down. 'Are you all right?' he said. 'Yes, but I damn near got hit. There's something going on down there. I saw something.'

'That dress of yours is an easy target,' Freddy said.

'Shut up.'

'Joanna dear!'

'We'll wait a few more minutes, then if it's quiet we'll beat it,' she said.

'I saw your dress. I thought it was blood.'

'I've got a bloody cut knee. Does that satisfy you, Freddy?'

He raised himself sufficiently to see part of the valley below. Then he moved closer to the path.

'Take care,' Joanna said. 'I saw some men moving down there just as the first shot whizzed up at me.'

'I can see three of the border guard down there. They're looking at a plough or a cart or something,' Freddy said.

'Are they Jordanian or Israelis?'

'I've no idea. Does it matter?'

'Not in the least. Anyway, they were firing up at me, and I was looking down the valley. I heard a sort of noise and then I saw two men coming out of the mist, then it looked as if one of them was dragging the other. Why did they fire at me?'

'I suppose they heard a suspicious noise, saw your dress and fired.'

'The second bullet went right over my head, quite close. I *felt* it.'

The two men, one dragging the other, were not two men, but Abdul and Barbara. They had reached the bottom of their hill and were about to cross the field that led straight to the hill they were to climb, into Israel, when Abdul saw distant shadows moving among some trees bordering the farthest side of the field. He stopped immediately. The stopping of the wheel-creaks must itself have sent suspicion to the alert ears of the guard. Abdul unharnessed himself from the cart and said to Barbara, 'Climb out.' She did so immediately. He took her hand and said, 'Run.' She ran, but not fast enough for him. Presently, he was half-dragging her. A shot was fired, resounding on another side of the hill to their left. Another shot, far away from them, followed it. Abdul stopped. They had got half-way up the hill they had descended. He pushed Barbara off the path, and told her to lie flat. Nothing else occurred, but below them they could hear voices. 'My sandals,' Abdul said. 'They've got my stock of sandals.'

'My legs have got scraped,' Barbara said, still in a daze. 'They feel awful.' She had felt no fear. There had been no time to feel anything.

She limped with him back to the house near the Potter's Field, passing on their way the monk at his door, feeding his chickens as if no shots had been fired.

When they had cleaned up Barbara's legs, which were less damaged than were the shredded toes of her shoes where they had been scraped from the dragging, and when Abdul had thrown cold well-water over his head, and they were able to sit down and speak in small gusts to each other or to themselves, it was plain that Abdul's pride, as well as his sandals, was lost.

Barbara said, 'I'm going to the British Consulate to give myself up. After all, what crime have I committed? I'm entitled to protection.'

Abdul said only, 'Quiet! I make a plan in my head.'

'No,' she said. 'The sensible thing for me to do is to go to the Consulate. I've had the pilgrimage, and that's what I came for, after all.'

'Yes, you had the pilgrimage, Miss. And what about me? What of us?'

'Must you go back? Can't you stay here?'

'Yes, and be a Palestine refugee in a camp, thank you so much, Miss. They look for me here, besides. I am known, and hated also. When the Arab hates he hates well. They say I'm an Israeli spy, as they say of you, Miss.'

'Oh, Abdul, don't call me Miss.'

He said, 'Look, Barbara, if you want to go to the British Consulate, O.K. But they ask you to talk, where have you been, and with whom.'

'I need not answer. They'll probably ask me the same in Israel.'

'In Israel they don't need answers from you to satisfy the police. In Jordan your embassy needs these answers, or they will be unwilling to help you. The Jordanians make difficulties unless they know where exactly you have been, and who it was with. They will never believe a pilgrimage, a fever. Who goes on a pilgrimage like this? You went like a spy, and they'll arrest Suzi and take my father's house at Jericho, and his wives, if you tell the facts. And if you don't tell the facts there is trouble for you from your own government. Who believes all this hiding for a pilgrimage?'

She said, 'Yes, I understand. You make trouble for me, I make trouble –'

'Who believes?'

'I understand. Abdul, let's eat something.'

'You have seen the mice?'

'What mice?'

'When we came in there was mice on the table eating this bread. You didn't see, but I did.' They had left their bread and cheese from the night before exposed on the table.

Barbara said, 'Where shall I put it? I'll throw it all out.'

'It goes for the chickens.'

She investigated for herself and found a covered tin box in the yard with a few crusts at the bottom. She tipped all the mouse-eaten food into it.

She came back to the kitchen and said, 'It's all gone, Abdul. Just in case we should reach the point of starvation and be tempted to eat it.' He was fully smiling again. He said, 'I'm going for food. I have good friends. Now I need to use your money also for another plan if I find one. So good-bye also to your traveller's cheques. Maybe I give you back a few in Israel.'

He already had her bank-notes in his pocket, where he had put them for safety before starting off with the cart. He had said at the time, 'We are safe. But in case we have to run we have to throw away all money and cheques, for always a captive with money is killed on the spot to shut him up.'

He said now, counting the cheque money, 'This is a great lot, many pounds, but Suzi will cash some as I do not deal in cheques with my friends. Suzi will have to cash, as these cheques may be traced. She'll keep them till we're out of it safely. Maybe I give you a little bit back, Barbara, if you marry me instead of your husband.'

Oh now I go and sing the plainchant
And bring to prayer the people of Abdul
Who are stealing now his sandals and leather goods in the field
We dance and sing although our servant has gone away
All the time past there was a servant in this house
But he died and the old monk has no man left
But I get from him a chicken to cook

And I will bring those grapes and lovely cheeses
And the coffee from Abdul's orange groves.

He said, 'It sounds better in the original language, but it's not too bad in English. With a guitar it's very excellent.'

She went upstairs to the camp-bed to sleep it off, and was still sleeping when he returned. And he woke her up, coming into the room with a bundle of clothes over his arm. He sat down in the horse-hair arm-chair and spread out his legs. He said, 'I got a lift in a very grand car, but I had to crouch not to be seen. I will one day be seen grand.'

She said, 'What are these clothes? They look like disguises.' She said, 'I don't think I want another disguise, Abdul.'

'It's all planned for four o'clock this afternoon. Come and eat a lot of food, and I tell you. This time is safe, because I smell this fact.'

This time the plan worked and they got into Israel safely. It was simpler and yet more terrifying than the attempted trek with the cart.

At half past three a car, driven by an Arab, arrived at the house. Barbara, drugged into a euphoristic near-trance by a very effective tablet that Abdul had given her, was dressed in a black nun's habit with a starchy white coif, the skirt slightly too short; she carried a black shopping-bag. She entered the car. Abdul followed, an Arab Franciscan friar in a brown habit, very handsome. They sat boldly in the back. Barbara examined once more the contents of the shopping-bag. A bottle of eau-de-cologne. A passport bearing a nun's photograph with an anonymous nun-like face slightly fatter and older than Barbara's – the name Sister Marie-Joseph Minton of the Holy Ghost Sisters, Paxton, Monmouthshire, England, the date of birth, 1920, and a pilgrim's visa. She had the passport by heart, and hoped she wouldn't need to put it to the test. Also in the bag were a rosary, four white linen handkerchiefs, a purse containing some English and some Jordanian coins, a missal, a book of religious offices, a small roll of cotton wool, a black cotton reel with a needle stuck through it, a yellow plastic thimble, a small tin box of blackcurrant throat pastilles, a pair of black woollen stockings, a small paper bag containing pictures of the Christian shrines in Jordan, an empty spectacles-case, a ball-point pen, and, for some reason, an empty soda-water bottle. In the cheerfulness of Abdul's drug Barbara examined these objects with great joy, marvelling at the genius of the collection. 'The only things that are wrong,' she said, 'are the absence of glasses to put in the case, and the absence of a sponge-bag and tooth-brush. Otherwise it's a perfect nun's outfit, and whoever did it is absolutely brilliant.'

'We had no time to look inside,' Abdul said. 'My friend that helped me, took this bag exactly as it stood.'

Barbara decided to leave the spectacles-case behind in the car. She felt very happy. Alexandros, at his shop door, did not recognize them. Abdul stared directly at the shop and she did too, but Alexandros observed nothing. Meantime, Barbara had noticed Abdul's head as he turned towards the car window. She said, 'What have you done to your head, Abdul?'

'It is shaved for tonsure of Franciscan friar,' he said heroically.

'I think you're a hero,' she said.

He said, 'It looks quite good, matter of fact. A few weeks, if I wear this tonsure around the place, many youths wear it also.'

They came to the Mandelbaum Gate, where a large crowd was gathered.

There she was very much afraid. Abdul was quiet, she was not sure whether from circumspection or anxiety. She remembered she was a nun, and must not show excitement. She rather regretted taking the drug, although she quite saw, later, that it had helped her through. The large crowd was not so large as it had seemed at first. As she pulled herself together she saw it was a pilgrim-group of about forty, attended by two priests. A separate group of five women seemed to be in a sensational buzz. Barbara looked hard at every head in the vicinity in case it should be Ricky's, and, nodding courteously to Abdul, moved aside to hear what the five women were discussing in such exclamatory tones. She perceived that they came from the north of England.

'Perhaps I should wait for her.' . . . 'Poor soul, the poor soul!' . . . 'No, she said, no, definitely to go on without her; it's the Lord's will, she said, it's the Lord's good will.' . . . 'Margaret, would you and I wait with her till she gets her things back?' . . . 'Poor woman, she was only two minutes having a shower-bath, and then she comes out of the cubicle and all her things gone.' . . . 'Not a mortal stitch to put on.' . . . 'The passport too.' . . . 'The police surely will get them back. Who'd want a nun's clothing, for the Lord's sake?'

Barbara moved back to Abdul, who stood politely behind the hubbub of the large group. 'What time is it now?'

'Five minutes to four.'

'And the pilgrimage doesn't go through till four.'

'Don't get excited.'

'But the police will be checking the passports. I've heard some women talking over there, about the nun whose clothing was stolen. Where did you get the stuff?'

'From a room in a convent where some Englishwomen were staying. My friend is the porter, which is a very fine post to hold. These clothes cost a great price.'

The crowd began to move forward. Barbara was in a hurry. Abdul touched her arm and shook his head. She held back humbly. 'It's two minutes to four,' Abdul said, 'so we are well ahead of time.'

'What time?' She thought he meant the time when the police could be expected to arrive.

'We are well ahead of four o'clock.' He was an admirable Franciscan. This gave her courage.

She saw one of the priests who attended the large group of pilgrims walk back from the front of the moving crowd, to help it to get in order. 'Have the bags gone through, Father Colin?' said a woman's voice.

'Yes, they've all gone ahead, don't worry.'

He looked for a moment at Abdul and Barbara, newcomers to him. Barbara now recognized him as the priest who had said Mass at the Holy Sepulchre while she endured the agonizing onslaught of her sickness. Barbara smiled cheerily at him and he gave her an unquestioning smile in return, including Abdul in it. Abdul nodded once or twice, severely, as befitted a Franciscan of the Holy Land. Then the priest was busy with his people again. As they came near to the Gate, Barbara, waiting her turn, was aware that some of the faithful were making way for her and for Abdul, and she remembered that they were objects of reverence and accepted the courtesies.

The Jordanian official said he hoped she had enjoyed her visit to Jordan 'where is many Christian faith'. Barbara said softly that it had been a great experience, and in the meantime the official looked at her visa, closed the passport and handed it back. She walked on with the crowd, not looking round for Abdul until she had to halt with the rest at the Israeli immigration hut. She saw him talking to the Jordanian official, explaining something. She looked away.

The Israeli official looked at her passport photograph and said, as he stamped her visa. 'The photographer might have done you better justice than that, Sister.'

'It's a matter of luck,' she said. She opened her shopping-bag for the customs clerk and he peered into it, jokingly. Through the door she saw Abdul joining the crowd, and as she left the hut he said, 'Wait for me.'

She waited, and again it seemed he was explaining something. At last he got through.

They followed the crowd, most of whom were now climbing into a waiting motor-coach. Abdul said, 'My visa wasn't quite right for the date, but I explained in Arabic to the Jordanian and in Hebrew to the Jew, that I am here for one day only and have now no time to get the correct visa. They are always impressed when a monk speaks their language.'

'Where are we now?' said Barbara.

'In Jerusalem. In Israel.'

'Already?' The drug carried her off. She started to run for it, all along the narrow streets of the Orthodox Jews. Abdul ran after her, and caught her. 'Wait, we'll get a taxi. Wait, please, we'll be arrested.' She wanted to run along the pavements of the sweet, rational streets. All the people in the shops had come to the doorways and the passers-by had stopped to stare at the astonishing thing, a running nun with a monk in pursuit. A small shrivelled man shouted up the street to a taxi which was passing diagonally. It turned towards them and they entered it with all their skirts bundling with them. 'I get you clothes to put on very soon,' said Abdul, cool and proud.

Three days after her return, when she had come back to the hotel after a long afternoon's shopping for some clothes in which to travel back to London, she found an envelope had been slipped under the door of her room. She had not been expecting any letter by this means, for Harry was already here with her, in the hotel.

It was a letter from Ricky, enclosing a photographed copy of

Harry's birth certificate. The letter was headed 'Ramdez Travel Agency, Jerusalem, Jordan'. It read:

DEAR BARBARA,

I have tried to locate you, but evidently you purposely eluded me. I now find you are returned to Occupied Palestine and the people of your origin.

Your defection from your school commitments has forced me to sell the establishment as a going concern. I cannot carry on without reliable assistance.

I wished to see you for a reason. This was to hand to you the enclosed photographic copy of a document which I located in Coventry after much search in parish registers, etc. It is a copy of the baptismal certificate of Mr Clegg, whom you say you had decided to marry. You will see from this that not only is he illegitimate (bearing the 'mother's name' without entry under 'father's name' is the significant point here), but he is also R.C. by birth, as you will see from an examination of the enclosed. Therefore, as the Romans do not allow divorce, I am sure you would wish to know in time that a marriage with Clegg would not be consonant with your Church, which, I am bound to say, compares unfavourably with other religions (e.g. Moslem) in this respect.

As you would not wish to act out of consonance with your principles, as you have frequently indicated, I am convinced you would wish to have this document, for Clegg's information as well as your own.

I trust I have done my duty and that you will find a man, as you appear to wish this after all these years. I trust a fuller and more grateful life awaits me after I have wound up the school.

Yours in anticipation of acknowledgement,

E. RICKWARD

Barbara saw immediately what Harry's birth certificate signified. She went along to Harry's room with it. He, educated in these matters by his recent experience in Rome, saw it too. 'But I never knew my mother was a Catholic,' he said. 'My aunts didn't tell me that. Of course, they weren't actually aunts at all. Perhaps they didn't know.' Manuscript-man that he was, he held the paper up to the light to see the water-mark. There was none. It was just a photographed copy.

She said, 'It's marvellous.'

He smiled. But he smiled more at Ricky's letter.

That evening they cornered a priest who was staying at the hotel, to confirm their assumption that Harry's previous marriage was now invalid. This was easy enough.

'Do they accept photographed copies in Rome?' said Barbara, 'or do we send for the original?' The priest had to corner another priest for the answer. The other priest was that Father Colin Ballantyne who had preached at the Holy Sepulchre and brought his pilgrimage through the Gate with Barbara. 'Yes, a copy is all right, of course,' he said. 'One can never get parishes to part with the originals.' He looked at Barbara again. 'Haven't we met somewhere before?'

She said, 'I came through the Mandelbaum Gate with your party on Monday.'

'Oh, is that where it was . . .' He still seemed puzzled, and they left him with the mystery.

Abdul Ramdez and Mendel Ephraim left Israel by way of Syria a few months later and managed to reach Tangier, where they opened a café.

Suzi married a lawyer in Athens.

Freddy remembered Suzi gradually, and especially on that day in Kensington Gardens when the red sun touched the skaters under the winter sky. He wondered, then, whether she was alive.

'You've got Gardnor's statement?'

'Yes. His wife's got away to Cairo, we hear. The Ramdez girl was arrested, probably shot. The police were keen to show willing.'

'Oh, well. At least you've got Gardnor.'

'Old Ramdez seems to have wriggled out of it. He's still going about.'

'Detestable fellow,' Freddy said.

And when it came at last to his wondering whether Suzi was alive, he didn't take steps to inquire, and was reminded again of that story of the man who went away for a holiday and left his dog chained up, and feared to return in case of what he should find.

Barbara and Harry were married and got along fairly well together ever after. They had one child, a girl, whom they fussed over continually. They saw Suzi many times in Athens and London. Her husband was not unlike Alexandros, but leaner and less large in manner.

Before he left Jordan Freddy bought the icon from Alexandros, who condoled with him formally, in Lebanese French, over the death of his mother, and, in Arab English, assured Freddy that there was no obligation for him to buy the icon.

'I'm afraid,' said Freddy, 'that I'm a little better off now.'

'Yes, the mother leaves to the son. The old must die. But she has had a life.'

Joanna said, 'Freddy, you simply aren't fit to travel, let alone face all those tragic details. There's nothing you can do now. Let your sisters cope.'

'I must see about Benny,' Freddy said. 'I must go home and see to poor Benny. My sisters will do nothing for Benny.'

'There's the Welfare State, you know.'

'I must see about her. I can't have her locked up in some lunatic asylum without seeing the actual place, at least.'

Before he left for Israel to collect his belongings and return home, Freddy walked round Old Jerusalem, up the Via Dolorosa, past the Temple site and the Dome of the Rock, locating the places of history that had become familiar to him, as well as those he had neglected to look into. He followed the ancient walls of the city and Temple, past the gates of historic meaning, sealed and barred against Israel – the Zion Gate, Dung Gate, Jaffa Gate, New Gate. Then St Stephen's Gate opened within the Old City to another medieval maze of streets – Damascus Gate, that gate of the Lord's triumphal entry into Jerusalem on Palm Sunday, and Herod's Gate. He walked round the city until at last, fumbling in his pocket for his diplomatic pass, he came to the Mandelbaum Gate, hardly a gate at all, but a piece of street between Jerusalem and Jerusalem, flanked by two huts, and called by that name because a house at the other end once belonged to a Mr Mandelbaum.